READER'S DIGEST

CONDENSED BOOKS

FIRST EDITION

THE READER'S DIGEST ASSOCIATION LIMITED
25 Berkeley Square, London W1X 6AB

**THE READER'S DIGEST ASSOCIATION
SOUTH AFRICA (PTY) LTD**
Nedbank Centre, Strand Street, Cape Town

Printed in Great Britain by Petty & Sons Ltd, Leeds

Original cover design by Jeffrey Matthews F.S.I.A.D.

For information as to ownership
of copyright in the material in this book see last page

ISBN 0 340 28393 9

Reader's Digest
CONDENSED BOOKS

THE ANGELS WEEP
Wilbur Smith

ALL THE DAYS
WERE SUMMER
Jack M. Bickham

WINNER HARRIS
Ian St. James

SADIE SHAPIRO,
MATCHMAKER
Robert Kimmel Smith

COLLECTOR'S LIBRARY
EDITION

In this Volume:

THE ANGELS WEEP

by Wilbur Smith (p.9)

It was the promise of great power and wealth that drew British men of spirit and adventure to Southern Africa towards the close of the nineteenth century. But as the white men conspired to win a bigger portion of the earth's riches, the conquered Matabele nation was gathering up its strength to strike back against the invaders of their bountiful land. An epic tale of action, excitement and danger.

all the days were SUMMER

by Jack Bickham (p.175)

The year is 1943. The place, Harmony, Ohio. And young Danny Davidson is wrestling with bewildering contradictions. He is expected to despise the German prisoners of war from the camp just outside town. But one of them has been disarmingly kind—and he's the only person who can save Danny's dog from almost certain destruction. Then the rains begin, and in the fight for survival that this deluge brings, Danny learns that patriotism counts for little when measured against the gift of compassion.

Winner Harris

by Ian St. James   (p.285)

Lady Fortune had always smiled on Sam Harris. He was London's most successful nightclub owner until unbelievably his world crashed around him, his hopes frustrated by a sinister and ruthless organization which would stop at nothing to achieve its ends.

Sadie Shapiro, Matchmaker

by Robert Kimmel Smith (p.431)

Sadie Shapiro, America's best-loved senior citizen and television personality, has found a new outlet for her unlimited energy—as a matchmaker. She has landed the task of finding mates for a trio of impossible-to-match clients. But Sadie does not know the word impossible, and no arrow from Cupid's quiver can equal her ingenuity as she sets out to smooth the course of love. A delightful story that will tug at the heart and warm our readers to this indomitable lady.

The ANGELS WEEP

A CONDENSATION OF THE BOOK BY

Wilbur Smith

ILLUSTRATED BY NEVILLE DEAR
PUBLISHED BY HEINEMANN

In the last five years of Queen Victoria's reign, dreams of an even greater Empire drove white men deep into the heart of Africa: men like Ralph Ballantyne, fearless in his ambition for wealth and power. Conflict with his old master Cecil Rhodes was, Ralph knew, inevitable. But what neither man had bargained for was that the sleeping might of the Matabele nation would one day awaken. This proud tribe was conquered, but not subdued—and the man urging his warriors to take up their spears was Bazo, Ralph's trusted friend.

Wilbur Smith's latest epic novel is the story of this bloody struggle for supremacy, as the black man and the white turned Africa's rich lands into a bitter battleground.

Three horsemen rode out from the edge of the forest with a restrained eagerness that not even weary weeks of constant searching could dull.

They reined in, stirrup to stirrup, and looked down into the shallow valley. Each stalk of the dry winter grass bore a fluffy seed head of a lovely pale rose colour, and the light breeze stirred them and made them dance, so that the herd of sable antelope in the gut of the valley seemed to float belly-deep in a bank of swirling pink mist.

There was a single herd bull. He stood almost fourteen hands tall at the withers. His satiny back and shoulders were as black as a panther's, but his belly and the intricate designs of his face mask were the startling iridescent white of mother-of-pearl. His great ridged horns swept back, curved like Saladin's scimitar, and his neck was proudly arched as that of a blood Arab stallion. This noble antelope had come to symbolize for Ralph Ballantyne this wild and beautiful land that now, in the year of 1894, bore the name "Rhodesia".

The great black bull stared arrogantly at the horsemen on the ridge above him, then snorted and tossed his warlike head. Sharp hooves clattering over the stony ground, he led his chocolate-coloured brood mares at a gallop up and over the far ridge—leaving the watching men mute at their grandeur and beauty.

Ralph Ballantyne was first to rouse himself and he turned in the

9

saddle towards his father. "Well, Papa," he asked, "do you recognize any landmarks?"

"It was more than thirty years ago," Zouga Ballantyne murmured, a little frown of concentration puckering his forehead, "thirty years and I was riddled with malaria." He turned to the third rider, the little wizened Hottentot, his companion and servant since those far-off days. "What do you think, Jan Cheroot?"

The Hottentot lifted the battered regimental cap from his head, and smoothed the little peppercorns of pure white wool that covered his scalp. "Perhaps—"

Ralph cut in brusquely. "Perhaps it was merely a fever dream."

The frown on his father's handsome features sharpened, while Jan Cheroot grinned with anticipation; when these two were together it was better entertainment than a cockfight any day.

"Damn it, boy," Zouga snapped. "Why don't you go back to the wagons and keep the women company?" He drew the thin chain from his fob pocket and dangled it before his son's face. "There it is," he snapped. "That's the proof."

On the ring of the chain, beside a bunch of keys, hung an irregular lump of quartz the size of a ripe grape. It was mottled like fine blue marble and starred through its centre with a thick wedge of gleaming metal.

"Raw red gold," said Zouga. "Ripe for the picking!"

Ralph grinned insolently at his father. "I always suspected that you picked that up from a pedlar's stall on the Grand Parade at Cape Town—and that it's only fool's gold anyway."

The scar on his father's cheek flushed from bone-porcelain to furious red, and Ralph laughed delightedly and clasped Zouga's shoulder. "Oh, Papa, if I truly believed that, do you think I would waste weeks of my time? What with the railway building and the dozen other balls I am juggling?" He shook Zouga's shoulder gently, the smile no longer mocking. "It's here—we both know it. We could be standing on the reef at this very moment, or it could be just over the next ridge."

Slowly the heat went out of Zouga's scar, and Ralph went on evenly. "The trick, of course, is to find it again. We could stumble over it in the next hour—or search another ten years."

Watching father and son, Jan Cheroot felt a small prick of disappointment. He would have liked to see them fight, now that Ralph was in the full prime of his manhood, almost thirty years of

10

age, and accustomed to handling with boot and fist the hundreds of rough men that he employed in his transport company. He was big and hard and strutty as a game cock, but Jan Cheroot suspected that the old dog would still be able to roll the puppy in the dust—the praise name that the Matabele had given Zouga Ballantyne was Bakela, the Fist, and he was still fast and lean. The two men seemed more like brothers, for Zouga's skin was clear and unlined, his eye quick and vital, and the faint lacing of silver in his golden beard might have been the bleaching of the fierce African sun.

"If only you had been able to get a sun sight—the other observations you made were all so accurate," Ralph lamented as they trotted down off the ridge into the valley. "I was able to go directly to every cache of ivory that you left that year."

"By that time the rains had started." Zouga shook his head. "By God, how it rained! We hadn't seen the sun for a week, every river was in full spate, so we were marching in circles. The only definite landmark we have to work on is the site of Great Zimbabwe. We marched eight days due westwards from the ruins."

"And Great Zimbabwe is there. Due east of us now." Ralph reined in his horse as they came out on the next ridge. He pointed at a rocky kopje, the distant blue summit shaped like a crouching lion. "The ruins are just beyond—I would never mistake that view."

For both father and son the ruined city had a special significance. There within the massive stone-built walls Zouga and Jan Cheroot had found the graven bird images that had been abandoned by the ancient inhabitants. Despite the desperate straits to which they had been reduced by the hardships of the long expedition, Zouga had insisted on carrying one of the statues away with him.

Then many years later it had been Ralph's turn. Though he had been pursued by the border impis of Lobengula, the Matabele king, Ralph had also won through to the deserted citadel, and spirited away the six remaining statues. All three men now stared at the far hills, silent with their memories.

"I still wonder what happened to the men who built Zimbabwe," Ralph said at last. "Were they the Queen of Sheba's miners? Was this the Ophir of the Bible? Did they carry the gold they mined to Solomon?"

"Perhaps we will never know." Zouga roused himself. "But we do know they valued gold as we do. It must be within a few miles of where we stand that Jan Cheroot and I explored the shafts that they drove into the earth. Perhaps it was on the next ridge. . . ."

The trio rode down into the valley that looked like a hundred others that they had crossed in the preceding weeks. Ralph was ahead of the others, swinging his mount to skirt a thicket of wild ebony, when abruptly he stood in the stirrups, snatched his hat from his head and waved it high.

"Tally ho!" he yelled. "Gone away!" And Zouga saw the burned gold flash of fluid movement across the far slope of open ground. "Three of the devils!" Ralph cried excitedly. "Jan Cheroot, you turn 'em on the left! Papa, stop them crossing the ravine!"

The two older men obeyed. None of them questioned for an instant why they should destroy the magnificent animals that Ralph had flushed from the ebony thicket. Father and son were both cattlemen, and they had suffered terrible depredations from the lion prides which infested the land. Ralph owned two hundred wagons, each drawn by sixteen draught oxen, while Zouga's huge estate, taken up with the land grants that the British South · African Company had issued to the volunteers who had destroyed the Matabele king's impis, was stocked with the pick of the captured Matabele breeding herds. Too often they had heard their beasts bellowing in agony in the night, and in the dawn found their ravaged carcasses. To both of them lions were the worst kind of vermin, and they were elated with this rare chance of taking a pride in broad daylight.

Ralph yanked the repeating Winchester rifle from the leather scabbard under his left knee as he urged the chestnut gelding into full gallop. The lion had been the first away, and Ralph had only a glimpse of him, sway-backed and swing-bellied, padding majestically on heavy paws into the scrub. The older lioness followed him swiftly at a bounding gallop, lean and scarred from a thousand hunts, and blue with age across the shoulders and back. However, the younger lioness, unaccustomed to men, was bold and curious as a cat, and she turned on the edge of the thicket to snarl at the pursuing horsemen. Her ears lay flat against her skull, her furry pink tongue curled out over her fangs, and her whiskers were as stiff as porcupine quills.

Ralph dropped his reins onto the gelding's neck, and the horse responded instantly by plunging to a dead stop and freezing for the shot. Ralph tossed up the Winchester and fired, and the lioness grunted explosively as the bullet thumped into her shoulder, angled for the heart. She went up roaring in a high somersault, then fell and rolled on her back, stretching out in a last shuddering convulsion before slumping into the softness of death.

Out on the right Zouga was pounding up the lip of the ravine, leaning forward in the saddle, and at that moment the second lioness broke into the open ahead of him, going for the ravine at a driving run. Zouga fired at full gallop, and the lioness collapsed and rolled like a yellow ball on the stony earth, shot through the neck a hand's span behind the ear.

"Bully for you!" Ralph shouted as he pumped a fresh round into the chamber of the Winchester. He kicked his heels into the gelding's flank and they charged up the slope shoulder to shoulder.

"Where is Jan Cheroot?" Zouga called. The bush was thicker ahead of them, and the thorn branches whipped at their thighs as they passed.

As if in reply they heard the clap of rifle fire on the left, and immediately afterwards the furious ear-numbing roars of the lion mingled with Jan Cheroot's shrill squeals of terror.

"He is in trouble!" Zouga called anxiously. They burst out of the thick scrub into fine open grassland. A hundred yards ahead Jan Cheroot was tearing along the crest of the ridge, his face a mask of terror, lashing his mount across the neck and shoulders. He had lost his rifle, and the lion was a dozen strides behind him, gaining with each elastic bound. Its heaving flank was bright with blood from a shot through the guts, but the round had not crippled the beast: rather it had maddened him, so that the solid blasts of sound from his throat sounded like thunder.

Ralph swerved his gelding to try and give himself an open shot— but at that moment the lion gathered itself to leap astride Jan Cheroot's panic-driven horse. It rose lightly into the air, and settled like a huge yellow bird on the horse's back, crushing Jan Cheroot beneath its blood-streaked body. At that instant, horse and rider and lion seemed to disappear into the very earth, and only a swirling column of dust marked where they had been.

Yet the roars of the enraged animal and Jan Cheroot's howls of terror grew even louder as Ralph galloped up to where they had disappeared. He jumped from the saddle with the Winchester in one hand, letting his own momentum throw him forward until he stood on the edge of a sheer-sided pitfall at the bottom of which lay a tangle of heaving bodies.

"The devil is killing me!" screamed Jan Cheroot. He was pinned beneath the lifeless body of the horse. It had broken its neck in the fall, and the lion was ripping the carcass and saddle, trying to reach Jan Cheroot.

"Lie still," Ralph shouted down at him. "Give me a clear shot!"

But it was the lion that heard him. It came up the vertical side of the pit with the ease of a cat climbing a tree, its glossy muscular hindquarters driving it lightly upwards. The jaws were wide open, the fangs long as a man's forefinger and white as polished ivory. Ralph could smell the rotten flesh taint of its breath, and flecks of hot saliva splattered against his cheeks and forehead.

Ralph dropped on one knee and fired, and pumped the loading handle and fired again, so swiftly that the shots were a continuous blast of sound. The lion arched backwards, hung for a long moment from the wall of the pit, and then toppled and fell back upon the dead horse.

"Jan Cheroot, are you all right?" Ralph called anxiously. There was no movement from the bottom of the pit. The little Hottentot was completely covered by the carcasses of horse and lion. "Jan Cheroot, can you hear me?"

The reply was in a hollow sepulchral whisper. "Dead men cannot hear—it's all over, they have got old Jan Cheroot at last."

"Come out from under there," Zouga Ballantyne ordered, as he stepped up to Ralph's shoulder. "This is no time to play the clown."

Ralph dropped a tethering rope down to Jan Cheroot, and between them they hauled him to the surface. The excavation into which he had fallen was a deep narrow trench along the crest of the ridge. In places it was twenty feet deep, but never more than six feet wide. Mostly it was choked with creepers and vegetation, but this could not disguise the fact that it had been dug by men.

"The reef was exposed along this line," Zouga guessed, as they followed the edge of the old trench. "The ancient miners simply dug it out and did not bother to refill."

"How did they blast the reef?" Ralph demanded. "That's solid rock down there."

"They probably built fires upon it, and then quenched them with water. The contraction cracked the rock." Zouga turned to the Hottentot. "Do you recognize this place, Jan Cheroot?"

"Yes, yes." Jan Cheroot clapped his hands with delight. "This is the same place where you killed the bull elephant—"

"—and the ancient dump will be just ahead." Zouga hurried forward to a low mound covered by grass and began to scrabble amongst the grassroots, picking out chips of white sugar quartz, examining each one swiftly and discarding it. At last he stood and wiped his hands on his breeches. "It's quartz all right, but the ancient miners must have hand-sorted this dump. We will have to find the old shafts if we want to see visible gold in the ore."

From the top of the ancient dump Zouga orientated himself rapidly. "The carcass of the bull elephant fell about there." He pointed, and to confirm it Jan Cheroot searched in the grass and lifted a huge thighbone, dry and white as chalk, and at last after thirty years beginning to crumble.

Zouga turned a quarter circle and pointed again. "The ancient shaft where we buried my old gunbearer will be there—but let him lie. There are other shafts along the strike." He turned away, and the others followed him. A hundred yards further on, Zouga stopped again. "Here!" he called with satisfaction. "The second shaft—there were four of them altogether."

The opening had been refilled with chunks of native rock. Ralph shrugged off his jacket, propped his rifle against the bole of the nearest tree and climbed down to the narrow blocked entrance. "I'm going to open it up," he said.

They worked for half an hour, prising loose the boulders and manhandling them aside until they had exposed the opening to the shaft. It was narrow, so narrow that only a child could have passed through it. There was no telling how deep it was for it was impenetrably black in the depths and it stank of damp, of fungus and of rot.

They peered into the opening with a horrified fascination.

"They say the ancients used child slaves in the workings," Zouga murmured. "We have to know if the reef is down there, but no grown man—" He broke off and there was a moment of thoughtful silence before Zouga and Ralph glanced at each other and smiled, and then both their heads turned in unison towards Jan Cheroot.

"Never!" said the little Hottentot fiercely. "I am a sick old man. Never! You will have to kill me first!"

RALPH FOUND a stump of candle in his saddlebag while Zouga swiftly spliced together three coils of rope, and Jan Cheroot watched their preparations like a condemned man watching the construction of the gallows.

15

"Since the day I was born, you have been telling me of your courage and daring," Ralph reminded him, as he tied the rope around Jan Cheroot's waist and led him gently back to the mouth of the shaft. "You, who have fought wild men and hunted elephant and lion—what can you fear in this little hole?"

"Perhaps I exaggerated a little," Jan Cheroot whispered huskily.

"You are not a coward are you, Jan Cheroot?"

"Yes." Jan Cheroot nodded fervently. "That is exactly what I am— and this is no place for a coward."

Ralph lifted him easily and lowered him into the shaft. His protests faded gradually as Ralph paid out the rope.

Ralph lowered the little Hottentot a little under sixty feet before the rope went slack.

"Jan Cheroot!" Zouga bellowed down the shaft.

"A little cave." Jan Cheroot's voice was muffled and distorted by echoes. "I can just stand. There are ropes, plaited grass ropes, and leather buckets—" Jan Cheroot broke off with an exclamation. "They fall to pieces when I touch them, just dust now." Faintly they could hear him sneezing and coughing in the dust he had raised, and when he called again they could hear the tremor in his voice. "Name of the great snake, there are dead men here—dead men's bones. I am coming up—pull me up!"

Staring down the narrow shaft Ralph could see the light of the candle flame wavering and trembling at the bottom.

"Jan Cheroot, can you see a tunnel leading off from the cave?"

"Yes, now will you pull me up?"

"Not until you follow the tunnel to the end and break a piece off the reef."

"Are you mad? I go no farther—not with dead men guarding this place."

"Very well," Ralph bellowed into the hole. "Then I will throw the end of the rope down on top of you and put the rocks back over the entrance!"

"I am going." Jan Cheroot's voice had a desperate edge, and once again the rope began slithering down into the shaft like a serpent into its nest.

"When they deserted these workings they must have sealed the slaves in the shaft," Zouga said. "That proves they were still working the reef and that they left in great haste." He paused, and cocked his head to listen. From the depths of the earth came the distant clank of a metal tool on rock. "Jan Cheroot has reached the working face."

However, it was many minutes more before Jan Cheroot's quavering and pitiful pleas came up to them. "Please, Master Ralph, I have done it. Now will you pull me up, please?"

Ralph hauled in the rope hand over hand, his muscles bulging as without a pause he lifted the Hottentot and his burden to the surface. "So, Jan Cheroot—what did you find?"

Jan Cheroot was coated all over with fine pale dust and he stank of the mushroom odour of long-deserted caves. With shaking hands he opened the flap of the saddlebag at his waist. "This is what I found," he croaked.

Zouga took a lump of raw rock from him. It had a crystalline texture that glittered like ice, marbled with blue and riven by minute flaws and fissures. The shattered fragments of shining quartz were held together by the substance that had filled every crack and fault line. This cement was a thin malleable layer of bright metal, which twinkled in the sunlight when Zouga wet it with his tongue.

"By God, Ralph, will you look at that!"

"Gold!" Ralph whispered reverently, and it sparkled at him, that lovely yellow smile that had captivated men almost from the time they had first stood upon their hindlegs. "Gold!"

To find this precious metal father and son had ridden far, had fought bloody battles, had helped destroy the proud nation of the Matabele and hunt their king, Lobengula, to a lonely death. Led by a sick man with a crippled heart and grandiose dreams, they had seized a vast land that now bore that man's name—Rhodesia—and they had forced the land to yield up, one by one, its riches. They had taken its wide pastures and mountain ranges, its forests of fine timber, its herds of sleek cattle, its legions of sturdy black men who for a pittance would work to gather in the vast harvest—and now at last they held the ultimate treasure in their hands.

"Gold!" Ralph said, for the third time.

THEY STRUCK THEIR PEGS along the ridge, cutting them from the living acacia trees, and they hammered them into the hard earth with the flat of the axe's blade. Then they built cairns of stone to mark the corner of each claim.

Under the Fort Victoria Agreement, which both Zouga and Ralph had signed when they volunteered to ride against the Matabele, they were each entitled to ten gold claims—though this did not apply to Jan Cheroot. He too had ridden into Matabeleland with Jameson's flying column, but he was a coloured man, and as such he could not share the spoils. In addition, both Zouga and Ralph had bought up a block of claims from the dissolute and spendthrift troopers of Jameson's conquering force, some of whom had sold claims for the price of a bottle of whisky; so between them they were entitled to peg off the entire ridge and most of the valley bottoms on each side of it. They worked through the heat of noon and by the light of the moon until sheer exhaustion forced them to drop their axes and sleep where they fell.

On the fourth evening they were at last content that they had secured the entire reef for themselves. There was no gap between their pegs into which another prospector could jump.

"Jan Cheroot, there is only one bottle of whisky left," Zouga groaned, and stretched his aching shoulders, "but tonight I am going to let you pour your own drop."

They watched with amusement the elaborate precautions which Jan Cheroot took to get the last drop into his brimming mug before he slurped up the first mouthful. Ralph retrieved the bottle, and ruefully considered the remnants of the liquor before pouring a dram for his father and himself.

"To the Harkness Mine." Zouga gave them the toast. "And to old Tom Harkness who gave me the map that led me to it."

Ralph carefully moved the whisky bottle out of the little Hottentot's reach, for Jan Cheroot had drained his mug already. He settled down luxuriously against his saddle. "Papa, I know just the right fellow to open up the workings for us. He is the best on the Witwatersrand goldfields. Before the rains break I'll have my wagons bringing up the machinery."

It was part of their agreement that Ralph would provide the men and machinery and money to run the Harkness Mine when Zouga led him to it. For Ralph was a rich man. Some said he was already a millionaire—though Zouga doubted that.

Nevertheless, Ralph had certainly been paid huge sums by Rhodes's British South Africa Company for providing the transport and commissariat for Jameson's expedition against Lobengula. He had also laid the telegraph lines from Kimberley to Fort Salisbury, and his construction gangs were at that moment laying the railway lines across the same wilderness towards Bulawayo, and now he was a half owner of a goldmine that promised to be as rich as any on the fabulous Witwatersrand. "Damn it," Zouga thought suddenly, "they might be right after all—the puppy might just possibly be a millionaire." His pride was tinged with envy. Zouga had worked and dreamed for much lesser reward. Apart from this new reef, all he had to show for a lifetime of striving was the estate of King's Lynn and Louise—and then he smiled. With those two possessions, he was richer even than Rhodes himself.

Zouga sighed and tilted his hat forward over his eyes, while across the fire Ralph still talked quietly, for himself more than for his father, conjuring up new visions of wealth and power.

IT WAS TWO FULL DAYS' ride back to the wagons, but they were still half a mile from the camp when they were spotted, and a joyous tide of children and dogs and wives came clamouring out to greet them.

Ralph spurred forward and leaned low from the saddle to sweep Cathy up onto the pommel, so violently that her hair tumbled into her face and she shrieked breathlessly until he silenced her with a kiss, holding it unashamedly while Jonathan danced impatiently around the horse shouting, "Me too! Lift me up, too, Papa!"

Ralph chuckled, then reached down and picked Jonathan up by one arm and dropped him behind the saddle. The boy wrapped his arms around Ralph's waist and demanded in a high piping voice: "Did you find gold, Papa?"

"A ton."

"Did you shoot any lions?"

"A hundred," Ralph laughed, and ruffled his son's thick curls.

Louise had followed the younger woman at a more sedate pace. Her hair was drawn back from her forehead and hung down to the level of her waist in a thick braid, emphasizing the high arches of her cheekbones. She stopped at the horse's head and Zouga stepped down from the stirrup and lifted the hat from his head, studying her gravely for a moment before he spoke. "Even in so short a time, I had forgotten how truly beautiful you are," he said.

As Ralph rode in through the gate of the high thornbush stockade, he looked about the camp with satisfaction. It was an elaborate camp—for this was Cathy and Ralph's home: like gipsies they moved to where the pickings were richest. There were four wagons outspanned under the tall arched wild fig trees on the bank of the river above the ford. The tents were of snowy canvas. One contained a galvanized iron bath in which one could stretch out full length, another smaller one held a hand-painted commode. There were horsehair mattresses on every camp bed, comfortable canvas chairs, and a long trestle table in the open-sided dining tent. There were canvas coolers for the champagne and lemonade bottles, gauze-screened food safes—and thirty servants to tend fires, to wash and iron, to cook and to wait upon the table.

"By God, it's good to be home—a hot bath, and you can scrub my back, Katie," said Ralph. Then he broke off, and exclaimed with surprise. "Damn!"

Parked at the end of the row of wagons was a closed coach, a vehicle with sprung wheels, the windows fitted with teak shutters. The body was painted a cool green, the doors were picked out in gold leaf and the high wheels piped with the same gold. There were leather steamer trunks strapped to the roof rack and, beyond the coach, in Ralph's kraal of thornbush, big white mules, all carefully matched for size, were feeding on bundles of fresh grass.

"You might have warned me," Ralph grumbled as he let Cathy down to the ground. He did not have to ask who the visitor was— this magnificent equipage was famous across the continent.

"You never gave me a chance," Cathy protested, and at that moment Zouga hurried in through the gate with Louise on his arm. He was as excited by their visitor as Ralph was irritated, striding eagerly towards the inner stockade of the camp.

Ralph dawdled deliberately. It was strange how all men came under the spell that their visitor wove. Ralph prided himself that he alone was able to resist it, although at times it required a conscious effort. Cathy tugged at his arm. "You know he wants to speak to you, Ralph," she urged, and, as Jonathan darted off to play, Ralph took Cathy on his arm, and sauntered into the inner stockade.

The canvas sides of the dining marquee had been rolled up, and there were half a dozen men seated at the long trestle table. In the centre was a hulking figure, dressed in an ill-fitting jacket of expensive English cloth that was closed to the top button. The knot of his necktie had slipped and the colours of Oriel College were dulled with the dust of the long road up from the diamond city of Kimberley.

Ralph was shocked by the changes that a few years had wrought on this ungainly giant of a man. The meaty features seemed to have sagged from his face, his colour was high and unhealthy. He was

20

barely forty years of age, yet his moustache and sideburns had faded from ruddy blond to silver, and he looked fifteen years older. Only the pale blue eyes retained their force and visionary glitter.

"Well, Ralph." The voice was incongruously high and clear. "How is my railway progressing, while you are enjoying yourself?"

"Ahead of schedule, Mr. Rhodes, and below budget." With a small effort Ralph broke the hypnotic gaze of those blue eyes and glanced at the men who flanked him.

On his right was the great man's shadow, small, narrow-shouldered and neatly dressed. Only his keen and acquisitive eyes gave the lie to his prim, schoolmasterly appearance.

"Jameson." Ralph nodded coolly at him, using neither Dr. Leander Starr Jameson's title nor the more familiar "Dr. Jim".

"Young Ballantyne." Jameson slightly emphasized the diminutive. From the first their hostility had been mutual and instinctive.

From Rhodes's left rose a younger man with a straight back and broad shoulders, an open handsome face and a friendly smile. "Hello, Ralph." His Kentucky accent was easy and pleasant.

"Harry, I was speaking of you this very morning." Ralph's pleasure was obvious, and he glanced at Zouga. This young American was the one that Ralph had chosen to operate the Harkness Mine. It meant little to Ralph that Harry Mellow, like most of the promising young bachelors in Southern Africa, already worked for Cecil John Rhodes—Ralph intended to find the bait that would tempt him away.

"We must talk later, Harry," he murmured, and turned to another young man seated at the end of the table. "Jordan!" he exclaimed. "By God, it's good to see you."

The two brothers met and embraced, and Ralph made no effort to hide his affection, but then everybody loved Jordan for his golden beauty and gentle manner.

"Oh Ralph, I have so much to ask, and so much to tell you." Jordan's delight was as intense as Ralph's.

"Later, Jordan," Rhodes broke in querulously. Jordan went instantly back to his seat. He had been Rhodes's private secretary since he was nineteen years of age, and obedience to his master's least whim was part of his nature by now.

Rhodes glanced at Cathy and Louise. It was well known that he was uncomfortable in the presence of females, and would not even employ a married man in a position close to his person. "Ladies,"

21

he said, "you have urgent chores to attend to, I am certain."

Cathy surreptitiously squeezed Ralph's hand, to calm his quick annoyance at Rhodes's presumption. Ralph might not be in his employ, but on this man depended the railway contract and a hundred cartage routes. Louise too was clearly piqued by the dismissal. There was a blue spark in her eyes and a faint heat under the fine freckles on her cheeks, but her voice was level and cool as she replied, for both Cathy and herself.

"Of course you are correct, Mr. Rhodes. Please excuse us."

Now Rhodes immediately turned to Zouga and began rapping out questions like the lash of a stock whip, but the attention with which he listened to the replies was evidence of the high regard he had for Zouga Ballantyne. Their relationship went back many years, to the early days of the diamond diggings at Colesberg kopje which had since been renamed Kimberley after the colonial secretary who accepted it into Her Majesty's dominions. Since then, Rhodes had employed Zouga as his agent at the kraal of Lobengula, for he spoke the Matabele language with colloquial fluency. After Dr. Jameson had led his swift and victorious strike against the king, Zouga had been responsible for rounding up the herds of Matabele cattle and redistributing them as booty. Rhodes would have appointed him Chief Native Commissioner to deal with the indunas, the Matabele war chiefs, but Zouga had preferred to retire to King's Lynn with his new bride, and had let the job go to General Mungo St. John. However, Rhodes still trusted Zouga as he did few other men.

"The country is booming, Mr. Rhodes," Zouga reported. "Bulawayo is almost a city already, and there are more than six hundred white women and children—a sure sign that your settlers are here to stay at last. All the land grants have been taken up, and many of the farms are already being worked."

"What about the minerals, Ballantyne?"

"Over ten thousand claims have been registered." Zouga glanced at Ralph. "Within the last few days my son and I have rediscovered and pegged the ancient workings I first stumbled on in the sixties."

"The Harkness Mine," Rhodes nodded. "Did you sample the reef?"

In reply Zouga placed a lump of quartz on the table, and the raw gold glistened so that the men around the table craned forward in rapt fascination.

"It will go fifty ounces a ton," Harry Mellow whistled softly. "How thick is the reef? How broad is the strike?"

Ralph shook his head. "I don't know. The workings are too narrow to get into the face."

"It's too rich," Harry murmured, fondling the sample of quartz. "I can't believe that it will be more than a few inches thick—"

"But if it is?" Rhodes demanded harshly.

The American smiled quietly. "Then you will not only control nearly all the diamonds in the world, Mr. Rhodes—but most of the gold as well."

His words were a sharp reminder that the British South Africa Company owned a fifty-per-cent royalty in every ounce of gold mined in this new land, and Ralph felt his resentment return in full force. Rhodes and his company were like a vast octopus that smothered the efforts of all lesser men.

"Will you allow Harry to ride with me tomorrow, Mr. Rhodes, so that he can examine the strike?" Ralph's irritation sharpened the tone of his request, so that Rhodes's big shaggy head lifted quickly, and his pale blue eyes seemed to search out his soul for a moment before he nodded. Then with a mercurial change of direction he shot his next question at Zouga.

"The Matabele indunas—how are they behaving themselves?"

This time Zouga hesitated. "They have grievances, Mr. Rhodes. The cattle are naturally the main source of trouble."

Rhodes cut him off brusquely. "We captured less than a hundred and twenty-five thousand head of cattle—and we returned forty thousand of those to the tribe."

Zouga did not remind him that the return was made only after the strongest representation by Robyn St. John—Zouga's own sister. Robyn was the missionary doctor at Khami Mission Station and she had once been Lobengula's closest friend and advisor. Robyn had warned Rhodes that famine would decimate the defeated Matabele, and might force the Imperial Government to revoke the Royal Charter under which Rhodes's company ruled the land.

"Still, the indunas claim they were given back only inferior beasts, the old and barren cows and scrub bulls."

"Damn it, Ballantyne, the volunteers earned the right to first pick from the herds. The indunas should understand that they are a conquered nation. Their welfare depends on the goodwill of the victors. They extended no such consideration to the tribes that they conquered when they lorded it across the continent."

"One of the reasons why we marched on GuBulawayo was to

23

protect the Mashona tribes from Lobengula's depredations," Jordan murmured.

"What else do they have to complain of?" Rhodes demanded.

"The company police—the young Matabele bucks whom General St. John has recruited are strutting through the kraals, usurping the power of the indunas, taking their pick of the young girls—"

Again Rhodes interrupted. "Better that than a resurrection of the fighting impis. Can you imagine twenty thousand warriors under Babiaan and Gandang and Bazo? No, St. John was right to break the power of the indunas. As Native Commissioner, it is his duty to guard against resurgence of the Matabele fighting tradition."

"Especially in view of the events that are in train south of where we now sit." Dr. Jameson spoke for the first time since he had greeted Ralph, and Rhodes turned to him swiftly.

"I wonder if this is the time to speak of that, Dr. Jim."

"Why not? Every man here is trustworthy and discreet. We are all committed to the same bright vision of Empire. What better time than now to explain why the company police must be made even stronger, must be trained to the highest degree of readiness?"

"No, Dr. Jim." Rhodes spoke decisively. "There will be another time for that." He turned to Jordan. "The sun is setting."

Jordan rose to charge the glasses. The sundowner whisky was already a traditional ending to the day in this land.

THE BRILLIANT WHITE GEMS of the Southern Cross hung over Ralph's camp, dimming the lesser stars, and sprinkling the bald domes of the granite kopjes with a pearly light as Ralph picked his way towards his tent.

He stooped through the fly of the darkened tent and sat down on the edge of the camp bed. He touched Cathy's cheek.

"I am awake." She whispered, for Jonathan slept just beyond the canvas screen. "What kept you so long?"

"The dreams and boasts of men drunk with power and success." He grinned in the dark and dragged off his boots. "And by God, I did my fair share of dreaming and boasting." He stood to strip off his breeches. "What do you think of Harry Mellow?" he asked, with an abrupt change of pace.

"The American?" Cathy hesitated. "He seems rather nice."

"Attractive?" Ralph demanded. "Irresistible to a young woman?"

"You know I don't think like that," Cathy protested primly.

24

"The hell you don't." Ralph chuckled as he kissed her. He lay down beside her and she snuggled against him.

"How would you like to have your sisters come down from Khami?" Ralph asked suddenly. "They enjoy camp life, but even more they like to escape from your mother."

"It was I who wanted to invite the twins," she reminded him sleepily. "You were the one who said they were too boisterous." She raised her head and looked at him in the faint moonlight that filtered through the canvas, aware that her husband always had good reason for even his most unreasonable suggestions.

"The American," she exclaimed in a fierce whisper. "Not even you would use my own sisters—you wouldn't, would you?"

He pulled her head down onto his chest again. "They are big girls now. How old are they?"

"Eighteen. But Ralph—"

"They never get to meet decent young men at Khami. Your mother frightens them all off. Ask them."

"You are awful, Ralph Ballantyne!"

THE VULTURES WERE STILL hunched in the treetops, although the bones of the lions had been picked clean, and their dark misshapen bodies against the clear winter sky guided Ralph and Harry the last few miles to the ridge of the Harkness claim.

"It looks promising." Harry gave his guarded judgment that first night as they squatted beside the camp fire. "You could have a reef that continues to real depth. Tomorrow I will mark out the spots where you must sink your prospect holes."

"There are mineralized ore bodies right across this country," said Ralph, "and I have the wagons and capital to grubstake a prospecting venture, and to develop the finds that are made. I like you, Harry, I think we would work well together—the Harkness Mine first, and after that, who knows?"

"Ralph." Harry shook his head. "I have already thrown in my lot with Mr. Rhodes."

Ralph sighed, and stared into the fire. "Under Rhodes you will never be your own man. You will always be a servant."

"*You* work for Mr. Rhodes, Ralph."

"I contract to him, Harry, but the profit or loss is mine. I still own my soul."

"—and I don't?" Harry chuckled.

"Come in with me, Harry. Find out what it feels like to give the orders instead of taking them."

"I'm Rhodes's man."

"When the time comes, we will talk again." Ralph rolled into his blanket and within minutes his breathing was slow and regular.

IN THE MORNING Harry marked the sites for the prospect bores with cairns of stone. By noon he had finished, and as they up-saddled Ralph realized it would be another two days before Cathy's sisters could arrive at the base camp from Khami Mission.

"Seeing that we have come so far, we should make a sweep out towards the east," he suggested. "God knows what we could find! Rhodes will be holding court in Bulawayo for the next month at least. He won't miss you."

Harry thought for a moment, then grinned like a schoolboy about to bunk his classes to raid the orchard. "Let's go!" he said.

They rode slowly, and at each river course they dismounted to pan the gravel from the stagnant green pools. Harry's enthusiasm increased with each mile, but by the third day they had reached the end of the outward leg of their eastward sweep, and even Ralph realized that it was time to turn back. They took one last look at the country that they must leave unexplored for the time being.

"It's beautiful," Harry murmured. "I have never seen a more magnificent land. What is the name of that range of hills?"

"That's the southern end of the Matopos, the sacred hills of the Matabele," Ralph said. "If I believed in witchcraft—" He chuckled with embarrassment. "There is something about those hills."

The first rosy flush of the sunset in the western sky was turning the distant hills to pink marble, while their crests were garlanded with fragile twists of cloud coloured by the softly slanting rays.

"There is a cave hidden in there where a witch who presided over the tribes used to live. My father took in a commando and destroyed her at the beginning of the war against Lobengula. They say—" Ralph broke off and studied the turreted range of rock with a thoughtful expression. "Those are not clouds, Harry," he said at last. "That's smoke. Yet there are no kraals in the Matopos."

"Then where is the smoke coming from?"

"That is what we are going to find out," Ralph replied, and before Harry could protest he was cantering across the plains towards the high rampart of bare granite that blocked off the horizon.

THE MATABELE WARRIOR sat aloof from the men who swarmed about the earthen kilns. He was lean, so that his ribs showed through the covering of muscle; his skin was burned to the deep midnight black of carved ebony, glossed with health, and blemished only by the old healed gunshot wounds on his chest and back. He wore a simple kilt and cloak of tanned leather, no feathers nor war rattles, no regimentals of fur nor plumes upon his head. He was unarmed, for the white men had made bonfires of the long rawhide shields and carried away the broad assegais by the wagon-load.

On his head the warrior wore the headring of the induna. It was of gum and clay, woven permanently into his own hair. This badge of rank announced to the world that he had once been a councillor of Lobengula, the last king of the Matabele: it declared his royal bloodline, the Zanzi blood running back pure and unbroken to old Zululand, a thousand miles away in the south.

Mzilikazi had been this man's grandfather; Mzilikazi, who had defied the Zulu tyrant Chaka, who had slaughtered a million souls on his terrible northward march to this rich and beautiful land, who had been the first to hear the myriad weird voices of the Umlimo, the witch and oracle of the Matopos.

Lobengula, son of Mzilikazi, had been the young man's uncle, and had appointed him commander of one of the élite fighting impis. But now Lobengula was dead, and his impi had been blown to nothing by the white men's Maxim guns on the bank of the Shangani River.

His name was Bazo, which means the axe. He had sat all that day, watching the Rozwi ironsmiths perform their mysteries at the smoking kilns. Now at last it was time to draw the smelting, and as the head smith freed the clay plug from the first kiln, a joyous shout of thanksgiving went up from the assembly at the bright glowing rush of the molten metal.

"The birth of the blades," Bazo whispered, and in his imagination he could already hear the dinning of the hammers as they beat out the metal, and the sizzling hiss of the quenching that would temper the edge of the broad stabbing spears.

A touch on his shoulder startled him from his reverie, and he looked up at the woman who stood over him.

She wore the leather skirt, decorated with beads, of the married woman. Although she had already suckled a fine son, her body was straight and hard, the skin smooth and drum-tight. Her neck was long and graceful, her nose straight and narrow, and her eyes slanted above the Egyptian arches of her cheekbones.

"What is it, Tanase?" Bazo asked with quick concern.

"Two riders," she said. "White men coming from the southern forests, and coming swiftly."

Bazo rose, quick as a leopard alarmed by the approach of the hunters. He lifted the buck-horn whistle that hung on a thong about his neck and blew a single sharp blast. Immediately the master smith hurried to him.

"How long to draw the rest of the smelting and break down the kilns?" Bazo demanded.

"Two days, oh Lord," answered the ironworker respectfully.

"You have until dawn—work all night, but screen the fires from the plain."

Bazo turned from him and strode up the steep incline to where twenty other men waited below the granite cap of the hill. Like Bazo, they were unarmed, but there was the warriors' arrogance in their stance as they rose to acknowledge their induna, and their eyes were bright and fierce. They followed him at a trot to a narrow cave in the base of the cliff. There Bazo drew aside the hanging creepers that screened the mouth and stooped into the gloomy interior.

Bazo gestured and two of his men went up to the end wall of the cave and rolled aside a pile of boulders. The slanting rays of the setting sun glinted on polished metal, lighting the secret arsenal of assegais. The two warriors swiftly passed the weapons down the line of men, until each was armed.

Bazo hefted the stabbing spear. The shaft was of polished wood, the blade was hand forged, long as his forearm and razor-sharp. He had felt naked until that moment, but now with the familiar weight in his hand he was a man again.

On the shoulder of the hill, Tanase waited for him on the ledge of rock which commanded a wide view across the grassy plains. "There," she pointed. Bazo saw two horses, moving at an easy canter. They had reached the foot of the hills and were riding along them, scouting for an easy route.

Bazo turned and looked back. The smoke from the kilns was dissipating, but there was still an hour of daylight left: "I must delay them until it is dark," he said. "I must turn them before they discover the path."

He went bounding down the steep pathway with twenty armed amadoda at his back. He stopped where the track narrowed and at a single gesture his men slipped off the narrow trail and disappeared into the boulders that stood tall on either hand. Then Bazo placed his assegai on a shoulder-high ledge beside the path. "If I cannot turn them, wait until they reach this place," he called to the hidden warriors. "Then do it swiftly."

It was a good ambush: in bad ground on a steep narrow track where a horse could not turn readily nor go ahead at full gallop. Bazo nodded to himself with satisfaction, then unarmed and shieldless he went springing down the track towards the plain.

"IT WILL BE DARK in half an hour," Harry Mellow called after Ralph. "We should find a place to camp. There must be a path." Ralph rode with one fist on his hip and a felt hat pushed back on his head, looking up the wild cliff.

"What do you expect to find up there?"

"I don't know—and that's the devil of it." Ralph grinned over his shoulder. He was unprepared and twisted off balance, so when his horse shied at the tall black figure, Ralph had to grab at the pommel to prevent himself going over, but at the same time he yelled to Harry, "Cover me!" His horse was rearing in a tight circle so he could not get his rifle up from its leather boot under his knee, and he swore helplessly, anticipating a rush of dark spearmen. Then he realized there was only one man, and that he was unarmed—and again he yelled, with even more urgency, "Hold it! Don't shoot!"

Ralph jerked the gelding down and then stared at the Matabele who had stepped so silently out of the crevice of a fractured granite block. "Damn you, I nearly shot you," he said. Then he caught himself, and this time demanded in the Matabele language, "Who are you?"

The tall man in the leather cloak remained absolutely still, the empty hands hanging at his side. "What manner of question is that," he asked gravely, "for one brother to ask another?"

Ralph stared at him, taking in the brow and the gaunt features, scored and riven by some terrible suffering. There was something familiar in the fierce dark eyes and the deep measured voice.

"Henshaw." The man spoke again, using Ralph Ballantyne's Matabele praise name, the Hawk.

Ralph shook his head in wonder. "Bazo, it is not you? Surely, it is

29

not you?" He jumped to the ground and ran to embrace the Matabele. "Bazo. My brother—my black brother."

Bazo accepted the embrace quietly, and at last Ralph stood back and held him at arm's length.

"At Shangani—after the guns were still—I thought you were dead. Your men were there—the Moles—I knew them by their moleskin headbands. I searched for you, rolling the dead men onto their backs to see their faces—but there were so many of them."

"So many," Bazo agreed, and only his eyes betrayed his emotion.

"And there was so little time to look for you," Ralph explained quietly. "The laager broke up and I had to leave."

"I was there," Bazo told him, and drew aside the leather cloak. Ralph stared at the dreadful scars, and then dropped his gaze. "I was lying amongst the dead men."

"And now?" Ralph asked.

Bazo shrugged. "What does a warrior do when the war is over, and the king is dead? I am a hunter of wild honey now." He glanced up the cliff where the last smoke wisps were blending into the darkening sky. "I was smoking a hive when I saw you coming."

"Ah!" Ralph nodded. "It was that smoke that led us to you."

"Then it was fortunate smoke, my brother Henshaw."

"You still call me brother?" Ralph marvelled gently. "When it might have been I who fired the bullets—" He did not complete the sentence, but glanced down at Bazo's chest.

"No man can be held to account for what he does in the madness of battle," Bazo answered. "If I had reached the wagons that day—" he shrugged, "—you might be the one who carried the scars."

"Bazo." Ralph gestured to Harry to ride forward. "This is Harry Mellow, he is a man who understands the mystery of the earth—who can find the gold we seek."

"Nkosi, I see you." Bazo greeted Harry gravely, calling him "Lord" and not allowing his deep resentment to show for an instant. His nation had been destroyed by the passion of the white man for that accursed yellow metal.

"Bazo and I grew up together on the Kimberley diamond fields," Ralph explained quickly. Then he turned impetuously back to Bazo. "Camp with us here. There is much to talk about."

"I have my woman and my son with me," Bazo answered.

"Bring them. Go quickly, before darkness falls, and bring them down into camp."

TANASE WAS WAITING for him with the boy carried on her hip, a roll of sleeping-mats upon her head and a leather grain bag slung on her back.

"It is Henshaw," Bazo told her, and heard the serpentine hiss of her breath.

"He is the spawn of Bakela, the white dog who violated the sacred places."

"He was my friend," Bazo said.

"You have taken the oath," she reminded him fiercely. "No white man can still be your friend."

"Tanase, we must go down to him. If he sees my wife and my son are with me, then there will be no suspicions. I have told my men to clear away the kilns and hide the weapons. Follow me." He turned back down the trail.

She followed him closely. "Do you not remember on the day that I met this man whom you call the Hawk, how I warned you? Before the powers of divination were torn from me by his father, I warned you against him, though you still called him 'friend'. In my vision I saw you high upon a tree."

"I remember."

There was a tremor in Bazo's voice now, for his beautiful young wife had once served the dark spirits in the secret cave in the Matopos, and she had become the Umlimo, the chosen one, the oracle.

It was Tanase, speaking in the weird voices of the spirits, who had warned King Lobengula of his fate: in her mystic trances she had been able to see through the dark veils of the future for the Matabele nation. However, these strange powers had depended upon her maidenhead remaining unpierced.

At the beginning of the war which the white men had carried so swiftly to Lobengula's kraal, a small band had detached from the main army led by Bakela, the Fist, a hard fierce man. They had ridden swiftly into these hills and galloped to the secret cavern of the Umlimo, for Bakela knew the power of the oracle, and how her destruction would throw the Matabele nation into despair. Bakela's riders had shot down the guardians of the caverns, and forced their way within. Two of them found Tanase, young and lovely, in the deepest recesses of the cave, and they had violated her until her screams had guided Bakela to them.

Then, strangely, this hard man had been overcome with compassion. Though he had ridden this dangerous road for the sole purpose of destroying the Umlimo, yet he drove his men off her. He must have known that with her virginity torn from her she had lost her powers, for he told her: "You who were once Umlimo, are Umlimo no longer," and he had turned and strode from the dark cavern, sparing her life.

She had told the story to Bazo many times, and he knew that though the mists of time had closed before her eyes she had once possessed the power of the Sight. Thus Bazo shivered briefly, and he felt the ghost fingers touching the nape of his neck as Tanase went on in her husky whisper.

"I wept, Bazo my lord, when I saw you up on the high tree—and while I wept, the man you call Henshaw, was looking up at you— and smiling!"

THEY ATE COLD bully beef straight from the tins, and then Ralph shared out his remaining cheroots to Harry Mellow and Bazo. Close at hand a hyena warbled and sobbed in the darkness, drawn by the firelight and the smell of food, while further out across the plain the lions were coughing throatily.

Tanase, with the child on her lap, sat at the edge of the firelight, aloof from the men, and they ignored her. It would have offended Bazo if they had paid undue attention to her, but now Ralph glanced in her direction. "What is your son's name?" he asked Bazo, and there was a heartbeat of hesitation before Bazo replied.

"He is called Tungata Zebiwe."

Ralph frowned quickly, but checked the harsh words that rose to his lips. "He is a fine boy."

Bazo held out his hand towards the child, and reluctantly Tanase let the sleepy child stagger to his father and climb into his arms. He was a dark toffee colour, with a pot belly and chubby limbs, naked except for bracelets of copper wire at his wrists and a string of beads around his waist. His eyes were owlish with sleep as he stared at Ralph. In the shadows Tanase hissed softly and reached out as if to take the child back, then dropped her hand again.

"Tungata Zebiwe," Ralph repeated. "The Seeker after Justice. That is a heavy duty to place upon one so young," he said quietly as he caught the mother's dark eyes. "You would make him an avenger of injustice inflicted before his birth?"

Then smoothly Ralph changed the subject. "Do you remember,

Bazo, the day we first met? You were a green youth sent by your uncle the king to work on the diamond fields. I was even younger and greener, and it was only later I found out that the reason Lobengula had sent young bucks like you to the fields was to bring home as many fat diamonds as you could steal!" They both laughed, Ralph ruefully and Bazo with a vestige of his youthful glee, and they chatted animatedly, recalling how they had worked shoulder to shoulder in the great diamond pit.

Then, abruptly, Ralph changed the subject again. "I have a son also," he said. "He is a year or two older than yours. They could be friends—as we are friends. You and I could work side by side once more," Ralph went on. "Soon I will have a rich goldmine in the forests yonder, and I will need a senior induna in charge."

"I am a warrior," said Bazo. "No longer a mine labourer."

"The world changes," Ralph answered softly. "The shields are burned and the assegai blades are broken. The eyes are no longer red, for the wars are finished. The eyes are white now, and there will be peace in this land for a thousand years."

Bazo was silent.

"Come with me, Bazo. Bring your son to learn the white man's skills. He will read and write, and be a man of consequence. Forget this sad name you have given him, and find another. Together he and my son will enjoy this beautiful land, and be brothers."

Bazo sighed then. "Perhaps you are right, Henshaw. As you say, the impis are disbanded. Those who were once warriors now work on the roads that Lodzi is building." The Matabele always had difficulty in pronouncing the sound of "R", thus Rhodes was "Lodzi". "When will you begin to dig for your gold, Henshaw?"

"After the rains, Bazo. But come with me now. Bring your woman and your son—"

Bazo held up one hand to silence him. "After the great storms we will talk again, Henshaw," he said quietly, and for the first time Tanase smiled with approval. Bazo was right to lull Henshaw with vague promises; she recognized that despite the direct gaze of his green eyes and his open smile, this young man was more dangerous than even Bakela, his father. And Bazo's words had a hidden meaning. "The great storm" was the secret thing that they were planning.

"First there are things that I must do, but once they are done, I will seek you out," Bazo promised.

BAZO LED UP THE STEEP narrow pathway through the granite hills, towards the secret valley of the Umlimo. Tanase and the boy followed behind him. The path ended abruptly against a sheer cliff; there was a thatched watchman's hut on a ledge just below the summit, and a quavering old man's voice challenged him. "Who dares the secret pass?"

Bazo stepped through the convoluted portals of granite and answered in an echoing bellow. "Bazo, son of Gandang, Bazo, Induna of the Kumalo blood royal."

The secret, narrow passage through the cliff twisted like a maimed serpent, abruptly debouching into a sweeping valley of lush green that was completely walled in by the high cliffs. In its centre was a tiny village of thatched huts, and beyond, in the opposite wall of the valley, the low wide opening of a cavern snarled like a toothless mouth. Neither Bazo nor Tanase spoke as they stared across at the sacred cave, but the memories came crowding back. In that cavern Tanase had undergone the frightful indoctrination and initiation which had transformed her into the Umlimo, and on the rocky floor she had suffered the cruel abuse that had stripped her of her powers; another being now presided in Tanase's place as spiritual head of the nation.

As they started down towards the village they were met by a weird procession of creatures, some of them barely recognizable as human: there were ancient withered crones, pretty girls with blank unsmiling faces, old men with deformed limbs who dragged themselves in the dust, and slim mincing youths whose mad eyes rolled back into their skulls—all of them decked with the gruesome paraphernalia of the necromancer and wizard. Bazo lifted his son high on his shoulder away from their prying hands, but Tanase was unperturbed, for this fantastic throng had once been her own retinue. Dancing and chanting, the horrible guardians of the Umlimo led the two wanderers into the village, and then disappeared into the thatched huts.

They were not alone, however. In the centre of the village stood an airy open-sided hut, and in its shade there were men waiting— some grossly fat, others skinny and stooped, but all of them wearing the black headring of gum and clay; all surrounded by an almost palpable air of dignity and authority.

Here assembled in the secret valley of the Umlimo were what was left of the leaders of the Matabele nation. All of them had sat upon the councils of King Lobengula, son of great Mzilikazi, and had been on the hills that fateful day when the king had stood before the assembled regiments and had faced the column of white soldiers. They had shouted the royal salute "Bayete!" as Lobengula poised his great swollen body on gout-distorted legs, and then had defiantly hurled the spear of kingship at the invaders. And these were the indunas who had led their men out to where the Maxim guns waited for them behind the plaited thornbush walls of the white men's laager.

In the midst of this distinguished assembly sat the three surviving sons of Mzilikazi, the most revered of all the indunas. Somabula, on the left, was the eldest; on the right was Babiaan, wise and brave. However, it was the man in the centre who rose from his ornately carved ebony stool and came out into the sunlight.

"Gandang, my father, I see you and my heart sings," cried Bazo.

"I see you, my son," said Gandang, his handsome face lit with joy.

"Baba!" Tanase clapped her hands respectfully before her face, and when Gandang nodded his acknowledgment, she withdrew quietly to the nearest hut, where she could listen from behind the thin reed wall. Tanase was still the interpreter of Umlimo and as such wielded great power. However, it was not for a woman to attend the high councils of the nation, an indaba such as this.

Then Bazo greeted his fellow indunas, beginning with Somabula and going slowly down the ranks, mourning their pitiful shrunken numbers. When he had done, Somabula rose, and because this was an indaba of the most weighty consequence, he began to recite the history of the Matabele nation. There were no archives to store this history: it had to be passed on orally to their children, and their children's children.

The story began in Zululand a thousand miles to the south, with the young warrior Mzilikazi defying the mad tyrant Chaka, and fleeing northwards from the Zulu might. It followed his wanderings, his battles, his growth from a fugitive to a great and mighty king. Somabula told of the subjugation of the surrounding tribes, the multiplication of the Matabele cattle herds until they darkened the sweet golden grasslands, the ascension of Lobengula to the king-ship. He reminded them how the regiments, plumed and befurred and carrying their great war shields, had paraded before the king like the endless flow of the Zambezi River; how the maidens danced at the Festival of First Fruits, bedecked with wild flowers and

35

beads. Listening to the telling of it, the indunas remembered how great had been the king, how fierce and warlike the young men— and they nodded and exclaimed in approbation.

Then Somabula sank down and Gandang rose from his stool. He was tall and powerful, a warrior in the late noon of his powers, his nobility and courage unquestioned, and as he took up the tale, his voice was deep and resonant. He told how the white men had come up from the south. They wanted to preach a strange three-headed god, they wanted to dig holes and search for the yellow metal and the bright stones. "The stone falcons were stolen from the sacred ruins of Great Zimbabwe," Gandang reminded them, "and the Umlimo warned Lobengula that there could be no more peace in the land until they were returned and that he could no more resist the white men than his father, Mzilikazi, had been able to." Thus the king had chosen the most powerful of all the white petitioners, Lodzi, the big blue-eyed man who was the induna of the white queen across the sea. Hoping to make him an ally, Lobengula had entered into a treaty with Lodzi: in exchange for gold and guns, he had granted him a charter to dig for the buried treasures of the earth in Lobengula's eastern dominions.

Sorrowfully, Gandang recited the long list of grievances against Lodzi, and the breaking of faith which had culminated in the clatter of Maxim guns and the destruction of the king's kraal at GuBula-wayo. Broken-hearted and sick, Lobengula had taken poison, and Gandang himself had laid the body in a secret cave overlooking the valley of the Zambezi, placing all the king's possessions around him. Finally Gandang had walled up the entrance and slaughtered the slaves who had done the work. Then he had led the shattered nation back southwards into captivity.

At the last words, Gandang's hands fell to his sides, and a desolate silence descended upon the gathering. Then one of the indunas in the second rank spoke. "Let us choose another king," he began.

Bazo interrupted him. "A king of slaves, a king of captives?" He laughed abruptly, scornfully. "There can be no king until there is a nation once again."

The ancient induna sank back, blinking about him miserably. "The cattle," he murmured, "they have taken our cattle."

"One-Bright-Eye sends unblooded young bucks of our own people to lord it in the kraals—" complained another. One-Bright-Eye was the Matabele name for General Mungo St. John, the

36

Chief Native Commissioner. "These company police are armed with guns. They laugh at the indunas and the tribal elders, and they take the young girls into the bushes—"

"One-Bright-Eye orders us to labour like dirt-eating slaves, digging his roads—"

"What must we do?" cried another, and then a strange thing happened. All of them, even Somabula, looked towards the tall scarred young man they called the Axe, and they waited expectantly.

Bazo made a sign with one hand and Tanase stooped out through the entrance of the reed hut. Clad only in a brief leather apron, she carried a roll of sleeping-mat in her arms. She knelt before Bazo and unrolled it at his feet.

In both hands Bazo took the assegai which had been concealed in the roll and held it high. It caught the light, and they all gasped. The design of the assegai was by King Chaka himself, its blade beaten out and polished to burning silver, and the shaft bound with copper wire and the coarse black hairs from the tail tuft of a bull elephant.

"Jee!" hissed one of the indunas, the deep drawn-out war chant of the fighting impis, and the others took up the cry.

Gandang sprang to his feet and the chant broke off as he made an abrupt gesture. "One blade will not arm the nation. One blade will not prevail against the little three-legged guns of Lodzi."

Bazo rose and stood facing his father. "Take it in your hands, Baba," he invited. "Feel how the heft of it can make a man of even a slave."

Gandang stretched out his hand. He could not resist the feel of the beautiful weapon and he stabbed into the air with it.

"There are a thousand like this," Bazo whispered. "By the time that the first rains falls, there will be five thousand more. At fifty places the smiths are at work—"

"Where?" Somabula barked. "Where are they?"

"Hidden in the caves of these hills."

"Why were we not told?" Babiaan demanded.

Bazo answered, "There would have been those who counselled caution and delay, and there was no time for talk. Now it is the task of each of you to rebuild the impis, and to make certain that they are ready when the spears are sent out."

"How will the spears reach us?"

"The women will bring them, in bundles of thatching grass, in rolls of sleeping-mats."

"Where will we attack? At the heart—at GuBulawayo?"

"No." Bazo's voice rose fiercely. "That was the madness which destroyed us before. We attacked into the strength of the enemy; we went in across good shooting ground to the wagons where the guns waited." Bazo broke off. "We must lurk in darkness," he continued, "and attack the white man in the dawn. We must wait for him in the bad ground and probe his flanks and his rear, then drift away like the morning mist at the first rays of the sun."

"This is not war," protested Babiaan.

"It is war, Baba," Bazo contradicted, "the new kind of war, the only kind of war which we can win."

"He is right," voices called from the ranks of indunas.

"When will it be?" asked Babiaan.

"That I cannot tell you," Bazo replied. "We must wait until the Umlimo sends for us."

THERE WERE PLACES where the scars had knotted into hard lumps in Bazo's flesh. The machinegun bullets had done deep damage. After hard marching or exercise the torn and lumpy flesh often seized up in agonizing spasms.

Kneeling beside him in the little reed hut, Tanase worked an ointment of fat and herbs into the twisted muscles of his spine and shoulder blades. Bazo groaned at the sweet agony of her hard fingers, and slowly he relaxed and the knotted muscles subsided.

"You are good for me in so many ways," he murmured.

"I was born for no other reason," she answered, but Bazo sighed and shook his head slowly.

"You and I were both born for some purpose which is still hidden from us. We know that—we are different—you and I."

She touched his lips with her finger to still him. "We will come back to that on the morrow," she whispered. "Tonight there is only us." Then she cradled his head against her bosom, and crooned to him like an infant, and she mourned for the man she loved, and for the need to goad him on towards the destiny that awaited them.

ON THE THIRD DAY the messenger of the Umlimo came down from the cavern to where the indunas waited in the village.

The messenger was a pretty girl-child with a solemn expression

and old wise eyes. Around her neck she wore a talisman that only
Tanase recognized, a sign that one day this child in her turn would
take on the sacred mantle of the Umlimo and preside over the
gruesome cavern in the cliff above the village.

Somabula rose to follow the messenger, his brothers and Bazo
with him. The child-witch took Tanase's hand, for they were sisters
of the dark spirits, and the two of them led the way up the steep
path.

The little party halted involuntarily at the mouth of the cavern.
The four indunas hung back and drew closer together, as though to
take comfort from each other. Those who had wielded the assegai in
a hundred bloody battles were fearful now as they faced the dark
entrance. As the two women stepped through the crumbling,
carved portals the four noble warriors crowded behind them, like
anxious children. Tanase and the child led them along the twisting
pathway with unerring familiarity, and came out at last above a deep
natural amphitheatre where an open fire burned, its smoke twisting
slowly upwards towards an opening high above. They went down
the rock steps to the smooth sandy floor of the amphitheatre, and at
Tanase's gesture the four indunas sank down gratefully and squatted
facing the smouldering fire.

The child crossed to the far wall and took some herbs from a big
clay pot. She threw a handful on the fire and immediately a great
yellow cloud of acrid smoke billowed upwards, and as it slowly
cleared, the indunas started and exclaimed with superstitious
dread. A grotesque figure faced them from across the flames, an
albino woman, with silver-white leprous skin. Her forehead was low
and sloped backwards, her mouth was wide and toadlike, and her
thickened forearms were folded across her naked belly and thighs.

"I see you, O Chosen One," Somabula greeted her. Despite
enormous effort of will, his voice trembled.

The girl-child was busy amongst the pots, and now she came to
the gross albino proffering the clay pipe she had prepared. The
Umlimo took the stem between her silvery lips, drew a slow lungful
and then let the aromatic smoke trickle out of her nostrils.
Immediately the heavy sweetish odour of wild cannabis carried to
the waiting men.

The Umlimo smoked quietly, expelling the smoke with explosive
exhalations, and the indunas watched her with such fascination that
they did not at first notice the soft scratching sound on the cavern

floor. It was Bazo who first started involuntarily with the shock.

Tanase's voice arrested him. "Do not move. It is dangerous," she whispered, and Bazo sank back and froze into stillness.

A scorpion was scuttling across the floor, the firelight glinting on its glossy armoured carapace. It reached the Umlimo, and then began to climb up her bloated white body towards her shoulder. The Umlimo remained unperturbed as the glittering creature crawled up her face until it stopped in the centre of her forehead, its long tail arched up over its horny back. She began to mutter and a rime of froth bubbled onto her lips.

"She speaks in the secret tongue of the initiates," Tanase murmured to Bazo. "She is inviting the spirits to enter and take control of her body."

The scorpion's long tail whipped furiously from side to side, and suddenly it struck, the rigid thorn burying itself deeply in her flesh. The Umlimo's expression did not alter—and the scorpion struck again and again, leaving little red punctures in the skin.

"She will die!" gasped Bazo.

"Let her be," hissed Tanase. "The poison will not harm her—it serves only to open her soul to the spirits."

The albino lifted the scorpion from her face and dropped it into the fire—and suddenly she uttered an unearthly shriek. Three or four wild voices seemed to issue from her throat simultaneously, each trying to drown out the others, until at last one rose above them. It was a man's voice, and it spoke in the mystical tongue, totally alien in its modulation and cadence, but Tanase quietly translated for them.

"When the noon sun goes dark with wings, and the trees are bare of leaves in the springtime, then, warriors of Matabele, put an edge to your steel."

The four indunas nodded. They had heard this prophecy before, for the Umlimo was often repetitive and always she was obscure.

Another voice now spoke, guttural, blurred, barely human. Tanase calmly translated.

"When the cattle lie with their heads twisted to touch their flank and cannot rise, then, warriors of Matabele, take heart, for the time will be nigh."

This time the words were slightly different from the prophecy they had heard before, and the indunas pondered silently as the Umlimo fell forward onto her face and lay like death. Gandang made as if to rise, but then a convulsion ran down her back, and her spine arched, her hideous face lifted, but this time her voice was childlike and sweet, and she spoke in the Matabele language for all of them to understand.

"When the hornless cattle are eaten up by the great cross, let the storm begin."

Her head sagged forward. "It is over," said Tanase. "There will be no more."

Thankfully, the four indunas rose, and crept back to the valley.

That night, Somabula repeated the prophecies of the Umlimo to the assembly. They nodded over the first two familiar riddles, as they had a hundred times before. "We will find the meaning when the time is appointed—it is always the way," they agreed.

Then Somabula went on to relate the new, third prophecy of the Umlimo: *"When the hornless cattle are eaten up by the great cross."* Only after they had all argued the hidden meaning did Somabula look beyond them to where Tanase sat holding her child under her leather cloak.

"What is the true meaning, woman?" he asked.

"Not even the Umlimo herself knows that," Tanase replied. "But when our ancestors first saw the white men riding up from the south they believed that their mounts were hornless cattle."

"Horses?" Gandang asked thoughtfully.

"It may be so," Tanase agreed. "Yet a single word of the Umlimo may have as many meanings as there are crocodiles in the Limpopo River."

"What is the great cross of the prophecy?" Bazo asked.

"The cross is the sign of the white men's three-headed god," Gandang answered. "My senior wife, Juba, wears that sign about her neck, given to her by the missionary at Khami when she poured water on her head. But is it possible that the white men's god would eat up their horses?"

So the discussion passed from elder to elder, while the watch fire burned low and over the valley the vast shining firmament of the heavens turned with weighty dignity.

RALPH BALLANTYNE had been wrong when he predicted to Harry Mellow that by the time they returned to the base camp Rhodes would have moved on to Bulawayo. That evening the tableau at the trestle table in the dining tent seemed unaltered since Ralph had last seen it, rather like a set of waxworks. Rhodes even wore the same clothing, dominating the tent with his expansive charisma.

He looked up as Ralph came into the tent. "Harry tells me your trip was a great success. He panned your crushings from the Harkness reef at thirty ounces a ton, that's thirty times richer than the best banket reef of the Witwatersrand. I think we should open a bottle of champagne. Jordan, don't we have a few bottles of the Pommery '87 left?"

Ralph lifted his glass to the toast, "The Harkness Mine," and the moment he had drunk he turned on Dr. Jameson. "What is this about the mining laws?" he demanded. "Harry tells me you are adopting the American mining code."

"Do you have any objection?" Jameson bristled.

"That code was drawn up by lawyers to keep themselves in fat fees in perpetuity. The new Witwatersrand laws are simpler and a million times more workable. By God, isn't it enough that your company royalty will rob us of fifty per cent of our profits? Your company owns the police force and the courts. And if I have a dispute with your company, who will decide it—the BSA Company's own magistrate?"

"I am sure we will have no need of the company magistrate."

Rhodes's tone was reasonable and placatory, but there was a steely blue flicker in his eyes as he raised his glass to Ralph. "To a deep mine and a deeper relationship," he said, and only one other person in the tent recognized it as a challenge.

Jordan Ballantyne knew these two men so well, loved both so dearly—he wanted to cry out to his brother, and restrain him from the folly of turning this brooding giant of a soul into an enemy. He had seen other men do just that, and be ruthlessly crushed. Jordan also knew on which side he would cast his lot if that dreaded confrontation ever forced a choice upon him—he was Rhodes's man, beyond brotherly ties and family loyalties, to the end of life itself. Now, as he sought desperately for some plausible excuse to break the tension between the two most important persons in his life, there came from beyond the fence the delighted cries of the servants, the hysterical barking of the camp dogs and the excited shrieks of women.

"It seems we have more visitors," Ralph said, and Jordan caught the smug expression on his brother's face as Cathy's sisters came into the inner stockade.

42

Victoria came first, on long shapely legs outlined beneath the whirl of her thin cotton skirts, bare-footed in defiance of all ladylike pretensions, carrying Jonathan riding on her hip. "Vicky! Vicky!" he was squeaking. "Did you bring me anything?"

"A kiss on the cheek and a slap on the behind," Vicky laughed, and hugged him. Her laughter was loud and gay and unaffected, her eyes were green and wide-spaced, and her skin had that lustrous silky English perfection that neither sun nor doses of anti-malarial quinine could mar. She would have been striking even without the dense tresses of copper-blonde hair that tumbled about her face and shoulders, and she riveted the attention of every man there, even that of Rhodes. She ran to Ralph for a kiss, then she tossed Jonathan to him and whirled away to run bare-footed down the tent and launch herself into Jordan's arms.

"Darling Jordan, how we have missed you!" she carolled joyously.

Ralph glanced at Rhodes, and saw his expression of shock and unease. He grinned and turned as the second twin came in arm-in-arm with Cathy.

Elizabeth was as tall as Vicky, but darker. Her hair was polished mahogany, her skin was sun-gilded, and there was a mischievous quirk to her lips and a measured candour in the gaze of her wild honey eyes. She kissed Ralph, and the contact was as brief but less sisterly than had been the elder twin's embrace.

"Mr. Rhodes, may I present my sisters-in-law," said Ralph with relish.

"Oh, the famous Mr. Rhodes," Vicky gushed theatrically, but there were sparks in her eyes. "It is such an honour to meet the conqueror of the Matabele nation. King Lobengula was, you see, a personal friend of our family."

"And our father sacrificed his life trying to help him," Elizabeth continued, "while your troops were pursuing him to his death. My mother—"

"Young lady, I am fully aware who your mother is," Rhodes forestalled her sharply.

"Then you will appreciate the gift that she asked me to present to you." Vicky reached into the deep pocket of her skirt and brought out a thin volume. She laid it on the table in front of Rhodes, and when he saw the title his heavy jaw clamped shut.

The book was entitled: *Trooper Hackett of Matabeleland* by Robyn Ballantyne, for the twins' mother wrote and published under

her maiden name. There was probably not a man in the
stockade who had not already read the slim volume: in six
months it had sold almost two hundred thousand copies, and
had been reviewed in almost every newspaper both at home
and abroad. It described the fictional adventures of Trooper Hackett
of the BSA Company expeditionary force, and his whole-hearted
participation in the slaughter of the Matabele, the pursuit and
shooting down of the fleeing survivors, the burning of the kraals, the
looting of Lobengula's cattle and the rape of the young Matabele
girls. It was little wonder, Ralph smiled to himself, that Rhodes
pushed the book away and wiped the hand that had touched it on
the lapel of his jacket.

"Oh, Mr. Rhodes," murmured Vicky, angel-faced and wide-eyed. "At the least you must read the inscription that Mama dedicated to you." She opened the flyleaf and read aloud. "For Cecil John Rhodes, without whose endeavours this book would never have been written."

Rhodes rose from his seat with ponderous dignity. "Ralph," he said quietly, "thank you for your hospitality. Dr. Jim and I will be getting on to Bulawayo, I think. We have spent too long here as it is." He looked across at Jordan. "The mules are well rested, Jordan. Can we be ready to leave this evening?"

It was a command. Rhodes did not wait for a reply, but stalked out of the stockade towards his own tent. The little doctor followed him stiffly, and the moment they were gone, the twins burst into tinkling laughter and hugged each other ecstatically.

"Mama would have been so proud of you, Victoria—"

"Well, I am not." Jordan was white-faced and shaking with anger. "You are ill-mannered and silly little girls, with no idea how dangerous a game you are playing!" He strode away from them, but paused for a moment in front of Ralph, his expression softening. "Nor do you, Ralph. Please be more careful—for my sake, if not for your own." Then he followed his master from the stockade.

Ralph pulled the gold hunter from the inner pocket of his waistcoat. "Well," he announced to the twins, "sixteen minutes to clear the camp. That must be a new record even for you two." He put one arm around Cathy's shoulders. "There you are, Katie my love. There is your home back again without a single stranger."

"That is not quite the case." Harry Mellow rose from the log he had been using as a seat and removed the slouch hat from his curly head. The twins stared at him for a startled instant, and then flashed each other a look of complete accord.

"You may present the young gentleman, Cousin Ralph," said Vicky.

WHEN THE MULE COACH drove through the outer gates of the stockade, there was one member of Rhodes's party who was not aboard.

"What did you tell Mr. Rhodes?" Cathy asked, hanging onto Ralph's arm as they watched the coach rolling away in the moonlight.

"I told him that I needed Harry for a day or two more." Ralph lit his last cheroot of the day and they began the leisurely stroll around the camp that was a ritual of their life together, the time when they talked over the day past and planned for the one ahead. "Actually I need him for longer than a day or two," Ralph admitted. "More like ten or twenty years."

"He is a man of many talents, your Harry Mellow."

"The chief of them is that he can spot gold in a filled tooth across a polo field. However, I have no doubts your little sisters cherish others of his accomplishments."

"I should send them to bed," Cathy murmured, as sounds of a banjo came from the inner stockade, accompanied by Harry's soaring baritone.

"Leave the poor creatures alone," Ralph admonished. "They have enough of that at home." And he led her away to their tent.

Ralph lay stretched out on his back on the camp bed, and watched his wife prepare for bed in the lamplight. "Come here, Katie!" he ordered at last, but she hung back provocatively.

"Do you know what I want?"

"No, but I know what I want."

"I want a home—with thatch and brick walls, and a real garden."

"You have the most beautiful garden in the world, and it stretches from the Limpopo to the Zambezi."

"A garden with roses and geraniums. Will you build me a home, Ralph?"

"When the railway is finished."

She sighed softly. He had made the same promise while he was laying the telegraph line—and that was before Jonathan was born, but she knew better than to remind him. Instead she slipped under the sheet, and for that moment his arms, as they closed around her, became for her a home.

THE WHITEWASHED WALLS of Khami Mission Station burned in the noon sunlight with eye-aching brilliance. The family dwelling, surrounded by wide shaded verandas, and roofed with thick dark thatch, stood a little apart from the church and its attendant buildings. From its front steps the gardens stretched down past a well to a little stream. Bougainvillaea, poinsettia and banks of phlox formed bright bold slashes of colour against a veld still brown from the long dry winter just passed; but nearer the stream fields of maize were tended by convalescents from the mission clinic, and

47

between the rows of corn the earth was hidden beneath the dark green leaves of new pumpkin plants. These fields fed hundreds of hungry mouths, the family and servants and sick and converts who came from all over the country to this tiny oasis of hope and succour.

On the veranda of the main house, at a bare hand-planed table, the family was seated at the midday meal. It was a meal of salted maize bread, and in the opinion of Vicky and Elizabeth, the grace that preceded it was disproportionately long for such frugal fare.

Dr. Robyn St. John had dutifully thanked the Almighty for his bounty but was now going on to point out to him that a little rain would help the pollination of the immature corn cobs. Her eyes were closed, her unlined features relaxed and serene. Her dark hair had the same russet highlights as Elizabeth's, but there was just a fine silver mist at her temples to betray her age.

"Dear Lord," she said, "in Your wisdom You have allowed our best cow, Buttercup, to lose her milk. We submit to Your will, which surpasses all understanding, but we do need milk if this little mission is going to continue to work to Your glory—"

"Amen!" said Juba from the far end of the table.

Robyn opened her eyes and smiled at her. She and this huge Matabele matron had been companions for many years, but it was only shortly before his destruction by the company's forces that King Lobengula had at last given his permission for Juba's conversion to the Christian faith.

Juba was the senior wife of Gandang, and she had borne him twelve sons, the eldest of whom was Bazo. Four of her younger sons had died in front of the Maxim machineguns. Nevertheless, as soon as that cruel little war ended, Juba had returned to Khami Mission and to Robyn.

Now she smiled back at Robyn. Her dark eyes sparkled with a lively intelligence, and her teeth were perfect and unblemished white. On her vast lap, within the circle of her arms, she held Robyn St. John's only son.

Robert was not quite two years old. Like many infants born of a mother on the verge of menopause, there was a quaint old-fashioned solemnity about him, and now he watched his mother's face as though he had understood each word she uttered.

"Dear Lord, Thou knowest of the great experiment upon which Thy humble servant will embark before this day ends, and we are certain of Your protection during the dangerous days ahead—"

At this, the smile faded from Juba's face. The twins looked up, troubled and unhappy. "You never told us it was to be today," Vicky protested.

"The young girl from Zama's kraal is a perfect subject. I expect her fever to peak before sundown."

"Please, Mama." Elizabeth jumped up from her seat and knelt beside Robyn with both arms around her waist. "It's so dangerous."

Robyn's expression softened a little, and she placed one narrow but strong brown hand on her head. "Sometimes we have to do things that frighten us. It's God's test of our strength and faith."

The previous year Robyn had, in her professional capacity as Medical Superintendent of Khami Mission, submitted a paper to the British Medical Association in which she set out the conclusions of twenty years' study of tropical malarial fever The august members of the British Medical Association had never forgiven Robyn for impersonating a man to attend medical school and obtain her medical qualifications and they read the first part of Robyn's latest paper on malarial fever with mild alarm. Her theory on the coincidence of parasite segmentation in the bloodstream and patient temperature-change could only add lustre to her reputation. Then with mounting joy they came to the second part, and realized that once more she had placed her reputation in jeopardy. Since Hippocrates had first described the disease in the fifth century BC, it had been an uncontested fact that malaria was transmitted by the foul night airs of swampy ground.

Robyn St. John, however, postulated that this was fallacy, and that it was transmitted from a sufferer to a healthy victim by the physical transfer of blood—then, incredibly, her paper went on to suggest that the carrier agents were the flying mosquitoes from marshy ground. As proof, she cited the discovery of the malarial parasite in the stomach contents of the insects.

The British Medical Association embarked on an orgy of derision. "There is not the remotest shred of evidence that any disease can be transferred in the blood," wrote one of her more charitable critics. "To look to the agency of flying insects to effect this mischief is not far removed from a belief in vampires."

Robyn's chin was up now as she addressed her family, and the strength and determination of her features was daunting. "Eat up your lunch," she said. "I expect you both to assist me in my work this afternoon."

BEHIND THE CHURCH stood the new ward that Robyn had built since the death of her first husband in the Matabele war, an open-sided godown with low walls and a thatched roof. Robyn's laboratory stood between the church and the ward. Shelves and a workbench ran around the adobe walls, and in pride of place stood Robyn's new microscope, purchased with the royalties of *Trooper Hackett*. Beside it was her working journal, a thick leather-bound volume in which she was now noting her preliminary observations.

"Subject: Caucasian female at present in good health," she wrote in her firm neat hand, but she looked up irritably as Juba spoke.

"You swore on oath to the great King Lobengula that you would care for his people after he was gone. How can you honour that promise if you are dead, Nomusa?" she asked, using Robyn's Matabele praise name, Girl-Child of Mercy.

"Juba is right, Mama," Vicky supported her. "You have deliberately stopped taking quinine and our own observations have shown the danger of blackwater fever is increased—"

"Enough!" Robyn slapped the table with the flat of her hand. "I am not going to die, and I will listen to no more."

"We won't try and stop you again," Elizabeth agreed. "But if you become dangerously ill, should we not fetch General St. John?"

Robyn leaped to her feet. "You will do no such thing, do you hear me? You will not go near that man."

"Mama, he is your husband," Vicky pointed out reasonably, "and Bobby's father."

Robyn's voice rang like steel from the scabbard. "You know I have forbidden discussion of him." She sat down and picked up her pen and for a long minute the scratching of her nib was the only sound in the room. When she spoke again, her voice was level and business-like. "You, Elizabeth, will write up the journal while I am incapacitated. I want hourly entries. Vicky, you will administer treatment, but not before the cycle has been established beyond any chance of refutation. I have prepared a written list of instructions in case I become insensible."

"Very well, Mama," the twins chorused.

"And me, Nomusa?" Juba asked softly. "What must I do?"

Robyn's expression softened. "Juba, just stay with me to give me comfort. You must understand that I am not breaking my promise to take care of your people. What I will accomplish with this work is an understanding of a disease that has scourged the Matabele."

"I wish there was another way, Nomusa."

"There is not." Robyn shook her head. "Come on children, we must be quick."

The black girl lay on her sleeping-mat against the low wall of the ward. Her skin looked brittle as parchment, her lips were grey and cracked, and her eyes glittered with the unnatural brilliance of the fever that was rushing down upon her.

Robyn pressed her hand into the girl's armpit, and exclaimed, "She is like a furnace, the poor child. I think this is the moment. Juba, take her shoulders while Vicky holds her arm."

The girl's bare arm protruded from under the blanket, and Vicky held her at the elbow while Robyn slipped on a leather tourniquet. Then Robyn picked up the syringe, found the vein immediately, and slowly withdrew the plunger, watching intently as the blood flowed into the brass barrel and showed through the glass inset. "I have taken two cubic centimetres," she murmured, as she withdrew the needle. "Give her the quinine now, Juba, and stay with her until she starts to sweat."

Robyn rose with a swirl of skirts, and the twins had to run to keep up with her as she crossed back to her laboratory. "Make a note of the time," Robyn ordered as she rolled up her sleeve.

"Seventeen minutes past six." Vicky looped the tourniquet around her mother's arm and began twisting it up tightly. "Oh, Mama!"

"Do be quiet, Victoria." Robyn fitted a fresh needle into the charged syringe, and without pause expelled the hot, fevered blood into her own vein.

"All right," she said. "If I am right—and I am—we can expect the first paroxysm in forty-eight hours."

THE FULL-SIZED BILLIARD table was the only one in Africa north of the Kimberley Club, and south of Cairo. It had been transported in sections three hundred miles from the railhead at huge expense, but the proprietor of the Grand Hotel had recouped his costs a dozen times over since he had set it up in his saloon bar. The table was a source of pride to every citizen of Bulawayo. It seemed to symbolize the transition from barbarism to civilization, that subjects of Queen Victoria should be striking the ivory balls across the green baize on the same spot where a few years before a pagan black king had conducted gruesome executions.

51

The crowd of spectators in the bar were nearly all men of substance, for they had won their grants and gold claims by riding in Dr. Jim's conquering column. They each owned three thousand acres of the veld, and many of them had already driven their claim pegs into the gold-rich surface reefs. Bulawayo was a boom town, and the spectators encouraged the two billiard players with raucous banter and extravagant wagers.

General Mungo St. John chalked his cue carefully and then wiped the blue dust from his fingers with a silk handkerchief. He was a tall man with wide shoulders and narrow hips, and his single eye had a predatory gleam to it, tawny and flecked like the eye of an eagle. The black cloth patch over the other eye gave him the air of a genteel pirate as he smiled across the table at his opponent. "Cannon and losing hazard off red," he announced calmly, and there was a roar of comment in which a dozen voices were offering odds against the play, and Harry Mellow tipped his head in reluctant admiration of the man's audacity.

There was a final flurry of bets, and then a silence fell over the crowded, smoky room. Mungo St. John lined up his white cue ball with his single bright eye. His face was grave as a professor of philosophy considering the riddle of the universe as he made a gentle practice stroke. Then he drew back the cue deliberately to its full travel, and at the instant that he launched the stroke the voice of a young woman cut through the tense silence of the watching men.

"General St. John—you must come quickly."

A voice with such lovely ringing tones could have turned every male head down both sides of the Champs Elysées, but in the billiard saloon of the Grand Hotel of woman-starved Bulawayo, it had the effect of a close-range broadside of grapeshot. The general's stroke had just made a perfect cannon and losing hazard, and a thousand pounds had been won and lost in those few seconds, but every man in the room was staring at the doorway in a kind of trance.

Mungo St. John calmly chalked his cue. "Victoria, my dear," he murmured, "there are times when even the prettiest young lady should remain silent."

"General St. John, my mother is dying."

This time Mungo St. John's head flew up, his single eye wide with shock. He let the wooden cue drop with a clatter onto the floor, and followed her out of the bar room at a run.

Harry Mellow tossed his cue to the barman, and shoved his way through the crowd. The twins' mother had until now ordered him off the Mission Station, calling him one of "Rhodes's hirelings". He would not miss this chance of seeing Vicky again.

By the time he reached the street, Mungo St. John, still in shirt sleeves, was mounted on a big bay mare. "Mr. Mellow," he called out to the tall figure in riding boots and breeches, "I would be obliged if you could see my stepdaughter safely out of town. 'I am needed at Khami." Then he put his heels into the mare's flanks, and she jumped away down the dusty street.

Vicky had already climbed into a rickety little cart drawn by two diminutive donkeys, with a mountainous black Matabele woman on the seat beside her. When she saw Harry waving at her she lifted her chin haughtily and shook up the donkeys into a dejected trot.

Vicky was sitting upright on the cart, looking straight ahead as they reached the outskirts of the town. "Tell me if you see him coming," she told Juba out of the side of her mouth, "but don't let him see you looking."

"He comes," Juba announced comfortably. "He comes like a cheetah after a gazelle."

Vicky heard the beat of hooves from behind, but she merely sat a little straighter. "Don't stare at him, Juba."

"He is so strong and impetuous—and he will make such fine sons in your belly."

"Juba!" Vicky flushed scarlet. "That is a wicked thing for a Christian lady even to think. I shall probably send him back anyway—" but before she could go on Harry Mellow reined in his gelding beside the cart.

"Your stepfather placed you in my care, Miss Codrington, and it is therefore my duty to see you home as swiftly as possible." He reached into the cart, whipped a long sinewy arm around her waist, and as she kicked and shrieked with surprise, he swung her up behind his saddle.

"Hold on!" he ordered. "Tightly!" and instinctively she threw both arms around his lean hard body.

Vicky's immediate confusion was dispelled abruptly by the realization that the gelding was in a flying gallop and at this pace the journey back to Khami would be brief indeed. "You are punishing your mount, sir." Her voice quavered and played her false. "Not so fast. My mother is not that ill."

"But you told General St. John—"

"It was just an excuse to get them together again. We should allow them a little time alone."

Harry reined the gelding down to a walk, but instead of relaxing Vicky tightened her grip around his waist. This was the only time in her entire life that she could remember being free from surveillance, without her mother or Juba or her twin being within earshot. It was an exhilarating sensation added to all the other unfamiliar feelings which assailed her, and the last restraints of her strict upbringing were swept away in this sudden reckless rebellious mood. She had loved Harry Mellow from the moment she saw him, and now she suddenly realized that she could have what she so dearly wanted, but only if she took bold action, and took it immediately.

"It is so hot in the sun," she murmured, and slowly Harry turned his head and looked into her green eyes. "I should like to rest for a few minutes in the shade."

He lifted her down from the saddle, and she stood close to him, without taking her eyes from his face. "The wagon dust has covered everything and left us no clean place to sit," she said. "Perhaps we should try further from the road."

She took his hand, and quite naturally led him through the soft pale knee-high grass towards one of the mimosa trees. Beneath its spreading, feathery branches they would be out of sight of any chance traveller upon the road.

MUNGO ST. JOHN'S mare was lathered in dark streaks down her shoulders as he drove her down towards the white Mission buildings. The mare's hoofbeats echoed from the hills, and Elizabeth's slim skirted figure appeared on the wide veranda of the homestead. She hurried down the steps into the sunlight to take the mare's head.

"General St. John—oh, thank God you have come." Tears were streaming down her cheeks. "It started as a game—Vicky and I wanted you to come because Mama needs you. She wasn't bad, just a slight fever. But now she is burning up with the girl's blood."

"Damn you, girl." Mungo seized her shoulders and shook her. "What has happened?"

Elizabeth gulped and her voice steadied. "She injected blood from a fever patient into herself."

"From a black girl? In God's name, why?" Without waiting for her reply, Mungo ran up onto the veranda and burst into Robyn's bedroom. He went over to the cot and looked down at the still figure upon it.

Robyn had wasted until the bones of her skull seemed to rise through the pale flesh of her cheeks and forehead. Her hair seemed dry and brittle as winter grasses, and as he leaned to touch her forehead a paroxysm of shivering took her so that her teeth chattered violently. Under Mungo's fingers her skin was almost painfully hot to the touch, and he looked up sharply at Elizabeth.

"Quinine?" he demanded.

"I have given her more than I should, one hundred grains since this morning, but there is no response." Elizabeth hesitated. "Before this Mama had not taken quinine for six weeks. She wanted to give the fever a chance to strike, and to prove her theory."

Mungo stared at her aghast. "But her own studies have shown that abstinence followed by massive doses—" He could not go on, as though the words might conjure up the spectre he feared most.

"Vicky and I tempted fate by telling you that Mama was dying."

"That's enough." He shook her gently. "Neither Vicky nor Juba are here, and you need help. Has she passed water?"

"Not since last night." Elizabeth shook her head miserably, and he pushed her towards the door.

"We must force her to take liquid. Get lemons from the garden, a bowl of sugar and a big jug of boiling water."

Mungo held Robyn's head while Elizabeth forced small sips of the steaming liquid between her white lips, and the icy chills that had racked her body gave way to a baking heat. Though she did not recognize Mungo or Elizabeth, she drank thirstily, choking in her eagerness. Mungo's hands were tender and gentle as he cupped her chin and wiped away the drops that dribbled from her lips.

"How much has she taken?" he asked.

"Over four pints," Elizabeth answered. She drew down the bedclothes—and then whispered huskily, "Oh, sweet God."

The skirts of Robyn's nightdress were sodden and the reeking stain was black, the drainage from kidneys that were trying to purge the bloodstream of anaemia. The malaria had been transmuted to something infinitely more deadly.

"It is what we feared," Mungo said quietly.

As they both stared helplessly at it, there was a commotion on the veranda and the door burst open. Victoria stood at the threshold. She was transformed, glowing from within, a young woman awakened for the first time to the wonder of love.

"Where have you been, Vicky?" Elizabeth asked. Then she saw the tall young man in the doorway standing possessively behind her twin. She felt no envy, only a small quick pleasure for Vicky, for her own love was for a man she could never have, and she had long ago resigned herself to that.

"What is it?" The glow had faded from Vicky's lovely face. "What has happened, Lizzie? What is it?"

"Mother has blackwater fever," Elizabeth answered flatly.

The twins had lived their lives on a hospital station. They both knew that the disease attacked only white persons, and Robyn's researches had linked that peculiarity to the use of quinine, which was restricted almost entirely to the whites. Robyn had treated fifty or more cases over the years, and only three had survived. The rest of them lay in the little cemetery beyond the river. Their mother was under virtual sentence of death.

JUBA HEATED ROUNDED river stones in the open fire and wrapped them in blankets. They packed them around Robyn's body, and then covered her with four karosses of wild fur. She fought weakly to throw off the covers, but Mungo held her down, and as the sun touched the treetops the fever broke and oozed from her marble-pale skin.

The temperature of her body plunged dramatically, and when the sweat had passed, Juba and the twins sponged her wasted body. When they finished, they called Mungo back from where he was sitting with Harry Mellow on the stoep of the Mission.

"I will call you if there is any change." He sent the women away and sat on the stool beside the bed.

Robyn sank slowly during the night, and seeing her in the dawn light Mungo knew she was dying. Then a soft rustle at the door made him turn his head. Robert, his son, stood in the door, his thick tangled curls flopping onto his pale forehead, his face owl-eyed from sleep. Slowly, a pace at a time, the child crossed to the bed, and hesitantly reached out to touch his mother's cheek.

"Mummy," said Robert. "Please don't die, Mummy."

Robyn opened her eyes. Glazed and sightless they flickered from side to side, and then miraculously focused on Robert's face.

"Listen to me," Mungo said harshly, and her eyes swivelled to him. "If you die," he said deliberately, "the child will be mine."

For the first time she recognized him. He saw the anger come alive in her eyes, saw the enormous effort that she made to speak as her lips formed a single soundless word, "Never!"

"Then live," he challenged her. "Live, damn you!" And he saw her begin to fight again.

ROBYN'S LIFE ROSE and sank to the dreadful tides of the disease, baking fever succeeding the icy chills, a long exhausted coma following the bursting sweats. At times she raved in delirium. Then for brief periods she was lucid. "Please, will you never let me be at peace?" she pleaded, her voice so low that Mungo had to lean over her to catch her words. "You know I cannot resist you—yet everything you stand for is an offence against my God and against the lost and leaderless people that have been given into my care." Then the disease would tighten its grip upon her and Mungo would rise, numbed with fatigue, to force Robyn to drink again. "Drink," he would whisper to her. "Drink, or die."

Sometimes in the noonday, when Robyn was resting between the onslaughts of fever, Mungo could sleep for a few hours until Juba or one of the twins called him. Then, as the fever began again, he would hurry to the bed and force her to go on fighting.

Sometimes he wondered at himself. He was well aware of the strange attraction he could still wield over women, and yet he had chosen this one—this one whom he could never possess, who hated him as fiercely as she loved him; who had conceived his son in a soul-consuming passion, yet kept him from the child with all her determination. She was the one who had demanded that Mungo marry her yet vehemently denied him the duty of a wife. Endlessly she had written to the newspapers denouncing almost every proclamation he made as Chief Native Commissioner. She was the most implacable and remorseless adversary he had ever known, and yet the thought of her dead desolated him, so that each time she sank he sank with her, and when she rallied, his spirits soared.

So it went on and on, without respite, day after day—until finally Elizabeth broke in on the few hours of deathlike sleep which he allowed himself. He heard the emotion that shook her voice and saw the tears in her eyes.

"It's over, General St. John," she said, and he flinched as though she had struck him across the face. Then he realized that Elizabeth was smiling through her tears. "It's over," she repeated. "Her water has cleared. She's safe. Thank God, she's safe."

By that afternoon Robyn was well enough once more to order Mungo St. John to leave Khami Mission.

"I cannot allow my son to come under your evil influence for another day. So far I have refrained from telling him that it was you and your ilk that waged unprovoked war upon the Matabele nation, and that you are the instrument of cruel oppression over them—but unless you leave, I will." Her voice crackled with some of its old force. "I order you to leave Khami immediately."

The effort left Robyn white and panting, and Elizabeth whispered to Mungo, "She might have a relapse. Perhaps it would be best."

The corner of Mungo's mouth twisted up in that mocking grin that Robyn remembered so well, and he gave her an exaggerated bow and strode from the sick room. Only then did she sink back against the bolster and turn to face the whitewashed wall.

At the crest of the hill Mungo St. John reined in his mare, and looked back at the homestead. Then he frowned, and lifted his chin to gaze into the heavens, for the northern sky was dark, as though a heavy curtain fell from the high heaven to the earth.

Mungo had never seen anything like this. It was not a cloud, for it had a peculiar density and body to it, and it reached in a great arc around half the horizon. Even as he watched, the fringes of the dark veil touched the rim of the sun and a vast shadow fell upon the land.

Now there was a sound, and the mare fidgeted nervously. A faint and distant sibilance gathered strength, became a deep humming flutter, and then with a low roar of million upon millions of wings, the twisting column of insects was upon him. It struck like a volley of grapeshot, driving into his face, the impact of each horny-winged body striking with numbing shock.

Mungo flung up his hands to protect his face, and the startled mare reared in terror. As Mungo snatched at the air, the flying insects were so thick that he caught one of them in his hand. It was almost twice as long as his forefinger, a glaring orange slashed with black. It kicked convulsively, piercing the skin.

"Locusts!" He looked up again, marvelling at their multitudes. "The third plague of Egypt." Then he swung the mare away and drove her at a gallop back down the hill towards the Mission.

The twins and servants were gathered on the veranda, paralysed with astonishment. He flung himself off the mare and ran towards them. "Get every person who can walk down into the fields. Take pots, drums—anything to make a noise, blankets to wave—come on!"

Then, with a suddenness that brought them up short, the air cleared and the sunlight was so white and blinding that they had to shield their eyes against it. The entire cloud of locusts had sunk to the earth: the trees were seething heaps of orange and black, and before their eyes the corn flattened under the onslaught.

They ran into the fields, a hundred frantic human figures, banging metal pots and flapping the coarse grey hospital blankets, and in front of each of them the insects rose in a brief puff of wings and resettled as they passed.

It did not last very long, less than an hour, then as abruptly as it had settled the great swarm roared spontaneously into the air. Once again an unnatural dusk fell across the earth, and a false dawn followed as the clouds thinned and winged away southwards.

In the empty fields the human figures stared about them in horror. They did not recognize their home. The maize fields were reduced to bare brown earth, the peach and apple blossom in the orchards was gone, and branches as thick as a man's wrist had snapped off under the clinging masses. There was no leaf nor blade of grass untouched in the wide swathe of destruction that the swarm had blazed.

JUBA TRAVELLED with two female attendants. There was a time, before the occupation by the company, when a senior wife of one of the great indunas would have had an entourage of forty women, and fifty armed amadoda to see her safely to her husband's kraal. But now Juba carried her own sleeping-mat balanced upon her head.

The two attendants, both young newly married women from Juba's kraal, followed her closely, staring in awe at the bleak and denuded land around them. The bare crippled trees were devoid of insect or bird life and the earth was crumbling into dust. The locust swarms had passed this way also.

They came up over a low rise. Gandang's kraal lay a mile down the bank of the Inyati River. The spring rains had not yet filled the river and the kraal itself seemed deserted, the cattle pens empty.

"They have taken the cattle again," said Kampu, the handsome young woman who stood beside Juba. She had been baptized by

Nomusa almost a full moon previously, and now she was most anxious to rejoin her husband, one of Gandang's nephews.

"No," Juba told her shortly. "Gandang will have sent the herds eastwards to find new pasture. Perhaps the men have gone with them."

"That is work for boys, not men."

Juba snorted. "Since One-Bright-Eye has taken their shields, our men are merely herdboys."

Juba's companions were shamed by the truth of her words. Their men had indeed been disarmed, and the cattle and slave raids which had been their main activity had been forbidden. At least their own husbands were blooded warriors, they had washed their spears in the blood of Wilson's troopers on the banks of the Shangani River in the one small Matabele victory of the war—but what would become of the younger men now that a whole way of life had been denied them?

"The women are still here." Juba pointed out the rows of workers replanting the brown denuded cornfields. "Let us go down."

The women saw them as they came along the river bank and ran shrieking with delight to greet them, jostling each other in their eagerness to make obeisance to Juba. They took her load from her, and two of her grandchildren came forward shyly to hold each of her hands. Then singing the songs of welcome the little procession filed up to the kraal.

Not all the men had left. Gandang sat on his carved stool of chiefship and Juba hurried to kneel before him with protestations of duty and devotion. He smiled at her fondly, and then as an extraordinary mark of his feelings for her, he lifted her with his own hand and seated her on the mat which one of his junior wives spread beside him. He waved the women and children away, and the two of them leaned their heads together and talked like the beloved companions that they were.

"Nomusa is well?" Gandang asked. He did not share Juba's deep love for the woman doctor at Khami Mission—in fact he viewed with deep suspicion this alien religion that his senior wife had adopted. It was Gandang's impi that had caught Wilson's little patrol during the war and slain them to a man, and amongst the corpses had lain the body of the woman missionary's first husband. There could never be love where there had been blood. However, Gandang respected the white woman for her unflagging efforts to champion and protect the Matabele people. "Has she thrown aside the evil spirits that she brought upon herself by drinking the girl's blood?"

"She did not drink the girl's blood," Juba tried to explain, but because she did not understand completely herself, her explanation was unconvincing and she abandoned the effort. "Bazo," she asked instead. "Where is he?" Her first-born son was also her favourite.

"In the hills with all the other young men," Gandang answered. "One-Bright-Eye sent word with his kanka that we must provide two hundred young men to work on the new goldmine in the south that belongs to Henshaw."

"You did not send the men?"

"I told his kanka—" the derogatory name for the Company Native Police likened them to the jackals that followed the lion for the scraps "—I told them that the white men had deprived me of my honour as an induna. Therefore I had lost the right to command my young men to dig the white men's holes for them."

"And now One-Bright-Eye comes?"

Juba spoke with resignation. She had watched the defiance and the confrontations before, and she was sick of wars and death.

"Yes," Gandang agreed. "Not all the kanka are traitors and one has sent word that One-Bright-Eye is on the road, with fifty men—and so the young men have gone into the hills."

"But you stay here to meet him?" Juba asked. "Unarmed and alone?"

"I have never run from any man," Gandang said simply, "never in my life."

Juba felt her pride and her love choke her as she looked into the stern handsome face. "Gandang, my Lord, the old times have passed. The sons of Lobengula work as houseboys in the kraal of Lodzi, the impis are scattered. Everything has changed, and we must change too."

Gandang was silent a long time, staring out across the river as though he had not heard her. Then he spoke. "The Umlimo has called forth an oracle. The nation will be free and great again—"

"The Umlimo sent the impis into the guns at Shangani," Juba whispered bitterly. "The Umlimo preaches war and death. There is a new god now, Jesus, a god of peace."

"Peace?" Gandang asked bitterly. "If that is the word of this new god, then the white men do not listen very well to their own."

61

Juba could not reply, and she bowed her head.

"The oracle of the Umlimo is in three parts," Gandang went on, "and already the first has come to pass—the darkness at noon, the wings of the locust, and the trees bare of leaves in the springtime—it is happening and we must look to our steel."

"The white men have broken the assegais."

"In the hills there has been a new birthing of steel. The forges of the Rozwi smiths burn day and night."

Juba stared at him. "Who has done this?"

"Bazo, your own son," Gandang whispered proudly. "And the impis are preparing in secret, relearning the skills which they have not yet forgotten."

"Gandang, I feel my heart beginning to break again. Must there always be war?"

"You are a daughter of Matabele, Juba—do you need to ask that question? There will be work for you when the prophecy of the Umlimo comes to full term. The women must carry the blades. They will be bound up in bundles of thatching grass, and carried on their heads to where the impis are waiting. The white men and their kanka will not suspect the women. It will be your duty to assemble the young women and to see them place the steel in the hands of the warriors at the time that the Umlimo has foreseen—the time when the hornless cattle are eaten up by the cross."

Then Juba lifted her head and looked deeply into Gandang's dark fierce eyes. "Forgive me, Lord. This time I cannot obey you. I cannot help to bring fresh sorrow upon the land. You must find another to carry the bloody steel."

She had expected anger, but she saw in his eyes something that had never been there before—contempt. Gandang stood up without another word and stalked away towards the river, and she wanted to run after him and throw herself at his feet, but then she remembered the words of Nomusa. "He is a gentle God, but the way He sets for us is hard beyond the telling of it."

Juba found she was trapped between two worlds and two duties—and she felt as though it was tearing her soul down the middle.

It was with relief that at last she looked up and saw her two attendants kneeling before her. She did not know how long they had been there, so rapt had she been in her sorrow and confusion.

"I see you, Kampu," she said, nodding at the girls. "And you too, Imbali—my little flower. What is it that makes you look so sad?"

"The men have gone into the hills," whispered Kampu.

"And your hearts have gone with them." Juba smiled at the two young women and they giggled and squirmed with embarrassment. How firm and nubile was their young flesh, how eager were their great dark eyes, how vast their hunger for all that life had to offer. Juba smiled again and clapped her hands.

"Be gone," she said. "Away with you. There are those that need you more than I do. Follow your men into the hills."

The girls squealed with delight, and throwing aside all ceremony, they embraced Juba joyously. "You are the sunshine and the moon," they told her.

Then they fled to their huts to prepare for the journey, and for a little while Juba's own sorrow was lightened. But at the fall of night when no young wife came to summon her to Gandang's hut, it returned in full strength, and she wept alone on her sleeping-mat until at last sleep overcame her.

FOR MANY SECONDS after waking, Juba believed that the screams of the women were all part of her nightmares. Then there was a crash as the door to the hut was broken open, rough men seized her and though she screamed and struggled, she was dragged naked into the open.

There were fifty of them there, all Matabele, but wearing a bizarre motley of traditional and European dress. Some wore patched moleskin breeches, and others tasselled fur aprons, and a few even sported hobnailed boots. All of them, however, were armed with a new repeating Winchester rifle, and wore a chain around the left arm above the elbow, which held a polished brass disc engraved with the words: "BSA Co. Police".

The sky was paling with the dawn and the police had piled fresh logs on the fire, so that Juba recognized the white man immediately: it was the cruel husband of Nomusa, and she shrank back instinctively into the crowd of wailing women before he could notice her. Mungo St. John was in a fury, bellowing at his sergeant, striding backwards and forwards beyond the fire, his single eye blazing.

"Enough!" A voice cut through the hubbub, and the tone and power of it commanded instant silence. "Let the women be."

Gandang stalked into the firelight. Though he wore only a short loin cloth, he was menacing as a prowling lion.

"What is it that you seek, white man, coming into my kraal like a thief in the night?"

St. John jerked up his chin and glared at Gandang. "You know what I come for. I want two hundred strong young men."

Gandang retreated immediately into the studied defensive obtuseness of Africa, which few Europeans know how to counter, and which infuriated a man like Mungo St. John. "Why do you want my young men?" Gandang asked. "They are content here."

The general's clenched fists shook with the effort of restraint.

"All men must work. It is the law of the white men."

"It is not the way of the Matabele," Gandang retorted. "The amadoda see no dignity nor great virtue in digging in the dirt."

Mungo St. John took a swift pace forward and slashed the riding whip into the induna's face.

Gandang blinked, but he neither flinched nor raised his hand to touch the shining welt that rose swiftly across his cheek. "My hands are empty now, white man," he said, in a whisper that was more penetrating than a bellow. "But they will not always be so." And he turned towards his hut.

"Gandang," Mungo St. John shouted after him. "Your men will work if I have to hunt them down and chain them like animals."

THE TWO GIRLS followed the path at a smooth swinging trot that did not unbalance the large bundles they carried upon their heads. In the bundles there were special gifts for their men, snuff and beads and lengths of calico that they had wheedled out of Nomusa's store at Khami Mission. They were both in high spirits, for they had passed out of the swathe of destruction left by the locust swarms, and the acacia forests were a golden yellow haze of spring bloom.

They skirted the base of a tall cliff, and without pausing to rest started up the natural steps of grey stone. Imbali was leading, and Kampu followed her closely into the angle where the path turned sharply between two huge boulders. Then Imbali stopped so abruptly that Kampu very nearly ran into her, and she hissed with alarm.

A man stood in the centre of the path. Although he was unmistakably a Matabele, the girls had never seen him before. On his arm sparkled a brass disc, and in his hand he carried a rifle.

Quickly Kampu glanced behind her. Another armed man had stepped out from the shaded angle of the boulder and cut off their retreat. The girls lowered the bundles from their heads and shrank closer to each other.

"Where are you going—pretty little kittens?" asked the kanka, smiling. His teeth were very white, but his smile never reached his eyes. "Lift your bundles, kittens, and lead us to the tomcats," he continued.

Kampu shook her head. "We go only to search for medicine roots. We do not understand what you want of us."

The kanka came closer. His hands were huge, and Kampu began to tremble as the thick and powerful fingers encircled her neck. "Take us to where the men are hiding," he demanded.

Kampu stared at him silently for a second, and then suddenly and explosively she spat into his face. "Kanka!" she hissed. "Traitor!"

The man never stopped smiling. "Watch the other," he told his companion, and he dragged Kampu off the path into the scrub. There was the sound of a blow, and the bushes heaved with their struggling.

The kanka guarding Imbali strained for a glimpse of what was happening, and with his attention so distracted, Imbali sidled quietly along the granite and then darted away. She had reached the angle of the pathway before the man turned and saw her. "Come back!" he shouted.

Imbali was fifty paces down the hillside, flying like a gazelle over the rough ground, driven by her terror. The man thumbed back the hammer of his Winchester, flung the butt to his shoulder and fired wildly. It was a fluke shot. The soft lead slug caught the girl in the small of the back, and she collapsed and rolled down the steep pathway, her limbs tumbling loosely.

The man slowly lowered the rifle. The other kanka had left Kampu, and they went down the path to where Imbali lay. Both of them stared at the dead girl.

"I did not mean it," the man said.

"We cannot let the other one go back to tell what has happened," his companion replied, and turned back up the pathway. The other man was still staring into Imbali's blank eyes when the second shot rang out, and as the echoes lapped away amongst the granite cliffs, the kanka stepped back onto the path.

"Now we must find a story for One-Bright-Eye—and for the indunas," he said quietly, and ejected the spent cartridge case from the breech.

THEY BROUGHT THE TWO GIRLS back to Gandang's kraal on the back of the police sergeant's grey horse.

The women were silent until the corpses were cut free, but as the bodies slid to the earth they began the haunting ululation of mourning, and their cries brought out gooseflesh down the arms of the sergeant. He kept his voice level as he spoke to Gandang.

"You have brought this sadness on your people, old man. If you had obeyed the wishes of Lodzi and sent in your young men, these women would have lived to bear sons."

"What crime did they commit?" Gandang asked, and watched Juba come forward to kneel beside the bloody dust-smeared bodies.

"They tried to kill two of my police—"

"Hau!" Gandang expressed his scornful disbelief, and for a long moment he stared at the sergeant with terrible eyes. "Look well at them, white man's jackal, remember this for all the days that are left to you."

"Dare you threaten me, old man?" the sergeant blustered.

"All men must die." Gandang shrugged. "But some die sooner and more painfully than others." And he turned and walked away.

GANDANG SAT ALONE in his hut, listening to the wailing of the women. He knew that Juba would come to tell him when the girls' bodies had been bathed and wrapped in ox skin, so he was not surprised when there was a soft scratching at the doorway.

Juba came to kneel at his side. "All is ready for the mourning, my husband."

He nodded, and they were silent for a while, and then Juba said, "I wish to sing the Christian song that Nomusa has taught me when the girls are put down into the earth. I wish also to place crosses over them."

"If that is the way of your new god," he agreed, and Gandang rose to his feet.

"Nkosi." Juba remained kneeling. "Lord, there is something else."

"What is it?" He looked back at her, remote and cold.

"I, and my women, will carry the steel as you bid me," she whispered. "I made an oath with my finger in the wound in Kampu's flesh. I will carry the assegais to the amadoda."

He did not smile, but the coldness went out of his eyes, and he held out one hand to her.

BAZO CAME DOWN out of the hills three days after the girls had been placed in the earth. There were two young men with him, and the three of them went directly to the graves with Juba guiding them. After a while, Bazo left the two young bridegrooms to mourn their women and he went back to where his father waited for him.

"It is a terrible thing," sighed Gandang.

Bazo looked up sharply. "Rejoice, my father," he said. "They have given us a bargain greater than we could ever have wished. For two lives—of no importance—we have kindled a fire in the belly of the nation. We have steeled even the most cowardly of our amadoda. Now when the time comes, there will be no hesitating."

"You have become a ruthless man." Gandang stared at his son.

"I am proud that you should find me so," Bazo replied.

"You do not trust the oracle of the Umlimo?" Gandang demanded. "She has promised us success."

"No, my father." Bazo shook his head. "She has told us only to make the attempt. She promised us nothing—it is with us alone to succeed or fail. That is why we must be hard, trusting nobody."

Gandang thought about that for a while, then sighed again. "Tell me what else there is to be done."

"You must order the young men to come down out of the hills and to go in to work as the white men are bidding. We must live under the white men's cloak like fleas, so close that he forgets we are there waiting to bite."

Gandang nodded at the sense of it, but there was a fathomless regret in his eyes. "I loved it better when we went out singing the praise song of the regiment, when we made our killing in the sunlight with our plumes flying—"

"Never again, Baba," Bazo told him. "In the future we will wait in the grass like the coiled puff-adder. We may have to wait a year or a lifetime—perhaps it will be our children's children who strike from the shadows. But it is you and I that will open the road for them to follow, the road back to greatness."

Gandang nodded, and there was a new light in his eyes. "You see very clearly, Bazo, and you are right. The white man is strong in every way except patience. We know how to wait."

ALL THE WINDOWS of the mule coach were open and the shutters were lowered so that Rhodes could converse freely with the men who rode in close attendance upon each side. They were the

67

aristocracy of this new land, only a dozen or so of them, who between them owned vast tracts of fertile country, sprawling herds of cattle, blocks of mineral claims beneath which lay dreams of wealth uncountable; and the man in the luxurious carriage was their head.

A private citizen, Mr. Cecil Rhodes enjoyed such wealth and power as was usually only commanded by kings. His company owned a land larger than the British Isles, he controlled the world production of diamonds through a powerful cartel, and he owned outright the mines that produced ninety-five per cent of those diamonds. His fortune was such that when, on a whim, he decided to pioneer the farming of deciduous fruit in Southern Africa, he had bought the entire Franschhoek valley for a million pounds. He was a privy councillor to the queen, and could speak directly to the men who steered the greatest empire the world had ever known. Added to all this, he was the elected prime minister of Cape Colony, sure of the vote of every English-speaking citizen and sure of most of the Dutch-speaking votes as well. Lolling on the green leather seat of his coach, dressed untidily in a rumpled high-buttoned suit, he was at the very zenith of his wealth and power and influence.

Now he raised his voice, calling in a high, almost petulant, tone. "Ballantyne," and Zouga Ballantyne spurred his horse up beside the window and leaned attentively from the saddle. Ralph Ballantyne, riding in the bunch, watched them talk with such interest that he neglected the lady riding beside him, until she tapped him on the forearm with her crop.

"I said, it will be interesting to see what happens when we reach Khami," Louise repeated, and Ralph's attention jerked back to his stepmother. She rode astride, the only woman he knew that did so, and though she wore ankle-length, divided skirts, her seat was elegant and sure. "Why on earth does Mr. Rhodes insist on going to the wedding?" Louise went on. "He must know what to expect from your mother-in-law."

"Well, firstly, he owns the land the Mission is built upon, and, secondly, he probably feels that the ladies of Khami Mission are depriving him of a valued possession." Ralph lifted his chin to indicate the bridegroom who rode a little ahead of the group. Harry Mellow had a flower in his buttonhole, and a grin upon his lips. "You know he fired him as soon as he realized he couldn't talk him out of it."

"Poor Harry—poor Vicky, what will they do?"

"Oh, it's all arranged." Ralph beamed.

"You?" she hazarded. "I should have known. In fact it would not surprise me to learn that you engineered the whole business!"

Ralph laughed and looked ahead, and his expression changed, like a gundog scenting the pheasant. The wedding party had ridden out past the last shanties of Bulawayo onto the broad rutted wagon road. Coming towards them was a convoy of transport wagons, so strung out that the furthest of them were marked only by columns of fine white dust rising above the flat-topped acacia trees. On the nearest wagon-tent the company name was already visible, RHOLANDS, the shortened form of "Rhodesian Lands and Mining Co." which Ralph had chosen as the umbrella for his multitudinous activities.

"Damn me," Ralph exclaimed happily. "Old Isazi has brought them in five days ahead of schedule. That little black devil is a miracle." He tipped his hat in apology to Louise. "Business calls. Excuse me, please." And he galloped ahead, swinging off his horse as he came level with the lead wagon, and embracing the diminutive figure who skipped at the flank of the bullock team brandishing a 30-foot-long trek whip.

"What kept you so long, Isazi?" Ralph demanded. "Did you meet a pretty Matabele girl on the road?"

The little Zulu driver grinned puckishly. "No, Little Hawk, I did not want to rob you of too much bonus money by bringing them in more than five days ahead." This was a gentle reminder of what Isazi expected in his next pay packet.

"There was never a driver like you, Isazi, and there probably never will be again."

"Hau, Henshaw, so I have taught you something—even if only to recognize true greatness." Isazi chuckled, and put the long lash up into the air with a report like a shot of cannon.

Ralph mounted and backed his horse off the road and watched his laden wagons trundle by. There was three thousand pounds of profit in that single convoy for him, and he had two hundred wagons, plying back and forth across the vast subcontinent. He shook his head in awe as he remembered the single elderly eighteen-footer that he and Isazi had driven out of Kimberley not so many years ago, purchased with borrowed money, and laden with goods that he did not own. "A long road and a hard one," he said aloud, as he kicked his horse into a gallop in pursuit of the wedding party.

It was almost an hour later that the mules hauled the coach up the steep track to Khami Station, and paused to blow on the level neck of ground high above the whitewashed church and its attendant buildings.

It seemed as though an army was encamped in the valley.

Jordan Ballantyne jumped down from the coach, shrugging off the cotton dustcoat that had protected his beautiful dove-grey suit, and crossed to his brother.

"What on earth is going on, Ralph?" he demanded.

"Robyn has invited half the Matabele nation to the wedding and the other half invited themselves," Ralph smiled. "Some of them have trekked a hundred miles to be here, every patient she has ever treated, every Christian she ever converted—and they have all brought their families and friends."

"But who is going to feed them all?"

"I sent Robyn a gift of fifty bullocks. Then they say that Gandang's wife, old fat Juba, has brewed a thousand gallons of her famous beer." Ralph punched his brother's arm affectionately. "Which reminds me that I have worked up a fair old thirst myself."

The road was lined on both sides with hundreds of singing maidens, all of them decked with beads and flowers, their skin anointed with fat so that it shone like cast bronze in the sunlight. "By God, Jordan, have you ever seen such a fine display," Ralph teased his brother, well aware of his prudish attitude to women, and Jordan blushed as the girls crowded about the carriage.

"Lodzi!" one of the girls called, and her cry was taken up by the others. "Lodzi! Lodzi!"

Then they recognized Zouga. "Come in peace, the Fist," they cried, and then to Ralph, "We see you, Little Hawk."

Zouga lifted his hat and waved it over his head. "By God," he murmured to Louise, "I wish the damned Aborigine Protection Society could be here to see this. They are happy and secure as they never were under Lobengula's bloody rule."

Ralph was looking over the girls' heads, noticing that there were very few men in the crowd, and a face caught Ralph's attention, a single solemn face amongst all the smiles.

"Bazo!" Ralph called and waved, and the young induna looked at him steadily, without smiling. "We will talk later," Ralph shouted, and then he was past, swept along by the throng.

When they reached the lawns the dancing black girls fell back, for by unspoken accord the lawns were reserved for the white guests. There were a hundred or so gathered below the wide thatched veranda. Cathy was there, slender and cool in a dress of yellow muslin with a flowered straw hat upon her dark head. Jonathan let out a shriek when he saw Ralph, and Cathy held his hand firmly as she led him through the crowd that surged forward to welcome the bridegroom. Then she froze and the colour drained from her face as Rhodes's bulk appeared in the doorway of the carriage.

"Ralph," she blurted, clinging to his arm. "What's he doing here?"

As she spoke Robyn St. John, drawn by the commotion, came out onto the stoep of the homestead. Her face was radiant with a smile of welcome for her latest guests, but the smile shrivelled when she recognized the man in the carriage and her face turned icy pale.

"Mr. Rhodes," she said clearly in the silence. "I am delighted that you have come to Khami Mission, because it gives me an opportunity to order you not to set a foot over my threshold."

Rhodes bowed. "Let us grant that your jurisdiction reaches that far," he agreed. "But this side of that threshold, the ground on which I stand belongs to the BSA Company of which I am chairman, and I should like to raise a glass to the happiness of the young couple."

"I assure you, Mr. Rhodes, that you will not be served refreshment at Khami," said Robyn hotly.

Rhodes nodded at Jordan, and he hurried back to the mule coach. In a flurry of activity camp chairs and tables were unpacked and as Rhodes and his party settled themselves, Jordan fired the cork from the first bottle of champagne and spilled a frothy deluge into crystal glasses. Huge golden Cornish pasties were served to whoever wanted them, and soon the veranda which had been crowded with guests was deserted, and around Rhodes there was a jovial throng.

"We will start cooking the sausage," Robyn told Juba furiously. "Get your girls busy. I'll back my sausage against Jordan Ballantyne's pasties to bring 'em back."

"And I'll put my money on Mr. Rhodes's champagne to keep 'em there," Ralph told her. "Can you match it?"

"I haven't a drop, Ralph," Robyn admitted.

With a single glance, Ralph caught the eye of one of the younger guests on the lawn, the manager of Ralph's General Dealer's shop in

Bulawayo. He hurried up to Ralph's side, listened intently to his instructions for a few seconds, and then ran to his horse.

"Where did you send him?" Robyn demanded.

"A convoy of my wagons arrived today. We'll have a wagon full of bubbly out here within a few hours."

"I'll never be able to repay you for this, Ralph." Robyn gave him a light kiss on the lips, before hurrying back to her kitchen.

RALPH'S WAGON hove over the hill at a dramatic moment. Jordan was down to his last bottle of champagne and the crowd had already begun to drift away. Isazi brought the wagon to a halt below the veranda, and like a conjuror drew back the canvas hood to reveal the contents. The crowd flocked away to leave Rhodes sitting alone beside his fancy coach.

By now copious draughts of warm champagne had made the men boisterous and the women sentimental, so a thunderous acclaim greeted the bride when she at last made her appearance on the Mission veranda. On her brother-in-law's arm, and attended by her twin sister, Victoria made her way across the lawn to the little Mission church. She was pretty enough to begin with, with her green eyes shining, but when she returned on the arm of her new husband, she was truly beautiful.

"All right," Ralph announced. "It's all legal—now the party can truly begin." And he signalled to the band.

By dawn of the following day, the party had started to warm up. The bride and bridegroom, reluctant to miss a moment of the fun, had not yet left on their honeymoon and were leading the dancing under the spathodea trees.

Rhodes, who had rested during the night in the mule coach, now emerged and, after a hearty breakfast, was moved to oratory. "My Rhodesians," he began—and his audience took it as an endearment rather than a claim to ownership, and loved him for it "—together you and I have made a great leap forward towards the day when the map of Africa will be painted pink from Cape Town to Cairo—when this fair continent will be set beside India, a great diamond beside a lustrous ruby, in the crown of our beloved Queen—" And they all cheered him, the Americans and Greeks and Italians and Irish, as loudly as the subjects of the "beloved Queen" herself.

"The Lord save us from jingoism!" Ralph groaned, and he wandered away down the valley carrying a bottle of champagne in one hand, and with his son perched upon his shoulder. Jonathan wore a sailor suit with a straw boater on his head, and he clicked and urged his father on with his heels as though he were astride a pony.

There were fifty head of slaughtered oxen and a thousand gallon pots of Juba's beer to account for down here, and the black wedding guests were giving the task their dedicated attention. The dancing was even more energetic than that under the spathodea trees, the young men leaping and twisting and stamping as the girls swayed and shuffled, and the drummers hammered out their frenetic rhythms.

Ralph sat Jonathan on the fence of the cattle kraal, and strode into the centre and sat himself in the heroic posture of the Niguni dancers. Bazo had taught him well when they were boys together, and now he raised his right knee high and brought his booted foot down on the hard earth with a crash, and the other dancers hummed in approbation. Ralph leaped and stamped and postured, and the women clapped and sang, and on the kraal fence Jonathan howled with excitement and pride.

His chest heaving, chuckling breathlessly, Ralph dropped out at last and lifted Jonathan back onto his shoulder. The two of them went on, accepting morsels of roast beef or a swallow of tart beer, until at last, standing aloof from the revellers, Ralph found the man he was seeking.

"I see you, Bazo," he said. He sat down and passed Bazo one of the cheroots for which they had both developed a taste so long ago. They smoked in silence, watching the feasting until Jonathan grew restless and edged away to seek more exciting occupation.

He was immediately confronted by a child a year or so younger than he was. Tungata, son of Bazo and great-grandson of great Mzilikazi, was stark naked except for the string of bright beads around his sturdy hips. His face was round and glossy, his eyes huge and solemn as he examined Jonathan with total fascination.

"What is your son's name?" Bazo asked, watching the child return Tungata's scrutiny with equal candour.

"Jonathan."

"What is the meaning of that name?"

"The Gift of God," Ralph told him.

Jonathan suddenly took the straw hat from his own head and placed it upon that of the Matabele princeling. It made such an incongruous picture that both men smiled involuntarily. Tungata gurgled with glee, seized Jonathan's hand and dragged him unprotestingly away.

The moment thawed the stiffness between the two men, and fleetingly they recaptured the rapport of their young manhood as they passed the champagne bottle back and forth. When it was empty, Bazo clapped his hands and Tanase came dutifully with a clay pot of bubbling brew, withdrawing as silently as she had come.

At noon she returned to where the two men were still deep in conversation, leading the two children by the hand. Ralph started violently when he saw his son. The child's beatific grin was almost masked by layers of grime and beef fat. The collar of his sailor suit hung by a thread, the knees were worn through, and he was covered with ash and mud.

"Oh my God," Ralph groaned, "your mother will strangle us both." He picked up his son gingerly. "I leave tomorrow to hunt buffalo. When will I see you again, old friend?" he asked Bazo.

"Tomorrow," Bazo replied softly. "I told you I would work for you again when I was ready. I am ready now."

VICTORIA HAD BEEN amazingly gracious in her acceptance of Harry's honeymoon arrangements.

"Ralph has this idea," Harry Mellow had explained shamefacedly. "He wants to follow up an African legend, at a place called Wankie's country, near the falls that Dr. Livingstone discovered on the Zambezi. I know how you looked forward to Cape Town, but—"

Vicky had simply taken Harry's hand. "Wherever thou goest, my love, Wankie's country, Cape Town or the North Pole—just as long as we are together."

The expedition was conducted in Ralph Ballantyne's usual style, with six wagons and forty Matabele to convey the two families northwards towards the great Zambezi River.

The weather was mild and the pace leisurely. The country teemed with wild game, the newlyweds were infectiously loving. They reached Wankie's country on the twenty-second day, and for the first time since leaving Bulawayo, the idyllic mood of the caravan bumped back to earth.

Under the reign of King Lobengula, Wankie had been a renegade and outlaw, but now he had brazenly set himself up as chieftain of the land between the Zambezi and the Gwaai Rivers, demanding tribute of those who came to trade or hunt. He was a handsome man in his middle age, with the air of the chief he claimed to be, and he accepted the gift of blankets and beads that Ralph presented to him with no effusive gratitude. Like a crocodile at the drinking place, he waited for Ralph to come to the real purpose of his visit.

"The stones that burn?" he repeated vaguely, his eyes hooded as he pondered, and then quite artlessly he remarked that he had always wanted a wagon. Lobengula had owned a wagon, and Wankie believed that every great chief should have one. He turned on his stool and glanced pointedly at Ralph's six magnificent Cape-built eighteen-footers outspanned in the glade below the kraal.

"That damned rogue has the cheek of a white man," Ralph protested later to Harry Mellow across the campfire. "A wagon, no less. Three hundred pounds of any man's money."

"But, darling, if Wankie can guide you, won't it be a bargain price?" Cathy asked mildly.

There was a discreet cough behind them. Bazo had come silently from the other fire, where the drivers and servants were bivouacked.

"Henshaw." Bazo spoke reproachfully to Ralph. "You told me that we had come here to hunt buffalo. Did you not trust me?"

"Bazo, you are my brother. But if I had spoken of the stones that burn in Bulawayo we would have had a hundred wagons following us when we left town."

"Did I not tell you that once I led my impi over these hills. If you had spoken to me—you would not have had to waste your time parleying with this unsavoury jackal."

Ralph stood up and seized Bazo's shoulders. "Bazo, can you lead us there? Can you take us to the stones that burn?"

Bazo nodded. "And it will not cost you a wagon," he replied.

They rode into a red and smoky dawn through the open glades in the forest. Ahead of them the buffalo herds opened to give them passage and closed behind them as they passed. The huge black beasts held their wet muzzles high, the massive bosses of horn giving them a ponderous dignity, and they stared in stolid astonishment as the horsemen passed.

The riders barely glanced at them, their attention fastened instead on Bazo's broad bullet-scarred back as he led them at an easy trot towards a low line of flat-topped hills. On the first slope they tethered the horses and climbed on foot, while above them an old baboon barked his challenge down at them. Though they ran at the slope, they could not keep up with Bazo, and he was waiting for them on a ledge under a cliff rising sheer to the summit. He made no dramatic announcement, but merely pointed with his chin. Ralph and Harry stared, unable to speak.

There was a horizontal seam, twenty foot thick, sandwiched in the cliff face. It ran along the cliff as far as they could see in each direction, black as night and yet glittering with a strange greenish iridescence in the slanted rays of the early sun.

"This was the only thing we lacked in this land," Ralph said quietly. "Coal to power the nation. Now we have it all."

Harry Mellow went forward and laid his hand upon it reverently. "I have never seen coal of this quality in a seam so deep—not even in the Kentucky hills." Suddenly he snatched his hat off his head and with a wild whoop threw it far out down the slope. "We are rich!" he shouted. "Rich! Rich!"

"Better than working for Mr. Rhodes?" Ralph asked, and Harry grabbed his shoulders and the two of them spun together in a yelling, stomping dance of jubilation on the narrow ledge, while Bazo leaned against the seam of black coal and watched them unsmilingly.

It took them two weeks to survey and peg their claims. Harry shot the lines with his theodolite, and Bazo and Ralph worked behind him with a gang of axemen driving in the pegs. On the fifteenth day they traipsed back to camp at the head of their bone-weary gang of Matabele.

Victoria, deprived of her new husband for two weeks, was as forlorn as a young widow, but at dinner the sparkle was back in her eyes as she hovered over Harry Mellow, replenishing his glass and heaping his plate with smoked warthog and scrambled ostrich egg.

Sitting at the head of the table, Ralph called to Cathy, "Break out a bottle of champagne, Katie my sweeting, we have something to celebrate," and he saluted them with a brimming glass. "I give you a toast to the gold of the Harkness Mine and the coal of the Wankie Field—and to the riches of both!"

They laughed and clinked their glasses and drank the toast.

"Let's stay here for ever," said Vicky. "I'm so happy. I don't want it to end."

"We'll stay a little longer," Ralph agreed, with his arm about Cathy's waist. "I told Dr. Jim we were coming up here to hunt buffalo. If we don't bring a few wagon-loads of hides back with us, the little doctor is going to start wondering."

"Ralph," Cathy sighed, "do you have to kill so many? If we go on killing like this—how long will it last?"

Ralph was startled. "What on earth are you talking about, girl?"

"When the animals are all gone, this will no longer be the land I know and love."

"Gone?" He shook his head in sympathy, as though for an idiot child. "Gone? By God, Katie, you saw the herds out there. They are countless, limitless. We could hunt every day and not scratch the surface. No, Katie, they will never go."

If anything, Ralph Ballantyne's estimate of the buffalo herds was conservative. Probably no large mammal had ever been so prolifically massed upon the earth's face in all of its history. From the infant Nile, southwards over the wide savannahs of eastern and central Africa, down to the Zambezi and beyond, the vast black herds roamed. They were very seldom hunted by the primitive tribes, being too swift and powerful for the bows and spears. The Arabs were not interested in such coarse game, and few Europeans had yet ventured into these remote lands. Even the huge prides of lion which followed the herds could not check their natural multiplication. Some herds, twenty or thirty thousand strong, were so dense that the animals in the rear literally starved, for the pasturage was destroyed before they could reach it. Weakened by their own vast multitudes, they were now ripe for pestilence.

The pestilence came out of Egypt, the same plague that Jehovah had inflicted on the Pharaoh of Egypt. It was the *Peste bovine*, the rinderpest, a viral disease which attacks all ruminants, but most particularly buffalo and domestic cattle. The stricken animals are blinded and choked by the profuse discharge from the mucous membranes. The discharge is highly infectious, and it persists on the pasturage over which the animal has passed long after its host has perished.

The course of the disease is rapid and irreversible. The mucous discharges are swiftly followed by diarrhoea, and when at last the animal goes down and no longer has the strength to rise, convulsions twist the horned head back and around, until in death the nose touches the flank.

The rinderpest passed with the speed of a gale wind across the continent, so that in places where the concentrations of buffalo were heaviest, a herd of ten thousand was wiped out in a single day. The carcasses lay so thickly on the denuded savannah that they were touching each other, and even the teeming flocks of vultures and packs of hyena could not devour the awful feast.

This gale of disease and death blew southwards, swallowing up the herds—until at last it reached the Zambezi. Even that wide stretch of swirling green water could not check the pestilence. It was carried to the far bank in the bulging crops of the vultures and carrion storks, and was scattered upon the pasture in the droppings that they voided in flight.

The dreadful gale had begun again, moving ever southwards.

ISAZI, THE LITTLE Zulu driver, was always the first awake in the laager. It gave him satisfaction to be alert and aware when others half his age still slept. Though it was still dark, he left his mat and wandered down to where the oxen were penned.

Isazi loved his bullocks as some men love their dogs. He knew their separate natures, their strengths and their weaknesses, those with great hearts and special intelligence. Of course, he had his favourites, like Dutchman, the black and white dappled lead ox that he had trained to come like a dog to his whistle and lead the others to their place in the span.

Isazi chuckled lovingly as he opened the thornbush gate of the temporary kraal and whistled for Dutchman. A beast coughed in the gloom. The sound struck a chill into Isazi's guts: a healthy bullock did not cough that way. He stood in the opening of the kraal, hesitating to go in. He had to force himself to go forward.

"Dutchman," he called. "Where are you, my beauty?" Then he recognized the bulky dappled shape. The bullock was lying down.

Isazi ran to it. "Up," he called. "Get up, my darling!" For a beast only lies down when it has given up hope.

The bullock heaved convulsively, but did not come to its feet. Isazi dropped to his knees. The neck was twisted back at an awkward unnatural angle, the velvety muzzle pressed into the flank. The muscles under the skin were convulsed as rigidly as cast iron.

Isazi ran his hands down the beast's neck, feeling the fierce heat of fever. He touched the cheek, and it was slick and wet. Isazi lifted his hand to his own nose. It was coated with a thick slime and the little Zulu gagged at the smell of it.

He scrambled to his feet, and backed away fearfully until he reached the gate. Then he whirled and ran to the wagons.

"Henshaw," he yelled wildly, "come quickly!"

"FLAME LILIES," Ralph Ballantyne growled, his face congested with blood as he strode angrily through the kraal. "Where are those bloody herdboys?" He stopped beside the twisted carcass of Dutchman, a trained wheeler worth £50. It was not the only dead ox. Eight others were down and as many more were sickening.

Isazi and the other drivers dragged in the herders.

"Haven't you ever heard of flame lilies?" Ralph shouted at the terrified children. "It's your job to watch for poison plants and keep the oxen off them. I'm going to thrash the skin off your black backsides to teach you."

"We saw no lilies," the eldest boy declared stoutly, and the others agreed, screaming at the cut of Ralph's whip as he laid it about him.

"Get the healthy animals into the span," shouted Ralph.

All thoughts of the buffalo hunt were now forgotten, and Ralph was forced to abandon half of the wagons before they trekked on southwards. Within an hour another ox had fallen in the traces, with its nose twisted back. They cut it loose and left it lying beside the track. Half a mile farther two more bullocks went down.

Then they began dropping so regularly that by noon Ralph was forced to abandon two more wagons. It was now clear to him that this was no ordinary case of veld poisoning. None of his drivers had seen anything to equal it. There was no precedent in the whole vast body of African folklore.

"It is a tagathi." Isazi gave his opinion mournfully—witchcraft.

"By God, Harry." Ralph led his new brother-in-law out of earshot of the women. "We'll be lucky to get even the one wagon home. We had better ride ahead and try to pick an easier crossing on the Lupane River."

Ralph and Harry rode side by side, both of them worried and anxious. They came out onto an open glade beside the river, and Ralph suddenly sat up very straight in the saddle. Moving in single file across the vlei were three huge dappled giraffe, the old bull leading a cow and a half-grown calf. The calf was swaying, turning in slow and elegant pirouettes, the neck twisting to one side and then to the other. Then, quite slowly, with a kind of weary grace, the calf slumped to the grass, and lay in a tangle of long limbs. The mother hovered anxiously for a minute or two, and then in the way of the wilderness, deserted the weak and went on after her mate.

Ralph and Harry rode up, almost reluctantly, to where the calf lay. Only when they reached it did they notice the fatal mucous

discharge. "That smell—the same as the oxen." Ralph
started, and suddenly realization dawned upon him. "A
murrain," he whispered. "Harry, it's some kind of plague, wiping out
everything." Under his deep tan, Ralph had turned a muddy colour.
"Two hundred wagons, Harry," he whispered, "almost four thousand
bullocks. I'm going to lose them all." He reeled in the saddle so that
he had to clutch at the pommel for his balance. "I'll be wiped out."

Then he whirled to face Harry. "I'm not finished yet, not without
a fight anyway. You'll have to bring the women back to Bulawayo
alone. I'm taking the four best horses."

"Where are you going?" Harry asked.

"Kimberley." Ralph had pivoted his horse like a polo pony, and was racing back towards the single wagon that had just come out of the forest behind them. Even as he reached it, one of the lead oxen collapsed and lay convulsed in the traces.

ISAZI DID NOT GO to the kraal the following dawn. He was afraid of what he would find. Bazo went in his place.

They were all dead. Every single bullock. They were already stiff and cold as statues, locked in that dreadful final convulsion.

Bazo shivered with superstitious awe. *When the cattle lie with their heads twisted to touch their flank, and cannot rise—*

"It is happening—just as the Umlimo prophesied."

He wanted to run from mine to farm, to where his comrades now laboured with pick and shovel instead of the silver blades, wearing their masters' ragged cast-offs rather than the plumes and kilts of the regiment. "Come, you diggers of other men's dirt," he wanted to say. "Come rehearse the war song of the Moles with me."

Then, with an effort, he masked his savage joy. It was not yet full term, there was still the third and final act of the Umlimo's prophecy to unfold, and until then Bazo, like his old comrades, must play the white man's servant.

RALPH BALLANTYNE STOPPED at King's Lynn, his father's estate. He threw the reins to Jan Cheroot, the old Hottentot hunter.

"Water them, old man, and fill the grain bags for me."

Then he ran up onto the veranda of the sprawling thatched homestead, and his stepmother came out to meet him. "Where is my father?" Ralph demanded, as he kissed her cheek, and Louise's delighted expression changed to match the gravity of his.

"In the north section. They are branding the calves."

"That's six hours' ride! I cannot spare the time to go to him." Ralph laid his hand on her arm. "There is some dreadful murrain sweeping down out of the north and killing everything. It hit my cattle on the Gwaai River, and we lost them all, over one hundred head in twelve hours—only the horses have not been touched yet."

"What must we do, Ralph?"

"Sell," he answered. "Sell all the cattle at any price, before it reaches us." He turned and shouted to Jan Cheroot. "Bring the notebook from my saddlebag."

He scribbled a note and gave it to Jan Cheroot. "Speak to nobody but my father. Tell nobody else of this thing. Go swiftly." And Ralph was up in the saddle and away before the little Hottentot was ready to rise.

Ralph circled Bulawayo to avoid meeting an acquaintance, and to reach the telegraph line well away from the main road. Ralph's own construction gangs had laid the telegraph line, so he knew every mile of it, and how most effectively to cut off Rhodesia from Kimberley and the rest of the world.

He tethered his horses at the foot of one of the telegraph poles and shinned up it to the cluster of porcelain insulators and the gleaming copper wires. He used a magnus hitch on a leather thong to hold the ends of the wire from falling to earth, and then cut between the knots. The wire parted with a singing twang, but the thong held, and when he climbed down to the horses and looked up, he knew that only a skilled linesman would detect the break.

He flung himself back into the saddle, and galloped towards the road. He changed horses every hour, and when it was too dark to see the tracks he knee-haltered the horses, and slept like a dead man on the hard ground. Before dawn, he ate a hunk of cheese and a slice of the rough bread Louise had put into his saddlebag, and was away again with the first softening of the eastern sky.

At midmorning, he cut the line in two more places and went on. The next day, fifty miles from the Shashi River, he met one of his own convoys coming up from the south. Ralph stopped only long enough to commandeer the overseer's horses and leave his own exhausted animals with him. He cut the telegraph lines twice more, on either side of the Shashi River, before he reached the railhead.

He came upon his surveyor first, a red-haired Scot working with a gang of blacks five miles ahead of the main crews.

"Did you get the telegraph I sent you from Bulawayo, Mac? I wanted you to hold a truck for me."

"Nowt, Mr. Ballantyne." The Scot shook his dusty curls. "Not a word from the north in days—they say the lines are down—but if you hurry, sir, there's a string of trucks going back today."

Five miles farther on Ralph reached the railhead. A green locomotive huffed columns of silver steam high into the empty sky, shunting the string of flat-topped bogies to the end of the glistening silver rails. Teams of singing black men levered the steel rails over the side of the tracks and as they fell in a cloud of pale dust, another team ran forward to lift and set the tracks onto the teak sleepers.

The boil of activity seemed incongruous in this bleak, desolate land on the edge of the Kalahari Desert.

Half a mile back was the construction headquarters, a box of wood and corrugated iron that could be moved up each day. Inside, the chief engineer was in his shirt sleeves, sweating over a desk made of condensed-milk cases. He jumped up nervously when Ralph entered. "Mr. Ballantyne, sir, we didn't expect you."

"Is the line to Kimberley open?"

"Yes, Mr. Ballantyne."

"Good. Get your operator to send this—"

Ralph stooped over the message pad and scribbled quickly.

"For Aaron Fagan, Attorney at Law, De Beers Street, Kimberley. Arriving early tomorrow 6th. Arrange urgent noon meeting with Rough Rider from Rholand."

Rough Rider was the private code for Roelof Zeederberg, Ralph's chief rival in the transport business. While the telegraph operator tapped it out on the brass instrument, Ralph turned back to his engineer. "All right, what's your rate of progress?"

For an hour they worked and argued and planned, until the locomotive whistled outside the shack. Ralph tossed his saddlebag and blanket roll onto the first flat car, vaulted up onto the bogie and waved at the driver. The whistle sent a jet of steam, the locomotive wheels spun and gripped, and the long string of empty cars began to trundle southwards.

Ralph found a corner of the truck out of the wind, and rolled into his blanket. "We have got to hurry. We have got to hurry," the wheels sang. And then, just before he fell asleep, the song changed. "The cattle are dying. The cattle are dead." But even that could not keep him awake one second longer.

THEY PULLED INTO the shunting yards at Kimberley sixteen hours later, at four in the morning.

Ralph slung his saddlebags over his shoulder and trudged up the De Beers road. There was a light on in the telegraph office. Ralph beat on the wooden hatch until the night operator peered out at him.

"I want to send an urgent telegraph to Bulawayo."

"Sorry, mate. The line is down—has been for four days."

Ralph was still grinning as he swaggered into the lobby of Diamond Lil's Hotel.

84

The Blue Diamond Suite, permanently reserved for Mr. Ballantyne, had one of the very few bathrooms in Kimberley with laid-on hot water. Two black servants stoked the boiler outside the window while Ralph lay chin-deep in scalding water. His steamer trunk was removed from the box room, and valets pressed the suits and tried to improve upon the perfect shine of the boots that they unpacked from the trunk.

At five minutes before noon, Ralph marched into Aaron Fagan's office. Aaron was a thin stooped man, with threadbare hair brushed straight back from a deep intellectual forehead. His nose was beaked, his mouth full and sensitive and his sloe-eyes aware and bright. They embraced affectionately, but Roelof and Doel Zeederberg did not rise as Ralph entered, nor did they make any attempt to shake hands. They had clashed too viciously, on too many occasions.

"So, Ballantyne, you want to waste our time again?" Roelof's eyes were quick with interest.

"My dear Roelof," Ralph protested, "I would never do that. All I want is that we should resolve this tariff on the new Rhodesian route before we put each other out of business. One of us should really buy the other out, and set his own tariffs."

The brothers glanced at each other involuntarily—and then Roelof made a fuss of relighting his cigar to hide his astonishment.

"You are asking yourselves why I want to sell out?" Ralph went on. "The truth is this—I need cash for the Harkness Mine."

The Zeederbergs had heard about the mine: the talk on the Johannesburg stock-exchange floor was that it would cost fifty thousand pounds to bring it into production. The lines of tension around Roelof's mouth smoothed out. "You had a figure in mind?" he asked.

By the following noon Aaron Fagan had drawn up the contract. It was very simple. The purchasers accepted the statement of assets, and the responsibility of all goods at present in transit. The seller gave no guarantee. The purchase price was in cash, and the effective date was that of the signature.

They signed in the presence of their attorneys, and then both parties crossed the street to the main branch of the Dominion Colonial and Overseas Bank where the cheque of Zeederberg Bros. was presented and duly honoured by the manager. Ralph swept the bundles of five-pound notes into his carpetbag, and tipped his hat.

"Good luck to you, gentlemen," he said and sauntered away.

Roelof Zeederberg massaged the bald spot on his crown uneasily. "I have this strange feeling," he murmured.

THE OFFICE OF THE De Beers Consolidated Mines Company was a magnificent edifice, a temple dedicated to the worship of diamonds. The open balconies on all three floors were laced with white grilles of delicate ironwork, the walls were of red brick and worked stone blocks, and the windows were of stained glass.

Ralph signed his name in the visitors' book and went up to the top floor.

The brass plate on the teak door at the top of the spiral staircase said only "Mr. Jordan Ballantyne", with no title to accompany it, but the grandeur of the office within gave some indication of Jordan's importance. The double windows looked out over the Kimberley mine, an excavation of almost a mile across, which each day was driven deeper and deeper still, as the miners followed the fabulous core of blue Kimberlite conglomerate downwards. Already that hole had delivered up ten million carats of fine diamonds, and Rhodes owned it all.

Ralph spun his hat onto the stand and turned to face the cloakroom door as Jordan came through it. He was in his shirt sleeves, drying his hands on a monogrammed towel, but he threw the towel aside when he saw Ralph and crossed to him with a cry of delight.

"Always the dandy," Ralph teased him.

No amount of brotherly familiarity could dim the fact that Jordan was still one of the most handsome men that Ralph had ever met. He was more than handsome, he was beautiful—and his evident pleasure at seeing Ralph heightened the glow of his skin and the lively sparkle of his green eyes. "And you," he laughed, "you look so brown and lean. What happened to that prosperous paunch?"

"I left it on the road from Rhodesia."

"Rhodesia!" Jordan's expression changed. "Then you'll have heard the terrible news." Jordan hurried to the leather-topped desk. "This message came through today, the first for almost a week."

He handed Ralph the flimsy, and he scanned it swiftly—it was from General Mungo St. John.

"Outbreak of cattle disease reported in north. Losses sixty per cent repeat sixty per cent. Company veterinarian recognizes symptoms similar to *Peste bovine,* also known as rinderpest. No known treatment. Urgently request authority to destroy and burn all cattle in central province to prevent southward spread."

While he feigned astonishment and shock, Ralph ran his eye swiftly down the remaining text. It was a rare opportunity to read a decoded BSA Co. report; the fact that Jordan had handed it to him at all was a measure of his agitation. There were lists of police strengths and dispositions, of trading licences and mineral claims. Ralph passed the sheet back to his brother with a suitably solemn expression.

At the head of the roster of new mineral claims filed in Bulawayo he had seen a block of forty square miles registered in the name of the Wankie Coal Mining Company, and Ralph glowed with hidden satisfaction. Harry must have got the women and Jonathan safely back to Bulawayo, and wasted no time in filing their claims. They were not yet confirmed, but Ralph would have to worry about that later. Right now, he had to concentrate on Jordan's apprehensions.

"Papa is right in the path of this thing—this rinderpest. And you too, Ralph. How many bullock teams do you have there?"

"None. I've sold every last ox and wagon to the Zeederbergs."

Jordan stared at him. "When?"

"Yesterday."

"When did you leave Bulawayo, Ralph? The telegraph lines— they were cut, you know, deliberately. In five places."

"Extraordinary. Who would have done a thing like that?"

"I don't even dare to ask." Jordan shook his head. "And on second thoughts, I don't want to know when you left Bulawayo, or whether or not Papa sold his stock as suddenly as you did yours."

"Come on, Jordan, I'll take you to dinner at the club. A bottle of bubbly will console you for belonging to a family of rogues—and for working for another."

UNTIL A MAN had become a member of the Kimberley Club, he could not consider himself truly to have arrived in South Africa. Ralph and Jordan's own memberships had been assured as soon as they came of age, for not only was their father a founder member, but he was also a holder of the Queen's Commission and a gentleman. These things counted at the Kimberley Club ahead of vulgar wealth.

The porter greeted the brothers by name, and put their cards up on the "in" board while the barman poured their drinks. In the dining room they both ordered from the carving trolley, juicy young lamb, served with parsleyed new potatoes.

Jordan declined the champagne that Ralph suggested. "I am a working man," he smiled. "My tastes are simpler than yours; something like Château Margaux '73 would suit me better."

"By God!" said Ralph. The vintage claret cost four times more than any champagne on the wine list. "Under that urbane veneer you are a true Ballantyne, after all."

They ate in contented silence for a few minutes, and then Ralph picked up his glass. "What does Mr. Rhodes think of the coal deposits that Harry and I pegged?" he asked mildly, carefully watching his brother's reaction. He saw the corners of Jordan's mouth quiver with surprise.

"Coal?"

"Yes, coal!" Ralph agreed. "Harry Mellow and I pegged a huge deposit of high-grade coal in the north. You must know about it, Jordan."

"What a fine wine this is." Jordan inhaled the bouquet. "A big, spicy perfume." Ralph stared at him, but Jordan would not look up.

"You know I can't say anything," Jordan whispered at last. "You would do better to consult our lawyers." He took the gold hunter from his fob pocket. "I should be getting back. Mr. Rhodes and I are leaving for London at noon tomorrow. There is a great deal to do before we go."

Ralph's jaw hardened as Jordan got up to leave. He knew his brother was hiding something. His eyes were cold as emeralds as he stubbed out his half-smoked cigar and strode out of the club.

"THESE GENTLEMEN are the legal advisers to the British South Africa Company." Aaron Fagan introduced individually to Ralph the men whom he privately referred to as the "wolf pack".

They did not look particularly lupine, the four soberly dressed men whose ages ranged from late thirties to mid-fifties. Each of them placed his pigskin folder of papers neatly in front of him, and then they looked up in unison from the long table. It was only then that Ralph recognized the wolf-like glitter in their eyes.

"In what way can we be of assistance?"

"My client is seeking clarification of the mining laws promulgated by the BSA Company," Aaron replied.

Two hours later Ralph was groping desperately through a maze of jargon and convoluted legal sideroads as he tried to follow the discussion. He sank lower and lower in his chair, placed his feet on the polished table and scowled at the lawyers opposite him, until Aaron Fagan asked: "Does that mean that in your opinion my client has not fulfilled the requirements of Section 27B Clause Five read in conjunction with Section 7 Bis?"

"Well, Mr. Fagan, we would first have to examine the question of due performance as set out in Section 31," replied the pack leader carefully. "In terms of that section—"

Ralph brought his boots down off the table with a crash. "I may not know the difference between one section and another," he announced violently, "but I do know a wagon-load of horse manure when I see one. And this, gentlemen, is grade-one horse manure."

"Mr. Ballantyne," one of the younger assistants protested. "Your insinuation—"

"It is not an insinuation." Ralph rounded on him. "I am telling you outright that you are a bunch of bandits. Is that still not clear? I want to speak to the head bandit. Where is Mr. Rhodes?"

At that moment a locomotive down in the shunting yards whistled. The sound only just carried in the silence which followed Ralph's question, and Ralph remembered Jordan's excuse for ending lunch the previous day.

"Aaron," Ralph demanded, "what time is it?"

"Eight minutes of noon."

"He was fobbing me off—the cunning bastard!"

Ralph whirled and ran from the room.

There were half a dozen horses at the hitching rack outside the De Beers building. Without checking his speed, Ralph decided on a big strong-looking bay and ran to it, ignoring the janitor's shouts as he vaulted to the saddle. It had been a good choice. The bay galloped strongly down the road towards the railway.

Rhodes's private train was already crossing the points at the southern end of the yards and running out into the open country. The signal arm was down and the lights were green and the locomotive, hauling four coaches, was picking up speed swiftly.

"Come, boy." Ralph encouraged the bay, swinging it towards the barbed-wire fence beside the track. The horse steadied himself, pricking his ears forward as he judged the wire, and they flew over it with two feet to spare. There was flat open ground ahead, and Ralph aimed to cut the curve of the railway tracks. Five hundred yards ahead, the locomotive hit the gradient of the Magersfontein hills and the huffing of the boiler slowed.

They caught it a quarter of a mile from the crest, and Ralph pushed the bay in close enough for him to lean from the saddle and grab the handrail on the last coach. He swung across the gap and scrambled up onto the rear balcony. When he looked back the bay was already grazing contentedly beside the tracks.

"Somehow, I knew you were coming." Jordan was standing in the door of the coach. "I even had a bed made up for you in one of the guest compartments."

Ralph turned quickly. "Where is he?" he demanded.

"Waiting for you in the saloon."

Rhodes was slumped in a buttoned calf-leather chair beside the wide picture window in his luxurious private coach. He looked tired and ill.

"Sit down, Ballantyne," he said. "Jordan, get your brother a drink."

Jordan placed a silver tray on the table beside Ralph while Rhodes addressed himself to a pile of papers in front of him.

"Do you know what is the most important asset of any nation, Ballantyne?" he said suddenly. "It is men. Young, bright men, imbued during the most susceptible period of their lives with the grand design. Young men like you, Ralph." Rhodes paused. "I am endowing a series of scholarships in my will. I want these young men to be chosen carefully and sent to Oxford University." For the first time he looked up at Ralph. "These men will be my living thoughts. Through them, I shall live for ever."

"How will you select them?" asked Ralph.

"I am working on that now." Rhodes rearranged the papers on his bureau. "Literary and scholastic achievement, of course, success at manly sports, powers of leadership. They will come from England, and from every corner of the Empire—even from America."

Ralph suppressed a smile, intrigued despite himself at this design for immortality.

"And after men?" Rhodes asked. "What is the next most precious asset of a new land? Diamonds, or gold?" He shook his head. "It is the power that drives the railways, that fuels the blast furnaces—the power that makes all the wheels go around. Coal."

Then they were both silent, staring at each other, and Ralph felt

90

every muscle in his body under stress, the hackles at the back of his neck rising in an atavistic passion.

"It is very simple, Ralph. The coal deposits in Wankie's country must be retained in responsible hands."

"The hands of the British South Africa Company?" Ralph asked grimly. "By what means will you take them? Legal or otherwise?"

"Come, Ralph, you know it is totally within my power to legalize anything I do in Rhodesia."

Ralph shook his head. "I want the coal deposits that I discovered and that I pegged. They are mine. I will fight you for them."

Rhodes sighed and pinched the bridge of his nose. "Let me point out a fact to you of which you are probably unaware. There are two company linesmen who have sworn an affidavit that they saw you cutting telegraph lines south of Bulawayo on Monday the fourth."

"They are lying," said Ralph, and turned to look at his brother. Jordan did not look up from the shorthand pad on his lap, and Ralph tasted the sourness of treachery on the back of his tongue.

"They may be lying," Mr. Rhodes agreed softly, "but they are prepared to testify under oath. And of course, any contract made under a deliberate misrepresentation can be set aside by a Court of Law. If Roelof Zeederberg could prove that when you signed your little agreement, you were fully aware of the rinderpest epidemic—" Rhodes did not finish. Instead he sighed again and rubbed his chin. "On the fourth your father, Major Zouga Ballantyne, sold five thousand head of breeding stock to Gwaai Cattle Ranches, one of my own companies. Three days later, half of them were dead of rinderpest, and the rest will soon be destroyed. Both your contract of sale and your father's could be declared null and void. Both of you could be forced to refund the purchase monies you received and to take back thousands of dead and dying animals. . . ."

Ralph's face was stony. With a jerky movement he poured the crystal tumbler half full of whisky and swallowed a mouthful.

The silence drew out, while Rhodes peered out of the window at the milky blue sky. Then quite suddenly he spoke again. "The choice before you is simple enough. Give up all claim to the Wankie coal deposits, and walk away still a rich man by any standards—or else I will destroy you and your father, utterly."

Calmly Rhodes met the ferocious hatred in the eyes of the young man before him. He was inured by now both to adulation and to hatred, for such things were meaningless when measured against

91

the grand design of his destiny. "You must understand that there is nothing personal in this, Ralph," he said. "It is in young men like you that I place my hope for the future. But I cannot allow anything or anybody to stand in my way. I know what has to be done, and there is so little time left in which to do it."

Ralph closed his eyes and fought off his murderous rage. When he opened his eyes again his voice was level and icy calm.

"I understand," he nodded. "In your place I would probably do the same thing."

"You will go far, young man," said Rhodes approvingly.

THE LOCOMOTIVE ROARED on into the night, lurching rhythmically as the ties clattered harshly under the steel wheels. Ralph sat by the window in his stateroom. He was still fully dressed, though it was three o'clock in the morning. The invitingly soft double bed behind the green velvet curtains had no attraction for him.

Ralph had sat through dinner at Rhodes's board, listening to his high, jarring voice parading a succession of weird and grandiose ideas. The only reason he had managed to control his emotions and keep a good face was the realization that he had uncovered a weakness in his adversary. Rhodes was so cushioned by his vast wealth, so blinded by his own visions, that he did not seem to realize that he had made a mortal enemy. If he did think at all of Ralph's feelings, it was to suppose that he had philosophically accepted the loss of the Wankie coalfields.

"I measure a man by the style in which he faces adversity," he had said. "You will do, young Ballantyne."

In that moment Ralph had come close to losing control, but then Rhodes had left the saloon with his bearlike gait, leaving the two brothers together at the table.

"I am sorry, Ralph," Jordan had said simply. "I tried to warn you once. You should not have challenged him. You should not have forced me to choose between you and him. We will reach the village of Matjiesfontein in the morning, and you can wait there for the northbound train to take you back to Kimberley."

Ralph glanced at the bed, and knew that he could not sleep, not even now when he was almost burned out with rage. Suddenly he wanted a drink, and he knew where to find it. At the far end of the saloon, behind double doors of intricate marquetry work, was an array of exotic spirits—that was where he could find oblivion.

Ralph opened the door and stepped out of his stateroom. The cold night air flicked his hair and he shivered in his shirtsleeves, and then weaved down the narrow corridor towards the saloon. He crossed the open balcony between coaches, clutching at the handrail to steady himself. As he entered the corridor of the second coach, one of the doors slid open ahead of him, and a shaft of yellow light outlined the slim graceful figure that stepped through.

Jordan had not seen his brother, and he paused in the doorway and looked back into the stateroom beyond. His expression was as soft and loving as that of a mother leaving her sleeping infant. Gently, with exaggerated care, he closed the sliding door. Then he turned and found himself face to face with Ralph.

Like his brother, Jordan was coatless, but his shirt was unbuttoned and his white feet were bare. He stood transfixed, rigid and pale, staring at Ralph with huge terrified eyes, one hand raised as though to shield his throat.

Suddenly Ralph understood. He remembered, when once he had jokingly suggested visiting a bawdy-house, how horrified his brother had been. Now it was he who recoiled in horror, unable to speak for infinite seconds, while they stared at each other.

Then at last Ralph regained his voice. "By God, now I know why you have no use for whores, for you are one yourself." He turned and tore open the door and ran out onto the balcony, looking about him wildly, like a creature in a trap. He saw the clean spaces of the open veld, and he swung down the steps and let himself drop into the night.

The earth hit him with crushing force and he rolled down the harsh scrub beside the tracks. When he lifted his head, the red running lights of the caboose were dwindling away into the south, and the sound of the wheels was already muted.

The dawn was an unearthly orange wash behind a crisp black cut-out of flat-topped hills. Ralph lifted his face to it, and he spoke aloud. "I swear I will have him. I swear that I will destroy this monster, or destroy myself in the attempt."

"MY FATHER KILLED a great elephant upon this spot. The tusks stand on the stoep at King's Lynn," Ralph said quietly. "And I shot a fine lion here myself. It seems strange that things like that will never happen again at this place."

Beside him Harry Mellow straightened up from the theodolite, and for a moment his face was grave. "We have come to conquer the wilderness," he said. "Soon there will be a high headgear reaching up into the sky, and if the Harkness reef runs true, one day a town with schools and churches. Isn't that what we both want?"

Ralph nodded. "It just seems strange, when you look at it now."

The low valleys were still blowing with the soft pink grasses, the tree trunks along the ridges silver in the sunlight, but even as they watched one of them shivered against the sky and then toppled with a rending crackling roar. The Matabele axemen swarmed over the fallen giant to lop off the branches, and a shadow of regret lingered in Ralph's eyes before he turned away.

"You have picked a good site for your quarters," he said, and Harry followed the direction of his gaze.

"Knobs Hill," he laughed.

The thatch and daub hut had a breathtaking view over the forest to where the southern escarpment dipped away into infinite blue distances. A tiny figure stood there, her apron a merry spot of tulip-yellow against the raw red earth which Vicky hoped would one day be a garden. She saw the two men below her and waved.

"By God, that girl has done wonders." Harry lifted his hat above his head to acknowledge the greeting, his expression fondly besotted. "Nothing upsets her—not even the cobra in the lavatory this morning—she just up and blasted it with a shotgun."

"Put her in a city and she'd probably be in tears in ten minutes."

"Not my girl," said Harry proudly.

They walked down the valley, while Harry pointed out the factors which had led him to choose the spot. A small gang of black men were clearing the collar area of the reef and Ralph recognized the tallest of them.

"Bazo," he cried, and the induna straightened up and rested on his pick handle.

"Henshaw." He greeted Ralph gravely. "Here you come to watch the real men at work." Bazo's flat hard muscles shone like wet anthracite. The old gunshot wounds had darkened, and one arm was twisted at an angle where the shattered bone had mended.

"Real men?" Ralph asked. "You promised me two hundred, and you have brought me twenty."

"The others are waiting," Bazo promised. "But they will not come if they cannot bring their women with them. One-Bright-Eye wants the women to stay in the villages."

"They can bring their women, as many as they wish. I will speak to One-Bright-Eye. Bring me your old comrades from the Moles, and tell them I will pay them well and feed them better."

"I will leave in the morning," Bazo decided. "And be back before the moon shows its horns again."

When the two white men moved on down the survey line, Bazo watched them for a while, his face inscrutable, then he looked at his gang and nodded. They spat on their palms, hefted the pickaxes and Bazo sang out the opening chorus of the work chant.

"Though our bodies are worn out, our hearts are constant."

"Jee!" came the soaring chorus, as the pick heads hissed downwards in unison, and with a crash buried themselves in the iron earth. Each man levered his pick head free and took one step forward as Bazo sang. And again the act was repeated, and a hundred times more, while the sweat was flung from their bodies and the red dust flew.

BAZO LOPED ALONG through the hills and valleys. His spirits were joyous, for he had not realized how much the labours of the last weeks had galled until he was released from them. Bazo had known the savage joy of fighting in the sunlight with his regimental plumes flying. He had won honours and the respect of his peers, and had sat on the king's council with the induna's headring on his brow. The drudgery of menial labour rankled the more for the glories that had preceded it.

The path dropped away towards the river. Bazo followed it down and stooped into the gloomy tunnel of dense dark vegetation, and then froze. Yet this was no enemy that came towards him down the narrow tunnel of bush, and his heart bounded almost painfully against his ribs.

"I see you, Lord," Tanase greeted him softly.

"Why are you so far from the village?" he demanded, as his lovely wife knelt dutifully before him, and clapped her hands softly at the level of her waist.

"I saw you on the road, Bazo, son of Gandang. I came to meet you alone, so we could be free for a while of your son's clamorous adoration and the eyes of the villagers." She raised herself, and with a kind of reverential wonder kissed his face, and said softly: "Bayete!"

It was the greeting that is made only to a king, and Bazo felt the insects of fear and superstition crawling on his skin. There still were things about his woman that disquieted him, for she had not been stripped of all her occult powers in the cave of the Umlimo.

"Oh Bazo, the bravest and the strongest, why do you start so at my words? You in whose veins runs the purest blood of Zani? Do you not feel the royal blood coursing in your veins? Do you not see the men of Matabeleland with empty hands entreat the spirits? 'Give us a king,' they cry."

"Babiaan," whispered Bazo. "Somabula and Gandang. They are Lobengula's brothers."

"They are old men, and the stone has fallen out of their bellies, the fire has gone out in their eyes."

"Tanase, do not speak so."

"Bazo, my husband, my king, do you not see to whom the eyes of all the indunas turn when the nation is in council? Do you not see how even Babiaan and Somabula listen when Bazo speaks?"

She laid the palm of her hand over his mouth to still his protests, and then Bazo suddenly took her in his arms and held her to his breast. "If I am the axe," he said, "then you are the cutting edge, for you are a part of me, and the sharpest part."

"Together, Lord, we will hack through anything that stands in our way," she answered fiercely, and then she pulled out from the circle of his arms and took something grey and fluffy from the pouch upon her belt. "I have a gift to make your brave heart braver and your will as hard as your steel. Wear this moleskin for the glory that was and that shall be again, induna of the Moles. One day soon, we will change it for a headband of spotted gold leopard skin, with royal blue heron feathers set upon it."

She took his hand and they started down the path together.

"WHAT IS THE MOOD of the people?" Bazo asked softly.

He had returned to the village to see the burning of hundreds of cattle carcasses—cattle that Mungo St. John had ordered to be destroyed. The black police had shot down beasts that, to the herdsmen, were their pride and very reason for existence. One-Bright-Eye's explanation that the animals could be carriers of the pestilence was meaningless to them.

"They are sick with grief," said Babiaan. "Not since the death of the old king has there been such despair in their hearts." Babiaan was the senior of all the old king's councillors, and it was not lost on the other indunas in the packed beehive hut that his tone was respectful.

"It is almost as though the white men wish to plunge the assegai in their own breasts," Bazo nodded. "Each cruel deed strengthens us, and confirms the prophecy of the Umlimo. Can there be one amongst you who still has doubts?"

"There are no doubts. We are ready now," replied Gandang.

Bazo shook his head. "We will not be ready until the third prophecy of the Umlimo has come to pass. When it comes, there will be no doubt in our minds. Until that time we must continue with the preparations."

One by one the indunas stood and each made his report. They listed the numbers of warriors that were trained and ready, where each group was situated and how soon they could be armed and in the field. When the last one had finished, Bazo gave the field commanders their objectives.

It was long after midnight before all of them had received and repeated their orders, and then Bazo addressed them again.

"Stealth and speed are our only allies. No warrior will carry a shield, for the temptation to drum upon it in the old way would be too strong. There will be no singing the war songs when you run, for the leopard does not growl before he springs. The leopard hunts in darkness, and when he enters the goat shed he spares nothing."

"Women and children?" asked Babiaan sombrely.

"Even as they shot down Kampu and Imbali," Bazo nodded. "When a wise man finds a mamba's lair, he kills the snake and crushes the eggs under foot."

There was something in his voice that made Gandang, his father, shiver: he recognized the moment when the power shifted from the old bull to the younger. Indisputably, Bazo was now their leader.

So it was Bazo who said at last, "The meeting is finished!" And one by one the indunas saluted him and slipped away into the night, and when the last was gone, the screen of goatskins at the back was pushed aside and Tanase stepped out.

"I am so proud," she whispered, "that I want to weep like a silly girl."

IT WAS A LONG COLUMN, counting the women and children almost a thousand human beings, strung out over a mile. Many of the men had brought more than one wife and some as many as four. The young girls carried rolls of sleeping-mats balanced upon their heads, the mothers had their infants slung upon their hips so that they could suckle while on the march, and Juba's high clear soprano led the singing.

Bazo came back along the column at an easy lope and fell in at Juba's side, greeting her respectfully. "The burdens of your young girls will be a little lighter after we cross the river. We will leave three hundred assegais concealed in the millet bins."

"And the rest of them?" Juba asked.

"Those we will take with us to the Harkness Mine. A place of concealment has been prepared. From there your girls will take them out a few at a time to the outlying villages."

"My son, I am troubled. Tanase tells me that all the white folk are to be killed with steel."

"All of them." Bazo nodded.

"Nomusa, who is more than a mother to me, must she die also, my son? She is so good and kind to our people."

Gently Bazo took her by the arm and led her off the path, where they could not be overheard. "That very kindness which you speak of makes her the most dangerous of all of them," he explained. "The love that you bear for her weakens us all. No, I tell you truly, if I were to spare one of them, it would be One-Bright-Eye himself."

"One-Bright-Eye!" Juba started. "I do not understand. He is cruel and fierce, without understanding."

"When our warriors look on his face and hear his voice, they are reminded once again of all the wrongs we have suffered, and they become strong and angry. When they look upon Nomusa, they become soft and hesitant. She must be amongst the first to die."

"You say they must all die?" Juba asked. She pointed ahead, where the path wound lazily beneath the acacia trees. There was a horseman cantering towards them from the direction of the Harkness Mine, and even at this distance there was no mistaking the set of his powerful shoulders and his arrogant seat in the saddle. "Look at this one who comes now! You have often told me how as youths you worked shoulder to shoulder, and ate from the same pot. Will you kill this man that you call your brother?"

"I will let no other do it," Bazo affirmed. "I will do it with my own hand, to make sure it is swift and clean."

"You have become a hard man, my son," Juba whispered.

Bazo turned away from her, and stepped back onto the path.

Ralph Ballantyne saw him and waved his hat above his head.

"Bazo." He laughed, as he rode up. "Will I ever learn never to doubt you? You bring me even more than the two hundred that you promised."

RALPH BALLANTYNE crossed the southern boundary of King's Lynn, but it was another two hours' riding before he made out the milky grey loom of the homestead kopjes on the horizon.

The veld through which he rode was silent and almost empty. Where once his father's herds of plump cattle had grazed, the new grass was springing up again dense and green and untrodden. Zouga Ballantyne had managed to sell off some small portion of his cattle herds before the rinderpest struck King's Lynn, but he had lost the rest and their bones gleamed like strings of pearls beneath the trees.

In the paddock below the big thatched house there were horses that Ralph did not recognize, and amongst them the unmistakable white mules of Rhodes's equipage. The coach itself stood under the trees in the yard, and Ralph felt his anger flare up when he saw it. He swallowed hard to control his burning hatred as he dismounted.

Two black grooms ran to take his horse as Zouga Ballantyne came out onto the wide stoep. Ralph ran up the steps and they embraced.

"Ralph, my boy." Zouga took his arm and led him down the veranda. Guarding the double doors were the immense tusks of the great bull elephant that Zouga had shot on the site of the Harkness Mine, and the two men passed between them into the dining room. Under the thatch it was cool and dark after the brilliant white glare of noon.

Zouga's empty chair was at the far end of the long table, and facing it down the long board was the familiar massive brooding figure that raised his shaggy head as Ralph came in. "Ah, Ralph, it's good to see you."

It amazed Ralph that there was no rancour in Rhodes's voice, and with an effort he actually smiled as he gripped the broad hand with its hard prominent knuckles.

The suave little doctor, Jameson, was appropriately at Rhodes's right hand, but the man on Rhodes's left was a surprising guest. It was the first time that Ralph had ever seen General Mungo St. John at King's Lynn, and he knew that there must be a compelling reason for his presence at the gathering. Ralph had always had a sneaking admiration for this romantically piratical figure, and this time his smile was genuine.

The stature of the other men at the table confirmed the importance and significance of the meeting. Apart from Jameson and St. John, there was Percy Fitzpatrick, a prominent representative of the Witwatersrand Chamber of Mines, the organ of the gold barons of Johannesburg. Beyond Fitzpatrick sat the Honourable Bobbie White, a handsome and pleasant young aristocrat, the type of Englishman that Rhodes preferred. He was also a staff officer and a career soldier. Next to him sat John Willoughby, who had ridden with Jameson's column against Lobengula. And at the end of the table, Ralph came face to face with his brother. He saw the desperate appeal in Jordan's gentle eyes. He gripped his brother's hand briefly, and then took the seat beside Zouga at the head of the table.

The animated conversation that Ralph had interrupted was resumed as the servants began to bring in the food. "They say that the Cape buffalo have been wiped out completely by the rinderpest," Dr. Jameson was saying. "What do you think, Major Ballantyne?"

"Their losses have been catastrophic," Zouga agreed, "yet I cannot believe they are now extinct. I suspect that somewhere out there are scattered survivors, the ones that had a natural immunity, and I believe that they will breed."

Rhodes changed the subject by turning to Ralph. "Your railway line—what is the latest position, Ralph?"

"We are still almost two months ahead of our schedule," Ralph told him with a touch of defiance. "We crossed the Rhodesian border fifteen days ago."

"It's as well." Rhodes nodded. "We will have urgent need of your line in a very short while." And he and Dr. Jim exchanged a conspiratorial glance.

Lunch was served and eaten, and then Zouga dismissed the servants and poured the cognac himself, while Jordan carried around the cigars. They all settled back in their seats as Rhodes began to speak.

"There is not one of you who does not know that my life's task is to see the map of Africa painted red from Cape Town to Cairo. We must have Africa—all of it—to add to our Queen's dominions. Already my emissaries have gone north to the land between the

Zambezi and the Congo Rivers to prepare the way, but all this will be of no avail so long as that ignorant old bigot, Paul Kruger, in his benighted little republic of the Transvaal, sits astride the richest stretch of the African continent like a hound with a bone."

They were all shocked by this bitter invective, and Rhodes looked around at their faces before he went on.

"There are thirty-eight thousand Englishmen on the goldfields of Witwatersrand—Englishmen who are responsible for every bit of civilization in the Transvaal, yet Kruger denies them the right to vote and taxes them mercilessly. He has given trade monopolies in all essential mining goods to members of his family and government. He is blatantly arming his burghers with German guns, and he is openly flirting with the Kaiser." Rhodes paused. "A German sphere of influence in the midst of Her Majesty's domains would for ever damn our dreams of a British Africa."

Although it was cool in the room Rhodes was sweating, and his hand shook as he reached for his glass. "I went to him, gentlemen. I went to Pretoria to see Kruger at his own home. He sent a message with a servant that he could not see me that day."

They had all heard the story, how President Kruger had sent a black servant to one of the richest and most influential men in the world with this message: "I am rather busy at the moment. One of my burghers has come to discuss a sick ox with me. Come back on Tuesday."

Dr. Jim intervened to break the embarrassed silence. "Mr. Rhodes has done everything a reasonable man could. To risk further insult from this old Boer could bring discredit not only on Mr. Rhodes personally, but on our Queen and her Empire." The little doctor paused and looked at each of his listeners in turn. "What can we do about it? What *must* we do about it?"

Rhodes shook himself, and looked at the young staff officer. "Bobbie?"

"Gentlemen, you may be aware that I have just returned from the Transvaal—" Bobbie White produced a sheaf of papers from a leather briefcase and passed a sheet to every man at the table.

Ralph glanced at his copy. It was the order of battle of the army of the Transvaal Republic. His surprise was so intense that he missed the first part of what Bobbie White was saying.

"—The fort at Pretoria is under repair and extension. The walls have been breached for this purpose and will be entirely vulnerable to a small determined force. As you can see from the paper before you, the Transvaal depends entirely upon its citizen commandos for defence. It requires four to six weeks for them to assemble into an effective force."

Rhodes turned to Fitzpatrick. "Percy?" he invited.

"You know what Kruger calls those of us whose capital and resources have developed his gold-mining industry for him? He calls us the Uitlanders, the Outlanders. You know also that we Outlanders have elected our own representatives—which we call the 'Johannesburg Reform Committee'. I have the honour to be a member of that committee and so I speak for every Englishman in the Transvaal." Fitzpatrick paused, then went on. "I bring two messages. The first is that we are determined and united to the cause.

"The second message is a letter signed by all the members of the Reform Committee. It is addressed to Dr. Jameson in his capacity as Administrator of Rhodesia, and it reads as follows:

Johannesburg

"Dear Sir,

The position of matters in this state has become so critical that we believe there will be a conflict between the Transvaal Government and the Uitlander population. A foreign corporation of Germans and Hollanders is controlling our destinies, and in conjunction with the Boer leaders endeavouring to cast them in a mould which is wholly alien to the genius of the British peoples. . . ."

Ralph sat bemused as the letter unfolded. This was not some boyish nonsense. These men were clearly plotting one of the most audacious acts of piracy in history. They were going to try to take by force of arms the richest gold reef in existence. He kept his expression calm with an enormous effort as Fitzpatrick went on.

"Under these circumstances we feel constrained to call upon you, as an Englishman, to come to our aid should a disturbance arise. We guarantee any expense you may incur by helping us, and we ask you to believe that nothing but sternest necessity has prompted this appeal."

At the head of the table, Zouga Ballantyne let out his breath in a low whistle, but nobody else spoke.

Everybody at the table waited for Rhodes, until at last he sighed heavily. "I much prefer to pay a man's price, rather than to fight him, but we are not dealing with a normal man here." His head turned towards Jameson, and the little doctor rode his chair back on its hindlegs and thrust his hands deep into his pockets.

"Five hundred rifles and a million rounds of ammunition are already in the De Beers mine stores at Kimberley," he announced. "We will need to send them into Johannesburg."

Ralph blinked. The plot was far advanced, further than he believed possible. They must have been busy for months.

"How will you transport them?" he asked.

"Ralph," Rhodes smiled. "You didn't really believe you were invited here for a social luncheon. Who is the shrewdest transport operator on the subcontinent?"

Ralph felt a sudden unholy excitement welling up within him. He was to be at the centre of this fantastic conspiracy, privy to every detail, and he knew intuitively that this was one of the opportunities that comes once in a lifetime.

"You will do it, of course?" A small shadow passed across the penetrating blue eyes.

"Of course," said Ralph quietly.

Reassured, Rhodes turned back to Dr. Jameson.

"We will raise a mounted force of around six hundred," Jameson went on, and he looked at John Willoughby and Zouga Ballantyne, both of them proven soldiers. "I have the approval of the British Government to maintain a mobile armed force in Bechuanaland, on the railway concession strip which runs down the border of the Transvaal. The force is for the protection of the railway, but it will be based at Pitsani, a mere one hundred and eighty miles from Johannesburg. We can be there in fifty hours, long before the Boers could raise any kind of resistance."

"What is the position of Her Majesty's Government?" Zouga Ballantyne asked. "Without their support it will all be in vain."

"As you know, I have just returned from London," Rhodes replied. "While I was there I dined with the Colonial Secretary. Let me just assure you all that Mr. Chamberlain and I understand each other. I can say no more at this stage—you must trust me."

It was at that moment that Ralph realized that it was feasible. Given Dr. Jameson's legendary luck, they could take the Transvaal with the same ease as they had seized Matabeleland from Lobengula. A billion pounds in gold, annexed to Rhodesia! The British

South Africa Company and De Beers Consolidated Diamond Company would become the richest and most powerful commercial enterprises on the face of the earth—and they were Rhodes's *alter ego*. At this thought Ralph's anger and hatred returned so fiercely that his hands trembled, and he had to place them carefully in his lap.

Zouga still probed for flaws and faults.

"Dr. Jim, will you be raising all six hundred men here in Rhodesia?" he asked.

Jameson nodded.

"With the rinderpest scourge having swept away their fortunes, there will be many young Rhodesians eager to enlist, and all of them will be good fighting men who rode against the Matabele," he said.

"Do you think it wise to leave this country stripped bare of its able-bodied men?"

Rhodes frowned quickly as he intervened. "It would be only for a few short months, and we do not have an enemy to fear, do we? The Matabele are a defeated and disorganized rabble. General St. John will set your fears at rest."

They all looked to the tall man at Jameson's side, and Mungo St. John removed the long cheroot from his mouth and smiled. "I have two hundred armed native police whose loyalty is unquestioned. I have informers placed in every large Matabele village who will give me warning of any stirrings. No, Major, I give you my assurance that the only enemy we need take into account is the obstinate old Boer in Pretoria."

Ralph watched their faces as they planned and argued, and suddenly he remembered that dawn over the barren desert, and the oath he had sworn there. If it were possible to destroy this giant of a man! Ralph felt the thrill of it humming through his blood, as he realized that this might be not only the chance for vengeance, but also the chance for a vast fortune. If the plot failed, then the shares of the gold-mining companies involved would all crash with it. A simple bear coup on the Johannesburg stock exchange could net millions of pounds.

He looked up when Rhodes repeated a question.

"I said, how soon can you leave for Kimberley to take charge of the shipments, Ralph?"

"Tomorrow," Ralph replied evenly.

Rhodes nodded. "I knew we could rely upon you."

THE RAILHEAD WAS FEELING its way up the escarpment like a cautious adder. It had left the swollen baobabs and yellow fever trees of the Limpopo basin far below and the forests were lovelier, the air sweeter, and the streams clear and cold. Ralph's base camp had moved up with the railhead into one of the secluded valleys, just out of earshot of the work-gangs' hammers.

The spot had many of the charms of the remote wilderness. In the evenings a herd of sable antelope came down to feed in the glade below the camp, and the barking of baboons roused them each dawn. Yet the telegraph hut at the railhead was only ten minutes' stroll away, and the locomotive bringing up the rails and sleepers from Kimberley delivered any luxuries that the camp required. In an emergency Cathy would have the railway overseer to call upon, while the camp itself was protected by twenty loyal Matabele servants—and Isazi, the little Zulu driver. The Harkness Mine was only thirty miles away, and Harry and Vicky promised to ride across every weekend.

"Can't we come with you, Daddy?" Jonathan pleaded. "I could help you—really I could. I'm four already."

Ralph lifted him into his lap. "One of us has to stay and look after Mama," he explained. "You are the only one I can trust."

"We can take her with us," Jonathan suggested, and Ralph had a vision of his wife and child in the midst of an armed and violent revolution.

"That would be very nice," Ralph agreed, "but what about the new baby? What happens if the stork arrives while we are all away?"

Jonathan scowled, for he was already developing a healthy dislike for this not-yet-arrived but eternally present little sister. Both parents managed to introduce her into almost every conversation, and his mother spent much of the time knitting and sewing or just sitting smiling to herself. She no longer went out riding with him, nor indulged in the rowdy romps which he enjoyed.

"Well, can I come with you when my baby sister is here to look after Mama?"

"I tell you what, old fellow, I'll do better than that. How would you like to go on a big boat across the sea?" This was the kind of talk Jonathan preferred, and his face lit up. "And when we get to London, we will stay in a big hotel and we will buy all sorts of presents for your mama—" Cathy dropped her knitting into her lap, and stared at him in the lamplight. "Then when we come back we will go to Johannesburg and we will buy a big house, with shining chandeliers and marble floors."

"And stables for my pony." Jonathan clapped his hands.

"And you will go to a fine brick school with lots of other boys." Ralph stood him on his feet again. "Now go and kiss your mother goodnight, and ask her to tuck you up in your bed."

Cathy hurried back from the nursery tent, moving with the appealing awkwardness of her pregnancy, and came to where Ralph sat in the canvas folding chair with his boots stretched to the blaze. She put both arms around his neck and with her lips pressed to his cheek whispered: "Is it true, or are you just teasing me?"

"You have been brave for long enough. I'm going to buy you a home that you didn't dare even dream about."

"Oh Ralph, I'm so happy I think I could cry. But why now? What has happened?"

"Something is going to change our lives. We are going to be rich."

"Can you tell me what it is?"

"No," he said simply. "But you only have a few months to wait, just until Christmas." And he picked her up in his arms and carried her carefully to the tent under the spreading wild fig tree.

In the morning Cathy stood with Jonathan beside her, looking up at Ralph on the footplate of the big green locomotive. Her heart swelled until it threatened to choke her.

"We always seem to be saying goodbye."

"It's the last time," Ralph promised her. "I'll be back just as soon as I can." The engine driver pulled down the brass throttle handle and the huff of steam drowned Ralph's next words.

"What? What did you say?" Cathy called as the locomotive began to trundle down the steel tracks.

"Don't lose the letter!"

"I won't," she promised, and she waved her white lace handkerchief until the curve in the tracks carried the train out of sight. The last mournful sob of its whistle died on the air.

Then, as she turned back to where Isazi and Jonathan waited, she slipped her hand into her pocket to check that the sealed envelope that Ralph had left with her was still safe. She drew it out and read the tantalizing instruction: "Open only when you receive my telegraph."

She bit her lip, fighting the temptation, and at last ran her fingernail under the flap and drew out the folded sheet.

106

"Upon receiving my telegraph, you must send the following telegraph immediately:

"To Major Zouga Ballantyne. Headquarters of Rhodesian Horse Regiment at Pitsani Bechuanaland.
Your wife Mrs Louise Ballantyne gravely ill return immediately Kings Lynn."

Suddenly Cathy was deadly afraid. "Oh my mad darling," she whispered. "What are you going to do?"

Elizabeth rose and began to gather up the soup bowls.

"You haven't finished, Bobby," she told her young brother.

"I'm not hungry, Lizzie," the child protested.

Elizabeth glanced at her mother, then dutifully stacked Robert's bowl with the others. None of the girls had ever been allowed to leave food, but she had learned not to protest at the unfairness of Robyn's indulgence of her only son. With the paraffin lantern in her other hand, she went out of the back door and crossed to the thatched kitchen hut.

"It is time she had a husband." Juba shook her head mournfully. "She needs a man in her bed and a baby at her breast to make her smile."

"Don't talk nonsense, Juba," snapped Robyn. "There will be time for that later. She is doing important work here. I could not let her go."

"The young men come out from Bulawayo one after the other, and she sends them all away," Juba went on.

"She's a sensible, serious girl," Robyn agreed.

"She is a sad girl, with a secret."

Robyn was about to protest, but she was interrupted by the sound of voices in the darkness outside. The flame of the lantern came bobbing back across the yard, and Elizabeth's voice rang out excitedly as she burst in through the door.

"Mama! Mama! Come quickly! Old Moses has come up from the village—he says that there are soldiers, hundreds of soldiers riding past the church."

"Juba, get Bobby's coat." Robyn took her woollen shawl down from behind the door. "Elizabeth, give me the lantern!"

Robyn led the family down the dark driveway, past the hospital

107

towards the church, with Bobby bundled up in a woollen coat riding on Juba's fat hip.

"There they are!" Elizabeth exclaimed. "Moses was right—just look at them!"

The starlight was bright enough to reveal the torrent of dark horsemen pouring down the road from the neck of the hills. It was too dark to see their faces under the broad brims of their slouch hats, but a rifle barrel stuck up like an accuser's finger behind each man's shoulder, silhouetted against the stars. The quiet was uncanny for such a multitude. No voice raised above a whisper, no orders to close up, not even the usual low warning, "Ware hole!" of massed horsemen moving across unfamiliar terrain in darkness. The deep dust of the track muffled the hooves.

"Who are they?" Juba asked with a thrill of superstitious awe in her voice. "They look like ghosts."

"Those aren't ghosts," Robyn said flatly. "Those are Jameson's tin soldiers, his new Rhodesian Horse Regiment."

The head riders reached the fork in the road below the church, and took the old wagon road towards the south. In the centre of the column were seven transport wagons drawn by mules, for the rinderpest had left no draught oxen. After the wagons came eight two-wheeled carts with canvas covers over the Maxim machineguns, then three light field guns. The tail of the column was again made up of mounted men, two abreast. It took almost twenty minutes for them all to pass the church, and then the silence was complete.

At last Robyn roused herself. "This stinks of Jameson—and his master," she murmured. "I wonder what devilry they are up to now." Then she led the little group back towards the homestead.

Juba let Bobby down from her hip, and he scampered back into the warm lamplight of the dining room as Elizabeth hurried off to the kitchen hut. The two women paused together on the stoep, close and secure in the love and companionship they bore each other. They looked out across the valley, in the direction in which the dark and silent horsemen had disappeared.

"How beautiful it is!" Robyn murmured. "I always think of the stars as my friends. They are so constant, and tonight they are so close." She lifted her hand as though to pluck them from the firmament. "There is Orion, and there is the Bull—"

"And there are Manatassi's four sons," Juba said.

Robyn hugged Juba closer to her. "The same stars shine upon us all, even though we know them by different names. You call those four white stars Manatassi's sons—but we call them the Cross. The Southern Cross."

She felt Juba start and then begin to shiver, and Robyn's voice was instantly concerned.

"What is it, my Little Dove?" she asked.

"It is cold," whispered Juba. "We should go in now."

Juba sat silent during the rest of the meal, but when Elizabeth took Bobby through to his bedroom, Juba caught Robyn's wrist. "Nomusa," she whispered. "I must go back to the village."

"Oh Juba, you have only just. returned. But whatever is the matter? You are shaking."

"I have a feeling, Nomusa, a feeling in my heart. No, do not speak," she pleaded. "I have so little time."

It was only then that Robyn realized that it was not the chill of night that was shaking Juba's vast frame. She was racked with sobs of fear and dread.

"You must go, Nomusa. You and Elizabeth and the baby. Take nothing with you, leave this very minute. Go into Bulawayo, perhaps you will be safe there. It is your best chance."

"I don't understand you, Juba. What nonsense is this?"

"They are coming, Nomusa. They are coming. Please hurry."

Then she was gone. She moved swiftly and silently for such a big woman, and she seemed to melt into the moon shadows under the spathodea trees. By the time Robyn had run down the veranda, there was no sign of her.

Robyn hurried towards the hospital bungalows, stumbling once on the verge of the path, calling with increasing exasperation.

"Juba, come back here! Do you hear me? I won't stand any more of this nonsense!"

She stopped at the church, uncertain which path to take.

"Juba! Where are you?"

The silence was broken only by the yipping of a jackal up on the hillside above the Mission. It was answered by another on the peak of the pass where the road to Bulawayo crossed the hills.

Robyn turned sorrowfully away, and walked through the darkness back towards the house. There was a light burning in Elizabeth's room, and as Robyn climbed the steps of the veranda, the door opened.

"Mama! What are you doing? I thought I heard voices."

Robyn hesitated. She did not want to alarm Elizabeth, but she was a sensible child.

"Juba ran off. There must be another witchcraft scare."

"What did she say?"

"Oh, just that we should go into Bulawayo to escape some sort of danger."

Elizabeth came out onto the veranda.

"Juba is a Christian, she doesn't dabble in witchcraft." Elizabeth's tone was concerned. "What else did she say?"

"Just that," Robyn yawned. "I'm going to bed."

"Mama, I think we should do as Juba says."

"What do you mean by that?"

"I think we should go into Bulawayo immediately."

"Elizabeth, I thought better of you."

"I have an awful feeling. I think we should go. Perhaps there is real danger."

"This is my home. Your father and I built it with our own hands. There is no power on earth that will force me to leave it," Robyn said firmly. "Now go to bed. We are going to have a busy day tomorrow."

"IT IS THE SIGN," whispered Tanase, crouched by the fire in the centre of the hut. "It is always the way: the meaning of the prophecy becomes clear only when the events come to pass."

"The wings in the dark noon," Bazo nodded, "and the cattle with their heads twisted to touch their flanks, and now—"

"And now the cross has eaten up the hornless cattle. The horsemen have gone south in the night. It is the third, the last sign for which we waited," Tanase exulted softly. "The spirits of our ancestors urge us on. The time of waiting is over."

"Little Mother, without you we would never have known what the white men call those four great stars. Now the spirits have other work for you. You are the one who knows where the white people are, you know how many are at Khami Mission."

Juba looked to her husband, and her lips trembled. Her dark eyes were swimming with tears. Gandang nodded to her to speak.

"There is Nomusa," she whispered. "Nomusa, who is more than a mother and a sister to me. There is Lizzie, my gentle sad Elizabeth—and Bobby, whom I carry upon my hip—"

110

Bazo looked at his father. "They are yours. You know what must be done."

Gandang nodded. Then Bazo turned back to his mother. "Tell me about Bakela, the Fist, and his woman. What news do you have of them?"

"Last week they were in the big house at King's Lynn."

Bazo turned to one of the other indunas who sat in the rank behind Gandang. "Suku! Bakela is yours, and his woman."

"Nkosi nkulu." The induna acknowledged the order, and no one queried that he called Bazo, "King!"

"Little Mother, where is Henshaw, and his woman who is the daughter of Nomusa?"

"Nomusa had a letter from her, three days ago. She is at the railhead with the boy. She carries an infant which will be born about the time of the Chawala festival. Henshaw may still be with her."

"They are mine," Bazo said. "They and the five white men who are at the railhead." He went on quietly allocating a task to each of his commanders, each farm and mine to be attacked, the telegraph lines to be cut, the native police to be executed; and when he had finished he turned to the women.

"Tanase, you will lead our women and children to the ancient sanctuary, in the sacred hills of the Matopos. The young boys will watch from the hill tops against the coming of the white men, and the women will have the potions ready for those of our men who are wounded."

Then the telling of it was over, and they waited for one thing more. The silence in the hut was strained and intense, the whites of eyes gleaming in faces of polished ebony, as they waited, and at last Bazo spoke. "So, on the night of this Chawala moon, let it begin. Then let the storm rage. Let the eyes turn red. Let the young men of Matabele run!"

"Jee!" hummed Suku in the second rank of indunas, and "Jee!" old Babiaan took up the war chant, and then they were all swaying together with their throats straining and their eyes bulging redly in the firelight with the fighting madness coming down upon them.

THE AMMUNITION was the most time-consuming of the stores to handle, and Ralph was limited to twenty trusted men to do the work for him.

There were ten thousand rounds in each iron case. The bulky

packets had to be broken down and repacked in waxed paper, one hundred rounds to the packet, then these had to be soldered into tin sheets before being packed into oil drums for transport. It was an onerous task and Ralph was pleased to escape for a few hours from the workshops of the De Beers Consolidated Mines Company where the work was being done.

Aaron Fagan was waiting for him in his office. "You are becoming a secretive fellow, Ralph," he accused. "Couldn't you give me some idea of what you expect?"

"You will learn that soon enough," Ralph promised, and put a cheroot between his lips. "All I want to know from you is that this fellow Silver is trustworthy. Can he keep his mouth shut?"

"He is the eldest son of my own sister," Aaron bridled. "I will stake my life on it."

David Silver turned out to be a plump young man with a pink scrubbed complexion, gold-rimmed pince-nez and hair glossy with brilliantine. He deferred courteously to his Uncle Aaron, and while Ralph briefly explained his requirements, he nodded his head brightly and made little sucking sounds of encouragement.

"Mr. Ballantyne," he said primly when Ralph had finished, "that is what we stockbrokers call a 'bear position' or 'selling short'. It is an entirely short-term speculative contract. I always make a point of mentioning this to any of my clients who contemplate entering into one. To be entirely truthful, Mr. Ballantyne, I do not approve of this type of speculation."

Ralph's eyes twinkled with amusement, but he said nothing.

David Silver puffed out his cheeks pompously. "The client enters the market and offers to sell shares of a specified company which he does not possess, at a price below the current market price, for delivery at some future date. Naturally, his expectation is that the shares will fall considerably in value before he is obliged to deliver them to the purchaser. From his point of view the larger the fall in value the greater will be his profit."

"Yes," Ralph nodded solemnly.

"On the other hand." David Silver's plump features became stern. "Should the shares rise in value the bear operator will incur considerable losses. He will be forced to re-enter the market and buy shares at the inflated prices to make good his delivery to the purchaser, and naturally he will be paid only the previously agreed price."

112

"Naturally!"

"Mr. Ballantyne, I think you should know that there is a buoyant mood in the market, in my view this is the time to buy gold shares, not to sell them. Will you tell me exactly what you have in mind?"

"I want to sell the shares of two companies short," Ralph told him. "Consolidated Goldfields and The British South Africa Company."

An air of melancholy came over David Silver. "You have chosen the strongest companies on the board. Those are Mr. Rhodes's enterprises. Did you have a figure in mind, Mr. Ballantyne?"

"Yes. Two hundred thousand shares," said Ralph mildly. "In each company."

David Silver sprang to his feet with such alacrity that his chair flew back against the wall with a crash. "But BSA is standing at twelve pounds and Consolidated at eight pounds. That is a transaction of four million pounds!" His pince-nez misted and his lower lip stuck out. "I will have to ask you to make a deposit."

"How much will you need?"

"Forty thousand pounds."

Ralph opened his cheque book and took a pen from the rack on the desk. The squeak of the nib was the only sound in the office, until Ralph sat back and fanned the cheque to dry the ink.

"There is just one thing more," he said. "Nobody outside these four walls, *nobody*, is ever to know that I am the principal in this transaction." Ralph's eyes were such a cold green that David Silver shivered.

IT WAS A TYPICAL Transvaal Boer homestead set on a rocky ridge above an undulating treeless plain. The roof was of rusty corrugated iron, and the whitewash was flaking from the walls; there was no attempt at a garden or lawn. A dozen scrawny speckled fowls scratched at the bare baked earth, or perched disconsolately on ruined farm equipment. As Ralph dismounted below the veranda, a pack of mongrel hounds came snapping about his boots.

"*U kom 'n bietjie laat, meneer.*" A man had come out onto the veranda and now held the door open for him.

"*Jammer.*" Ralph apologized for being late and stooped through the door into the windowless living room. It smelled of stale smoke and dead ash from the open fireplace. The floor was covered with rush mats, and there was a single table of crudely fashioned wood. The only book in the room lay open on the bare table top, an enormous Dutch Bible with a leather cover and brass bindings.

Eight men sat down the length of the table, not one amongst them younger than fifty years old, for the Boers valued experience in their leaders. Most of them were bearded and all of them wore rough hard-worn clothing. Ralph sat down and every head turned towards the figure at the far end of the table.

He was the biggest man in the room and monumentally ugly. His beard was a grey scraggly fringe, and his face hung in folds, the speckled skin darkly burned by the fierce African sun. One eyelid drooped to give him a crafty, suspicious expression and his toffee-brown eyes were bloodshot and inflamed. His people called him Oom Paul, Uncle Paul, and held him in only slightly less veneration than they did their Old Testament God.

Ralph watched him intently as he began to read aloud from the open Bible before him, and he thought of the legend that surrounded this strange man.

Paul Kruger had been nine years old when his father and uncles had packed their wagons and gathered their herds and trekked northwards from the Cape, away from British rule. The year had been 1835 and on that hard trek Paul Kruger became a man, at an age when most boys are still playing with kites and marbles. He became, by necessity, an expert marksman. He was also a skilled horseman and developed an almost mystical affinity for the veld, and the herds of fat-tailed sheep and multi-hued cattle that were his family's wealth. Like a Matabele majiba, he knew every beast by name, and could pick out an ailing animal from the herd at a mile distant.

At sixteen, he was entitled, as a citizen of the new Boer Republic of the Transvaal, to ride off two farms—each approximately sixteen thousand acres, as much land as a horseman could encircle in a day. They were the first of the vast land holdings he acquired and held during his lifetime. At twenty he was a field cornet, an elected office which was something between magistrate and sheriff. To be chosen at such tender years by men who venerated age, marked him as somebody unusual. After having fought every warlike tribe south of the Limpopo River, after having burned Dr. David Livingstone's mission on the suspicion that he was supplying arms to the tribes, after having fought even the rebellious Boers of the Orange Free State, he was made Commandant-in-Chief of the

114

army, and still later the President of the Transvaal Republic.

It was this indomitable, courageous, devout and cantankerous old man who now lifted his head from the Bible, and finished his reading with a simple injunction to the men who waited upon him.

"Fear God, and distrust the English."

The men around the table charged their pipes, watching Ralph with closed and guarded expressions. Once the oily blue smoke had veiled the air, Kruger spoke again.

"You asked to see me, *mijn heer?*"

"Alone," said Ralph.

"These men I trust."

"Very well."

They used the simplified Dutch which the Boers called the taal, the language. Ralph knew that Kruger could speak English with some fluency, but that he would not do so as a matter of principle, and Ralph had learned the taal on the diamond diggings.

"My name is Ballantyne."

"I know who you are. Your father was the elephant hunter. A strong man, they say, and straight—but you," and now a world of loathing entered the old man's tone, "you belong to that heathen, Rhodes." Kruger shook his head slowly. "Do not think I have not heard his blasphemies. He will pay for them one day, for the Lord has commanded 'Thou shalt not take my name in vain.'"

"Perhaps that day is already at hand," said Ralph softly. "And perhaps you are God's chosen instrument."

"Do you dare to blaspheme, also?" the old man demanded sharply.

"No." Ralph shook his head. "I come to deliver the blasphemer into your hands." And he laid an envelope on the table. "A list of the arms he has sent secretly into Johannesburg, and where they are held; the size of the force gathered on your borders at Pitsani, and the route they will take to join the rebels in Johannesburg."

Every man at the table had stiffened with shock; only the old man still puffed calmly at his pipe. "Why do you come to me with this?"

"When I see a thief about to break into a neighbour's home, I take it as my duty to warn him. We are white men living in Africa. We have a common destiny. We have many enemies, and one day we may be required to fight them together."

Kruger's pipe gurgled softly, but nobody spoke again for fully two minutes, until Ralph broke the silence.

"Very well then," he said. "If Rhodes fails, I will make a great deal of money."

Kruger sighed. "All right, now I believe you, for that is an Englishman's reason for treachery." He picked up the envelope in his brown gnarled old hand. "Goodbye, *mijn heer*," he said softly.

CATHY HAD TAKEN to her paintbox again. She had begun a study of the trees of Rhodesia, and already had a considerable portfolio of them. Her new hobby helped fill the dreary days when Ralph was away, and this morning she had found a beautiful spreading tree on one of the hills above the camp.

Cathy was busy sketching the upper branches when she heard a voice calling in the thick bush.

"Yoo hoo!" she yodelled, and the telegraph operator came sweating and scrambling up the steep hillside. He was a dismal shrimp of a man, with a bald head and protruding eyes—but he was also one of Cathy's most fervent admirers. The arrival of a telegraph for her was an excuse for him to leave his hut and seek her out.

He waited adoringly as she read the message.

PASSAGE RESERVED UNION CASTLE LEAVING CAPE TOWN FOR LONDON MARCH 20 STOP OPEN ENVELOPE AND FOLLOW INSTRUCTIONS CAREFULLY STOP HOME SOON LOVE RALPH

"Will you send a telegraph for me, Mr. Braithwaite?"

Cathy wrote out the message, recalling Zouga Ballantyne to King's Lynn, on a sheet of her sketch pad, and Mr. Braithwaite clutched it to his chest like a holy talisman.

"Happy Christmas, Mrs. Ballantyne," he said, and Cathy started. The days had gone by so swiftly. She had not realized that 1895 was so far gone, and suddenly the prospect of Christmas alone in the wilderness, another Christmas without Ralph, appalled her.

"Happy Christmas, Mr. Braithwaite," she said, hoping he would leave before she began to cry. Her pregnancy made her so weak and weepy. If only Ralph would come back. . . .

PITSANI WAS NOT a town nor even a village. It was a single trading store, standing forlornly in the flat sandveld on the edge of the Kalahari Desert. To the east, however, it was only a few miles to the frontier of the Transvaal Republic.

The country was so flat and featureless and the scrub so low that

116

the rider could see the trading store from a distance of seven miles, and around it the little cone-shaped white tents of an army encamped. He had pushed his horse mercilessly along the thirty miles from the railway at Mafeking, for he bore an urgent message. His name was Captain Maurice Heany.

The sentries picked up his dust from two miles out, and when Heany trotted into the camp of the Rhodesia Horse, all its senior officers were already gathered at the command tent. Dr. Jameson himself came forward to shake his hand and lead him into the tent where they were screened from curious eyes.

Zouga Ballantyne poured Indian tonic into a dram of gin, and Heany drank gratefully before looking up at the little doctor.

"Well then, out with it, man," Jameson ordered.

"It's not good news, Dr. Jim. Mr. Rhodes is utterly determined that you must remain here until after the Reform Committee has captured Johannesburg."

"When will that be?" Jameson demanded bitterly. "Just look at these!" He picked up a sheaf of telegraph flimsies from the camp table. "A new telegraph every few hours, advising delay."

"There is one other thing that you should know." Heany hesitated. "It does seem that the Boers are aware that something is afoot. They are making certain preparations. It is even possible that they have already called out their commandos."

"If that is the case," Zouga said softly, "then we have a choice. We can either move immediately—or we can all go home to Bulawayo."

Dr. Jameson jumped up from his canvas chair and began pacing up and down the tent with quick jerky little strides. He stopped at the opening of the tent and stared out towards the eastern horizon beneath which lay the great golden prize of the Witwatersrand. When at last he turned back to face them they could see that he had reached his decision.

"I am going," he said.

"I am going with you," said Zouga, and Willoughby nodded.

"Good! Johnny, will you call the men out? And Zouga, will you see to it that the telegraph lines are all cut? I don't want ever to see another telegraph again."

"THEY'VE GOT JAMESON!" The cry echoed through the elegant hush of the Kimberley Club. The consternation was immediate and overwhelming. Members boiled out of the bar and the reading room into the marbled lobby, and surrounded the news crier, some lining the banisters and shouting their queries down the stairwell.

The bearer of the news was one of the prosperous Kimberley diamond buyers, and such was his agitation that he had forgotten to remove his straw boater when entering the club portals. Now he stood in the centre of the lobby, reading excitedly from a copy of "The Diamond Fields Advertiser", the ink of which was so fresh that it smeared his fingers.

"Jameson raises White Flag at Doornkop after sixteen killed in fierce fighting. General Cronje accepts surrender."

Ralph Ballantyne had not left his seat in the dining room, although his guests had deserted him to join the rush into the lobby. He signalled the distracted wine waiter to refill his glass while he waited for them to return.

They came trooping back, led by Aaron Fagan, like a funeral party returning from the cemetery.

"The Boers must have been waiting for them—"

"Dr. Jim walked straight into it—"

"What on earth did the man think he was doing?"

"Ralph, your father is among the prisoners!"

For the first time Ralph showed emotion. He snatched the paper from Aaron's hand, and stared at it in agony. "That's not possible!"

Somebody else was yelling in the lobby. "Kruger has arrested all the members of the Reform Committee—he has promised to have them tried for their lives."

"The gold mines!" another said clearly in the ensuing silence, and instinctively every head lifted to the clock on the wall above the dining-room entrance. It was twenty minutes to two. The stock exchange reopened on the hour. There was another rush, this time out of the club doors. Some members shouted impatiently for their carriages, while others set out at a determined trot towards the stock-exchange buildings.

The club was almost deserted. Aaron and Ralph sat alone at the corner table, Ralph still holding the list of prisoners.

"I cannot believe it," he whispered. An image came into his mind of Zouga Ballantyne in a white shirt, his hands bound behind his back, regarding a rank of riflemen in front of him with calm green eyes. Ralph pushed his plate away from him.

At that moment the club secretary came out of his office ashen-faced, and stood in the doorway of the dining room.

"Gentlemen," he croaked. "More terrible news has just come through. Mr. Rhodes has offered his resignation as prime minister of Cape Colony. He has also offered to resign from the chairmanship of the Charter Company, of De Beers and of Consolidated Goldfields."

"Ralph." Aaron was staring at him across the table. "The bear transaction, you sold the shares of Charter and Consolidated short, and your position is still open."

"I HAVE CLOSED all your transactions," said David Silver. "I averaged out BSA shares at a little over seven pounds—that gives you a profit, after commission and levy, of almost four pounds a share. You did even better on the Consolidated Goldfields transactions, as they were the worst hit in the crash." David Silver looked at Ralph with awe. "It is the kind of killing which becomes a legend on the floor, Mr. Ballantyne. The total is one million and fifty-eight pounds eight shillings and sixpence. After the one that Mr. Rhodes paid to Barney Barnato for his claims in the Kimberley mine, it is the largest cheque ever drawn in Africa, south of the equator—what do you say to that, Mr. Ballantyne!"

Ralph looked at Aaron in the chair behind the desk. "Just be certain that cheque can never be traced back to me."

"I understand," Aaron nodded, and Ralph changed the subject.

"Has there been an answer to my telegraph yet? My wife is not usually so slow in replying. I must get her down here, where she can have expert medical attention. She is within two months of her time."

"I'll send my clerk to the telegraph office." Aaron crossed to the outer office to give his instructions, as David Silver respectfully took his leave. He had to shoo his nephew out of the door.

"Poor David," he murmured, as he came back to the desk. "His very first millionaire—it's a watershed in any stockbroker's life."

Ralph did not smile. "My father—"

"I'm sorry, Ralph. There is nothing more we can do. He will go back to England in chains with Jameson and the others. They are to be imprisoned in Wormwood Scrubs until they are called to answer the charge."

"What will happen to them? It's a capital offence—"

"Oh, no, Ralph, I am sure it won't come to that."

Ralph stared moodily out of the window, for the hundredth time castigating himself for not having anticipated that Jameson would cut the telegraph lines before marching on Johannesburg. The recall that Cathy had sent could not have reached Zouga and he had ridden into the waiting Boer commandos with the rest of them.

Ralph looked up expectantly as the clerk came into the office.

"Has there been a reply from my wife?" The man shook his head.

"Begging your pardon, Mr. Ballantyne, sir, there has not." The clerk gulped. "But there has been a message from Tati on the Rhodesian border. A rider got through this morning. He seems to have been the only survivor—"

"Survivor!" Ralph stared at him. "What does that mean? What on earth are you talking about?"

"The Matabele have risen. They are murdering all the whites in Rhodesia—man, woman and child!"

"MUMMY, DOUGLAS AND SUSS aren't here. There is nobody to get me breakfast." Jonathan came into the tent while Cathy was still brushing out her hair.

"Tell one of the grooms to go down and fetch them, darling."

"The grooms aren't here either."

Cathy stood up. "All right, then, let's go and see about it."

They stepped out into the dawn. Overhead the sky was a lovely dark rose colour, and the bird chorus in the trees above the camp was like the tinkle of silver bells. The campfire had died to a puddle of grey powdery ash.

Cathy crossed to the kitchen hut. It was deserted. She frowned with annoyance, and then looked up as the doorway darkened.

"Oh Isazi," she greeted the little Zulu. "Where are the servants?"

"Who knows where a Matabele dog will hide himself when he is needed?" Isazi asked contemptuously. "They have most likely spent the night drinking beer and now their heads are too heavy to carry."

"You'll have to help me," said Cathy, "until the cook gets here."

After breakfast Cathy called Isazi again. "I want to go down to the railhead. I hope there is a telegraph from Henshaw. Will you put the ponies into the trap?"

There was a little frown of concern on the old Zulu's wrinkled features. "The horses—they are not in the kraal."

"Where are they, then?"

"Perhaps one of the mujiba took them out early. I will go and see if I can find them."

120

"Oh, it doesn't matter." Cathy shook her head. "It's only a short walk to the telegraph hut. The exercise will be good for me," and she called to Jonathan. Swinging her bonnet by its ribbon and with Jonathan skipping beside her, she started along the track that led around the side of the hill towards the railhead.

Jonathan noticed it first. "It's so quiet, Mama," he said, and they stopped to listen. There was no clangour of hammers on steel.

"That's strange." Cathy held her bonnet up to shade her eyes from the low sun. There was a pile of teak sleepers at the railhead and a smaller bundle of steel rails. The sledgehammers and shovels were in neat stacks where the shift had left them at dusk the night before. There was no human movement.

"Where is Mr. Henderson, Mama?" Jonathan asked, his voice unusually subdued. "Where are Mr. Mac and Mr. Braithwaite?"

"I don't know. They must still be in their tents."

The tents of the white engineer and his supervisors were just beyond the square iron telegraph hut. There was no sign of life around the neat pyramids of canvas, except for a single black crow which sat on the peak of one of them. Its hoarse cawing reached them faintly, and as Cathy watched, it spread its black wings and flapped heavily to earth.

Suddenly Cathy shivered, and Jonathan shrank against her legs.

"Mummy, I'm frightened."

"Don't be a silly boy," Cathy told him firmly, and dragging him by the hand, she started down the hill.

By the time she reached the telegraph hut, she was panting. She did not know what prompted her to leave Jonathan at the steps of the veranda, but she went up alone to the door and pushed it open.

Mr. Braithwaite sat beside his table. He was staring at her with pale popping eyes, and his mouth hung open. "Mr. Braithwaite," Cathy said, and at the sound of her voice there was a hum like a swarm of bees taking flight, and the big cobalt-blue flies that had covered his shirt front rose in a cloud into the air, and she saw that his belly was a gaping mushy red.

Cathy backed away slowly out of the door. She felt her legs turn rubbery under her; she almost tripped on the steps, and sat down heavily. "I want you to be a brave little man," she whispered, as Jonathan ran to her.

She realized what had caused the hideous mutilation of the corpse in the hut. The Matabele always disembowelled their victims. It

121

was a ritual that released the spirit of the dead man, and allowed it to go on to its valhalla rather than return to haunt the slayer. This was the work of a Matabele war party.

"Where is Mr. Henderson, Mummy?" Jonathan demanded shrilly. "I am going to his tent."

The big burly engineer was one of Jonathan's favourite friends, and Cathy caught his arm. "No, Jon-Jon—don't go!" she pleaded. "Let Mummy think."

The missing servants had been warned, of course, as had the Matabele construction gangs. They knew that a war party was out, and they had faded away. The renegades would have struck at dawn, for it was the favourite hour. They had caught Henderson and his foreman asleep in the tents. Only the faithful little Braithwaite had been at his machine.

The telegraph machine—Cathy started up—the telegraph was her one link with the outside world.

"Jon-Jon, stay here," she ordered, and crept back towards the door of the hut. She steeled herself, and then glanced into the interior. One quick look was enough. The telegraph machine had been ripped from the wall and smashed into pieces on the floor.

She reeled back and leaned against the iron wall beside the door, clutching her swollen stomach with both hands. The service train from Kimberley was due late that afternoon, ten hours from now, and she was alone, except for Jonathan. Cathy reached for him and clung to him with the strength of despair, and only then realized that the boy was staring through the open doorway.

"Mr. Braithwaite is dead!" Jonathan said matter-of-factly. "They are going to kill us, too, aren't they, Mummy?"

"Oh Jon-Jon!"

"We need a gun. I can shoot. Papa taught me."

A gun—Cathy looked towards the silent tents. She did not think she had the courage to go into one of them—and then a shadow fell over her and she screamed.

"Nkosikazi. It is me." Isazi had come down the hill as silently as a panther. "The horses are gone," he said, and she motioned him to look into the telegraph hut.

Isazi's expression did not change. "So," he said quietly. "The Matabele jackals can still bite."

"The tents," Cathy whispered. "See if you can find a weapon."

Isazi went with a lithe swinging run, ducking from one tent

opening to another, and when he came back to her, he carried an
assegai with a broken shaft. "There are no guns. The Matabele have
taken them."

"There are guns at the camp," Cathy whispered.

"Come, Nkosikazi." He lifted her tenderly to her feet, and
Jonathan manfully took her other arm.

The first pain hit Cathy before they reached the thick bush at the
edge of the cut line, and it doubled her over. They held her while
the paroxysm lasted, and the little Zulu was grave and silent. Then,
at last, they went on up the track. Isazi was watching the forest on
both sides and he carried the broken assegai in his free hand.

Cathy gasped as the next pain caught her, and she went down on
her knees in the dust. When it passed, she looked up at Isazi.

"They are too close together. It is happening. Take Jonathan to
the Harkness Mine."

"Nkosikazi, the train—"

"The train will be too late. You must go. Without a horse, I could
never reach the Harkness."

He did not move.

"If you can save him, Isazi, then you save a part of me. If you stay
here, we will all die. Go. Go quickly!" she urged.

Isazi reached for Jonathan's hand, but he jerked away.

"I won't leave my Mummy." His voice rose hysterically. "Daddy
said I must look after my Mummy."

Cathy gathered herself. It took all her determination to perform
the most difficult task of her young life. She hit Jonathan
openhanded across the face, back and forth, with all her strength.

The child staggered away from her, the vivid crimson outlines of
her fingers rising on the pale skin of his cheeks. She had never
struck his face before.

"Do as I tell you," Cathy blazed at him furiously. "Go with Isazi
this very instant."

The Zulu snatched up the child, and looked down at her for a
moment longer. "You have the heart of a lioness. I salute you,
Nkosikazi," and he went bounding away into the forest, carrying
Jonathan with him. In seconds he had disappeared.

Only then did Cathy let the sobs come shaking and choking up
her throat. She thought of Ralph, and she had never loved nor
wanted him the way she did at that moment. It seemed that she had
used the last grain of her courage to strike her only child, and to

123

send him away. Then from somewhere deep within her she found the strength to rise and hobble on up the path.

At the heel of the hill, she looked down at the camp. Her home, her only home—it looked so welcoming, so safe. She struggled on, until, unbelievably, she reached her own tent, and again her legs gave way beneath her.

She crawled painfully across the floor, her hair tumbling down, and groped her way to the wagon chest at the foot of the big camp bed. The lid was so heavy that it took all her strength, but at last it fell open with a crash. The pistol was tucked under the white bed-covers that she had hoarded for the home that Ralph would one day build for her.

It was a big service Webley revolver. It needed both her hands to lift it. She sat with her back against the chest, her legs straight out in front of her, and she held the pistol in her lap.

She must have dozed, for when she started awake, it was to hear the whisper of feet against the bare earth. She looked up. There was the shadow of a man silhouetted by the slanting rays of the sun against the white canvas of the tent like a figure in a magic lantern show. She lifted the pistol—and the man stepped through the flap.

"Oh, thank God." Cathy let the pistol fall into her lap. "Thank God it's you," she whispered and let her head fall forward, the thick curtain of her hair parting.

Bazo looked down at the tender nape of her neck. He wore only a kilt of civet tails, and about his forehead a band of moleskin. In his left hand he held a broad stabbing assegai. In his right he carried a knobkerrie like the mace of a mediaeval knight.

The handle was three feet long, and the head was a ball of heavy wood stubbed with iron nails. When Bazo swung the knobkerrie, all the strength of his wide shoulders was behind the blow, and his point of aim was the pale nape of Cathy's neck.

Two of his warriors came into the tent and flanked Bazo, and they looked down at the crumpled body on the floor of the tent. One of them changed his grip on the assegai, ready for the cutting stroke. "The woman's spirit must fly," he said.

"Do it!" Bazo said, and the warrior stooped.

"There is life within her," he said. "See! It moves yet."

"Still it!" Bazo ordered, and left the tent, striding out into the sunlight.

"Find the boy," he ordered his men. "Find the white cub."

124

THE DRIVER OF THE locomotive was terrified. They had stopped for a few minutes at the trading post at Plumtree siding, and he had seen the bodies of the store keeper and his family lying in the front yard. But Ralph Ballantyne had thrust the muzzle of the rifle between his shoulder blades and marched him back to the cab, forcing him to go on northwards. They had come all the way from the Kimberley shunting yard with the throttle wide open and with Ralph himself, bare-chested and sweating in the furnace glare, shovelling the lumpy black coal into the firebox.

As they came roaring around the bend between the hills and saw the iron roof of the telegraph hut, Ralph clambered onto the side of the cab to peer ahead. His heart leaped joyfully when he saw movement around the hut—and then he recognized the doglike shapes of hyena, squabbling over what they had dragged out of the tents. It was only when Ralph started shooting that they scattered.

Ralph ran from the hut to each tent in turn, and then back to the locomotive. He scrambled up the side of the cattle truck behind the coal buggy, let down the door and led four horses out of the truck, one already saddled. He paused only long enough to cinch the girth, and then swung up into the saddle with the rifle still in his hand. "Wait here!" he shouted at the driver.

"I'm not going to wait," the driver yelled. "God Almighty, those murdering niggers will be back any minute."

"If my wife and son are here, I'll need to get them back. Give me one hour." Ralph asked.

"I'm not waiting another minute. I'm going back." The driver shook his head.

"You can go to hell, then," Ralph told him coldly.

He kicked his horse into a gallop, and dragging the spare mounts on the lead rein behind him took the track up the side of the kopje towards the camp. Before he turned the angle of the hill, he glanced back over his shoulder. The locomotive was already huffing back along the curve of the rails towards the south. Now, as far as he knew, he might be the only white man left alive in Rhodesia.

Ralph galloped into the camp. "Cathy!" he shouted, as he dismounted. "Jon-Jon! Where are you?"

The camp had been looted, Jonathan's clothing was scattered and trampled into the dust. Cathy's portfolio of drawings had been thrown down and had burst open, the paintings of which she was so proud were torn and crumpled.

Ralph ran on to their living tent, and ripped open the flap.

Cathy lay on her back with her unborn child beside her. He fell on his knees and tried to lift her, but her body was stiff as a statue carved in marble.

Ralph backed away, and then flung himself out of the tent. "Jonathan!" he screamed. "Jon-Jon! Where are you?"

He ran through the camp like a madman. When he found no living thing, he stumbled into the forest, up onto the slope of the kopje. "Come!" he yelled into the silent forest. "Come and find me also!" And he stopped to fire the Winchester into the air, and listen to the echoes go bounding away down the valley.

At last he could run and scream no more, and slowly he turned and went down the hill, moving like an old man. At the edge of the camp he stopped and peered at something that lay in the grass, then stooped and picked it up.

He turned it over and over in his hands, and then balled it into his fist. His knuckles turned white with the strength of his grip.

What he held was a headband of softly tanned moleskin.

Still holding the scrap of fur in his hand, he went into the camp to prepare his dead for burial.

THEY SQUATTED in long silent ranks in the long grass below the crest of the hills. It was strange to sit upon the bare earth during the waiting time. In the old days they would have sat on their shields, the long dappled shields of iron-hard oxhide, squatting upon them not for comfort but to hide their distinctive shapes from a watchful enemy. It was strange also not to be decked out in the full regimentals of the Inyati impi, the plumes and furs and tassels of cow-tails, the war rattles at ankle and wrist. They were dressed like unblooded boys, with only the kilt about their waists—but the scars upon their dark bodies and the fire in their eyes gave the lie to that impression.

Gandang felt himself choking with a pride that he once thought he would never experience again. He loved them, he loved their fierceness and their valour, and though his face was quiet and expressionless, the love shone through in his eyes.

"Baba!" they called him in their soft deep voices. "Father—we thought we would never fight at your shoulder again. Those of your sons who die today will be for ever young."

Across the neck of the hills a jackal wailed mournfully and was

126

answered from close at hand. The impi was in position, lying across the Khami hills like a coiled mamba, watchful and ready.

There was a glow in the sky now, and as the sun pushed up and gilded the treetops a wild pheasant called from the hill."Qwaali! Qwaali!" The penetrating cry was a characteristic sound of the veld, and only a sharp ear would have detected anything strange about this one.

Gandang rose to his feet at the sentry's signal. "The leopard comes," he said quietly, and stalked up to the vantage point from which he could look down the full length of road that led to the town of Bulawayo. There was an open coach and a troop of eleven horsemen upon the road. The figure that led them was unmistakable, even at this distance. The height in the saddle, the alert set of head, the long stirrups.

"Hau! One-Bright-Eye!" Gandang greeted him softly. "I have waited many long moons for you."

GENERAL MUNGO ST. JOHN had been awakened three hours before dawn by a man who had escaped from the trading store on the ten-mile drift. He had been stabbed through the thigh and his left arm was broken by blows from a knobkerrie. He had ridden into town clinging to his horse's neck with his good arm. "The Matabele are out!" he was screaming. "They are burning the farms!"

By first light there were fifty wagons formed into a laager in the market square. All Bulawayo's women and children had been brought into the laager and put to work making bandages and baking bread against a siege. The few able-bodied men that Dr. Jameson had not taken with him into the Transvaal were swiftly formed into troops, and horses and rifles were found for those who lacked them.

In the midst of the confusion, Mungo St. John had commandeered a fast open coach with a coloured driver, picked out the best mounted troop of horsemen, and using his authority as Acting Administrator given them the order, "Follow me!"

Now he reined in on the crest of the hills above Khami Mission and shaded his single eye. "Thank God!" he whispered. The thatched roofs of the mission that he had expected to see billowing with smoke and flame stood serenely in the quiet green valley beyond. "Forward!" he shouted, and spurred away down the track, with his troopers clattering behind him.

127

Robyn St. John came out of her laboratory, and as soon as she recognized the man that led the column she placed her hands upon her boyish hips and lifted her chin angrily. "What is the meaning of this intrusion, sir?" she demanded.

"Madam, the Matabele tribe is in full rebellion. They are murdering women and children, burning the homesteads. I have come to take you and your children to safety."

Robyn took a step backwards protectively, for Robert had come to hang onto her skirts. "The Matabele are my friends," she said. "I have nothing to fear from them. This is my home, and I do not intend leaving it."

"I do not have time for disputation, madam," Mungo said grimly. "Elizabeth!" he bellowed, and she came onto the veranda of the homestead. "The Matabele are in revolt. We are all in mortal danger. You have two minutes to gather what your family may need—"

"Take no heed of him, Elizabeth," Robyn shouted angrily. "We are staying here."

Before she realized his intention, Mungo had backed his horse up towards the laboratory doorway, stooped from the saddle and caught Robyn about the waist. He swung her up over the pommel of the saddle, walked his horse alongside the coach and with a heave of his shoulder dumped her in a flurry of petticoats onto the back seat. "Robert," he ordered his son, "go to your mother, immediately!"

The child scampered to the coach and climbed into it as Elizabeth ran out onto the veranda with a bundle over her shoulder.

"Good girl!" Mungo St. John jumped down to boost her into the coach, and then vaulted back into the saddle. "Troop, march," he ordered, and they wheeled out of the yard.

The coach was in the rear of the column. The ten troopers were in double ranks ahead of it, and five lengths out in front of them again rode Mungo St. John. How noble and dashing he looked, Elizabeth thought, how easily he sat his horse, and when he turned to look back at the coach how reckless was his smile. There was only one other man in all the world to match him. But that thought was sinful, and she put it away quickly, and to distract herself looked back down the hill.

"Oh, Mama!" she cried. "Look!"

The Mission was burning. The thatch of the church stood in a tall beacon of leaping flame. Smoke was curling out of the homestead,

128

and as they stared in horror, they saw tiny dark figures carrying torches of dry grass. One of them stopped to hurl his torch onto the roof of the clinic.

"My books," whispered Robyn. "All my papers. My life's work." She and Elizabeth clung to each other like lost children.

Their little column reached the crest of the pass, and without a pause the weary horses plunged down the far side—and the Matabele appeared simultaneously from both sides of the track. They rose out of the grass in two black waves, and the humming roar of their war chant swelled like the sound of an avalanche. The troopers had been riding with their carbines cocked, the butts resting on their right thighs, but so swift was the rush that only a single volley rippled down the column. Then as the horses reared and whinnied with terror the troopers were dragged from their saddles and stabbed through and through. The warriors were mad with blood lust, swarming over the bodies, snarling and howling.

Only Mungo St. John, five lengths ahead of the column, broke clear. He had taken an assegai thrust through the side, and the blood streamed down one leg of his breeches, but he still sat high in the saddle. He looked back over his shoulder, over the heads of the Matabele and straight into Robyn's eyes. It was only for an instant, and then he wheeled his horse, and drove back into the mass of black warriors, riding for the coach.

He fired his service pistol into the face of a warrior who leaped to catch his horse's head. "I'm here!" he shouted to Robyn. "Don't worry, my darling—" and then a warrior stabbed him through the belly. He doubled over and his horse went down, but miraculously Mungo St. John rose to his feet and stood foursquare with the pistol in his hand. His eye patch had been torn from his head, and the empty eye socket glared so demoniacally, that for a moment the warriors fell back. Then Gandang stepped out of the press, and the two men stood face to face for a long second. Mungo tried to lift the pistol, but his strength failed him, and Gandang drove the silver blade through the centre of Mungo St. John's chest.

Gandang stood over the body and pulled the blade free. There was a terrible silence as the amadoda formed a ring around where Mungo St. John lay upon his back, his features still twisted into a grimace of rage, his one eye glaring at the enemy he could no longer see. Then one by one, the warriors lifted their heads and stared at the huddle in the open body of the coach.

Their eyes were glazed with the killing
madness, and blood splattered their arms and chests
like a macabre war paint. The ranks swayed like prairie
grass in the breeze, and in the rear a single voice began to hum,
but before it could spread, Robyn St. John rose to her feet and from
the height of the coach looked down upon them. The hum died out
into silence as Robyn reached forward and flicked the reins, and the
mules started forward at a walk.

The Matabele watched her and still not one of them moved. Then
Gandang, senior induna of the Matabele, stepped off the track, and
behind him the ranks of his amadoda opened. The mules passed
slowly down the lane between them.

Robyn stared straight ahead, holding the reins stiffly. Just once as
she drew level with where Mungo St. John lay, she glanced down at
him, and then looked ahead again. Slowly the coach rolled on down

the hill, and when Elizabeth looked back, the road was deserted.

"They have gone, Mama," she whispered, and only then did she realize that Robyn was shaking with silent sobs.

Elizabeth put her arm around her shoulders, and for a moment Robyn leaned against her. "He was a terrible man, but, God forgive me, I loved him so," she whispered. Then she straightened up and urged the mules into a trot towards Bulawayo.

RALPH BALLANTYNE rode through the night, taking the direct path through the hills rather than the broad wagon road. The spare horses were loaded with food and blankets that he had salvaged from the railhead camp, and he led them at a walk over the rocky terrain, husbanding them for whatever efforts lay ahead of them. He rode with his rifle across his lap, loaded and cocked, yelling his despair into the silences of the wilderness. "Jonathan! Jonathan!"

When the dawn came he watered the horses at a stream and let them graze for a few hours, and at midmorning he up-saddled and rode on again. He knew that in daylight there was greater danger of running into a Matabele patrol, but the prospect had no terrors. He found himself welcoming it. Deep inside him he had found hatred and anger as he had never believed was possible.

An hour after noon, he climbed the ridge where Zouga had killed the great elephant and looked down onto the Harkness Mine. The buildings had been burned. On the far ridge the walls that Harry Mellow had built for Vicky were still standing, but the empty windows were like the eyes of a skull, the roof beams stark and blackened. The gardens were trampled, and the lawns were strewn with the debris of two young lives—the brass bedstead with stuffing bursting out of the torn mattress, the chests of Vicky's dowry broken open and the contents scorched and scattered.

Farther down the valley the mine store and office had been burned also, and in the trees about the burned-out buildings roosted hundreds of hunchbacked vultures. Ralph rode down off the crest and almost immediately found the first bodies: Matabele warriors, he saw with grim satisfaction, who had crawled away to die of their wounds. Harry Mellow had held out better than the construction gang at the railhead.

Ralph dismounted behind the ruins of the mine store and tethered the horses with a slippery hitch, ready for a quick run. Holding his rifle high, he stepped carefully through the ash and debris towards the corner of the building. When he reached the corner he peered around the wall.

There were two hundred yards of open ground between the burned-out store and the open mouth of the No. 1 shaft that Harry had driven into the side of the hill. The ground was heaped with dead warriors, piles and drifts of them. Most of them had been ripped by the birds and the jackals, but others were untouched.

"Good for you, Harry my boy," Ralph whispered.

Ralph was about to step into the open, when his eardrums cracked at a passing shot, so close that he felt his own hair flap against his forehead. He reeled back behind the shelter of the wall. The bullet must have missed by an inch or less, good shooting for a Matabele sniper. They were notoriously poor marksmen.

He had been careless, stupidly presuming that the impi had finished its bloody business and gone on. Now he crouched low and ran back down the length of the burned building to where one corner of the stone wall had collapsed. Carefully he peered out over the bloody ground. They were well concealed, probably in the bush above the mineshaft.

Then with a start of surprise he realized that the mouth of the shaft had been barricaded, blocked with baulks of timber and what looked like sacks of maize. They were in the mineshaft, but that didn't make sense, he puzzled. Yet it was confirmed immediately. There was a vague shadowy movement in the throat of the shaft, and another bullet sang off the lip of the wall under Ralph's nose.

He ducked down. Then he filled his lungs and bellowed. "Harry! Harry Mellow! It's me, Ralph."

There was a faint answering shout, and Harry Mellow was racing towards him, jumping over the piles of dead Matabele. They met halfway, and embraced with the violence of relief, wordlessly pounding each other's backs, and then before he could speak, Ralph looked over the American's shoulder. Other figures had emerged from behind the rude barricade. Vicky, dressed in men's breeches and shirt, with a rifle in her hand and at her side the diminutive Isazi. Another even smaller figure ran ahead of them both. The child ran with both arms pumping, and face screwed up.

Ralph caught him up and hugged him to his chest, pressing his unshaven cheek against the boy's velvet skin. "Jonathan," he croaked, and then his voice failed. The feel of the child's warm body, and the milky puppy smell of him was almost too painful to be borne.

"Daddy." Jonathan pulled back his head, and his face was pale and stricken. "I couldn't look after Mummy. She wouldn't let me."

"That's all right, Jon-Jon," Ralph whispered. "You did your best." And then he was crying with terrible dry hacking sobs.

THOUGH HE HATED to let the child out of his arms for a moment, Ralph sent Jonathan to help Isazi feed the horses. Then he drew Vicky and Harry Mellow aside.

"Cathy is dead," he told them. "I don't want to say any more."

Harry held Vicky while she wept and when her first sharp grief was over, Ralph went on, "We can't stay here. We have a choice, south to the railhead, or Bulawayo."

"Bulawayo may be burned and sacked by now," Harry pointed out. "But if anyone is still alive there, then they'll need fighting men to stay that way."

"My mother and my family will be at Bulawayo. This is the land of my birth—I'm not running away," Vicky said. She wiped the wetness off her cheeks. "If you go there, I'm coming with you."

Ralph nodded. He would have been surprised if she had agreed to go south.

They took the wagon road northwards, past the little one-man goldmines and the homesteads where men and their families had begun to carve a life out of the wilderness. Some of them had been taken completely by surprise, the corpses still clad in the remnants of their nightclothes. Others had sold their lives dearly, and the dead Matabele were flung in a wide circle around the burned-out buildings. Once they found dead amadodo but no white bodies, and there were tracks of horses and a vehicle heading out northwards.

"Please God they got away—" Ralph said.

Vicky wanted to take the old wagon road, past Khami Mission, but Ralph would not do so. "If they are there, it's too late. You've seen enough. If they got away, we'll find them in Bulawayo."

So they rode into Bulawayo in the early morning of the third day. The barricades opened to let them pass into the huge central laager in the town square, and the townspeople thronged around the horses shouting questions.

"When are the soldiers coming?"

"Did you see my brother—he was at the Antelope Mine?"

"Have you any news?"

When she saw Robyn waving to her from the top of one of the

wagons in the Market Square, Vicky wept again for the first time since leaving the Harkness Mine.

Elizabeth jumped down from the wagon and pushed her way through the crowd to Ralph's horse. "Cathy?" she asked. Ralph shook his head and saw his own sorrow reflected in her dark eyes.

Elizabeth reached up and lifted Jonathan down from the front of the saddle. "I'll look after him, Ralph," she said softly.

THE FAMILY WAS installed in a corner of the central laager where, under Robyn's and Louise's direction, the single wagon had been turned into a crowded but adequate home. On the first day of the rising, Louise and the little Hottentot Jan Cheroot had brought the wagon in from King's Lynn. Alerted by the desertion of the Matabele labourers and servants, they had taken time to pack the wagon with essentials, and thus the family did not have to rely on the charity of the townsfolk, unlike so many others who had arrived with only a lathered horse and an empty rifle.

Ralph set off across the laager to find a member of the siege committee, and it was after dark when he got back to the wagon. Elizabeth had bathed both Jonathan and Robert, and now as they ate their dinner at the camp table, she was telling them a story that made their eyes big as marbles in the lamplight. Ralph smiled his thanks at her, and summoned Harry Mellow with an inclination of his head.

The two men sauntered off, while Ralph spoke quietly. "The siege committee seem to be doing a good job—but nobody has yet thought of anything but defence. I've given them the first news that they have had from outside the territory since the rising began. They were delighted to think that their plight is known in Kimberley and they seemed to think that was as good as a couple of regiments of cavalry on their way already."

"It will take months to get troops up here. How many have the savages murdered?"

"There are hundreds of scattered farms and mines out there. We have to reckon on five hundred men, women and children dead."

They walked on in silence to the far end of the laager, and Ralph spoke quietly to the guard who challenged him there.

"All right, Mr. Ballantyne, but keep your eyes open. Those murdering heathen are all over."

Ralph and Harry passed on through into the deserted town. The

135

thatch and daub shanties were dark and silent, and the two men walked down the dusty main street until the buildings petered out and they stood staring out into the scrubland.

"Listen!" said Ralph. A jackal yipped down near the Umguza stream, and was answered from the shadows of the acacia forest out in the south.

"Jackal," said Harry, but Ralph shook his head.

"Matabele." Ralph was staring out into the veld, and he was teasing something in his hands like a string of Greek worry beads. "There are probably twenty thousand fighting bucks out there. Sooner or later, when they have massed their impis, they will come."

"What are our chances?"

Ralph wrapped the thing he held in his hand around one finger, and Harry saw it was a strip of drab fur. "We have got four Maxim guns, but there are six hundred women and children—and out of the nine hundred men, half are not fit to hold a rifle. The best way to defend Bulawayo is not to sit in the laager and wait for them."

"What are you going to do, Ralph?"

"I am going to get together a group of men who know the tribe, and the land—those who can shoot straight and talk Sindebele well enough to pass as natives. We are going to go out there, wherever they are hiding, and we are going to start killing Matabele."

THERE WERE SHRIEKS of delight as Judy set about her husband with her baton. The children in the front row clapped their hands as the blows cracked upon Punch's wooden head and his grotesquely humped back, and the bells on his cap jingled.

Swimming valiantly against the mainstream of sentiment, Jon-Jon's face was outraged, and as red as Punch's nose. "Hit her back!" he howled, bouncing up and down. "She's only a girl!"

"Spoken like a true Ballantyne," Ralph laughed, at the same time forcibly restraining his son from leaping into the fray.

Elizabeth sat beyond Jon-Jon with Robert on her lap, her face radiant with a childlike joy as she egged Judy on to further excesses. It drew Ralph's attention from the puppets, and he watched her covertly over Jonathan's curly head. Her enjoyment was natural and unashamed, and he laughed again in sympathy.

The sketch ended to Jonathan's vast satisfaction with Judy being led away to some richly deserved fate by a policeman in Mr. Peel's blue helmet. He sat on his father's shoulder as the audience dispersed across the laager chattering like a flock of starlings. Ralph and Elizabeth walked in silence.

When they reached the wagon, the children scampered away. Half-heartedly, Elizabeth made to follow them, but stopped and turned back to him when Ralph spoke.

"I don't know what I would have done without you. You've been wonderfully kind." He hesitated. "Without Cathy—" He saw the pain in her eyes and broke off. "I just wanted to thank you."

"You don't have to do that, Ralph," she answered quietly. "Anything you need—I'll always be here to help." She started to speak again, but her lips trembled and she turned away sharply and followed the two boys into the wagon.

ISAZI BROUGHT IN fourteen men. They were all Zulus from the south, drivers and wagon boys from the Zeederberg Company who had been stranded in Bulawayo by the rinderpest. Jan Cheroot brought in six more, all of them Cape boys, with mixed Bushman and Hottentot blood, like Jan Cheroot himself. They were all good men, fluent in Sindebele.

Ralph had paid siege prices for a bottle of whisky, and he took it hidden under his coat to where Isazi and Jan Cheroot sat away from their men. They sipped in silence for a while, all of them staring into the campfire flames, letting the warmth of the spirit spread through their bodies.

At last Isazi began to speak quietly. "Gandang and his Inyati impi are still waiting in the Khami Hills. He has twelve hundred men, all blooded warriors. Babiaan is bivouacked below the hills of the indunas with six hundred." Quickly Isazi recounted the positions of the impis, and the mood of their warriors.

"What of Bazo and his Moles?" At last Ralph asked the question that concerned him most.

Isazi shrugged. "We do not have word of them. I have my best men in the hills, searching for them. Nobody knows where the Moles have gone."

Ralph poured out some more whisky, and as he cupped the mug in his hands his mind went back to the afternoon and the puppet show they had watched, to the laughter of the children, and to those women and children who were not there—who had perished under the Matabele assegais.

His voice was rough and ugly. "Their women and children," he said. "They will be hidden in the caves and the secret valleys of the Matopos. Find them!"

THERE WERE FIVE small boys under the bank of the stream, all stark naked, and covered with slick yellow clay. They laughed and squabbled good-naturedly as they dug the clay out of the bank and packed it into crudely woven reed baskets.

Tungata Zebiwe, The Seeker After Justice, was the first to climb out of the stream, lugging the heavy basket to a shady place where he squatted and set to work. He took a handful of clay from his basket and rolled it into a thick soft sausage between his pink palms. Then he moulded it, forming the humped back and sturdy legs, the head on its thick neck set at a proud angle.

He sat back and studied it with a critical eye. "Inkunzi Inkulu," he hailed his creation. "Great Bull!"

Tanase watched him from the shadows. She had come silently down the path through the thick bush, and now she was reluctant to interrupt this magical moment. In the menace and smoke of war, it seemed that joy and laughter had been forgotten. It needed the vision of a child to remind her of what had once been—and what might be again.

Then Tungata looked up and saw her, and came to her carrying the clay bull with shy pride. "See what I have made for you, Umame."

Tanase took the offering. "He is a fine bull, and he will breed many calves," she said, and she felt a suffocating weight of love overwhelm her, so that the tears scalded her eyelids. She did not want the child to see it.

"Come," she told him. "We must go up to the cave."

He skipped beside her on the path, up to the cave in the base of the cliff. There were almost five hundred persons living in this place, one of the secret safe places of the tribe, where the women and the children were sent when war or some other catastrophe threatened the Matabele. Though the valley was steep and narrow, there were five escape routes, hidden paths scaling the cliffs or narrow clefts through the granite, which made it impossible for an enemy to trap them in the gut of the valley.

Juba was at the far end of the shelter, and when she looked up and saw Tanase and Tungata her smile split the great round of her face.

"My mother," Tanase knelt before her respectfully. "I must speak with you. Bazo has sent for me. There is dissension amongst the indunas. Bazo needs the words of the Umlimo made clear. Without that the struggle will fail. We will lose all that we have won so dearly."

"Then you must go, my child. Tungata is safe here. I will look after him. When do you leave?"

"Immediately."

Juba sighed and nodded. "So be it."

Tanase touched the child's cheek. "Obey your grandmother," she said softly, and like a shadow she was gone.

TANASE PASSED THROUGH the granite portals that guarded the valley of the Umlimo. As soon as she entered the little cluster of huts in the bottom of the valley, she was immediately aware of the tension that hung over the place like a sickly miasma over a fever swamp.

She could feel the anger and frustration in Bazo when she knelt before him and made her obeisance, and before she rose she had noted how the indunas had drawn into two separate groups. On one side were the elders, and facing them the young and headstrong were ranged about Bazo.

She crossed the space between them and knelt before Gandang and his white-haired brothers, Somabula and Babiaan.

"I see you, my child." Gravely Gandang acknowledged her greeting, and then abruptly he broached the reason for her summons. "We wish you to speak on the meaning of the Umlimo's latest prophecy."

"My Lord and father, I am no longer an intimate of the mysteries."

"You understand more than anyone outside that dreadful cave," Gandang said impatiently. "Listen to the words of the Umlimo—and discourse faithfully upon them."

She bowed her head in acquiescence.

"The Umlimo spake thus: 'Only a foolish hunter blocks the opening of the cave from which the wounded leopard seeks to escape.'" As Gandang repeated the prophecy, his brothers nodded at the accuracy of his rendition.

"There is more," Gandang continued. "The Umlimo spake a second time: 'The hot wind from the north will scorch the weeds in the fields, before the new corn can be planted. Wait for the north wind.'"

All the indunas leaned forward eagerly.

"Speak to us of the meaning," Gandang told her.

"The Umlimo's words are never clear at once," Tanase answered. "But I can read meaning into the parable of the foolish hunter who hesitates in the entrance of the cave." Gandang frowned as he guessed the slant of her reply, but she went on calmly. "Would not the brave and skilled hunter go boldly into the cave where the animal lurks, and slay it?"

One of the elder indunas hissed with disagreement, and sprang to his feet. "I say that the Umlimo has warned us to leave the road to the south open, so that the white men may leave this land for ever," he shouted, and immediately Bazo was on his feet facing him.

"The white men will never leave. The only way to rid ourselves of them is to bury them. If you leave the south road open, it will certainly be used—by the soldiers who march up it with their little three-legged guns."

There were angry cries of denial and encouragement.

"I say to you that *we* are the hot wind from the north that the Umlimo prophesied, *we* are the ones who will scorch the weeds."

The shouts that drowned him out showed just how deeply the nation's leaders were divided, and Tanase felt the blackness of despair as Gandang rose to his feet.

"We must give the white men a chance to leave with their women. We will leave the road open for them to go—and we will. wait in patience for the miraculous wind from the north that the Umlimo promises to blow our enemies away—"

Bazo alone had not squatted respectfully to the senior induna, and now he did something that was without precedent. He interrupted his father.

"You have given them chance enough," he said, and his voice was full of scorn. "You have let the woman from Khami and all her brats go free. I ask you, my father, is what you propose kindness or is it cowardice?"

Gandang looked at Bazo across the small space that separated them, which was a gulf neither of them would ever be able to bridge again. Though he was still tall and erect, there was a sorrow in his eyes that made him seem as old as the granite hills that surrounded them. "You are no longer my son," he said simply.

"And you are no longer my father." Turning on his heel, Bazo strode from the hut. First Tanase, and then one after another the young indunas stood up and followed him out into the sunlight.

THERE WAS NO DOUBT that he was a wizard. He was a little fellow, painted in the most marvellous colours, zigzags of crimson and white and black across his face and chest.

When he first appeared out of the bush beside the stream in the secret valley, Tungata and his companions were frozen with terror. But before they could recover their wits sufficiently to run, the little painted wizard uttered such a string of cries and grunts, imitating horse and eagle and baboon, that their terror turned to fascination. Then from the sack over his shoulder, the wizard dug out a huge lump of rock sugar candy. He sucked it noisily, and the children who had not tasted sugar in weeks drew closer and watched him with glistening dark eyes.

Then Tungata edged forward, snatched a proffered lump of sugar and scampered back. The little wizard laughed in such an infectious manner that the other children swarmed forward to grab at the fresh lumps of candy. Surrounded by laughing, clapping children, the little wizard climbed the path up the side of the valley to the rock shelter.

The women, reassured by the happy children, came to crowd about the little wizard.

"Who are you?" the boldest asked him. "What is in the sack?"

In reply the wizard drew out a handful of coloured ribbons, and the younger women shrieked with feminine vanity.

"I bring gifts and happy tidings," he cackled. "Look what I bring you."

There were steel combs, and small round mirrors, a little box that played sweet tinkling music—they crowded about him, utterly enchanted.

"Gifts and happy tidings," said the wizard. "The spirits of our forefathers have come to aid us. They have sent a divine wind to eat up the white men, as the rinderpest ate up the cattle. All the white men are dead!"

"The Amakiwa are dead!"

"The town of Bulawayo is empty of white men, and all these wonderful things are there for all to take, as much as you will. But hurry, all the men and women of the Matabele are going there.

141

There will be nothing left for those who come after. Those who want them must follow me!"

"Lead us, Little Father," they begged him. "We will follow you."

The women snatched up their little ones, called to the elder children and hurried after the wizard, down towards the end of the narrow valley.

"Follow me, people of Mashobane!" he chirped. "Your time of greatness has come. The prophecy of the Umlimo is fulfilled."

Tungata, almost hysterical with dread that he would be left behind, hurried down the length of the rock shelter, until he saw the huge beloved figure squatting against the wall of rock.

"Grandmother," he squeaked. "The wizard has pretty things for us all. We must hurry!"

THE STREAM HAD CUT a narrow twisted exit from the valley, with high cliffs on each side. Compressed into this chasm the stream fell in smoking cascades of white water, before debouching into a shallower wider valley in the lower foothills. Here, the gradient became more gentle as the path emerged into the quiet valley below. Rainwater had scarred the side of the lower valley with deep natural entrenchments, and one of these afforded an ideal emplacement for the Maxim.

Ralph had two of his troopers set it up, with two thousand rounds of ammunition stacked beside the weapon. While Harry Mellow cut branches of thornbush to screen the Maxim, Ralph paced off the ranges in front of the entrenchment and set up a cairn of loose stones beside the footpath. "Set the sights for three hundred yards," he told Harry.

Then he gave his orders to each man, making sure there was no misunderstanding. "When Jan Cheroot reaches the cairn, the Maxim will fire. Wait for the Maxim, then open up on the back of the column, and move your fire forward."

They nodded, and Ralph returned to where Harry Mellow was preparing the Maxim. From the pouch on his hip he took the strip of mole fur and bound it carefully about his right arm above the elbow.

"Ready!" Harry looked up at Ralph.

"Now all we have to do is wait."

They waited in the sunlight, and it beat down upon their naked backs until the sweat poured. They waited while the sun made its noon, and began to slip down the farther side of the sky. Then,

142

abruptly, Ralph raised his head, and at the movement a little stirring rippled down the line of marksmen lining the lip of the entrenchment.

From the entrance to the gorge a diminutive figure came dancing. The weird pattern of coloured paints disguised Jan Cheroot's features, but there was no mistaking his sprightly step, and the way he carried his head at a birdlike angle. He scampered down the path towards the stone cairn which Ralph had built, and behind him came the Matabele. So eager were they that they crowded three or four abreast, and jostled each other to keep pace with the Pied Piper that led them.

"More than I had hoped," Ralph whispered. Harry Mellow did not look at him, but his eyes were stricken as he stared fixedly over the sights of the Maxim.

"Ready," Ralph grated.

Jan Cheroot reached the cairn, and then with a miraculous twinkling movement, he disappeared as though a pitfall had sucked him in.

"Now!" said Ralph. "Open fire!"

"I can't do it," whispered Harry.

"Damn you!" Ralph's voice shook. "They slit Cathy open and tore my daughter out of her womb. Kill them, damn you!"

"I can't." Harry choked, and Ralph seized his shoulder and dragged him backwards. He dropped down behind the gun and grabbed the double pistol grips. With his forefingers he hooked the safety locks open, pressing his thumbs down on the chequered firing button. The Maxim gun began its hellish fluttering roar, and the empty brass cartridge cases spewed in a bright stream from the breach.

Peering through the drifts of blue gunsmoke, Ralph slowly traversed the gun from left to right, sweeping the pathway from the mouth of the gorge to the stone cairn, and from each side of him the repeating Winchesters added their thunder to the din. The gunfire almost, but not quite, drowned out the sounds from the valley below.

JUBA COULD NOT keep pace with the younger women, nor with the racing children, and she lagged farther and farther behind, with Tungata urging her on anxiously. "We will be too late, Grandmother. We must hurry."

Before they reached the gorge at the end of the valley, Juba was wheezing and staggering, her rolls of shining fat wobbling. "I must rest," she panted, and sank down beside the path as the stragglers streamed past her.

Tungata waited, hopping from one foot to the other with impatience. "Oh Grandmother, just a little farther—"

When at last she rose again and hobbled along the path, they were the very last in the file, but they could hear the laughter and chanting far ahead, magnified by the funnel of the gorge. Tungata ran forward, and then drawn by his duty, skipped back to seize Juba's hand again.

"Please, Grandmother—oh please hurry!"

Twice more Juba was forced to stop. They were all alone when the two of them came around the bend of the narrow gorge and looked out between the high granite portals into the open sunlit grassy bowl beyond. The pathway through the yellow grassland was thick with people, but the column had come against an obstacle and the head of the line was bunching and milling.

Juba heaved her bulk upright and hobbled towards the welcoming warm sunlight. At that moment the air around her head began to flutter as though a bird had been trapped within her skull. For a moment she thought that it was a symptom of her exhaustion, but then she saw the masses of human figures ahead of her begin to swirl and tumble.

Although she had never heard it before, she had listened when the warriors who had fought at Shangani described the little three-legged guns that chattered like old women. Armed suddenly by reserves of strength that she never believed she possessed, Juba seized Tungata and blundered back up the gorge.

RALPH BALLANTYNE sat on the edge of his camp bed. There was a lighted candle on the upturned tea chest that served as a table, and a half-filled whisky bottle beside it. The bottle had been full half an hour before. He shook his head to try to clear it, then he picked up his pen, dipped it and wrote. "War makes monsters of us all."

Ralph reached for the bottle again, but knocked it on its side, and the golden spirit glugged into a puddle on the lid of the tea chest. He fell back on the bed and closed his eyes, his legs dangling to the floor and one arm thrown over his face protectively.

Elizabeth had put the boys to bed in the wagon, and crawled into

144

the bed below theirs, careful not to disturb her mother. Now she lay on her side under the woollen blanket, and her eye was level with the laced-up opening in the canvas hood. She could see the candle still burning in Ralph's tent, but in the corner of the laager the tent that Harry and Vicky shared had been in darkness for an hour.

She closed her eyes and tried to force herself to sleep, but she was so restless that beside her Robyn St. John sighed petulantly and rolled over. Gently Elizabeth eased herself out from under the blanket. She picked up her shawl from the lid of the chest, and clambered silently down to the ground.

With the shawl about her shoulders, she sat on the disselboom of the wagon. The night was warm, and the laager almost silent. Two of the sentries met at the nearest corner, and their voices murmured for a while. Then they parted and she saw the silhouette of a slouch hat against the night sky as one of them passed close to where she sat.

The candle still burned in Ralph's tent, and it was past midnight by now. The flame drew her as though she were a moth. She rose and crossed to the tent silently, lifted the flap and slipped inside.

Ralph lay on his back on the steel bed, his booted feet dangling to the ground, and one arm covered his face. He was making an unhappy whimpering sound in his sleep. The candle was guttering, and the smell of spilled whisky was sharp and pungent.

Elizabeth crossed to the tea chest and set the fallen bottle upright. Then the open page of the journal caught her attention, and she read the big uneven scrawl: "War makes monsters of us all."

It gave her a pang of pity so sharp that she closed the leatherbound journal quickly, and looked at the man who had written that agonized heartcry.

Squatting beside the bed, she undid the straps of his boots, and then taking them one at a time between her knees, she pulled them off. Ralph muttered and rolled away from the candlelight. Gently Elizabeth lifted his legs and swung them up onto the bed, and he groaned and curled into a foetal position.

"Big baby," she whispered, and smiled to herself. Then she could resist no longer and she stroked the thick dark lock of hair off his forehead. His skin was fever-hot, moist with sweat, and she laid her palm against his cheek. And then she sensed the moment when he became conscious.

"Cathy!" he said hoarsely. "My Katie! I missed you so!" He looked

145

at her uncomprehendingly for a long moment, and then she saw the change in his eyes.

"Not Cathy," she said softly. "It's Elizabeth." She took his hand. "I love you. I have always loved you—I will always love you."

JORDAN BALLANTYNE stood beside his father on the platform of the Cape Town railway station. They were both stiff and awkward in the moment of parting.

"Please don't forget to give my very warmest regards to Louise."

"I am sure she will be pleased," said Zouga. "I have not seen her for so long—" he broke off. The separation from his wife had drawn out over the long months of his trial before the Lord Chief Justice, and a special jury.

The Lord Chief Justice had shepherded the reluctant jury towards the inevitable verdict of guilty, and he had his way.

"The sentence of the Court, therefore, is that as to you Leander Starr Jameson, and as to you John Willoughby, you be confined for a period of fifteen months' imprisonment; that you, Major Zouga Ballantyne, have three months' imprisonment."

Zouga had served four weeks of his sentence in Holloway, and with the balance remitted, had been released to the dreadful news that the Matabele had risen in Rhodesia and that Bulawayo was under siege. The voyage across the Atlantic had been agonizing, with no word of Louise or King's Lynn. Only when the Union Castle mailboat had docked that morning in Cape Town Harbour were his terrible anxieties relieved.

"She is safe in Bulawayo." Jordan had answered his first question. Overcome with emotion, Zouga had embraced his youngest son.

They had lunched together in the dining room of the Mount Nelson Hotel and Jordan had given his father the latest intelligence from the north. "Napier and the siege committee seem to have stabilized the situation. They have got the survivors into Bulawayo—and Ralph with his irregulars, the Ballantyne Scouts, has given the rebels a few bloody knocks to keep them at a wary distance.

"Of course the Matabele have an absolute free run of the territory outside the laagers. They do as they please, though strangely enough they do not seem to have closed the road to the south. If you can reach Kimberley in time to join the relief column that Spreckley is taking through, you should be in Bulawayo by the end of the

146

month, and Mr. Rhodes and I will not be long in joining you. As you
probably know, Major-General Sir Frederick Carrington has been
chosen to command the imperial troops, and Mr. Rhodes and I will
be going up with his staff."

Father and son faced each other awkwardly on the platform, as
the guard blew his warning whistle.

"Mr. Rhodes asked me to inquire whether you would still be good
enough to act as his agent at Bulawayo?"

"Please tell Mr. Rhodes that I am honoured by his continued
confidence."

They shook hands and Zouga climbed into the coach.

"I hope you have a safe journey, Papa."

Leaning from the carriage window as the train pulled out of the
platform, Zouga studied the receding figure of his youngest son. He
was a fine-looking young fellow, tall and athletic, and yet there was
something incongruous about him, an aura of uncertainty and deep-
rooted unhappiness. "Damned nonsense," Zouga told himself, and
he pulled up the window by its leather strap as the locomotive built
up speed.

JORDAN BALLANTYNE cantered up the driveway towards the great
white house that crouched on the lower slopes of the flat-topped
mountain. He was pursued by a feeling of guilt, for a year ago it
would have been unthinkable for him to neglect his duties for an
entire day. Every day, Sunday and public holidays notwithstanding,
Rhodes had needed him close to hand.

Now, there was a subtle change in their relationship. It had not
been entirely necessary for him to spend the whole of that day with
his father—he could have been back at his desk within a few hours,
but he had tried to force an acknowledgment of his own indis-
pensability. Instead Rhodes had barely glanced up from the London
newspapers.

"Take a few days if you like, Jordan. Arnold will be able to handle
any paperwork that might come up. It will give him a chance to use
that new-fangled Remington." Rhodes took a childlike pleasure in
having his correspondence printed out swiftly and neatly on the
caligraph, and Jordan had not yet mastered its noisy keyboard,
chiefly because Arnold monopolized the machine.

Now Jordan reined in the big glossy bay at the steps to Groote
Schuur's back stoep, dismounted, and hurried into the house. He

took the back stairs to the second floor, and went directly to his office. There was a note on top of his desk, weighted down with the silver ink well.

"See me as soon as possible. C.J.R."

Jordan felt a leap of his spirits. He picked up his shorthand pad, knocked on the communicating door and went through. "Good evening, Mr. Rhodes. You wanted to see me?"

Rhodes did not reply at once, but went on making corrections to the typed sheet in front of him. He was almost totally grey now, and the pouches below his eyes were a deep purple colour. His jowl had thickened, his eyes were red-rimmed and their messianic blue was blurred and diluted: all this deterioration in the six short months or so since Jameson's disastrous raid.

Rhodes had not slept for five nights after hearing the news, and Jordan had lain awake in his own room down the passage and listened to the heavy tread back and forth across the floor. Then long before dawn Rhodes would ring for him and they would ride for hours upon the slopes of Table Mountain, returning to the great white mansion to face the latest renunciations and rejections, to watch a life's work crumble inexorably about them.

Then Arnold had arrived as Jordan's assistant. His official title was second secretary, and Jordan had welcomed his assistance with the more mundane details of running the complex household. He had accompanied them on their visit to London in the aftermath of Jameson's misadventure, and remained firmly by Rhodes's side on the long return journey.

Arnold now stood attentively beside Rhodes's desk, and with the rancid taste of envy, Jordan recognized that Arnold possessed the clean blond good looks that Rhodes so much admired. His demeanour was modest and frank, and it was more and more obvious that Rhodes took as much pleasure and comfort in having him nearby, as he had previously taken from Jordan's presence.

Jordan waited quietly by the door, until Rhodes handed the corrected sheet to Arnold and looked up.

"Ah, Jordan," he said, "I wanted to warn you that I am advancing the date of my departure for Bulawayo to next Monday. I think my Rhodesians need me."

"I will see to it immediately," Jordan nodded. "We will take the express to Kimberley, of course?"

"You will not be accompanying me," said Mr. Rhodes flatly.

"I do not understand, Mr. Rhodes." Jordan made a helpless little gesture of incomprehension.

"I require utter loyalty and honesty in my employees."

"Yes, Mr. Rhodes, I know that." Jordan nodded, and then slowly his expression became uncertain and disbelieving. "You are not suggesting that *I* have ever been . . ."

"Get that file please, Arnold," Rhodes ordered. "Give it to him."

Arnold silently came across the thick carpet, and offered a box file to Jordan, and as he reached for it Jordan was suddenly aware of a flash of vindictive triumph, so vicious as to sting like the lash of a whip across the face. It lasted for only a blink of time, but it left Jordan feeling utterly vulnerable.

He opened the folder. There were at least fifty sheets in it, and each was headed "Copy of Original". There were stockbrokers' buy-and-sell orders for huge numbers of shares in De Beers and Consolidated Goldfields. Then there were copies of statements from half a dozen banks, and a dozen or so entries on the statements had been underlined in red ink.

Transfer to Rholands—£86,321 7s. 9d.

Transfer to Rholands—£146,821 9s. 11d.

The name of Ralph's company shocked him. "I don't understand—" He looked up at Rhodes.

"Your brother entered into a series of large bear transactions in the companies which were most drastically affected by the failure of Jameson's enterprise. It would appear that he has made profits in excess of a million pounds, and that he and his agents have gone to extreme lengths to disguise and conceal these machinations."

"Mr. Rhodes, he is my brother, but I cannot be held responsible—"

Mr. Rhodes held up three sheets of writing paper, and proffered the top one to Jordan. "Do you recognize this?"

Jordan felt himself blushing agonizingly. He had written the letter in the terrible spiritual travail following the night of Ralph's discoveries and brutal accusation in the private Pullman coach from Kimberley.

"It is the copy of a private letter that I wrote to my brother—" Jordan could not lift his eyes. "I do not know what possessed me to keep a copy of it."

A paragraph caught his eye, and he could not prevent himself rereading his own words. "There is nothing I would not do to convince you of my continued affection, for only now when I seem to have forfeited it am I truly conscious of how much your regard means to me." He held the sheet possessively. "This is a private and intimate communication."

"You do not deny that you are the author, then?"

"It would be vain for me to do so."

"Indeed, it would," Rhodes agreed, and passed him the second sheet.

Jordan read on down the page in mounting bewilderment. The handwriting was his, the words were not; but so skilfully and naturally did they continue from the first page, that he found himself almost doubting his own recall. What he was reading was his own agreement to pass on confidential and privileged information related to the planning and timing of Jameson's intervention in the Transvaal. The entire page was a skilful forgery.

"That your conspiracy was successful, we know from the rich fruits your brother harvested," said Rhodes wearily, a man so often betrayed that this had no longer the power to wound him. "I congratulate you, Jordan."

"Where did this come from?" The page shook in Jordan's hand. "Where—" He broke off and looked up at Arnold, standing behind his master's shoulder.

"I see." Jordan nodded. "The letter is a forgery, of course."

Rhodes made an impatient gesture. "You agreed it was yours."

"Not this page, not this—"

Rhodes's expression was remote, his eyes cold and unfeeling. "I will instruct the bookkeeper to issue you a cheque for three months' salary in lieu of notice, though I am certain you will understand my reluctance to provide you with a letter of recommendation. I would be obliged if you could remove yourself and your belongings from these premises before my return from Rhodesia."

"Mr. Rhodes—"

"There is nothing further that we have to discuss."

RHODES HAD NOT SPOKEN to Jordan again after that final confrontation. Arnold had relayed two brief instructions, and Jordan had retained his dignity and resisted the temptation to hurl recriminations at his triumphant rival. He had only seen Rhodes from his window as he climbed into the coach for the railway station.

150

Now Jordan was alone in the great deserted mansion. He had ordered the servants to leave early, and had personally checked the kitchens and rear areas, before locking up the doors. He moved slowly through the carpeted passageways carrying an oil lamp in both hands, wearing the Chinese silk brocade dressing gown that had been Rhodes's personal gift to him on his twenty-fifth birthday. He was on a pilgrimage of farewell about the great house, and the memories that it contained.

He had been present from the very first days of the renovation of the old building, and it was he who had suggested the motif for the mansion, a stylized representation of the stone bird from the ancient ruins of Rhodesia, the Falcon of Zimbabwe. The likeness of the great raptor decorated the banisters of the main staircase. It was worked into the polished granite of Rhodes's huge bath, it formed a fresco around the walls of the dining room, and four replicas supported the corners of Rhodes's desk.

The bird had been a part of Jordan's life from as far back as his earliest memories reached. The original statue had been taken by Zouga Ballantyne from the ancient temple, one of seven identical statues that he had discovered there. He had left the other birds lying in the ancient temple enclosure, and taken the best-preserved example.

Almost thirty years later Ralph Ballantyne had returned to Great Zimbabwe, guided by his father's journal. Ralph had found the six remaining statues lying in the ruins just as his father had left them. Ralph had come prepared. He had loaded the statues onto the draught oxen he had brought with him and, despite the attempts of the Matabele guardians to prevent him, had escaped southwards with his treasure. In Cape Town a syndicate of businessmen had purchased the relics from Ralph for a substantial sum, and had presented them to the South African Museum in Cape Town. The six statues were still on display to the public there. Jordan had visited the museum and spent an hour standing transfixed before them.

However, his own personal magic was embodied in the original statue his father had discovered, which throughout his childhood had ridden as ballast over the rear wheel-truck of the family wagon, during their wanderings and travels across the vast African veld. Jordan had slept a thousand nights above the bird, and somehow its spirit had pervaded his own and taken possession of him.

Financially reduced, Zouga had been forced to sell the bird to Rhodes, and the boy had been desolated, until the opportunity to enter Rhodes's service arose. Then the emptiness of his existence was filled with not one but two deities, the raptor and Cecil Rhodes.

Now he had lost the lodestone of his life, and irresistibly he was drawn towards the statue for the last time.

Slowly he descended the curve of the main staircase to the lofty hall below. The light of the lantern that he carried sent grotesque shadows fluttering like gigantic bats against the high carved ceiling. Jordan set the lamp upon a heavy table like a ritual lantern upon a pagan altar. He stepped back and slowly raised his head.

The original stone falcon of Zimbabwe stood in its high niche, guarding the entrance to Groote Schuur. Seeing it thus it was not possible to doubt the power that invested the graven image. It seemed that the prayers and incantations of the long-dead priests of Zimbabwe still shimmered in the air about it, that the blood of the sacrifices streamed from the wavering shadows upon the marble floor, and that the prophecy of the Umlimo invested it with separate life.

Zouga Ballantyne, the first white man to reach Zimbabwe, had heard the prophecy from the Umlimo's lips and had faithfully recorded it in his journal. "The white eagle will war with the black bull until the stone falcons return to roost."

Jordan looked up at the bird's proud, cruel head, at the sightless eyes which stared blankly towards the north, towards the land which men now called Rhodesia, where the white eagle and the black bull were locked in mortal conflict, and he felt as though he were caught up in the coils of destiny. In the lamplight his face was tinged with a faint greenish sheen as though it had been carved from ice.

He lifted the ceramic lamp from the table, and held it high above his head with both hands.

"Forgive me," he whispered. "I cannot leave you or him. I have no place to go." Then he hurled the lamp against the panelled woodwork of the wall.

The lobby was plunged into darkness for a moment, as the flame of the shattered lamp fluttered to the very edge of extinction. Then a ghostly blue light skittered across the spreading pool of oil, and suddenly the flames burned up strongly and touched the long velvet curtains that covered the windows.

Still kneeling before the stone statue, Jordan coughed as the dense, swirling smoke enveloped him. The image of the falcon high above him slowly receded, dimmed by the tears that filled his eyes and by the dense swirling smoke.

Then one of the heavy curtains burned through, and as it fell it spread open like the wings of an immense vulture. The fiery wings covered Jordan's kneeling figure and their weight bore him face down to the marble floor.

Already asphyxiated by the dense blue smoke he did not even struggle. Within seconds the mound of crumpled velvet was transformed into a funeral pyre, and the flames reached up joyously to lick against the base of the stone falcon in its high niche.

"BAZO HAS COME DOWN from the place of the Umlimo at last."

"Are you sure of this?" Ralph demanded eagerly, and Isazi nodded.

"I have sat at the campfires of his impi, and with my own eyes have seen him."

"Where is he, Isazi? Tell me where I can find him."

"He is not alone." Isazi was not about to spoil the dramatic impact of his report by prematurely divulging the bare bones of fact. "Bazo has with him the wildest and most reckless of the young indunas, and they have brought their amadoda, three thousand of the fiercest and finest. They say that the old indunas have decided to await divine intervention and to leave the road southwards open for the white men to depart, but with Bazo and his witch-woman Tanase at their head, the impis are as dangerous as the gut-stabbed lion. I tell you, Henshaw, that Bazo is the serpent's head. Cut it off and the body dies."

"God damn you, Isazi," Ralph snarled at him, "tell me *where* he is."

Isazi looked pained and deliberately took a little snuff. "He is very close," he said. "He lies with his three thousand amadoda in the Valley of the Goats."

Ralph looked up at the segment of old moon that hung low over the darkened laager. "Four days to new moon," he murmured. "If Bazo plans to attack us here—then it will be in the dark of the moon."

"Three thousand men," Harry Mellow murmured, "and there are fifty of us."

"We will take them," said Ralph Ballantyne calmly. "We will take them in the Valley of the Goats, two nights from now, and here is the way we will do it."

BAZO PASSED FROM one watch fire to the next—and beside him moved the slim and exquisitely graceful figure of Tanase. The flames picked out in harsh detail every line and crease that suffering had riven into his face. Around his forehead was bound the simple strip of moleskin; he did not need the feathers of heron and paradise widowbirds to place the seal upon his majesty. His scars were the only regalia of honour that he wore.

Tanase's beauty was even more poignant when seen beside his ravaged features. Yet as she stood at Bazo's shoulder in the firelight, her gaze was fierce as any warrior there, and she looked up at her husband with a ferocious pride as he began to speak. His voice was not raised, not strained, but it rang clearly to the highest part of the natural rocky amphitheatre, and the dark masses of the warriors that filled the bowl stirred and sighed at the words.

"I offer you a choice," Bazo said. "You can remain as you are, amaholi, the dogs of the white men, or you can become once again amadoda. You have heard the fainthearted tell you that if we do not dispute the southern road, then the white men will pack their wagons and go meekly down that road to the sea. But they were wrong, and now they are proven so. Lodzi has come," said Bazo, and there was a sigh like the wind in the grass.

"Lodzi has come," Bazo repeated. "And with him the soldiers and the guns. They gather now at the head of the iron road that Henshaw built and soon, very soon, they will be in Bulawayo. You and your sons will toil in the white men's mines and herd the white men's herds—"

A growl shook the dark ranks like a leopard when it is roused.

"But that is not to be," cried Bazo, stamping his right foot, and the waiting warriors strained for every word. "For we will eat up the laager at Bulawayo."

Standing before them in the old way, Bazo gave them their order of battle, and squatting in the black mass of half-naked bodies, his hair covered by the feather headdress and his face and body plastered with a mixture of fat and soot, Ralph Ballantyne listened to the detailed instructions.

"At this season, the wind will come from the east, so from the east we will come also. Each one of you will carry upon his head a bundle of thatch grass and the green leaves of the msasa trees," Bazo told them, and anticipating what was to come, Ralph felt the nerve ends in his fingertips tingle with shock.

"A smokescreen," he thought. "That's a naval tactic."

"And as soon as the wind rises," Bazo continued, "we will build a great fire. Each of you will throw his bundle upon it as he passes, and our smoke will blind their gunners."

Ralph imagined how it would be. The warriors would be emerging from the impenetrable bank of smoke, swarming over the wall of wagons, three thousand of them coming in silently and relentlessly. The Maxims would be almost useless in the smoke, and the broad-bladed assegais the more effective weapons at such close range. A vivid image of the slaughter burned into his brain, and his rage came strongly to arm him as he stared down into the amphitheatre at the tall figure laying out the terrible details of the massacre. But even in his rage Ralph shouted with the other amadoda, and hummed the wild war chant, his features as contorted as theirs, and his eyes as wild.

"The indaba is ended," Bazo told them at last. "Go now to sleep for the morrow."

RALPH BALLANTYNE lay beneath his fur kaross and saw the watch fires dwindle, listening to the camp settle into sleep about him. They had withdrawn into the narrow reaches of the valley. Here, the Valley of the Goats was a broken rocky defile, choked with thick thorn scrub, so that the impis could not concentrate in one place. They were spread out in pockets, fifty men or so in each small clearing. The darkness became more menacing as the last fires died into powdery grey ash, and Ralph gripped the haft of his assegai and judged his moment.

It came at last, and Ralph drew back the kaross stealthily. On all fours he crept to where the nearest warrior lay, groping gently for him. His fingers touched the bare warm skin of an arm. The warrior started awake at his touch and sat bolt upright.

"Who is it?" he asked in a thick guttural voice, rough with sleep— and Ralph stabbed him in the stomach.

The man screamed. The cry bounded from the rocky sides of the valley, cutting through the silences of the night watch, and Ralph bellowed with him. "Devils! Devils are killing me!" He rolled over and stabbed another warrior, so that he yelled with surprise and pain.

"There are devils here!"

At fifty other watch fires down the valley the men of Ballantyne's scouts were stabbing and screaming with Ralph.

"Defend yourselves, there are ghosts at work!"

"Tagati! Witchcraft! Beware the witches!"

"Run! Run! The devils are amongst us!"

The three thousand warriors, every one of them steeped from childhood in superstition and witchlore, awakened to the screams and panic-stricken cries of men face to face with the devil's legions. They seized their weapons and struck out in terror, yelling with fright, and the comrades they wounded struck back at them. The night was filled with running figures that collided and stabbed and cried: "Hah! Hah! The devils are killing me!"

"The valley is haunted!"

"Run! Run!"

Then from the head of the valley rose such a monstrous iron-lunged braying, such a cacophony that it could only be the voice of Tokoloshe, the great demon himself. It was a sound that drove terrified men over the last frontiers of reason, into the realms of witless pandemonium.

On his hands and knees, Ralph crawled down the narrow pathway, keeping below the level of the slashing spears, and when he stabbed up at the frantic figures of running men, he aimed for the belly rather than the killing stroke, so that the men that he maimed added their cries to the uproar.

From the head of the valley, Harry Mellow blew another blaring blast on the brass foghorn, and it was echoed by the screams of men blundering up the sides of the valley and escaping into the open grassland beyond.

In the first few minutes hundreds of fleeing warriors, most of them unarmed, had escaped from the valley, and each second they were followed by others, men who would have unflinchingly charged into the smoking muzzles of machineguns, but who were reduced by fear of the supernatural to mindless panicstricken children. Their cries faded with distance, and now at last Ralph heard the voice for which he had waited.

"Stand fast, the Moles!" it roared. "Stand with Bazo. These are not demons." And Ralph crept towards the sound.

156

In the clearing ahead of him a campfire flared up, and Ralph recognized the tall figure with the slim woman at his side. "This is white men's trickery," she was crying. "Wait, my children."

Ralph ran through the dense scrub to them. His voice was rough and hoarse, disguised by dust and tension. "Lord Bazo, I am with you! Let us stand together against this treachery."

"Brave comrade!" Bazo greeted him with relief as Ralph loomed out of the dark. "Stand back-to-back to form a ring, and call out to other brave men to join us."

Bazo turned his back to Ralph, and drew Tanase to his side. It was she who glanced back and recognized Ralph as he stooped.

"It is Henshaw," she screamed, but her warning came too late. Before Bazo could turn back to face him, Ralph had changed his grip on the assegai to use it like a butcher's cleaver, and with a single stroke he hacked across the back of Bazo's legs, just above the ankles. Bazo collapsed onto his knees, both legs crippled, as the Achilles tendons parted.

Ralph seized Tanase's wrist, jerked her out of the circle of firelight, and hurled her headlong to earth. Holding her easily, he placed the point of the assegai against her stomach. "Bazo," he whispered to the crippled warrior. "Throw your spear upon the fire, or I will cut your woman open as you did mine."

THE SCOUTS USED the first glimmerings of the new day to move slowly down the valley in an extended line, finishing off the wounded Matabele. While they worked, Ralph sent Jan Cheroot back to where they had left the horses to fetch the ropes.

"The Matabele have scattered back into the hills," Jan Cheroot reported when he returned. "It will take a week for them to find each other and regroup. We lost four men, but we counted over two hundred Matabele."

"Get ready to pull out," Ralph ordered. "What remains to be done will not take long."

Bazo sat beside the remains of the fire. His arms were bound behind him with thongs of rawhide, and his legs were thrust straight out in front of him, the slow blood oozing from the deep gashes above his heels.

Tanase sat beside him, bound like him with her arms behind her back. She spoke to Bazo without moving her lips, in the way of the initiates.

"What is the business of the ropes, Lord? Why do they not shoot us, and have done?"

"It is the white man's way, the way that conveys the deepest disrespect. They use the ropes on criminals."

"Lord, on the day I first met this one you call Henshaw, I dreamed that you were high up on a tree and he looked up at you and smiled," she whispered.

"They are ready now," said Bazo, and turned his head to her. "With my heart I embrace you. You have been the fountainhead of my life."

"I embrace you, my husband. I embrace you, Bazo, who will be the father of kings."

She went on staring into his ravaged face and she did not turn her head when Henshaw stood tall over them and spoke in a harsh tortured voice.

"I give you a better death than you gave to the ones I loved."

THE ROPES WERE of different lengths, so that Tanase hung slightly lower than her lord. Her long heron neck was twisted sharply to one side, so that she still seemed to listen for Bazo's voice—Bazo, whose swollen face was lifted towards the yellow dawn sky.

Ralph Ballantyne's face was lifted also as he stood at the base of the tall acacia tree in the bottom of the Valley of the Goats looking up at them. In one respect Tanase's vision was unfulfilled—Ralph Ballantyne did not smile.

SO LODZI CAME, and with him came Major-General Carrington and the guns and the soldiers. The women and children danced out from the laager at Bulawayo with bouquets of wild flowers for them, and wept with joy.

The senior indunas, squabbling amongst themselves and awed by the massive show of military force, withdrew their impis from the vicinity of Bulawayo. The Imperial troops sortied in great lumbering columns and swept and shelled the valleys and the open land. They rode their horses to exhaustion, chasing the elusive black shadows that flitted through the forest ahead of them. The weeks dragged on and became months, and the soldiers tried to starve the Matabele and force them into open battle, but the indunas took refuge in the Matopos Hills where the guns and the soldiers dared not follow them.

It was an inconclusive, cruel little war, that drew on and on. The military officers who were conducting the campaign were not businessmen, they did not think in terms of cost efficiency, and the bill for the first three months was a million pounds sterling. The bill was for the account of Mr. Cecil John Rhodes and his British South Africa Company.

In the Matopos Hills, the indunas were forced towards starvation, and in Bulawayo, Rhodes was forced just as inexorably towards bankruptcy.

THE THREE RIDERS moved in a cautious, mutually protective spread. Jan Cheroot rode point, fifty yards ahead, his little woolly head turning tirelessly from side to side as he searched the bush. Behind him came Louise Ballantyne, delighting in her escape from the confinements of the Bulawayo laager. She turned to look back every few minutes, her lips parted in a loving smile, for she was not yet accustomed to having Zouga with her once again, and she had constantly to reassure herself. Zouga was fifty yards behind her, sitting easy and straight in the saddle, and he answered her smile.

In that extended order they rode up from the grassy plains, under the high arched branches of the msasa trees, and as he reached the crest Jan Cheroot stood in his stirrups and shouted with relief and delight.

Unable to contain themselves, Louise and Zouga cantered forward and reined in beside him. "Oh, thank you, Lord," Louise whispered huskily, and reached across for Zouga's hand. "It's a miracle."

Ahead of them the mellow thatch of King's Lynn basked comfortably in the sunlight. It seemed to be the most beautiful sight either of them had ever looked upon.

"It must be the only homestead in Matabeleland that wasn't burned." Zouga shook his head in wonder.

"Oh come on, my darling," Louise cried, with sudden ecstasy. "Let's go back to our home."

The house had been looted. They could not have expected less, but the books were still there, and Zouga's journals, the record of his life, meticulously handwritten and illustrated with drawings and coloured maps. "It would have truly broken my heart to have lost these," he murmured, piling them carefully on the library table and stroking the red Morocco covers.

The silver was lying on the dining-room floor, some of it battered, but most of it intact, and there was still crockery and glassware on the kitchen shelves, though all the pots and knives had been stolen and the doors to the pantry and store rooms had been broken off their hinges.

"It won't take much to fix," Zouga told Louise. "I can't believe how lucky we've been."

Louise went out into the kitchen yard and found four of her red Rhode Island hens scratching in the dust. She called Jan Cheroot from the stable and begged a few handfuls of grain from the horses' feed bags they had brought with them. The hens came in a flutter of wings to be fed.

Then Jan Cheroot dusted off the chairs and table on the front stoep and unpacked the picnic basket they had brought from Bulawayo. They drank fine Constantia wine and ate cold Cornish pasties, while Jan Cheroot regaled them with anecdotes of the exploits of Ballantyne's Scouts.

"There were none like us," he declared modestly. "Ballantyne's Scouts! The Matabele learned to know us well."

"What happened to all your heroes?" Zouga asked. "The war still goes on, and we need men like you."

"Master Ralph changed," said Jan Cheroot, darkly. "From the day we caught Bazo at the Valley of the Goats, he wasn't interested any more. He never rode with the Scouts again, and within a week he had gone back to the railhead to finish building his railway. They say he will drive the first train into Bulawayo before Christmas."

At that moment, from the back of the house came the sudden shriek and cackle of alarmed poultry. Zouga jumped to his feet and reached for his rifle. "Jan Cheroot, go around the back of the stables," he said urgently. "I'll come from the other side. Louise, be ready to run for the horses if you hear a shot." And the two men slipped away silently down the veranda.

Zouga ducked around the corner, and sprinted down the whitewashed wall that protected the kitchen yard. Above the cacophony of terrified chickens and the flapping of wings, he heard a voice say in Matabele, "Hold that one! Do not let it go!"

Almost immediately a half-naked woman ducked through the doorway beside Zouga, carrying a chicken in each hand. Zouga knocked her to the earth with the butt of his rifle and he leaped over her body into the kitchen yard.

160

Beside the kitchen door stood Jan Cheroot. He held his rifle in one hand and in the other the skinny, struggling body of a small black boy.

"Keep a hold on him, but don't hurt him," Zouga told him, and he turned back to examine his own prisoner.

She was an elderly Matabele woman, almost on the point of starvation. She must once have been big and heavily fleshed, for her skin hung loosely upon her in folds and wrinkles, and as Zouga caught her arm and marched her back into the kitchen yard he could feel her bones through the wasted flesh. The boy too was skeletally thin, each rib poking through the skin, and his head seemed too big for his body.

"The little devil is starving," said Zouga.

"That's one way of getting rid of them," Jan Cheroot agreed, and at that moment Louise stepped into the kitchen doorway.

Her expression changed the instant she saw the black woman. "Juba," she said. "Is that you, Juba?"

"Oh Balela," the Matabele woman whimpered. "I had thought never to see the sunshine of your face again."

"What now!" said Zouga grimly. "We have caught ourselves a pretty prize, Jan Cheroot. The senior wife of Gandang, and this puppy must be his grandson! I didn't recognize either of them; they are on their last legs."

Louise searched the saddlebags and found a battered tin of bully, as well as more Cornish pasties. Tungata Zebiwe sat in his grandmother's lap and ate with the total dedication of a starving animal, stuffing the food into his mouth with both hands.

"That's right," said Jan Cheroot sourly. "Fatten him up now, so we have to shoot him later." And he went off sulkily to saddle the horses for the return to Bulawayo.

"Juba, Little Dove," Louise asked, "are all the children like this?"

"The food is finished," Juba nodded. "All the children are like this, though some of the little ones are dead already."

"Juba—is it not time that we women put an end to the foolishness of our men?"

"It is time, Balela," Juba agreed. "Time and past time."

"WHO IS THIS WOMAN?" Rhodes asked, in that exasperated high-pitched voice that betrayed his agitation, and he peered at Zouga with eyes that seemed to have a new prominence.

161

"She is the wife of Gandang, the senior of all the indunas," Zouga told him. "She has brought a message from the hills."

"I don't suppose there is anything to lose by talking to them," Rhodes shrugged. "This business will destroy us all if it goes on much longer. Tell this woman to take a message back to the indunas that they must lay down their arms and come in to Bulawayo."

"I'm sorry, Mr. Rhodes," Zouga told him, "they won't do that. They have had an indaba in the hills. The indunas have spoken, and there is only one way. They want you to go to them."

"Me—personally?" Rhodes asked softly.

"'We will speak only to Lodzi, and he must come to us unarmed. He may bring three other men with him into the Matopos, but none of them must carry a weapon. If they do, we will kill them immediately.'" Zouga translated the message that Juba had brought, and Rhodes closed his eyes and covered them with the palm of his hand.

"In their power," he wheezed painfully. "Alone and unarmed, completely in their power."

Outside in the hot dusty noon, a bugle sang the advance, and there was the distant sound of a cavalry troop leaving the laager— hooves and the rattle of the lance butts in their hard leather boots.

Rhodes dropped his hand and stood up. "Can we afford to trust them?" he asked.

"Can we afford not to, Mr. Rhodes?"

THEY LEFT THE HORSES at the place that had been agreed, in one of the myriad valleys in the granite hills. Zouga Ballantyne led from there, taking the twisted narrow footpath through dense brush, looking back every few paces at the shambling, bearlike figure that followed him. Rhodes's face had taken on a bluish mottled appearance, and he was sweating heavily.

Close behind Rhodes followed the two others that the indunas had stipulated. One was a journalist, and the other was a doctor, for Rhodes realized that the assegais of the Matabele were not the only threat he faced on this gruelling journey. The shimmering heat of the Matopos Hills made the air above the granite surfaces dance and waver.

The scrub pressed in closely on each side of the track, and once Zouga saw a branch tremble and stir when there was no breeze. Then the path turned sharply into a vertical crack in the highest

162

point of the granite wall. Here Zouga waited for Rhodes to reach him.

"Do you think they will come, Ballantyne?" he gasped, wiping his face and neck with a white handkerchief.

Farther down the valley, from the thickest bush, a robin called and Zouga inclined his head to listen. It was a most convincing mimicry. "They are here before us, Mr. Rhodes. The hills are alive with Matabele." He looked for fear in the pale blue eyes, and he found none. "You are a brave man, sir."

A smile twisted the swollen, disease-ravaged face. "A pragmatic one, Ballantyne. It's always better to talk than to fight."

"I hope the Matabele agree." Zouga returned his smile and they went on into the shadowed vertical crack.

Below them was a circular valley in the granite ringed by high ramparts, and bare of any cover. In the middle of the basin was a low anthill, a raised platform of hard yellow clay. Instinctively the little group of white men made their way down towards it.

"We might as well make ourselves comfortable," Rhodes panted, and sank down upon it. The other members of the party sat on each side of him.

Only Zouga remained on his feet. This was the heart of the sacred hills of the Matabele, their stronghold in which they would be at their bravest and most reckless. It was folly to come unarmed into this place, to throw themselves upon the mercy of the most blood-thirsty tribe of a cruel wild continent. So Zouga stood with his empty hands clasped behind his back, and turned slowly upon his heel, surveying the wall of rock that hemmed them in.

"Well, gentlemen," he said quietly. "Here they are!"

Without a sound the impis rose from their concealment, and formed a living barricade along the skyline. They stood rank upon rank and shoulder to shoulder, completely encompassing the rocky valley.

It was impossible to count their multitude, impossible even to guess at their thousands, but still the silence persisted as though the white men's eardrums were filled with wax.

"Do not move, gentlemen," Zouga cautioned them, and they waited in the sunlight while the silent impassive impis stood guard about them. Now no bird called and not the lightest breeze stirred the forest of feather headdresses.

At last the ranks opened and a little group of men came down the path. These were the great princes of Kumalo—but how they were reduced: they were all of them old men, starved to the thinness of pariah dogs, with the warriors' muscles stringy and wasted, and their old bones showing through. Gandang led them, and behind came his half-brothers Babiaan and Somabula, and the other indunas of royal blood, wearing the headrings of honour and carrying the broad silver killing blades and the tall rawhide shields.

Ten paces in front of Zouga, Gandang stopped and grounded his shield, and the two men stared deeply into each other's eyes.

"I see you Gandang, Son of Mzilikazi," Zouga said at last.

"I see you, Bakela, the one who strikes with the fist."

And behind Zouga, Rhodes ordered calmly, "Ask him if it is to be war or peace."

Zouga did not take his eyes from those of the tall emaciated induna. "Are the eyes still red for war?" he asked.

Gandang's reply was a deep rumble, but it carried clearly to every induna who followed him, and it rose up to the massed ranks of warriors upon the heights.

"Tell Lodzi that the eyes are white." He stooped and laid his shield and assegai upon the ground at his feet.

THE MIX WAS FIFTY-FIFTY, half river clay dug from the bank of the Khami and half yellow anthill clay, made more adhesive by the saliva of the termites which had carried it up to the surface. The clays were puddled in a pit beside the bottom well; two of the mission converts cranked up each bucketful and spilled it into the mixing pit, another two shovelled in the clay and a dozen naked black children made a game out of trampling the clay to the correct consistency.

Then, under Robyn St. John's supervision, the clay was packed into oblong wooden moulds, and carefully turned out onto beds of dry grass at the drying ground.

There were thousands of yellow bricks lying in long lines in the sun, but Robyn had calculated that they needed at least twenty thousand for the new church alone. Then of course they would have to cut all the timber and cure it, and in a month's time the thatch grass in the vleis would be tall enough for cutting.

Robyn straightened and placed her muddied yellow hand in the small of her back to ease the cramping muscles. She looked up at the burned-out ruins of the Mission, and the prospect of all that grinding, unremitting labour gave her a deep and exciting sense of anticipation. She felt as strong and alive as the young medical missionary who had first stepped onto this unforgiving African soil almost forty years before.

"Thy will be done, dear Lord," she said aloud, and the Matabele girl beside her cried happily, "Amen, Nomusa!"

Robyn smiled at her, and was about to bend once more to the brick moulds when she started, shaded her eyes, then picked up her skirts and ran down the track towards the river. "Juba!" she cried. "Where have you been? I have waited so long for you to come home."

Juba set down the heavy load she carried balanced on her head. "Nomusa!" She was weeping as she hugged Robyn to her.

"Stop crying, you silly girl," Robyn scolded her lovingly. "You will make me start. Just look at you! How skinny you are—we will have to feed you up! And who is this?"

The black boy dressed only in a soiled loin cloth came forward shyly.

"This is my grandson—Tungata Zebiwe. I have brought him to you so that you can teach him to read and to write."

"We will, but we have got a lot of work to do first," Robyn said firmly. "We have to start again, Juba, and build it all up from the beginning."

"I ADMIRE THE GRANDEUR and loneliness of the Matopos, and therefore I desire to be buried in the Matopos on the hill which I used to visit and which I called the "View of the World", in a square to be cut in the rock on the top of the hill and covered with a plain brass plate with these words thereon:- 'Here lie the remains of CECIL JOHN RHODES'."

So when at last the pumping of his diseased heart ceased, Rhodes came to Bulawayo once more along the railway that Ralph Ballantyne had laid. The special saloon coach in which his coffin rode was draped with purple and black, and at each town and siding along the way, those whom he had called "My Rhodesians" brought wreaths to pile upon the coffin. From Bulawayo the coffin was taken on a gun-carriage into the hills, and the pure black bullocks that drew it plodded slowly up the rounded egg-shaped dome of granite that he had chosen.

Above the open sepulchre stood a tripod gantry, with block and chain at the peak, and around it was a dense throng of elegant gentlemen, uniformed officers, and ladies with black ribbons on their hats.

Then, farther out, there stretched a vast black sea of Matabele, twenty thousand come to see him go down into the earth. At their head were the indunas who had met him near this same hill to treat for peace. There was Gandang, and Babiaan and Somabula, all of them very old men now. Gathered at the head of the grave were the men who had replaced them in real power, the administrators of the Charter Company and the members of the first Rhodesian Council. Ralph Ballantyne was amongst them with Elizabeth beside him.

Ralph's expression remained grave as the coffin was lowered on its chains into the gaping tomb, and the bishop read aloud the obituary that Mr. Rudyard Kipling had composed:

> "It is his will that he look forth
> Across the world he won,
> The granite of the ancient north,
> Great spaces washed with sun.
> There shall he patient take his seat
> (As when the death he dared)
> And there await a people's feet
> In the paths that he prepared."

As the heavy brass plaque was lowered into position, Gandang stepped out of the ranks of the Matabele, and lifted one hand.

"The father is dead," he cried, and then in a single blast of sound, like the thunder of a tropical storm, the Matabele nation gave the salute they had never given to a white man before.

"Bayete!" they shouted as one man. "Bayete!"

The salute to a king.

THE FUNERAL CROWDS dispersed, slowly, seemingly reluctantly. The Matabele drifted away like smoke amongst the valleys of their sacred hills, and the white folk followed the path down the face of the granite dome.

Ralph helped Elizabeth over the uneven footing, and he smiled down at her.

"The man was a rogue—and yet you weep for him," he teased her gently.

166

"It was all so moving." Elizabeth dabbed at her eyes. "When Gandang did that—"

Ralph paused on the lower slope of the dome and looked back up at the peak.

"Yes. He fooled them all, even those he led into captivity. Now he's dead at long last, but his company still governs us. I have work to do yet, work that may take the rest of my life."

Then he chuckled. "I told Isazi to bring the carriage round to the back of the hill. We'd best go down now before Jon-Jon drives him completely out of his mind."

He took her arm and led her down to where Isazi had parked the carriage in the shade, and from a hundred paces they picked up the piping of Jonathan's questions and speculations, each punctuated with a demanding:

"Uthini, Isazi? What do you say, Isazi?"

And the patient reply: "Eh-heh, Bawu. Yes, yes, Little Gadfly."

EPILOGUE 1980

The Minister for Trade, Tourism and Information in the Cabinet of the newly-elected Government of Zimbabwe walked briskly along one of the narrow gravel pathways that meandered through the lush gardens of State House.

His four bodyguards followed him at a respectful distance. They were all former members of his old ZIPRA cadre, each of them a hardened veteran whose loyalty had been tested a hundred times. Now, however, they had changed the camouflage dungarees of the bush war for dark business suits and sunglasses, the new uniform of the political élite.

The daily pilgrimage on which the minister was intent had become a ritual of his household. As one of the senior cabinet ministers, he was entitled to luxurious quarters in one of the annexes of State House. It was an easy and congenial walk from there, through the gardens, past State House itself, to the indaba tree.

State House was a sprawling edifice with white walls and gables, arched in the tradition of the great homes of the Cape of Good Hope. It had been built on the instructions of that arch-imperialist Cecil John Rhodes, and his taste for the big and barbaric showed in

167

the design. His sense of history and his own immortal place in it showed in his choice of the site for the State House. It was built on the spot where Lobengula's kraal had once stood before it was destroyed by Rhodes's marauders when they rode in to take possession of this land.

Beyond the great house, not two hundred paces from its wide verandas, stood a tree, a gnarled old wild plum enclosed and protected by a fence of iron palings.

This tree was the object of the minister's pilgrimage. He stopped in front of the iron palings, and his bodyguards hung back—so as not to intrude on this private moment.

The minister stood with his feet apart and his hands clasped lightly behind his back. He was dressed in a navy blue suit with a light chalk stripe. It was one of a dozen that Hawkes and Gieves of Savile Row had tailored for him during his last visit to London, and he wore his expensive Western clothes with the same élan as his forefathers had worn the blue heron's feathers and royal leopard pelts.

He removed the gold-rimmed Polaroid glasses from his face, and as part of his personal ritual read the inscription on the plaque that was riveted to the palings.

Beneath this tree Lobengula, the last King of the Matabele, held his court and sat in judgment.

Then he looked up into the branches, as though in search of his ancestors' spirit. The tree was dying of old age, some of the central branches were black and dry, but from the rich red soil at its base new shoots were bursting into vibrant life.

The minister saw the significance of that and he murmured to himself, "They will grow as strong as the great tree once was, and I also am a shoot of the old king's stock."

His lips moved in a silent supplication. Then he replaced his gold-rimmed glasses, and turned back to where his car was waiting.

It was a black bullet-proofed Mercedes 500. There were four police motorcycle outriders and a second smaller Mercedes for his bodyguards.

The small convoy drove very fast down the three-kilometre-long jacaranda-lined driveway that Cecil Rhodes had designed as the approach to his State House, across the main commercial section of Bulawayo, flying through the red lights at the junctions, past the town square where the wagons had laagered during the rebellion when Bazo's impis had threatened the town, and at last turning off sharply and drawing up in front of the modern three-storeyed museum building.

There was a red carpet laid down the front steps of the museum and a small gathering of dignitaries, headed by the Mayor of Bulawayo—the first Matabele ever to hold that position—and the curator of the museum.

"Welcome, Comrade Minister, on this historic occasion."

They escorted him down the long corridor to the public auditorium. Every seat was already filled, and as the minister mounted the platform the entire gathering stood and applauded him, the whites in the gathering outdoing the Matabele as a positive demonstration of their goodwill.

The minister had an immense presence, and without yet uttering a word, he transfixed them with his smoky unwavering gaze.

"My people have a saying that was passed down from the wise ones of our tribe," he started in his deep rumbling voice. "It is this: 'The white eagle will war with the black bull until the stone falcons return to roost.'"

He paused a moment, letting his words hang between them, heavy with portent. Then he went on.

"I am sure all of you here know the story of how the bird statues of Zimbabwe were seized by Rhodes's plunderers, and carried away southwards across the Limpopo River."

He strode to the curtained-off section at the back of the speakers' platform.

"My friends, my comrades." He turned to face them once more. "The stone falcons have returned to roost!" And he drew aside the curtains.

There was a long breathless silence and the audience stared avidly at the serried ranks of tall soapstone carvings that were revealed.

There were six of them, those that Ralph Ballantyne had lifted from the ancient stone temple. The one that his father had taken on his first visit to Zimbabwe thirty years before had burned in the pyre of Groote Schuur. These six were all that remained.

Each bird crouched on top of a plinth that was ornamented by a pattern of intermeshed triangles like the teeth in a shark's jaw.

The statues were not identical, some of the columns supported crocodiles and lizards that crawled up towards the bird image that

169

surmounted it. Some of the statues had been extensively damaged, chipped and eroded, but the one in the centre of the line was almost perfect.

The bird was a stylized raptor, with its long bladelike wings crossed over its back. The head was proud and erect, the cruel beak hooked and the blind eyes haughty and unforgiving.

It was a magnificent and evocative work of primitive art, and the crowded auditorium rose as one person in spontaneous applause.

The minister reached out and touched the head of the central bird. His back was turned to his audience so that they could not see his lips move.

"Welcome home," whispered Tungata Zebiwe. "Welcome home to Zimbabwe, bird of my ancestors."

Wilbur Smith

No one is better qualified than Wilbur Smith to write an epic novel on the creation of Rhodesia. Not only is he the most popular novelist ever to emerge in Southern Africa, but he was born and bred in the land to which Cecil Rhodes gave his name almost one hundred years ago.

Wilbur Smith was brought up in Southern Rhodesia, and was expected to take over his father's engineering business. Instead he gambled on literary success and won far more handsomely than he could ever have foreseen. As with many authors, his first work was repeatedly rejected, until characteristically he risked everything on a single throw. He spent two years on one huge novel on the South African gold rush. It was based partly on his grandfather's tales of carrying supplies to Witwatersrand, partly on his own reading and partly on his childhood on the family cattle ranch. The novel was called *When the Lion Feeds*. It was immediately a great success, a giant first step on his triumphant climb to the top of the best-selling league.

Twelve novels and fifteen years later Wilbur Smith decided that he would, through a trilogy of novels, return to the period and style of his first big bestseller. He would tell the story of the white pioneers who first found the land of his birth. In *A Falcon Flies* and *Men of Men* he traced the early adventures of the Ballantyne family. For *The Angels Weep* he saved the great historic scenes of how the British finally wrested possession of the land from the Matabele.

Wilbur Smith, however, is more than a simple storyteller. His sense of history, in particular his appreciation of the enduring strength of the African tribes, is reflected in the brief epilogue which closes this story. He sees the creation of Zimbabwe as an inevitable step in Southern Africa's return to a pace that suits the Matabele temperament. The great continent cannot, he believes, be converted permanently to the Western way of life.

all the days were SUMMER

a condensation of the book by

Jack M. Bickham

Illustrated by Stuart Bodek   Published by Robert Hale

It is 1943. Wartime. A time, according to young
Danny Davidson, when every German is the
enemy. And around Harmony, Ohio, the enemy
is present in force—there are four hundred of
them in a prisoner-of-war camp outside town.
Most of the townsfolk are of Danny's mind, and it
takes only two small incidents to bring passions
to the boil. Yet, when guards at the camp are
ordered to shoot to kill, Danny is among the first
to protest. Amazingly, a German has shown him
great kindness, has taught him the special care
that can save Danny's beloved dog, Skipper.
A far greater peril than the German prisoners is
needed to bring the town to its senses. And by
then Danny has learned other lessons: that a
boy's father can sometimes be right, and that
love is worth the price, no matter what. A story
as full of warmth and colour as the last summer of
childhood that it describes.

CHAPTER ONE

In my heart, all the days of my youth were summer. And the summer that always dominates, the summer of my revolt against my father, of all the terrible things that happened, of my German friend—the summer of my Skipper—was in 1943.

One night in the spring of that year, my father told us at the supper table that we were moving to the country. He tried to say it casually, his lean face lit by a little smile, as if he were announcing a picnic. But his hand holding a fork was shaking slightly, and so I knew it was a momentous decision. My mother appeared calm. But for my sister, Aggie, and me there had been no warning. We were stunned.

Aggie, seven, had been drinking her milk. She almost dropped it, and when she managed to put it down, she had a wide milk mustache that made her look even more shocked. "The country!" she gasped. "You mean leave *home*?"

"We'll have a new home," my father told her. The smile remained on his lips, but I could see the strain in his face. He was tall, thin, his dark hair combed back, suspenders broad and dark against his white office shirt, his navy and white dotted bow tie askew. "It's a nice house, Agatha, on a farm with ten whole acres, a little orchard and a creek. We'll have a huge victory garden this summer. Won't you like that?"

Aggie stared at him, and her big eyes welled up. "I like it here!" she said, and started to bawl.

My father looked like he had been shot. "Oh now—" he began.

My mother stepped in. "That's all right, George." She addressed herself to Aggie. "That's enough of that, young lady. You just sit up and eat your green beans."

"I don't like green beans!" Aggie wailed. "And I don't like it in the country! There are lions and bears in the country!"

"Cows, too," I said. "Vicious ones that bite."

"Danny!" Mother snapped. She was the loveliest woman in the world, blond, with vivid blue eyes, and I adored her. But when her amazing eyes glinted as they did now, I knew to shut up. She leaned over Aggie and said something more to her. Aggie started straightening up. Mother gave her her spoon. Aggie put some beans in her mouth as if they were hemlock.

"Now that's better," my mother said, giving me another dirty look. "We're going to have a wonderful time in our new home, aren't we, Danny?"

"Yes, ma'am," I said.

"What it's all about," my father told us, "is that I'm taking a new job. I don't know if you've heard it or not, Danny, but we're starting to get some German prisoners of war in this country—"

"He doesn't understand that, George," my mother said softly.

"I'm twelve!" I protested. "I understand *all* about it!"

My father grinned. "Anyway, there's a new prisoner-of-war camp south of Columbus, near the little town of Harmony. I'm going to be supervisor of the guards," he said with quiet pride.

"You mean you're going in the army?"

"No," he said with the faintest irritation. Although he was almost forty, and an inner-ear complaint had made him ineligible for service, he had felt odd about being home when others were away at war. I instantly regretted bringing this up. But he went on. "There

176

will be a few soldiers. But most of the guards will be civilians . . . some full time, some part time. And I'll supervise all of them. It's a big, responsible job, Danny."

"You'll be great at it," I said enthusiastically. "It sounds real dangerous!"

"It won't be. They screen the prisoners. Any hard-core Nazis are put in a heavy-security camp. These men are just ordinary soldiers. Of course they are still the enemy, but . . ."

"When do we move?" I asked.

"In a week or so."

This was even more startling. "A week! What about school?"

"There's a very nice school in Harmony, Danny. You and Agatha will transfer there and not miss more than a day or two."

I sat back in my chair. Supper was roast and potatoes with brown gravy, always my favorite, but even that didn't look so good all of a sudden. I would miss my pals at school. "Will I get to see any of the firing squads?" I asked dubiously.

My father's head jerked. "Firing squads!"

"When some of those Krauts get out of line."

"Danny!" my mother exclaimed, shocked.

"Well, Mom, Germans are all just a bunch of killers."

"Now, Squirt," my father said in his lecture tone, "the prisoners are people just like the rest of us. They fought in the German army and they got captured."

I stared at him in consternation. "Dad, these guys ran over Poland and blitzkrieged France, and bombed London. If you're a good American, you hate 'em—and the Japs even more."

"That's not so," my father told me. "The Geneva Convention—"

"It says to treat prisoners decent," I piped up, "but it doesn't say you can't hate their guts."

"I don't want to hear that kind of remark," he said sharply.

My father's sudden soft talk was confusing. I knew my duty as a good citizen was to hate Germans and Japanese. "We'll have a normal life down there," he said. "We might even get a chance to buy the house and farm, if things work out."

Puzzled and at a loss, I did not reply.

"Agatha, I know you've wanted a cat," my father continued. "I imagine we'll be able to have several on a farm. And Danny, I know you've wanted a dog. Well, on ten acres we'll need one, don't you think?"

Owning a dog had always been my dream, but it had been forbidden on a tiny city lot. At the mention of cats, Aggie brightened up immediately. My reaction, although I hid it, was the opposite. This sounded like a bribe, which meant all was not so peaches-and-cream as my father and mother were letting on.

But Aggie began babbling happily about kittens, all thought of uprooting forgotten. Girls, especially at age seven, were so dumb! One curse of being nearly a man was being able to see through things. I almost wished I were not so sophisticated.

ON THE NEXT SUNDAY we visited our new home for the first time. It seemed an enormous journey from the west side of Columbus. We drove slowly because our 1936 Chevrolet was using a lot of oil, and oil was almost as hard to get as gas. A cool gray rain forced us to close the car windows on the intoxicating fragrances of the greening fields. Finally we reached a little town with a brick street. It did not strike me as much: many very old, tall houses with big front porches, a few stores and filling stations, a bank, a post office, a couple of grain elevators, and a greenhouse with a war sign in the window: LOOSE LIPS SINK SHIPS.

"Well, what do you think of Harmony?" my father asked.

"Why, it seems like a very nice place," my mother said.

I looked at Aggie. She was slumped on the seat, with two fingers in her mouth. She sucked them only when she was upset.

After a few more miles we crossed a metal bridge and then slowed. I saw broad farm fields in the distance. Trees lined the narrow road. Then we turned onto a gravel driveway and parked in front of a small one-story white house with a green roof. The rain had abated. We got out and walked up onto the porch.

The first thing that struck me was the stillness. Except for the distant wind and the cry of birds, there was nothing: no traffic, no neighbors' voices, no radios—just quiet. It seemed spooky.

178

My father swung open the creaky screen and unlocked the door. We went into a large vacant living room. Its bare wooden floor was dusty, the pale yellow wallpaper faded. A few water stains showed on the ceiling. Beyond this room was the dining room, with a door at the back going to the kitchen, and a hallway to the right leading to bedrooms. In the kitchen, the linoleum was broken, and the cabinets had been painted a garish yellow green. My father kept up a running commentary.

"Have to repaint in here, of course. Looks like we might need new washers on those faucets, too. Say, won't this enclosed porch be nice for storage? Now through here, kids, we've got the bathroom and the bedrooms. Agatha, this one is yours. You'll get to see the road. Isn't that neat? Danny, this one is for you. You'll have plenty of space for your model airplanes."

I followed numbly. In truth, the house looked horrible. Everything was filthy and in need of repair. The windows in my room looked as though they hadn't been washed in a hundred years, and I could just guess who would get to make them shine again. The room was larger than the one I had in the city, but I didn't like it. It was too . . . square or something.

Outside, we explored like troopers from a foreign land. There was a small barn with rock walls and some hay inside. A fallen fence marked an old garden plot, with a well nearby. Struggling through weeds, I found cherry, apple and peach trees, and some strawberries and raspberries. The last I discovered the hard way, by getting tangled up in their stickers.

"Get out of there, Danny!" my mother called.

"I want to go on down and see the creek."

"All right, but hurry. We're going back." With that she took Aggie's hand, and turned up a weedy slope toward the house; my father walked with them.

I got out of the stickers and went down the hill. I could hear water and smell it. Elms and maples formed a canopy overhead. I climbed over a fallen tree, startling a cottontail who hopped away on a zigzag course. My heart was thumping. If I got a dog, I thought, we could hunt with my BB gun.

Farther downslope I came to the creek—about ten feet wide and only a few inches deep—rippling over earth and yellow pebbles. Its high banks were shaggy with winter-killed vegetation. A Baltimore oriole flew away in fright as I half climbed and half fell down

179

the bank. I accidentally stepped in the water, going into ooze over my shoe top. The water was shockingly cold. Now I was in trouble, I thought, but my fascination with a real creek, and being alone in such wilderness, made worry a distant thing.

I walked along the edge of the water. Spiders scampered in the sunlight, and a frog flopped into the creek at my approach. There were still dark rain clouds nearby, and I heard thunder. I examined a piece of rotted timber carefully, dug up some bottle caps and found an old medicine bottle. I was having a great time, but the thunder repeated and I knew it was time to get back.

The banks were so high that I did not think I could climb out. Walking ahead in search of an easier way, I turned a slight bend and saw a large concrete drainage pipe jutting out of the earthen wall of the creek. It was about five feet in diameter, and a steady trickle of water issued from it and tumbled down about three feet to make crystalline sparkles in the creek below.

I scrambled up to the big pipe and peered inside. It seemed to go back into the earth forever. Dank, frightening air issued from those depths. It was pitch-black. I got a knee on the rough concrete lip and heaved myself in. Awkwardly straddling the stream that burbled from the depths, I took a few confident steps inward. The cold closed around me. I saw nothing whatsoever ahead. Be brave, I told myself sternly.

Each step became more difficult. I thought about the strange odor. Sewer gas? Would they eventually find my skeleton in here? I looked back; the opening seemed a mile away. Suddenly panic hit me. *What if the thing collapsed?* I hurried back toward the circle of daylight and tumbled out onto the creek bank with a sense of intense relief. My nerves began to return to normal.

This, I thought, promised a great adventure. The pipe must lead somewhere. I would have to explore it. But I would need a flashlight and string to leave a trail behind me in case there were puzzling forks deeper inside the tunnel.

"Danny!" I heard my mother calling distantly.

I managed to scramble up the hill toward the house. My parents and Aggie were waiting for me. The weeds had pulled most of the mud from my shoe, and they didn't notice it was wet.

"Don't go off like that," my father scolded mildly. He pointed at the clouds. "It's about to rain again. We're leaving."

We climbed into the car and took off. We had gone less than a mile when we encountered tall, obviously new fencing with barbed wire along the top. Through the trees we could see several bleak old brick buildings on a hill, and a scattering of raw new wooden construction. "What's that, Daddy?" Aggie piped up.

"It used to be a private school," my father said. "Now it's the new camp where your daddy is going to work."

No one replied. The rain had resumed, and the place was grim and forbidding. I did not know why at the time, but I shivered.

And they say there is no such thing as premonition.

CHAPTER TWO

The days before we moved were filled with tension and excitement as we all packed boxes and barrels. My mother had her best friends over for coffee. She was in unfailing good spirits, and it was only when I managed to catch her unawares that I saw her pause over some item and get a wistful look in her eyes.

My father's last day at the plant where he had spent many years was a Friday. He came home a bit early, gray-faced and worried, but when he saw me watching him, he smiled at once. He and mother prattled about last-minute packing. Aggie watched them and sensed their tensions, too. Later I found her in her room, hugging her rag doll and sucking her fingers.

The movers came on Monday. Now Aggie ran around, calling and laughing to make echoes in the cavernous house, as the men took out the final items. My mother diligently swept the barren floors, while my father, with me at his heels, went to the basement to make sure nothing had been forgotten. He looked at the spot where his workbench had been, then walked over to the huge cylindrical coal furnace that had always been his nemesis. A faint smile on his lips, he reached down to the iron grate handle and shook it briefly, making the familiar rattling sounds that had awakened me so often on frigid mornings. "I'll never have to do that again anyway." Then he tousled my hair. "You know, Squirt, I guess I always wanted to live on a farm."

"How come you waited till now, then?" I asked.

"I don't know." He took a deep breath. "When you're a man, you go where the work is. I think you're too young to remember, but we've had some hard times."

181

"I remember when I was little," I said, "and you took your lunch to work. One day there wasn't any work. You came home and ate your lunch at the kitchen table."

"You remember that, do you?" He looked off into a private distance, this man I adored. "Well, I was lucky to get out of the factory and into the office. They helped me a lot down there." For an instant his eyes were filled with uncertainty, but then he shook himself. "Going to night school helped, too. A man makes his own opportunities. Nobody owes you a living."

"Isn't that what moving to the country is all about?"

"Exactly," he said brightening. "Come on. Let's get going."

We went upstairs. The movers were finished. Aggie was already out in the car with her doll. My father and I found my mother looking at the space in the kitchen where the refrigerator had been. She was crying without sound. My father put his arms around her. I went outside, pretending I didn't see.

BY EARLY EVENING the moving van had deposited everything at the little country house. We had a cold supper. Then we got busy cleaning and unpacking. My father was hooking up the stove, Mother was putting dishes in the cabinets and Aggie was swinging in the old porch glider. I clung to the top of the ladder in my new room, draping kite string from wall to wall in order to hang my model airplanes. Just as I stuck myself with one of the pins, someone pounded loudly on the front door. Holding my tongue against the hole in my thumb, I climbed down. My father's voice, and that of another man, came from the living room.

I went in as my father introduced my mother to the man who had come to call. He was a colonel in the army, thick-waisted and graying, with metal-framed spectacles, several service ribbons on the blouse of his dark winter uniform, gleaming brown riding boots, and a little leather quirt in one hand. He clicked his heels sharply and bowed slightly from the waist. "A pleasure, Mrs. Davidson! I look forward to working with your husband."

"It's very kind of you to call, Colonel Thatcher," my mother said.

"Think nothing of it." Colonel Thatcher's eyes roved the room. He spied me. "And who might you be, soldier?"

"I'm not a soldier," I told him. "I'm a civilian. I'm Danny."

He chuckled. "Well, you'll be a soldier soon enough, I wager, and then the army will make a man of you, eh?"

"No, sir. I aim to be in the air corps."

He strode over to me, boots thudding, and tapped me lightly with his whip. "Bully!" He turned to my parents. "A bright lad! I pity the Germans when his generation enters the fray."

"My heavens," my mother said softly. "It's not going to last that long, is it?" The dismay was clear in her eyes.

"Madam, we are dealing with fanatics. Our air power will have to demolish their homeland before Germany surrenders. We'll need the mightiest invasion ever mounted to conquer the fortress continent. And once that is accomplished, we still face those yellow people in the Pacific. The war may last into the 1950s!"

Mother looked at me fearfully. We were doing the same mental arithmetic. I imagined myself flying a P-38, shooting down hundreds of Nazi Messerschmitts. Her imaginings were clearly not as happy. "Oh, Colonel," she said, "that's a terrible prospect."

"We must prevail. And for those of us charged with keeping rebellious prisoners in line, our sense of duty must never falter." He glared at my father. "Working together, Davidson, we can handle it."

"I hope so, sir," my father said. He looked pale and drawn.

The colonel began pacing, hands behind his back, holding his quirt. "The first shipment of prisoners arrives in three days. My detachment is not at strength, with twenty-four enlisted men and two officers. We have thirty-seven civilian employees. You'll have precious little time to shape them up, but they must be ready. I've called a general meeting for oh eight hundred hours tomorrow. You will be ready to make out duty rosters, I assume?"

My father looked stunned. "We just started moving in—"

"Everything has been accelerated," Colonel Thatcher snapped. "This is war. We have no choice but to be ready. It means all of us must expect extra duty. You understand, of course."

My father took a rag from his pocket and began wiping his hands. "It looks like I'd better get at those rosters."

"Bully," the colonel said, slapping his thigh with his quirt. "Security is of the essence, Davidson. Remember that. I intend to live up to the laws of the Geneva Convention, but we must never forget these people are the enemy. I will run this camp the military way. I expect no less from you or the other civilians."

"Dad will do his part," I piped up. "You can count on me, too."

The colonel stared at me. "Oh, I can, eh?"

"I hate Germans," I told him proudly. "If any of them try to get loose, I'll help. I'm a crack shot with a BB gun."

"Well, my boy, you'll never have to test your resolve locally. We'll keep them in line at the camp. Maybe kill a few for you."

"Colonel," my mother said huskily, "I think this child has heard quite enough talk about this terrible war."

The colonel looked sharply at her. "Of course, madam. I applaud a mother's point of view." He patted my head and turned back to my father.

"I expect we'll get along well. I can see you have things to do here, but the war effort must take priority. We are helping to make the world safe for democracy."

"Yes, sir," my father said respectfully.

The colonel bowed stiffly to my mother. "I trust you will enjoy your new quarters, madam." He walked to the door, then looked back at my father. "I suppose you have no side arm for your own use?"

"No. I—"

"One will be issued. Good day."

We stood at the front windows and watched him vault heavily into the rear seat of his jeep. A young corporal started the engine. As the jeep went down the road, two little flags with silver eagles fluttered on the front fenders. I looked at my mother and father. She seemed worried. He was grim.

"Are you really going to carry a gun?" my mother asked.

"Oh, maybe not. And if I do, it will be for appearances' sake. There's no danger, Elizabeth! I told you that."

"That's not what he just said, George."

"Well, he's an army man. You know how they are."

I left them to go work in my room. Later Aggie came in, dragging an old flannel blanket and sucking her fingers.

"If you don't stop that," I said, "you'll get buckteeth."

"Don't care," she said around her fingers.

"Aggie, you're in school now, for cripes' sake! Grow up!"

She looked at me with those big eyes and began to cry. Instantly contrite, I knelt to hug her. "Hey. There's nothing to be scared of. School will be just fine."

"Nobody will like me," she sniffled.

"*Everybody* will like you! You're a really neat girl."

I consoled her as best I could, and after a while she smiled and

184

padded off to bed. It was getting late. I put on my pajamas.

That night I awakened many times, sitting upright from some vague dream, confused in this new room of strange shadows and unknown dimensions. Every time I came back to reality I saw the dim light from the kitchen, where my father sat hunched over rosters and ledger sheets, preparing for the morning. At six am my mother roused me and Aggie and nagged us into getting ready for school. The bus came by the house at seven twenty, and we boarded. Aggie squeezed my hand so tight it hurt. For all of us our new lives had begun.

THE SCHOOL BUS trundled into Harmony and crossed a bridge over the Big Walnut, the slow-flowing creek, as broad as a river, that bisected the town. We stopped in a graveled parking area beside a long, low, modern-looking school building with lots of glass. There were kids of all ages everywhere. Aggie and I got off the bus. The driver nudged me, pointing to a green metal door in the side of the building.

"You're new, ain't you? The office is to the right."

Thanking him, I dragged Aggie inside to a large office where several women were rushing around. I got someone's attention and handed over papers from our old school. After consultation, one of the women took Aggie's hand. "Come with me, dear, and we'll introduce you to your new teacher. My, that's a pretty dress!" Aggie went off looking like she was being taken to the electric chair. There was enormous bustle in the halls, and then everyone seemed to disappear.

I sat on a chair against the wall. Finally a tall woman with gray hair came out of an inner office.

"What are you still doing here?" she demanded.

"Waiting for someone to tell me where to go," I said.

She scowled at some papers. "You're the new boy. You're in room one twenty, Davidson. Land! You're late! Hurry."

I rushed out, heading in the direction she'd indicated. All the classroom doors were closed, and I heard kids doing the pledge of allegiance. Sweat bolted out of every pore on my body. I turned a corner looking for 120, and there stood Benny Harrison.

Not that I knew him then, of course. But I knew he was someone important. He was standing beside a closed door, leaning against the wall, one booted foot resting behind him. He was not large, only a bit taller than I, and slender. But everything about him said *tough!* He was wearing a tight pale blue T-shirt and cutoffs. His battered lace-up boots almost reached the knee. I had never seen anyone wear them with short pants before. He had a round beanie-type hat on his head, with badges and trinkets sewn all over it. Picking his teeth with the small blade of a pocketknife, he turned narrowed eyes to me, saying nothing.

"Is this one twenty?" I asked breathlessly, pointing to the door with the number 120 on the opaque glass.

"What's it look like, stupid?"

I reached for the doorknob. He stopped me with the hand that still held the knife. "What's your name?"

"Danny Davidson, sir."

"You're new here."

"Yes, sir."

He stared at me for a long moment. I was chilled to the soles of my feet. There was violence behind those icy eyes. I didn't move a muscle. Finally he let his hand drop.

I opened the door and went in. Everyone turned toward me, and at the front of the room a gray and massive woman with the face of George Washington paused in what she had been saying.

"Yes?" she said to me.

"I'm Danny Davidson," I croaked.

"You're late," she snapped. "Not a very good start, is it?"

"No, ma'am."

"Come over here."

I approached her. Everyone was judging me. My flesh crawled.

"Class," the woman said, a hand heavy on my shoulder, "this is Danny Davidson and he comes to us from the Columbus schools. Danny, tell us something about yourself!"

I looked at her, strangled. "Well, I—my parents and I live in

186

the country—" Someone snickered and there was general shuffling. Sweat stung my eyes. "We just moved, see. My dad—"

"No, no, no. What about you?"

"Well . . ." My mind raced. All I could see was a blur of faces. I had to say something. "I—I guess I like school all right. I make model airplanes. I'm a great football player because of my exceptional speed—" All the girls were grinning and nudging each other. I stopped, realizing how stupid I sounded.

"What do you play?" the teacher asked helpfully.

"Ma'am?" My mind had shut off. I wished I were dead.

"Play!" She smiled. "What do you play?"

"Well, I've got a mouth harp—"

The room erupted in laughter. Over it, the teacher chuckled. "In football, Danny! What position do you play?"

Mortified, I saw how I had erred. "Halfback," I choked.

"Good. I'm your new teacher, Mrs. Broadus. Now—"

The door opened. My earlier antagonist came shuffling in, still picking at his teeth with the knife. Mrs. Broadus whirled, fire in her eyes. "Benny Harrison, get that hat off your head!"

Benny tossed his beanie on the floor and stepped on it, staring insolently back at her. There were snickers.

"Pick it up and go to your desk! Put that knife away!"

Benny obeyed, slouching down a far aisle. He took a playful swing at a smaller boy, who almost fell, dodging the blow. Benny slumped into his seat and cocked one foot on the desk.

"Sit up right!" Mrs. Broadus snapped. He obeyed again, giving her a killing look.

Mrs. Broadus sighed and returned her attention to me. "You see that empty desk under the windows? That's your place." I went there and sat down gratefully.

"Now," Mrs. Broadus said. "We were starting our geography lesson. Can anyone tell me what the main crop is in Brazil?"

"Brazil nuts?" Benny Harrison asked hollowly.

Mrs. Broadus marched to her desk and picked up a dunce cap made of construction paper. "Up here," she ordered, pointing to a tall stool in the front corner.

Benny Harrison slouched up the aisle. He climbed onto the stool, beanie in hand. Mrs. Broadus rammed the dunce cap on his head. "Now sit there and be quiet!"

Benny Harrison sat staring out at the class. Mrs. Broadus, after glaring at him, turned her back. He removed the dunce cap and put on his beanie. She pretended she didn't see. I didn't blame her. He was the toughest kid I had ever seen.

At first recess I located Aggie's room, then saw her happily playing with some girls her own age outdoors. I would have preferred to find a hole to crawl into rather than face my peers, but signs at the doors said everyone would exercise outside except during bad weather. I went to meet my fate.

It was a large playground. In a graveled area the smaller kids were gathered around swings and teeter-totters. The seventh grad-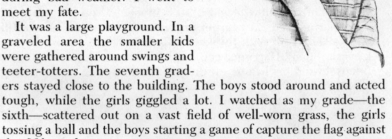ers stayed close to the building. The boys stood around and acted tough, while the girls giggled a lot. I watched as my grade—the sixth—scattered out on a vast field of well-worn grass, the girls tossing a ball and the boys starting a game of capture the flag against the fifth grade.

At this point rough hands grabbed my arms and propelled me across the playground. Looking around frantically, I saw that I was held by two of my classmates, a stocky, sandy-haired boy a few inches taller than me, and an even bigger dark-haired kid with pimples. I knew from observation that morning that they were the ringleaders of the class, if Benny Harrison was left out of the equation. "Lemme go!" I said, struggling as they bore me along.

"Shuddup," the stocky boy growled. They hauled me down to an isolated spot outside the gym and pushed me against a wall. "I'm Bill Sheehan," the stocky boy said. "This is Phil Inright. Now. What do you think you're doing here?"

"I'm going to school," I said, scared.

Sheehan sneered. "I guess you think you're a stud, down here with the country yokels."

"*No!*"

Sheehan grabbed a handful of my shirt. "We don't like kids from Columbus. So you're on probation here. Understand?"

I struggled. My shirt tore. Some instinct took over. I hit Sheehan in the face. It was not a hard blow, but he was so shocked that he let me go. Inright growled and lunged. I ducked him and ran. They chased me until I skidded to a halt. Standing in front of me was Benny Harrison.

I stopped, sure I was dead. He stared slit-eyed at me, legs spread, hands on his hips.

Behind me, Sheehan and Inright thundered up. They, too, saw Benny and stopped. He stared at them. They froze for a count of three, then fled without a word.

Benny Harrison had not moved. His gimlet eyes swiveled to mine. "Okay, kid. You're saved."

I stared at him in wonder. I could only utter, "*Why?*"

"You punched Sheehan. He's bigger than you. I liked that."

Relief flooded through me. "Thanks! I really—"

"On the other hand," Benny Harrison cut in coldly, "maybe I just wanted to save you for myself." He ejected some spit from between his teeth. The school bell sounded. "You better hurry," he said in a tone that clearly implied the difference between us.

CHAPTER THREE

In Columbus my afternoons had followed a pattern. When I got home, I changed clothes and sat down at my desk to work on a flying model while listening to the Zenith. "Stella Dallas" and "Lorenzo Jones" were among my favorites and provided a time reference while I cut out and pinned the balsa-wood members to the model blueprint. At five "Jack Armstrong" came on.

In this country, however, it was clear the pattern would be different. The bus did not get Aggie and me back home until after four. My room, like much of the house, was still a wreck. Our mother met us at the door with cookies and a list of orders. The new Stuka model would have to wait.

Supper was ready as usual at six, but my father did not arrive until almost seven. He came in smiling cheerfully but looking worn down. He kissed my mother. "Everything all right?"

"Fine," she said. "Hurry and wash. Supper is ready."

At the table, he told Mother that the camp was physically ready, assuming the plumbers worked all night. He had met with the army officers and all the civilian guards. They were going to be shorthanded, and the truck drivers who would take prisoners to work on farms in the area would have to double as watchmen.

"It's really a massive puzzle," my father said. "The colonel says we'll never have as many men as we ought to. I not only have to make out the duty rosters, plan sick fill-ins and make sure all the spots are covered; I also have to write up rules and regulations, devise an accounting system and rotate work equitably to the various farms. I'm afraid starting the garden will have to wait, honey."

"We'll start it," my mother said. "Don't worry about that."

They looked at each other, Aggie and me forgotten.

"I still think I did the right thing," my father told her. "When Finnegan got the promotion, I had to leave the company. This job could lead to something, Elizabeth. I can move up in the government service. And I'm working for the war effort. It isn't much, but I'm not just a four-F."

"You were *never* just a four-F," my mother replied, her bright eyes angry. "You went to that company as a part-time stocker, and you worked hard and studied at night to learn accounting. Without that, they could never have changed production to bayonets that quickly. Even if you hadn't had a health problem, they would have kept you out of the service to help hold things together. What you're doing now is even more important. I don't want to hear that four-F talk again!"

He stared at her, his tired face slack, and then slowly he smiled. "Hey," he said. "Do you know what?"

"What?" she asked crossly.

"You're great."

It was her turn to smile. "Eat your supper."

He looked at me. "You'd better eat up, too. We have an errand to run later."

"Errand?" I echoed.

"Well," he went on slowly, "it seems that the colonel's shepherd had some puppies. They're weaned now."

I stared at him and my heart began thumping. "Yeah?"

"Yeah," he said. "So I thought if you wanted, we might drive back to the post after supper and look the pups over. If you find one you like, we could bring it home."

190

"*Yow!*" I yelled.

My mother dropped her fork. "Don't ever scream like that at the supper table again!" But she was laughing when she said it.

Aggie looked disgusted. "When do I get my kitten?" she asked.

My father's grin threatened to split his face. "I thought you'd never ask, Agatha. Maybe, if you check the box out in the back seat of the car, you might find something to interest you."

Aggie's eyes widened. Then she was off the chair like a bolt. The back screen door slammed as she rocketed out.

"You didn't," my mother said.

"I did," my father answered.

Outside, Aggie started squealing with delight. Moments later she exploded back into the kitchen. Under each arm was a furry gray ball with staring eyes and a swishy tail.

"Oh, Daddy!" she cried. One of the kittens squirmed away and jumped onto the table where it promptly turned Aggie's milk over. The other kitten dashed under the stove. It was glad pandemonium.

After supper my father helped with the dishes as usual, while I waited impatiently. When he had first mentioned getting a dog, it had seemed only a mythical possibility. But now it was *real*. The farm suddenly looked better to me.

Finally the dishes were done, and my father turned to my mother. "We won't be gone long," he promised her. He motioned to me, and I followed him out to the car.

Darkness had already come on. My father started the engine, then eased the gearshift into low and released the clutch slowly. I had never seen him mistreat any piece of machinery, and the car was the object of his gentlest attentions. We pulled out onto the road, accelerating easily. The lights of the house faded behind us. "So is school all right?" he asked after a while.

I thought of my new enemies, Bill Sheehan and Phil Inright, and the specter of Benny Harrison. "Oh, sure," I lied. "Fine."

"Fine," he repeated. "That's fine, Squirt."

We drove along new fencing, shiny in the headlights. After what seemed like a long time, we turned onto a gravel driveway. Ahead was a tall gate with barbed wire and a wooden guard shack, not yet painted. From the shack marched a soldier in uniform with a rifle. Was I impressed!

My father rolled down his window as the soldier approached. "We're here to see the colonel, Sergeant."

191

"You're expected, sir," the guard said. He swung the gate open. As we drove by, he snapped to attention and saluted.

"Wow! They salute you, Dad?"

My father smiled, embarrassed. "I wish they wouldn't."

"Have you got a gun yet? Can I see it?"

"A revolver. But I just shoved it in my desk drawer."

"Wow! I bet those old Germans won't try anything here!"

"Danny, I hate to disillusion you, but it's no big thing. The prisoners coming here are people just like you and me. For them the war is over. Dangerous captives have been screened out and sent elsewhere. I've got an idea that if we left the front gate open, these guys would close it to make sure nobody wandered off."

"You make it sound like it's nothing."

"We've got to take care of them, keep track of them, keep them working on the farms," he told me slowly. "It's a vital job. But don't think this is a Tyrone Power war movie. It isn't."

I was disappointed. "Well, you'd do better in a war than Tyrone Power anyway."

He laughed, something he seldom did. "Okay, pay attention now. The big wooden building is the mess hall, see? These two brick ones are where the men will sleep. Over there, that's the old school gym. We'll use it, too."

We passed more new construction, then halted at a great old mansion with a new flagpole. Lights blazed in every window.

"This used to be the schoolmaster's house," my father explained. As we got out, the front door of the mansion opened, and the colonel came to greet us. He was still in uniform, the jacket off, tie gone, boots replaced by house slippers. He looked vastly different with skinny legs at the end of his riding pants.

"Here you are, Davidson!" he said loudly. "Good!" He turned to me. "Ready to get a good guard dog, son?"

"I thought you had puppies," I said.

· He grunted a little laugh. "Ha! Yes. Pups now, and the good Lord only knows what traveling man was the father! But they're all going to be big rascals." He scowled at me. "We'll need good guard dogs with all these Huns around here."

I didn't say anything. The colonel frightened me a little, but I also saw that there was something theatrically false about him. I didn't know how to handle this combination of perceptions.

The colonel led us into the house and through a series of great echoing rooms filled with packing crates. In the kitchen, we met his wife, a gray-haired woman with eyes like slate. She gave us a wintry smile and stood aside while the colonel took us onto the back porch. An enormous German shepherd bitch rose from the shadows and barked once, making me jump back a step.

"*Down*, Helge!" the colonel roared. He pointed to the far side of the porch. "Over there!" The big dog slunk across the floor and lay down obediently, watching me with sullen eyes. The colonel went to the shadowy area and pulled a rug-padded carton with one side cut away into the middle of the floor. Out spilled a tiny explosion of puppies.

"Look at that!" my father said, laughing.

There were five of them, three brown, one brown and white and one almost all black. They cavorted around the colonel's legs, yipping and rolling over each other. I bent, to be engulfed by them. They jumped and nipped at my hands, almost scaring me. The little black fellow ran around in circles, whining.

"Good stock," the colonel said, picking up a brown one to show to my father. "Did you see the size of their paws?"

The little black puppy stopped running in his aimless circles and sort of leaned against my foot. I picked him up. He stared at me with enormous dark eyes and whined again. I held him close. His skinny tail began to wag, and his rough tongue mopped my face.

"Hey!" I giggled. "Stop that!" He only licked me more frantically, wriggling as if trying to get inside my shirt.

"Running an ad in the Harmony paper Friday," the colonel said. "They'll go fast then."

I put the black puppy down and picked up a brown one. This one nipped at my fingers playfully, hurting me slightly with his sharp little milk teeth. The others all gamboled over the floor, wrestling. The black puppy scurried around my feet, nudging me pitifully. I put the brown pup down and picked my dog up again. He repeated his frenzied, joyful act. I got the giggles again.

"What do you think, Squirt?" my father asked, grinning.

It was no contest. "This black one!" I said.

The colonel scowled. "Runt of the litter."

"Are you sure, son?" my father asked.

I hugged the puppy closer. "Yes!"

My father sighed. "Well, it's your dog." He reached into his pocket and took out three dollars. "There you are, Colonel."

The colonel counted the money carefully. "You understand, Davidson, that I'll get twice this when I advertise."

"Yes, sir," my father said respectfully. "We appreciate it."

"Yes, sir," I said. "We sure do!"

"Think nothing of it," the colonel said grandly. He glanced at his watch. "Almost twenty-one hundred."

"Perhaps you'd stay for coffee?" the colonel's wife asked from the doorway. She gave me a smile. "I have some cookies."

I looked at my father. He hesitated.

"I'm sure they want to get their new pup home, Gladys," the colonel said. "And we've a big day tomorrow, eh, Davidson?"

"Yes, sir," my father said. "We'd better get going, ma'am."

When we arrived home, I showed my puppy to Mother and Aggie. Then I brought in a big box from out back and put it in a corner of my room with a piece of rug in it. My father found an old pan suitable for water, and we put that in the box, too.

"What are we going to call this little rowdy?" my mother asked, watching the pup fall into his water pan.

"Skipper. I've had his name picked out forever," I admitted.

She kissed me. "Well, I know it's asking a lot, but you're already late for bed and tomorrow is a school day."

"Oh, Mom, if I could just stay up a little while—"

"Young man, it won't work. Scoot!"

Reluctantly I obeyed. After all the lights were out and the vast country silence had enveloped the house, Skipper began to whine in his box. I told myself that I was sparing my parents the noise, and fumbled over to him in the dark. I carried his wriggling, furry little body back to bed with me. He cuddled against me and was immediately happy.

You're going to be the greatest dog in the world, Skipper, I thought. I had never been so excited. It took hours to fall asleep. I had no inkling of what lay ahead for Skipper and me.

EARLY IN THE MORNING I rigged up a little pen beside the house with some boards and chicken wire, and put Skipper inside it. He ran around aimlessly, sniffing the ground and bumping his nose against the boards. I petted him and put in his water pan, some leftover meat-loaf scraps and stale bread. He ignored the food. Reluctantly I left to catch the bus with Aggie.

The morning went well enough. Benny Harrison was on the

194

dunce stool again. After recess Mrs. Broadus said, "Benny, I'll give you a chance to return to your chair. Did you study your lesson last night?"

"No." Benny sneered.

Mrs. Broadus was trying hard. "Well, if you can answer this question, you can return to your seat. Who was President during the Civil War?"

Benny looked at her unblinkingly, his eyes slitted and cold. A smile quirked the corner of his mouth. "Mussolini?"

Mrs. Broadus raced to her desk and pulled out a heavy yardstick. "All right, Benny! Hold out your hands."

He held them out. *Crack!* Down came the yardstick, right across his outstretched knuckles. *Crack!* His hands turned beet red. I flinched; he did not quiver or change expression. Breathing hard, Mrs. Broadus stared at him. "Now will you behave?" Benny just returned her stare. Defeated, she stormed back to her desk.

I was in awe of him. Was he tough! Somehow, though, he did not frighten me the way Bill Sheehan did. Of all the boys, Sheehan was the only one I recognized as truly evil. We all teased the girls, but he pulled their hair really hard and seemed to enjoy seeing tears in their eyes. Even Phil Inright and Jimmy Cantwell, the two biggest boys in the classroom, did not have that air of real viciousness. Sheehan was cruel and he was sneaky. And if he had not already picked me as a special target, I assured his attention that day at lunch recess.

We were in the playground, and a game of capture the flag was under way again. The fifth graders, who far outnumbered us, had gotten the flag out of our territory once, capturing two of our boys in the process. With Sheehan in the middle, we huddled to plan our attack. "Okay, big shot," he said to me. "You bragged about how fast you are. Let's see you go get the flag."

"By myself?" I asked.

"That's the way the game is played, kid."

"Maybe what we need is strategy," I said, thinking fast.

"Like what?" Sheehan was scornful. All eyes were on me.

I raised my head and looked across into enemy territory. A scheme formed in my mind. I ducked back. "What if I run down this side? Some of them will chase me. Then Jimmy starts going like mad for the center. They'll think the first attack was a diversion, and the real one is in the middle!"

"And you both get captured," Sheehan said.

"No, no! While we're being chased, you and Phil are on the other side of the field—strolling along the edge like you weren't in the game, see? Then when Jimmy and I are both getting caught, you and Phil run in from the trees at the far end, get the flag and come back with it!"

Sheehan's eyes became sober. "We never tried that."

"It will work!" Jimmy Cantwell said. Everybody in the huddle started jumping around, getting excited.

"Okay," Sheehan said grimly. "We'll try it."

We broke the huddle and ranged along our line. The fifth graders faced us, scattering over the field. Children from other rooms wandered freely in the area, making the players only a part of the human mosaic. I walked to one side, then turned and dashed into enemy territory. I wanted to be very sure everyone saw my intentions.

No one responded at first. Then there was a sharp cry, and I saw some boys running to cut me off. I pretended fear and scurried back toward the line. They started to close. I turned on my speed but saw to my real horror that they were faster. There were other cries in the distance. I turned a second to see Cantwell lumbering through the fifth-grade middle. Boys converged on him. He dodged and fell, just as a couple of them tackled me.

Spitting dirt and grass, I was dragged to the enemy rear. Cantwell was already there. I looked to see if Sheehan's main attack had gained the flag; alas, it waved brazenly in the wind. And coming at me, fifth graders pinioning both his arms, was a muddy Sheehan. They shoved him into the capture circle.

"Idiot!" he screamed at me. "Moron! Nobody *ever* captured me before."

Without warning, he hit me. There was a sharp flash of pain in my mouth as I sat down hard. Then I tasted blood, and a tooth that had been loose almost went down my throat. I spat it into my hand and looked at it. I was dazed.

Sheehan danced around me, thumbing his nose with his right fist. "Come on! Fight!"

"I don't want to fight!" I protested. He looked absolutely stupid, but I was terrified.

"Aw, Bill," Cantwell said, "he didn't mean nothing."

"*You* want to fight?" Sheehan demanded, dancing around

Cantwell, a crazy, cruel look in his eyes. "Come on, you fat slob!"

Distantly the bell began ringing. The other boys ran for the building. "Come on, coward!" Sheehan taunted, returning to me.

I sat in the grass, hating myself, unable to move. Sheehan dropped his hands. Some of the mad glaze left his eyes. He looked down at me with infinite disgust. "I'll finish you off later," he said, before running back to class.

I got up shakily. There was blood on my shirt and hands. I held my handkerchief to my mouth as I limped toward school and went into the boys' room to clean up. Standing inside, smoking a cigarette, was Benny Harrison.

"What happened to you?" he demanded.

I swallowed and began to tell him. As I did so, his hard face grew even harder. He tossed his cigarette butt into the toilet, flushed it and walked out. When I got to class, he was already on the dunce stool, staring into his own private universe.

I went to my seat. My mouth hurt, but it had stopped bleeding. I did not dare look at Sheehan. The arithmetic lesson flew by. After we did art, the bell rang for the afternoon recess. I went to the bathroom again to get the blood out of my shirt. When I returned to class, Benny Harrison, his face a little pink, came in right behind me. He perched on the stool. Mrs. Broadus closed the door. Sheehan was not back.

A minute later he came in holding a handkerchief to his nose. He had been crying and blood was all over his face. The room hushed. "What happened to you?" Mrs. Broadus asked.

Sheehan's strained eyes darted. "I fell down," he said.

There was a commotion. Mrs. Broadus took him to the principal's office. When he came back, he sat quietly through the last hour of school, blinking at his textbook. After the final bell I did my best to avoid him, but as we all marched toward the exits with teachers monitoring us, Sheehan was next to me. His eyes were bright with rage. "I'll get you," he whispered.

"*Why?*" I demanded. "I never did anything to you!"

Mrs. Broadus nudged me with her yardstick. "No talking!"

Outside, the line loosened as we followed school traffic guards to various streets and buses. I looked around for Aggie and instead saw Benny Harrison. He trotted up beside me, the gewgaws on his cap jingling.

"What did he say to you just then, kid?"

"He said he'd get me."

Benny sighed. "Well, I guess you'll have to fight him, then."

"Did you punch his nose during recess?"

"Sure."

"Because he knocked my tooth out?"

"Sure."

"Why, Benny?" I asked, unbelieving.

"I dunno." He looked like he was casting around for a reason. "You got class. I seen that right away. I guess I just like you. Don't worry about it. Maybe I'll change my mind."

We waited at the corner for the guard to block traffic. I saw Aggie hurrying behind us. Benny hesitated.

"You smoke, kid?" he asked.

"No," I told him.

"I didn't think so. See you." He turned and ran off.

When I got home, I immediately went to Skipper's pen and started talking to him. He was ecstatic. I took him out and put him on the grass, and he ran a few feet, then hunkered down and whined. I examined him carefully but found nothing wrong with his paws. The order of the day was to start on the garden plot, so I put a string around his neck and took him with me, tying him to the remains of the fallen fence. I got the shovel and hoe from the barn and set to work. Getting the weedy patch ready to plant was going to be a very big job.

Within a few minutes my mother came down the slope, the wind whipping her thin dress. She gave me a sunny, quizzical smile. "Hello, stranger. Why didn't you come in and let me know you were home?"

"Well, I wanted to get started on this right away, Mom."

She walked closer and saw my face. She stared. "Your lip is all swollen!"

"I fell down," I lied. "I knocked out that loose baby tooth, see?" I stuck a finger in my mouth and gaped for her.

She sighed. "You're all right?"

"Yessum."

"This garden is an awfully big job, Danny. If your face hurts, I don't want you out here. We can work on it tomorrow."

"I'm fine. Really. And I've got Skipper to keep me company."

She went back to the house. I dug for a while, my progress impeded by the fact that I couldn't stand on the shovel and make

198

it go in all the way, as I had seen my father do. I had to hack at the ground, then turn over small amounts of dirt at a time. I sat down, out of breath. Skipper whined. I crawled over and lay beside him in the grass.

"You want to run around?" I asked, untying the string.

Skipper ran a few paces, then hunkered down, whining.

"What's the matter, you old dummy?" I asked.

He ran toward me. I held out my hand. He fell over it, scrambled, found it and began licking frantically. His tail was going a mile a minute. In my mind something about the way he had *fallen over* my outstretched hand linked with his behavior last night on the colonel's porch and his stumbling through the water pan. A coldness gripped my midsection as I held him up in front of me, staring into his brown eyes.

"Are you all right?" I asked softly.

He wriggled madly, trying to catch me with his pink, darting tongue. But I held him fast, transferring his weight to my left hand. Freeing my right, I drew it back and made a sudden sharp gesture at him. He did not flinch.

Heart pounding now, I put the puppy down. He leaned against my foot, rubbing. I backed up, leaving him alone in the grass. He hopped to his right and to his left, then stopped, going down on his belly. He whined. Creeping, I knelt about ten feet in front of him and held out my arms. He was panting. He seemed to stare right at me but did not move.

"Skipper," I said.

With a glad little bound he jumped toward me, beside himself with joy. I held him close to my face. His eyes stared back, but now I knew with a sickening certainty that they did not see.

Skipper was blind.

I will never know how long I squatted in the grass, holding the pup. I wanted to cry, but I couldn't. Sheer shock made thought impossible. I examined Skipper repeatedly, hoping that somehow I was wrong. I tried more sharp gestures in front of his face and got no reaction whatsoever. All the while he was wriggling and licking my face. He was perfect in every other way, and the most terrible thing was how happy he seemed. Evidently he had been born blind and knew no other condition.

At first I was angry at the colonel. He had done it on purpose, I thought. But then I realized that *I* had picked Skipper from the litter over the mild objections of both the colonel and my father. My own choice was a puppy who would never live a normal life— if he lived at all.

My next thought was of my father's reaction when he found out. He would either demand that we return Skipper, or simply destroy him. The newspaper ad had not yet run; the other puppies were still available. I imagined the colonel giving us one in exchange. Then *he* would kill Skipper. I could practically hear him. "A blind dog is no good to anyone. I'll shoot him myself." The prospect filled me with horror, and I hugged Skipper closer.

"They aren't going to hurt you," I crooned as he licked me.

But how could I prevent it? I wasn't going to keep him, was I? My dream had been of a fine dog who would play with me, help me hunt rabbits and go with me to school sometimes, so that Bill Sheehan would know that he must never touch me again. What good was a blind puppy?

With a burst of angry resentment I tossed Skipper to the ground. He yelped with pain and rolled over. Then he took a few meaningless steps and went to his belly, in a gesture of helplessness that now made perfect sense to me.

"Oh, you dummy," I murmured, hurrying to pick him up again.

No, Skipper must not be returned to the colonel. If I could keep his blindness a secret for a while, then the other puppies would be adopted. After that I could pretend shock when my family noticed his blindness. Maybe they would have mercy on him.

It seemed the best plan I could come up with. But then a danger occurred to me. If I admitted the problem now, there would be a new puppy, a whole one . . . the one I had always dreamed about. But if I waited and deceived everyone, the other pups would be sold. I might still lose Skipper, and with him all my chances of having any dog for a long time.

The thought stopped me momentarily. I looked at Skipper again. He was such a fat little mutt. Holding him close, I could have sworn he was grinning at me.

"I ought to play it safe," I told him softly. "If I try to save your worthless life, I might lose *everything*." His pink tongue darted out and caught my nose. "Quit that!" I groaned. "Oh, Skipper, you don't play fair. Stop!"

He would not. With sheer joy he lathered my face. I hugged him closer. The decision was made.

200

CHAPTER FOUR

The German prisoners began arriving the next day, and all weekend more trainloads came in. Something had gone wrong, and instead of a couple of hundred, as anticipated, there were almost four hundred captured German soldiers in the camp by Sunday afternoon. My father was there night and day, making arrangements for new building construction. Saturday afternoon, however, he took time off to drive us into town.

Harmony was stirred up. The weekly paper had featured a news account of the prisoners' arrival and an editorial pleading for calm and cooperation with camp officials. My father said the merchants who made big sales to the camp backed the installation. Everyone else was either flatly against it or simply scared. I saw one sign reading, TAKE THEM TO FORT KNOX.

"They wouldn't be so excited if they could see those poor devils," my father said. "We'll have to have a daily shuttle to Fort Hayes for medical treatments if doctors aren't assigned here permanently."

"Have the prisoners been mistreated?" my mother asked sharply.

"Not really. But they've been through a war, Elizabeth. Some of them have suffered wounds, a lot of them are malnourished. They're thousands of miles from home, not sure what's going to be done to them, with no money, no cigarettes, nothing. And the colonel didn't help their spirits any by having them stand formation this morning."

"What did he tell them?"

"He read them the riot act. Listed things that a man could be put into solitary confinement for, explained that the guards have live ammunition." My father sighed. "It was rough. But things will work out. I've visited with some of the prisoners already. A surprising number speak English. They don't want trouble."

We had pulled into the grocery store parking lot. My father reached for his wallet and handed a bill to my mother. "Maybe you could get me four extra cartons of cigarettes."

"Four!" she said. "People will think we're hoarders. What on *earth* are you going to do with that many cigarettes?"

My father looked at her, his smile crooked. "Well, I thought a few of the prisoners might get a smoke anyway."

"You'd give a smoke to a German?" I burst out, shocked.

"Squirt, I've told you. They're people. Just like us."

"Not like us," I said indignantly. "We didn't run over France! Look, we've got to be tough. You start letting people push you around and there's just no end to it."

"Treating someone with decency is not a sign of weakness."

"You give any sign you might be weak," I said, "and they're liable to just run right over *you*." I was dimly aware that we might be talking about two different things now. Being tough with the Germans was suddenly all mixed up with my own desperate need to defeat my fear of Bill Sheehan.

My mother seemed to think it was time to intervene. "Are you taking Danny to the shoe store now?" My brown oxfords were through on the right sole and almost through on the left.

"We'll go there right away," my father said as she got out.

A trip to the shoe store was always a big event, and despite my worry about Skipper, I had given the matter considerable thought. When my mother took me shopping, she would only let me bless her decisions. With my father it was different, and as we entered the store I saw what I wanted immediately: a pair of dark lace-up boots like Benny Harrison wore.

"Those," I said as soon as the clerk had measured my foot.

"*Those?*" my father repeated incredulously.

"They'll be real practical for work and school," I said.

My father looked at them. They were as ugly as Benny's, with thick black soles and heels, and a flapped side pocket where a man could carry a knife. "Your mother would never let you wear them to church. You'd have to polish up these old oxfords."

"Okay!"

"How much are they?" my father asked, hefting the boots.

"Four eighty, sir," the clerk said. "We're clearing them out."

I waited in agony. My father sighed. "Try them on."

I tried them. They were stiff and heavy, and they hurt my feet. I said I would wear them. I clomped out feeling tougher already, and tried walking like Benny did.

My mother took one look and had a fit. But a sale was a sale. When we got home, I found an old beanie a little like Benny's. Hunting up some buttons and a wheel off a model, I got busy sewing. The hat didn't turn out as well as Benny's, but I was proud of it. After my father had hurried back to the camp that evening, I felt it was safe to take Skipper out. I wore the new boots, but after we had walked a few hundred yards, I stopped and went barefoot. The boots had already raised five raw red blisters.

My greatest concern that weekend, however, was Skipper. The next day when I let him out of the box to change the papers, he did not sink to his belly as he had on earlier occasions. Tail wagging, he sallied across the room—right into the leg of my desk. He fell sideways, fat little legs sprawling, then got up and walked into the wall. Shaking his head, he looked pitifully into his own private darkness and wet on the floor.

I carried him outside, so no one would notice that he couldn't navigate. Taking him beyond our garden, I put him down in the ankle-high grass. He sniffed it with interest and wandered away.

"You'll learn, boy," I told him encouragingly. "You've got a great nose, right? And you can learn sounds, too." He rolled in the damp grass, playing, and biting at his own tail, which he could not quite reach. I laughed and watched, and then fell silent.

He got up and stood still, one floppy ear cocked. He took a few tentative steps, moving in a half circle. I remained silent. Hopelessly lost, he began whining. He was less than ten feet from me.

"Here I am, Skipper," I said, patting my hands together.

His tail began wagging a mile a minute. He went off in the wrong direction, and I hurried over to scoop him up. He went wild with pleasure. Hugging him tightly, I said, "You'll be fine!" But *how*?

A start had to be made. Carrying Skipper to the little barn, I looked around at rusty bits of metal and broken tools left by some former occupant. Hanging from a nail was a thin leather strap with a fastener at one end. I measured the strap around Skipper's neck and punched in some holes with my pocketknife. It made a usable collar. Then I found a three-foot piece of stout string for a leash.

"Okay, boy," I said. "Let's practice." Skipper walked to the end of the leash and flipped over backward. I tugged him onto his feet again. Pulling, I managed to get him to walk in a crooked line. There was a rotting barrel beside the door. "Look out—" I started.

Too late. He walked into the barrel. For a moment I felt utter despair. Even with the leash, every obstacle became an impossible hazard. But there had to be a way. There had to.

I FELT A NEED to take my mind off Skipper, and the afternoon loomed vacantly. Planning further exploration of the drainage pipe into the creek, I had gotten new batteries for my flashlight and a ball of kite twine. Now I put Skipper in his box, and avoiding detection by my mother, I set off alone.

Fresh greenery concealed the stickers in the raspberries, and I encountered them painfully again. I scrambled down the steep bank, one boot slipping into the creek again, and proceeded to my left. Rain had raised the water level temporarily, bringing down all sorts of new and interesting debris, including a soggy orange crate, some beer bottles and two old tires. I inspected the tires, hoping to find a red inner tube for a rubber gun. I was disappointed. Going on, I found the pipe virtually hidden from view by new spring weeds.

Climbing inside with confidence, I was again struck by the cold, dank odor. I braced myself and switched on my small flashlight. It penetrated about a dozen paces into the gloom, illuminating wafting strands of horrible whitish gas. I tied one end of my kite twine to a bush at the opening, then started along, unwinding the string.

Things went well at first. I had gotten used to the gassy odor, but I was sweating despite the low temperature. I kept thinking that I could (a) get lost, (b) get caught in a flash flood or (c) meet a hideous creature. But I hunched along anyway.

After a while I paused to rest and looked behind me—the opening was a pinprick of brilliant sunlight. I felt like an outcast from the real world. Here, I was doomed to the life of a mole. Mole Man! It sounded like a great idea for a comic strip. To get the feel of it, I switched off my flashlight, felt the darkness close around me— and got the light back on quickly. I set my teeth and pressed on, laying out more string behind me.

Another hundred paces, and the tunnel began to bend to my right. When I glanced back, there was no longer any trace of the outside world. I was feeling homesick. I kept going, my footsteps in the hard leather boots the only sound.

Up ahead I heard something else and froze, holding my breath. A vague rumbling. It did not sound like running water or wind. It was some kind of great, vast, *horrible* movement, and I was not far from whatever it might be. I had come a very long way. My legs ached, and I was almost out of string.

"You might as well go ahead," I told myself softly. "You won't be satisfied till you know what it is." I inched forward another few paces. The flashlight flickered and went yellow in my hand, almost going out. Thought vanished. The next thing I knew, I had turned and was running for my life. Gasping for breath, I didn't stop until I tumbled out of the sun-flooded opening onto the wet dirt.

After I regained my composure, I looked back up at the pipe. It certainly did not look frightening from here. "Now you've got to do it again!" I told myself disgustedly.

But not today.

ON MONDAY, true to my plan, I wore my new boots and took my beanie in my lunch pail. Once Aggie was in her classroom, I put the beanie on. Jimmy Cantwell met me in the hall.

"Who do you think you are?" he demanded.

I gave him my Benny Harrison tough look. "Who's askin'?"

Cantwell punched me in the stomach and waltzed into class.

The bell rang. I staggered in after him. Most students were at their desks, and Mrs. Broadus was at the blackboard, but she glanced over and saw me. Her expression went fierce, and she came across the room like a Sherman tank. With one swoop she knocked my beanie off and propelled me toward the dunce stool. "What do you think you're doing, coming to school looking like that?" she demanded. "Get up there! You want a hat? You'll get one!" She crammed the dunce cap on my skull.

At recess Cantwell punched me again, and Inright shoved me down. Fighting tears, I got up and shuffled to the building. Benny Harrison was there watching. I gave him an accusing look, silently asking why he had stopped championing me.

"Kid," he said, "it comes with the territory. You wear the uniform, you better be prepared to fight."

At the end of the day Mrs. Broadus did not return my beanie, and I did not ask for it. Once home, I removed the boots, surveyed the raw blisters and got out my old tennis shoes. They were too small this year. I put them on anyway.

For the next few days my secret about Skipper remained secure. I worked in the garden and began to get a large portion of it weeded and the earth broken a few inches deep. I kept Skipper close beside me at all times. Everyone else was so busy that he passed casual muster, giving me a false sense of security.

In the fields of the big farm across from our creek, the captured Germans had been at work for two days. It had been exciting at first, seeing the trucks unloading prisoners in dark fatigues, carrying shovels, hoes and rakes. A handful of guards looked on, but the prisoners broke rows without incident. As I worked in our garden that Thursday, I paid no attention to them until I became aware that someone was watching me.

I looked up and saw a tall, slender man in the dark fatigues standing nearby. A second prisoner was behind him, and a soldier with a rifle brought up the rear. The first prisoner had buckets in his hands. He had close-cropped hair, a large nose and a crooked smile. He was perhaps my father's age.

"We were told we could get water," he said in a thick accent.

I scrambled back, looking around for a rock. "Get away from me! My dad is important! You try anything and you'll be sorry!"

The second prisoner came up beside the first. Shockingly, he didn't look much older than I was, and he seemed so skinny and sad in his oversize fatigues that I felt sorry for him. Then I thought, You can't feel sorry for these guys! They're the enemy!

The first German was watching me closely, with a grave, kind expression. "There is nothing to fear, young man."

"I know who you are. You're Germans."

The older man exchanged glances with the boy beside him. "He is perceptive." They both smiled.

It made me mad. I caught Skipper's leash and pulled him away. He ran after me and blundered into a fence post.

The older man registered dismay. "The puppy. He is blind?"

"What's it to you?" I shot back.

"Poor puppy," he said softly, coming over to pet Skipper, who went crazy licking his hands and rolling over. The German chuckled and held Skipper's head to look into his eyes. "Yes. Blind. What a pity."

"He can be trained," I snapped.

"Of course he can," the German answered.

I was stunned. "He can? Really?"

"Of course. I had a dog, Heidi, blind like this one. *Ja.*"

I forgot to hate him. "Like Skipper? How long did she live?"

"A blind dog can have a fine long life."

"How long *did* she live?" It was terribly important.

The soldier strode up. "Hey, kid, can we draw some water?"

"Right over there," I told him, pointing to our well, and returned my gaze to the German.

His smile was sad. "She may still be alive—if the bombers have not struck my home near Munich."

"You mean she didn't die from being blind?" I asked excitedly.

"No. I am a—" He raised his eyebrows. "I was a veterinarian. It is hard to train such a dog, but it can be done. Your dog, if he lives, will always require special care."

"How do you train him?" I demanded. "What do you do first?"

"Come on!" the soldier said sharply.

The German flinched and started to turn away with the buckets. Then he glanced back. "Teach him to come to the sound of your voice and to walk with the leash close to your side."

"Come on, come on!" the soldier said.

I sat in the garden and watched the men filling their buckets from the old outside well. I was excited beyond belief. The German did not seem like a liar. I had new hope.

As they started back across the yard toward me, I saw that the German limped badly. His face was intent on his task, as if it was difficult for him. On impulse, I intercepted him. "What's your name?" I asked, and then, seeing that that might sound impolite, added, "I'm Danny Davidson."

His heavily lined face broke into another smile. He put down his buckets and extended his hand. "I am Rudi Gerhardt."

The soldier hurried over. "I'm not telling you again, Gerhardt! Move it!"

He picked up the buckets. "I would like to talk to you, but we must hurry now. Perhaps there will be another day."

"And maybe you can tell me more about training Skipper!"

"If there is a way we can have time, of course."

He walked away then, downhill to the creek. It seemed a very great moment. I had met my first German prisoner, and suddenly Skipper's future looked brighter.

I raced back to the garden and sat down with the pup. Taking the leash, I tugged on it gently. "Skipper," I said firmly, "here." He came to me. The training had begun. I was not going to give up now, even if it meant collaboration with the enemy.

CHAPTER FIVE

That night we had our first real guests. My mother flurried through the house, brushing at imaginary specks of dirt. A pot roast produced an indescribably lovely aroma. My father came home early

208

and immediately went to the bedroom, returning in a fresh white shirt and different bow tie. Following orders, I took a bath and then put on my school clothes. Aggie was sitting in the living room, dressed in her best pink pinafore, white hose and sandals. No one had told us the names of the guests.

At about ten minutes before seven a car sounded in the front. "They're here," my father called.

Getting out of a black Cadillac sedan were a rotund man in a dark suit, a small woman with gray hair and Bill Sheehan!

"What's *he* doing here?" I gasped.

"Who?" my father replied. "Oh. You mean the boy? You ought to know him, Danny. He's in your grade at school."

"I know him," I said, strangled.

"Let's all be on our best behavior," my mother said. "The Sheehans are very nice people. We want to be friends with them."

There was a rap on the door, and my father opened it. During the confusion of greetings Bill and I glared at each other. He was wearing Sunday clothes and looked more uncomfortable than I felt. Everyone sat down. I chose the windowsill across the room from Bill.

Mr. Sheehan mopped his prodigious forehead. "Nice place you folks have here."

"We're just getting it fixed up," my mother told him.

Sheehan rolled his eyes around. "Well, that's obvious, but you've made progress. My bank owns the mortgage, you know."

"I didn't know," my father said, smiling as if amused.

"Farmers and Citizens owns most of the mortgages in these parts," Sheehan said. "If you ever buy, we'll be doing business."

Mrs. Sheehan chirped, "It will be a very nice area again, I'm sure, once those Germans are gone."

"There isn't really any danger," my father told her.

"No danger! How can you say that?"

"Now, Effie," Sheehan said. He looked at my father. "I've explained repeatedly that the camp means real financial help for Harmony. We all know you people are doing everything in your power to make the camp secure, and for the sake of business you won't hear any of us speaking publicly against it."

Mrs. Sheehan shuddered. "It makes me nervous being even this close." She looked at my mother. "How do you stand it?"

"Stand it?" my mother repeated slowly. "Well, I don't really think there's much danger. The prisoners are under guard. And if they escaped, where would they go? They're probably glad to be safe where they are."

"That's the ticket!" Sheehan said. "Exactly the right line for public consumption!" He winked at my father. "Excellent, George! Between us, we'll get through this in fine shape."

My mother stood up. "Excuse me. I have to see to things in the kitchen."

"I'll help, dear," Mrs. Sheehan said, and followed her.

Sheehan glanced their way, then leaned his ponderous weight closer to my father, lowering his voice. "I sympathize, George. Keeping a woman happy in the danger zone. Believe me, it's a patriotic thing to do. Anything we can do to help, don't hesitate." He turned to me. "And when your dad is working, you keep a sharp eye out. Know where all the guns are. If any of those Krauts come near the house, stack them up like cordwood!"

"Those prisoners aren't going to try to escape!" my father said.

"I hope you're right, George. But it doesn't hurt to be ready— and for those Germans to *know* we're ready. There's a loaded gun near every doorway in Harmony. If they do try anything, you won't have to rally your guards, just send for the hearse."

My father's face was strained. "That isn't going to happen."

"I hope not. But when you talk to those Germans, remind them that we're all good Americans. There are no sympathizers here. Even the old German families are loyal. We've checked them out very, very carefully. There are a lot of us just aching to strike a blow for freedom—and reduce the cost to the taxpayers at the same time." Sheehan grinned a wolfish grin. "You understand?"

"Yes," my father said huskily. "But—"

Sheehan turned to me. "I understand you and Bill are pals."

I hesitated an instant. "Yes, sir," I said.

Why had I agreed with him? My impulse had been to blurt out that he was crazy. I glanced at Bill, who sat watching me with a hint of his father's wolfish grin, and then at my father. He looked puzzled, and worried, and sad. Why had either of us allowed this man to say outrageous things?

My mother came in to announce the meal was ready. In addition to roast we had potatoes, carrots, salad and fresh-baked bread, topped off with apple pie. It was a delicious feast.

Afterward the women returned to the kitchen to stack the dishes.

210

Aggie tagged along, jabbering. The men went into the living room, where my father lit a cigarette while Sheehan puffed a large dark cigar. He seemed to be making a serious effort not to mention the camp. Instead, everything he talked about reeked of money. My father suggested I show Bill my room. I had no choice. The two of us went down the hall.

Bill looked around at the models on strings. He flipped one contemptuously, making it gyrate. "All dime models."

"I've made fifty-cent models, but I gave them away," I lied.

"Yeah. I'll just bet you did."

Before I could reply, Skipper made a noise in the carton partly hidden behind the bed.

"What's that?" Sheehan asked, walking over. "Hey. A mutt."

"Be careful," I said quickly. "He's little."

Sheehan picked him up. Skipper frantically licked his face. "Yuk!" Sheehan put him on the floor. Skipper dashed headlong into a leg of my desk, rattling it. He yelped in pain.

"What's wrong with that dog?" Sheehan asked.

"He's fine," I said, picking Skipper up and holding him close.

"Lemme see," Sheehan said.

"No!"

He tugged at Skipper. "I'll just look, for cripes' sake." I had to let go or Skipper might have been hurt. Sheehan held him up and looked into his eyes. Then he put him on the floor. Skipper took a few steps and hunkered down, whining. Sheehan moved as if to kick him. Skipper did not react at all.

Sheehan looked at me, surprise in his pale, cruel eyes. "Do you know this mutt is—"

"I know," I said. "But nobody else does. I'm training him."

Sheehan stared at me a moment then started for the door.

"Bill," I whispered, "please don't tell anybody! All I need is a few more days."

Sheehan glanced back at me. "Kid, you're nuts." He hurried out into the hall. A moment later I heard his voice loud in the living room. "Dad! Come and see! Danny's got a mutt, and it's blind as a bat!"

IT WAS MUCH LATER, and I was alone in my room, when my father tapped gently on the door. I was sitting on my bed in my underwear, holding Skipper. A shaft of light fell across both of us. My father came in and sat beside me. He didn't speak, and neither did I. Aggie had gone to bed, and my mother was still in the kitchen. I was crushed by humiliation and fear.

The scene had been far worse than I could have imagined. My father and Mr. Sheehan had come at once after Bill's summons. My father had examined Skipper and looked at me in shocked disbelief.

"A shame," Mr. Sheehan rumbled. "Have to be put to sleep, of course."

"No!" I screamed angrily, forgetting all politeness.

"No choice," Sheehan told my father, as if I weren't there.

"Maybe it can be fixed," my father said.

The discussion went on and on. Sheehan did not think blindness in a dog could be repaired. I said I could train Skipper. My father said he had never heard of that. Sheehan said dogs could be put to sleep with no pain. My father got that sad look of perplexity he sometimes got when dealing with me and said we would discuss it later. We all went back into the living room, where I squirmed for an hour while Bill smirked at me. When they left, I fled to my room. Then I heard my mother and father talking quietly alone.

"He knew it?" my mother had said loudly at one point.

I wished I was the Sub-Mariner or the Green Lantern, so I could do something to Bill Sheehan for this. But mostly I held Skipper, feeling his intense body heat. They can't kill you. You're mine. I love you.

Now, at last, my father spoke in the dimness. "How long have you known, Squirt?"

"Since the other day."

My father sighed. "When did you plan to tell the rest of us?"

"After I had him trained."

"Son, think about Skipper. He's blind. He'll never be able to see the sky, or chase a rabbit, or run in the woods. He's crippled. Do you think he would want to stay alive like that?"

"If I was blind, I'd hate it, but I'd still want to live."

"Dogs aren't like people."

"He loves me. He's growing. He doesn't want to die."

My father took a slow, deep breath. "If you let him go now, it will hurt for a while. I know that. But you'll get over it. You can have another dog—"

"I don't want another dog! I want Skipper! I can train him! I won't let him be a nuisance."

"It's not us I'm worried about," he said despairingly. "It's you. Don't you see you're just asking for all kinds of heartache?"

"I don't care! I want him!"

"Squirt," he said heavily, "you're just not old enough to make this decision. It's going to have to be made for you."

I began to cry. He went on slowly as I tried to stifle my sobs. "You know, Danny, the one thing a father and mother would like to do is keep their children from disappointments, but they're there. It's the way it always is. Life isn't all joy. You start out scared and you end up scared."

"What were you ever scared of?" I choked.

He put a hand on my shoulder. "Of not being smart enough. Of not getting ahead. Of not being able to take care of your mother and you kids. Of changing, or staying put. Of not being liked. Of failure." He gently squeezed my neck. "Most people, Squirt, are scared more than half the time."

"But you're great," I told him. "You always know everything."

He sighed again. "Squirt, if you try to train Skipper and it doesn't work, he's going to be miserable. Maybe God just didn't intend to let Skipper grow up that way."

"Oh, Dad," I said, "please don't have him put to sleep. He won't be miserable. I'll take care of him. Honest I will! Just give me a chance! Please!"

He did not reply. He sat there stroking my hair. I smelled his tobacco and the linty odor of his clothing. There had been very few times like this because he had always been so busy. I wanted to say how much I loved him. Yet I knew that any moment he would take Skipper from me and carry him away.

He did not. He sat quiet for a very long time. Skipper squirmed a little in my lap, and then slept.

Finally my father stood up. He looked tired and enormously sad. "What if you fail, Squirt? It's going to be harder on you then. You'll be more attached to him. Are you really ready to risk that much more pain?"

"He'll be great, Dad. You'll see. I'll teach him *everything*."

He seemed ready to say more. Then with another sigh he left the room, closing the door softly behind him.

I put Skipper down inside his box. He walked around a little, splashing in his water pan. Then I heard him slurping a drink. He's learned that already, I told myself. He'll be fine.

213

Pulling back the sheet on the bed, I stretched out. Somewhere in the house my mother and father were talking quietly. By the tone I could tell that my mother was asking questions, my father calmly trying to reassure her. He was on my side. This realization came to me so clearly, and with such force, that I cried again. Skipper was still in the box beside me. I was going to have a chance!

I thought, too, about Rudi Gerhardt. He had not seemed vicious. And his companion had looked like a scared kid.

This was all very complicated for me. I was supposed to hate Rudi, but I knew he could help me train Skipper. That presented me with a choice, and I had no doubt what my choice would be. I felt I might have just taken the first step toward becoming a traitor to my country.

COLONEL THATCHER was, if anything, methodical, and his duty rosters ordered that identical crews work the same farm areas over and over. My father had said that our outside well was always available for prisoners' use, under proper watch. For these reasons I soon had an opportunity to talk with the man I had begun to consider "my German."

"You are teaching Skipper to know your voice?" Rudi asked.

"Yes," I replied. "His tail always wags when I talk to him."

"Good. He must learn commands." Rudi frowned, thinking. "'Come.' This is number one. Always: 'Come.' No other word. Except his name. He must obey."

"This morning he came right at my voice, but there was a chair in the way, and he bonked himself good."

Rudi smiled faintly. "Then *you* must learn. Never say to come unless the way is clear between the dog and you."

"That might not be so easy," I said.

"It was never said to be easy."

"I'll try."

"Good. Now another command is 'Stay.' At that he must sit down and remain exactly where he is."

"That's going to be even harder! He wants to run around all the time." I looked at Rudi. "I don't know if I can do this."

"If you want to badly enough, you can. Discipline. It is the only way a dog such as this one can live. He has no eyes. You are his vision. He must be taught to obey your voice and trust it as though it were his own eyes."

214

"I don't know how to make him obey," I admitted.

"Repetition. Tell him a thousand times. Tell him one million times. Always the same. He will learn."

"What if he won't?" I asked despairingly. "I had him on the front porch. I pulled on the leash. I said to come. He knew where I was. But he wanted to play. He went in the other direction and fell clear off the porch like a dodo bird!"

"When he disobeys," Rudi told me, "you must punish him. Speak sternly. He will learn the tone. If he is very bad, shake him by the neck. That is how a mother teaches her pups."

"I get mad," I said.

"Of course. But you must never give in to the anger. When he is good, reward. When he disobeys, punish."

I tried. Oh, how I tried. I would take the puppy into the side yard and put him on the leash I'd made. He had begun to learn that he was safe within its confines, but he liked to stay at the end of it, as if the tug at his neck gave him a center. I would pull on the leash. "Skipper, come." More often than not he ignored me completely.

"Skipper! Come!" Wagging his tail, he nuzzled the grass.

I pulled the leash harder, stretching his neck. "Come. *Come.*" He fought, writhing, almost getting an ear through the collar. I grabbed him and shook him roughly, making him cry. I had to be hardhearted.

"Now we'll try it again," I said in my stern voice. He walked to the end of the leash.

"*Come.*"

Perhaps by accident, he gamboled my way. I hugged him and took a piece of a cookie from my pants pocket. He slobbered all over me with pleasure.

"You're going to learn," I told him, "if it kills us both."

There were some heavy spring rains, and the creek behind our house ran high and fast, scattering debris along its banks. Later, when the sun was out again, the prisoners came to clear the channel to prevent flooding upstream. When I got home from school I found them there, and Rudi was with them. Soon a shrill whistle gave the men a break, and I pulled Skipper to where Rudi had slumped on a wet fallen log.

"The dog grows," Rudi said, smiling. He looked thin and tired. "The training?"

215

"I must be making progress. I've told him to come two million times already."

"Good!" Rudi chuckled.

"He sure is hard to walk on the leash, though," I said.

"Then you must also begin teaching him to heel."

"What's that?"

"To walk at your side at all times on command."

"Oh, he'll never learn that!"

Rudi stood up. "May I?" he asked, reaching for the leash.

I gave it to him, and he made little kissing sounds, tugging Skipper to his feet. He wrapped the leash around his fist, making it so short that Skipper could only stand comfortably when it was extended directly downward. "Heel," Rudi said. "Heel."

He started walking slowly, murmuring softly in German. Skipper fussed and struggled. He tried to run ahead, and swung into the air. Then he hung back, getting dragged along in the wet earth. Rudi kept repeating the command softly. Skipper gave up and moved alongside him to ease the tug of the leash.

"He's learning it!" I cried. "How did you do that?"

"I gave him very little space in which to make a mistake. If he will not walk, drag him gently. He will learn to heel with his coat lightly brushing your leg. Later, even without the leash, he will walk the same."

"You must know everything there is to know about dogs! Did you really have a blind dog in Germany?"

"Of course."

"Do you miss her?"

"Yes."

"Where did you get captured?"

"In Africa. Near a town whose name I never knew."

"Was Africa nice?"

"Nice?" He seemed puzzled. "No."

I was surprised. Africa had always sounded terribly exciting to me. "Do you like it in America, then?" I persisted.

He looked at me thoughtfully. "It is not relevant."

"Look," I said, suddenly worried. "How do I know I can trust you?"

"Trust? I do not understand."

"You're German. I'm American. We're enemies. But you're helping me with Skipper. You haven't tried to kill me once!"

216

"*Mein Gott!* Why should I want to'injure you? A soldier goes to fight because it is his duty and he must obey. A soldier does not kill women or children—civilians who are not fighting."

"Yeah! Tell me more about your bombers, then!"

Rudi looked inexpressibly sad. "Yes. But now this is different. You can trust me, Danny. I want nothing from you."

"I still feel like it's risky," I admitted.

"Of course it is. To trust someone is always a risk."

"Then why should I do it?"

"Because you are a good boy and you cannot help yourself."

The guards sounded whistles. One said, "Back to work *Schnell—*hurry." Rudi turned away.

"What was it like in Africa?" I called after him.

He looked back. "Hot. Sand. Very dry."

"What was it like in Germany?"

"Green. Cool. On the hills, forests. Across the fields from my home there was a white castle on the hillside. I walked my dogs there. Children came. We sang."

"Come on, come on," the nearest guard snapped.

Rudi limped away. I watched him thoughtfully. It seemed very strange to hear of green fields, and a castle, and the singing of children from this man. It was hard to square it with Stukas, and the blitzkrieg, and storm troopers, and Hitler. I wondered if only the nice Germans got captured.

THE WORK ON THE CREEK took several days, and in that time I managed several more meetings with Rudi. Sometimes the guards were suspicious and watched us as if we were co-conspirators. Most of the time they were vigilant but relaxed. On one visit Rudi brought me a whistle he had carved out of wood. When I blew it, I heard no sound, but Skipper's ears perked up. And so I learned about sounds that dogs hear but humans cannot. On another day he took a stick and drew a diagram in the dirt of a slipping clasp I could make, to leave Skipper tied to a stake so he would not tangle himself up.

"He needs more exercise than you can give him," Rudi said. "You see how large his paws are. He is going to be a fine big dog. In six weeks he will be large enough to go wherever he wants, even if you hold on to his rope. By then he must be trained to do what you tell him. Or he will drag you away."

217

I looked at Skipper, still roly-poly with fat, but beginning to get longer legs. "He always comes now. He's smart. He's going to be fine."

"I hope so. Yes. There is one other thing . . ." Rudi looked into the distance, seemed to reconsider and stopped. He frowned. "Sometimes a dog with such a disability turns mean."

"Skipper would never turn mean! He likes everybody!"

"This kind of dog is very loyal to a person . . . a small group of persons. His heart is deep, but not wide. You should watch him for signs of viciousness. If this starts to happen, you must punish him severely. If you ignore it, the results could be very bad."

We squatted in silence and watched Skipper nervously walk the length of his rope. Something else had been on my mind, and I considered whether to ask it. Curiosity won out. "Is it okay in the camp, Rudi? I mean, do they treat you all right?"

"Fine," he said soberly. "The food is good. Good place to sleep. You do your work and not cause trouble, it is fine."

"Are you glad you got captured? So you don't have to fight anymore?"

His eyes hardened. "*Nein*," he snapped, and for an instant he was angry with me.

"You act like you want Germany to win this war!"

"Do you want America to win the war?"

"Sure! I love my country!"

"I love my Germany. The same. It is the duty of every man to fight for his fatherland."

"You love Hitler? People like that?"

He sighed. "Sometimes your country has leaders you do not like. But it is still your country. You still love it. My unit was in the desert. For three days we fought. Cut off. With no food and no water. Finally, no more bullets. Our tanks, burning. Our commanders, all dead. Some of us fought with knives." He gave me a fierce look. "When I am captured, it is because I am injured, there is no more way to fight."

It was too much for me. I could not understand his point of view. "When the war is over," I said, "will you go back?"

"Of course," he said quickly. Then his eyes dimmed. "If there is a Germany remaining."

"There will be, Rudi. You'll get to go back."

He smiled. "Yes. We will think that, eh?" He got up stiffly and limped back to his comrades. I saw one of them give him a sullen look and a burst of German. Rudi shrugged and walked past him. Several of them glanced toward me with angry eyes.

"IF YOU ASK ME," Jimmy Cantwell said one day at recess, "what they ought to do is go out with a bunch of grenades and just blow the whole camp up."

"Or use the Krauts for bayonet practice," Bill Sheehan growled.

We were hanging around near the school building, waiting for the signal to return to class. Of the half dozen in the group, everyone except me leered at the prospect.

"My dad says there's going to be trouble," Cantwell went on. "And he's ready for it. You oughta see the guns we got. If the prisoners escape, we'll get our chance, boy."

Sheehan turned to me with his instinct for the jugular. "Your old man works there. Has he killed any of them yet?"

"There hasn't been any trouble. They do good work on the farms, my dad says."

"Probably poisoning everything," Phil Inright observed.

"I bet your father gets to beat up on those Krauts," Sheehan said with relish. "Boy, would *I* make them bleed!"

Everyone else nodded. I knew I should keep my mouth shut, but as usual I did not. "They're not all that bad," I said.

"What?" Sheehan said, incredulous. He put his fists on his hips. "Are you some kind of Nazi?"

I began to sweat. "All I said was, they're not all bad guys. A lot of them are just kind of ordinary."

"Is your old man sweet on Nazis, too?" Sheehan asked. "How'd he get that job, anyhow? Write to Hitler?"

My face flamed. "Don't talk about my dad like that!"

"How come he ain't in the army? Too old?" Inright asked.

"He's four-F," I said. "He's got something wrong with him."

"Probably flatfeet." Cantwell grinned. "And a coward."

"Yeah," Sheehan said. "Like father, like son, huh, Flatfoot?"

"You take it back," I said weakly.

"You want to make something of it?"

I looked at him, torn between anger and fear. He scrambled to his feet, dancing around, head ducked behind his shoulder, thumbing his nose. He looked so foolish that I might have laughed if I had not been terrified. "I don't want to fight," I said thickly.

219

Behind us, the school bell clanged loudly.

Sheehan bounced a fist off the top of my head. The pain rocked me. "You'll fight, Flatfoot," he said. "Sooner or later."

Back in class, I went through the afternoon sure that they would get me afterward. Benny Harrison was my only hope, and I scrambled to get into the departure line beside him. We marched behind the school guards to the street crossing where he would go his way and I would board the bus.

"You're going to have to fight him," Benny told me without preamble.

"Fight who?" I asked as if surprised.

"Don't give me that crap. You know who."

"I don't want to fight him."

"He's not so tough. You can probably lick him."

"What if I don't?"

"Then he'll probably kill you," Benny said philosophically.

"I don't know anything about fighting."

"Didn't you have to fight in Columbus?"

"That was different. I started in school there, and I was always one of the guys."

"Well, here the new kid fights. That's the way they run it."

We crossed the street. The buses were waiting. I looked at Benny. "Are there books about fighting?"

"Kid, you don't learn fighting in no book. You come to my house someday after school. I'll give you a lesson."

"Would you do that? Gosh!"

"Sure," Benny said, his hard eyes flicking over the crowd. "You could come stay the night. My old lady won't mind."

"Thanks, Benny! Thanks a lot!"

He shrugged, making the trinkets on his cap jingle, and sauntered off.

WHEN MY FATHER GOT HOME that evening, he was excited and upset. It seemed that two prisoners had walked away from their work detail near Grove City. They had not been missed until the truck got back to camp.

"We're trying to keep it quiet," he said, "but we've notified Fort Hayes and the governor's office. The state police are looking too."

"But where do they think they can go?" my mother asked, her face pale.

"God knows," my father said grimly.

As it turned out, however, the escape had been a comedy of errors. The two prisoners had been in a washroom at a tourist rest stop when the trucks pulled out for the next job. Finding themselves abandoned, the forty-six-year-old man and twenty-year-old boy had been in a panic. They hitchhiked with an unsuspecting farmer into Grove City. There they had gone to the police station to surrender, but all the police had been working a funeral. They sat on the porch for three hours, because the funeral ran into the supper hour, then they had been "captured" by a drugstore owner waving a Colt .45, and two farmers with shotguns. The prisoners were shaking all over when the soldiers got them back to camp.

Late that night in our living room, we heard this story from the colonel, who was not amused. My father smiled with relief when he had finished telling us.

"All's well that ends well," my father said.

"Possibly," the colonel snapped. "Nevertheless, this demonstrates laxity in our security. I intend to issue new directives. In the event of an escape, guards are to shoot to kill."

My father looked shocked. "But this was an accident."

"Granted. However, we must consider the psychological effects both on the prisoners and the populace at large. A strong statement, showing we won't hesitate to take the most severe action, will prevent a real escape. And it will reassure the citizenry of Harmony."

"I'm afraid, sir," argued my father, "that such an order might increase tension. It could cause resentment among the prisoners. They've behaved very, very well. Also, instead of reassuring the populace, it might fan fears—make the danger sound greater than it is."

The colonel glowered. "I disagree. Stern action, Davidson; that's the ticket. I've made my decision. We'll stand formation at oh seven hundred tomorrow and I'll announce it personally."

My father and mother unhappily saw him to the door. When his jeep drove away, my parents came back into the living room, where I sat with plans for a new model airplane.

"He'll cause trouble," my father said. "That town is an armed camp just aching for it. *Damn!* We've bent over backward to be fair. The men have respected us for it. But some of those prisoners are tough. Give them mistreatment as an excuse . . ."

221

"Isn't there some way you could stop the colonel?" I asked.

My father looked surprised. "No. How?"

"Couldn't you tell his boss at Fort Hayes that the colonel is doing wrong?"

"No. Of course not. You owe loyalty to your superior."

My thoughts were full of Rudi working in front of trigger-happy guards. "Don't you owe the prisoners something, too, though?"

"You don't understand this."

"I think you ought to go tell the general."

"And lose my job?" my father said sharply, angry.

I looked at him, and it was my turn to be shocked. My dad was afraid for his job, *afraid of the colonel*.

"I burned my bridges when we came out here," he said, half to me, half to my mother. "I can't go off half-cocked and risk everything!"

"Of course you can't," my mother said. "I'm sure it will be fine, George. Really."

He did not reply. Quietly I gathered up my plans and went to my bedroom. I was shaken. My own father was going to be a party to a bad thing. I did not know how to deal with this. I sat watching the airplanes turn on their strings and wondered what trouble lay ahead for all of us.

CHAPTER SIX

Colonel Thatcher made his hard-line speech to the prisoners the next day. Almost at once his action began to backfire, as my father had feared. That day a prisoner was late returning to work detail after drawing water. A soldier pushed him. The prisoner attacked. The guard knocked him out with the butt of his rifle. Later two other men got into a fight. Civilian guards intervened with bayonets, and one of the prisoners ended up in hospital with a serious wound in his abdomen. The colonel decreed ten days in solitary confinement for both the prisoner who had attacked the guard and the unwounded man who had been fighting.

Meanwhile, word of the "escape" to Grove City went through Harmony like wildfire. At my school, we heard a story from Jimmy Cantwell that German submarines were everywhere off the east coast, and that radio messages had been sent to all prisoners to break out and get to New Jersey, where rubber boats would pick them up.

Another story, repeated solemnly by Phil Inright, had it that prisoners were to seize their captors' weapons and fight their way into control of nearby towns and cities, creating island fortresses all over the United States.

That same week there was a big practice air-raid blackout in central Ohio. It had been well publicized and was being taken very seriously, for everyone here *knew* that Columbus and its environs would be a prime target when the Luftwaffe struck. Columbus, after all, had the Bolt Works, Timken Roller Bearings, Fort Hayes and the Columbus General Depot, a huge army facility where saddles and gas masks from World War I were still in storage. To outsiders Columbus might not look like a major target, but local people knew. And Harmony, just on the outskirts, was clearly vulnerable.

Elaborate plans had been made for the blackout, and they were posted everywhere in town on the afternoon I went home with Benny Harrison for my long-awaited boxing lesson. We had left the school and walked east, through the small business district to the river.

Here the Big Walnut wended its way through town, grassy banks punctuated by railroad tracks, metal industrial buildings and grain elevators. The steel bridge carried both cars and pedestrians, and we could feel it vibrate from traffic as we crossed. The Big Walnut was almost a hundred yards wide below. "It's a big old river," I observed.

"Creek, really," Benny corrected. "But wait until it floods."

"It floods?" I said, thrilled.

"Not for years, but it once covered the whole business district." He grinned fiendishly. "If it does that again, bang! There goes the school!"

We walked on to his house, one of a dozen on a dirt street behind a sprawling junkyard. An old Ford rusted into the weeds in his side yard. On a rickety swing on the front porch sat a heavy, smiling blond woman wearing shorts and a halter.

"This your friend?" she asked, putting down a bottle of beer.

"Yeah," Benny said. "Danny Davidson, this is my old lady."

His mother winced as she untangled long pale legs and got to her feet. She tugged at her short shorts, making herself more presentable. "Hi, Danny. Tell him he ought to respect his mother. 'Old lady' indeed!"

"Pleased to meet you, I'm sure," I said, shaking hands.

"Real nice manners. Why can't you be like that?" she asked Benny.

"Aah, baloney," he growled.

"It's kind of warm, boys. Do you want something to drink?"

"Yeah!" Benny grinned. "How about a coupla beers?"

She gave him an affectionate swat, took us into the house and poured us green Kool-Aid. I looked around the kitchen in fascination. Every inch of drainboard was covered with dirty dishes. The trash can brimmed with empty beer bottles.

"You go to school with Benny?" his mother asked me.

"Yessum," I said. "We're in the same room."

"That's nice," she told me. "Are you a class officer, too?"

I glanced at Benny, not wanting to mess up his lie. "No, ma'am."

"Well." She beamed. "You stick with my Benny, and if he ever gets tired of being president, maybe he'll fix you up in some high office." She sighed. "It's time for me to go to work. No rest for the wicked." She gave me what I could only interpret as a strangely flirtatious glance and left the room.

"What a dodo," Benny muttered.

"That's no way to talk about your mom!" I told him.

"You can feed her anything and she'll believe it," he said disgustedly. "You know where she works? Downtown in a beer joint. She says she waits tables, only once I went there and looked in. She wears this frilly costume, with her top practically hanging out."

"Benny!"

"Well, it's true. My old man left her. One day I'll take off, too."

"You shouldn't say things like that! She loves you!"

"Kid, you got a lot to learn. In this world nobody loves you. It's dog eat dog, and the devil take the hindmost."

"I could never believe that, Benny."

"Yeah! And that's why you spend so much time on your butt in the playground. Now drink up. We'll go out back and see if we can't teach you a few things about beating people up."

We went into the backyard, which was a patch of barren earth bounded by a rusty metal fence. Benny squared off in the middle of the dirt.

"The first mistake most people make," he told me, "is trying to

224

be nice. In a fight you don't be nice. If you can stay out of a fight, good. But if you can't, what you want is the shortest fight possible. Now. With a little guy, you move in fast and aim for the nose. He'll bleed like crazy and run off. With a guy a lot bigger, you look for a brick and hit him right between the eyes, and then run."

"What if he catches you?" I asked.

Benny shrugged. "Then you get beat up. That happens sometimes. But let's talk about a guy your own size, like Inright."

"Inright is a foot taller!" I protested.

"He's blubber, too. Okay. Now. The other guy dances around, getting ready. The trick is, you don't wait. You attack." He assumed a fighting stance. "I'm Sheehan. What are you going to do?"

I wanted very much to please him and learn. I rushed him. He made a sharp little movement, and something painful exploded on my chin. I saw yellow stars and sat down in the dirt.

Benny looked down at me thoughtfully. "I forgot to mention, you don't just run in with your hands at your sides. You cover up and you hit with your fists. Okay. Try again."

I got up slowly. He danced around me. It occurred to me that this had to be one of the world's great insane spectacles, *me* attacking Benny Harrison. I hesitated. Before I knew what was happening, he bounced against me. I found myself sitting in the dirt with blood in my mouth.

Benny helped me up. "I said attack *first*. Even a dopus like Sheehan will get you if you stand around. Try again."

I rushed, a wild anger in me. He caught my blows against his hands. "Good!" he coached, as my left uppercut almost didn't get blocked. "Don't look around for cheers, man! Just remember to *keep your guard up!*" Wham! Down I went. He reached to help me up. "I'm sorry, kid. You got to—"

I lashed out with my foot. It caught him low in the abdomen, and he staggered back, doing his own pratfall in the dirt. I stared, horrified. Now he would kill me.

His grimace changed to a grin that went from ear to ear. "Great!" he told me. "Boy, that really hurt! And it came natural to you! There might be hope for you yet!"

He scrambled up, brushing himself off. "Let's go again."

I got up and faced him.

"Of course, you did make one bad mistake. You had me," he said, easily parrying a left and popping me lightly on the nose. "For a few seconds I was defenseless. That was when you should have finished me off."

"I could never hit a guy when he's down. It's—"

He blasted me on the side of the head, then wagged a stern finger at me. "Don't talk stupid," he said. "The purpose in a fight is to get it over. You get a guy down, you cream him, right?"

"Right," I muttered, and bounced another punch off his elbow.

We went at it a while longer. When we were both breathing hard and sweating, he suggested we quit. We went into the house to his room. The bed was unmade, and clothes were all over the floor. He had a few flying models on strings, and another on a card table in an early stage of construction.

"What do you think?" he asked, flipping a Hurricane with his finger.

"Real nice," I said carefully. In truth it was an awful-looking model. He had done well enough up to gluing the tissue-paper skin on the body and wings, but then everything had gone wrong. The paper was much too loose and all wrinkled. I very politely didn't mention it.

"Actually," he said, staring at the model. "I don't know how guys get the paper strung over the fuselage so tight and smooth. I try and it wrinkles on me. Maybe you noticed."

"Yes, I did. Well, how much water do you spray on?" I asked.

He looked blank. "Water?"

"You don't know about spraying water on the tissue paper after it's glued, so it shrinks?"

He made a face. For the next hour I demonstrated. He watched in silent amazement as I glued paper on a wing he had finished, then sprinkled tap water onto the tissue. It sagged even worse at first, but after we put it on the sunny windowsill, it began to shrink and tighten. By luck it was one of my best efforts, and when it dried, the thin paper stretched over the balsa-wood members like the finest steel.

Benny stared in disbelief. "Plain old water," he said. "You're all right, do you know that? You are really smart."

"It's just a trick," I said modestly.

Later we listened to the radio awhile. Out of the refrigerator he produced some bread and cold meat, and we ate sandwiches on the front porch, watching traffic go by. Darkness came. At ten the town's sirens wailed for the air-raid blackout, and we made sure all the lights were off, then climbed up on the roof to watch. There were a few stars overhead. We could make out the river and the city buildings beyond. We could not see a light, only the occasional glow of a cigarette on someone's porch. In the vast silence people could be heard talking softly, as if the Germans would hear if they raised their voices.

It thrilled me, to tell the truth, seeing how well Harmony complied with the blackout regulations. German bombardiers would not find Columbus tonight. I was proud to be an American.

"I hope the war don't end too soon," Benny said thoughtfully.

"Some people say ten or twenty years."

"I hope so. I want to go."

"You want to be in it, you mean? I guess we all do. It's an honor to fight for America."

"I could be a hero," he said. "People might get to know my name."

"People know your name already."

"I'm nothing," he said. "My old man run off, and my old lady works in a beer joint. I can't even learn."

"Well, Benny, if you didn't act the fool in class—"

"No," he said somberly. "I tried. For a long time. I did." He tapped his forehead. "There's something wrong upstairs."

"Aw!"

"There is. I look at a page, and the letters scramble up on me. I don't even know whether to start frontward or backward. So I said the hell with it."

"Benny, if you've got an eyesight problem, maybe a doctor could help."

"Fat chance."

"Did you ever tell anybody?"

"No. Never. And if *you* ever tell anybody, I'll kill you."

"I won't, Benny, not if you don't want me to. But—"

"Nope," he said firmly. "It don't matter. I'm nobody, anyhow. As long as I act like I won't learn, nobody will ever know I can't. Maybe the war will last long enough for me to be a hero."

I did not reply. Here I was with one of the most feared guys in our entire school, and he was nothing like he appeared on the surface. In a way, I saw, he was like Rudi, my German. He had complicated my life. I almost wished I were still stupid, the way I had been when I first came to Harmony. Then I had hated all

Germans, and knew people like Benny Harrison were nothing but trash. It had been so very simple. Now I had to try to judge people one at a time, rather than in bunches. Life was never going to be easy for me again.

AS JUNE NEARED, Skipper was still growing wonderfully. His parentage was clear now, and it had been nearly purebred shepherd. He was black, with typical shepherd tan on his shoulders and along the sides of his neck. A collar of silvery white adorned his throat and chest, and there were more touches of white on his large bushy tail. His ears stood straight when he was listening, head erect, every muscle taut with attention. When he ran and put his front paws on my shoulders, as he loved to do, he staggered me.

His training had worked out better than I had hoped. He came promptly to the sound of my voice. If I told him to stay, he stayed— at least until he thought I was out of view. He had begun to heel properly.

In addition, he was learning things on his own. In the yard, when freed, he now knew how to walk around the entire house, sniffing furiously and coming back precisely to the stake that held his rope. If he wandered out toward the driveway and encountered gravel beneath his paws, he tried to reverse his course. In the house, he had learned how to leave my room, come out through the hall, carefully pick his way around my father's chair and move to his favorite spot under a window, where he lay for hours, listening.

I was enormously proud of him, and as I counted down the days until school would be out, I imagined the expeditions we would take.

"We'll have a great time, Skipper!" I told him, nestling my face in his luxurious fur. "You're going to like it!"

TWICE DURING THE WARMING DAYS of early June I went home again with Benny Harrison. On the second occasion he took me a different way. I found us standing across the street from a grocery store.

"You want to learn something, kid? Come on and I'll show you how to hook stuff," Benny said.

I was startled. "No," I said huskily. "I . . ."

"All right." He sneered. "Just stand there, then."

Before I could reply, he was walking jauntily across the street.

I watched him enter the big A&P. It was Wednesday, a busy time. Many farmers' trucks were in the parking lot.

Benny was inside for a long time. I sweated, knowing he had been caught. I watched for the police car to come and take him away. It was agony for me. Had I betrayed him by refusing to go with him? Would he tell the police I was his cohort, and would I go to jail, too?

After an eternity the door of the A&P swung back, and Benny walked out as jauntily as before. In his hand he had a small sack of peanuts. He popped them into his mouth singly as he watched traffic, crossed the street and joined me.

We walked around the corner and headed for the bridge. "Boy!" I exclaimed. "You really had me worried! But you paid for the peanuts, right? I mean, you walked out eating them."

"Sure," Benny said. "You always pay for *something*."

I looked at him, afraid of what his words meant. With a smirk he dug into his left pants pocket. To my horror, out came a slightly mangled Hershey bar and a package of jelly beans. He thrust them at me, then brought out some Pall Malls from his right pocket. He slit the pack, took a cigarette, cracked a match on the seat of his corduroy knickers and started smoking.

At that moment a vast shadow descended on us from the rear. A big rough hand seized my arm, the other hand grabbing Benny so hard that the cigarette fell out of his mouth.

The big man, his face red and contorted with anger, was wearing a tag identifying him as the store manager. He slammed us against the wall of a building and grabbed the cigarettes and candy in a single motion.

"Have you punks got a sales slip for this stuff?" he demanded.

IT WAS ALMOST FIVE O'CLOCK before my father, his face ashen, strode into the police station. Sitting on the wooden bench beside the door to the cells, I felt my soul shrivel.

The police chief was grim. "Benny was being watched," he told my father. "This time they caught him with the goods."

The store manager, he went on, was convinced that I had not taken part in the stealing and might not even have known what Benny was up to. The manager was going to press juvenile charges against Benny, but it had been agreed that I deserved the benefit of the doubt. I was being released in my parents' custody.

The chief turned to me. "This time you were lucky, Danny. We know you now. Get in trouble again and it's curtains. Do you understand that?"

"Yes, sir!" I choked. "I'll never even go near the A and P again!"

"Choose your companions more carefully, you hear? Boys like Harrison are no good. Do you understand that?"

"Yes, sir! I sure see now that he's no good!" This cowardly statement seemed to satisfy both the chief and my father.

The chief frowned at me. "Very well. You're free to go."

My father gripped my arm and marched me toward the door. Just as we reached it, Benny's mother rushed in, wearing a raincoat over a shockingly skimpy costume. Rouge made her face garish, and she was crying, tears streaking her mascara. For an instant our eyes met. I said nothing. I heard her weeping voice, the chief's dully angry response. The door closed that world behind us.

In the car, my father drove in irate silence until we were on the highway. My pulse thudded in my skull. I felt like I might throw up. *Nothing* had ever been this bad. I had shamed my parents. I had denied Benny. I was the worst kind of worm—a sneak and a coward.

"Well?" my father said at last, his voice tight. "What do you have to say for yourself?"

"I didn't know what was going on," I said abjectly.

"Don't give me that," he snapped, in a tone he had never used before. "Maybe you didn't steal anything, but you would have the next time. Why were you hanging around with that kid?"

"I didn't know he stole stuff. I didn't even *like* him . . . very much. He just asked me if I would help him with models."

He thought about that, driving. Finally he said, "Your mother doesn't have to know. Something like this would kill her."

"I'm sorry," I said, crying. "I didn't mean anything—"

"I don't want any of your apologies! If I ever, ever—get another call from the police about you, son, I won't go in there after you. If you want to be trash, then you can be trash. But your mother is a fine woman. Your sister is a wonderful little girl. You won't drag them down, or me. You'll go to BIS alone."

I was so frightened that my tears stopped. Boys Industrial School was a buzzword for terror. Only the worst went there. It was one step away from the penitentiary in Columbus.

"You'll get no allowance until further notice. You'll clean the

231

barn and do it *right*. No radio for a month. Is that understood?"

"Yes, sir," I mumbled.

He sighed. "I don't know what you had in mind, hanging around with a kid like that. Benny's had his chance, Squirt. He's lost it. You got another chance. If you let this be a lesson to you, maybe you can still be the kind of fine young man I know you can be." He glared at me. "Understood?"

"Yes, sir!"

He breathed deeply. "All right, then."

The next day I went to school, dreamlike, as if it were a normal day. Of course Benny was not there. I pretended not to notice. But at recess it all came out.

"Wonder where old Benny is," Jimmy Cantwell said.

"Ain't you heard?" Sheehan chuckled. "He's in jail. Caught hooking stuff at a store. My old man told me."

"Good grief," Inright said softly. "I knew he was tough, but—"

"He wasn't so tough." Sheehan sneered. "He just talked tough. All he ever was was a punk, my old man says. BIS is good enough for him. And any of his buddies," he added, looking at me.

Silent, on the edge of being afraid and ashamed, I looked down at my too small tennis shoes. It had been one thing to betray Benny with adults. This was even worse.

"I never thought it would happen," Cantwell said.

"He had it coming," Sheehan remarked. "He was no good, all blow and no show, just trash. Good riddance to bad rubbish, right, Flatfoot?"

I looked up at him, intent on keeping quiet. But his gloating expression drove me over the edge. "You dopus," I said.

Sheehan's head jerked back. "*What* did you say?"

"Benny is worth a hundred of you!"

Sheehan began dancing around. "You want to make something of it, Flatfoot? You want to put up or shut up?"

Whether it was conscious or instinctive I will never know. Perhaps I simply could not handle any more. Sheehan was thumbing his nose when I rushed him. My first blow caught him squarely on the mouth, and the second caught his right eye. He yelped and staggered backward, falling. I piled on top of him, pounding at his face with both fists.

"I give!" he yelped, covering up. "I give! I give!"

I stopped hitting him and, shaking all over, got to my feet. Jimmy

Cantwell and the others looked like statues with big round eyes. Sheehan was trying to wipe mud off his clothes. I faced him with my fists ready. "You want more?"

"You hit me when I wasn't looking." He dabbed at his bloody nose. The class bell sounded. I turned and walked away.

As Mrs. Broadus started the history lesson, my arms and legs trembled and I felt sick. But I had faced Bill Sheehan! You were right, Benny. Never let them get set. And now, I thought, my troubles at school were over.

I was allowed to think that during afternoon recess, when we played capture the flag without incident. When I went back to my desk, however, my tablet had been opened and someone had printed a message in red pencil, with a picture of a dagger dripping big drops of blood. I read it with a new feeling of nausea: WE WILL GET REVENJE. YOU WILL DIE. THE BLOODY HAND GANG. It was a really stupid note. But I shivered all the same.

CHAPTER SEVEN

If school went along badly, and I was haunted by thoughts of Benny Harrison, my work with Skipper provided joy and even elation. He was large now, all legs and big paws, and he walked obediently close by my side with or without the leash.

We had even learned a game. I found a rubber ball with a bell that rattled within its hollow center. Skipper learned to chase it and bring it back to me, tracking it down swiftly and unerringly by its jingling, then homing in on my encouraging voice. I had to be very careful where I threw the ball. Once he ran headlong into a corner of the porch. Another time he collided with a clothesline post. For if I threw the ball, he galloped after its sound, trusting that nothing stood in his way. I loved playing the game with him. It made life seem almost normal.

If there was a bane to Skipper's existence, it was Aggie's pair of cats. When he was asleep in the shade beside the house, they crept up and cuddled beside him, kneading his fur with their claws as if he were their mother. He would wriggle and yawn, but never snap. If a fly made one of his ears twitch, both cats would be on him in an instant, wanting to play with his ears. Aggie thought it was very funny.

"One of these days," I growled, "Skipper will bite those cats in two."

"Skipper?" Aggie trilled. "Oh, Danny, don't be so *silly!*"

With us he was the most loving, docile creature imaginable, but he was becoming a good watchdog. At the sound or scent of a stranger approaching, he made a terrific racket. People did not know he was blind and probably harmless. He looked fierce. It was not until the man from the electric company came one afternoon that I learned Skipper might truly be fierce.

We had been playing wtih the ball and now lay side by side in the shade near the house, resting. I was sweaty and itchy from grass, and Skipper panted, his tongue lolling out. The yellow electric-company truck came slowly down the highway. I watched it, idly tickling Skipper's ears, which he liked. When the truck turned into the driveway, Skipper's ears pricked up.

"Wonder what he wants," I said.

Skipper stared directly at the truck, just as if he could see. The engine was shut off, and a tall man got out from behind the wheel. As he walked across the driveway toward us, his feet crunched the gravel. I felt Skipper tense under my hand.

"Hello, son," the man said. "Is your mama inside?"

Without warning, Skipper exploded into action. He crossed the space to the man in a twinkling, and leaped. "What the—" the man yelled hoarsely, dodging.

Skipper missed him and landed heavily in the gravel. Scrambling up, he wheeled around. I saw his fangs bared. A low, vicious growl came from his throat.

"Call him off, kid!" the man said, terrified.

Skipper lunged again. The man threw up his arm; in his hand was a steel-clad record book. I heard Skipper's teeth clash on the metal. The man staggered and fell. Skipper whirled around.

"*Skipper!*" I screamed. "Skipper! Heel! *Heel!*"

He stopped dead. The growl coming from his throat sent chills down my back. "Heel!" I repeated, and clapped my hands.

Skipper trotted obediently to me, his old self again. I locked my fists in his shaggy hair. "It's okay, mister!"

"Tie him up," the serviceman said huskily. I led Skipper around to the post and roped him securely. The man got up, dusted himself off and went muttering to the front door.

I was amazed. I remembered what Rudi had told me about

disabled animals becoming vicious. If I had not been there, what would Skipper have done? From now on he would have to be watched more closely. But I also saw that he had obeyed me instantly under the worst possible circumstances. Although I was shaken, I was proud of him.

ON THE LAST DAY OF SCHOOL we were released early, but a mix-up meant an hour's wait for the buses. It gave me time to do something I had been wanting to do. I ran across the bridge and up the street, breathing hard, to Benny Harrison's house.

The porch swing was empty, and the house looked deserted. Nevertheless, I rapped loudly on the door. I heard nothing. I was about to turn away when it opened. Benny's mother, a robe wrapped around her, looked out at me.

"Hello, Mrs. Harrison. I'm Benny's friend. Remember?"

"Why, yes," she said. "Danny, isn't it?" She wiped her eyes as if she had been crying. "Would you like to come in?"

I knew I didn't have much time, but I had to know. I went in and sat down in the wreck of a living room. She offered cookies. I refused. "Mrs. Harrison, how's Benny?"

Her lips set. "Why, Danny, he's doing just fine. He's now at Boys Industrial School." She gave me a hectic, false smile. "He mentioned you last weekend when I went to see him."

"Is he really all right, Mrs. Harrison? Is he *really*?"

"Why, yes," she told me. "He has regular classes, and they also have nice things like shop, where a young boy can learn a trade."

"Will you tell him I came by? And that I did what he taught me to Bill Sheehan?"

She frowned. "To Bill Sheehan? Will he understand that?"

"Yessum. He will."

"All right, Danny. It was very sweet of you to come."

As I started out the door, she hugged me. I kissed her cheek. Her breath caught, and tears started in her eyes. She did not speak. I hurried down the steps and away from the house. When I looked back, she was still in the doorway. She waved. And I waved back.

Hurrying toward school, I was crossing Main Street when a truck pulled up in front of the Harmon Ice Company. The gates of the truck were let down, and half a dozen prisoners climbed out, four guards with them. Mr. Harmon emerged from his office, handed out ice tongs and opened the heavy doors of the cooler building.

235

The prisoners trooped in. Harmon, a stocky man with shaggy eyebrows, stood by glaring. When the prisoners came out, each was carrying a fifty-pound cake of ice. As they hefted them into the rear of the truck, one man stumbled slightly, and the heavy cake of ice fell, hitting Mr. Harmon's leg. He danced back, his face contorting. He shoved the prisoner and said something. The prisoner dropped his tongs and pushed Harmon. Just as Harmon snatched another pair of tongs off the wall, two soldiers rushed over and grabbed both men. Angry words were exchanged. Then the soldiers hustled the prisoners into the truck.

As the truck engine started, a man ran from the service station next door with a rifle in his hands. Another man came out of the barbershop across the street, and although he was not armed, his anger was clear. The truck lurched into motion and lumbered down the street.

For a moment I did not move. It had been a very near thing. If the soldiers had not acted swiftly, blood would have been spilled. For my father this could only mean more trouble.

AS A RESULT OF that incident on Main Street, a meeting was held in our living room the following evening. Colonel Thatcher was there, along with Mr. Sheehan, Mayor Gump and Sheriff Lockwood. The atmosphere, even as my mother served iced tea and cookies, was tense. The colonel kept prowling the room. Mr. Sheehan sat with his fat legs spread, fanning himself with a magazine. Gump was a wizened older man and owner of a hardware store. He looked permanently soured on the world. He and the sheriff sat stolidly, unhappy. At the dining-room table, pretending to read, I was able to see and hear everything.

"We appreciate your offering your house," the colonel told my father. "Obviously we have a problem."

"The guards' reports are clear," my father answered. "It was a minor incident. Nothing serious happened."

"I was on the street within seconds," Sheehan retorted. "I saw one of our businessmen with a gun. I tell you, Davidson, we came within a hairsbreadth of tragedy!"

My father looked pale and drawn. "That may be. But it was not any fault of the prisoners."

"People want them Germans out of here," Mayor Gump said. "We don't want 'em running wild in our town."

"They're not running wild," my father said patiently. "A prisoner dropped a piece of ice, hitting Mr. Harmon. He—"

"We all know what happened, Davidson," the colonel broke in. "It was a mistake for that truck to be in town."

"Possibly," my father conceded. "However, we need to remember that the prisoners did not threaten the town. If anyone caused trouble, it was Mr. Harmon."

Sheehan scowled. "You sometimes seem to forget, George, that those Germans are soldiers of the Third Reich. Under different circumstances they would still be killing our boys."

"Gentlemen," Colonel Thatcher interrupted, "it won't accomplish anything to argue. Clearly the populace must be reassured. The prisoners must be forced to see that they are in no position to strike back, whatever the provocation. In the first place, Mr. Mayor, I am issuing a directive that trucks bearing prisoners will no longer stop in, or even drive through, your community. As to the prisoners involved yesterday, disciplinary action will be taken."

My father reacted as if he had been slapped. "Like what?"

"Extra work details. Suspension of allowance for cigarettes and other personal needs until further notice."

"Is that fair?"

"Face it, Davidson: when those men come into contact with locals, remarks will be made. That's human nature. The men have to know that any response will result in punishment."

Sheehan said, "We can see the paper gets a story on that."

"All guards," the colonel added, "will be issued additional instructions. They will tolerate *no* misbehavior by any prisoner. If necessary to prevent a disturbance, they will shoot to kill."

"Kill a few," Mayor Gump said. "That'll straighten 'em out!"

Colonel Thatcher turned to my father. "I expect you to make sure the guards understand the new orders. I have noticed astonishing laxity on the part of some of them. I expect them to carry their weapons on duty. You, too. I want to see you wearing your side arm when you're out in the compound."

My father's face twisted. "I can't predict how everyone will react to this, Colonel. None of us knows our new guards well. They might seize this as an excuse—"

"Davidson, if you spent more time worrying about your responsibilities and less being a bleeding heart on behalf of enemy soldiers, we would all be a lot better off."

There was an instant of total silence. I saw my father's stricken expression, and the look of shock that crossed Sheehan's face. The colonel seemed oblivious of his cruelty. He glanced at Sheehan. "I will make our position clear when I speak next week to the chamber of commerce. In the meantime, it is incumbent on law officials to issue similar statements emphasizing the harsh action that will be taken if any civilian causes trouble."

"I'll see the police chief," Sheriff Lockwood said. "We'll get out a statement of our own."

"Good." The colonel looked around. "Anything further?"

My father started to speak, thought better of it, then shook his head as he again changed his mind. "We're overreacting. By doing all this, Colonel, you're crowding the men; something really serious will happen."

"Davidson," Colonel Thatcher said heavily, "it was a blow to me when I was given this assignment. By background and inclination I should be a combat soldier. But this is my duty, and I intend to carry it out. Your job is to follow my orders."

Sheehan got up. "Well, gentlemen, that covers it."

There was handshaking, and then they went out to their cars. My father stood on the porch, watching them go. My mother remained in the kitchen. I did not know how much she had heard.

I met my father coming back inside as the last car droned into the night. His eyes were empty and remote. Then he saw me standing there. "Well, Squirt," he said.

My mother came in. She had heard. "What do you think?"

He shook his head. "I think it's an awful mistake."

"Why didn't you make them not do it?" I demanded.

"How could I?" he shot back.

"Danny," my mother said with soft warning.

But I was not to be swayed. "You're in charge of the guards! You could have told the colonel you wouldn't do it! Those prisoners aren't going to hurt folks! They're tired, and homesick, and scared. The people in town are just dummies."

"Danny!" my mother repeated in quite a different tone.

My father tousled my hair. "When you're a man, Squirt, you follow orders."

"That's not being a man! That's being a coward!"

He stiffened. "Go to your room."

"Dad, I—"

"I said go to your room! I'm not taking any more tonight, especially from a boy who doesn't know what he's talking about!"

He had betrayed me. None of us, not even my friend Rudi, could count on him. And now if worse things happened, he would be as much a cause as anyone. I ran so they would not see my tears.

"You shouldn't have shouted at him," I heard my mother say.

"Are you going to get on me, too?" my father said sharply.

I closed the door of my room then, and could hear only the murmur of their voices. Skipper's tail thumped, and I petted him. I sat on the bed, sniffing and thinking.

It was going to be a lonely summer without Benny. If I could not count on my father, whatever I did I was going to have to do on my own. For some reason I thought again of that ghastly pipe in the bank of the creek. Maybe I can't do much about most things, I thought. But I could do something about that. And if I got killed, I thought spitefully, it would serve them right! Tomorrow I would explore it all the way. It did not seem very scary in the safety of my bed.

THE NEXT MORNING it was quite a different matter. With my ball of string and flashlight in hand, I climbed into the tunnel. I started bravely enough, but as the cool vapors closed around me, my resolve began to slip. A steady stream of water rippled through the pipe, causing me to walk like a subterranean crab. I gritted my teeth and told myself I would not look back. If I didn't have the guts to explore this dumb old pipe, what was there left for me?

Soon I reached the point where my nerve had failed me last time; I heard the distant rumble and paused, sweating. You've come this far, I thought. Keep going! Gulping a breath, I did so.

The air became danker and heavier as I proceeded. The grayish walls seemed to vibrate with the rumble; I began to think it was machinery of some kind and felt a little better. At this point my dwindling ball of string became a few loose strands and then ran out.

I crabbed ahead. I had not gone more than another twenty paces when the tunnel branched into three passageways. This was a real problem. I must not get confused. I decided to bear right at every branch, and then I could always get back by going left. Shaking my flashlight to make it a little brighter, I waddled into the right-hand tunnel. I was sweating heavily. How long was this pipe?

The rumbling was beating in my eardrums. I came to another branching, into four more tunnels. Again I took the rightmost one. But I had gone only a few steps when it became hardly more than five feet in diameter, forcing me to bend sharply at the waist to keep going. I was really upset now. I shone the flashlight ahead anxiously—and saw a dead end. There was nothing but solid rock wall. The tunnel simply stopped.

I turned and backtracked. At the first intersection I went right, and the tunnel again became smaller. I stopped and thought about it, my heartbeat louder than the rumbling now. I should have turned left. I went back to the junction. In the sprayed light of the dying flashlight, all four tunnels looked identical. Be calm, be calm, I told myself.

The new branch I'd chosen narrowed abruptly, just like the others. I was wrong again. Panic was taking over. I told myself I was every kind of dopus, and then some. But what to do?

I decided grimly to keep going. If this tunnel, too, dead-ended, then perhaps all of them did except the one that led back home. I would just keep walking until I found my way out—or died!

Still lecturing myself to be calm, which was now impossible, I continued. The tunnel curved again. I went on, muttering prayers. I turned the corner, and up ahead was something that startled my eyes—distant light! I ran, splashing in the stream of water, until I reached a narrow shaft, which marked the end of this tunnel. The shaft went up to a beautiful, thrilling patch of bright sky. And on the wall, leading up to a metal grate, was a steel ladder. I climbed it with frantic speed. Reaching the grate, I tried to peer out, but could see only the edge of something big and metal against the summer sky. It had to be the machine that filled the tunnel with its rumble. I caught a breath of air and heaved, but the grating did not budge. Then I heaved again with all the strength left in me.

The grating popped out of its rusty socket, showering me with dirt. I shot my head up, gulping the blessed fresh air. The machine was some kind of generator; it hulked beside an old brick building, which somehow looked familiar. Turning my head, I saw that I had come out of a manhole at the edge of a sprawling paved courtyard that was filled with men in dark fatigue clothing. German prisoners!

Before I could recover from my surprise at coming up inside the camp, some of the men saw me. Several ran toward me, grabbed my arms and helped me climb out.

"Gosh, fellows, thanks a lot!" I gasped. "I—"

Someone put a rough hand over my mouth, cutting off my words, and propelled me swiftly across a blurred terrain to a barracks. I was tossed down rudely on the nearest cot. The door slammed, then reopened as more Germans rushed in. I struggled, but the man holding me kept his hand over my mouth. All my old fears rioted. The prisoners had taken me prisoner.

The Germans babbled excitedly in their own tongue. The door swung open again and about a dozen more prisoners boiled in. One was older and evidently a senior officer. He looked at me as if he were going to have a stroke, then unleashed a barrage of German at the man holding me in a fierce grip. I figured they were going to tear me limb from limb.

The officer turned to a lanky blond fellow of perhaps twenty and issued some orders. He in turn came over and stiffly addressed me. "What haf you done to come into zis place?"

"I was exploring the tunnel!" I said the moment my captor removed his hand from my mouth. "I didn't know where I was coming up! Honest!"

The soldier repeated my words in German, and the officer barked a reply. The soldier turned to me again. "How many ozzers know of zis tunnel?"

"Nobody!" I said. Then I thought, if they know I'm alone, they'll kill me. "Just me and my pals," I added. "And if I don't get right back home, of course they'll send the army."

There was another heated consultation in German. My overwhelming impression now was that these men were terrified. I did not know what that meant for me.

The door opened once again, and in came a familiar figure.

241

"Rudi!" I cried with relief. "Tell these guys to lemme alone!"

Rudi, ashen, hurried over. The older man snapped something, and Rudi jerked to attention. They had a sharp exchange. Rudi knelt to hold my hand. "Be calm, Danny." He looked far from calm. "What have you done? You came out of the sewer?"

"I was exploring, Rudi, honest! The tunnel forked, and I got mixed up. I saw this manhole, and climbed out, but I didn't mean to bother anybody, *really!*"

Rudi patted my hand and turned to the officer, explaining in German. The officer barked something back, clearly worried.

Rudi turned to me. "How many others know of the sewer?"

"Nobody!"

Rudi reported this to the officer, who smacked his forehead and rolled his eyes toward heaven.

"This is a very dangerous thing you have done," Rudi said.

"I knew that when I got lost!"

He registered surprise. "Not for you. For us. You have discovered the sewer which leads out of the camp."

I tumbled. "It's your escape hatch!" I whispered. "Oh, Rudi, just let me go, and I'll never tell! I won't!"

"Escape? Do you think we are mad? We found this sewer almost at once. It had been overlooked. But we do not want to escape. In France or Africa, yes. Even in England, yes. But in America, where would we go? *Mein Gott!* Those people in the town would kill us! Yet we could not tell your colonel what we had found, for he would have said we were trying to escape. So we have told no one. Not even all of us inside know. A few idiots might try to use the sewer and bring down trouble on the rest of us."

I began to understand. They were in the middle of an insane game here. They really did want to stay in the camp. And they couldn't admit knowledge of the escape route for fear of what might happen. I had poked my head up right in the middle of their secret.

Rudi and the officer had another exchange. Two others joined in, but the officer snapped an order and they shut up, stony-faced. Then Rudi lifted me down off the cot. "We are taking you back to the sewer," he said. "You must never tell anyone about this, or we would be in grave trouble."

"I promise, Rudi! I do!"

Rudi said something to the officer, who in turn gave a long speech in German. There were questions. Some men hurried out.

242

A conspiratorial air filled the barracks. Rudi took my hand and led me to the door.

Outside, several prisoners were now standing well away from the barracks, waving their arms and yelling at each other. To my astonishment, I saw one push another. The two men tangled and went down on the pavement. The others began shouting, and guards ran to intervene.

At that moment Rudi propelled me out the door, and we dashed into the shadows of the brick building. Some men hauled back the manhole grating, and Rudi climbed down inside. The others thrust me in after him. He went down the ladder with me pressed against his chest.

His flashlight was much better than mine, and despite his limp, he ran, dragging me through the maze like it was a straight line. Minutes later, breathing hard, he'd brought me to the place where the pipe disgorged water into the creek.

He knelt in the water and handed me down. "You must never do this again," he said severely. He was badly out of breath.

"I never will!" I promised.

He turned back to the sewer. I listened to his receding footsteps. Then I looked around the creek. A bird sang. The sky had puffy clouds. I could hardly believe it. The world, I thought, was truly crazy.

CHAPTER EIGHT

For days things were very quiet on the farm. I worked every morning in the garden, hoeing around the sprouting beans, lettuce, radishes, potatoes, spinach and corn. There was no rain, so I hauled our old hose out of the barn and watered the hard, cracked earth. I kept my mouth shut about my sewer adventure.

"I tell you one thing," my mother said one morning when I went out with my dog, having him heel through the kitchen. "That animal thinks the sun rises and sets with you."

"Sure he does. He ought to. I'm his best pal."

I was trying to teach Skipper "right" and "left" commands, but progress was slow. Whenever I sensed that one of us was losing patience, we wrestled; the signal for that game was for me to grab him around the neck and tumble to the grass. He tried to get free.

I held on. He shook and dragged me around. When I slipped loose, he piled on top of me, mauling me with his lethal teeth. Once in a while he hurt me a little, although he never broke the skin. On those occasions I popped him on the nose with my fist, lightly, and he looked stunned and repentant. Then I had to love him for five minutes before he got over his hurt feelings.

We liked to take walks. Usually we went down the hill to the creek and the heavy brush. Because the weather was now humid and very warm, Skipper drank from the creek until his belly hung down. I always wondered why he liked the water there better than that in his pan until one day I lay on the mossy bank and tried it myself. It was spring-cold, making my teeth ache, and tasted brightly of iron. It was delicious. Sometimes I lay very still after I had drunk, so the minnows and tadpoles would swim back into view.

Then, suddenly, we had a week of heavy rains, and north of Columbus there was some flooding. When we went to the grocery that weekend, I was startled to see the Big Walnut running bankfull. Sunday was sunny and warm. But new debris had piled up in the creek, and the following week a handful of prisoners came to clear it again. Rudi was among them. Although the guards watched us with a sullen intensity, we managed to talk during the rest period.

"Are you okay?" I asked him. "They're not feeding you bread and water, are they?"

Rudi's rare grin came, showing bad teeth. "Your father is in charge, *ja*? He would feed us bread and water?"

"The colonel would. They oughta send him to fight the Japs."

"I am sure many would be pleased at that."

"My dad is scared of him," I said.

"Of the colonel? He is a very formidable man."

"He's a dopus. When I grow up, I won't be scared of anybody."

"I hope that is true, Danny."

"I won't be like my dad anyway."

Rudi's face lengthened. "You must never speak disrespectfully of your father."

"But he lets the colonel do anything he wants!"

"The colonel is the commandant. Your father is powerless."

"He's as bad as Bill Sheehan's dad. They act like you're criminals!"

244

"You will not speak disrespectfully of your father!" Rudi snapped. I stared, shocked by his sudden harsh tone. Instantly the hardness vanished from his eyes, and he smiled. "It is not the way of things."

"Even if he's wrong?"

"Especially if he is wrong, he needs your support. If a father cannot have the support of his own son, what does he have left?" Rudi shook his head. "And the colonel and your father are not entirely wrong if they are stern with us. It is a matter of war."

"I'll be glad when it's over! I don't understand it very well!"

His smile returned. "We are alike, then."

"What are you going to do when it's over?"

"I hope to go home. Open my business again. Train dogs. Try to make them well. Danny, I have something for you." He reached into his pants pocket and unrolled a beautifully braided leather leash. One end formed a hand loop, and on the other was a metal snap for the collar.

"Wow!" I felt its oily softness. "Where did you get this?"

"I made it. The snap is from a broken canteen. The leather I peeled from a belt." He raised his floppy shirt to reveal a length of rope holding up his pants. "See?"

"It's a beautiful leash."

"It is strong," he told me. "It will never break." Absently he patted his upper left shirt pocket. Almost simultaneously the guards blew their whistles. It was time to resume work.

"Thank you very, very much," I said.

"It's nothing." He got up and walked away.

The men worked through the afternoon, and although I did not get a chance to visit with Rudi again, I watched him from our garden. Again I saw him absentmindedly pat his shirt pocket. When I saw him take a cigarette from another prisoner, I understood. He was out of cigarettes. Now there was something I could do for him.

That Saturday when we all went into town to shop, I had my life's savings, almost a dollar, in my pocket. As I often did, I visited the drugstore—most times it was to look at models or comic books—while my parents were in the grocery.

No other customers were there, and the owner, Mr. Epperman, was behind the soda fountain. I marched up to the sales counter and waited for him to cross the store to me and peer over the glass top, which was stacked high with items. "Yes, sonny?"

"Pack of Pall Malls, please," I said.

"You've got to be kidding," he replied.

"My dad hurt his foot," I said. "He can't come in."

"Well, sonny, I'm sorry, but we don't sell fags to children. He'll have to come in his own self."

"He's sure gonna be mad," I said, skulking over to the rack with the model planes.

"No opening those boxes to look at the planes!" he called.

I stared at the colorful cardboard boxes, hardly noticing them. I was determined to repay Rudi's kindness. There was only one way. Picking out a P-40 model, I went back to the high counter. Mr. Epperman looked over his glasses at me. "What do you want this time?"

"Here," I muttered, handing up the model.

"Thirteen cents," he said.

I gave him a quarter. He turned to the register. I slipped a pack of Camels into my pocket.

He handed me my change and my model. "There you go."

"Thanks," I said, starting for the door.

"Hey, sonny?" he called.

Oh, no, I thought. Caught! I looked back. "Yes, sir?"

"Sure you don't want to try for a beer?" he cackled.

I could feel my heart thumping as I walked out. I got the cigarettes home and hid them in my desk.

A day or two later I saw Rudi and some of the other prisoners working in a field up the road. Hiding the pack in my pants, I hiked there and stood at the fence. When a break came, Rudi limped over.

"Hello!" he said. "It is hot." He wiped his face on a rag.

"I got something for you," I said. I dug out the cigarettes.

He took the pack, examined it and looked gravely at me. "Where did you get these?"

"I bought 'em."

"They would sell to one so young?"

"Well, I know the man at the store."

"You are not in trouble over this?"

"No! Why should I be in trouble? Go ahead. Smoke one!"

Rudi put the pack in his shirt pocket. "I will not smoke one today. I will tomorrow," he said soberly, extending his hand. "Thank you."

I shook his hand. "What are friends for?" I asked.

FOR FOUR DAYS it rained almost continuously. The creek came out of its banks. The garden lay flattened, a slick of black mud.

"If it doesn't break soon," my father said at the supper table, "we'll have some serious flooding. They're getting ready in town. Thousands of empty sandbags have been delivered to the gym, and they're talking about evacuating the flats."

"If the creek out back gets much higher," my mother said, "I'm going to start worrying about *our* evacuating."

"Oh, I don't think it will affect us. We're on good high ground. Harmony is a different matter."

"It worries me anyway."

"The first time we get a break, I'll get a crew out here again to deepen the channel and to clean up that bend and any other areas that impede the current."

"Why don't they work the same way on the Big Walnut to make it stop flooding?" I asked.

"They are, bit by bit. But that's a mighty big project."

"What do they do if it just keeps raining?"

"It's a very serious thing, son. Harmony was founded in a curve of the river by a couple dozen families. But now the town has grown, so that the business section is just below the curve. During the big flood in the '30s, the river took a shortcut, eliminating the bend. If it does that again, it will cover downtown."

"Sandbags won't help that much!"

"The plan is to pile them on the banks along the curve. Hold the water back there, and the worst they'll have is minor flooding down around the park."

The more my father talked, the more serious things sounded. He explained that the normal level of the river through Harmony was fourteen feet, and at present it stood at seventeen. The serious flooding of the 1930s had started when the river spilled over its banks at the nineteen-foot level. Channel work since then had extended the spill point to twenty feet precisely. The town leaders had been to the statehouse in Columbus, trying to get help in case the rain kept coming. The governor had pledged as many national guardsmen and state policemen as he could spare. But there were already floods north and east of Columbus, and around Dayton. Ohio River towns were preparing for that mighty waterway to rise dangerously.

The rain continued through the night, but slacked to drizzle by

247

morning. The creek had tumbled trees and trash on the lower slope, and water gleamed in the fields beyond. The rushing brown torrent made ugly foam along its edges, tugging away chunks of earth in little avalanches. My father left for work at eight, and was back by ten. "We're going to clear the creek out before the rain picks up again," he said.

It was exciting when the truckload of prisoners pulled into the driveway. Aggie and I watched from the front window. Although the sky was swollen, the rain had stopped. About a dozen prisoners climbed out with their shovels. In addition to the driver, there were three other guards. I did not see Rudi at first, but then I spied him in the group as they came around the house. In the bedroom, Skipper heard them and started going crazy.

My father, who had gone outside to speak to the guards, came back in. "Squirt, tie Skipper outside, where he can bark his head off without breaking everybody's eardrums."

By the time I had tied Skipper to his stake, the work detail had gone down the slope. From the house I could not see them at all. My father came out wearing rubber boots, and a raincoat that swirled in the breeze. "Want to go with me?" he asked.

"Yeah!"

"Get your boots on. Hurry."

I rushed to the back porch and buckled on my galoshes. When I rejoined my father and we started away, Skipper began whining.

"Not this time, Skipper. All we need is for you to fall in."

We mushed past the garden and into the little orchard that sloped toward the creek. The roar of the water came to us before we could see it. When we did get it in view, I was numbed by how broad it had become where it boiled around the bend. The prisoners were freeing debris that had piled up to form a dam across the channel. Others, with big saws, were cutting down several willows that the rushing water had undermined.

It was hard, muddy, dangerous work. My father and I watched for some time. Overhead, the thick clouds parted a bit and a few stray shafts of sunlight came through. It seemed a good omen. I watched Rudi shoveling debris away from the bank. He looked tired, and his limp was more noticeable. I felt sorry for him.

"Dad, don't you think it's time they got a rest?"

"The head guard decides that, son."

I checked over the guards. Three were civilians, older men

248

standing aside with their rifles, at ease, merely watching. The fourth was a tough-looking sergeant. He had slab features and vigilant eyes. With his carbine slung over his shoulder, he moved from place to place, his putteed boots heavy in the muck, giving an instruction here and pointing something out there. When he gestured at Rudi to work faster, I knew I did not like him.

The work at the curve was finished. The crew moved nearer the house, clearing more debris from the bank. There were larger breaks in the clouds now, and the sun gleamed on water everywhere. "Maybe the weatherman is wrong again," my father said as he shaded his face with his hand. "He says more rain tonight."

I sat on a soggy stump. "I'm getting tired. I bet these guys would like a rest by now."

My father looked at me a moment, then signaled the sergeant, who strode over to us. He was a grim, unsmiling man, all business. "Yes, sir?"

"Sergeant, isn't it about time for a break?"

"Sir, there's a lot to be done."

My father's jaw set. "Give them ten minutes' rest, Sergeant."

"Yes, sir." The sergeant blew his whistle. "Ten minutes!" he barked. He stood beside a tree, hands clasped rigidly behind his back in parade rest, angry about the break.

I watched as the men sank down thankfully. Rudi took my pack of cigarettes from his pocket. He lit one, looked toward me and raised his hand in a slight salute. I signaled him to join us, but he smiled and shook his head.

"Are you waving at one of the prisoners?" my father asked.

"Yes. Rudi Gerhardt. He's my friend. Over there."

"Your *friend*?"

"He's in the gang that works in this area. He noticed Skipper, and he told me how to train him. He knows everything about dogs. He had a blind dog himself."

My father was puzzled. "A prisoner? I'll be damned," he said softly. "Which one is he?"

"Hey, Rudi!" I waved. Rudi nodded in response.

My father started toward him, picking his way among the others. I followed closely. Rudi got nervously to his feet and came to a semblance of attention.

"I understand you and my son are friends," my father said.

Rudi smiled. "Yes, sir. It is so. You have a very fine boy."

249

My father was watching him with quiet intensity. "You gave him some pointers about the dog?"

"Yes, sir. I am—I was a veterinarian in Munich."

"What barracks are you in, Rudi?"

"Six, sir."

"And you had a blind dog?"

"One much like Danny's, sir. *Ja.*"

My father looked at me. "No wonder you knew how to teach him to obey. I never thought you could do it. But you did. Now I begin to see how."

"It was easy, with Rudi giving me tips," I said.

Rudi shook his head. "Not easy, sir. Your son put in more hours than you can imagine. It required a heroic effort, sir."

My father looked at Rudi and me for what seemed a long time. He appeared at a loss. "Are you being treated all right, Rudi?"

"Yes, sir. Fine."

The sergeant had begun pacing. "It looks like time to get back to work," my father said. "Maybe we can talk later."

"It would be my pleasure, sir."

My father led me back across the worksite. The sergeant's whistle shrilled. Work resumed. At lunchtime the prisoners and guards ate out of their metal boxes. We hiked back to the house to eat. The weather had continued to improve, and my mother needed groceries. Since my father wanted to remain here, it was agreed that she and Aggie would drive to Harmony.

After they departed, my father went to the barn for the ladder. Setting it against the side of the house, he climbed onto the roof with hammer, and nails, and tar paper. He tacked down the tar paper over a spot that had been the source of a slight leak. Finally he climbed down. He said there were other places that looked suspicious, but he could not fix them alone.

"I'll help," I said.

"You on that roof? Not on your life."

"Rudi will help you, then," I suggested eagerly.

"That's not a bad idea. And he can pay Skipper a visit."

"Great! He's never seen how we do the game with the ball."

Skipper pulled at his rope, whining again, as we headed off. I told him to be patient, and we went down the hill through the mud, the hot sun making it seem like steam was rising around us.

When we reached the worksite, my father spoke to the sergeant.

He signaled a civilian guard, who walked over to Rudi. They spoke, and Rudi started toward us, the guard at his side.

"Rudi doesn't need a guard," I told my father.

"Humor the sergeant," my father said. "Besides, he can hold the ladder."

Rudi reached us. "You need some help at your house, sir?"

"Some roofing has blown loose. I can't hold it in place and nail a new piece down at the same time. Can you give me a hand?"

"Of course. It is permitted to smoke while we walk?"

My father lit a Chesterfield for himself and gave Rudi one. We started up the hill with the guard trailing us.

"Wait till you see the game with the ball, Rudi!" I told him. "Old Skipper catches it before it bounces twice!"

"Then does he bring it back to you?"

"Sometimes. Other times he makes me take it from him."

Rudi chuckled. "I think the dog believes he has taught you a game."

"I'm going to find the ball to show you!" I ran ahead through the brush, allowing them to walk along at their slower pace. I was deliriously happy. My father had met Rudi, and had given him a cigarette. That showed how much he liked him. In the future there might be other odd jobs around the house, and Rudi would come more often. Everything was going to be better now.

As I passed the garden, I heard a sharp yelp of pain from Skipper. Hurrying faster, I rounded the corner of the house.

The first thing I saw was two bicycles—a red Fleetwing and a battered blue Roadmaster—parked in the driveway. Next I saw Skipper, turning around and around at the end of his rope. He was whining, baffled and hurt.

Then I saw Sheehan and Inright nearer the house, out of Skipper's reach. Sheehan had a handful of small rocks. As I watched, he took one and hurled it at Skipper. It hit Skipper in the hindquarters, and he danced in pain, yelping again. Sheehan was laughing.

"*Stop that!*" I yelled.

They both saw me. Inright took a step backward. Sheehan held his ground, tossing another rock lightly in his hand.

I ran to Skipper and threw myself down beside him, hugging his neck. "It's okay, Skipper! They won't do it anymore!" I buried my face in his thick fur. "You're safe now, boy!" He twisted around

251

with intense relief, licking frantically at my face.

A rock stung my back. I scrambled to my feet and faced them.
Sheehan must have seen something in my eyes, because he
dropped the rocks and started to
turn away. Inright was already
walking to his bike. Now Sheehan
broke into a run after him.

I was unhinged—filled with
rage over helpless Skipper. My
legs had never carried me faster,
as I chased them. I saw Inright
get on his bike and start to pump
away. Sheehan got a leg up, but
was off balance and staggered. I
crashed into him, knocking both
him and the bicycle over. The impact jarred me, but I was punch-
ing blindly, and the blows were landing. I hit him in the eye and
the nose and we rolled over, fighting. Behind us, Skipper was
barking as I had never heard him bark before.

Sheehan managed to stick his fingers in my eye. I yelled and fell
back, and he was on top of me instantly. He hit me hard, but lost
his balance. I kicked him and rolled over on top of him, swinging
hysterically.

"You won't *ever* pick on a dog again," I panted, hitting him on
the chin. "You think you're so tough, but you're just a big bully.
I'm gonna show you."

"I give!" Sheehan cried. I was aware of adults rushing toward us,
but I kept swinging. "I give, Flatfoot!"

I stopped hitting him, but held my fist ready. "You promise?"

He kicked me off, picked up a rock and piled on top of me. Rudi
had reached us. He tried to separate us. We were both punching
wildly. Rudi grabbed Sheehan's arm and pulled him away. Sheehan
swung around awkwardly, and something popped in his shoulder.

"*Ow!*" Sheehan screamed, going limp in Rudi's grasp. "You killed
me! You broke my arm! Help! Help! He's killing me!"

The guard rushed up behind Rudi. I saw how completely he had

252

misunderstood. He raised his rifle in a lethal position.

"*No!*" I cried. "He's—"

Too late. The butt of the rifle crashed into Rudi's skull and he went down like a feed sack.

Horrified, I stared. The guard looked down at Rudi, then at Sheehan, who was writhing like he had been tortured. My father ran up. The guard bent over Rudi as if to hit him again.

I attacked the guard, screaming, and beating him with my fists in such fury that he actually staggered backward. Then my father was there, grappling with me, lifting me bodily into the air.

"Calm down!" he ordered. "Calm down!"

"You've killed him!" I shrilled at the guard. "You've killed my Rudi! I'll get you for it if it's the last thing I ever do!"

WE USED THE CAMP TRUCK to hurry Rudi to the small clinic in Harmony. My father and I rode in the back with him, and his blanket-wrapped form did not move during the hard, jouncing trip. I think that I was on the edge of hysteria. My father kept his arm around me.

"He's going to be all right, Squirt," he told me. "You see? He isn't bleeding. It doesn't feel like his skull was fractured."

"I hate this town!" I retorted. "And everybody in it! I'm going to get even!"

Bill Sheehan and Phil Inright were in the front with the guard, who was driving. When I had last seen him, Sheehan had still been writhing in pain. Someone had said that his shoulder might be dislocated. "I hope it's been torn out by the roots!" I had screamed.

When we reached the clinic, my father hurried inside. Moments later I peered out and saw the guard helping Sheehan, who was weeping and grimacing, through the glass doors of the entryway. Then my father and a heavyset nurse rushed out with a stretcher on a dolly of some kind. A doctor followed. The three of them managed to get Rudi out of the truck and onto the stretcher. The doctor and nurse wheeled him inside. My father lifted me down and we entered close behind.

In the lobby of the building, a dozen patients, older people, sat on the periphery. Beyond the vacant reception desk was a hallway that led to treatment rooms. Phil Inright sat in a chair nearby. I heard Sheehan hollering. Phil looked scared.

My father took me to a chair beside him. "Are you all right?" he asked Inright.

"Yes, sir, I guess," Phil said huskily.

My father looked around grimly. "I've got to make a few phone calls." He dug into his pocket. "You boys want a Coke or something?"

"No!" I said. How could he think about Cokes at such a time?

He went to a phone booth on the far side of the lobby. Inright cracked his knuckles. "Boy! Bill is hurt bad."

"I hope he dies," I snapped.

"He'll be in a lot of trouble if you tell about him chucking rocks at your dog, Danny. His dad is real mean to him sometimes. Maybe we could just say—"

"Listen, Phil," I hissed, squeezing his arm as hard as I could. "If you lie to protect Sheehan, I'll beat you up every day of your life!" He looked pale. "I mean it," I told him. "I'll go find Benny Harrison and have him get you!"

"I'll tell the truth! We didn't mean any harm."

"That's a lie right there. Sheehan came to beat me up. And he dragged you along to watch."

"Your dog started growling when we rode up."

"So you had to throw rocks at him?"

"I didn't think it would hurt your dumb old dog!"

I almost hit him then and there. "Just remember what I told you. You tell the truth, or you'll wish you were dead!"

"I will! I will!"

My father came back and sat down beside me. He gave Inright a cold glance. "Your father is on the way. I also talked to Mr. Sheehan and Colonel Thatcher. Now all we can do is wait."

I sat in agony, swinging my legs. From outside came a roll of thunder, signifying that the weatherman had not been wrong after all. The older folks in the room waited, covertly watching us or reading ancient copies of *The Saturday Evening Post*.

The doctor finally came out and walked over. My father stood up to greet him with the expression of a man bracing himself.

"The boy has a dislocation and possible muscle damage," the doctor said. "He'll be all right, but we want more X-rays. The German has a slight concussion, but he's conscious now."

"Rudi's okay?" I said with intense relief.

The doctor ignored me. "We want to send them both to Columbus. The boy will probably need a shoulder cast, but he ought to be ambulatory in an hour or two. The German should be observed overnight, just as a precaution."

The front door swung open. Mr. and Mrs. Sheehan boiled in. Mrs. Sheehan's hair was in curlers. She was crying. "My baby!" she wept. "Where is my baby?"

"He's in the treatment room—" the doctor began.

"What happened?" Sheehan demanded angrily. "A boy goes bicycle riding and is attacked in broad daylight by a Nazi! I—"

"It was hardly that way," my father cut in. "The prisoner was trying to separate your boy and mine. They were fighting."

"Fighting!" Sheehan's bulging eyes rolled to me. "Were you picking on Bill again? You ought to be disciplined severely. George, this is not the first time there's been trouble between these boys. I hope, now that something serious has happened, you'll take effective action!"

"I never picked on him!" I said. "He picked on me!"

"Not long ago my son came home from school all muddy after you had attacked him without provocation—"

"That's a lie!"

Mrs. Sheehan wailed. "I want to see my boy!"

"This way," the doctor said, and they followed him.

My father stared at me. "It's a lie!" I repeated, frantic.

"Did you knock the Sheehan boy down at school?"

"Yes! But—"

"I don't know where this will end," he broke in. "First you're thick as hops with that delinquent. Then this. You were always a good boy. What's happened to you? Since we moved to Harmony you've been nothing but trouble."

It was the worst possible time to lose my composure, but my universe was crumbling. I could not help it. The tears rolled. "Dad, it's not that way at all! He was the one!"

The front door swung open again and a burly man wearing a butcher's apron came in, thick arms swinging. "What's happened?" he demanded.

"Pop," Phil gasped, "Bill Sheehan got hurt, but he's going to be okay! I'm fine!" He looked scared to death.

"What happened?" the man repeated, glaring at my father.

"I'm George Davidson. You must be Mr. Inright." He held out his hand.

The man ignored it. "I know who you are. You're the one coddling those Nazis out there. What have you got to do with this?"

"The Sheehan boy was hurt at our place."

Mr. Inright wheeled on his son. "What were you doing out there?" His fists balled. I thought he was going to hit Phil.

Phil looked dreadful, eyes wide, face the color of bread dough. "We went for a ride. We"—he glanced fearfully at me—"we stopped at Danny's house. Nobody was around . . ." Phil hesitated. He was torn between fears.

"What happened?" his father insisted.

"Then he came up," Phil said, pointing at me. "And he started punching Bill. I wasn't doing nothing. This German ran up and pulled Bill away from the fight, only he hurt Bill."

"A German hurt him? Davidson, what was a German doing where he could attack innocent kids?"

"There was a work detail," my father said. "It wasn't quite the way your boy told it."

"Don't call my son a liar!"

"I'm not. He's just excited. I saw the last part of the fight. The prisoner merely tried to break it up."

The man was shaking with anger. He was big, powerful and nearly out of control. He grabbed Phil's neck roughly and started to turn him away from us.

"Wait!" I said. "He hasn't told all of it!" I looked at Phil imploringly. "Phil, tell him the rest of it. Please."

Phil was trembling. His father had him clamped in a harsh grip.

256

"Is there more?" Mr. Inright growled. "Do you know what will happen if you lie to me?"

"Yes, sir!" Phil's eyes rolled back. "There wasn't any more."

They headed for the door. "I'll talk to you later!" Mr. Inright flung back at my father.

My father looked down at me. I had seldom seen him so angry. "I didn't beat up on Bill Sheehan," I said. "He beat up on me. All I did was hit back, the way Benny taught me."

"Benny Harrison again? Sit down and be quiet!" There was a tone in his voice I had never heard before. It was contempt.

SOMEHOW WE FOUND my mother in town. There was a grim ride back to the house. The work crew was gone. Rain came down steadily.

My father said he had to go to Columbus to see how Rudi and Bill Sheehan were. When he started to leave, I did not ask if I could go; I simply climbed into the front seat beside him.

The drive to Columbus was made in frigid silence. The hospital was a great, gloomy red-brick building on the city's south side. We parked and hurried through the rain. My father made inquiries, then we walked down a long, glistening corridor. Up ahead, past a nursing station, I saw a soldier with a rifle standing beside a closed door. The colonel was pacing up and down. When he saw us, he hurried over.

"This is terrible, Davidson," he said tightly. "The worst."

"How are they?" my father asked.

"The Sheehan boy was put in a shoulder cast and sent home. Looked like he was still in a lot of pain. Our prisoner is in there. They say they'll release him tomorrow morning . . . A prisoner attacking an innocent child! The parents are beside themselves, and I can't say I blame them. This is going to make things even more difficult for us."

"All Rudi did was pull the boys apart. It was an accident."

"By godfrey, I don't care what you want to call it! This is the last straw! What were you doing anyhow, Davidson, with a crew on your property?"

"They were clearing the creek. You signed the work order."

"That child-butcher didn't attack the boy at the creek. It was in your front yard! What was he doing there?"

"He was going to help me fix a leak in my roof."

"Work on personal property? That's a clear violation of regulations, Davidson."

My father's jaw set. He didn't say a word.

The colonel said, "We'll transport the prisoner to the camp in the morning. He'll be interviewed and put in the stockade. There will be a hearing about your participation in all this. Now I must attend a meeting in Harmony." He turned and strode toward the exit.

I stared at my father. He stood stiff, in shock. "It wasn't the way they said," I told him.

"Danny, haven't we had enough from you today?"

"Just ask Rudi, Dad!"

He thought about it, then squared his shoulders with resignation. He turned to the soldier blocking the hospital-room door. "We want to go in for a minute, Private."

"Sir! My orders are to admit only medical personnel."

"Private, do you know who I am?"

"You are the civilian overseer for all guard personnel, sir!"

"Don't you think you'd better get out of our way, Private?"

The young soldier looked at my father for a moment. Then he stepped smartly to the side. "Sir!" he said.

The room was dimly lit. In the lone bed, Rudi lay in a sea of white sheets. There was a thick gauze bandage around his head. He was almost as pale as the bedding.

"Are you all right, Rudi?" I whispered.

He nodded, smiling faintly. "Dizzy only. Fine."

"That guard was a dopus," I said. "I'll get even with him—"

"All right, Squirt," my father put in. "That's enough."

Rudi looked at my father. "The other boy?"

"His shoulder was hurt, but he's home now. In a cast."

Rudi's face twisted. "*Ach!*"

"There will probably be charges."

"Because I hurt the boy. Yes. I understand."

"Rudi, what were they fighting about? Did you see?"

"No. When I turned the corner, they were already fighting. I was afraid one would get hurt. The other boy had a rock in his hand."

"The Sheehan boy had a rock?" my father asked.

"He was throwing rocks at Skipper," I said. "That's what I've been trying to tell you!"

258

"I didn't hear the Inright boy tell his father that."

"He was afraid his dad would kill him, probably."

"So you saw the Sheehan boy hitting Skipper with rocks."

"Yes. And Skipper was crying. He didn't know what was going on because he's blind and all. I just— Sheehan calls me Flatfoot, Dad, and he always picks on me. That's why I got Benny to teach me how to fight. When I saw Sheehan doing that, I just hit into him. That's the truth, Dad! I swear it!"

He put his hands on his hips. "Well, it explains a lot of things. I'll look into it." He sighed. "I don't know how much good I'll do. If those boys lie, their parents will believe them, not you or me. I can just imagine what they're saying in Harmony right now."

"You can make 'em see the truth, Dad!"

"I don't know, Squirt. But you can be sure I'll try."

My relief was so deep it was almost painful. I looked at Rudi, and he winked at me. On impulse I leaned over the bed and kissed him. His cheek was rough with stubble.

"Such a boy!" he said softly. "Such a boy!"

My father put his arm around me. I let go and bawled like a baby.

CHAPTER NINE

The rain came down steadily all night. When my father left for the camp in the morning, water was standing in our front yard, and the creek behind the house was creeping close to the garden. We had pans under three leaks that had now developed in the roof. I put on my slicker and took Skipper out briefly, leading him back into my room, where he shook himself vigorously, spraying everything in sight. I cleaned that up and went to the living room, where my mother was ironing. The Zenith was playing on the table.

"And now the news at eight," the announcer said. "On the local scene, new downpours have caused flooding in central and south-central Ohio. About two hundred residents were evacuated in Chillicothe during the night. In West Jefferson, power has been off since midnight. Officials warn that forecasts of up to another six inches of rain in some areas will mean heavy local flooding. The Big Walnut is rising fast and could threaten Harmony and other towns to the south within forty-eight hours."

"Mom! He said—"

"Hush, Danny! Listen."

"In Harmony, Mayor Gump has ordered emergency action along the notorious curve in the river. City and county crews have already begun filling and placing sandbags. A town meeting has been called for three o'clock today."

"It's going to flood!" I said excitedly.

"Maybe not," my mother said. But she looked worried.

Skipper appeared in the doorway and padded slowly, unerringly, into the room. He veered slightly to avoid my father's chair, then started toward his favorite spot under the west window. My mother and the ironing board were in his way.

"You'll have to go around, Skipper," my mother said.

He stopped at the sound of her voice and waited, tongue lolling. His tail wagged. "Skipper," I said, "here."

He walked toward me. I grasped his collar and led him past the ironing board and to the window area. He turned around once, sniffing to orient himself, and then lay down.

"I suppose I'll never be able to rearrange the furniture." My mother sighed.

"He can relearn it," I told her. Just then Aggie came in with the two cats trailing behind her. The cats immediately ran across the room and attacked Skipper's ears. His tail thumped. He closed his eyes and shook his head lazily, trying to make them stop.

It rained steadily all morning. At noon my father drove home and ate his lunch at the kitchen table. He was grim.

"The Big Walnut is over eighteen feet," he told us. "They've started to sandbag on both sides around the curve. The governor is sending in a few reserves—state police and national guardsmen; he can't spare many because a lot of towns are facing the same thing. They're asking for volunteers. I'm going to a town meeting at the fire station at three o'clock."

"Are the prisoners going to be used?" my mother asked.

"The colonel volunteered them. It's idiotic, but the city fathers refused, community feeling being what it is. Yesterday capped things off. I understand the stories are pretty wild. With a few more retellings, we'll have had a mass breakout."

"Is Rudi all right?" I asked.

"He's fine. I saw him in a detention cell at the camp."

"It's not fair, putting him there!"

260

"We'll sort that out later. The flood takes precedence now."

"George," my mother said, "I think all of us ought to come into Harmony with you this afternoon."

"Why?" He was surprised.

"Go look at our creek."

He got up and went outside. When he came back he was grimmer. "I don't think it will go much higher, but you're right. No sense anyone being stuck out here. . ."

"Can the kitties go?" Aggie piped up.

"Yes. The kitties can go."

"And Skipper?" I chimed in.

He sighed. "And Skipper, yes."

The rain drummed down hard while we prepared in a carnival atmosphere. Aggie ran in and out of her room at least twenty times, asking if she could take such and so. The cats were everywhere but on the ceiling. My father dressed in heavy work clothing, and we all put on slickers. By the time we set out, it was well past two o'clock.

Along the way we saw many signs of flooding. When we crossed the Big Walnut, the muddy water was within two feet of the pavement, boiling with ugly foam. We could feel the bridge trembling as we drove over it. Farther along, a little creek had spilled onto the highway, and water sloshed under the fenders and running boards. When we reached higher ground again, everyone breathed easier. The clouds overhead were low, and lightning veined them periodically.

Townspeople were flocking toward the fire station for the meeting. When we arrived, we saw that officials had packed chairs wall to wall, but these were already occupied, so our family stood in the back. More people were still trickling in when we saw Mr. Sheehan, the police chief, the sheriff and Mayor Gump enter through a side door and sit up front. The mayor waved his hands for quiet, and the roar of voices began to subside. "Mr. Sheehan," the mayor told us, "is the chairman of the emergency committee. We'll hear from him."

Sheehan got up. "I don't have to tell any of you that we have a serious problem. The level of the water out there right now is about eighteen feet eight inches." There was a chorus of groans.

"What does that mean?" someone called.

"Trouble. The flood in the 1930s crested at nineteen feet."

"Then we're about to get flooded again?" he was asked.

"Not necessarily," Sheehan said. "For one thing, there's been a lot of work on the banks since 1933. For another, we've already placed layers of sandbags all along the banks, and work is moving fast. The governor has promised us more manpower if he can find it. We're getting some help from the penitentiary and from BIS. If the rain lets up, we can stay high and dry."

"How fast is the river rising?"

"It's been coming up about one inch every two hours. That means," Sheehan went on over some hubbub, "it could be as high as twenty feet by tomorrow this time. But by then we should have another foot or two on the sandbags."

Voices rumbled everywhere. Someone called, "What's the highest it can go and not flood downtown?"

"We figure," Sheehan replied, "we can stay ahead of it to the twenty-three-foot mark. That gives us quite a margin. Barring some tremendous new rain upstream, we can make it—if everyone pitches in. We've got emergency kitchens set up at the school, and workers will be able to rest and sleep in the Porterfield warehouse near the river. For any families that need evacuation, the chief has a list of people who will put them up. Harmony has been through crises before, and we'll get through this one, too, as long as we all pull together."

After that the meeting was over, and we walked to our car. When we reached it Skipper started barking. I spoke to him through the almost closed window and he calmed down. The cats were on the back shelf behind the rear seat.

My father unlocked the doors. "I'm going down to the river to take a look. It's only a couple of blocks. Do you want to stay here?"

My mother nodded. "We'll wait in the car."

"Can I go?" I asked.

He hesitated. "Okay. You can go."

"Me!" Aggie said excitedly.

"Absolutely not. You stay with your mother."

The rain came down lightly as we walked east toward the river. The area looked like a battleground. The streets were covered with sand and dirt spilled from trucks; two dump trucks, empty from unloading, rumbled past us. Cars were parked helter-skelter near sawhorse barricades.

We moved around the corner of an old brick warehouse, where

262

we got our first broad view. What had been grassy strips and a gentle river meandering north to south, was now a world of turgid water. The river was already at the top of the banks, which were built up with rows of brown sandbags. Mounds of sand were every-where. Grayish figures of men were shoveling it into more bags while other men passed them in a continuous line to still others on the banks, who were stacking them. Men were slipping and sliding in the colossal quagmire.

The river itself appeared enormous. Brown, raging, it seemed to race past us. I saw an entire tree, leaves still fresh, carried rapidly downstream. Men in yellow raincoats—supervisors—yelled orders. I saw one worker throw down his shovel, walk over to a parked truck and collapse in a heap against one of its tires. There was a Red Cross truck a block north. A line of men appeared to be getting coffee.

"Well, Squirt," my father said quietly, "that's what a flood looks like." We walked back uphill to the car, where Mother and Aggie waited with the pets. "It's bad," my father told them as he started the car.

We drove to the corner of Main Street and turned left. Poking along in traffic, we reached the edge of town. Ahead we saw a melee of cars and trucks, and flashing red lights. Cars were turning around and coming back. We inched to the front of the line. The red lights were on a highway patrol car. A trooper, rain steaming off his jacket, peered in the window at us. "I'm sorry, folks. You have to go back."

"We live out this way," my father told him.

"I'm sorry, sir. The bridge just went out up ahead. No way you're going to get through tonight, I'm afraid."

My father somberly backed around. If we tried to get home by going through Circleville, it would take a couple of hours.

"*Now* what do we do?" my mother asked. Her voice had a tinge of hysteria in it.

"We'll just find out where they're putting people up."

It took a while. Many others had been blocked from their homes. There was a small crowd at the fire station when my father went in. Finally he came out holding a slip of paper.

The home we were sent to belonged to an elderly couple named Henderson. They were very nice. Mrs. Henderson said we could keep Skipper and the cats in the garage. Aggie and I took them out there and found it cozy and dry. We got a carton for the cats, which they wouldn't stay in, and an old piece of rug for Skipper. When I told him to stay there, he curled up obediently, but I saw him cock his ears trying to follow the sounds of our departure.

In the house, which was very old-fashioned, Mrs. Henderson served us sandwiches and tea. Mr. Henderson talked a lot about the railroad and being retired. They had been in Harmony during the earlier flood. They said it had been awful.

After we ate, my father left to go and help at the river. My mother herded Aggie and me upstairs to the bedroom the Hendersons had given us. I didn't know what to do, so I just sat on the old canopy bed and swung my legs, making the springs creak. I thought of Skipper in the garage. I knew he was probably scared. I was scared, too.

IN THE DEAD OF THE NIGHT, with rain beating lightly on the roof of the strange house, my father crept into the room. I was awakened by my mother's whispers to him. She turned on a lamp, and I saw him hanging up his wet muddy clothes.

"It's coming up faster than they expected," he told her softly.

"Is it going to be all right?" she whispered back.

He shook his head and said nothing.

As he got into bed with us, I felt the cold radiating from him. In moments his breathing became steady and deep. My mother turned out the light again. I went back to sleep.

In the morning we were up early. The rain had stopped, although clouds still hung low over the town. Mrs. Henderson prepared a mammoth breakfast.

We sat around the big dining-room table and ate while listening to the radio. There was flooding not only in Ohio but in parts of Indiana and Kentucky.

"Today and tonight will tell the tale," my father said. "The water level was way over nineteen feet when I left last night. But now the rain is slacking off. It's going to be touch and go."

"If it's stopping, the river will go down," I said.

"Not necessarily," he explained. "The rain that falls here raises the river *below* Harmony. We have to worry about the weather upstream."

"That's the way it was in '33," Mrs. Henderson told us. "When the river went over its banks, the sun was shining!"

"I'll get back down there," my father said. "I'll call and let you know how it looks."

"That won't be possible," Mr. Henderson said. "I'm afraid the telephone is out."

My father sighed.

"I'll go with you," I said. "Then I'll come back with the message." I had been dying for an excuse to see the latest for myself. My parents somewhat reluctantly agreed. I rushed out to the garage and leashed Skipper, who was frisky after a night in unfamiliar surroundings. He obeyed me perfectly, however, heeling as we walked downtown.

Our first stop was at the fire station. We found Mr. Sheehan and Colonel Thatcher among the officials 'in the command center. A couple of soldiers were operating radios that seemed to broadcast .mostly static, and others were studying maps.

"Heard about your predicament, Davidson," the colonel said. "Just as well you're here. We need every man we can get."

My father looked at Mr. Sheehan. "Does that mean we're going to use the prisoners?"

Sheehan ignored the question. "The river is rising a lot faster. We're almost at twenty feet. At the present rate we'll be over twenty-three feet within six or seven hours. We may not even get the sandbag walls that high. The workers are all exhausted. Some of them are in the clinic to recuperate."

"Then why not use the prisoners?" my father asked.

"As we've said, community feeling against it is too strong. We're not using them."

"Is community feeling stronger against the prisoners than against downtown being flooded?"   .

Sheehan's jaw set angrily. "We're getting the word out to evacuate a twelve-block area. Not many people living in it. Stores, mostly. The property damage will be terrible." He sighed. "I don't know if the town will ever be the same."

"I'll go down and see if I can help," my father said. .

"Oh, George . . . ." Mr. Sheehan seemed embarrassed. "Hardly a time to discuss this, but at home last night I had a talk with my son. Bill said he threw a rock at the dog here. I want you to know I don't blame your boy for whatever happened."

"That's why they were fighting," my father said.

"Yes. Well, I guess your boy misunderstood. Bill says the dog was watching him suspiciously, and Bill thought that he would attack."

"Is that what he said?" I piped up. "That Skipper was watching him suspiciously?"

"Yes."

"That's real strange, then!" I said triumphantly. I knelt beside Skipper and held his head up so Mr. Sheehan could get a clear look at his eyes. "You see these eyes? Skipper is *blind!*"

Sheehan's expression went blank. "Yes! I remember the night at your house now!"

"And he was tied up," I added. "That's why I was fighting Bill."

"It looks like I have another talk coming with my boy," Sheehan said in a low voice.

"That wasn't the only misunderstanding," my father told him. "Rudi Gerhardt's actions have also been misinterpreted."

Sheehan ran his hand through his hair. "I just can't talk about it anymore now! We're trying to save a town!"

"All right." My father was angry. "What do you want me to do?"

"You can get a report from the crew bosses on how many men there are in each section. Any other messages they have, you can bring back. We're having trouble with our communications here."

My father turned to me. "Go back to the Hendersons' and say there's no immediate danger. I'll try to be there by lunchtime."

I followed these orders, as far as they went. I gave Mother and the Hendersons the message. But I was anxious to see the latest for myself. So after telling them the news, I started down the steps.

"Where are you going?" my mother called sharply.

"Back down there," I replied, hoping she would think I was still following orders.

I was very busy looking innocent. "Heel, Skipper," I commanded. And it worked! She let us leave again.

The lightest drizzle started coming down on us as we hurried along Main Street and toward the river. At Front Street, a man standing at a barricade hailed us as we went by.

"Where do you think you're going, kid?"

"I just saw Mr. Sheehan," I said. "I'm carrying messages." Strictly speaking, it had not been a lie. I had seen Sheehan, and if I saw my father, I intended to tell him the other message had been delivered. Making sure Skipper heeled, I walked into what looked like a combat zone.

The river was noticeably higher than it had been yesterday.

Looking across its turgid expanse, I saw places on the far side where water had filled acres of lowland. At the Red Cross station around the river bend, a long line of workers waited for coffee. Below me, some buses had BOYS INDUSTRIAL SCHOOL painted on their sides. The workers near the buses were clearly boys, struggling to relay the heavy sandbags to the top of the makeshift levee. I knew I was already in trouble, but my curiosity led me on. I crossed a storage area for some kind of farm machinery and went along a cobbled street to the river.

Down here it was warmer, the stink of the flood everywhere. The pavement was slick underfoot from spilled sand and seepage. Supervisors were urging boys along, although they were clearly exhausted; some were no bigger than I, and I was surprised that they could even lift the heavy bags. To one side, a small group of tough-looking kids were resting on a heap of filled bags. I scanned faces, and then my heart turned over.

"Hey, kid," Benny said wearily. He was slumped on some bags, smoking a cigarette. He was wet and muddy and he looked older.

"Benny," I said, "are you all right?"

"Sure." He grinned, showing a gap where one of his front teeth had been. "Some flood, huh? Maybe it'll get the school."

"I saw your mom," I told him. "She said you were okay."

"Yeah. She comes down sometimes, blubbers."

"Are they really treating you all right?"

He looked at me for what seemed a long time. "Sure," he repeated finally, without the tough tone. "They're teaching me how to be a mechanic."

"Hey. That's great, Benny."

"Your mutt looks good. He still blind?"

"Yes. But he's learned everything fine. Say hello, Skipper."

Skipper wagged his tail.

Benny smiled. "I had a dog once. Only the guy that owned him came and took him back."

"When you get out, maybe you can have one."

"The old lady is taking me somewhere else when I get out. There ain't likely to be no dog."

"You might get one, Benny. You never know."

His eyes became boyish. "That would be neat, wouldn't it?"

A burly man in a brown uniform strode up, carrying what looked like a short baseball bat. "Okay, guys! Back to work!"

Benny, like the others, scrambled up. "See you, kid," he said.

"I hope you do good as a mechanic, Benny."

He showed the gap in his teeth again. "Are you kidding? I ain't gonna be no stupid mechanic. I'm gonna be a bank robber."

"Move it, Harrison!" the big man ordered angrily.

"Aah, your mother's mustache," Benny growled under his breath, and moved along with his pals.

I watched him trudge back to the top of the levee. A bigger boy took a sandbag from another and staggered under its weight. Benny shook his head patiently, grabbed the bag and hurled it to the next person in line. Benny was all right. They weren't going to get him down, ever.

CHAPTER TEN

I wandered north along the levee. There was a sort of command post where crude wooden steps had been built up to the top of the sandbag wall. I climbed them and found a platform without railings that extended over the rushing water. A yellow and red post protruded from the muddy river. Large black numbers were painted on it. The lowest one I could see, about six inches above the water, was twenty-one.

Feeling the platform tremble beneath my feet, I clung tightly to Skipper's leash and looked around at the river, frighteningly wide and wild. To my left, it curved half a mile away, details hidden by the haze and continuing light drizzle. To my right, it went under the bridge, past a grain elevator and warehouses. I wondered how anyone imagined this battle could be won. Although there were many workers, they were stretched thin. On the far side, the fight had already been partially lost. The low ground was swamped more than it had been only minutes earlier.

A hand grabbed my shoulder painfully, turning me. It was my father. Mr. Sheehan, Mayor Gump and Colonel Thatcher were coming up the steps behind him. My father looked terrifically angry. "Don't you know you could fall off this thing and get yourself *killed*?" he yelled at me.

"I was being careful!" I protested.

Mayor Gump walked forward to get a view of the numbers on the post. "Look at that!" he exclaimed excitedly.

"Up two inches in less than thirty minutes!" Sheehan said.

"All that rain in Columbus last night. It'll go to twenty-five feet." For an instant no one spoke. Harmony was doomed. As if to punctuate that certainty, the platform trembled again.

"I don't see what more we can do," Sheehan said. "We'll have to pull everyone back to safety, Mr. Mayor."

"There's one more thing to do," my father told them sharply. "I mean our prisoners. They might still save the town, damn it!"

"We can't afford," Mayor Gump said shrilly, "to have our community ruined by—"

"Look!" my father said heatedly. "Every man we've got out here is exhausted! But the people in Columbus said it's not raining up there now. If we could just hold through today, the river might start to recede. We've got almost four hundred fresh, strong men out at the camp! Are you going to let Harmony go under, or are you going to put aside your hate and make this one last try?"

Sheehan replied slowly, "We have no assurance we can win anyway."

"If you don't try using our men, you know you're lost!" my father retorted.

Mayor Gump looked at Colonel Thatcher. "How long would it take to transport them?"

"Two hours," the colonel snapped.

Mayor Gump told Sheehan, "I'm willing to go along with—"

Sheehan cut in. "Get them, Colonel. It's our only chance."

The colonel turned to my father. "There's a telephone line open at the fire station, Davidson."

"Yes, sir!" my father snapped, heading for the steps. "You come with me!" he barked at me. We rushed down the steps, and I had to run to keep up with his long strides as we hurried uphill toward the fire station.

"Dad!" I panted. "Dad!"

"What?" he answered, distracted.

"Make sure they let Rudi out to come, too!" I begged.

"I don't know about Rudi." He scowled. "The people are afraid of these prisoners. If Rudi is recognized. . ."

"What do they think he would do? Escape?"

"He might. Any of them might."

I simply could not hold it back any longer. "They could have all escaped any time they wanted to, Dad."

269

"Don't talk nonsense. There's no time."

"There's a sewer system under the camp," I told him. "It dumps out in the creek just below our house. I explored it and climbed right up inside the camp."

"You?" His eyes were bulging. "What happened?"

"The prisoners grabbed me. They knew about the sewer right from the start, but they were afraid that if they told you or the colonel, they'd be in trouble. They were scared to death I would tell. But I didn't. And I wouldn't be telling now if it wasn't for Rudi. *He* knew, Dad."

"When did all this happen?" my father asked huskily.

"Right after that iceman hit a prisoner, and the meeting at the house when they all said how dangerous the prisoners were."

My father stared. His expression changed from disbelief to amazement, and then his mouth began to twitch. He bent over and began to choke. Then he began to laugh. The tears rolled down his cheeks. "All our wonderful security!" he managed. "And you—it's too good!"

I watched him laughing, and everyone around us stared as if he had gone mad. "So what about Rudi?" I demanded.

"I'll let him come," my father choked, still convulsed with laughter. "I'll let them all come." He banged me on the back. "Squirt, you're priceless! Come on! I've got to make a phone call." Still laughing, he led me away.

AFTER HE MADE HIS CALL, my father told me to go to the Henderson house, report what was happening and stay there. I obeyed the first part of his instructions but not the second.

"What are you doing here?" he demanded almost two hours later when he caught me serving coffee at the Red Cross station.

"They need help!" I told him, and thrust a cup at him. He rolled his eyes heavenward, took the coffee and hurried away.

The rain let up at noon just as the first prisoner trucks started arriving. Guards piled out, then the Germans; some of the prisoners began yelling orders in their own language. The other workers looked on dully, not fully comprehending. The guards got out of the way. Prisoners formed squads and ran into position. Bags were passed at a record pace. With new men on the line, we were deluged at the coffee station as haggard farmers stumbled up for a brief rest.

270

The trucks continued to rumble in and disgorge more men. Within an hour the prisoners were about the only men active on the lines. Engines coughed into action when prisoners, of their own volition, manned graders to move piles of sand closer to the levee. Fresh rows of sandbags piled up on the wall.

Thunder rolled overhead and the light rain resumed; the word was that it was not falling to the north. The prisoners took no rest breaks, and the guards, who had long since put down their rifles, worked side by side with the men. I heard reports second-hand. The water was at twenty-two feet. It had been holding steady, but now it was rising again.

By four o'clock I was exhausted. Some women appeared at the Red Cross station with fresh-baked doughnuts. I let them replace me on the coffee line, untied Skipper, who'd been waiting outside, and went searching for Rudi and my father.

There was just too much going on to find either of them easily. New truckloads of sand were being delivered. The levee had sprung some leaks, and men were trying to patch things up. I saw Mayor Gump and Mr. Sheehan on the observation platform. Sheehan spied me at the same moment and waved for me to join them. Puzzled, I climbed up the steps.

"Son, where's your father?" Sheehan asked worriedly.

"I don't know. I think he's working upstream."

"Find him. Get him back here." Sheehan pointed at the marker post jutting out of the muddy water nearby. "It's still rising."

I looked. It read twenty-three. "What can my dad do?"

Mayor Gump said, "We have to start evacuating parts of downtown. Your father has to get some prisoners together to help people move. We'll wait here to talk with him about it." The mayor's face worked. "Tell him . . . there isn't a moment to lose."

I looked upstream and spied my father perhaps a hundred yards away. He was atop the levee, issuing orders to prisoners. The roar of the river and all the confusion between us made signaling him impossible.

I plunged down the slippery wooden stairs of the observation platform and into the muddy chaos below. Pulling Skipper along on his leash, I ran the distance, arriving badly out of breath. The wall here was broader at its base than on top; I knew my father was up there, but I could not see him.

"Dad!" I called. My voice was swallowed up.

There was no time to lose. With Skipper coming after me, I scrambled up the slimy, gritty wall of bags. Reaching the top, I saw my father directing some prisoners who were stacking fresh bags in a fault in the levee. Staggering on the uneven bags, I hurried toward him.

"Dad, Mr. Sheehan said—"

"What are you doing here, Squirt? This whole thing is shaky!"

I dropped Skipper's leash. "Skipper, stay." I went forward to my father. "Dad, Mr. Sheehan and the mayor want to see you right away! They said that they need some prisoners to help evacuate the—"

I got no further. I had reached my father's side, and just as he stretched a steadying hand toward me, I stepped on a sandbag perilously near the edge. The bag shifted under my weight. I lost my balance. I think I yelled as I tried to catch his hand. I missed. My feet slid from under me and there was a sickening instant of fall, and then I tipped over the edge, tumbling out over the water.

"Squirt!" I heard my father cry despairingly.

I hit the shockingly cold water. My eyes were open, and all I saw for a moment were swirling brown bubbles. I tasted the muddy water, choking. Then I bobbed up, being turned rapidly around by the current. The force was terrifying, whirling me out away from the sandbag wall. I saw my father's face above me, etched in shock and fear. He was shouting something. I fought the current, but I was never a good swimmer.

"Help!" I yelled. And then, "Skipper!"

At the top of the wall a blur of tan and black moved. I saw my dog leap off the wall. He plunged into the water with a great splash. His head came up; his sightless eyes seemed frightened.

"Skipper! Here, boy! This way! Help!"

He heard me and swam strongly toward me. We were both being carried with horrifying speed downstream. Behind us, at least two men hit the water, trying to catch us, but we were already out of range. I was dimly aware of other men yelling and running atop the wall, now more than thirty feet away. I was mainly watching Skipper. I kept yelling. He swam head up, fighting the river.

My head went underwater. I started to strangle, and fought with all the remaining strength in my arms and legs. The cold had begun to sap me. I went under again and choked, almost vomiting. I was not going to make it. The river was too strong.

"Skipper!"

He was close. With a final brave lunge he reached me, banging his thick, matted wet fur into my face. I clutched his coat. Instantly his strength flowed through me. I felt the powerful motions of his legs as he started working to keep us both afloat. It isn't fair, I thought. I'll just drown him, too. But I was helpless without him. I clung, coughing and fighting for air.

We hurtled along at great speed. I could not see clearly but knew when we flashed by the raised observation platform. Men on top hurled a coil of rope through the air toward us. Releasing one hand, I lunged for it—and missed. I felt the stout rope brush my flailing legs as we were carried past.

Skipper, blind, knew none of this. His head was up, and he was gasping for air. My weight kept tugging his muzzle into the water, but he kept going valiantly, raising us both higher again. I saw to my despair that his efforts were actually carrying us farther into the center of the raging stream, away from the levee. I tried feebly to tug at him, to make him move toward the bank. It was no use. The current turned us completely around so that for a moment all I saw was the vast turgid expanse of the river, and then the bridge far ahead, and then, blurrily, the sandbag wall again. A terrifyingly huge tree sailed close to us.

"Skipper, go to the right!" I pleaded. "To the right!" But this was not an order he had learned. He knew it was my voice in his ears, the weight of my body tugging him downward in this terrible, unfamiliar universe. All he knew how to do was fight for our lives, and he was doing that with everything in him.

We turned again in the current. The big tree missed us and was a little ahead. Skipper made a choking sound and began swimming more spasmodically. I saw men leaping into the water off to our left. Then we spun around again, and more men were hitting the water up ahead of us. My hands were knots of pain in Skipper's thick fur. How was he keeping us up?

Without warning, something big and dark loomed into my vision—the great broken end of a log. The water drove it down upon us. I felt the shuddering impact as it hit Skipper's side, sending both of us under for a few seconds. Then we popped back up again, and I saw bright red in my dog's fur, and his blood splashed onto my hands. Skipper's movements were disconnected now. I could feel his strength go, the river start to take us under.

Voices yelling in German dinned in my ears; I fought to get my head up again with my last ounce of energy. There were faces in the water all around me. I recognized Rudi. Strong hands bore me up. Ropes hissed into the water around us, and more hands grasped my body. I saw Rudi grab a rope, felt it snake around my middle, sawing at me roughly.

The ropes pulled us toward the embankment. Perhaps I lost consciousness for a few seconds, because the next thing I knew, men were reaching down from the top of the wall and pulling me and the others out of the water. I was slung bodily onto the slippery, blessedly solid sandbags. I choked, retching. Hands pounded my back painfully, and I vomited. Rudi, hugging me, sat me up. Water streamed off of us.

"You are safe!" he told me. "You are safe!"

My father broke through the wall of bedraggled men around us. He, too, was soaked and wild-eyed. Seeing me, he threw himself to his knees and hugged me. "Thank God!" he rasped. "You're okay now! You're—"

"It was Skipper, Dad." I shuddered. "Skipper held me up. He saved my life until the guys could—" I stopped suddenly, sitting bolt upright. "Skipper?"

Rudi jumped to his feet. "The dog?" he yelled at the other men. With an oath he pushed them aside, opening a view to the rushing river. He stared. The river was empty of life.

"Skipper!" I screamed despairingly.

"Downstream!" Rudi told the men. "Run and look everywhere! Pass the word!"

Men scrambled, shouting. My father stared at me. "He'll be all right."

"A log hit us," I said. "Find him, Dad! He's hurt! Go help! Please!"

"I can't leave you, Squirt—"

"Dad!"

He let go of me then and hurried away. I sat hunched over, teeth chattering. But the chill went deeper than my aching body. They had to find him. They had to. It was forever before my father came back. His face told the story.

"We'll keep looking," he said. "He could have crawled out— might have gone farther downstream. We'll have people looking until we find him."

275

I did not speak. There were no words. I stared at the horrid river, its emptiness. The cold shook me from head to toe, and I knew.

He was gone.

THE RIVER CRESTED LATE that day at twenty-three feet four inches. The levees held. Harmony was saved.

I was not there when the workers finally saw the river start to recede and a great cheer went up along the battle line. I had been rushed to the Henderson house, where I was covered with high-piled blankets and fed tea and toast until I fell into an exhausted sleep.

In the morning the skies were cloudy, but without new rain. My father sternly ordered me to remain in bed and hurried downtown. My mother sat in a rocker and gently made sure his orders were obeyed this time. Aggie sat on the edge of the bed, watching me. The Hendersons poked in and out, trying to cheer me. I felt feverish and inconsolable.

After a few hours my father came back. He entered the bedroom cautiously, as if afraid of what he might find. My mother quietly left the room, taking Aggie with her. I put down my "Captain Marvell" comic.

"Well," my father said wearily, sitting on the bed, "it's down below nineteen feet. Looks like we won."

"*Won?*" I repeated bitterly.

"Squirt, I wish there was something I could say."

I stared at him, waiting to hear verification of what I already knew. "We've searched both banks. We had Boy Scouts go as far down as Circleville. We've looked everywhere."

"He's dead," I said. "I killed him."

My father's face twisted. "You didn't kill him."

I looked at him. There was nothing to say.

He smoothed the hair off my forehead. "It's okay to cry, you know."

I continued to stare, dry-eyed.

"Sometimes," he said gently, "it helps."

I picked up my stupid comic again. I looked at the brightly colored pictures and meaningless words. There was nothing inside me but a vast, echoing cold.

There were whispered consultations. The doctor came, and then

276

I heard more whispers in the hallway. Beyond the windows the sun beamed. I knew my parents were worried, but that was meaningless, too. I closed my eyes and again felt the cold thickness of Skipper's fur in my wet hands and saw the bright splash of his blood. His blood was on my hands.

IN THE NEXT WEEKS my family tried very hard. I stayed indoors at home, worked in desultory fashion at a model and cleaned out every memory of Skipper. I took his box to the trash dump, pulled his stake out of the yard, hurled his ball as deep as I could throw it into the woods.

"Maybe we could get another dog," my mother said one night at supper. I could only stare. I thought she was insane.

I hated it, the way they watched me, pretending to be cheerful, as if nothing were wrong. I stayed away from them as much as possible, in my room or sitting hidden inside the mouth of the drainage pipe that led to the camp. News registered on me, as when the bridge was repaired, or when the civic celebration of the town's deliverance from the flood was scheduled for late summer. But nothing really affected me.

"You have to let it go, darling," my mother told me one day. "You have to go on."

"Why?" I shot at her bitterly.

They made me go with them to the civic celebration. Main Street was roped off around the park, and more than half the town turned out. Under the hot sun a band played patriotic songs and twirlers twirled. The mayor made a speech and so did the colonel. There were American flags for everyone, whirligigs for the children. A squad of the German prisoners attended, standing stiffly at attention during the speeches and then staying to themselves near their truck.

In his speech Mayor Gump made it sound like our prisoners were all really Americans who got their birthplace mixed up. There was a lot of cheering over this. It sounded wrong to me. In my solitude I had pondered it. I knew that most of our prisoners were good men, victims of politics. I knew that their efforts had probably saved the town. But Nazi Germany was still a fact. Some of these men had voted for Hitler. They were not all good men. This confused me, but in my present state of mind it was just another puzzle that I would never understand.

277

Rudi was among the prisoner honor group. I saw him glancing at me repeatedly during the climax of the ceremony. This involved unveiling a marble obelisk about six feet tall, with a bronze plaque that commemorated the flood.

On the bottom of the plaque were the names of all the German prisoners who had helped save Harmony. The mayor said that the obelisk would stand forever, like the American way of life. Everyone applauded, and then the band played "The Stars and Stripes Forever."

Afterward people milled around. I refused an ice-cream cone. My parents edged me toward the truck where Rudi and some other prisoners were standing.

"So," Rudi said with a faint smile. "I hear you have been sick."

"I'm fine," I told him.

"You are thin."

I shrugged.

"We have something for you," Rudi said. He signaled to one of his companions, who went to the back of the truck. He took out a fairly large carton, the top open, and carried it to Rudi. Smiling, Rudi reached into the box and took out a squirming little black German shepherd puppy.

He thrust it toward me. "For you."

I pulled back in horror. "No!"

Rudi's smile faded. He continued to hold the wriggling pup. "But he is for you. From us. With our gratitude."

"I'll never have another dog! I don't want any other dog!"

"Squirt," my father said huskily, "take this puppy. You—"

"No! I don't want the responsibility! I don't want to love something and lose it again!"

"You must love again," Rudi told me. "This is living."

"I don't have to and I won't! Ever! It's all a gyp!"

My mother put her arm around me and knelt beside me. Her eyes were filled with concern. "Darling, you loved Skipper. That—"

"And I *killed* him!" I cried.

"You gave him life," my father said.

"I gave him nothing! All I did was get him killed!"

"He was blind. You gave him your love and you made his one summer a paradise. Squirt, don't you see? Because of you, he had far, far more than most animals do, even if they live to be a hundred! You gave him a grand life, son, and he gave his life back for you."

I stared at them in turn, then at the squirming little puppy still in Rudi's outstretched hands. I wanted no more of this pain, no more of such risk. But something beyond words—something in the love for me that radiated from each of them—penetrated into the cold of my depths, and I felt a great clotted pain deep inside begin to break loose.

Rudi extended the puppy closer. "Take him. See? He loves you already. Neither one of you can help yourself."

Without my willing it, my hands reached out. Rudi thrust the puppy into my arms. I tried to harden my heart. The little dog went into convulsions of joy, licking my face frantically, nipping at my ears.

I buried my face in his rich puppy fur and hugged him against me so tightly I thought I would pull his warmth completely inside my own body. And then, suddenly, I was weeping as I had never wept in my life.

Holding my new dog, my new Skipper, I cried with a racking sense of relief and salvation. The warmth of new life inside me felt like the heat of the sun itself.

EPILOGUE

In the fall the prisoners were moved to another work camp in Kentucky, and my father's new job took us to Washington. It was many years before I visited Harmony again. The small obelisk still stood, the bronze plaque green gray with the years. I went to see the old school, but it was gone, replaced by a building of steel and grass.

I found Jimmy Cantwell in his drugstore; he told me that Bill Sheehan was president of the bank now, and that Phil Inright, when a high school senior, had died in a terrible car accident. He had heard that Benny Harrison was in the army, a career man much decorated in Korea.

Our old house in the country was still there. They had a garden in the same spot where we had tried to grow one. As I stopped the car, an Irish setter ran out and barked at me, and I saw a boy in the side yard, swinging in an old tire. I drove on.

My own business, that of a reporter, took me many places in the next years, but it was not until the late 1970s that I finally went to Germany. My wife confessed she considered me a fool to consult the telephone directory in Munich, as there were many Gerhardts. But only one was listed as a veterinarian in a nearby community.

On a sunny Sunday afternoon we drove out of the beautiful city into the rolling countryside. Up an isolated mountain road we found a house with a steep Bavarian roof and window boxes ablaze with geraniums.

As I got out to open the car door for my wife, a stooped, gray-haired but unmistakable figure came around the house from the garden. Beside him, closely at heel, was a handsome shepherd who might have been the twin of my own long-lost Skipper, or the dog who replaced him in my life if never entirely in my heart.

"You see?" I told my wife. "He is still alive. He had to be."

She walked beside me toward the old man. His smile had not changed in the slightest.

"Welcome," he said. "I have been waiting for you."

We clasped hands.

Jack Bickham

Jack Bickham is no stranger to Reader's Digest Condensed Books. Two of his previous novels, *Baker's Hawk* and *Dinah, Blow Your Horn*, have already appeared in these pages, both to enthusiastic receptions.

Like Danny Davidson, the young hero of *All the Days Were Summer*, Bickham grew up in Columbus, Ohio. When he was a teenager his grandmother introduced him to the best-selling western novels of Zane Grey and thereafter he faithfully spent his pocket money on them at the local book shop. At seventeen years of age he began writing westerns himself. At first, he admits, he "didn't sell a lick." But he stuck with it. Today he is the widely published author of a·variety of books, including *The Apple Dumpling Gang*, which was made into a Walt Disney film.

Why are Bickham's books so popular? Perhaps the answer lies in what he tells the students at the University of Oklahoma, where he teaches journalism. "The job of the novelist is to say something affirmative about the human condition . . . that life is worth living."

In *All the Days Were Summer*, Bickham explores one of his favourite themes: the almost inevitable conflict between father and son as a boy moves into manhood. An experience from his own childhood served as the inspiration for the tunnel episode. "There was a sewer pipe in my neighbourhood," he explains with a chuckle. "But I was the kid who was too cowardly to go beyond the first turn."

Jack Bickham and his wife live in Norman, Oklahoma. Now that three of their four children have grown up and moved away from home, he has selected a small bedroom for his study. There, at an old rolltop desk, he writes his quota of ten pages every day.

Winner Harris

A CONDENSATION OF THE BOOK BY
Ian St. James

ILLUSTRATED BY BRIAN SANDERS
PUBLISHED BY HEINEMANN

Winning came naturally to Sam Harris.
His career might have had modest beginnings
but, as the owner of London's most glamorous
nightspot, Winner Harris had definitely reached
the top—and that's where he was determined to
stay, especially when pressure was exerted on
him to sell up. But even he was powerless
against the anonymous forces ranged against
him, and eventually his world crashed.

Yet, two years later, he was back fighting to re-
establish himself in London's glittering casino-
land. The stakes were high, far higher than
Harris realized as he challenged the might of the
international syndicate known as "the Pipeline"
Soon the trail of kidnappings, fear and torture
led to a tiny village in Sicily, and threatened not
only his life, but the lives of the beautiful and
vulnerable women close to him.

Chapter 1

It was still raining when the cab turned into Holborn. Water streaked the windows soaking up dust as it ran down the glass, so that peering out was like looking through bars. Last time the bars had been real. My last glimpse of the Old Bailey had been through the rear window of a Black Maria, handcuffed to a policeman. But that was two years ago.

We trundled westwards in the cab: into Trafalgar Square, along Pall Mall, into Piccadilly and along past the Ritz. For a moment I was tempted to stop for a drink, or to look in at Annabel's before lunch. But the moment passed. I wasn't ready to face that yet. The suit I wore felt uncomfortable and I knew it was important to look smart when I went back. When I went back! That was all I had thought about for months. Going back and taking the West End by storm the way I did before. But according to my solicitor, Lewis Collins, it would be harder this time.

I had just been to his office for an accounting session—to find out how I stood financially. When the business went into receivership my entire investment in it was lost: Kay had half the proceeds from the sale of Ashley Grange as part of her divorce settlement and my half went on personal guarantees and legal costs, along with most of my bank account. I had discovered Collins's greed too late, when I had already given him power of attorney over my affairs. Now all I had left was the mews cottage, and a cash balance at the bank of eight thousand, three hundred and twenty-eight pounds.

Besides, there was another complication. Collins had had the police onto him. They'd written to him a few weeks ago, and their letter read, in part: "Should Mr. Harris endeavour to re-open a casino in the Metropolitan area, we feel it proper to warn you that we shall most strenuously oppose the granting of a gaming licence to him, on the grounds that he is not a fit and proper person to hold such a licence." And Chief Inspector Davis had phoned to make sure there were no misunderstandings. The police would oppose the granting of a licence to me, or any associate of mine.

Lack of money was bad enough but a concerted effort by the police to keep me out of the gaming trade was worse. Hell, it was the only business I knew. Could they do that? I remembered the sneer on Davis's face when he climbed out of that Black Maria. *Davis* could do it—one way or another.

We drove through Hyde Park, not the most direct route to Battersea but the way I wanted to go, and the cabby was ready to oblige a fare-paying customer. Then we turned east along Oxford Street and back through Soho. For a while I forgot about Davis. I just drank in the sights. London has always been my place. When I was a kid all I ever wanted to be was someone important in London. It never mattered at what—just as long as the place was London. Now every street is alive with memories. There's not a restaurant worth mentioning where I haven't eaten, not a bar where I haven't had a drink, or a decent nightclub I haven't owned, or had a share in, or been on the verge of buying at one time or another.

Finally we drove across the river to the other world of Battersea. There I paid the cabby and went in search of Jack Green—who was where I expected him to be, in the bar of The Blue Posts. His face split into a grin like a crescent moon when he saw me, and he gripped my hand until my bones ached. He never said anything, not even hallo. He just stood there grinning, looking me up and down, until he raised his glass: "Cheers, Sam," he said, and I might just have come back from the Gents instead of two years in Brixton.

I could say a lot about Jack Green but he might read this one day and it would embarrass him. The truth is we are as close as two men can be. We grew up together in Battersea: same school, same girlfriends, same mob in the army, and when we came out we even went into the same line of business—restaurants and clubs and pubs. We nearly became partners at one time, but it never worked

286

out. In 1964 I gave Jack the money to start his restaurant—sixty thousand pounds, which was a lot of money in those days. But I had it then. I just wrote a cheque and said it was for old times' sake. Of course Jack insisted on repaying me and a year later he did, though he needn't have done, not as far as I was concerned. Odd, the way things work out. I was worth over a million then, and all Jack had was his two little pubs in Battersea. Now I was as good as broke and Jack owned The Blue Posts and The Golden Lion and his restaurant, plus a bit of property in the West End. He ran a Rolls-Royce and I didn't even have wheels. He had a beautiful wife and I was divorced.

"I expected you earlier," he said.

"I stopped in to see Collins."

He pulled the kind of face people pull when they smell bad fish. "Hope you took a witness."

"No need. Not this time. It doesn't take two people to listen to a catalogue of disasters."

"Money?" he asked softly. "Cleaned you out did he?"

I smiled. Jack has never trusted lawyers, least of all Collins. I said: "And worse. Davis phoned him. Apparently the police will oppose any application I make to get my licence back."

Jack smiled sadly. "That was always on the cards. I knew Davis was spreading the word. He was in here last night. Five minutes before closing time. Full of himself. He left a message. Said you'd never run a casino again—not while he's on the force."

I whistled. Spreading the word was right. If Davis had called on Jack, where else had he been? "Did Davis say anything else?"

"Never had a chance. It was closing time then so I saw him off the premises. Nothing personal, I said—just I've got my own licences to worry about."

"Watch yourself Jack—he's a spiteful devil."

"Don't we know it," he said. Then he leaped from the stool. "Come on, Sam, let's go home to lunch."

Jack's car was outside. Not many in Battersea own a Rolls-Royce and it would have excited envy in most. But I never met anyone envious of Jack. Most of the locals are downright proud of him. They know he is rich, stinking rich by their standards, but they don't mind that. He is a character, larger than life and twice as colourful. As far as Battersea is concerned Jack is "local boy makes good" and unlike others they could name he never moved to a posh part of

London—he just stayed in Battersea and turned The Dog's Home into an institution.

As restaurants go, The Dog's Home is unique. There's not much to it from the outside. It's on the corner of two rows of terraced houses—those tall, thin, four-storey town houses which sprang up in London a hundred years ago. Jack bought four of them with my money in 1964. Then he gutted them and made them into one building inside. People thought he was mad when he talked of opening a classy restaurant in a place like Battersea. Then it came to the sign going up. The Dog's Home! What a name! How can you serve a classy cordon bleu meal in a place called The Dog's Home? But Jack just shrugged: "Battersea Dogs Home is known the world over. It's almost the only famous thing in Battersea. So I'm paying a tribute to my old home town."

Inside, The Dog's Home is like a series of salons—that's the only way I can describe it. No single room has more than six tables; but the rooms are interconnected by tall double doors and the effect is amazingly graceful. And Jack's furnishings are all antiques. After dinner people adjourn to the sitting rooms—full of chaises longues and stuffed ottomans—to play backgammon or chess, or just sit around drinking. And talking, of course. The talk is something you always remember after a night at The Dog's Home.

Jack and his wife Maria live there. They have a couple of rooms on the top floor. It's more a way of life with him than a way of earning a living. The only thing he cares more about is Maria. When we went in she took one look at me, gave a little cry of welcome, and threw herself into my arms.

Jack's got an eye for beautiful things, but Maria is the loveliest. Pale skinned and raven haired with lips which curve provocatively. That day she was dressed in a cotton shirt and black velvet trousers. She had the figure of a young girl, which wasn't bad for a woman I knew to be thirty-five. "Oh Sam—it's so *good* to see you." She touched my face, tracing the line of my jaw the way a sculptor might examine a subject before starting work.

"No scars," I said, a shade self-consciously.

"None that show anyway." She kissed me, muttered something softly in Italian, then took my hand. "Sam, come and meet my cousin Lucia. She's here on holiday."

Only then did I see the other girl. She sat watching us, her legs crossed and one arm draped along the back of the Victorian sofa.

Her brown hair was kept in place by a tortoiseshell comb, her skin was bronzed that honey gold which people acquire on the Riviera, and her simple white dress emphasised her tan.

She shook hands with a cool, firm grip. "Hallo, Sam." Her voice was low pitched, almost husky, with the sort of smoky timbre you sometimes hear in a nightclub singer.

"Well—" I said, foolishly awkward. "This *is* a surprise. *Two* beautiful women to greet me."

Maria laughed. "Come on, let's eat." At the door she stopped and looked up at me. "Oh Sam, it's just so *good* to see you—so very good." Then she hugged me again.

IT WAS FUN, that lunch. Good food, chilled wine, two beautiful women, Jack—it was like coming alive again. Jack regaled us with stories about his clientele and we did a fair bit of reminiscing about the good old days. Afterwards we moved into the big sitting room for coffee. "I was at Rex Place last week, Sam," Maria said. "Gave the place an airing and restocked your booze cupboard."

Kay had left me and the mews cottage at the same time—while I was languishing in Brixton. I said: "Thanks—but you shouldn't have troubled."

"No trouble. I took your suits to be cleaned. They're back now, hanging in your wardrobe. And I gave the place a tidy up—cleared out the cupboards and so on." She picked at a loose thread in her trousers, and when she looked up she was blushing. "Anyway, Lucia gave me a hand. She did most of the cleaning."

Her red cheeks startled me. I wasn't sure what to make of them, so I just mumbled my thanks again.

We chatted for a while longer, which was selfish of me because I knew Jack and Maria usually slept for an hour in the afternoons—most people do when they're up until three or four every morning. But eventually I summoned up the energy to leave. Jack asked my plans for the evening. I said I would look around town. "Meet up with a few people. See what's changed—that kind of thing."

"Take Lucia," Maria suggested. "She'd love to go. We haven't shown her the nightlife yet. It's difficult—dragging Jack away from this place—"

"*No!*" Jack startled us. "Not tonight." He must have caught our expressions, because he shrugged and looked away. "I mean, not the *first* night. It'll be best for Sam to wander round by himself."

It was an awkward moment. I tried to make a joke of it by saying to Lucia: "You've found a big brother. I'll persuade him I'm a reformed character if you'd like to come?"

She hesitated for a split second, then smiled. "I'd love to—but not tonight, I'm washing my hair—"

"Come to lunch tomorrow, Sam." Maria put her hand on my arm. "Make the arrangements then."

My disappointment must have shown. Lucia smiled as she touched my hand goodbye. "Till tomorrow," she said. "I look forward to it."

So I said goodbye, and followed Jack downstairs. He insisted on lending me his car and I was about to drive away when he said: "Do me a favour, Sam. Don't worry about cash. When you're ready let me know. I've got the best part of a hundred grand not doing much at the moment."

"Partners?"

"I'd like that," he said solemnly. "But I've got enough on my plate. If you can sort your licences out why not use the money to get going again? Pay me back when you feel like it."

What can you say to something like that? I punched him on the arm and promised to think about it. Then I drove back to the West End. I was a bit wary about going to the mews. The place held too many memories. Kay would fill every room. The beginning of our married life had been spent there, and it had been a happy time, despite what happened afterwards. But—memories or not—the cottage was all I had left, so it had to be faced.

Rex Place is just behind Park Lane. A hundred years ago the carriage trade stabled their horses there. Now all the little boxes have been converted into tiny dwellings, each with a flower box windowsill. Mine was standard size: a tiny entrance hall, sitting room, a kitchen-diner, and an opening under the stairs euphemistically called a study. Upstairs was a bedroom and a bathroom and that was the lot.

Once inside I knew why Maria had blushed. Everything was different. Only the desk and the filing cabinet remained in their place in the alcove—nothing else was the same. Jack and Maria had refurnished it from top to bottom. Upstairs my clothes were in the wardrobes—but nothing there belonged to Kay. Her photograph had gone from the dressing table and not even an old scarf remained to remind me of her. She might never have lived there.

I telephoned Maria and thanked her for her thoughtfulness, and afterwards I spent a long time in the shower, getting the smell of Brixton out of my pores. Good food and lovely women are not all you miss in jail. Apart from the loss of the big freedom, you miss all the little ones—simple things like enjoying a shower in privacy, the smell of decent soap, or the feel of proper bath towels.

I planned my evening as I dressed. The people I would meet, the places I would visit. Only when I fumbled with my cuff links did I realize how nervous I was. Being accepted back was the most important thing left to me. Ten years ago I had been rich and successful. Now, at forty-two, I had to start again from scratch.

Looking back I realize what a fool I was. Jack had seen it coming—which was why Lucia had been kept out of things that first night. But at that moment I was so full of the welcome Jack and Maria had given me that I was blind to everything else. So by eight o'clock I was behind the wheel of the Rolls, dressed in a dinner jacket, looking forward to the evening ahead of me.

It was disastrous. I went to The Lucky Seven first. I knew Charlie Dyson from the old days. He had been my head waiter at Winston's before branching out on his own. But minutes after I arrived Charlie came into the bar and asked me to leave. I was astonished. "Leave? But Charlie I only just got here—"

"Your membership expired," he said, stony faced. "The doorman shouldn't have let you in." I never stayed to argue. What was the point? Dammit, I only went to see how he was! I climbed back into the car, hot with temper, and drove away.

When I reached The Captain Morgan in Piccadilly, the doorman had never seen me before, so he delayed me in the foyer while he sent for Ron Brown. But Ron was nowhere to be found and with no one to vouch for me I was refused admittance. Then at Gaston's I was turned round in my tracks by two big fellows who appeared either side of me as I crossed the threshold. Six strides took us back to the Rolls. To take them both on was asking for trouble. I climbed back into the car and drove away.

I went to see Tony Fields at The Green Door. Tony was in a big way of business, not as big as I once was but big enough. He stood me a drink and though he seemed genuinely pleased to see me I sensed he was uncomfortable. He was sympathetic about the trial and went on to talk about some of the things that had happened while I was inside. A company called Tuskers had bought my club and restaurant chain from the Receiver—for about ten per cent of what they were worth. I knew that, of course. But who were Tuskers?

"Who's running the show, Tony? Anyone I know?"

He shook his head: "They came from nowhere. Provincial crowd—started in Cardiff, I think. Never thought they had the bread to buy half the West End—but that's what they're doing."

We had another drink, and eventually he said, "Word's out on you, Sam. It's as simple as that. Everyone's had a touch of the frighteners. Anyone helps you and he'll be in dead trouble."

"Who says so? Chief Inspector Davis?"

He shrugged. "Davis ain't helping—but he's not the real pressure." He finished his drink. "A lot's changed, Sam. Matter of fact I'm thinking of getting out."

"Come off it, Tony—the casinos are taking a fortune. Those Arabs still lose an oilwell a night."

"Casinos are OK. But the restaurant and club trade is down." He hesitated for a long moment. "And most of us are bled dry for protection just to open the door at night."

I whistled. There was no point in beating around the bush so I asked how much he was paying.

He spread the fingers of both hands. "Every week," he said.

Ten thousand *a week!* I tried to imagine his cash flow. "What about the police? Have they been asked to help?"

"Eric Blockley asked. And a week later he was killed."

"I read about that. Wasn't he killed in a boating accident?"

"That's what the papers said. They also said you were guilty of a brutal crime. I never believed that either."

I was grateful for that and said so. He was getting a bit fidgety by this time, but I pushed him to answer a couple more questions. "Who's putting the bite on, Tony?"

He shook his head. "We never see the same man twice. They're well organized."

I took a deep breath, then asked: "You serious about selling?"

"I'd like to—that's the truth. Trouble is finding a buyer. It ain't easy. There's only one outfit buying—" He pulled a face. "Correction—at the prices they're paying, that's stealing."

"Tuskers?" I guessed, and when he nodded I asked: "Tony, would you sell to me? If I could raise a decent price?"

His eyes filled with a look of complete incredulity: "You're not listening, Sam. Don't you understand? Word's out on you. I'm not even supposed to sell you a *drink*." He paused. Then his face slowly relaxed into a smile. "Besides, what's the point? Word is the police will oppose a dog licence with your name on."

I was too sick to smile. Two years ago a door had shut me in prison. Now another one was keeping me out of the West End.

Tony put an arm across my shoulder. "Something will break for you, Sam. It's got to—a man like you—"

"Sure, Tony."

He ushered me away from the bar and into the foyer. I drove around town for the next hour. Just round and round. Miles and miles of flashing neon, dozens of clubs and bars and restaurants owned by people who had been friends of mine. I cursed them all and turned west back to Rex Place, feeling sorry for myself and thinking it was a hell of a way to spend my first night of freedom.

Once back in the cottage I flung my jacket over a chair and went out to the kitchen to make some coffee. I was too agitated for sleep and the night stretched ahead of me like an empty road. But I had plenty to think about.

I STARTED IN BUSINESS when I came out of the army. Jack Green and I were demobbed on the same day and we were both full of plans for the future. National Service had wasted two years of our lives and we were in a hurry to make up the lost time.

Along with my savings I had a starting capital of nearly ninety pounds, and a week later I went into business. Sam's Place I called it. It was nothing to look at—a crack in the wall at the cheaper end of Oxford Street. Still, Charlie Forte had started with a milk bar in Regent Street and he wasn't exactly starving. Sam's Place measured twenty feet by six and a half. It was going to be a sandwich bar. Lunchtime trade only—take-away sandwiches for clerks and typists. I did the place up myself, painted the walls and ceiling. Funny how hard you'll work when you want something badly enough. My old Mum was alive then and I lived with her in Battersea. I used to get up at four in the morning and go straight to Smithfield, where I would buy joints of ham, pork and beef at good prices, and take them home to Mum to cook. Then I went to Covent Garden and bought tomatoes and lettuce and cucumbers. Butter and cheese came from a local wholesaler, and bread and doughnuts were delivered to Sam's Place at half past eight every morning. That was when the real work started. The idea was to get everything ready by eleven. Then I made a cup of coffee and waited for the rush. And rush they did—you would never believe how much food an eight-stone typist can put away.

At about three o'clock I used to shut the door, hang up the closed sign and make sure everything was clean for the morning. Then I cashed up. It was the best part of the day, so I left it until last—to give me something to look forward to while I was scrubbing the floor.

Generally I got home to Battersea at about half past four. Mum would have cooked the roasts so my first job was to slice the cold meat for the morning. Then I snoozed for an hour before going out again. I worked as a barman in the evening at The Jolly Friar in Buckley Street. The wages paid my "running costs", so that everything I made at Sam's Place was ploughed back into the business. Four years later I had nine little sandwich bars—all round the West End and into the City. I was twenty-four—and on my way.

It was 1961 when I sold the lot—for a hundred thousand. I had saved a fair bit too, so at the beginning of '62 I was worth the best part of a hundred and thirty thousand, and all in cash.

I quit my job at The Jolly Friar then. I had only kept it on for the experience it gave me: doing their ordering had taught me all about stock control and things like that—at least as far as the licenced trade was concerned. I could even read a balance sheet—and write books up to trial balance, so all in all I was beginning to feel like a proper businessman.

Jack and I went to Paris to celebrate. He had bought a half share in his first pub by then—The Blue Posts. Neither of us had been abroad before and we couldn't speak a word of French. But what a time we had! And once back in London I took a long look at the nightlife. Compared with Paris it was as lively as a Sunday School.

It took me months to make my next move, because I wanted to be *sure*. Something told me nightclubs were my big chance and I was afraid a mistake would ruin it. So I spread my risk in the end, and opened two places within six months of each other—and a third nine months after that.

Winston's was a lunchtime club for young businessmen who were making money and needed somewhere to take their clients. I spent forty thousand doing it up, put a ticker tape in the lobby, hired my chef from Simpson's and a commissionaire from

Sandhurst—and went into business. Within a month I had two thousand members.

Jennifer's was very different. It was a disco at the bottom end of Carnaby Street. We had strobe lighting and hairy two-hundred watt amplifiers, and a few dim corners for lovers. It's old hat now but it was as fresh as a daisy then.

But I was still gearing myself up for the big one. Both of my ventures were generating cash and I still had a chunk of capital to invest—but investing it was going to require the biggest decision of my life. Eventually I found what I was looking for in Regent Street. The Point of View opened on New Year's Eve 1963, and the swinging sixties really roared into town. I gave a party for just about every celebrity in London and my old Mum came up from Battersea. She wore a new frock and had her hair fixed, and I gave her a rope of pearls to commemorate the occasion—so she wandered around smiling at people, just like the Queen Mum, and had a lovely time. Jack came too, of course, with his new girlfriend, a slim, dark-haired Italian beauty by the name of Maria.

We made the headlines in all the gossip columns the next morning—even had pictures in a lot of them. Full of stories about Swinging Sam Harris and how the jet set was coming to London. I thought it was terrific. Mum started a scrap book of press cuttings and the future looked golden.

Then, halfway through April, Mum died. I used to get home to Battersea at about half past four most mornings, later sometimes. Mum would snooze during the afternoons and evenings, and wait up for me with a cup of tea. It was crazy really. I had more than fifty waiters working for me then, but Mum *had* to make me a cup of tea.

Well, one morning in April, when I got home, she was dead. She was sitting in front of what was left of the fire, and I thought she had dozed off at first, but as soon as I touched her I knew she was dead. The shock hit me like a hammer. We had always been close—Mum and I. Dad was killed when we were bombed out in the war, and Mum brought me up single-handed, so life had never been easy.

I pulled myself together eventually. Then I went round the corner to phone the doctor. And Jack, of course. He arrived ten minutes later, with a half bottle of brandy in his overcoat pocket. We sat drinking until the grey light of a Battersea morning crept into the kitchen. The doctor came and went—and two days later I buried Mum at the little cemetery near Chelsea Football Ground.

It's all so long ago now. Looking back I'm glad she died when she did. I was on my way up then. She had lunched at Winston's and been to Jennifer's and had a few dinners at The Point of View. And she was so *proud* of it. Thank God she never lived to see me charged with murder—or sat through the trial at the Oxford Assizes—or listened to the judge pass sentence on me.

Chapter 2

I slept badly that first night back at Rex Place and woke with a splitting headache. But the simple act of making coffee cheered me up. After all, Rex Place was a sight better than Brixton Prison. If I had problems at least I was free to do something about them. So within an hour I had shaved and dressed, and was ready to start thinking about my future.

A prison record may not automatically disbar a man from holding a gaming licence, or even one to sell spirits—but it doesn't help. In both cases licences are issued by magistrates and the applicant has to prove himself a "fit and proper person" to hold such a licence. My trial had left me disillusioned with lawyers. But my application for licences would be heard by magistrates—so, as I had finished with Lewis Collins, I was back in the business of hiring lawyers.

Tomlinson saw me at eleven o'clock. A tall, thin man of about sixty, he chose his words carefully, like an old fashioned schoolmaster. Of course, he knew who I was. Lawyers follow court cases the way most men follow football. He listened attentively as I told him my side of things. Now and then he asked a question and noted my answers on a pad. Eventually I had told him all there was to tell, and it was his turn to speak. "How old are you, Mr. Harris?"

"Forty-two."

"You're still a young man. Full of energy. Experienced in life and in business. Why not try something else?"

"Because the casino business is what I know best."

He raised his eyebrows. "Oh, come now. Business is business."

"Are you saying I'll never get back?"

He hesitated at that; lawyers always seem to when you ask a direct question. "I'm saying it's unlikely. If the police lodge a strenuous objection the magistrates are bound to take note of it."

"But it's not the police—it's Davis."

"Who happens to be a policeman—and a fairly senior one." He steepled his fingers and looked at me severely. "You have just finished a term of imprisonment and Chief Inspector Davis was largely responsible for bringing the prosecution—"

"Not entirely *responsible*. But his manoeuvering had a lot to do—"

"That's as may be," Tomlinson said with surprising forcefulness. "But the fact is that you pleaded guilty. It's all very well to condemn the practice of plea bargaining now, but now is too late."

I glowered but said nothing. So he went on: "It seems to me that there is a good deal of personal animosity between you and Chief Inspector Davis."

"Bloody right. So what about my licences?"

He sighed, as if I was behaving like an obstinate schoolboy, and in truth I was beginning to feel like one. "You must realize by now that a plea of guilty means exactly what it says. An admission of guilt. And the police will make a meal of that, believe me. What more proof, they will ask, do the honourable magistrates require to find this man unsuitable?"

It was all very depressing but I was determined not to show how I felt. I said: "So we're in for a fight. I knew that anyway. I want you to set up a meeting with the best QC you can get. Let's go in with all guns firing. The bigger the guns—"

"The more resounding the defeat," he interrupted, and there was no doubt about whose defeat he meant. He looked at me steadily. "Then you're quite determined to go ahead—whatever my advice?"

I nodded cheerfully, but in case I broke into a smile, he said: "It will cost money. I don't wish to be indelicate but . . ."

I took the bank statement Collins had given me from my pocket. It was all the money I had in the world, but whoever said justice is cheap never fought battles in the law courts of London. I said: "A thousand should cover it, shouldn't it?"

He thought for a moment, then nodded. So I wrote him a cheque.

He came downstairs to say goodbye. "All in all it will take five to six weeks. I'll make immediate inquiries about retaining a QC. Meanwhile, I'll apply for a hearing—which will get it on the lists." He moistened his lips. "Unfortunately that will also put the other side on notice of our intentions, so no doubt the police will take a special interest in your affairs. Discretion had better be your watchword. Keep out of trouble yourself and don't mix with any undesirable characters." His severe look melted to a wintry smile.

"In the unlikely event of you obtaining licences, you'll have to put up with more than the usual amount of police scrutiny. Your new club will need the Archbishop of Canterbury as headwaiter and the Queen of England on the cash desk."

Tomlinson had been far from encouraging. But after driving around for a while I began to feel more cheerful. So what if it was hard to start again? When had life been easy? Jack was willing to stake me and Maria was still fond of me, so I couldn't be *all bad*, despite the cold shoulder around town last night.

I drove Jack's car down to Battersea and went to The Golden Lion. When I arrived Jack was at the bar talking racing with some cronies of his. I waited until they had drifted away, then I said: "You might have warned me."

He grinned. He knew what I meant. "Last night? What difference would it have made? You'd have gone anyway."

"You had any trouble from this protection mob?"

He shook his head. "Battersea's a bit out of the way for them. There's really only me down here, and I'm small fry—those boys are catching bigger fish."

We finished our drinks and left The Golden Lion. In the car I asked him about Tuskers.

"Welsh, I think. Leastways they've got some clubs down in Cardiff." He pulled out to overtake a cyclist. "Buying your lot from the Receiver got them started in the West End. Since then they've gone from strength to strength. Must have plenty of cash behind them." Jack seemed to lack curiosity to an extent which amazed me. By the sound of it Tuskers were getting bigger every day, yet as far as he was concerned they could be operating in Moscow.

"About the money," I said. "The hundred thousand. You were serious weren't you?"

"Ever know me joke about cash?"

"Thanks." Then I told him about my meeting with Tomlinson, and about what I planned to do.

He pulled up outside The Dog's Home just as I finished. "And this Tomlinson?" he asked. "He reckons you're wasting time and money, does he?"

I nodded, knowing I had to ask if he thought so too, even though I might not like his answer—but someone lending you a hundred thousand is at least entitled to an opinion. He climbed out of the car and locked the door. "What I think doesn't matter," he said, leading the way in. "The money's yours anyway. Sam Harris will come again—whatever the odds."

Maria and Lucia were in the big sitting room upstairs. Maria kissed me and Lucia smiled hallo from across the room. "Come on," Jack said happily, "let's have a drink before lunch."

Nobody can be depressed when Jack's in a good mood, especially when Maria is sharing it with him. And when I wasn't laughing I was watching Lucia—and trying not to show it. She was as delicate as— I don't know what. As lace, as a fresh rose, or Dresden china. Yet she had this *sureness* about her. Whenever she looked at me I sensed some hidden knowledge, some awareness of what was going on which she was withholding from me. Enigmatic, but not off-putting—in fact just the opposite.

So I spent a happy hour, laughing at Jack's stories and admiring Lucia—while all the time warning myself against her. After all, I was nearly broke. It was time to fight—not a time to be distracted by someone like Lucia. And I was just resigning myself to that when she turned and asked: "Where are we going tonight?"

I thought she was talking to all of us for a moment, then I realized she meant just me. "Tonight?" I repeated stupidly.

"I washed my hair *last* night—remember? Didn't you say something about showing me the town?" She looked away. "But of course, if you've made other arrangements . . ."

"No," I said quickly. "No, I haven't made other arrangements. It's just that—well London is closed as far as I'm concerned. I've been warned off."

Lucia's eyes opened a mile wide as she teased me. "The whole of London is closed? You must be a *very* wicked man."

We all laughed and it gave me a chance to think of where I might take her. Eventually we settled on a show and supper afterwards, and despite my earlier reservations I looked forward to it.

I left The Dog's Home at about half past three. There's a theatre booking office in the Hilton so I took a taxi there first, to see what tickets I could get at short notice. Luckily they had two cancellations for a revue at the Garrick, and with the tickets safely in my pocket I took the cab on to Rex Place.

Once back in the little sitting room I got to thinking about what Tomlinson had said. It concentrated my mind on the case we had to present to the magistrates. No doubt Davis would paint me as the biggest rogue ever to walk the streets of London, whereas we had to show my trial and prison sentence as being quite unrepresentative of my life as a whole. Of course when I met the QC in chambers I would explain the background, but I wondered if I couldn't do better than that.

I brewed a pot of tea, collected a scrap pad from the desk, settled into an armchair, and began to search my mind for anything which might help.

RUNNING A NIGHTCLUB is an education. At least it was for me. The Point of View was my university. It was there that I grew up, matured, and smoothed enough of the rough edges to acquire a certain amount of what they call polish. I said "Harris" instead of "'Arris" and could tell good wine from bad. And I had become a fair businessman, even though I say it myself. So I suppose I was turning into what I always wanted to be—"someone important in London."

On the other hand Jack wanted a quieter life. "Bigger doesn't always mean better," he would say and although I tried to persuade him to come in with me he decided not to. Halfway through '64 I gave him the money for The Dog's Home and shortly afterwards I was invited to invest in the casino business.

Legitimate gambling arrived in London with the Gaming Act of 1961, after which casinos became part of the nightlife scene and big business. *Very* big business.

I'm not really a gambler—unless you count being a business-man—but a hell of a lot of rubbish gets talked about gambling. When I started running casinos, I came in for stick from all sorts of quarters. Of course some people do become gambling addicts, but I'm damned if I'll accept it's criminal to run a casino because it encourages the habit. You may as well say anyone who serves a pint of bitter encourages alcoholism.

Anyway, four years after The Point of View opened its doors for the very first time, I had a phone call one day from a man named Charlie Weston. I knew him slightly; he was a member of Winston's among other things, and an occasional visitor to The Point of View. He said he had some business to talk about so we fixed a meeting for eleven the next morning, and I thought no more of it.

He arrived with a whole team of people: a lawyer, an architect, and a merchant banker. After shaking hands I arranged them on chairs around my office and asked Weston what was on his mind.

He was older than me, but not by much. I was thirty then and he

300

was maybe thirty-six. I knew he was fairly big in the haulage business—he never stopped boasting about it at Winston's—but apart from that I knew little of his background. He was a well-built man about six feet two and broad with it—strong and rough, with a handshake like a coal crusher.

That meeting lasted six hours! I had sandwiches and drinks sent in from the club, and innumerable pots of coffee, until, at about five o'clock, we had talked ourselves to a standstill. What it amounted to was this: Charlie had just bought into two casinos and had obtained the necessary licences to open a third, at the bottom end of Park Lane. After Charlie had shown me copies of the latest accounts to prove what a viable business he had acquired, the merchant banker took over. His bank had been making a study of the leisure industry—and here were the figures. They confirmed my gut feeling that the casino business had growth written all over it. Then the lawyer explained that they were looking for a partner. The idea was that Charlie and I merge our businesses, then float a public company and sell a chunk of our stock to the investing public. That would give us the cash to finance the new venture, and after that everything would come up roses.

What impressed me was the proposed new board of directors. Lord Hardman was to be chairman, and the others would be the Earl of Darlington, Lew Douglas, Charlie and me. Hardman was blue-blooded business, owning outright the oldest firm of wine merchants in the country, Darlington was on the board of the merchant bank and Lew Douglas owned a string of hotels. But it was more than that. They wanted me—a boy from Battersea—to run the whole show as managing director.

We discussed a whole lot of things. I was surprised to learn that Charlie Weston knew Hardman quite well. Their backgrounds were totally different, but Charlie ran a fleet of road tankers to transport Hardman's wine in bulk, and the two had come to know each other through business.

Jack brought Maria over to dinner that night. He thought I was mad even to consider it. "What's in it for you?" he wanted to know. "You've already got everything you want. Your own business, money, the good life. What more do you want?"

"I dunno, but I've got to think about it. This could be big—the biggest there is."

"You're out of your mind." He sounded disgusted. "Those guys will give you so much trouble you'll wish you were back in Oxford Street making sandwiches."

Maria looked concerned, but I patted her hand and said, "I'm a big boy now. I can look after myself."

We floated Apex Holdings on 2nd April 1967. The shares were over-subscribed three or four times, so the underwriters made a killing and I was officially a millionaire—at least on paper. I was thirty-one years old and life had never been sweeter.

I was given my head. Board meetings were a formality. Hardman presided with a light touch and was invariably the first to propose the acceptance of my report each month. There was rarely any dissension. They were all experienced businessmen and as long as the figures were coming out right they were happy to let me get on with it—and running Apex proved to be little different from running my own venture. The scale was bigger, that's all.

Mind you, I worked all hours God sent, but bit by bit I assembled a strong team of people. Of course I made mistakes, who doesn't? Luckily none were too serious because we prospered overall.

It was at the end of a very busy twelve months that I met Kay. Apex were sponsoring a number of races at Ascot, principally the Apex Gold Cup, and we had a permanent box for entertaining VIPs. Lord Hardman came down for the third day of the meeting, and brought his daughter.

I wasn't immediately attracted to her. I was working when we met—being host at these business things demands concentration. So all I saw then was a girl of medium height, with golden hair and blue eyes, who raised her glass and said something—but the words were lost in the general chatter.

After the last race was over people began to gather their things for the journey to town. We were a party of twenty and a fleet of cars waited to convoy us back to London. I had just sent a message to Tom, my driver, to bring the cars round when Kay excused herself from the people she was with and came over to join me. "Still giving orders, Mr. Harris? Doesn't the boss ever relax?"

"The name's Sam. And I never give orders. It's better to ask."

She looked down at the racecourse. The crowds were still milling around, saying goodbyes or making arrangements to meet again later. She turned back to me and put one hand on my lapel. "It's my birthday. I'm having a party tonight—will you come?"

There was nothing aggressive in her manner, but her directness was unusual, as though she went through life taking whatever she wanted as if it were hers *by right*. I tried to imagine her kind of party. Our backgrounds were light years apart. I had called at the Hardman country home once, and nobody left there without being impressed. Hardmans through the ages looked down from the walls and their ghosts paced the terrace at night.

"I'm afraid I'm working," I said, then added more diplomatically, "My business plays havoc with my social life."

"Don't you have managers? You don't have to lock up, balance the books at the end of the night—that sort of thing?"

I smiled. "No, not these days."

"Then come when you finish. I'll expect you," she said simply. "Will you have eaten or shall I see you for dinner?"

There seemed no way of avoiding it without seeming boorish. "I won't be finished until about ten—" I began, but she cut me short.

"Dinner will be waiting for you." She thrust a card into my hand just as her father came over to join us. "Au revoir, Mr. Harris," she said. "It's been a perfect day—" she lowered her voice "—and it's not over yet."

Back in the West End I said goodbye to my guests and went home to change for the evening. I had developed a routine by then: I would call on each of our clubs and restaurants between eight and midnight, though never in the same order, stay for a drink, answer any queries, and then move on.

I left for Kay's place in Chelsea at nine forty-five, expecting the worst and cursing myself for being talked into going. The meal would be one of those buffet affairs—how else could she keep dinner for me at a party?—the wine would be undistinguished and the guests would be the crowd of chinless wonders who make up the upper-class party set. I promised myself to stay an hour.

But when the cab drew up outside the address she had given me the place was in darkness. There were no signs of a party at all. Puzzled, I asked the cabby to wait while I rang the bell. Perhaps it was a joke? It seemed bloody silly and my temper was rising when the door phone squawked in my ear: "Come up, Sam—I'm on the first floor." The automatic lock buzzed and the door moved open an inch, so I paid the cabby and went in.

It was a well-appointed house. Thick carpet drifted upwards from the wide hall onto the sweep of the staircase. Kay was waiting for me on the landing—and she took my breath away.

That fact alone needs explaining. After all, nightclubs and casinos draw beautiful girls like moths to a flame. I was no stranger to attractive women, so what was so *special* about Kay?

Sensuality, I think. She was neither pretty nor beautiful, at least not in the accepted sense. She had a superb figure but although her face was striking, it was certainly not beautiful. Yet she was the most *feminine* woman I ever met.

That night she wore grey satin, and the neckline of her dress plunged deeply, caught itself together at the waist and then reached down to the floor. Any movement revealed a long leg up to the thigh. She wore silver slippers and I guessed—correctly as it turned out—nothing else.

She kissed me lightly on the cheek. "How like you to be exactly on time." Taking my arm she led me into a large room, graciously furnished to serve as combined sitting and dining room. "Downstairs belongs to Father," she explained. "But up here's all mine."

I sat on a sofa and watched her pour me a drink. I raised the glass. "Happy Birthday."

"It is, isn't it?" she said curiously. "I've prepared Chinese by the way. I hope you like it."

"That's fine." I looked round the room, vaguely puzzled. "Where are the others? Am I the first?"

She seemed surprised. "What others? There's only you and I. Do you mind?"

"No—I don't *mind*. But I thought you said a party."

"We're having it. Relax. Enjoy yourself." She laughed. "Have another drink before I fix dinner."

Dinner was superb. Kay was a brilliant cook. We drank *sake* with the meal and as the evening passed, the talk became more personal. "Why aren't you married?" she asked me.

"Oh, I don't know. I've been too busy I suppose. Besides I've never wanted to get married."

"And you always do what you want." She poured the last of the wine into my glass. "You are dynamic, and positive, and you do exactly what you want. Most people don't. They lack the courage."

It was all very flattering. I asked: "And what kind of courage do you have?"

She grinned. "Oh, yours of course—but a lot more of it."

I laughed and conceded the point. But it must be easy to be dynamic and positive if you were as rich and vivacious as she was.

305

"But seriously," she said, "you ought to get married."

"What on earth for?"

"You're a man in a hurry, Sam. A winner. And you need a wife for the next steps. And a house—with your wife presiding over dinner parties. An elegant background to impress the fat cats—prove you're here to stay, not a flash in the pan."

I wondered how much of this had been gleaned from her father. Edgar Hardman was a blue-blooded old bastard, but he was also the shrewdest businessman I knew. And he *was* my chairman. I asked: "So I should settle down? Buy some carpet slippers? Get a dog?"

"Not all on the same day. But I still want you to get married."

"And you always get what you want?"

She smiled her radiant smile and leaned across to kiss me lightly on the lips. "That's already established. Shall we take our drinks across to the fire?" After that the talk became steadily more intimate and of course we ended up in bed, where I discovered that cooking was Kay's *second* most polished accomplishment. I awoke at around six the following morning to the realization that, once again, she was moving gently into my arms. "By the way," I murmured, holding her off for a moment. "Just how old were you yesterday?"

She took ages to reply, but eventually she said, "Twenty-two years, four months and seventeen days."

"Funny kind of birthday."

"I thought it was lovely." She nibbled my ear. "Besides, some things should be celebrated more than once a year."

And they were. We married five months later. I bought Rex Place and we were very happy to begin with—ecstatically so during the early months. I was busy at Apex, while Kay was looking for "our place in the country". The mews cottage suited me but Kay wanted something larger, something grand, somewhere she could entertain, give weekend parties. Eventually she found Ashley Grange. It was an impressive house, standing in sixty acres of farmland.

"But when am I going to be here?" I asked, when we drove down to see it.

She stroked my neck. "It's only an hour down the motorway. Less if you hurry. And I'll be waiting for you."

She had planned the first party even before the builders had finished decorating the place. I remember asking who was to be invited. "Winners," she said simply. "People like you. Don't worry, darling—you'll love them."

And so the pattern was established. Anyone who made the headlines came to Ashley Grange. Tennis players, racing drivers, pop singers—they all beat their way down the M4 to our place.

After Kay "opened" Ashley Grange, which is more or less what it amounted to, the early hours of most mornings found me driving down the motorway. But after about a year it became too much, so I arranged for Kay to spend two nights a week at Rex Place. But people were always staying at Ashley Grange and it was increasingly difficult for her to get up to town—so I grew accustomed to spending a couple of nights a week alone at Rex Place.

I was too busy to ask if I was happy. What is happiness anyway? I was building Apex into the biggest company of its kind in Europe. My working day was a long one but I enjoyed every minute of it. And as for life with Kay—well, we adapted. We had little time to ourselves. Dinner at Ashley Grange was rarely for less than ten, and most of the diners would be house guests. Kay arranged their comings and goings without reference to me. They did their best to amuse me when I was at home, but they were her friends, not mine.

I remember going home once. It had been an easier day than most and I left the West End before the rush hour, arriving at Ashley Grange at about five thirty. Four strangers were using the tennis court and screams of excitement came from the swimming pool. I parked the Rolls next to some other cars and crunched across the drive and into the house. Kay was in the drawing room, pouring a drink for a dark-haired man, tanned and athletic-looking, dressed in casual clothes and decorated with a lot of personal jewellery.

"Hi, Winner." She kissed me and turned to make the introductions. "Come and meet Marcel."

That was when I met Marcel Faberge for the very first time. He was a song writer with a hit in the charts.

"Marcel can't stay for the party," Kay said. "I've spent the afternoon trying to change his mind, but he insists on leaving in half an hour's time."

The Frenchman murmured something about an early morning recording session in Hamburg and having to be at Heathrow for a seven o'clock flight. I said it was a shame, and we chatted until his taxi arrived. His case was already packed and we went to the door to say our goodbyes. He kissed her hand. "Kay, what can I say about the past two days? It's been an experience to treasure."

After he had gone I finished my drink and then went up to change. Kay joined me in the shower. "What about your guests?" I asked.

"They don't own me," she said, and for the very first time I wondered if they sometimes did.

THE BELL STARTLED ME. I thought it was the door at first and it took a few seconds to realize it was the telephone. When I answered Lucia said: "Have we still got a date tonight?"

"*Oh Lord!*" It was half past seven! I had arranged to collect her from The Dog's Home at seven. The show at the Garrick started at eight! My notes lay scattered over the sitting-room carpet and I still had to change for the evening.

"Look Lucia—I've been working on something—I hadn't realized —look, I'm *very* sorry." It sounded so inadequate. I tried again. "It'll take me ten minutes to wash and change, but by the time I get there—"

"I'll get a cab to your place," she said. Then she paused. The tone of her voice changed. "Unless you'd rather not bother—"

"I've got the tickets. And booked a table at Oliver's." The latter wasn't true but it would be by the time she reached Rex Place. "And I'm looking forward to it."

"Obviously," she said acidly. "Well, if you're quite *sure*—"

"Positive."

"Then I'm on my way."

As it happened Lucia had trouble in getting a cab, so it was almost eight thirty when she arrived. She had looked beautiful earlier, but dressed to go out she was sensational.

"Look, I've made a bit of a mess of things—"

"I can see that," she said, looking at the scraps of paper still littering the floor.

I started to collect them up. "I booked for a show," I began, then we both said together, "but it's a bit late now." We laughed, and I relaxed. "Let's have a drink here and replan the evening."

"Fine."

She handed me a few sheets of paper which had found their way onto the chesterfield. "Is this what you were working on?"

"Yes—sort of. I had an idea earlier and got a bit carried away with it." I mixed her a Bloody Mary, while telling her about the kind of case I would have to present in the magistrates court.

When I finished she said: "Sam, that sounds *terribly* important. May I read what you've written?"

I hesitated. Not everything remembered had been set down but there was enough to indicate what I felt about Kay. It was too private, too revealing. But there was another reason for hesitating— the warmth in her eyes might be damaged by a snub, and I felt in need of friends. So I mumbled: "Well, if you're really interested—"

"Of course I am." Her voice told me to trust her. I settled in a chair and watched her decipher my scrawl. When she finished she looked up and tapped the notes: "When have these to be finished?"

I shrugged. "Tomlinson is making an appointment with counsel as soon as possible. Which probably means next week."

She turned to the last page. "You're only as far as the end of the sixties. You've a long way to go . . ." She looked serious, as if thinking about something else. "Do you have a typewriter?"

"There's a portable by the desk. I'm not sure—"

"Well, let's go out to dinner and come back here afterwards. You should write some more. These notes are vital. I'll take everything down in shorthand and type it up later."

Of course I protested, but she was determined to do things her way, and after a while I gave in. We chatted for another half hour and then left for Oliver's. I hailed a taxi in Mount Street and as I climbed in a car pulled out behind us. I had no reason to pay particular attention, and what with Lucia chatting happily beside me I forgot about it, or at least I did until later.

Oliver's is in Dover Street, on the corner. The ground floor entrance leads into the bar and beyond that to the restaurant, with a tiny dance floor in the middle. Above is an open gallery, which turns the dance floor into a central courtyard. I had used the restaurant before but not often, so I felt there was a good chance of not being recognized. Our table overlooked the dance floor. The food was good, the wine excellent, and Lucia looked ravishing. Brixton Prison seemed a lifetime away.

During the meal I tried to get to know her. After all, she knew a lot about me whereas I knew next to nothing about her—only that she was Maria's cousin. She told me some things quite easily. For example she had been educated in Geneva and New York, as well as Milan, which explained why she didn't have an Italian accent. But she was more reticent about others. She was expensively dressed but she gave no hint as to where the money came from, and she

309

casually mentioned a man's name when talking about Geneva, and another when talking about New York—but the impression given was they were just good friends, nothing more. I was glad about that, despite my determination not to become involved.

Suddenly—astonishingly—someone banged into my shoulder so hard that I was almost knocked out of my chair. I grabbed the table to steady myself. "What the hell—"

A man staggered drunkenly, lurching as he pointed at me. "Harris, isn't it?" he shouted, slurring the words. "*Winner* Harris?"

"What the devil do you think you're doing?" I snapped, conscious of Lucia's startled expression.

"It *is* Harris!" the man roared. "Don't bloody pretend it isn't! So they've let you loose again, have they?" He was well built, in his mid forties, smartly dressed but for the loosened tie. I had never seen him before in my life. "Get up, damn you," he shouted.

Two waiters rushed over and tried to restrain him, but he shook them off contemptuously. "You owe me fifty thousand quid, Harris. That's what I lost when Apex went up the shoot. *Fifty thousand!*"

One of the waiters grabbed the man's arm and tried to pull him away from the wreckage of our table, but the man knocked him away and shouted: "You're a swindler, Harris. A *bloody swindler!* A crook. A filthy damn crook and a murderer! MURDERER!" He sent the other waiter spinning and came at me with fists flying.

Whoever he was he was no fighter. His left arm looped wide and I stepped inside and hit him twice, once below the heart and again on the point of his jaw as his knees buckled. A woman screamed at a nearby table and a moment later others joined in. The headwaiter arrived and the whole place erupted into pandemonium. The man at my feet never moved. Flash bulbs popped and the gloom of the restaurant cracked open with the flashes of light.

The next half hour was a nightmare. Lucia was magnificent. She delivered some very sharp sounding Italian to the staff in general, then helped usher people back to their tables. A police car arrived within minutes. Chief Inspector Davis, of all people, stepped through the entrance. He gave me a sour look but refrained from speaking immediately. Instead he directed the man with him to begin taking statements and interviewing people.

The odd thing was that the man who attacked me was not to be found, yet nobody remembered seeing him go. And the waiters said he was a stranger, they had never seen him before. He had arrived ten minutes before the incident and gone straight to the bar to have a drink until some friends joined him. After which nobody took any notice until he appeared on the gallery with me.

Eventually Davis came over to me. "I ought to run you in, Harris," he growled. "Assault. Causing a disturbance."

"Really? Well this time I've got witnesses—so just you try."

He flushed angrily. I thought he *would* arrest me for a moment—witnesses or otherwise. Then he leaned forward so that only I could hear him. "You're trouble, Harris. Out thirty-six hours and in a punch-up. Do us a favour and go and play somewhere else."

"Someone should straighten you out, Davis. You're supposed to protect the public—not persecute them."

"Take my advice," he growled back. "Get out of town."

"When I'm ready. Right now I'm ready to take this young lady home. If you've quite finished?"

He turned and walked away.

Chapter 3

I overslept the following morning. After taking Lucia by cab to The Dog's Home I had gone back to Rex Place and straight to bed, but not to sleep. The events of the evening were too vivid in my mind for that: the man who had attacked me in the restaurant, the photographers who had apparently been waiting. Then I forgot about them and thought of Lucia instead. Finally I dozed off, until the telephone woke me at ten o'clock.

It took me a moment to recognize the voice: "Tomlinson?"

"You've seen the newspapers, I suppose? What the *devil* are you playing at?"

I shifted the phone to the other ear and swung my feet onto the floor. I was still only half awake. Not that Tomlinson cared. He was barking: "You'd better get across here straight away."

It took me forty minutes and he was still simmering when I arrived. His secretary left a pile of press cuttings on his desk, gave me a funny look and then scuttled off to make some coffee.

I picked up the top one. It was from the *Express*. A photograph showed me with raised fists, standing over the man in the restaurant. Two waiters looked on, while in the background Lucia's lovely features were caught in an expression of alarm. The headline read: "Winner Harris is back in town!" All the papers carried the same story, except for the *Mail*, which broke the pattern with a shot of Lucia descending the gallery staircase, and a story speculating on the identity of "Winner Harris's lovely new girlfriend".

Tomlinson barely gave me time to read them: "Well?" he demanded. "You undertook to stay out of trouble. Only *yesterday* for Heaven's sake! And now *this!* I'm waiting for an explanation."

Tomlinson's attitude sparked my temper. It took self-control not to have a go at him, but something told me I would need him before this mess was cleared up. "All right—let's calm down. Any undertaking given by me was abided by. Trouble is we didn't get an undertaking from the other side."

"What *other* side?"

"The other side who attacked me in a restaurant. It was a put-up job—can't you see that?"

"*Mr. Harris,*" Tomlinson said. "You claimed it was a put-up job when you were last in trouble. Now you're in trouble again—and *again* it's a put-up job. Is that what you're asking me to believe?"

"One—" I ticked the points off on my fingers. "A man attacks me in a restaurant. He attacked *me*—not the other way about. Witnesses will testify to that. Two—he came there for that *express purpose*. He arrived, had a drink until the staff forgot about him, then he came looking for me. Three—"

"That's supposition!" Tomlinson said sharply.

"Like hell it is. He wasn't *led* upstairs. He wasn't *shown* to a table by a waiter. He came *looking* for me. Three—at least two people in that restaurant had cameras. When was the last time you took your camera out to dinner? *Think about it!* Two people there expected to photograph something. And when they did they delivered prints to every paper in Fleet Street."

I was still ticking points off. "Four—the man who attacked me vanishes afterwards. He's a mystery. Even the photographs don't show his face, just his body crumpled on the floor. And five—Chief Inspector Davis seems to have been standing by in the wings."

Some of the anger faded from his face: "Well . . . put like that—" He cleared his throat. "I may have been wrong about you, Mr. Harris. In which case I apologize."

I sighed. An apology was irrelevant. I said: "Forget it. You were angry because it makes your job harder. This won't help our case with the magistrates one little bit, will it?"

"I'm afraid not." He steepled his fingers and moistened his lips in that characteristic way of his. Then he spoke slowly and carefully: "Even though it appears not to have been your fault, I think it probably destroys what slender chance we had with the magistrates. Violence seems to follow you around, Mr. Harris."

I stood up and walked to the window. I knew what he was saying. Pull out now. Tony Fields's words came back to me: "*I'd like to get out, Sam*—" Would I feel that if I got my licences back? Maybe all I was doing was trying to recapture the past. . . .

I sighed and walked back to my chair. "I don't know how much I want my licences back. But this pressure—intimidation if you like— that's something else. Whatever I do next is for *me* to decide. Dammit, I *won't* be pushed!"

"So we go on?"

"Yes." I glared defiance across the desk, half expecting him to say I was wasting my time and money. But instead he gave his wintry smile and said he had arranged to see counsel at the end of the following week. "And yesterday I sent off our application for a court hearing. They'll get it this morning." He tapped the newspapers. "After reading these over breakfast."

I shrugged. "Who's the QC?"

"Tim Hastings," he said, and watched for my reaction. Even *I* had heard of Hastings. His reputation for cross examination scared most people rigid even before they took the stand. "Ten thirty on the twelfth at his chambers. Perhaps you'd call here first, say at ten, and we'll go round together."

I nodded. Then I told him about the stuff I was writing at Rex Place. He listened politely, but when I finished he said, "I don't guarantee he'll read it."

"No? Well you get it onto his desk before we meet and say I'll be bloody angry if he doesn't know it off by heart."

The telephone was ringing when I returned to Rex Place. It was Lucia, reaffirming her willingness to play secretary. I looked at the pile of notes and breathed a sigh of relief. Time was short if Tomlinson was to read them before passing them to Hastings. But I hesitated about involving Lucia further.

"Have you seen the papers?"

"Sam Harris's lovely new girlfriend? Don't worry, I'll come in disguise."

"Maybe you shouldn't come at all?"

"I won't, unless you want me to," she said quickly.

A better man would have stopped her there; someone less selfish would have turned her away rather than risk her getting hurt. But I felt in need of company and the prospect of *her* company was especially appealing. I said: "Of course I want you to come."

Afterwards I made coffee and sandwiches, and then settled down to work on the notes. Reviewing my life had taken on a new urgency. Only *part* of it was to provide Tomlinson with material. Now there was another reason. I felt like a running man, looking back over his shoulder. Who was trying to push me out of the West End? And why?

CASINOS ARE MACHINES for making money and we made a packet at the end of the sixties. We had moved into betting shops by acquiring a chain of forty from a company called Winwright. It was a heady time and hardly a week passed without mention of Apex Holdings in the financial press. And while I made news in the "heavies", Kay became the darling of the gossip columnists. She was England's number one party-giver by then and it seemed that nothing could stifle people's curiosity about the lives of the rich. Kay became a willing target. She was articulate, outspoken, and very photogenic. "Winner's Wife" they called her.

Business continued to flourish well into the seventies—at least for Apex Holdings. The money passing across the green baize tables around the West End made London the gambling capital of the world. It was the classic case of being in the *right* business in the *right* place at the *right* time. Winner Harris had it made. I was what I always wanted to be—someone important in London.

But the takeover attempt in '75 caught me napping. True we were making huge profits, but Apex stock had never been the most sought after in the City. So when somebody started to buy our shares in a big way it caught me off guard. On 2nd May our shares opened at a pound seventy-five, and six hours later the price had risen to two pounds twenty. Somebody *big* was buying—and buying in large enough blocks to send the price through the ceiling.

I spent the whole of the following morning telephoning our brokers, while Edgar Hardman called up half of the City. But all to no avail. Another bout of heavy buying took the price through the two pounds fifty barrier, but try though we did, we failed to discover the identity of the bidder.

314

The next day was a Saturday, so mercifully the market was closed. I had stayed in town overnight and was drinking a solitary cup of coffee for breakfast when the telephone rang. "My name is Corrao," he said after I confirmed I was speaking. "I would very much like to meet you. Rather urgently if possible."

"In what connection?" I asked brusquely, still worrying about the report in the *Financial Times* open in front of me.

"It concerns Apex Holdings, Mr. Harris. And the events of the past forty-eight hours."

That cleared my brain faster than the scalding hot coffee. "Who are you representing?"

He laughed softly. "An interested party."

Stalemate. His attitude irritated me, but I knew I had to meet him. I *had* to find out who was buying our shares. But I tried to sound unconcerned. "I suppose that *might* be possible—a meeting I mean. Perhaps if you called me on Tuesday or Wednesday—"

He laughed again. "Better make it sooner than that. After all, a few more days trading on the Stock Exchange could change the circumstances of our meeting dramatically."

It was an open threat. They would continue to buy until they obtained control. I sighed. "When had you in mind for a meeting?"

"Why not now? Join me for breakfast. I'm at the Hilton. The Kennedy Suite." We met half an hour later. He was a trim little man, dressed in black mohair and a pyjama-striped shirt. Dark hair was pasted across the crown of his head as neatly as a bathing cap, and he sported a thin moustache. Smoked glasses hid his eyes.

He poured coffee. "People I represent are interested in acquiring control of Apex Holdings, Mr. Harris. I am authorized to make a very generous offer for your shares."

"Are you going to tell me who is behind all this?"

He jerked his head. "I'm afraid not. That would exceed my brief."

"The Stock Exchange have issued a recommendation on take-overs," I said carefully. "Anyone holding more than ten per cent should declare their interest—and their intention."

He smiled. "You just said it all, Mr. Harris—a recommendation."

I gave up. "So what are they offering?"

"Two forty-five. It's a very good offer."

It was. Two forty-five was less than the inflated price on the Exchange but that was just for mopping up smaller interests. The price was inevitably lower for a big block of shares.

315

I thought about the others. Between us we controlled a third of the voting shares—Hardman, Charlie Weston, Lew Douglas, Darlington and myself. When we put the merger together and floated the public issue we had signed an agreement saying that none of us could dispose of any shares without the consent of the others. I wondered how they would feel now? Hardman and Darlington and I would reject almost any offer because of the growth potential, but I was not so sure about Douglas or Charlie Weston. I reached a decision and decided to bluff. "I'm sorry but my shares are not for sale. Neither are those of my co-directors."

He drummed the fingers of his right hand on the table. "My people spent a lot of money on Apex stock last week. They won't like being stuck with a minority holding."

"Then tell them to sell."

"On a falling market? They'd take a loss. A very big loss. They won't like that either, Mr. Harris."

"Tough luck," I said cheerfully.

His eyes were hidden behind the dark glasses, but he was obviously watching me. He said: "We haven't time to bargain. I'll go to two fifty-five but not a penny more. I suggest you accept our offer and tell your colleagues to do the same."

His arrogance was astonishing. His blatant threat made me see red and I snapped: "You can suggest whatever you damn well like. The answer remains the same."

"You have until Monday to change your mind," he growled. "I suggest you consult your colleagues before giving me your final answer."

"I'll do that, but don't hold your breath—you've had our answer."

Never have I seen a man fly into a rage so quickly. "You're making a big mistake," he snapped. "This thing of ours is too strong for you. We shall take Apex, Mr. Harris. *One way or another!*"

I had listened to all the threats I could take for one morning, so I left—and I never did find out who Corrao was working for, though I spent a deal of time thinking about it.

We had a board meeting the next day. They were all there—Edgar Hardman, Darlington, Lew Douglas and Charlie Weston. It was a Sunday but the emergency demanded that we met before the market re-opened. I outlined the details of my meeting with Corrao, and I knew I had a fight on my hands as soon as I finished.

"It's a bloody good offer." Lew Douglas waved his cigar with

316

excitement. "Take the money and run, eh? Two fifty-five can't be bad." He was already working out his profit on a scratch pad.

Charlie Weston was inclined to agree. "Justifies the initial investment. An excellent return. I wonder who he's acting for."

"Who gives a damn," Douglas said. "As long as he's got the cash."

"Sam?" Edgar Hardman cocked his head, inviting my opinion. He was a tough old bird. Carried himself like a soldier. Strong square jaw, blue eyes, brusque upper-class voice—but never any *side* to him. He and I had always got on, even before I married his daughter. "Sam," he said, "what do you make of it?"

So I began my argument—how two fifty-five was a good price *now* but that Apex would be worth a lot more by the end of the year. Casinos were like geese laying golden eggs—and only fools sold those. But Douglas was adamant. "What you're saying is all very well, but it's only a forecast. Cash in the hand, Sam—can't beat it."

It went on like that for another hour—Darlington wavering, Weston and Douglas for accepting, Edgar prodding for ideas. Perhaps it was inevitable that Lew Douglas and I were on opposite sides. He and I had never got on. He was too flashy for my liking, and a loudmouth to boot. His father had built up the string of hotels which provided Douglas with his fortune, and Lew himself had been over-indulged, overfed and over-valued since he was born. There was a streak of greediness in him which I found offensive.

Suddenly Edgar Hardman put forward his astonishing suggestion. "Look, I'm sorry you feel this way, Lew," he said, "so I'll make you an offer. I'll guarantee your shares will be worth more than two fifty-five in a year's time."

Douglas was caught off guard. We all were. "Guarantee *how?*"

Edgar shrugged. "Sign a note if you like—guaranteeing you three pounds say, in twelve months' time."

It was a gigantic vote of confidence in me—but a hell of a way to buy peace in the board room. Then Charlie Weston asked: "Does that offer stand for the rest of us?"

He spoke quietly but it was like a bomb going off. Edgar under-writing Douglas's corner was one thing—Douglas only owned fifty thousand shares. Charlie Weston owned ten times as many. Under-writing his end could cost Edgar *one and a half million pounds!*

Edgar stiffened. "Do I take it that you'd like it too?"

Charlie grinned. "I just can't bear to see Lew get the better of me. He's getting a hell of a good deal—I'd like it too."

318

I immediately protested and to his credit Darlington supported me. We said Edgar would be mad to even consider it. It was a ludicrous risk, and all so damned unnecessary. But our words fell on deaf ears. "Very well then," Edgar said frostily. "You've got the same deal as Lew." He turned to Darlington. "How about you?"

"Don't be a bloody fool, Edgar. You know me better than that. If you and Sam want to reject this offer, I'll go along with you."

I was very unhappy about the whole business. I tried to pursue it there and then, but Edgar declared the meeting closed and left immediately afterwards. And when I phoned the next day he just dismissed it—told me to forget it and concentrate on running Apex. Of course I never *forgot* it—but after that so much was happening at Apex that it did slip my mind at times.

The only thing which gave me any pleasure was in giving Corrao his answer—and after that the takeover battle *really* started. We did all the usual things—full page advertisements in the financial press: profit forecasts, anticipated growth, that kind of thing. The actual battle only lasted a month. By then most shareholders had decided to hang on to their shares and the price stabilized—and some weeks after that Corrao's nominees started to sell. The price slipped back then, and we reckoned they must have lost half a million pounds. Not that we cared. We were jubilant, basking in the joy of victory as life returned to normal. Except we got it wrong. Life never returned to normal. It was merely the lull before the storm.

I WAS STILL thinking about Corrao when the doorbell rang. Lucia had said to give her an hour or so and a quick look at my watch said it was about her time. I hurried to greet her, but I faced empty air when I opened the door. A letter lay inside, on the mat, and a cab was easing quickly away from the kerb.

I was still staring after it when a flame-red Mini turned into Rex Place. The driver's window was down and Lucia smiled up at me as she drew alongside. I opened the door and she unwound onto the pavement—five feet eight of curves knitted into a black sweater and ski pants. The casual brush of her lips on mine suggested a relationship established months instead of hours. She ducked back into the car and collected a wicker basket from the back seat. "Dinner," she announced, turning towards the front door.

I closed the door and watched her carry the basket into the kitchen. "Where did the car come from?" I asked.

"Rented." She came back. "Important letter?" she asked.

"It must be. Someone paid a cabby to deliver it."

I opened the manilla envelope. Three pieces of paper were in it—if you count an airline ticket as a piece of paper: British Airways, first class to Sydney, *one way.* The other two were press cuttings, one from the *Telegraph* and the second from Sydney's *Morning Star.* The story from the *Telegraph* was eight months old and carried the headline: "London Club Owner dies in river accident". Eric Blockley smiled up at me, next to a photograph of his wrecked cabin cruiser. The Sydney story was more recent. "Gambling booms down under" it said, and along the bottom had been typed: *"Go Winner— before your luck runs out."*

Lucia buried her head in her hands and whispered, "Mary Mother of Christ, please help us."

I was on the telephone to Tomlinson a minute later. "Can you get over here? I've got some—" I struggled for the right expression, "I've got some new material which you ought to see." I expected him to protest, claim other appointments or pressing engagements, but he agreed to come with barely a moment's hesitation.

I telephoned British Airways. "Some friends of mine promised to book me a flight to Sydney. On—on the second." *The second was Saturday!* They really were in a hurry! "Look I'm sorry to be a pest but they've probably forgotten all about it and it's vital I catch that flight."

The girl said: "May I have your name, sir, and I'll check with reservations." I told her and waited. A minute later she said: "Mr. Sam Harris. You have a reservation on our flight KL629, Mr. Harris. Departure 0900 from Heathrow on Saturday the second."

I sighed with mock relief and then said. "Look, can you tell me where it was booked? If I knew where the ticket was booked I would know whom to thank. I mean it would be one guy in Manchester, but a different one in Birmingham—see what I mean?"

"Hold the line." Her voice was cooler now. I was becoming a nuisance. I tightened my grip on the telephone until she returned. "Your reservation was made at our office in Victoria this morning."

"Victoria? Victoria, *London?* This morning?"

"Right on all counts," she said wearily.

"Did they—did *he*—pay by cheque? You see if I had his name—"

"Your ticket was bought for cash, Mr. Harris."

"*Cash?* Isn't that unusual?"

320

She said: "You must have some very rich friends, Mr. Harris," and hung up.

Then the door bell rang. It was Chief Inspector Davis—with a friend.

"Come in," I said. "I was just about to send for you."

"An invitation from Winner Harris," Davis murmured. "That *is* an honour." Lucia came in with coffee just then, and I made the introductions. After she had put the coffee on a low table she seemed uncertain about what to do next.

"I'll fetch some more cups," she said, and fled to the kitchen.

"Keep her out of this, Davis," I said with an edge to my voice.

"Out of what?" he inquired mildly.

We were still glaring at each other when Lucia returned with the cups. She must have heard what was said because she said: "Sam, if you don't need me perhaps I could start typing the notes?" She turned to the desk. "Are these them?"

The little Olivetti was in its case next to the desk. She picked it up. "OK to work upstairs? It will be more comfortable than the kitchen."

We watched her go and Davis asked: "Writing a book, Mr. Harris?"

"Rogues I have known. You've got the star part."

The other man said: "That could be construed as an offensive remark. We could arrest you for that."

"What's your name?" I asked coldly.

"Evans—Detective Sergeant Evans."

"Listen, Evans. Someone took a swipe at me yesterday. *Now* I'm getting threatening letters—and all you talk about is arresting *me* for offensive remarks. Get your priorities right or I'll be shouting offensive remarks at the chief commissioner."

Davis blinked. "Threatening letters?"

The airline ticket and press cuttings were still on the coffee table. "Delivered by taxi," I said. "Read them yourself."

They were still huddled over the press cuttings when Tomlinson arrived. I relieved him of his coat and took him in. "The police go around in pairs in this town," I explained. "Battersea gets constables but we get the top brass."

The effect of the introduction was quite startling. Tomlinson looked downright angry and Davis seemed vaguely apprehensive, as if he had been caught in the act. Certainly he moderated his

321

attitude towards me. "Have you any idea who might have sent this?" he asked, casting an anxious glance at Tomlinson.

"How about you? You're always telling me to get out of town."

Tomlinson broke it up. "The question is, what are you going to do about it? I cannot stress too strongly—"

"Are you asking for police protection?" Evans interrupted.

What *was* I asking for? I certainly could live without the law on my doorstep. I said: "I want you to find the source of this intimidation—"

Davis snorted. "Intimidation! We've nothing to go on have we? You could have fabricated this stuff yourself—"

"You're crazy!"

"You've even got a typewriter in the house. You could have typed that message yourself."

I threw my hands into the air and looked at Tomlinson for support. He was furious. He sat bolt upright, his face even whiter than usual. "May I ask why you called here today, Inspector?"

"To get a statement signed about last night," Davis snapped. Then he remembered he was speaking to Tomlinson so he moderated his tone. "But if it's inconvenient we could make an appointment."

"Mr. Harris's written statement will be with you tomorrow," Tomlinson said crisply. "Now, unless you have any other query?"

Davis and Evans swapped glances, but they knew they were beaten. So they contented themselves by making a few notes and asking additional questions. Then they asked to take the press cuttings and the airline ticket, plus the envelope of course—and after collecting a receipt Tomlinson showed them out. When he came back he was blazing angry. "Being your solicitor means I represent you *at law*, Mr. Harris! Which includes the police. You refuse to answer *any* questions without me being present. That's your right and by Heavens you are going to insist on it."

It took him ten minutes to cool down. Meeting Davis had been a good thing for Tomlinson. It had brought him into the fight—pushed him into my corner. When we finished working on my statement, he asked me to call at his office in the morning to sign it. Then he said: "I think I'll try for an earlier meeting with Hastings. If he can spare the time, could you make Monday at eleven?"

"Yes, I think so."

"What about the notes you are working on—will they be ready?"

322

I thought of Lucia. "I'll have them ready by Friday morning."

"Good, get them round to me then, will you? I'll have a look at them before sending them on to Hastings."

I thanked him and, after letting him out, I went upstairs. Lucia was standing at the window, looking out into Rex Place. It was dusk outside and the room was grey with shadow, but I saw the typewriter on the dressing table beside a neat pile of paper.

Lucia turned as I entered the room. "Everyone gone?" I nodded. "I've been reading the life and times of Sam Harris." She was frowning over the last sheet of paper. "This man Corrao?" she said. "What did he look like?"

I cast my mind back over the years. "Short and thin, about five six, weighing a lot less than me. Black hair, dark glasses."

"Anything else?"

I shrugged. "That's not bad going. I only met the guy once."

"Think Sam—it is *important*."

"Why?" I asked, thinking instead of Tomlinson. "The lawyers won't be interested in—"

"Forget the lawyers," she said sharply. "Concentrate on Corrao. Try Sam—was there *anything else* about him?"

I stared at her, wondering what she meant. "What about his hands, Sam?" she prompted. "Was there anything special about his *hands?*"

Suddenly I went cold. I knew what she meant. I saw Corrao back in that hotel suite, sitting at the breakfast table. Buttering a slice of toast *with one hand*. His right hand. Then he did the same with the marmalade. He poured the coffee with his right hand, put the pot down, picked up the cup and passed it to me—*all with his right hand*, just as if his left was paralysed or something.

I looked at Lucia's excited expression. How had she known? And what the hell did she mean— *"forget the lawyers"?*

"His *hands*, Sam. Do you remember them?"

I was as cold as the grave. Cold with a sudden fear. Fear of betrayal. "Yes, I remember. And I remember something else. How calm you were at Oliver's after the fight. Calm, like a nurse, like a professional. And I remember you saying these notes are vital. But not for the lawyers, apparently?"

I looked at her, hating myself for distrusting her. I forced the words out, made myself ask: *"Who are you, Lucia?"*

She sat perfectly still, but even from across the room I sensed the

323

tension in her body. Before she could move I heard a step on the stairs and a moment later the bedroom door opened. "Good evening, Mr. Harris. No, don't move—please remain as you are."

I watched in amazement as another man entered. I swung back to Lucia. *She knew them!* From the look on her face they were friends of hers. "You heard?" she asked the first man.

He nodded, without taking his eyes away from me.

The world, *my* world, was going mad. Heard? How? Us, talking together in that little room? Lucia had helped refurnish the cottage. Refurnished it with hidden microphones? I took a deep breath and asked: "Who the hell are you?"

"My name's Henderson. Attached to the Home Office." He produced a wallet and flicked a plastic identity card in front of me.

Lucia asked: "What happens now?" She spoke to him, not me.

The man called Henderson said: "Headquarters." He shrugged, dismissing the questions in her eyes. "It had to happen, sooner or later." He looked at me. "You're coming with us, Mr. Harris. Don't be alarmed. You'll be quite safe, well looked after. My colleague will help you pack an overnight bag."

"Am I being arrested?"

He smiled, faintly amused, then he shook his head. "You'll be back here within a day or two."

Lucia said: "Sam, it's all for the best—please believe me."

But I was incapable of believing anyone by then. "I'm not going." I swung back to the two men as they came towards me. "Look, what the hell is this all about? How did you get in here anyway?"

Henderson smiled. "There's no cause for alarm, Mr. Harris." He moved a pace nearer, reaching out to take hold of my elbow. "Let's be sensible. There are two of us and only one of you."

I lashed out but he rode the punch like a professional fighter. Then his mate wrapped himself over my back like an overcoat. I struggled and shouted, but I was no match for both of them, and a minute later I was being forced into a chair as my sleeve was pushed up above the elbow. Lucia was pleading: "Sam, it's all for the best. Really it is."

I was telling them to go to hell, but it made no difference. The needle went in just the same. Suddenly my body felt heavy and the lights went dim in the room. Then all I could see was the ceiling, reducing in size, as big as a tablecloth one minute, then as small as a postage stamp. And then I blacked out.

Chapter 4

It was morning when I awoke, and the curtains were drawn back. I propped myself up in the strange bed and looked about me. It was a large room, comfortably furnished with a dressing table, two armchairs and a wardrobe. Wall-to-wall carpet followed the shape of the bay windows. Regency-striped wallpaper rose to a high ceiling. It was an old-fashioned, country-house kind of room.

A cock crowed in the far distance. That was the only sound. No traffic noise, no transistor radios. A dull hangover buzzed at the back of my eyes but apart from that I felt well enough. I crossed the room to the windows which overlooked a kitchen garden: neat rows of bean sticks and cabbages. Thirty yards away a shed nestled against a high brick wall and beyond that ploughed fields were criss-crossed with hedgerows and the occasional tree.

The door was locked but I expected that. People had taken a lot of trouble to bring me here. Doors would stay locked until they told me why. And *they* included Lucia. She had sat there and let them do it! Watched while they had stuck a needle in my arm.

My clothes were in the wardrobe. I washed and shaved, dressed and combed my hair. I felt no fear, which surprised me at first. Then I realized I was too angry to be afraid. So when the door opened I was ready for anything.

"Morning, old boy," said the man called Henderson. "Glad you're an early riser. We've a busy day ahead of us."

"Doing what? Jabbing people with needles?"

He smiled. "Nothing so exciting, I'm afraid. Talk mainly. But you'll meet some interesting people."

"Where the devil are we?"

"Headquarters," he said simply. "Really it's better for you if you don't know where it is." He smiled again. "Shall we go down to breakfast?" We crossed a wide landing to a sweeping staircase grand enough for Fred Astaire to dance down. Wood-panelled walls were decorated with military crests, and two suits of armour stood to attention in the hall below. It was a bit like Edgar Hardman's pile at Wickham Manor, but more institutionalized. More like a club than a home—especially the dining room.

Three men were already eating at the end of a long table when we arrived. Heads turned and conversation stopped as Henderson ushered me in. I just had time to notice the silver serving dishes on the sideboard, and french windows which opened onto a terrace, when the man at the head of the table rose to greet me.

"Mr. Harris," he shook my hand warmly. "My name's Llewellyn. It's a pleasure to meet you." He was a tall, straight-backed man of about sixty, dressed in tweeds. Thinning grey hair, strong blue eyes, a clipped military moustache and a very firm handshake. "Let me introduce two of my colleagues—Bill Kaufman and Enrico Bonello."

Then he steered me to the sideboard. "Have some breakfast. Ham, eggs, bacon, it's all there. Or smoked haddock if you prefer? Coffee and tea—just help yourself, eh? Make yourself at home."

Henderson grinned and passed me a plate. Make yourself at home seemed odd words for a kidnapper, but it seemed best to go along with them—at least for the time being. I carried a heaped plate back to the table and sat opposite Kaufman. I wondered if Lucia was in the house.

Kaufman speared an egg with a forkful of sausage and munched happily while staring at me. He was a pleasant-faced man in his early forties, sandy-haired and green-eyed. He even had freckles. "You ever shoot craps in those casinos of yours?" he asked.

"Some," I said. "But blackjack and roulette were more popular."

"French roulette or American?"

"French."

He shook his head. "House gets better odds with American."

"You in the business?"

He looked surprised. "Me? Hell no, just a punter. Craps is OK, though—it's the only game I can win."

I nodded and concentrated on my food, repeating their names over and over again—Bonello and Kaufman, Llewellyn and Henderson—trying to establish a common denominator, but without success. For a start three different nationalities were involved—British, American and Italian—and their conversation was of no help. What talk there was confined itself to the weather or food, and except for Kaufman's opening inquiry about the casino business, my presence went largely ignored.

Eventually Llewellyn suggested we got down to business. I wondered what would happen if I said no. But I was more nervous than I was letting on, and I was curious about where this was all leading. We assembled in the room next to the dining room. It was almost as large, and laid out for a conference. A top table butted onto a longer one to form a T shape. Water jugs and glasses flanked pads and pencils. A small cinema screen was set into one wall.

"Perhaps you'd care to sit here?" Llewellyn stood behind a single chair at the end of the longer table. "As you are guest of honour."

I sat down and Llewellyn walked to the other end of the room. He took the central place at the top table, flanked by Kaufman and Bonello, exactly opposite me. "Make yourselves comfortable," he said, lighting a stubby briar pipe. "It's going to be a long session and I'm not quite sure where to begin."

"Why not start by introducing yourselves?" I snapped. "You've told me the names, Llewellyn, but not *who* you are. Or *what* you are."

Kaufman said: "Relax, Sam. This is going to be hard for you. We've a lot to tell you. When we finish you're going to have to make a big decision. A very big decision. So listen real good, huh?" He smiled, then turned and looked across Llewellyn to Bonello. "Enrico, why don't you start? After all, it began at your end."

Bonello nodded sadly. Watching him, I was reminded of Charles Aznavour. The same wiry frame, brooding unhappy eyes. "I don't know how much you know about Sicily, Mr. Harris," he said. "Most people only know of it as the home of the Mafia. That curse was almost stamped out before the war. Cesare Mori fought the Mafia to a standstill in the twenties. Mussolini trampled them underfoot in the thirties. But then the war came and afterwards—" he shrugged. "The Mafia was back in Sicily, stronger than ever."

Why tell me? I thought. But I remained silent. He screwed a cigarette into a holder and sat playing with it, rolling it in his fingers. "No offence is meant to my American friends when I say they helped the Mafia regain power in Sicily. When the Allies invaded, the Mafia facilitated their advance. One capo-mafia in particular, Don Calogero Vizzini, was of such great help that in the immediate post-war years he became the American adviser. Oh, I don't blame the Americans—how could they be expected to sort the goats from the sheep on one little island?"

He put a light to his cigarette. "Old style Mafia like Vizzini ran Sicily until the early sixties—"

Suddenly Kaufman interrupted: "Fix that date in your mind, Sam. The early sixties. You're in London laying the foundations of your business empire, while in Sicily—"

"—Vizzini was still in power," Bonello said quickly. "Vizzini worked in the shadows, dispensing favours, granting protection, wielding political influence. But then came a new generation of young mafiosi, who flaunted their wealth and importance. And when the young mafiosi clashed with the old, the streets of Sicily ran with blood. For example, in Palermo alone fifty-six people were shot dead in two months in 1962."

"1962, Sam," Kaufman said with strange emphasis. Then he turned back to Bonello. "Tell him about the family, Enrico."

"I was just about to," Bonello said, faintly irritated. "A man named Vito lived in Milan. A northerner, important, successful—a businessman from an old family. When he was young he studied in Rome and became friendly with people who owned land in Sicily. One summer before the war his friends invited him to stay in Sicily, and during his visit he met the daughter of one of their neighbours. The two young people fell in love and wanted to marry. Vito took his young bride back to Milan. There he inherited the family construction business. They had a child. They survived the war and even prospered from it. Afterwards they seemed set to live happily ever after. But the wife, Franka, had kept something secret from her husband. That her family were Mafia—and she kept this from him until June 1952. She had to tell him then. There was a power struggle between the two largest Mafia families. Many people were killed, among them Franka's parents. Her brother, Guiseppi Serracino, fled to the hills with his two small children—a boy and a girl who was just a few months old. Somehow Guiseppi got a message to Franka in Milan. Would she take the baby girl and bring her up as her own. When Franka told Vito the whole story he listened, forgave her, and agreed to take the child. Their own child, also a girl, was about seven at the time. Luckily she took to the new baby, and Vito and Franka grew to love the child as their own.

Bonello looked at me. "I'll remind you of what I said earlier, Mr. Harris. The early sixties in Palermo were a bloodbath. Guiseppi had long since returned from the hills to establish himself as capo-mafiosi. God knows Guiseppi was vicious enough—but his son!" Bonello threw up his hands. "Fiore was the wildest of all. He was a *butcher!* Finally, with the carabinieri hounding his every move, Palermo got too hot for Fiore—so he fled to Milan."

"1961, Sam," Kaufman said sharply.

Bonello continued swiftly. "In Milan, Fiore made no effort to contact Vito and Franka. After all, he barely knew them and the child they loved as their own—Fiore's own sister—had been a baby when he last saw her. No, Fiore submerged into the underworld. Within a year his protection rackets spread to the construction industry—and Vito was the biggest builder in Milan. And he *refused* to pay protection money. Vito was a brave man, Mr. Harris. He fought like a tiger. He even formed his own security corps to guard his properties. Fires would break out, work would be wrecked, materials looted. But *still* Vito fought. Until on the fourteenth of January 1963, he went to a site on the outskirts of the city. The site was supposedly guarded by twenty of his own people, but when he arrived they could not be found—and Fiore was waiting for him."

Bonello paused to eject a half-smoked cigarette from its holder. He stubbed it into an ashtray and his voice took on a harsh new note as he finished his story. "I arrived on that site the following morning. Of course I was younger then—not in charge, you understand—but *I* was the one who cut Vito's body down from the scaffolding. Every inch of his body had been mutilated. . . ."

His voice tailed off. Nobody moved. We sat in silence, watching Bonello as he struggled with his emotions. I risked a glance at the others. They were all the same, perhaps not displaying the same degree of personal misery as Bonello, but grimly tense and determined. The common denominator was there now—in their faces. And Bonello had said he wasn't in charge. Did that mean that he was a policeman of some kind? Were they *all* policemen of some kind?

My imagination struggled with the picture of Bonello handling that terrible corpse. I shuddered—at the exact moment the cigarette holder snapped in Bonello's hands. It broke the spell. He looked up at me and said: "Terrible though that was, it was not the end of the story. Vito had fought with the courage of a tiger, but his wife was to fight with the demented fury of a wounded tigress. She took over Vito's business and ran it herself." He paused, shaking his head. "Franka was unique, Mr. Harris. Proud, beautiful, determined and—" a smile played briefly at the corners of his mouth, "—and stubborn. People wanted to help, believe me, but Franka would have none of it. It was *her* fight and she fought it until she went broke. Finally she had only one property left. An apartment building. Vito's staunchest workers fought the world to finish that project. Franka was spitting in the eye of her husband's murderers and it was something to be proud of. But the humiliation was too much for Fiore. A week before the apartment block was due to be opened, Franka was kidnapped and—and taken to a basement—"

His voice dropped to a whisper. "And what they did there was, was—." His head shook from side to side, as if denying some terrible knowledge. "It took eight hours for her to die."

The horror of what he had said filled my mind. I was stunned. Sick to the pit of my stomach. Bonello sat with an expression of disgust now on his face, fumbling through his pockets for a cigarette until Kaufman passed him a pack. Then he puffed thoughtfully on a new cigarette.

"Enrico," Llewellyn said gently. "Why not get some fresh air?"

Bonello nodded and walked towards the french windows and out onto the terrace. Beyond the terrace I could see Lucia, carrying a basket of cut flowers over the crook of her arm. She made such a perfect picture that she might have belonged there—as if the setting had been designed for her. Bonello had seen her too. He hurried across the garden, calling her name. She turned, startled at first, then glowing with a smile when she saw who it was.

"She's the child Vito and Franka adopted," Llewellyn said, following my gaze. "And he's Vito's brother."

"Vito's brother?"

"They're a remarkable family," Kaufman said.

Lucia and Bonello strolled towards us, arm in arm. Suddenly she looked up and saw me watching her through the window. She halted at the bottom of the terrace, confused for a moment, then she unlinked her arm from his, climbed up the steps and entered the room. She stopped a yard away, her face anxious as her eyes met mine. "Please forgive me, Sam." Our hands touched. "For—for deceiving you." I suppose I could have forgiven her anything. She must have seen it in my face because when she drew away she simply said: "Thank you."

As Lucia sat down next to me at the table, Henderson handed Kaufman an envelope. He opened the flap with his thumb, read the letter quickly and passed it to me. "It's from Tomlinson," he said casually. "That statement for Davis. Sign it, and we'll get it back to him."

Tomlinson! "Is Tomlinson in on this?" I asked. "Is he—one of you?"

"Hell, no." Kaufman shook his head. "But we couldn't have him all steamed up about your appointment, so we phoned his secretary. Said you couldn't make it but you'd send a messenger." He shrugged. "Sign it, Sam—we've other things to talk about."

But I wasn't buying that. Not *that* easily. "How did you know I was meeting him?"

Kaufman smiled. "Rex Place. You made the arrangements there, remember? The whole place is wired. We can even hear you brush your teeth." Tiny spots of colour appeared on Lucia's cheeks. *So I had been right!* What had seemed preposterous last night was perfectly true. No wonder she had wanted to discuss the notes there—Kaufman had heard every word we said.

I never even bothered to read Tomlinson's statement—just scrawled my signature and handed it back to Kaufman.

At that moment Bonello reappeared at the door. Llewellyn said, "If you've had enough fresh air I think we ought to continue. We've a lot to talk about."

Kaufman resumed by saying: "We'll go back to Enrico's story later. Meanwhile remember the dates will you, Sam. They're important. Vito was murdered in 1963, right? The same year you opened The Point of View. A critical year for the Mafia. Police were moving against them in Italy like never before. We were hounding them in the States." He paused, as if struck by a sudden thought. "By the way, the name Joe Valachi mean anything to you?"

"No."

He smiled briefly. "Valachi was a convicted trafficker in heroin. In June '62 he was doing a stretch in the Atlanta Penitentiary when he sang his heart out to the FBI in exchange for State protection. Robert Kennedy called it the biggest breakthrough ever made in combating organized crime. He was Attorney General at the time, and going after the mobs in a big way. The Mafia faded. Sure, they still control heroin imports into the States, but now they let the blacks and Puerto Ricans run the wholesale market. The Mafia took a step backwards."

I fidgeted uneasily. The whole thing frightened me. "Look, this has nothing to do with me. I have never been involved—"

"Sam!" Kaufman shouted. "Will you let us finish, for God's sake?"

Llewellyn scraped his pipe into an ashtray. "The point is that for the first time in history the Mafia came under simultaneous pressure in the United States and Italy. Mafia families reacted differently. In particular some emigrated to Britain."

331

"The Mafia in England?"

Bonello answered. "Yes, Mr. Harris. For example, Milan was too small to hide Fiore Serracino. I had been given a squad of five hundred men to fight the Mafia and, in particular, to catch the man who murdered my brother and his wife. But Fiore slipped through our net and returned to Sicily, and from there he was smuggled to Malta aboard a fishing boat. He acquired Maltese papers, a passport, a new name—and after that he went to live in Cardiff."

Cardiff? A note of warning jangled in the back of my mind, but before I could pursue it Llewellyn said: "Of course we never knew that until much later. . . . The Maltese had controlled the vice trade in Cardiff for years but we were gradually cleaning them up. Until Fiore Serracino arrived, in the late sixties. We didn't know it was him then, but suddenly the vice trade became a lot better organized, and the rackets started to grow bigger."

"That's an understatement," Kaufman interrupted. "We found out later that Serracino organized some sort of conference in Cardiff. An organization called the Pipeline was set up there—and believe me, the Pipeline is some organization."

Llewellyn nodded. "By the early seventies the Pipeline was operating illegal activities in various parts of the country. Mainly at ports—Portsmouth, Harwich, Southampton. Suddenly the Pipeline was everywhere. Except we never recognized it—we just put it down to a general increase in criminal activity."

Kaufman cleared his throat. "Sam, have you ever heard the expression—'this thing of ours'? Strictly translated from the Italian it means 'our thing'—Cosa Nostra."

Cosa Nostra! Kaufman's interruption somehow stirred my memory.

"You've heard it then?" Llewellyn asked quickly. "You've had contact with the Mafia?"

"Am I being accused of—?"

"Corrao was Mafia," Kaufman snapped. "Remember Corrao? The man who tried to buy Apex Holdings?"

"Corrao?" The name reminded me. He had said, *This thing of ours is too strong. . . .* "So what?" I struggled to sound normal. Was that why I was being told all this? Because they thought that I was connected with the Mafia? "I mean, I never did business with him. I only met him once. You must know—"

"What do you think of the West End now?" Kaufman changed

course unexpectedly. "A lot has changed, hasn't it? And I'll tell you why. Because the Pipeline has started to take over."

I remembered Tony Fields—"*A lot's changed, Sam.*" Why was I sweating? My mouth was dry and I reached for a glass of water.

Kaufman said: "It's big, Sam. And getting bigger."

"So why tell me? It's *not* my story, Kaufman. It's nothing to do with me—"

"You became involved when they tried to buy Apex." Kaufman suddenly lost his temper. "They know you. Corrao's orders were to take Apex without hurting you. *Without hurting you, Sam.* Why?"

"How the hell do I know? You've got it wrong. You're trying to implicate me in something I know nothing about—"

"The men running the Pipeline *know* you," Kaufman insisted. "The top man knows you. He's a friend of yours—we're certain."

"You said that man Fiore Serracino runs it. I never met—"

"I *never* said that. Serracino's not the top man—at most he's three or four in the chain. We've been trying to break the Pipeline for seven years now. And the nearest we ever got is the tenth man in the chain. He told us Corrao was part of the Pipeline. And he told us Corrao's orders as far as you were concerned."

I was really frightened now. "So ask Corrao—don't ask me."

"Corrao was nine in the chain. He disappeared. So did number eleven. It's part of the system. If we pick a man up the contacts on either side of him vanish within hours."

I shook my head. "I still don't *understand*. This has nothing to do with me. Nothing—"

"Why did they try to take Apex without hurting you?"

"I don't know! I'm *not* involved and by God I never will be."

Kaufman snapped back: "We'll see about that. Take a look at this film, buddy boy." He leaped from his chair and crossed to the windows. He shouted over his shoulder at me as he drew the curtains: "Take a *good* look. Then say you're *not* involved."

Before I could answer a disembodied voice came from the loudspeakers. "Sam Harris? *Winner* Harris, you mean? Yeah, I knew him. We did bird together in Brixton."

I was still trying to place the voice when his image appeared on the screen in the far wall. A middle-aged man sat in an armchair, and I recognized him. I mean I knew his face—placing him, putting a name to him, was something else.

The man said: "Hard bastard, Harris. Most of us stayed clear of

333

him. He got special treatment in Brixton. Worked in the library, nothing manual, know what I mean? But a real hard case."

The film changed to a thin-faced, foxy-looking man, fumbling through his pockets for a light for his cigarette. "None of us knew Harris well," he said. "Kept himself apart too much for that. But those rumours about losing all his money were rubbish. Harris was looked after in the nick. Any trouble and the screws closed ranks round him like a private army—and that costs money, take it from me. Harris ain't broke and he ain't alone neither. He had some sort of set-up working for him on the outside. The West End's not my scene mate, but I'll tell you this—Harris will be back, he ain't called Winner for nothing, is he?" The man smiled his thin, crafty grin and put a light to his cigarette. "Best bloke to talk to is Micky Blisset. He got closer to Harris than anyone."

I watched in amazement. *None of it was true.* Memories of people met in prison flickered through my mind. I *had* worked in the library, but apart from that it was a pack of lies. But Micky Blisset's name rang a bell. I shared a cell with him once, for about eight weeks. Then he was there, up on the screen.

"People could never make head nor tail of Harris," he said. "Well, he was never your average villain, was he?" Blisset shrugged. "But Harris is still big time, and it's true about people working for him. And about the list of names. I don't know who's on it or where it gets kept—but he's got it all right. I asked him about it once. 'Insurance,' he says. 'Anything happens to me and that list gets published. There's names on there to blow this thing of theirs right open. But I don't want to bust these boys, Micky,' he said. 'I want to join them. That list is my way of buying my way back in.'"

Then the screen darkened and went blank. Kaufman swished the curtains open and the sweet normality of daylight flooded back into the room. I still felt bewildered. "It's a bloody pack of lies. Who *were* those men?"

Kaufman said softly: "There are ten of those men, Sam. They all did time in Brixton. They started coming out three months ago. At staggered intervals. They're all spreading the same story."

"No wonder I'm treated as a leper. They've got to be stopped."

Kaufman shook his head. "We can't do that. You see—they are undercover agents. They're spreading that story on our say so."

I could hardly believe my ears! None of it made sense. Then Kaufman added: "We've set you up, Sam."

I gripped the arms of the chair, half rising to my feet. "You bastards! *BASTARDS!* Who the hell are you anyway?"

"My name is Kaufman. William Kaufman, United States Bureau of Narcotics. And *you* are the best chance we've ever had. Our best hope of breaking the Pipeline is to nail the top man. They call him The Ferryman. And he knows you. Which means you know him—"

"You're wrong. Completely wrong—"

"You wouldn't know him for what he is," Kaufman interrupted. "He's too clever for that. This isn't some tin pot outfit, Sam. This is narcotics. You got any idea how big *that* is? Like fifty *billion* dollars a year in the States. Like as much again across Europe—"

"It's *not* my story," I said stonily.

"Those men *made* it your story." Kaufman pointed to the screen. "Those men say you've got a list of names, Sam. And the Pipeline believes it—they've already taken the bait. They misjudged you to begin with. Thought they could frighten you off. Stop your licences, send you flight tickets. But you're staying, Sam."

I remembered the looks around town. Fear? Hostility?

Kaufman nodded grimly. "You ever had any experience of heroin?" I felt the blood rush to my face and I had a great deal of trouble in meeting his eye. "Yeah, well," he growled, "we'll talk about that later. But I'll tell you something. This country is being used as a clearing house for heroin on its way to the States. The Pipeline is by far the biggest drug-smuggling operation ever encountered—and the man running it knows you, Sam. Knows you've served your time, knows you're out—and he *thinks* you've got a list of names. So now what's he going to do?"

I remembered Vito Bonello and shuddered.

Kaufman smiled. "He's got to *negotiate*, Sam. The Ferryman ain't going to damage you—not until he's sure about the list."

"You're mad. I don't have a list."

"Neither do we. Not a complete list. But we've got bits and pieces. Cells of the organization. We could wrap up Southampton, Hull and several other places. But they're merely distribution centres for narcotics. Raiding them wouldn't cut the Pipeline—"

"They'll make contact," Llewellyn said. "All you have got to do is insist on meeting the top man."

"Just like that," I said sarcastically.

"Sure, just like that." Kaufman nodded. "They'll pass you up the line. Shall I tell you why? Because you'll threaten them. Tell them

335

that for every day's delay you'll blow one of their operations. Starting with Southampton. Anonymous tip-off to the police—"

Llewellyn put in: "But it's the Pipeline itself we're after. We know it starts in the Middle East and North Africa—we *think* it runs through Sicily—but what we don't know is how they land the stuff here and then transship to the States."

I looked at the faces around the table. "So I'm to be used as bait? Staked out—like a tethered goat? What if I say no?"

Kaufman's eyes flashed with temper. "Get your head together and *listen*. Don't you want to know who framed you? Who *ruined* you? And we're dealing with narcotics pouring into this country like water through a sieve. This country can't build drug dependency clinics fast enough—you know that? Hard drug addiction is growing at the rate of at least twenty per cent per annum."

"A heroin addict reduces his life expectancy to five years," Llewellyn said mildly.

"If he's lucky," Bonello interrupted. "Some of the stuff on the streets now has been cut with brick dust, detergent or even strychnine. Shoot that in your arm and you die even quicker."

Kaufman smiled. "You say *no* any time you want, Sam. But let me tell you something. Since you left Brixton we've had a team of men covering you. Sixteen of them. Plus Lucia. She's a colleague of Bonello's and she's *good*. We've watched over you like a baby. If you're with us that team stays put. If you're not—" he shrugged. "Like the book said, Sam, we had to make you an offer you couldn't refuse."

Chapter 5

So much more happened that day. They kept after me, hour after hour, obsessed by a sense of urgency—there was information they had to tell me and information I had to tell them, and all within the space of a few hours. It was essential for me to be in position tomorrow, back at Rex Place, waiting to hear from the Pipeline.

At one point Llewellyn revealed the scale of the operation. "Your release date was planned months ago. More than two hundred operatives are in position now—in London, New York, Milan—"

"And all because of your story, Sam," Kaufman interrupted. He was transferring various items from a briefcase onto the table in front of him. Even from where I sat I recognized the Apex Minute Book, and I saw a file marked *Transcript of Trial*.

"Your story," Kaufman repeated. He waved a hand at the paperwork in front of him. "I've got most of it here. I've read it a hundred times, discussed it with dozens of people, checked a million details—and you know something? One item puzzles me."

I shifted in the chair and said nothing.

"Or perhaps I should say one *person* puzzles me," he said. "I've thought about it a lot. Imagine you—fighting to save your business. You never knew it but you were fighting the Pipeline. Casinos are good meeting places—channels to launder the Pipeline's money. They wanted yours, and you gave them a hell of a battle. What was your *wife* doing while all this was going on?"

"Why?" I puffed on my cigarette. "Kay is not relevant—"

"Dammit! I'll decide that. Will you get that into your head? You can't hold back on *anything*. And don't give me that mule-eyed look. It cuts no ice with me. I'm not your defence counsel."

"What's that supposed to mean?"

"As if you don't know. Like I spent a day grilling the bastard. Trying to find out why in God's name you pleaded guilty."

"You had *no right*—"

"Shove it! It's over and done with. I did it, that's all that matters. Want to know what he told me?" Kaufman lowered his angry face to within inches of mine. "That you clammed up whenever his questions got within a mile of that precious wife of yours! Well, clam up on me, buddy boy, and I'll break every bone in your body!"

Then he slammed a glossy photograph face up on the table in front of me. It was a picture of Kay. Naked. On a bed. She was not alone, but I wasn't there. I closed my eyes. Oh God, would the nightmare never end! "Where—where did you get that?" I asked.

"We committed a burglary early this year. Oh, not us personally. Members of staff. Cracked a safe and took some valuables, just to make it look good. What we were really looking for escaped us, but in the process we came across that photograph."

Llewellyn leaned forward slightly. "We'll tell you whose house it was later, I promise—but meanwhile we must get the rest of your story. It's vitally important. In fact the man whose safe we took the photograph from is the man we suspect of running the Pipeline."

"We *know!*" Kaufman shouted. "We don't suspect. But knowing and nailing the bastard are two different things."

I hardly heard him. I was wondering who else had seen the photograph. Gloated over it.

"OK, Sam," Kaufman sighed. "You sent Corrao away with a flea in his ear. But what happened then?"

It was like the lull before the storm—that summer in '75. Not that it began as a storm. Occasional squalls perhaps, but not a storm. There was a fight at The Point of View on a Saturday night, then a spot of bother at Winston's a few days later. And some kids were caught smoking pot at Jennifer's the following week. None of the incidents were big in themselves, but they seemed to mount up. I thought it was a run of bad luck at first. Then the whispering campaign started—rumours that Apex was going broke.

Start rumours in a business like ours and it's like a run on the bank. No gambler likes to think the kitty will be empty when his win comes up. So our business suffered—especially the betting shops which took a real beating. Six months of that . . . well, the writing was on the wall. Even though I refused to read it.

Running Apex turned into a nightmare. And board meetings became a farce. Only Edgar Hardman gave me unqualified support, the others seemed to lose interest. It brought home to me how much the takeover battle had unsettled things. Charlie Weston had wanted that deal, and I had blocked it. And Lew Douglas felt the same. I was facing ruin, and if Apex collapsed Edgar might be ruined as well. That weighed with me as much as anything. He and I had become very close.

By then I was working a sixteen-hour day, often seven days a week. Constant emergencies kept me in town, and I hadn't seen Kay in weeks. But despite the worry and the strain I always thought we would win in the end. At least I did until my problems started with Kay—and then life came apart at the seams.

When she put on "the party of the year" at Ashley Grange, the papers were full of it. And full of speculation about my absence. But she and I had argued bitterly two days before, so I sulked in my tent at Rex Place and let her get on with it. And after the party she started to hit the town, to accept invitations back, so that within a short while she became one of the leading lights on the celebrity circuit.

Some of the celebrities worried me. That French songwriter, Marcel Faberge, was always hanging around, along with a couple of

338

acolytes—Marvin Brooks, a black American, and a Corsican called
Pipo Martinez. Faberge, Brooks and Martinez. They had collabo-
rated in writing a musical which was enough the rage then to make
them instantly newsworthy wherever they went. And where they
went, Kay went too. Always the *four* of them. I put up with it—but
I never liked it.

One night they came to the casino on Park Lane. They had been
to the opening of a new show, then on to a party afterwards, and
they were all a bit high. I was at The Point of View when they
arrived, but I was sent for when the trouble started. Faberge's luck
was out. He lost a few hundred at baccarat and the other two fared
little better, and when their cash ran out they asked to change a
cheque for five thousand pounds. Of course Paul Hammond—my
man running the club—knew who they were, so he cashed the
cheque. After which they gambled like drunken sailors and lost the
lot within an hour. Then they went back to Paul for more.

I had arrived by this time. It took a moment to get rid of my coat
and to spot Kay amid the crowd of people gathering in the salon.
Paul was a good operator and his technique was generally successful. "Gentlemen," he was beaming, "it's just not your night. Lady
Luck is riding against you—why not leave it until tomorrow?"

"Are you refusing us?" Faberge asked bluntly.

"I know when to look after my friends," Paul said smoothly.
"You'll wake up in the morning and thank me."

"I'll thank you for more chips and less chat."

Paul smiled, parrying the insult like a fighter riding a punch. "I've
just had an idea," he said. "Why not come back tomorrow night? Be
my guests for dinner—then your luck might change and—"

Faberge swung him round angrily. "We came here to gamble, not
to stand round gabbling all night. You do like I say or I'll start
believing what I've heard about this place."

Paul went white as a sheet. "And just what *have* you heard about
this place?" he asked softly.

Faberge mimicked him in a high falsetto voice. "And just what
have I heard about this place? Sam Harris is a crook. The tables are
rigged. Apex is on the rocks. . . ."

Nobody saw the actual punch. All they saw was the look of
concern on Paul's face as he held Faberge upright. Faberge went
green at the gills and gasped for breath, then Paul got him pointed
in the direction of the office. Kay arranged Faberge's arm across her

shoulders and took some of the weight of his sagging body. "Marcel, are you all right? Darling—"

I said: "He'll be fine in a minute, Kay. He needs a breath of fresh air, that's all. Don't crowd him too much."

She jumped at the sound of my voice. Brooks and Martinez were edging away, but by this time three of Paul's people were shepherding the entire party across to the office. One of them murmured "heart attack" which added authenticity to the look of concern on Paul's face—and a moment later we were mercifully out of the salon and into the office. Martinez realized what had happened. "You *hit* him, man. In front of all those people—"

Paul dropped Faberge like a sack of potatoes and sank his fist into Martinez's midriff. Martinez buckled as he clutched himself. Paul turned an inquiring glance at Brooks but the negro pretended to be busy helping Faberge into a chair. I grabbed Kay's arm and hurried her into the next room, closing the door after us.

She was white and frightened. "What's happening to my friends?"

I was blazing angry. "Forget your bloody friends. What's happening to your husband?"

"You're asking *me?*" she demanded. "Why ask me? I don't have a *husband*. I have an empty bed. I have phone calls."

"At least you know where I am. You know I'm working—"

"I'm sick of it, Sam!" she shrieked. "Sick of waiting, sick of pretending that being Winner's wife is the best thing since—"

"For God's sake! Will you listen to me. Sit down a minute and—"

"I don't want to listen! Why should I listen? You never—"

Suddenly an explosion of sound next door rocked the place. The partition wall shivered as something smashed into it. There was a shout of pain, followed by the sound of a chair being knocked over. Kay screamed. "What are they *doing?* For God's sake—is this what you do? Beat people up when they come out for a little fun—"

"*Fun?* That was fun? Attacking my reputation—"

Another shattering thump drowned the rest of my words. The noise from the other room was deafening. Kay set off for the door but I pulled her back. "Kay, will you *sit down!* Stay here a minute while I see what the hell's happening in there—then we'll talk—"

"I don't want to talk. Can't you understand that?"

The door opened and Paul poked his head round the corner. "Boss, can you spare a minute?" He stopped at the sight of us struggling. Then he mumbled: "I'm sorry but—"

341

"For God's sake, Paul! Can't I have a minute's peace?"

He flushed and withdrew just as another terrible crash rocked the place. I turned back to Kay. "We've got to talk—" But even as I made one last attempt to reach her, the shouts next door rose to a new pitch. I went across to the door and wrenched it open.

The room was full of people. Martinez was backed up against the far wall, struggling helplessly in the clutches of two uniformed policemen. Faberge and Brooks were on a sofa, flanked by two other policemen. And Paul was arguing with Chief Inspector Davis.

I shouted: "What the hell goes on here?"

The room went suddenly still. Paul stopped talking in mid-sentence, and Chief Inspector Davis turned slowly to face me. "Ah, Mr. Harris."

Martinez giggled. "Mr. *Winner* Harris."

"Martinez's been caught in possession, Boss. He claims he got the stuff here," Paul explained.

Davis opened his hand to show me three badly made reefers. "This club is a pick-up point for drugs."

I took a deep breath and looked at Martinez. One glance said he was lying. God in heaven—a blind man could see that! He was causing trouble, any way he could. I got a tight grip on my nerves. "One man's word, Inspector." I threw a withering glance at Martinez. "The word of a junky. You'll have to do better than that."

Davis shrugged. "I've got the evidence here." His fingers closed over the reefers. "All I need to close this place down."

"Your evidence is against him," I nodded at Martinez, "not against the club."

"We'll see about that," Davis said grimly.

It took half an hour to get rid of Davis and the boys in blue. They took Martinez away with them, and Faberge and Brooks left at the same time—muttering assurances about bail to Martinez, while threatening action against the club, Apex Holdings and Winner Harris in particular. I went back to the other office, wondering how on earth to deal with Kay in her present mood. But she had left, by the other door. I was stunned. I know I wasn't thinking straight, but I had expected her to wait. Dammit, we had to sort things out!

I went to Rex Place, telling Paul where to contact me in an emergency. There was no sign of Kay at the mews so I telephoned Ashley Grange and Mrs. Jones, our housekeeper, answered. I told her to ask Kay to call me the minute she got in and after that I suppose I dozed off. I must have done because the post startled me when it fell through the letterbox. I phoned Mrs. Jones again, but Kay had not been home all night.

I was worried sick until the papers arrived—then I read all about it. The more sensational of them ran the story on the front page. There was even a picture of Martinez leaving the club, flanked by policemen. And a photograph of Kay leaving the police station an hour later. It was a toss-up which was the bigger story—"Martinez on drugs charge", or "Winner's wife puts up bail"

I was at the office by eight and on the phone to Lewis Collins an hour later. He sent one of his people to the court for me and phoned back afterwards to tell me about it. "Martinez got a suspended sentence," he growled, "plus a Mickey Mouse fine and costs. If you ask me, magistrates are far too lenient—"

"Was Kay there?"

"You bet! Kay was there—*Fleet Street* was there—and you couldn't move outside the court for TV cameras. I just hope to God she never said anything, that's all."

So did I. It was the end of the morning by this time. For once I had no lunch appointment and I was glad of it. I fidgeted through the paperwork on my desk, waiting in vain for Kay to call. When I phoned Ashley Grange again there was no answer at all. That worried me until I realized it was Wednesday. Mrs. Jones went to her sister's on a Wednesday. I tried to work out where Kay would go. Eventually I was too tired and worried to think straight so I decided to go to Ashley Grange. Kay would *have* to return there at some time, and I planned to be there when she did.

I called Tom, my chauffeur, and asked him to collect me. Some twenty minutes later we were on the motorway, heading for Ashley Grange. It was five past five when we arrived. Funny remembering that now, but I suppose those next few minutes will live with me until I die. I remember a great sense of relief at the sight of Kay's blue Jaguar slung carelessly across the drive, as if she had parked in a hurry. Tom asked what time I wanted him in the morning, I said to phone me before leaving town, then I sent him on his way.

I walked across the drive and into the house. The smell of pot was everywhere. The drawing room was drenched in it. Kay's mink was thrown across the back of a sofa, and her shoes were kicked under a chair. I checked the other rooms: they were all empty. Then I went upstairs. I heard the sounds as I reached the half-landing. I sprinted up the rest of the stairs two at a time. Then I was through the doors into the master bedroom.

A man should never see some sights. Shock etches the details into his brain for the rest of his life. Seeing Kay like that—on the bed with the three of them—was that kind of experience. I couldn't believe it. One of Kay's arms was turned towards me. Even as I turned my eyes away I saw the blue bruising on her inner arm. The kind of bruising which comes with a needle.

Emotion overrides judgment at such moments. Disgust. Anger. Pity. *Self-pity?* You react without knowing it. My hands closed round Faberge's throat, forcing his head back, trying to snap his neck. Then, suddenly, pain exploded behind my ears as something hard crashed down on my head. Another blow, a taste like iron in my mouth, a red mist, and then unconsciousness.

By the time I came round the local doctor had sewn nine stitches into my scalp. Mrs. Jones stood by the bed, her hands screwing a handkerchief into a ball. "Oh, thank heavens," she said. "I thought you was dead, sir. I got back at six. The front doors were wide open, things all over the place. I was that frightened."

The doctor came in from the bathroom. I got the rest of the story while he checked me out for concussion. Apparently the signs elsewhere were of a burglary. Some of Kay's clothes were missing and a good deal of her jewellery, some silver had gone, that sort of thing. "Amateurs," said the doctor. "That's what the police think. There's a sergeant downstairs now, but you've no need to see him until the morning if you don't want to."

I lay there thinking about Kay. God, she had to be sick to do what I had seen. What would drive her to something like that? My absence? Boredom? *Drugs?* Most of her crowd were into the occasional joint, cocaine—*but mainline heroin?*

I groaned and the doctor looked at me carefully. "Head ache? I'm afraid it will for a while," he smiled sympathetically. "They must have been worried about you, though. They put a pillow under your head after they busted you."

Kay did that. I nearly said it. I smiled and thanked the doctor for his help. After that they let me doze for a while, until about an hour later when Mrs. Jones came back with a bowl of hot soup.

"Lord Hardman is downstairs," she said. "He's asking to see you, if you're up to it."

I was up to it but I didn't want to see Edgar. He would ask

344

questions about Kay. But it would be better to face him now. Make up some story, then send him on his way. I said: "Dammit, Mrs. Jones, I only had a bump on the head. You'd better send him up."

Edgar arrived in a mood of embarrassed agitation. "Doc says you'll be all right by the morning. Bit shaken up, eh?"

"I'm OK."

His blue eyes searched my expression. "Burgled? Knocked on the head? Man should have a wife around at a time like this." He looked at me carefully. "The local CID asked where she was by the way. Dunno why, but I said the first thing that came to my head—said she was at my place in town. Damn silly of me really."

I wondered how much he knew. He stood up and crossed to the window. It was almost dark outside, the fag end of twilight. He peered out while he talked to me over his shoulder. "Mind you, daresay the police read the papers, just like the rest of us."

Edgar was fishing. Clearly he was as worried as I was. He swung round. "God in Heaven, Sam, she's in some sort of trouble, isn't she? What the *devil's* going on? You're here with stitches in your head. Papers are full of nonsense. Where the devil is she?"

"I—she's out—she'll be back later—"

"Then I'll wait. It's high time I had a word with my daughter—"

"I'd rather you didn't. Wait, I mean. Really. Best for me to—"

"You don't want me hanging around because you've no idea when she'll turn up! You've no bloody idea where she is either. But I'll find out—*by God* I will! And I'll tan the backside off her when I get my hands on her. She's not too old for that you know—"

"For God's sake, Edgar—"

But he slammed the door shut as he went out. I could hear him stamping down the stairs. It was too late in the day for Edgar to play the Victorian father, but he wasn't hanging around to hear it from me. Soon his car was crunching ripples in the driveway.

I wrapped myself into a dressing gown and went downstairs. Mrs. Jones made me a pot of coffee and I sent her off to her flat at the other end of the house. I carried the coffee into the study and sat down. It was going to be a long night, waiting for news of Kay—and wondering what the hell to do about her when I got it.

KAUFMAN PICKED UP the photograph from the table. I saw Kay again, on that bed. Kaufman slid the photograph back into a large brown envelope and handed it to me.

"It's yours, Sam. To do with what you want."

It was such an unexpected gesture that it took me by surprise, but before I could say anything he returned to his chair.

"Faberge was a pusher, Sam," he said. "He got out of his depth with his gambling losses and had to make a quick buck."

Llewellyn said: "I imagine that it was some hours after this—er, this incident that you were found in circumstances which eventually led to you being charged with murder?"

I nodded.

"And remember this," Kaufman said: "The man running the Pipeline ruined you. Indirectly he ruined your wife, too, because the stuff Faberge was hawking was Pipeline material. Directly and indirectly the Pipeline cripples a thousand lives a day. And the man running it is a friend of yours."

"But you're not going to tell me his name?"

"But we are. That's why we're here. We tell you what we know, and in exchange you tell us what you know. Like, for example, all the things you *forgot* to tell the police before your trial."

I thought about it. Whether he knew it or not, Kaufman's remark about the supply of drugs to Faberge touched just the right nerve. The clock can never be put back—but if ever I laid hands on the man who put heroin within reach of an animal like Faberge! "You promise to give me The Ferryman's name?"

"We'll do better than that. We'll *prove* he is The Ferryman. And remember this—we set this whole deal up so that he has to come to you. And when he does . . ." Kaufman opened and closed his hand, "we'll put him away for the rest of his life."

Lucia cleared her throat. "And Fiore Serracino with him."

There was a long silence after that. I hated the thought of having to relive old nightmares, but knew I *had* to. So I took a deep breath and told them the rest of the story.

I SAT IN THE STUDY for hours. My head throbbed from the crack it had taken and my nerves felt as raw as an open wound. I chain-smoked and drank a gallon of black coffee—and chased the coffee with a whisky or two. I didn't know what to do. Rightly or wrongly, I've never felt the need for advice, I've always made my own decisions. But I felt the need then—especially when Edgar telephoned.

"She turned up yet?"

I almost said yes. I nearly said she was at home and in bed asleep. But Edgar in his present mood would have demanded to speak to her. And failing that he would have arrived—breathing fire and brimstone. "No," I said. "Not yet."

"It's two o'clock! *Two o'clock!* Sam—where the devil is she?"

"Two isn't late. She's probably on her way home—trouble with living in the country it takes hours—"

"Don't give me that. Something's happened. I don't know what but I *know* something has."

It took me a long time to get rid of him. I had been fairly strung up to begin with, but after dealing with Edgar my nerves were completely wrecked. He was so convinced that Kay was in danger.

I sweated it out. I thought about calling the police. But the situation was already too complicated for that. What with the faked burglary and Edgar's lie about Kay's whereabouts—plus the possibility of the police finding her in possession of drugs. . . .

Then, at three thirty, the telephone rang. I answered, half expecting it to be Edgar. But all I could hear was the sound of someone crying. It was an eerie, weird sound. Not tears of grief, or fear or pain—but of utter *hopelessness.*

"Kay? Kay? *For God's sake!* Is that you?"

"Don't . . . don't hang up . . . *please* don't . . ."

It's hard to remember how I felt. I was so mixed up. Part of me was angry, but part of me was so relieved that I nearly cried with her. "Kay, pull yourself together! Where the hell are you?"

"Oh Sam—you're *all right!* Thank God . . . you're all right . . ." Her voice shook and tailed off, racked by sobs.

I shouted: "Kay—where are you, for God's sake?"

"Don't . . . don't shout . . . don't hang up, Sam . . . please . . ."

"Okay, okay—I am *not* hanging up. But you've got to tell me . . ."

"Just . . . just talk . . . talk to me, Sam . . . please. Oh, thank God you're all right. I thought . . . I thought . . ."

She was crying again, but the words came through in gulps. "Sam, I'm so frightened . . . everything's got out of hand . . . they're insane . . . really insane . . . ."

"Where—are—you?"

"Don't shout . . . please . . . you promised not to shout."

I bit my tongue.

Then she said: "I'm at . . . at the boat. You know the phone box? Up the lane? I'm there. Oh Sam, it's so dark and . . . and—"

"What the hell? Why—why *there* for God's sake?"

"Marcel wanted to see someone—"

"Where are the others?"

"Brooksy went over to The Fisherman . . . the place Lew Douglas owns . . . They said we were going to have a party . . . breakfast on the river—except something's gone wrong . . . and Sam . . . *I'm scared out of my mind!* Marcel is hopped up to the eyeballs and . . ."

"Get out of there, Kay." I panicked and started to shout. "Get out. D'you hear me? Can you drive? Are you OK to drive?"

"The car . . . it's round by the boat . . . Marcel would see me. Oh Sam, he'll *kill* me if I run out now."

I tried to visualize the phone box. It was up the lane about fifty yards from the river. A deserted, country lane. "Calm down, Kay," I said, "calm down. . . . Can you see any houses?"

"No . . . it's too dark to see anything . . . trees . . . the lane . . . oh God! *They're calling me.* Marcel will kill me if—"

The line went dead.

It took me three minutes to dress. The boat was fifteen miles away, maybe twenty. I pulled a pair of trousers over my pyjamas, grabbed a sweater and an old jacket, socks and shoes. A moment later I was out of the back door, running across to the garage. Then I skidded to a halt. Kay had taken the Jaguar. The Rolls was in London. *How was I going to get to the boat?*

The Mini! We had an old Mini! Kay used it sometimes for the odd bit of shopping in the village. I switched on the light in the garage, and saw it in the corner. *The key was in the ignition!* The engine turned once—then coughed and died on me. I took a deep breath and tried again. A splutter—and she started!

I switched off, staggered out into the garage. A weapon? Tools on the wall. I threw a heavy spanner onto the back seat, did a racing start down the drive, bouncing gravel as high as the windscreen. And all that time I kept asking myself—how long had I been?

That bloody boat! I had bought it the summer before. Hardly used the damn thing! But Lew Douglas owned one and, after spending a convivial day in his, Kay said what fun it would be to have one of our own. Even then nothing would have come of it if Douglas hadn't poked his nose in. He phoned me a week later—he had this friend who was going abroad. "Got a *smashing* boat, old boy. Just down river from The Fisherman." So Kay went over, and I heard all about it that night. "Darling, it's an *investment*. Lew says they appreciate like mad. So we could have a lot of fun without it costing a penny."

Oh God—*how long had I been?* Half an hour at least. And I still wasn't there. Another mile. The lane straightened. The phone box would be soon—round the next bend perhaps? Nothing—no phone box. Another bend. *The phone box!* There—on the left. Empty. I hit the horn in case Kay could hear.

Three boats. Mine was the middle one. I stopped the Mini, switched off, sat listening. Nothing. I got out. The night was as black as pitch. No sign of the Jaguar. No sign of *anything*. "Kay," I shouted.

Wind hurled my voice back into my face. A bird screeched and crashed its wings against the upper branches of a tree. It started to rain. I caught the glitter of the black water ahead. The night shifted and rustled all round me.

I turned back to the car and collected the heavy spanner from the back seat. "Kay," I shouted again, at the top of my voice.

Then I heard the laughter. High pitched like a woman's, but *not* a woman's. "Oh man! See who just came? The Winner Man himself. Go home, Winner Man. Ain't nothing for you here."

Martinez must be on the boat. I was standing on the jetty now, which was about eight feet wide. The boat was tied up down one side. Slowly my eyes adjusted to the darkness. The grey light coming off the river helped. Now I could make out the shape of our boat, could even identify the cockpit. If I could edge down to the end of the jetty I would be able to see into the cockpit.

"Stop fooling around, Winner Man. Go home, before you get hurt."

I wondered if he could see me? Surely not. The shore was behind me, whereas the light of the river was behind him—what light there was. I had the advantage. Even so I hesitated. I wiped the sweaty palm of my left hand against my trousers and transferred my grip on the spanner. Every step I took down the jetty took me further into the misty light coming off the river. The wind howled, the river hissed and gurgled, and Martinez jeered and catcalled.

I reached the bow of the boat and shouted: "I've come for my wife, Martinez. Send her out and—"

Suddenly Kay's screams rose above Martinez's sneers, above the wind. I dashed down the jetty. My foot caught a coiled rope and I stretched my length alongside the boat. I saw Kay struggling in the

349

cockpit, fighting Faberge, Martinez was on the deck behind them. Then I was shouting: "Jump, Kay—for God's sake, *jump!*"

Faberge turned at the sound of my shout. It was enough for Kay to scramble free. She threw herself across the gap between the boat and the jetty, landing a yard from me, her knees buckling as she fell. But I was up by then, swinging the spanner in a wide arc. The heavy steel cracked against bone and Faberge screamed with pain. My free hand found Kay's arm and I was dragging her back along the jetty. But then I dropped the spanner. I cursed as it fell with a clatter. Martinez whooped with triumph, and scuttled forward on the boat. He cleared the prow and landed on the jetty. *He had reached the shore ahead of us.* We were cut off.

Kay was trembling violently. I doubt I was much better. Falling over had opened the cut on my head, and the neck of my sweater was sticky with blood. "Where's Brooks?" I panted.

"Not back . . . he went to The Fisherman."

Martinez shouted: "Hey—Marcel. We got 'em trapped, man."

Faberge shouted some kind of reply. I saw his silhouette in the cockpit. He was hugging his right shoulder with his left hand. I knew I had to act fast, before he recovered. I cupped my hand to Kay's ear, pitching my voice against the wind. "The Mini's on the road—key in the ignition—take it and *go*—"

"No, Sam . . . *NO!*" I smacked her face hard. Every split second counted. Already Faberge was hunting for a boathook in the stern of the boat. Martinez would rush me any moment. I grabbed Kay's hand and started to run towards him.

I was at the prow of the boat before Martinez launched himself at me. His knee thumped upwards into my groin, but he was at the wrong angle to get any force behind it. Not that he had any real chance anyway. I was fighting like a madman, kicking wildly, lashing out with both fists. And by the time Faberge arrived with that boathook Martinez and I were rolling over and over, a foot or so from the water's edge. The wind shrieked louder than ever—and when I looked up Kay had gone.

It's all a bit hazy after that. I *know* Martinez fell into the water. I may have shoved him, I probably did. There was a hell of a splash but Faberge was coming at me with that boathook by then. I was backing up against the boat, trying to avoid his lunges, when I saw something behind him—on the river.

There was a skiff, very low in the water, with three men in it. The

350

prow of the skiff nosed up to the jetty just as Faberge lunged with
the boathook. I ducked, and it was a moment or two before I had a
chance to look again. One man was holding the skiff steady, and the
man behind him stood up in the boat—he looked as if he was about
to throw something. Then Faberge caught me across the head with
that boathook and—and, well I don't remember much after that.

THERE WAS A LONG SILENCE when I finished. They were thinking
over what I had told them. It was impossible to judge whether they
believed me. Llewellyn sucked on his empty pipe. Kaufman sat
staring at me, with his chin cupped in his hands. Bonello scratched
his head and watched smoke drift upwards from his cigarette.

Finally Llewellyn cleared his throat. "The police arrived at twelve
minutes past six that morning. You were unconscious. They never
knew about your wife. Martinez had drowned. The police autopsy
says he struck his head when he fell in the water. And Faberge was
dead, with a knife in him."

I nodded. There was nothing to add.

Kaufman lit a cigarette. "Forget what you said in court, Sam. Just
for the record—did you kill Faberge?"

I had already told them so much more than had come out at the
trial. "No," I said quietly. "I didn't kill Faberge."

Llewellyn murmured: "I assume the light was too bad for you to
give a positive description of these men in the skiff?"

I looked at him sharply and said: "The light was behind them—
what light there was. All I saw was their silhouettes. But the man
standing up in the boat was a big man I think. And . . ."

I can see him now. I'll always be able to see him. Just his outline,
his left leg forward and his body half turned towards me. His right
arm was bent, and his left arm was stretched out in front to balance
himself. Light glinted on something in his hand. His left hand, not
his throwing hand. That's what caught my eye I think, that sudden
glitter of light.

Kaufman rubbed his chin when I finished. "OK, Sam, we'll file it
away for now. And the man Brooks? You never saw him?"

"No. But we all know what happened to him, don't we?"

"We know what happened to him *later*," Kaufman corrected.
"Not what happened to him that night."

I nodded. There was nothing more. I had told them all I knew.

Kaufman bent his head over his papers. "So let's go on from there.

Six in the morning and the place is swarming with cops. You're out cold and Faberge and Martinez are dead. Then what happened?"

I sighed. I had a very strong feeling that Kaufman knew what had happened then. But there seemed no way to avoid telling him the rest of the story.

I WAS IN HOSPITAL when they arrested me. I never knew it but Kay was downstairs in the Special Care Unit. She had wrapped the Mini round a tree and was unconscious for three whole days.

They let me sleep the clock round—and when I awoke they arrested me, and charged me with the murder of Marcel Faberge. Too stunned to say much, I felt like death warmed up and must have looked it. Then I collapsed.

I was in another hospital when I came round, this time in prison. The following morning I was taken to Didcot Magistrates Court and remanded in custody. Lewis Collins made application for bail, but he was refused. Then he asked that I be given permission to visit Kay in hospital. But the police opposed that as well—so the magistrates handed down another refusal.

I was taken to Aylesbury Prison then. Collins arrived about two hours later and we were given privacy and a chance to discuss the charge levelled against me. I told him about Faberge and the others being at Ashley Grange—but not what they had been doing. I just couldn't bring myself to talk about it. It made things damned awkward because like all deceptions it led to complications. For instance Collins wanted to know how I got the bang on the head—the one which took nine stitches to fix. I waffled a bit, but in the end I had to admit I had been knocked cold in a fight before Faberge had left.

Collins knew I was being evasive and he got angry. "Listen, Sam. Not only are you charged with murder, but the police are very hostile towards you. What's got into you, anyway?"

I mumbled some sort of answer, but he was far from satisfied. He looked at his watch. "I've got to get back to town now, but I'll be back tomorrow and I'll want to know exactly what happened."

Life was a series of shocks after that. Like breakfast the next morning—a rasher of greasy bacon and a mug of greasier cocoa. A screw yelling at me to make my bed. One lavatory for a hundred prisoners—with no door, no seat and no toilet paper. Prison clothing—stiff, discoloured underwear, shoes worn by a hundred prisoners before me. And always that prison smell that clings to your hair and settles deep in your pores.

Edgar Hardman came to see me the next morning. A prison guard stood by the door to take notes of everything we talked about. Edgar looked tired and haggard, and about ninety-nine years old. I asked if he had seen Kay.

He nodded: "Just left the hospital. She's still in intensive care. Multiple fractures of the skull, a broken leg, fractured pelvis. Still unconscious of course. But the doctors aren't *too* worried. I'm going back to the hospital from here."

"Stay with her, Edgar. And give her my love when she comes round."

He offered me a cigarette, glanced at the guard, then fixed me with a look which said to keep quiet until he finished. "The police have been to see me, Sam. About Kay being in town with me the other night. Silly misunderstanding when I called at your place earlier in the evening. I was on my way back from Wickham Manor, so I thought I'd give her a lift up to town. But, as you know, she had left already—she was actually waiting for me when I got home."

I was lost for words. The screw glanced up curiously. I could *feel* his suspicions. I was damn sure he would guess some kind of message was being passed. Edgar's face twisted into a smile. He said: "Of course, as soon as I told her about the burglary at your place and you getting a knock on the head, she wanted to get back. Good job you phoned when you did, I can tell you—otherwise she would have left there and then. As it was she left at crack of light in the morning, you know. Before I was up. Of course I thought she had the Jaguar—not that little Mini—didn't find that out till later."

My brain meshed into gear. I marvelled at the way he had swept up all the loose ends. Everything had been explained. And what was more natural for Kay to have left at crack of dawn to get back to an injured husband. It seemed foolproof.

When he left I was moved into the maximum security block, which is where I remained for my entire stay in Aylesbury. After Kay emerged from her coma, Edgar kept the police at bay with a battery of physicians and lawyers. Then he moved her to a private nursing home. By the time she did make a statement it tallied with Edgar's exactly. I had already decided to keep Kay out of it, but now I had no choice—or rather the only alternative was to call Edgar and Kay liars in open court, and I would never do that.

I told Collins everything on his next visit—*everything*. We were talking in an empty cell, without a screw taking every word down, and I was anxious to know how I stood, what sort of chance I had.

Collins paced up and down, smoking. "You realize what's happened? Your father-in-law has sold you down the river."

"Rubbish. He's just worried about Kay. And I want her kept out of it too. Edgar knows that—he's trying to protect both of us—"

"Funny way of showing it."

"Suppose it all came out? What good would that do? Gives me an extra reason for being mad enough to kill Faberge, that's all."

"And you *didn't* kill him?"

"Lewis, I just told you. That's exactly what happened. When I blacked out Faberge was only too alive—"

"OK, OK—I had to ask, that's all." He avoided looking at me. I knew he thought I was lying. After a moment or two he scratched his head. "Only two people can vouch for your story," he growled. "One is your wife and we all know what she's saying. The other is this black guy, Brooks. And he's disappeared. Vanished. Unless the police are holding him."

"You mean in prison?"

"No, I mean under wraps. Holding him for the trial. To refute your evidence."

"Can they do that?"

"They can do anything, Sam. I've never known them so prickly. This guy Davis is getting them all steamed up."

"Inspector Davis? The Club Squad Davis?"

Collins nodded. "Did you ever do anything to that man? Think carefully, it's important."

I scowled. "Davis is always on my back. I hate his guts."

"It's mutual, Sam, believe me. Davis got at the local law even before we were in front of the magistrates. He fed them a tale about you being a bad influence in the West End, an out-and-out villain. Davis is making a career out of bad-mouthing you."

"But if we know this we can stop him surely?"

"How? What we know was told me over a few drinks by the local law. A few drinks and—" Collins rubbed his thumb and index finger together. "A half bent copper telling tales out of school is one thing. The same copper in court is a different animal."

It was a gloomy meeting. They mostly were, with Collins. I felt very depressed and tried to talk myself out of it by saying that things

354

couldn't get worse. But that was a mistake. They got worse the very next day, when a Receiver was appointed at Apex Holdings. We had a bank overdraft like most other businesses, well covered by assets, and there was nothing to worry about in normal circumstances. But these weren't normal circumstances. The bank had panicked because of the bad publicity and had appointed a Receiver over our heads. It was the beginning of the end for Apex. When a Receiver is appointed the directors automatically lose their authority. The sole charge of the business rests with the Receiver—and he sets about turning assets into cash to repay the bank in double quick time.

Meanwhile Lewis Collins was worrying about all sorts of things— but mainly about money. My income had ceased the moment the Receiver walked into Apex, and although I was comfortably off my money was tied up in Apex shares—now of dubious value—and in Ashley Grange and Rex Place, and various possessions—motorcars, antiques, paintings, that bloody boat, things like that. I was able to realize about twenty thousand, which seemed to keep him happy for the time being. But that was about all he was happy about.

A few friends came to see me in Aylesbury. Jack of course, but not Maria, although she always sent her love and wrote frequently. Edgar came to see me—but only twice after his first visit. Prison upset him and I can't say I blame him. But Kay never came. Nor did Charlie Weston or Lew Douglas—or anyone else from Apex.

It took them five months to bring me to trial. Collins was busy spending my money, but there was little to show for it. He had not found Brooks, nor any proof of the existence of the skiff or the men in it, nor had he found out anything discrediting about Inspector Davis. A month before the trial Collins engaged a QC and told me he was planning a conference three days later.

I shrugged and waited for Collins to deliver the rest of the news. "Sam," he said, "this story of yours—you know we can't sell it to the court. It's Kay's account which screws us. Hers and her father's. So suppose we use their story for our own ends."

I took one of his cigarettes but when I put a match to it I noticed my hand tremble. Then he surprised me by saying: "Wouldn't amaze me too much if you got it wrong. What with that crack on the head and everything. Suppose it happened like this. Ashley Grange was broken into, right? You got thumped on the head. OK, let's stick to that because the police have accepted it. Your housekeeper goes to bed, you speak to Kay on the phone at her father's place—

then you get to worrying. What were the burglars *really* after? Then you remember some important papers you left on the boat—say you were working on them the previous weekend, something like that. In the end you worry so much that you get dressed and go over to fetch them. Then you run into Faberge and Martinez."

"But—but what the hell were *they* doing there?"

He shrugged. "Who knows—who *cares?* They had a grudge after that business at the club. We can bring witnesses to confirm that. Maybe they were planning to scuttle your boat out of spite. Hell Sam, they're dead—they won't trouble us."

"And what about the car? If Kay had the Mini, how in God's name was I supposed to get there?"

"In the Jag. It was by the boat when the police arrived."

That, at least, was news to me. I certainly hadn't seen it. I sat thinking over what he had said. I hated the thought of telling a pack of lies. On the other hand I was afraid to tell the truth.

Collins pressed on. "Sam, don't you see—it's a much better story. Without the papers to rescue, what motive did you have for going to the boat? There's only the police's answer to that—you went there to fix Faberge and Martinez once and for all. On the other hand if you remember it *this* way—you ran into them, they attacked you, and whatever happened then was self defence. Got it?"

I'm not very proud of my answer. I simply asked: "Will it work?"

He grinned. "My advice is give it to Malcolm Gerrard. He's our QC. A good man. Expensive of course, but—" he shrugged.

I signed another promissory note.

A week before the trial, Brooks turned up. A farmer had been ploughing his fields not far from the boat, and had unearthed the remains of a black human body. They were the remains of Archie Brooks. Of course the newspapers never actually said I was involved. In fact, with my trial less than a week away, they were careful about even mentioning my name. But Collins was in despair about it and I wasn't exactly over the moon.

After that we went to trial. That was another shock because it was the first I heard of *plea bargaining*. It's not supposed to happen in Britain, but according to Collins it happens all the time. The first inkling I got was at eleven o'clock, in my cell below the courtroom. Battle should have commenced at ten and I was wondering what the delay was about when Collins came to see me.

"Gerrard's had a long session with the prosecution. There's a chance of a deal," he said excitedly. "They'll drop the charge of murder and go for manslaughter—if we agree to plead guilty."

"*Guilty?* Lewis, I never killed him. Can't you get that into your head? I never killed the bastard—"

"Sam, listen a minute. Gerrard's convinced the most you'll get for manslaughter is six years. And six could mean three with remission. Sam, it's a *breakthrough*. Until now we've been fighting the possibility of life. It's one hell of a step forward—"

"*Step forward?* Lewis, I didn't kill him—"

"I've got to get back upstairs," he said looking at his watch. "Just thought you'd want to know what was happening. Sam—it's your first offence. The way Gerrard's dealing there's even a chance of a suspended sentence. You might not even *go* to jail."

He left me to stew. Dammit, I was *innocent*. Why the hell should I plead guilty? It was a hell of a decision. Part of me wanted to fight all the way—try to prove my innocence. But the prospect of freedom made me giddy. If I could get out *now*—there was still a chance of saving Apex and of getting it back from the Receiver. Collins was back within fifteen minutes—wanting my answer. With a heavy heart I agreed to plead manslaughter. He looked pleased, patted my back and left me to wait in my cell.

My trial only lasted an hour. As soon as the judge summed up I knew Collins had been over-optimistic. I *knew* I would be sent to prison. So I was prepared for the sentence when it came. Six years. The policeman motioned me to turn and go back downstairs to the cells, and just as I did so I looked up, to see Kay watching me.

I stopped dead in my tracks. Kay was in the front row. She looked tanned and well. The policeman pushed me from behind and I stumbled down the top two stairs. I craned my neck, resisting the policeman's pushing hands on my shoulders. I wanted to go back, for a last look, a final word. I could still see Kay's face, framed in the opening at the top of the stairs. "Kay," I shouted.

A man reached over to pat her shoulder. He stood up behind her, resting both hands on her shoulders. I couldn't see his face. Then the policeman kicked my legs from under me and I fell down the rest of the stairs—and Kay had gone.

KAUFMAN STOOD UP when I finished. He crossed to the windows, and stood there, hitching up his trousers and staring moodily out across the terrace.

"Well, well, well," he growled to himself. "What do you know? What *do* you know?"

"It all fits," Llewellyn said, "like pieces of a jigsaw."

"And how," Kaufman said. Then he jerked his head in my direction. "That poor schmuck never knew what hit him."

I walked to the sideboard and poured myself a scotch. It was a relief to have finished, even though it left me feeling on edge. I said: "Didn't you say something about an *exchange* of information? It's been a bit one-sided so far. It's your turn, Kaufman. Where's all this proof you promised? The name of the man running your precious Pipeline—the man I'm supposed to know."

Llewellyn cleared his throat. "Two men run the Pipeline—possibly three. Serracino is one, of course. He organizes the procurement of heroin throughout the Middle East. The distribution end is run by the man known as The Ferryman, and we think a third man liaises between him and Serracino."

"And The Ferryman is the man I'm supposed to know?"

"Sure you know him," Kaufman said. "That's why we had to use you. You're the best chance we ever had of penetrating the Pipeline." He turned to Bonello. "Tell him about the man we had in Sicily."

Bonello raised his sad eyes to mine. "Two years ago," he said, "one of our agents succeeded in confirming that part—if not all—of the Pipeline was organized from Sicily. He worked alone, constantly in danger as he probed deeper. Then one day he overheard a name—how and where we never found out. He was discovered and chased—because that name was important. He got as far as his hotel room in Palermo. Got as far as reaching me on the telephone. Then they shot the lock off the door and murdered him—but not before he screamed one name down the line to me, Mr. Harris—and we believe it was the name of The Ferryman."

Kaufman swung back to me. "We started digging after that. On the face of it this man was a respectable English businessman. Then we found out his connection with you. Bear in mind that we already knew Corrao's instructions were to take Apex without hurting you. So now we had another link. Eventually we committed a little burglary at a house in Chelsea. *His* house. Still nothing—except for that photograph. So we ask ourselves—what's a man like *this* doing with a photograph like *that?*" Kaufman pointed a finger at me. "And now we get your story. You were framed and you know it. Not necessarily the murder—maybe that was an added bonus, but everything that led up to it. Come on, Sam—wake up! He was putting you away. They wanted Apex, but you fought too hard. Maybe originally he meant to give you a break for his daughter's sake, but you left him no choice. He knew you wouldn't contradict the story he gave the police. And once you got suckered into that there was no way you could get out clean—"

"Rubbish! He was protecting Kay—"

"Like hell! With that photo in his safe? What sort of father is that? You think it was there for the family album? He'd have used it against you if the murder rap hadn't done the job for him."

"You can't *possibly* be right—"

"I'm right, buddy boy. Some poor agent screaming his last breath down a phone ain't telling lies. One name he got out—and *that name was Hardman.* That's the man running the Pipeline. That's the man who *ruined you!* Your precious father-in-law—"

"I don't believe—"

"You don't want to believe. But you've got twelve hours to wise-up because tomorrow you're going down the Pipeline. And The Ferryman is there waiting for you. He's already made contact—"

"Contact?"

"We got a girl answering your telephone at Rex Place. Edgar Hardman has called three times in the last two hours. Sounds like he's damned keen to see you."

Chapter 6

They drugged me when they took me from the big house. Oh, not the way they did before—there was no struggle this time. After a meal they put something in my drink. At least I think they did because I was wide awake one moment and struggling to keep my eyes open the next. And the next I knew was waking in my bed at Rex Place.

I heard a noise downstairs, from the kitchen. I wrapped myself in a dressing gown and crept down into the hall. It was Jack, breaking eggs into a frying pan. "Are you the last?" I asked. "Or are there more surprises later?"

Not that I was really surprised. Something in the back of my mind said Jack was involved. He *had* to be. How else could they have bugged the place? How else could Lucia have been ready and waiting? Jack *must* have known—and so must Maria.

He managed a self-conscious smile as he poured coffee into cups. "Sorry about not telling you. Kaufman made us promise. Said it would only be for a couple of days."

I shovelled sugar into the coffee. "How long have you known?"

He moved a pan on the stove. "How long haven't I? Maria told me her story before we got married. Her parents were Vito and Franka, you know. Anyway, Enrico came to see us six or seven months ago. Lucia put him on to us. We thought it was a social visit at first—but then he took us to meet Kaufman. Kaufman needed my cooperation so he had to tell me what he was up to. About old Hardman running the racket over here—"

"That's rubbish. I told them that yesterday."

He shrugged. "Kaufman and Enrico are professionals, Sam—they know what they're doing."

I shook my head stubbornly.

He flipped eggs onto a warmed plate, added rashers of bacon from under the grill, and brought them to the table. "Well anyway—they reckoned Hardman needed a shove if they were to nail him. Kaufman figured if Hardman thought you knew about the Pipeline he would do one of two things. Either invite you to join, or—" he drew a finger across his throat.

Despite everything I had to smile. It was just so damn stupid to think of Edgar killing me. I changed the subject. "What about this lot? Where do you fit in?"

"Right next to you," he grinned. "It was part of the deal."

"Deal?"

He shifted on his seat. "The rumours about you started the day you went inside. People said you were taking the rap for someone else. That's what gave Kaufman his idea. I think. He argued that the Pipeline might suspect you of knowing something and come looking for you. Doing things Kaufman's way made sure—but, well, he persuaded me that the benefits to you justified the risk—"

"*Benefits?*"

He stood up and crossed to the larder—a big, walk-in job, lined with shelves. He pushed the back of the larder and *it swung open.* I saw a short passage, with two doors at the end. Jack grinned at my astonishment. "You left that way the other night."

Henderson and his mate! *That* was how they got into the cottage!

360

Jack closed the wall again and returned to the table. "One door leads to a house in Wells Court, and the other goes next door."

"Wells Court?" I said weakly, trying to take it all in.

"It backs onto here. Kaufman's got a sort of Field HQ there. Radio communications and all sorts of stuff. And the front bedroom next door is like a film studio. All the comings and goings of Rex Place are filmed. Twenty-four hours a day, infra-red equipment, the lot. And of course the whole place is bugged."

I began to realize what Kaufman had meant by watching over me like a baby. "And you *agreed* to all this?"

He flushed. "Not immediately. It was a hell of a decision. But after a week I began to see Kaufman's argument. That the mob *might* come looking for you—and, well you'd have a better chance with all this." He waved a hand as if we were sitting in the middle of an armoury. "And there was another reason, perhaps the biggest. Kaufman promised he'd get you out twelve months early."

So *that* was it. I had wondered about that. Collins had reckoned on three years. But I assumed I had been such a docile prisoner that some extra remission had come my way. Jack was watching me with such an anxious look that I reached over and punched his shoulder. "Thanks, Jack—I'd have done the same for you."

He brightened. "Of course," he said. "I dealt myself in—why should you have all the fun."

"But you can't get involved. What about Maria—"

"Gone away. Staying at a safe house in the country. Kaufman fixed it. Two Special Branch men, and a housekeeper to look after her." He was grinning again. "The pubs can run themselves and The Dog's Home is closed—we bought the place next door and the builders are in extending the place—so it's all fixed."

I was telling him he was mad when the door bell rang. It buzzed once, then twice, and ended with an extra long burst—like a snatch of morse code. Jack's grin broadened. "That's Lucia. She's our secretary—and maybe your girlfriend. The cover story is that you met her at our place and offered her a job."

Lucia kissed me when I opened the door. It wasn't a peck on the cheek, either. I was just relaxing into it when she pulled away. Two men were about a yard behind her, one with a raised camera. The man with the camera said: "Any statement, Mr. Harris?"

Lucia snuggled into my side and answered before I got my breath back. "No statement, boys—and before you ask, we're just good friends." She drew me across the threshold. As she closed the door she said: "If we're going to do this every morning, can you shave first? You've got a chin like a pot scourer."

"If I shave now, can we try again?"

"I can wait," she said drily.

I went upstairs to dress and when I came down they were all in the kitchen. The larder door was open and Kaufman was at the table. "What about Tomlinson?" I demanded, having just remembered him. "Isn't he busy making appointments with counsel?"

"Yeah, it's a pity about Tomlinson." Kaufman rubbed his jaw thoughtfully. "Fact is you took us by surprise—moving that fast. We reckoned you'd dump Collins but we never expected you to hire a new lawyer that quickly."

I felt pleased. It made me feel less of a robot programmed by Kaufman's computer. Kaufman checked his watch. "Ten o'clock. Henderson should be with Tomlinson now. He's got a letter from the Home Office. The police will be instructed to withdraw their objections at the appropriate time. You'll get your licences back—when all this is over."

Jack grinned and I didn't know what to say.

Then Kaufman launched into a lecture on "procedure"—what I *was* and *was not* to do. I was never to go out alone. Lucia would answer the telephone. If anyone asked to meet me I would arrange to see them at Rex Place or in a public building. "The main job is to stop them snatching you," he said. "That's what they'll try to do. But don't worry, our people will be covering you wherever you go. Like I said, Sam—we're watching over you like a baby."

Even so I jumped when the telephone rang in the sitting room. We listened as Lucia chatted up another reporter. Kaufman smiled. "Relax, Sam—Hardman will call soon. Remember the procedure that's all—leave the rest to us."

Events proved him right. It was ten forty when the telephone rang, and Lucia's face was flushed with excitement when it popped round the door. "It's Lord Hardman," she said, looking at me.

I avoided Kaufman's eye. We followed Lucia into the sitting room. An extension had been fitted to the telephone on the desk— *and* some kind of intercom. Kaufman reached for the extension and nodded to me. "Edgar?" I said into the telephone.

"*Sam!* I've been trying to reach you for days! Tried half a dozen times yesterday. Sam—how *are* you?"

He sounded exactly as I had remembered him. The same old Edgar. I said: "I'm fine, Edgar—and you?"

"All the better for hearing you. Dammit, Sam—why haven't you called? I was hoping to hear, you know—"

I felt guilty. He was giving me the kind of welcome Jack and Maria had given me the day I came out. *The day I came out*—three days ago! *Only three!* I said: "I'm sorry, Edgar, I was planning to call you today. Meant to yesterday but I had meetings all day and—"

"Never mind that now—you're excused. Sam—it's splendid to hear you. When can I see you? Are you free for lunch today?"

Kaufman was nodding and mouthing "procedure" at the same time. I felt like a traitor, but I said: "Lunch is fine, Edgar."

"Great! The Club then—about twelve thirty?"

The Club? Kaufman's lecture rang in my ears and I said: "Edgar— I can't—not the club. I mean, I've—" I was making a mess of it. I sensed Kaufman stiffen with alarm. I gulped, then said: "Look, Edgar, do me a favour. Be *my* guest today, will you? Problem is I must be in Hampstead at half past two for another appointment. There's a good restaurant out there—The Hunter's Tower, you must know it. Could we meet there?"

"Hampstead? Hunter's Tower, you say?"

"That's right. Edgar, if you wouldn't *mind*—"

"*Mind?* Why the hell should I? Half past twelve then—all right?"

I was sweating when I replaced the receiver. Kaufman grinned and passed me the handkerchief from his top pocket.

"That was swell, Sam—just swell. Handled it like a pro." He took my elbow. "Come on, now, you gotta be briefed before you go to work."

And we went back to the kitchen where I received my instructions, just like any other spy.

THE HUNTER'S TOWER sits high up on Hampstead Heath. I propped up the counter in the Turret Bar and looked out of the window. The view outside was a bit special: across Hampstead to the West End, with the City office blocks on the sky line. Closer at hand I saw our taxi in the car park. Or rather, Kaufman's taxi. Our driver, Watkins, was downstairs now, in the other bar. He wouldn't leave before me, any more than Henderson would, now immersed in his *Financial Times* at his corner table.

Across the room two lovers held hands. Apart from them and

Henderson and the man behind the bar, I had the place to myself. Which is why I had chosen this place. It was never busy at lunchtimes, and I could be sure of a quiet corner.

Suddenly Edgar Hardman stood in the doorway. But I had to look twice to recognize him. He had aged ten years since I last saw him—his back was bent and his mane of grey hair had turned white.

I went forward to meet him. His eyes lit up when he saw me and his greeting was every bit as cordial as I might have expected. I told the story we had agreed upon—a friend would pick me up after lunch for us to go on to our meeting together. This was to provide an excuse in case Edgar suggested we went on elsewhere.

Early conversation at reunions is always a bit stilted and ours was no exception. I tried to follow Kaufman's advice and make Edgar lead the conversation, but apart from the occasional dry comment, he was taciturn. And although Kay must have been in our thoughts—I had heard no news of her since our divorce—we both avoided her name. The headwaiter collected our orders and we had a drink before going through to the dining room. From the corner of my eye I watched Henderson select a spot near the entrance before resuming his study of the share prices.

Edgar picked at his food with the appetite of a sparrow. It saddened me to watch him. I remembered Edgar from the old days—full of life and authority. Now he was a shadow of his former self. And just as he had changed, so too it seemed had our relationship. We had been good friends once, but now we had to struggle to find things to say to each other.

As we neared the end of the main course, Edgar raised his glass with approval. I had ordered a Mouton Rothschild. He swallowed slowly and set his glass back on the table. "It still exists," he said, "the quality trade. Only wish we still did it—but Charlie Weston moved us down market. Most of our stuff is plonk these days. He controls Hardman's Wine now, of course."

I was more than surprised. "I didn't know that. How—why?"

He shrugged. "That damn silly deal I did with Apex. Guaranteeing the share prices, remember? Seemed safe as houses at the time. But when the Receiver sold it off—well, I had to settle with Weston and Douglas." Edgar sighed. "Business is business. I don't blame them especially, but I could have done with more time."

"So what happened?" I asked.

He was embarrassed. "I settled with Douglas for cash," he said.

364

"He's sold up here, you know—lives abroad—extended his hotels in the Mediterranean, I think. But—well, I owed Charlie Weston a million and a half. Takes some finding, Sam. I couldn't raise it without liquidating, so Charlie accepted shares in the wine business. He's been our bulk carrier for years, you know, so he knows a bit about it. He was quite decent on the whole—the shares were transferred at a fair price, and that was that."

"So what are you left with?" I asked grimly.

He reached across and patted my arm. "Don't worry about me, Sam. They kept me on as chairman and I still own five per cent of the business. I'm still rich, by some people's standards."

A waiter cleared our plates away. I was about to say something but Edgar waved me down. "Anyway, let's not waste time talking about my business. It's yours I want to talk about."

I said "yes" to the waiter about coffee and when I turned back Edgar was saying: "This rubbish in the papers. About you going back into the club business. You can't *possibly* be serious. *They* won't let you go back, surely you realize that?"

I froze. Kaufman could not—*must not*—be right. I stared at him. I could not believe what I heard. "Who are *they*, Edgar?"

Instead of answering he sat back in his chair and looked nervously round the room. Only two tables were occupied: the lovers on one, Henderson on the other.

"Dammit, Sam, there must be something else. Another line of business—" He cursed as he fumbled with his cigarettes. He was actually *trembling*. "Sam—it's not that I've anything *against* clubs— but—but, well I was rather hoping *we* might do something together. I know I'm not as well off as I was, but—well I would like to help you get started again."

Was that all it was? Edgar rallying to help? The gesture of a friend? "That's very nice of you, Edgar, but—"

The waiter arrived with a pot of coffee and Edgar fidgeted until the man went away. "It would be fun," he said. "Working together again. Any business you like except clubs—"

"Edgar, is something the matter?" I asked bluntly. He was frightened, I was sure of it. "Something's worrying you," I said. "Edgar, just now you said *they*—who are they?"

"Sssh, Sam—*please*." He looked round the room again. "Not here, Sam—we can't talk now."

"Edgar, you can tell me, surely?"

"I *must* tell you," he said with sudden determination. "Ever since January I've waited to tell you. But we can't talk now—your friend will be here in a minute—"

"Jack? He can wait in the bar downstairs—"

"They'll be closing—besides you have your appointment." He seemed more in control of himself than a minute earlier. He checked his watch. "And I ought to be going."

I cursed under my breath. Jack's involvement had been Kaufman's idea—now I *wanted* to go on and Jack's arrival would prevent it. "Why not come back to my place now?" I suggested. "We could talk for a while longer, in privacy—"

"But your appointment—" He broke off, looking over my shoulder.

I turned and saw Jack in the doorway. He waved and began to thread his way between the tables to where we sat. I turned to Edgar. "Tonight then?" I said urgently. "Come round for a drink—"

Jack grinned down at us. I made the introductions. The waiter arrived with our bill. *Damn!* There was so much I wanted to know. "Tonight, Edgar," I pleaded. "Any time to suit you."

We stood up. I put some notes on the plate and indicated that the waiter should keep the change. Jack turned for the entrance, and then Edgar said: "About eight then—will that be all right?"

I sighed with relief. "We've a lot to talk about," I said, with a hand on his elbow.

He knew I meant Kay. Or at least in part. There was a flash of pain in his eyes, followed by that haunted, worried expression. We rode down in the lift, turned towards the exit which opened onto the car park, then walked through the doors into the pale sunlight. Edgar's chauffeur was waiting outside.

Then I heard the shouting. *"Down! For God's sake, get down!"*

I turned and saw Henderson ten yards away. His knees were bent and his right hand was thrust forward, supported by his left. He looked like a cop in a TV film, and the gun in his hand was blazing away at the bushes under some elm trees. As I swung back I saw splashes of red on Edgar's coat. His eyes opened wide, his knees buckled and he fell backwards. Then Jack hurled me to the ground.

I heard a wildly revving engine and felt my face cut by flying gravel as our taxi skidded to a halt in front of us. The driver screamed to get inside. We threw ourselves through the open door. Watkins leaped out, crouched like Henderson—fired twice at the bushes, shouted something, threw himself back up behind his wheel, crashed into gear—and almost stood the cab on its side as he swerved away. I saw Edgar's chauffeur face down on the gravel, the back of his head covered with blood. Then I got a hand to the door and slammed it shut.

IT TOOK US a long time to get back to Rex Place—but then it would, the way we went. Edgware, Harrow, across the Western Avenue at Hanger Lane and down into Ealing—then along the Uxbridge Road to Shepherds Bush and up the Bayswater Road. It was procedure: someone gets hit, you scatter. When we reached Marble Arch Watkins said: "We're going in the back way. Wells Court. When we get there walk straight up the path to the front door. It will open as you reach it. Go straight in—but don't run or do anything daft. You got that?"

I said yes. Jack scowled out of the window. He had barely spoken for the last half hour. Being involved in a shooting is a frightening experience, but he looked more angry than scared. I was angry too—angry with Kaufman and his senseless suspicions about Edgar. And now Edgar was dead.

We turned into Mount Street and a minute later we were there—number fifteen Wells Court. I had been curious about the place earlier but I couldn't care less now—I was too bloody anxious to get hold of Kaufman and tell him what I thought of his half-baked ideas.

It was a very short path to the door but it seemed a very long way. Any second I expected the crack of a rifle. My spine tingled where it would shatter under the impact of a bullet. But the door opened as we reached it and a second later I was inside, with Jack on my heels.

He brushed past me to lead the way. The room was at the back of the house, quite large, bigger than the sitting room at Rex Place. Half a dozen easy chairs were set in a semi-circle facing a desk. Three reel-to-reel tape recorders were bracketed to one wall, and the long table against the far side was littered with telephones. Kaufman rose from behind the desk as we entered. Llewellyn watched us from an armchair.

"You great, stupid bastard!" Jack roared at Kaufman. "You said Sam would be safe. So how *safe* was he today, Kaufman? If I hadn't knocked him down he'd be dead now."

"Back off will you!" Kaufman shouted back. "You know what was out there today? A professional hit man, complete with Schneider

303 and telescopic sights. Well, *he* won't be worrying us again, but don't kid yourself—if they had wanted Sam no fancy heroics from you would have saved him." He waved at a chair. "Sit down, Sam. You look white as a sheet. You wanna coffee or something?"

"No," I said, "I don't want coffee."

Llewellyn frowned. "Surprising turn of events, eh?"

"Not for me," I said coldly. "I never thought Edgar was your mysterious Ferryman."

Kaufman flushed. "How many innocent men get whacked by hit men? Hardman being killed don't change a thing. He was in this up to his back teeth. Maybe someone down the line got ambitious. A struggle for power? Happens all the time—"

"That's your explanation, is it?" I sneered.

"I don't have an *explanation*. But I've told you what we *do* have. That fancy photo locked up in Hardman's safe. A man ripped apart as he shouts Hardman's name down an open line—"

"He was frightened. *Terrified!* He was going to tell me—"

"Yeah? Well, he ain't now." Kaufman slapped the flat of his hand down on the desk. Then he sighed heavily, like a man trying not to lose his temper. "OK, Sam, cool down. Now let's hear about your conversation with Hardman."

It took an hour and a half for them to debrief me, and when we had finished Kaufman walked heavily to the table and picked up a bottle of Johnny Walker. "Want a slug, Sam?"

I accepted gratefully and Kaufman handed me a glass, then reached across the desk to push a button on the intercom. When Lucia answered he asked: "Anything happening?"

"No visitors, but the phone's been busy. Press mainly—they've picked up the angle that Hardman was Sam's ex-father-in-law. They want Sam's comments. I said that Sam is shocked and very upset— and he's not taking any calls until tomorrow."

Kaufman nodded approvingly. "Nobody suggested Sam was there when it happened?"

"No, nobody," Lucia confirmed. I wondered how my name had been kept out of it. My face had appeared in the morning papers so one of the waiters might have recognized me.

"Anything else?" Kaufman asked.

"A man called Darmanin keeps calling. He sounds very upset and says he needs to speak to Sam urgently."

Kaufman looked at me. "You know any Darmanin?" When I shook

my head he said: "Probably a reporter. You ask what he wanted, Lucia?"

"Yes—but he'll only discuss it with Sam."

Kaufman shrugged. "OK—we're coming through." He switched off and stood up. "Come on, Sam—let's go home."

He led the way into a passageway—and then we came out into the larder at Rex Place. Cooking smells closed round me like memories from another world. *My* world. Kaufman sniffed with approval. "Don't tell me—let me guess. Spaghetti bolognaise?"

Lucia turned from the stove. "It's ossobuco—and it won't be ready for hours yet."

"That's just fine." Jack went to the bathroom while Kaufman and I went into the sitting room. "What's the frown about?" Kaufman asked.

I shook my head. "So much has happened. I'm still trying to fit it together. Coming out of gaol—seeing Jack and Maria again—meeting Lucia . . ." My mind reeled as I tried to retrace the sequence of events. *Three days!* Could it really be only *three days?* Then another thought struck me. "Davis," I said. "What about Davis?"

"What about him?"

"He's bent. He was always at me in the old days. And he *still* is."

Kaufman smiled. "We know all about Davis. Someone paid him a bundle to lean on you. He never actually *did* much—just harassed you with a lot of official muscle, that's all."

"That's all? You try living with it." Then I realized what he had said. "Paid him—*who* paid him?"

"Are you kidding? Can't you guess?" Kaufman shrugged. "Fifty thousand in three undeclared bank accounts—one in a false name. Davis earned plenty making your life a misery—"

"He's *still* at it. He's still on the force. He's—"

"Listen, Sam—putting Davis away won't break the Pipeline. When we move we want the whole works—the Pipeline *and* the men running it."

Just at that moment the telephone rang and Lucia crossed the room to answer it. She gave the number, listened for a moment, then said: "Yes—hello, Mr. Darmanin—I'll check if he's in."

Kaufman switched on the loudspeaker extension and we moved to the desk together. "Hello—Sam Harris here."

"Mr. Harris—my name is Darmanin." The voice paused as if to

give me time to recognize the name. When I remained silent the voice continued: "My son is—my son *was*—Tony. He worked for a friend of yours until—until this afternoon."

It took me a moment to realize what he meant. Then I blurted it out. "Your son was the chauffeur?"

"Yes, yes," the voice said impatiently. "Can you see me now— tonight?" I wondered why. Kaufman was busy writing on a scratch pad when Darmanin said: "I—I *must* see you. My courage will fail by the morning, or—or the Pipeline will kill me, too."

I heard Lucia's sudden intake of breath. Kaufman swore softly and wrote "meet him" and "procedure" on the pad. As calmly as I could I asked: "Where are you, Mr. Darmanin?"

"Greek Street. Number fifty-one. I run a bar. The Lantern. It is closed tonight but I live upstairs."

Kaufman wrote "fetch in cab" in large letters.

I said: "Look Mr. Darmanin, I can't get over myself—but I'll send someone in a cab. He'll be with you in ten minutes—"

"I must see *you*—"

"You will—I'm sending someone in a cab to bring you to me. Then nobody need know we've ever met. It's safer—understand?"

"Yes—but—"

I hung up. Kaufman prodded a button on the intercom. "You get all that?" he asked, and Henderson said "yes" from the operations room next door.

Kaufman said: "Get down there. Take Watkins in the cab and have a back-up car behind you." He switched off, flushed with excitement. "It's beginning to break. Didn't I tell you. Stir the pond up real good and all sorts of stuff floats to the surface."

"And that man," I said, "sounded *very* frightened."

"He did, didn't he? *That* man—running a nothing special bar in Soho—whose son Hardman employed as a chauffeur. I wonder—"

"He's Maltese," Jack said unexpectedly. He had just returned from the bathroom. "Darmanin is a Maltese name."

As soon as he said it I knew he was right. Soho was full of Maltese. I was about to add something when I saw the expression on Lucia's face. She said: "Fiore Serracino used Maltese papers to get into the UK at the end of the sixties. He lived in Cardiff amongst the Maltese. He would have made contacts—"

Kaufman snapped the button down on the intercom. "What have we got on that chauffeur?"

Llewellyn answered. "The prelims came across the teleprinter ten minutes ago. Tony Darmanin, aged twenty-five. Single, lived with his father in Greek Street. Occupation chauffeur. Maltese nationality, been here three years. No police record, clean driving licence." He paused. "That's all so far."

Kaufman thanked him and switched off. He peered at his watch under the light from the table lamp. "How far away is Greek Street?"

I shrugged. "Fifteen minutes—depends on the traffic."

"It's nearly seven." Kaufman looked at me. "What time did—"

"Nearly *seven?*" Jack checked his watch. "Hell! I promised Maria I'd phone her at six. She'll be worried sick. Look, I'll just give her a quick call—"

"Make it upstairs will you," Kaufman nodded at the telephone on the desk. "I want the outside line kept free here. We've installed another one upstairs. The green handset."

Jack walked to the door. I said: "Give Maria my love."

"Not likely. She talks about you too much as it is."

"It's happening, Sam." Kaufman carried his glass across the room. "I can *feel* it. We've rattled the bastards."

I nodded. "Like the Czechs rattled Hitler before the war. The next week he walked all over them."

Then the telephone rang again. Lucia went white when she answered it. She stood perfectly still. And when she covered the mouthpiece she was trembling. "It's Corrao," she said, "Pietro Corrao. At least, he *says* he is."

We moved for the desk together, bumping into each other. Kaufman put a hand on my arm as I reached for the telephone, but I brushed him aside. "Hello—Sam Harris speaking."

A jeering laugh burned a hole in my memory. "Hallo, Winner," he said. "How does it feel to be a free man again?"

Hatred made my mouth go dry. Corrao! I *hated* him.

"Winner? Still there, Winner?"

"Yes, I'm here Corrao. What do you want?"

Kaufman shot me a warning look, aware of my temper.

"Now, Winner," Corrao scolded, "that's no way to greet an old friend—besides I thought you wanted to meet me. At least, that's what everyone's saying."

"Then everyone's got it wrong," I snapped. "I want the organ grinder, not the monkey. I want a meeting with The Ferryman, and

I want it fast. So fast that I'll blow one of your operations every day you delay. Starting tomorrow. You might not know it, but Southampton is important to the people you work for. And it will mean a lot to the police tomorrow. You got that?"

"That's a big mistake—"

"Come off it, Corrao. Tell them it's Hull the next day. You want me to go on? I can, you know—I've got a list as long as your arm."

"I doubt that—"

"Do you? Well, you explain it to your masters when the police hit Southampton tomorrow."

Corrao's voice was strangulated with temper. "Listen, Harris. You'll get your meeting, but at a time and place of our choosing. And I'll *guarantee* you won't give a single name to the police."

The open threat! Like three years ago. But it was no bluff then— he had carried it out. I hesitated and he sensed my uncertainty because he laughed. "Why not talk it over with your new partner?" he suggested. "I'll call back in an hour's time. Ciao, Harris." Then he put the phone down.

I stared at Kaufman. "He knows about you."

"Like hell—" Kaufman scowled, interrupted by the intercom.

"Trouble, I'm afraid," Llewellyn said. "Watkins has reported in. Darmanin was shot by a sniper as he answered the door. The light was behind him—made a perfect target. Henderson's on his way back."

"Is Darmanin dead?"

"He wasn't killed instantly. But he's dead now."

Kaufman swore violently, just as the door opened and Jack came in. He looked troubled and preoccupied—but he managed a tired smile for Lucia as he slumped into an armchair.

"How was Maria?" she asked.

Jack shrugged. "She and the housekeeper went shopping in Bristol. They weren't back. I'll call again later."

"I'm going next door," Kaufman said sharply. "Sam, come with me. Jack, you stay with Lucia and wait for Henderson to get back."

I was half led, half pushed into the kitchen. Then Kaufman crossed to the larder and was running down the passage with me on his heels. Llewellyn was no longer in the big back room. Another man had a telephone under his chin and was writing furiously.

Kaufman snapped: "Get the safe house on the line."

The man looked surprised. "They just came on. About ten minutes ago. I'm talking to them—"

"Switch that loudspeaker on. No, don't bother, I'll do it myself." Kaufman flung himself behind the desk and flicked a button on his telephone. "Kaufman here—what's happened down there? Where's—"

"Hook, here, Mr. Kaufman. It's bad news I'm afraid."

"Tell me," Kaufman growled, staring at the telephone.

"Mrs. Green and the housekeeper went shopping in Bristol. They parked the car in an underground car park—"

"Parked the car? *Who* parked it? How many men did you have on this?"

"Ray Peters parked the car. He stayed with the car while Harry Hall accompanied the ladies shopping—"

"Just *one man* went with them? Is that what you're handing me?" Kaufman's head was in his hands. "Go on—what happened?"

"They shopped, had tea out, Harry stayed with them all the time. Then, before they returned to the car, the ladies went to the loo. Harry waited outside. After fifteen minutes Harry got worried—"

"*Then* he got worried! God in heaven! Two girls go to the can and he *lets* them go. Why weren't women assigned to this—"

"Harry went in after twenty minutes," the voice said hurriedly. "There—well, there was another entrance. The housekeeper was out cold. Chloroform. There was no sign of Mrs. Green."

Kaufman groaned.

"Harry rushed down to fetch Ray Peters, but Peters wasn't there. At least not in the driver's seat. We only found the body minutes ago, in the boot. Harry never thought to look there—"

"Get on with it, Hook," Kaufman said in a voice cold with fury.

"Well, we've pieced together part of what happened," Hook continued grimly. "Two men dressed as ambulance attendants commandeered a lift. They held the doors open and refused access to public and staff—then two nurses arrived pushing a patient in a wheelchair. They went straight to the basement car park where they wheeled the patient into the back of a white van."

"Oh God!"

"Yes—well—exactly. Anyway, when Harry couldn't find Ray, he went back up into the store to phone in."

"There was no RT?" Kaufman's astonishment threatened to render him speechless. "There was no RT in the automobile?"

374

"It was the housekeeper's own car. A Mini. We thought it would be less conspicuous."

"And the white van?"

"No sign of it yet, sir. But we've put out a full-scale search: road blocks, the airport—it happened less than an hour ago."

Kaufman moaned. His head was in his hands again and when he lifted his eyes he made no effort to hide his despair. "Listen, Hook," he said softly. "You pass the word. Peters is the lucky one. Peters is dead. Maria Green got sucked down the Pipeline an hour ago. If they touch a hair of her head, I'll have *all of you*."

Chapter 7

We were still in the big back room at Wells Court. Kaufman was halfway through another drink and I had poured myself one with shaking hands. Jack had gone nearly crazy when he had learned what had happened to Maria, and was now asleep, heavily sedated.

The other man had left, and Llewellyn had returned. Nobody said a word. We were still sitting like that when the door opened and Henderson came in, looking like a refugee from a traffic accident. Blood splattered his shirt front and most of his jacket. "It's not mine," he said. "It's Darmanin's."

Kaufman looked up. His expression was no longer angry. "Have a drink," he said. "Then tell me about it."

Henderson was surprised—either by Kaufman's tone or the invitation itself. He looked from Jack to me. I poured him a scotch. He downed half of it and collapsed into the chair next to mine. "What a bloody awful day," he said.

His eyes closed and I could almost feel him trying to relax. Then he resumed. "There was nothing I could do for the old man. He had caught it in the guts. He thought I was you. Said he had heard all sorts of rumours about me—Sam Harris, that is. I asked what he knew about the Pipeline. He kept saying he knew nothing but his son knew *everything*. It was all very garbled. He was trying to take a ring off his finger. He said I should take the ring to his son. His *other* son. He runs a bar too, called The Oyster. He kept saying the son knew *everything* about the Pipeline." Henderson paused. "And then the poor devil died on me." He reached into his pocket. "That's the ring. Diamond, I think, but I'm no expert."

It was diamond. A man's gold ring, with a square face in which small diamonds had been set in a Maltese Cross design. Not that I paid much attention. I was too appalled by Henderson's story, especially as it so swiftly followed the news about Maria.

Kaufman used the stub of his cigarette to light another one. "Where's this bar? What's it called—The Oyster?"

"Watkins is trying to find it in the telephone directory."

"And the sniper?" Kaufman asked.

Henderson shrugged. "You'll have to ask the back-up boys. All I know is he got away. He must have been on the roof opposite. I reckon he could see into Darmanin's flat from there. That's what he was after—Darmanin coming to the door just made it easier."

Llewellyn's growing impatience had been marked by a series of muffled curses. Suddenly he snapped. "First, Hampstead. Then this kidnap thing and now another shooting in London. Four killings in one day! I tell you quite frankly—"

A squawk from the intercom stopped him. Kaufman touched a button and Lucia's voice sounded strained as she said: "It's Corrao calling back, for Sam."

Every eye in the room looked at me. One of the recorders switched itself on with a click. I sprang across to the desk and grabbed the telephone. "Corrao—is that you?"

He laughed. "Well, Winner? Did you have your little chat with Jack Green? How's his wife by the way? Did you ask him?"

At least he did not know about Kaufman. The partner he had referred to had been Jack. I gritted my teeth: "Get on with it, will you?"

Corrao chuckled. "You won't learn, will you, Winner? Ask and you shall receive. Threaten and . . . well, you see what happens."

"Where's Maria? You listen to me, Corrao—"

"No! You listen. You wanted a meeting. Well, you'll get it, but on our terms. Start understanding that and your partner's wife might stay alive."

"Listen, Corrao—I'll make a deal—"

"Begging, Winner?" His voice hardened. "Our terms, Winner, not yours. Now listen carefully because I'll only say it once. You are invited to a meeting in Sicily in two days' time. Be in Alcamo at the Café Cordina in the Piazza Ciullo at eight o'clock in the evening. And Winner, make sure you bring that list—"

Sicily? Fiore Serracino? The Sicilian connection out in the open?

Kaufman signalled me to keep talking and somehow I stumbled on. "Why two days? Why not sooner? I want a meeting now—"

"Two days because we say so," Corrao snapped. "Goodbye, Winner. See you in the Piazza Ciullo—"

"Wait! For heaven's sake—what about Maria?"

"She'll be there. Our terms, Winner. Your partner's wife in exchange for you. Bring him with you. Just you and Jack Green— and the list, of course."

Then he hung up. Kaufman jabbed the intercom. "Was that enough? Could you trace—?"

"Lost him, Mr. Kaufman. Another minute maybe and—"

"Damn." Kaufman cut him off. He looked at Llewellyn. "Sicily," he whispered, and I could see the fear in his eyes.

IT WAS THE LONGEST night of my life. Nobody got any sleep except Jack. Bonello and Lucia were at a meeting with the Italian ambassador. There was a chance, apparently, of putting forty men into Alcamo, armed to the teeth but totally invisible.

Kaufman, however, was still obsessed with his theory that the best route to the Pipeline lay buried in my memory, so we picked up from where we left off yesterday. It seemed futile at times but we kept going. Working stopped me breaking out in a cold sweat at the thought of what might be happening to Maria. Bristol and elsewhere were being torn apart in an effort to find her.

Kaufman was forever trying to find a link back to Edgar. How often did Hardman visit the clubs? Was he a heavy gambler? Who were his friends?

"You're wasting time. You're wrong—*really wrong!*"

"Yeah? Two things Sam. That fancy photo in his safe at Chelsea—"

"Edgar was at his wit's end. I *know* the man. Perhaps someone was blackmailing him. It's the only explanation . . ."

Kaufman shook his head. "If you accept blackmail you must take what goes with it. Which is that Hardman knew *something.* If blackmail comes into this it's because someone found out Hardman's connection with the Pipeline. Now that would really give a blackmailer some leverage."

I rubbed my eyes as if trying to get a clearer picture of what was in his mind—or what might have been in Edgar's mind.

"And another thing," Kaufman drove on relentlessly. "I got this little scene buzzing round my brain. A scruffy hotel room in

Palermo. A man's through to Bonello on the phone—someone starts shooting the door down—the man on the phone screams—shouts a name—then he's cut down in a hail of bullets." Kaufman paused to ram the point home. "And the name he shouts is Hardman. That's all—just one word—one name—and that name is Hardman."

We came back to that every time. It was unanswerable. At midnight, Kaufman called a break and we went upstairs to find Henderson. He was in a room with some sort of computer terminal. Another man occupied one of the chairs, checking names on a typewritten list. Henderson himself looked close to exhaustion.

"Well?" Kaufman said.

Henderson sighed. "A club in Fulham called The Oyster. Three bars in London called The Oyster Shell. Two pubs in East Anglia called The Oyster Catcher. A bar in Birmingham called The Oyster Room."

"And?" Kaufman offered his cigarettes.

"Nothing so far." Henderson nodded at the computer screen. "But the list gets longer all the time."

"Anything else?"

"Immigration are checking their Maltese section. So far they've come up with forty-two Darmanins registered in London alone." He smiled, but not enough to dispel his air of weariness. "Darmanin is beginning to seem like the Maltese equivalent of Smith."

"What's happening to the names?" Kaufman asked.

"Being classified—given names, ages, occupations—" he broke off with a gesture of exasperation. "There's another complication. Children of mixed British and Maltese parentage can choose—British *or* Maltese. So our man may not be registered as an alien."

"I don't see the problem. Get the Passport Office to run a check on all Darmanins holding a British passport."

"It is midnight," Henderson said. "The Foreign Office gave us a very frosty answer an hour ago. Llewellyn is sorting it out now."

Kaufman grunted. "All right. Keep me posted."

It had turned two o'clock when Llewellyn came in. I had the impression that he wanted me out of the way—to have a private word with Kaufman. But I settled deeper into my chair, so he had no choice but to get on with it. Finally he withdrew an envelope from an inside pocket. "This was found at Wickham Manor. Stuffed at the back of a drawer in Hardman's desk."

Kaufman reached for the envelope and extracted a letter from the already unsealed flap. He raised his eyes to me in a curiously revealing gesture, as if he too would have preferred my absence. Their secretive attitude infuriated me. Kaufman turned his attention back to the letter. He read quickly, and then—when I guessed him to be halfway down the page—he gave a start of surprise. After which he read more slowly. Finally he looked up. "Read it, Sam. It's addressed to you anyway." Then he turned to Llewellyn. "Let's check on Henderson—bring a drink with you."

I doubted they were going to see Henderson. They wanted to discuss the letter, and perhaps leave me alone to read it. *It was dated January!* Even as I saw it I remembered Edgar in the restaurant—"Ever since January I've wanted to tell you."

And on the twenty-eighth of January, Edgar had written:

> I doubt I'll ever send this. I'm safe enough writing it now—I cannot post it anyway, not until you are released. The prison censorship officers would have a fine old time with it. So I've a while yet to make up my mind about sending it—and a while longer to screw up my courage to talk to you about it.
>
> Sam—Kay is dead.

I dropped the letter as if it had burst into flames. Kay was dead! All that vitality, that zest for life—gone, gone for ever. I drank the scotch which Kaufman had provided, then sat staring into space thinking of Kay—mourning her. Even in Brixton I had guessed I would never see her again when the divorce went through. But *dead?* I was stunned by the shock of it. I reached again for the letter.

> She never told me what happened that night—with Faberge and Martinez—but I gather she was involved. She went to pieces after the trial, you know. I never told you but the hospital found traces of heroin in her blood after she crashed the car that night. There were lots of questions, but nothing came of it.
>
> I wanted her to go into a private clinic, but she wouldn't have it. I tried to reach her but she was jumpy as a tick with me and I couldn't stand the people she was with.
>
> Anyway, a few weeks later she told me about the divorce. I was shocked. I tried to talk her out of it, but then she told me something else. That she needed money, a lot of it, and a divorce settlement was the only answer. Of course I asked what the money was for but she refused to say another word.

She avoided me after that. I tried to keep in touch, but I was having the devil's own fight with the Receiver at Apex, and I had the wine business to think of. But I knew your divorce had gone through because there was a bit in the papers about it. Then about a month after that Kay phoned me late at night. She was at Rex Place, and I knew she was in trouble. It took me twenty minutes to get there and that wasn't a moment too soon. She had taken an overdose of something and was barely conscious.

It was a ghastly business, but it was a turning point. We got her into some hush-hush clinic at Beaconsfield. Sam, I can't describe the hell she went through but I swear she was over it when she came out. She came to live with me then, in her old flat upstairs. I wanted to keep an eye on her and keep her away from her old crowd at The Fisherman. I expected trouble at first, but as she grew stronger she seemed to like living there.

By then the fight with the Receiver was as good as lost and I was at my wit's end. A few weeks ago I got the old crowd together again to try to work out a last-ditch stand. But Charlie Weston and Lew Douglas had washed their hands of it because of that damn fool undertaking of mine. Charlie Weston really got under my skin. So I said if he wouldn't at least try to save Apex then I would cancel my contract with his haulage firm for the shipment of our wines. A bit to my surprise he was much more helpful after that—and even Lew Douglas made a few constructive suggestions. It's all so much wasted effort now because I've just heard that the Receiver has sold out over our heads—but I want you to know that I tried.

That night Kay asked me if Apex could be held together until you came out. I had to say I was beginning to doubt it, but I told her how the meeting had gone, about me leaning on Charlie Weston and all the rest of it. We talked for about an hour, then she made some coffee and we went to bed.

In the morning she announced she was going on holiday. It must have been a sudden decision because there was no mention of it the night before. When I asked where, she said anywhere in the Med— just as long as she got some sunshine. Well, it was the usual bloody January in London and had I not been so busy I might have gone with her—wish to God I had now, but there it is. Oh, and another thing— she told me to stop worrying about Apex because she felt sure it would turn out right in the end.

Then something rather strange happened. She gave me a large

brown envelope and asked me to look after it. I had to promise not to open the damn thing, just keep it in the safe until she returned. She said it really ought to be destroyed but it had cost too much for that—and just knowing it was there was enough to remind her of how much she had lost. I couldn't make head nor tail of it, but I put the envelope in the safe for her—just to humour her.

Well Sam, now comes the hardest part of all. A week ago I had a phone call from a man called Rogers in Tunis. He wouldn't go into details, other than to say it concerned my daughter and he was afraid it was bad news, and could I get out there immediately? I was there the same day as the call. Not that it mattered—Kay was dead before Rogers picked up the telephone.

Rogers runs some kind of fishing business. He's English—a sly, ferret-faced man, as oily as a grease rag. His Arab fishermen had found Kay drifting in an open boat—somewhere in the Gulf of Hammamet. How she came to be in that boat is a mystery. Rogers found my name and address, enough to know she was my daughter—so he phoned me instead of going to the police. His fishermen all vouched for his story—I questioned them myself. And there was something else—Rogers found a hypodermic—and some heroin.

I wish to God you had been there, Sam—to share the decision. Even now I wonder if I did the right thing. But it seemed to me that we've had enough of the bloody newspapers to last us a lifetime. Rogers offered to bury her at sea and keep his mouth shut. He wanted money naturally, but not a fortune. Well, to my mind it made as good a final resting place as any.

It's taken the best part of a bottle of Remy to get this letter this far—so I may as well finish it. Sam, I did what I thought was best for Kay—please believe that. But back here in England, well, I'm not so sure. Life is more complicated. For a start, the house was broken into while I was away and that envelope has gone missing. I don't know what was in it, but Kay's words keep coming back to me—about it costing too much to be destroyed. Is it too preposterous to imagine Kay being blackmailed? God alone knows what about—but it may explain her desperate need for money last year.

I'm damned if I know what to do next. All her old crowd seem to have dropped her but somebody is bound to ask about her sooner or later. What the hell do I say? That she's living abroad, I think—and hope nobody pursues it. But it's a terrible worry.

Sam—try to remember all the good things about her. I know the pair of you had troubles at the end, but she wasn't a bad girl, spoiled I know, but that was my fault not hers—and she sorted herself out in that clinic. She was settling down to wait for you—I'm sure of that—and now this terrible thing has happened.

Kaufman left me alone for a long time. Long enough to recover from the shock of Edgar's letter, but never long enough to get used to the concept of murder. Before my trial, murder had been something involving other people, headlines in a newspaper—now I was surrounded by it. Even for a loner like me people—*some* people—were important. Kay, Edgar, Jack and Maria were . . . *had been* . . . the cornerstones of my life. Now two were dead and Maria was in mortal danger. Reminding myself of that helped me concentrate—made me think of other people—so that when Kaufman returned at three thirty I was ready for him.

He bustled into the room. His tie was loosened and he conveyed the air of a man who has been hectically busy. There was a determined set to his jaw and a look of subdued excitement in his eyes. He picked Darmanin's diamond ring up from the desk and tossed it from hand to hand as he looked at me.

I pointed to the letter. "How much of it did you know?"

"Not much. We knew your ex-wife had disappeared. And we suspected Hardman of knowing a lot more than he was telling."

"But he was *not* The Ferryman. Even you must admit—"

"Now hold on—maybe I was less than completely right about Hardman. But that letter begs more questions than it answers."

"Such as?"

"Such as what was your ex-wife *doing* in Tunis? Come on, Sam—the Pipeline runs through Tunis."

"For God's sake! Don't you ever stop?"

"Listen, knucklehead—your ex-wife is dead. So is your pal Hardman and there's no telling what's happening to Maria. And in two days' time . . ." he checked his watch, "correction—*tomorrow*—you go to Sicily with a fifty-fifty chance of getting your head blown off. You think *now* is a good time to stop?"

"But you'll *find* Maria . . . I mean, the search, there's still time—"

"Forget it, I'll give you a thousand to one, unless . . ." he jabbed his finger in my direction. "Unless you remember something real good in the next two hours."

I was still digesting that when Llewellyn arrived. He sat on the

382

edge of the desk and tapped his knee with what was obviously a British passport. "Your ex-wife went to Malta. Not Tunis." He handed the passport to Kaufman. "We came across this at Wickham. Hardman must have brought it back with him."

Kaufman riffled the pages. "Just her date of arrival. No departure . . . no re-entry elsewhere." He glanced at Llewellyn. "This place she was found—how far is it from Malta? This Bay of something . . ." he reached for Edgar's letter.

"*Gulf* of Hammamet," Llewellyn corrected. "About two hundred miles. Sicily is even closer . . ." He paused. "That's an idea. Hardman employs a Maltese chauffeur and his daughter makes a sudden trip to Malta. Do you think there's a connection?"

Kaufman raised the diamond ring. "Find Darmanin's son and you'll get your answer . . . unless the Pipeline finds him first."

It went very quiet after that. I concentrated on the ring in my hands. A vague idea touched the corner of my mind. The ring . . . Malta . . . Kay had gone to Malta? *FABERGE!* His name exploded in my mind. I began slowly. "When I was fighting Faberge that night, after Martinez had gone into the water, Faberge was swinging that boathook like a claymore when this skiff appeared. The man standing up—something in his left hand caught the light. But it wasn't *in* his hand, it was on it. He wore a ring on his left hand . . . that's what sparkled."

I met the scepticism in Kaufman's eyes, and hurried on before he had a chance to interrupt me. "The man in the skiff killed Faberge," I said with slow conviction. "And he wore a ring on his left hand. And when Kay was sitting behind the dock when I was sentenced at Oxford she was crying and a man reached over to comfort her. He rested his hands on her shoulders. I couldn't see his face, but he wore a diamond ring on his *left* hand."

Kaufman massaged his jaw. "Faberge knew someone who wore a ring like that? Is that what you're saying?"

I hesitated. "Kay said Brooks had gone to The Fisherman. Lew Douglas owns The Fisherman. He spends a lot of time there . . . so did Kay . . . you read Edgar's letter. Brooks met Lew Douglas that night. Douglas is a flashy dresser. I bet—"

"OK, suppose you're right," Kaufman interrupted. "Are you saying that Faberge knew Lew Douglas and that he was the man in the skiff?"

"It all fits," I said excitedly. "Kay was always talking about parties she'd been to at The Fisherman with Faberge and Brooks. Listen, Edgar said Kay was spending a lot of time at The Fisherman at the time that she needed the money. That bastard Douglas was blackmailing her. Brooks must have taken the photograph to him that night. He *must* have."

"You don't know that. It was hours before Kay called you."

Llewellyn cleared his throat. "You are assuming, Mr. Harris, that your ex-wife only behaved that way on the one occasion. There may have been others."

Blood rushed to my face. Of course he was right—it was *possible*. I was trying to think of a counter-argument when he interrupted. "I'm going to phone Bristol," he said, rising to his feet. "Then I'll look in on Henderson." He went out.

I remembered something else. "You know Douglas has sold up here and left England? Edgar said he was expanding his hotels— somewhere in the Mediterranean. Tunis is in the Med. So is Malta, so is Sicily. And Kay was found murdered somewhere between the three of them. Why don't you find out where Douglas has his hotels?"

Kaufman stared at me. "You're guessing, Sam. Douglas is clean. We investigated him when you were in Brixton and Apex was in Receivership. The finger had been pointed at you so we dug into your background, which included screening your associates."

"But suppose he owns a hotel in Malta?" I grabbed Edgar's letter from the desk. It took me a moment or two to find the place. Then I said: "Edgar told Kay about meeting Darlington and the others. The following morning she took off—"

"To see Lew Douglas?" Kaufman said sarcastically.

"She went to see him about Apex. She tried to save it."

"But why Douglas? Why not Charlie Weston—he was the biggest stockholder?" Kaufman stared at me, then shook his head. "Just now you had Douglas blackmailing her—now she's running to him like he's her big brother."

"But she *might* have gone to see Douglas. He was part of her crowd."

Kaufman swore and reached for the intercom. "I want the Lew Douglas file. Especially I want to know where his hotels are."

"I've got the digest on Douglas's affairs here, if that's any help?" came Henderson's reply. "Er—you do *know* Douglas is dead, don't you?"

384

I felt my knees weaken with the shock. Kaufman said: "When did Douglas die? And how?"

"Natural causes, apparently—heart attack, last February, at his hotel in Gozo. That's an island next to Malta."

Kaufman stared at me. He shook his head and was still shaking it when he turned back to the intercom: "What comes next?"

"Douglas also owned a part interest in a hotel at a place called Sousse. Then another in Salerno."

"Sousse? Where's that?" Kaufman reached for a pencil.

"It's in Tunisia, on the Gulf of Hammamet. Salerno is in Italy, just south of Naples."

Kaufman scowled at me as he flicked off the intercom. "Wipe that look off your face. All we got is Douglas doing business in the Mediterranean. And now he's dead. You make a case out of it and you'll likely be disappointed."

But my mind kept going back to Kay and The Fisherman Hotel on the river. I was *sure* Douglas had blackmailed Kay. And Douglas had been mixed up with Faberge . . . and Faberge had been involved in the Pipeline . . . so why not Douglas too? He had a hotel in Malta . . . Kay had gone to Malta . . . Edgar's chauffeur had *come* from Malta.

"This hotel at Sousse," I said quickly. "Douglas owned a part interest. Can we find out who owned the rest of it?"

Kaufman frowned. "Maybe—it might be in the file. Alternatively . . ." he hesitated, as if wondering whether to confide in me. "We've got a man on his way to Tunis now, to find this Rogers—maybe he could check locally—" He broke off as Henderson entered the room.

It was at least two hours since we had visited Henderson in his upstairs room, and there was a marked change in his appearance. The look of despair had vanished. Instead he grinned from ear to ear as he crossed to the drinks tray. Kaufman's narrowed eyes followed him all the way.

"You've found Darmanin, haven't you?"

Henderson nodded. "I've even got the telephone number." He poured himself a generous drink. "His name is Salvio. Salvio Darmanin. And his bar is exactly where you would expect to find it."

"In Soho?" I guessed.

"No," Henderson beamed. "At a place called Rabat. In Malta."

Chapter 8

I had adjourned to the kitchen at Rex Place. Jack was awake by now, and I would have given a lot not to see the terrible suffering on his face. As I messed about frying bacon and eggs, I remembered him yesterday morning. How pleased he had been with everything. And now, twenty-four hours later . . . the Pipeline had snatched Maria . . . Edgar was dead. . . .

We had just about finished breakfast when the door opened. Kaufman entered, followed by Lucia and Llewellyn. Lucia immediately crossed the room to kiss Jack and take his hand in hers.

Kaufman had shaved during his absence; now he looked more or less normal, if you discounted the dark circles under his eyes. "We're going to Malta," he said to me. "Make contact with this kid Darmanin. We'll cross to Sicily from there. There's a flight—"

"Who's we?"

"Me, you and Jack—"

"I'm not going anywhere. Neither is Jack," I said as calmly as I could. "Listen. Whenever you make arrangements someone gets hurt. I followed your precious procedures when I met Edgar. Result? He was shot dead. And I arranged to meet Darmanin the way you wanted it—he was murdered too. Maria stays down in the country on your say so—and she gets kidnapped—"

"OK, Sam," Kaufman interrupted. "Back off. I know it looks like a leak but I know the people we got working here. That *cannot* be the explanation. You'll just have to take my word for it—"

"I'm not taking your word for anything. From now on we're told everything—then *we* decide—"

Jack gave me an alarmed look. I knew what he was thinking. He was afraid I would refuse to go to Alcamo. He was damn near right, too. Anyone but Maria and I would have refused.

Kaufman watched me carefully. "OK, Sam, here's what we do. There are no scheduled direct flights to Sicily. Most people go to Rome and connect there. That's the obvious way and the Pipeline will stake that route out. But another way is to fly to Malta, cross on the ferry to Siracuse—then drive across Sicily to Alcamo—"

"Why the performance?"

"Let me finish, will you?" Kaufman said heavily. "Two people who look like you and Jack will be on today's noon flight to Rome.

They'll use your names and travel on your passports. Tonight they'll stay in Salerno, hire an automobile and leave for Sicily first thing in the morning—in plenty of time to reach Alcamo by eight tomorrow evening. We think they'll be tailed. A back-up team will be behind them anyway. Meanwhile we go to Malta on a charter flight. If Darmanin knows as much as his old man claimed—"

"If."

"Sam—we need *something* to trade." He stopped short of saying "trade as well as you", but that's what he meant.

"Passports are being prepared now. Jack comes with me—and you and Lucia are a honeymoon couple."

"Lucia! She's coming—"

"You're going to Sicily, remember?" Kaufman pointed his finger at me. "You know any languages?"

Lucia joined in. "You and I will travel together, Sam. The Pipeline will be watching for you and Jack. It's better cover this way."

I nodded. I could see the sense in that—even if I didn't like it. "Why the decoys?" I asked eventually. "After all, Corrao wants us in Alcamo—"

"You'll be there," Kaufman nodded grimly. "But it won't harm for them to watch the front door as we come through the back window."

I stared at him, wondering how much I could take on trust and what alternative I had. "I want that list," I added slowly. "The entire list—everything you've got on the Pipeline."

"You'll have it," Kaufman agreed. "It's being prepared now."

Jack raised his head. He looked at me. "All right, Sam?"

I took a deep breath. "All right," I said. I hoped to God it was.

THE TRAVEL ARRANGEMENTS went smoothly enough. Lucia and I were taken by Watkins in his taxi to an office in Manchester Square. I was separated from Lucia and photographed in a cubby-hole of a place which served both as studio and darkroom. In another room I submitted to being re-clothed in a safari suit and suede shoes. It reminded me of that first day in prison. People made decisions about me as if I weren't there.

Lucia and I were married the previous day. At the Marylebone Registry Office. At least, that's what the marriage certificate said. Except my name was Samuel Howard and hers had been Lucia

Portelli. Kaufman went through the documentation with me at ten fifteen. Apart from the marriage certificate, there was a UK driving licence with one endorsement, a Diner's Club card, an Access card, and membership of the AA. A bill from a garage in Fulham said they had serviced my car and a receipt from the Savoy Hotel confirmed that Mr. and Mrs. Howard had begun their honeymoon there.

Kaufman tucked them into a worn pigskin wallet and turned to the rest of the items on the desk. Two torn ticket stubs from a West End theatre, airline tickets, traveller's cheques, and a hotel reservation at the Grand Verdala Hotel, Malta. "That's about it," he said. "It's not full cover, but it will do."

I was putting the stuff into my pockets when Lucia entered, followed by the man who had dressed me up for a safari. Lucia looked cool and casual in a cream trouser suit. "You can kiss the bride," Kaufman grinned.

Lucia smiled and stood next to me. Then the little tailor opened a packet of confetti and threw it all over us. "It's in your luggage as well," he said happily. "It takes days to get rid of—pops up all over the place."

I brushed confetti out of my hair.

"The car's ready," the little man said to Kaufman.

Kaufman nodded and looked at Lucia. "Stay in your hotel room until eight o'clock. Then make your way to The Oyster Bar. I'll meet you there. OK?"

"Where's Jack?" I asked.

"Getting kitted out. You'll see him on the aircraft—but don't acknowledge either of us—remember that."

A black limousine took us to Luton airport. When we arrived the driver found a porter for our luggage, then touched the peak of his cap. "Have a pleasant journey, Mr. Howard." The girl at the check-in desk said something similar. "Your flight will be called in fifteen minutes, Mr. Howard."

"This Howard business will take some getting used to," I grumbled to Lucia.

"Imagine what it's like for Mrs. Howard. Come on Sam, buy your wife a drink. And for heaven's sake, don't look so worried. We're on our honeymoon, remember?"

The flight was crowded with holidaymakers. Lucia and I were among the first to board the aircraft. I kept a sharp look-out for Kaufman and Jack. Ten, fifteen minutes passed without sign of

388

them. Then I saw Kaufman, leading a man by the elbow, a man who wore dark glasses and carried a white stick. *JACK!*

We dozed for most of the journey. The plane landed in Malta at three o'clock—four o'clock local time. I craned my neck to catch a glimpse of Kaufman. A steward gave him a hand in hoisting Jack to his feet. He faced me for a second, but his eyes were masked by the dark glasses. Then something else caught my eye. Kaufman carried a burgundy-coloured briefcase in his left hand, sunlight glinting on the security chain attached to his left wrist. Was that the list? Tomorrow night my life could depend on it—my life, Maria's life and perhaps Jack's as well.

Walking out into that sunshine was like entering a furnace. My eyes were dazzled by the light reflected from the white airport buildings. We collected our baggage and cleared customs, and by then Jack and Kaufman had vanished.

"Are they staying with us—I mean at the same hotel?"

Lucia was unsure. "I don't think so. Anyway my guess is Kaufman has arranged to meet someone else before going to The Oyster Bar. That's why we are to stay at the hotel until eight."

It was the only explanation available. I had to accept it.

We found a cab and fell into the back seats. The road leading away from the airport climbed slowly through parched countryside, with lots of yellow-brown grass and outcrops of rock.

The Grand Verdala is set high up, on the edge of Rabat. It is a big, square, modern hotel, and air-conditioned. I signed us in as Mr. and Mrs. Howard and we were shown to our room. Lucia studiously ignored the huge double bed and crossed to the balcony. Half of Malta lay spread out below, with the sea shimmering a few miles away. She looked out at the view. "They say you can see Sicily from Malta—on a clear day."

I smiled. "Seeing it from here is fine—it's going there that worries me."

She managed a faint smile in return. "Try not to worry. Enrico is organizing some help."

Bonello! I had forgotten about his meeting with the Italian ambassador in London.

"You mean the cavalry arrive in the nick of time?" I said.

A colossal explosion drowned her reply—I grabbed her without thinking and pulled her away from the balcony. We fell back onto the bed. Then there was another explosion, and another followed by

389

the chatter of machinegun fire and a screaming noise like the whistle of bombs.

But Lucia was laughing! "Sam, it's *all right*. It's a festa, to honour a Saint. People celebrate with fireworks and firecrackers, and processions and bands."

We listened to the thuds and bangs until the noise faded and died. Lucia kicked off her shoes to snuggle into my side. A feeling of tenderness existed between us, but not—for the moment—of passion. We were both very tired, and I dozed off.

The bedside telephone woke me. "Finished your siesta?" Kaufman asked. The bed beside me was empty. My watch said seven thirty.

"I'm down in the bar," he said. "You going to keep me waiting all night?"

"I thought we were supposed to meet at—"

"Changed my plans."

"I'll be right down."

He hung up. The bathroom door opened and Lucia emerged. She was still wearing the suit she had travelled in, but she looked cool and refreshed. I guessed she had showered and I wished I had time to do the same before going down to meet Kaufman.

The Verdala bar had a pianist who played Chopin in one corner. The sky outside had turned a darker blue. Kaufman sat on a sofa twenty yards away, talking to another man. But the man wasn't Jack. He was dark-haired, and in his early thirties.

"Ah—Mr. and Mrs. Howard," Kaufman rose to his feet. "May I introduce Lino Cassar." He beckoned a waiter and ordered a Bloody Mary for Lucia and a scotch for me. "Lino works for Enrico in Rome," he murmured as the waiter departed, "but he's Maltese by birth. He's come down here to help us out."

Lucia had been right. Kaufman *had* arranged another meeting. "Where's Jack?" I asked.

Kaufman shrugged. "Tired after the journey. He's sleeping."

Cassar brushed a hand through his hair. He said: "Enrico called me in the early hours of this morning. I located Darmanin and left a man watching him, then I went to this hotel in Gozo. An examination of the register was most illuminating."

I *knew* I had been right! "That's where Kay went in January."

Lino Cassar nodded.

Kaufman said: "And our man in Tunis found Rogers. Frightened him to death, but he stuck to the story he told Hardman—about the burial at sea and all the rest of it."

I had never doubted that Edgar had written the truth, so I paid little attention. "So what's happening? Any news from Bristol?"

Kaufman shook his head. "Nothing positive yet. Our people are following up leads . . . maybe we'll have some news later tonight." He stood up to go. "But I'll tell you something. This guy Darmanin had better come across . . . we ain't got time for subtleties."

NIGHT HAD FALLEN with surprising suddenness. A fat full moon shone amid a million stars. But it was still hot. Hot and noisy. Most of Rabat's streets were now closed to traffic because of the festa, so Lucia and I walked to The Oyster Bar. Kaufman had insisted on leaving a few minutes before us, as he was anxious to preserve our cover. The bar was in the square. So was the church. All we had to do was follow the crowd, or so a cab driver told us. Street vendors shouted from stalls selling nougat and cheese cakes while a man stood on the back of a cart and cut a huge swordfish into steaks with the aid of a saw. Coloured lights were strung across narrow streets little wider than alleyways. Flags and bunting hung from every window, plaster saints stood on wooden plinths at twenty-yard intervals, the sound of church bells competed with the crackle of fireworks and the raucous blaring of a brass band.

The noise was overpowering. Lucia clung to my arm as we swept along on the tide of humanity. I looked in vain for Kaufman and Lino Cassar. Finding them, finding *anyone*, would have been impossible in that crowd. The sky turned yellow and green and red as another cluster of fireworks soared high above the house tops.

In the square Lucia tugged my arm and pointed to a neon sign which proclaimed The Oyster Bar to be open for business. It took fifteen minutes to reach it—though I doubt the square was more than thirty yards wide. We arrived breathless. The only entrance to the bar appeared to be a hanging curtain of strings of beads. I drew Lucia behind me and we passed through the screen to find ourselves at the top of a flight of stone steps, curving down to reveal a cellar bar much larger than the entrance suggested. The main room accommodated at least a dozen tables, and archways opened on either side to reveal others—a few occupied by men playing cards. A bar counter ran the length of the far wall, while giant fans overhead turned slowly enough to leave the flies undisturbed.

Noise from the square faded to a buzz which murmured like surf on a distant beach.

Kaufman was at the bar, listening to Lino Cassar next to him. I steered Lucia to the counter, where we sat far enough away from Kaufman not to be with him but close enough to hear his every word. An old woman glanced up from rinsing glasses in a sink, and the barman asked what we were drinking.

I ordered. Kaufman beat a tattoo on the counter with a coin. "I'd like a word with the owner," he said loudly. "Salvio Darmanin. It's a personal matter. Is he around?"

The old woman just stared at Kaufman. Finally she said: "Salvio cannot be disturbed." She withdrew her red hands from the water and dried them on a stained towel. "He's had some very bad news."

I stifled my gasp of surprise. Bad news! Darmanin knew about his father and brother. But of course he would—even if the police had not informed him as next of kin, *somebody* in the Maltese community in London would have contacted him.

Kaufman, on the other hand, showed no sign of surprise. "I know," he said softly. "That's what I want to see him about." He tapped the counter again, but not with a coin this time—Darmanin's diamond ring was in his hand. "This was given me by a friend of mine," he said. "The man who gave it him was dying—but he said to bring it to Salvio Darmanin."

The old woman gasped and reached out—but Kaufman avoided her. He slipped the ring onto his finger, closed his hand, then offered his fist for inspection. The old woman was mesmerised by the ring. With a sigh she shuffled to the back of the bar and vanished behind the strips of plastic which screened the opening. I heard her climbing some stairs, pausing on each step to catch her breath.

Lino Cassar slid down from his stool. He moved casually, as if stretching his legs, but I knew what he was doing. Counting the house, just as I was. Eight of them, not counting the old woman, all in their sixties, some even older. Except for one, sitting alone, reading a newspaper. Something told me that he was the man Cassar had left to keep an eye on Darmanin's movements.

At that moment the screen parted behind the bar. The young man who entered was dark-haired and brown-eyed, and he hopped along on a pair of aluminium crutches. Some people are clumsy on crutches, but this one was as agile as a mountain goat. He reached our side of the counter with surprising speed and as he passed I

392

Winner Harris

noticed his left leg was bent at the knee, and his left foot never touched the ground. "Which one of you has the ring?" he demanded.

Kaufman turned to face him. "Are you Salvio Darmanin?"

"What if I am?" Darmanin's manner was defiant. Everyone in the bar was watching.

Kaufman regarded Darmanin steadily. "Is there somewhere we can talk—in private?"

"So that you can kill me too?" The onlookers gasped, and several stepped forward.

"Nothing like that," Kaufman said softly.

"Let me see the ring." Darmanin took the ring and held it up to the light to see better. A half-suppressed sob muffled his cry of pain. Then he erupted into a torrent of Maltese—turning to his audience, shouting, indicating first the ring and then Kaufman, as if asking them to witness something.

Kaufman cocked his head attentively to Lino Cassar. I guessed Cassar was translating Darmanin's excited Maltese, but I was too far away to hear Cassar's words. Everyone was talking at once. Kaufman stretched out a hand as if to correct a misunderstanding— but Darmanin misinterpreted. Planting his right foot firmly on the floor, he balanced his weight, and swung the right crutch upwards as an extension of his arm. The solid aluminium pole caught Kaufman across the face, knocking him sideways.

Cassar called out to Darmanin, obviously disputing what had been said. Men shouted back, and Darmanin started to hop towards the steps at the entrance as Kaufman fought to free himself of restraining hands.

"Darmanin! Wait—you're wrong! Quite wrong—" he shouted. But his words were drowned in a babble of noise.

Darmanin reached the foot of the steps.

"Sam," Kaufman shouted. "Stop him. He knows something—he thinks we're from The Fisherman."

I understood nothing. The Fisherman? Lew Douglas owned The Fisherman. *Had* owned The Fisherman. Kay had spent a lot of time there. But what on earth had that to do with Darmanin?

"Stop!" I shouted—but Darmanin was already mounting the curved steps with that curious hopping gait of his. I avoided outstretched hands and dodged round a table. Lucia was a pace behind me. Two men blocked my path. I elbowed one, ground my

393

heel into the other's instep. Darmanin had already disappeared up the spiral staircase. At the other end of the bar Kaufman and Cassar were throwing punches to drive a path through the onlookers. The man with the newspaper joined in, intercepting the barman and throwing him to the floor. Lucia was already on the third step by the time I reached the bottom one. Kaufman was treading on my heels, while Lino Cassar was shaking off another man a yard behind. Then we were climbing up into the roar of the crowd in the square.

It took me a second or two to catch sight of Darmanin's head as he bobbed among the crowd. He was ten or twelve yards away. I shouted to Kaufman and plunged into the mob. Lucia was to my left. I tried to get a hand to her but she was too far away. It should have been easy to catch him—he was a cripple and we were all reasonably fit. But although the crowd pressed on all sides, gaps seemed to open for Darmanin—perhaps because he *was* a cripple, or perhaps simply because he was a local whom everyone knew.

I risked a glance over my shoulder. Kaufman was perhaps eight yards behind, separated by a dozen or more people. His face was yellow in the glare from the fireworks. He shouted something, but should have saved his breath. I looked ahead, craning my neck for that telltale hop which identified Darmanin—and cursed when I realized he was drawing away from me.

I saw him scuttle up some steps, and through a door. I hurried after him, gaining on him. The door led into a paved courtyard, fringed by palm trees and decorated with coloured lights. The whole place was crowded with people, but not as tightly packed as the square at the front of the church. I could even run, if you count two steps forward and one sideways to avoid a collision as running. But even so Darmanin managed to stay twenty yards ahead of me. He swung along on his crutches, throwing an occasional look backwards. It was like a sequence from a dream—that running dream where you end up spinning through space.

Darmanin was descending some steps to the street. People blocked my path. I bumped and barged my way through. When I reached the top of the steps I was clutching my side with stitch. There was no sign of him. The street below was crowded with a procession. Choirboys in white surplices carried a forest of candles, followed by men in scarlet robes trimmed with gold, and others dressed in blue, all carrying richly embroidered banners. And

behind them a squad of twenty men heaved and strained under a huge gold statue.

Then I saw Darmanin. He had crossed the street and was on the opposite corner. We saw each other in the same instant. He turned and scuttled down a side street.

When I looked back there was no sign of Lucia—or Kaufman or Lino Cassar. But to wait for them, would mean losing Darmanin. I barely hesitated. I was down the steps and waiting for a break in the procession, dodging church officials. The side road was no more than an alleyway, dark and empty, with shuttered houses on either side. I cursed aloud. I had no torch, no weapon—and I was alone. The alley made a sharp turn to the right. I eased round the corner, pressed tight against the wall. Suddenly twelve yards ahead, a door opened on a latch. A shaft of light splashed across the cobblestones for a split second but long enough to see the splinter of light reflected down the length of an aluminium crutch. Then the door closed softly.

It took me a minute to make up my mind. I left the door open behind me so that if Kaufman and Lino Cassar were following down the alley, they would see it. I stepped into a tiny walled garden. Lemon trees flanked a narrow path. The dense black bulk of a building loomed up in front of me, its shuttered windows visible in the moonlight. I crept forward, step by step along the path. A yard from the house a twig snapped behind me. I turned quickly. I remember crying out, remember the coppery taste of blood—and falling.

WHEN I RECOVERED I was in a room with a very high ceiling, white-washed plaster, supported by heavy timbers. I tried to sit up. Lucia restrained me with gentle hands. I brushed her aside to prop myself upright. My surroundings came into focus. Lino Cassar was talking. Darmanin sat awkwardly, with his chin crooked at a strange angle and an expression of pure terror on his face. A necktie had been knotted round his throat. The other end was attached to the trigger of a shotgun . . . and Kaufman held the shotgun, both barrels pressed into Darmanin's neck. A sharp movement— almost *any* movement—and Darmanin's head would be blown off his shoulders.

Kaufman glanced my way. "Easy boy—everything's under control."

Lucia dabbed my head with a flannel. "It's stopped bleeding, but you could do with a stitch in that cut . . . Thank God we were only a few minutes behind you."

Beyond Kaufman heavy bolts were rammed into place across a big wooden door. The shutters were closed at the windows. A man lounged in a chair, with another shotgun cradled in his lap. It was Cassar's man, the one from The Oyster Bar.

"What's happening?" I asked.

Kaufman's gaze remained fixed on Darmanin's face. "Lino's laying it on the line," he said grimly. "Telling him what happened to his old man—and what will happen to him unless he cooperates."

I swung my feet off the sofa and lowered them slowly to the floor.

Suddenly Darmanin screamed: "*Is-sajjied* will kill me if I tell you."

Cassar translated. "*Is-sajjied* means The Fisherman."

"He'll kill you anyway," Kaufman snapped brutally. "He's already murdered the rest of your family. What more proof—"

"But I kept quiet," Darmanin protested. "We *all* kept quiet. Don't you understand? Why did he do it? Why—"

Kaufman jerked the gun. "You are dead unless you cooperate. Your chances of being alive this time tomorrow—"

"I *am* cooperating. I *will* cooperate," Darmanin pleaded. "But you must help me." Lino Cassar cut in with a burst of Maltese, his voice persuasive. God knows what he said but it certainly helped because a moment later Darmanin embarked on his story. His head moved back so that the gun no longer pressed into his skin.

"*Is-sajjied* came to see us three years ago. We . . . we ran a garage then, in Balzan. My father, my brother and me. Repair work, panel beating, the usual things. My brother was the best mechanic in Malta. And I was the best panel beater . . . trained by the British REME. Everyone said I was the best, you can ask—"

"I'll take your word for it," Kaufman said.

"He wanted some work done . . . in Sicily. It was unusual . . . to do work in Sicily, but he explained they lacked the skills—"

"Panel beating?" Kaufman sounded doubtful.

"And welding . . . welding to very high standards. Seams had to be invisible. *Is-sajjied* was very exacting. He even gave me a test—"

"Go on," Kaufman grunted.

Darmanin's white face strained into a faint smile. "I was to take a team of four men to Sicily. For three weeks. The pay was good, very good. We went over on the ferry—to Siracuse." His speech was almost normal now the shotgun was no longer pressed into his windpipe. "A transit van took us to where we were working. It was hard work—difficult, tiring, long hours. We worked non-stop, never went out, stayed at a farmhouse next to the garage. The day we finished he came to inspect our work. It—"

"He? You mean this fisherman?"

"*Is-sajjied*. The Fisherman. It is the only name we know him by. It is not necessary to know a man's name to take his money."

"Is that right?" Kaufman sounded bored. "OK, so he inspected the work—then what?"

"It was all good. He passed it. Joey Grech, one of my men, drove on the way back to Siracuse. Just the five of us in the transit. *Is-sajjied* told us to follow his Mercedes. Well, we set off, but Joey had trouble keeping up with the Merc—through the mountains, all twists and turns, hairpin bends—" Darmanin shuddered. "It wasn't Joey's fault. He was trying to catch the Mercedes. But . . . we took this tight bend, high in the mountains . . . and there was this truck—parked right across the road. Joey never had a chance. The road was narrow and . . . and we crashed through the railings—"

Kaufman looked at him. "Go on."

Darmanin would have preferred not to. "It was a very long drop," he said. "The van hit the mountainside on the way down. The passenger door next to me buckled and burst open . . . and I was thrown out. Then . . . then the van blew up, like . . . like a bomb. . . I fell near a road . . . the same road just lower down. A man and woman were running towards us. My leg was all twisted up. Then *Is-sajjied* drew up in the Merc. He and the man with him argued with the man and woman about what to do with me. But the woman was a doctor, on holiday with her husband. She insisted on her husband driving to the hospital in Palermo, while she nursed me in the back of their car. I am a cripple today, but without her I would have lost my leg—"

"You would have lost your life," Kaufman sneered. "*Is-sajjied* and his buddy would have finished you off like your workmates. Didn't you ever figure that out?"

Darmanin stared. "I was in hospital for weeks. *Is-sajjied* paid for everything. He was very good. And in return I was to forget about the work we did. He gave the money the men had earned to their families in Balzan—and Joey's widow got five thousand pounds."

"And it wasn't even Christmas," Kaufman said sarcastically. "OK, and what did Santa Claus bring you?"

Darmanin looked uncomfortable. "He . . . he promised to look after me . . . me and my family. We were to work for him occasionally and be protected . . . as long as I kept quiet. We sold the garage . . . the work was too heavy anyway, what with this leg and everything—so I bought The Oyster Bar and this villa."

"And your pa and brother—what did they get out of all this?"

"Tony always wanted to go to London. So *Is-sajjied* got him a job there. And he bought my father a little bar in Soho."

I stiffened. "*Is-sajjied* got your brother his job?"

"With his partner—Lord Hardman."

I went cold. I couldn't believe it. Edgar was *innocent!* Dammit, even Kaufman had been halfway to believing that last night.

I was about to say something else but Kaufman interrupted. "This work in Sicily," he said to Darmanin. "Tell me about it."

Darmanin looked terrified. "No!" he shouted. "Nobody was to know. *Is-sajjied* said—"

Kaufman's open left hand cracked across Darmanin's cheek, knocking his head backwards. "Forget what *Is-sajjied* said. He said he'd look after you, didn't he? He *murdered* your family—"

Darmanin screamed: "How do I know that? How do I know who you are—"

Kaufman hit him again, harder. "This job in Sicily," Kaufman growled. "Tell me about it?"

Darmanin looked on the verge of passing out. "We . . . we worked on the wine tankers. We fitted a second skin."

"How's that again?"

"The wine tankers. Hardman's Wine. They all have a second skin. Inside the main body. Each tanker carries two separate loads at the same time. The inside container carries most of the volume and is directly accessible through the two filler caps on top. That's because English Customs men use dip sticks to check the load. What they don't know is that all they are measuring is the inner tank. There's a two-inch gap between that and the outside shell. An extra cargo can be carried within that gap."

Kaufman frowned. "Can't you *see* the gap—with the filler caps off?"

Darmanin shook his head. "It's a sealed unit at the top. You need different filler caps. Put one filler cap on and you pump out the main

399

tank. Put another filler cap on and you pump out the cavity between the walls."

We had discovered the Pipeline!

I tried to calculate the capacity of a two inch gap the length and circumference of a tanker lorry. But a sum like that would have defeated me on the best of days—let alone when I had taken a crack on the head.

The frown stayed on Kaufman's face. "You're telling me that even if a tanker was impounded and pumped dry—all you would get would be the contents of the inner tank?"

Darmanin nodded. "That's all you *could* get—without the special filler caps."

Kaufman picked his teeth. Nothing in his expression betrayed his excitement. All was quiet for a moment, then he said: "You must have known your work had an illegal purpose."

Darmanin hesitated. "There is a saying in Sicily. See nothing, hear nothing, say nothing—and you live to be a hundred."

"Is that right?" Kaufman looked at him coldly. "Pity your pa and brother can't hear you say that."

"*Is-sajjied* promised," Darmanin said indignantly. "We would be unharmed if we kept quiet. We *did* keep quiet. We did every-thing—"

"What did your pa and brother have to do with this cosy little arrangement?"

"Not much. My father's bar was used as a pick-up point for parcels, that's all. And Tony kept tabs on Lord Hardman. If he went anywhere out of the ordinary Tony phoned my father to let him know, and he passed the information on, that's all. *Oh Madonna!* Why *kill* a man for doing what he is asked to do?"

So that was it. The chauffeur had passed the word about Edgar meeting me at The Hunter's Tower. *Both* sides had been watching Edgar. Poor Edgar.

"This man," Kaufman was saying, "*Is-sajjied*. Why was he called that? Was he a fisherman?"

Frightened though he was, Darmanin couldn't hold back a smile. "With his money? You should have seen the villa behind the farmhouse in Sicily. A swimming pool, servants—everything."

"And it belonged to him?"

Darmanin shrugged. "He stays there. But he lives in Gozo."

I sat bolt upright. Kaufman shot me a warning look—but I got my question in first. "He was English?" I said with sudden understanding. "He was English—not Maltese? This *Is-sajjied*—"

Darmanin seemed surprised. "Yes, an Englishman. Very rich."

"Did he wear a big ring on his left hand? A diamond ring?"

"You *know* him!" Darmanin's face contorted with fear. "It's a trick—all these questions. *Is-sajjied* sent you to trick me—"

"No," I protested. "He's dead. His name was Lew Douglas and he died—"

"*LIAR!*" Darmanin spat at me, "Liar! I saw him a week ago—"

Suddenly there was a noise at the door. A slap, then a slopping sound, as if someone had thrown a bucket of water over the outside of the house. Lino Cassar rushed to the door. Then he slipped. There was a gap beneath the door, and water was coming through, covering the tiles like a flood tide.

"Oh God!" Kaufman used both hands to untie the necktie at Darmanin's throat. "Hit the deck!"

Then there was a *whoomph* and the *water* caught fire. "Gasoline!" Kaufman shouted. Darmanin screamed and hopped towards the far wall, knocking Lucia aside. Cassar stumbled back, beating flames out on his trouser leg. The smell of petrol was everywhere now. "Get those bolts drawn back!" Kaufman roared. "For God's sake—they'll be too hot to touch in another minute!"

Everyone was coughing. Kaufman threw himself at the big wooden door and started to attack the three bolts. The shutters to the right of the door suddenly burst into flame. Kaufman was bent double, dragging at the bottom bolt, coughing and swearing in equal measure. "Don't open the door," he panted, "but get those bolts drawn back. Quick, Sam—*quick.*"

Flames licked the curtains at the other window. We were all spluttering, but Kaufman was almost totally overcome by a fit of coughing. We helped him into the hall first, through a door in the back wall, and I was about to turn back into the room when Lucia stopped me. An open door opposite revealed the kitchen. She filled a saucepan while tugging the scarf loose from her throat. Then she turned and threw the pan of water all over me. She thrust the scarf into my hands. "Put that over your face."

I ran back into the room. Even before I reached the bolted door the heat was overpowering. Hairs scorched on my hands. I backed off, half turned and I then reached for the middle bolt. It was already half clear—Kaufman had managed that much. And the others were completely clear. I yelped with pain as my fingers touched scorching metal. A split second later I was hacking away with my shoe—using the heel as a hammer. The bolt came free! Thank God! Knock the latch up, don't open the door, just knock the latch upwards. God! *I'm on fire!*

I turned away, blinded. Then Lino Cassar was dragging me through the smoke and into the hall. I was spluttering, nose running, eyes streaming, gasping for air. Lucia was saying to me: "Keep still while I get your shoe back on."

"Stop him!" Kaufman roared. "For God's sake stop him!"

My vision cleared just in time to see Darmanin lurch through the outside door at the end of the passage into the street. As Darmanin ran out, he looked back at us. Then his head split open. I never even heard the shot. All I heard was Kaufman shouting: "Stupid bastard! Goddam *stupid* bastard!"

Then Cassar's man kicked the door shut.

"Oldest trick in the world." Kaufman was sprawled on the floor next to me. "Bomb one entrance and they run out the other way. Oldest trick. . . . God, I *tried* to stop him—"

Lino Cassar swung back to me. "We're leaving—same way we came in, through the garden door. Come on."

I was coughing as badly as Kaufman, but Cassar pulled me upright and pushed me towards the door. I flinched as the heat hit me. The wall opposite was a solid barrier of flame and smoke. Wooden beams crackled overhead and sparks showered down everywhere.

Bent double, Cassar reached the unbolted door, and heaved. The wall of flame parted, smoke swirled everywhere—billowing into our faces with the draught. But Cassar was through to the garden; rolling into a ball and coming to rest beneath a lemon tree, his automatic already in his hand as his eyes scanned the surrounding walls. I landed beside him and Lucia fell over me, while Kaufman staggered to a halt a yard away. Behind us the flames leaped upwards to the bedroom windows and the glare from the house lit the garden as had the fireworks earlier.

"The sniper's gone," Cassar panted, craning his neck and swivelling round to look up at the flat rooftops.

"He got what he came for," Kaufman grunted.

I heard bells in the distance. Someone had raised the alarm; the fire brigade was on its way. "Get to the automobile," Kaufman gasped, and a moment later we were back in the alleyway, hurrying away from the scene as quickly as possible. The alleyway opened into a small square. Cassar had his keys out and in very short order Lucia and I were clambering into the back of a Toyota saloon. Cassar gunned the engine and Kaufman said: "Get back to the boat—fast."

"Our clothes are at the hotel," Lucia said.

"We daren't go back there now." Kaufman turned. "Lino's boy will have his work cut out explaining that lot to the cops."

"Where's Jack?" I asked.

"On the boat, don't worry."

Cassar took his eyes off the road to glance at Kaufman. "If you're lucky it takes less than four hours to Siracuse. Fifty miles. But Enrico might want to land further round the coast."

"Is Enrico here?" Lucia asked in surprise.

"Arrived from Rome at eight o'clock," Kaufman told her.

I looked out of the window. We were already out of the town and into the country. The sea glistened a couple of miles away, glimpsed between a gap in the trees. Kaufman swivelled round to Lucia. "What about that? Narcotics men all over the world train tracker dogs to sniff the stuff out and Hardman brings it through in sealed tankers. Wait till Enrico hears that."

When Lucia failed to reply Kaufman twisted back again and looked out of the front window. "Damn stupid kid, Darmanin. He could have taken us there. This farmhouse, next to a garage—"

"But did you hear what Darmanin said?" I said bitterly. "Douglas is still alive—he's *still alive*—"

"*Is-sajjied* is alive! That's all we know—"

"Rubbish! He set Tony Darmanin up to spy on Edgar. Of course it's Douglas—"

Lucia interrupted. "*Is-sajjied* couldn't be The Ferryman could he?"

Cassar shook his head. "No. The Ferryman is based in London."

Kaufman was looking to the front. When he spoke it was in pursuit of his own theories. "Yeah, that's how they knew you were meeting Hardman all right. The chauffeur told them. And as for Maria—well the papers were full of you and Jack going back into business, so they picked it up from them. Then they tailed Maria, slipped those incompetents at Bristol, then *zap!*"

"But why kill the chauffeur?" Lucia asked. "And his father—"

"They didn't kill him," Kaufman said. "Henderson did."

Lucia caught her breath.

"He asked me to keep it quiet." Kaufman shrugged. "It'll be on his record, of course. He caught the chauffeur in the crossfire. They identified the slug. That's why he was so upset about the kid's old man. Once the kid was killed his family had to be wasted. The Pipeline couldn't risk them staying quiet."

Through the windows the moonlight showed a narrow road bumping downhill to a tiny harbour. The open doors of a café splashed yellow blotches of light across the waterfront. It was only ten o'clock but I was desperately tired.

The *Miranda* was a large boat, moored right at the end of the quay, well away from the handful of fishing boats. Lino Cassar drove right up to her. I saw Bonello standing at the rails, with Jack next to him. I breathed a sigh of relief.

We said a hurried goodbye to Lino Cassar, and scrambled up the walkway. Jack showed me to my cabin. He was ashen with worry. "Maria is in Corsica," he said. "They're almost certain."

"Corsica?" I sat down quickly on the bunk.

"They reckon she was taken to France in a crate. Smuggled out in a *crate*, Sam! Urgent pharmaceuticals, from a well-known company, on a special charter flight. And by the time customs had checked with the company the plane had left. Anyway, they've traced her to an airstrip just outside Marseilles. There was a light aircraft there and . . . well, Bonello thinks they've flown her to Corsica."

"But why Corsica? I don't understand—"

"Bonello reckons they'll take her across to Sicily tonight, by boat." I was silent at first, relieved that the kidnappers hadn't been panicked into killing Maria. But putting my thoughts into words was difficult. Jack rocked back and forth, running a hand through his hair. "A crate, Sam . . . like a coffin—"

"*Not* a coffin," I said as firmly as I could. "Jack, it proves she's still alive and unharmed. They said they'd produce her tomorrow night to swap for me—they *said* they would—"

"Oh God! I don't know what to think . . ."

After that I talked non-stop, trying to persuade him that Maria would be unharmed. And I think he believed me in the end.

I was so busy talking that I hardly noticed the motion of the deck beneath our feet as we put out to sea. I stared into the night and watched the lights of Malta recede. The next land we would sight would be Sicily.

Chapter 9

It was rougher than I imagined, but then I've been brainwashed by the travel brochures, which show the Mediterranean as a continuous expanse of blue water. The surface of the sea boiled like a witch's cauldron and smashed tons of black water over the bows of the *Miranda*. Life, however, was snug and warm in the saloon below. The remains of a meal of lampuki littered the table in the mahogany-panelled dining saloon. I had eaten well. We drank *rapitala* and strong black coffee and I fought the urge to go to sleep.

Kaufman had done most of the talking, telling Bonello about Rabat. Now he asked: "Anyone likely to interfere with us? Sicilian coastguard—anyone like that?"

Bonello showed his surprise: "*La Finanza?* We are bound for Castellammare. *La Finanza* never interferes with boats there. Castellammare has the most spectacular coastline in the world. But it has never been developed. And why? Because Castellammare is the bridge between North Africa and the States, my friends. At night the boats unload their cargoes of drugs, arms, diamonds . . ."

"And victims?" Jack asked bitterly. "Is that where they'll land Maria?"

Bonello looked at him. "Perhaps," he said sadly.

"Well, if we know that—" Jack's frustration boiled over.

"There's no chance of an intercept now," Kaufman said firmly. "Who would help us? Sicilians? Sicilian police? Those who are not *owned* by the Mafia are afraid of them. I'm sorry Jack."

"So you're going to let it *happen?* Let them get away with it?" Jack thumped the table.

Lucia reached across and placed her hands on Jack's clenched fist. "At the meeting tomorrow night you will be taken to Maria for the exchange to be made. That's what it's all about. They won't harm her and we'll get her out—you'll see."

Jack stood up. "I'm going on deck for a breath of air." He glared at Kaufman as he crossed to the door, then slammed it behind him.

Kaufman rubbed the mark on his face made by Darmanin's crutch. "Poor bastard," he said softly.

"He's worried out of his mind," I said.

"We'll work something out by morning. We've found out a hell of a lot." Kaufman looked round the table. "We know, for instance, that they're shipping liquid heroin out in tankers." He turned to me. "Do you know anything about making heroin?"

I shook my head.

"Then I'll simplify. The base is opium, of course. Poppy. Not the oriental or common poppy, but PSL. Papaver Somniferum. You cut an incision into the green seed capsules of a PSL poppy before they ripen. White latex appears—like on a rubber tree. It hardens and turns brown after about fifteen hours. Cut a field of PSL and you can smell the aroma for miles."

"Wouldn't that give you away?" I asked.

"They're not *growing* it in Sicily," Kaufman snapped.

Bonello explained. "PSL is grown quite legally in many countries. Greece, Turkey, Bulgaria, even Russia."

"Someone," Kaufman interrupted, "the Pipeline—now imports the latex into Sicily and processes it there."

"Is it difficult—making the stuff?"

He nodded. "The latex is just the first step. That has to be made into a morphine base, which in turn is made into heroin. You need a pulverizer, vacuum pumps, a drying room—but the real difficulty is acetic acid. Know what that is?" I shook my head again. "It smells like vinegar. Processing morphine creates a tremendous amount of acetic acid. Two problems—one, the smell while you're making it, and two, getting rid of it."

Bonello frowned. "Do you think there's a connection with the wine rackets?"

"Who knows? Every racket overlaps another in Sicily. Every cellar is its own chemical plant in Alcamo."

Bonello explained to me: "Wine doctoring is big business. Very big. Every year Sicily exports more wine than can possibly be produced from the grape harvest."

Kaufman cut in. "And where you're going—Alcamo—is the centre of the wine rackets. Like I said, come harvest time and every cellar becomes a . . ." He dried up, in mid-sentence, as if struck by a sudden thought.

Then, very slowly, in an almost awe-struck voice, he said: "Every cellar becomes a chemical plant. *That's it!* By God—that's the cover!" He swung round to Bonello. "Don't you see? They've gone into the manufacturing business. They're actually making heroin in a winery. What do you think?"

Bonello took his time answering. "The smell would certainly be

406

disguised in a winery. Many have a vinegary smell. And as for getting rid of it—you might even disguise it as wine vinegar and export it in tankers—if you had the transport of course."

Kaufman enjoyed his moment of triumph. His excitement buoyed us all up for a while. I listened to their technical discussion on heroin but after half an hour I was just too tired to absorb any more, and Kaufman suggested I turn in. "What about Jack?" I asked.

"Enrico will look after him."

I said my goodnights and dragged my aching body back to the tiny cabin. Undressing was painful—blisters had appeared down the entire length of my left arm. I swore, rolled onto the bunk, and pulled a sheet over me.

I SLEPT SO SOUNDLY that the steward had difficulty waking me next morning. On deck the sun was already warm, with the promise of a hot day. The Mediterranean was calm again. We were running parallel to the shore, about two miles out. Bonello had been right about his spectacular coastline.

The others had started breakfast, though without much enthusiasm. The atmosphere in the saloon was strained. Bonello said good morning, but with a frown on his face—and Lucia looked washed-out and ill. Jack managed a brave grin, but he avoided my eye. Only Kaufman was eating a cooked breakfast and even he was playing with it. "Want something to eat?" he asked.

"Just coffee." I helped myself.

Neither Kaufman nor Bonello had shaved and I wondered if they had worked through the night. Kaufman said: "Sorry about waking you, but we've plenty to talk about—and Jack was getting anxious."

I went cold. "What's happened? Have you heard something about Maria?"

Kaufman shook his head, but the atmosphere still puzzled me.

"Something's happened all·right," Jack said bitterly. "Kaufman's just been telling us his plan."

I sat down slowly on the bench next to Lucia. They all avoided my eye now, not only Jack. "Perhaps we had better get started," I said.

Kaufman cleared his throat. "Hardest thing about these jobs is deploying the troops," he said. "The trouble with a place like Alcamo is that newcomers stand out like sore thumbs. The locals suspect all strangers. Part of the mentality. Right, Enrico?"

Bonello nodded. "It was the first thing to worry us."

407

Kaufman continued: "For the past five weeks a film company has been working in the hills around Alcamo. Location shots for a spaghetti western—the place is supposed to be Mexico. Enrico found out about it in London. The point is people have become accustomed to seeing this film crowd around the place—dressed as Mexican soldiers, cowboys, that sort of thing. And technicians rushing about in jeeps loaded with equipment."

He paused to look at his watch. "At eleven this morning a charter flight arrives from Rome with more men and equipment. Except these are *our* men and *our* equipment. We can put forty armed men on the ground without exciting local suspicion. And the kind of surveillance stuff we need, radio gear, microphones, can be used openly." He gave me a quick look of satisfaction. "Didn't I say we'd have an army of people looking after you? Enrico will join the film unit at noon. That gives us eight hours to pinpoint the place you and Jack will be taken to from the café—"

"Maria will be there," Jack interrupted furiously. "It's too dangerous. If these people even *suspect*—"

"We're trying to locate the place, that's all," Kaufman said.

"What about the real film crew?" I asked. "What will they say when your mob turns up?"

Bonello answered. "The flight bringing our people in, will take the real crew out. Filming has been transferred to Italy." He rubbed his thumb and forefinger together. "Everyone gets a bonus from the Italian government. Don't worry, they'll be happy."

"I'm glad someone is," I said. "So what happens then? If your men start this afternoon they've got damn all time. Besides, what are they looking for?"

"They're looking for that farm Darmanin went to—a farm next to a garage, with a big house in the background—a villa, with a swimming pool—and preferably next to a winery." Kaufman pointed his finger at Bonello. "Find me that and I'll find you Maria."

"You can't be sure—" I began.

"Who's sure?" Kaufman asked. "My God, we've got to start somewhere." He stood up and crossed to a cupboard and dipped inside. When he turned round he was holding the wine-coloured briefcase I had seen him with at the airport. "The list, Sam," he announced. "Your job is to trade this list for Maria's release—"

"*Trade it!* How the hell can I do that? Once they've got us they'll take it by force—"

"You've got another ace, you must say you've left a copy of the list in London. Unless you contact your associates every two hours your organization will take over—"

"They'll never fall for that!" Jack roared.

"They'll play for time," Kaufman lashed back angrily. "They want to find out how much Sam knows. They've heard the rumours— they need to know what sort of organization he's got—"

"They'll find out from *him*," Jack snapped, pointing to me. "They'll nail the poor devil to the floor finding out."

"Not to begin with, they won't," Kaufman contradicted. "The first priority is to get Maria out. If you're convincing, Sam—"

"No chance," Jack said angrily.

"Sam?" Kaufman said, and everyone looked at me.

It took some thinking about. Eventually I said: "I think you're wrong, Jack. I think they will release Maria—after all, she'll have served her purpose."

Kaufman sighed with relief, but Jack just stared at me. "Ask him what happens next," he said.

I looked at Kaufman and he nodded. "OK, let's go through the sequence of events. One—Corrao makes contact, then takes you both to this house. Hopefully that will verify Maria's whereabouts. Two—you negotiate her release with Jack. Three—she and Jack return to the *Miranda*. All right so far?"

I nodded.

"We'll be tailing you all the way," he said. "Let's say they take you to this farmhouse. Fifty minutes after Maria and Jack come out we storm the place." He saw the look on my face. "Sam, we'll get you out of there—"

"Dead!" Jack shouted. "*Dead!* They'll murder him first!"

"Will you shut up!" Kaufman snapped. He swung back to me. "We've got forty highly-trained men. And they're equipped with stun grenades—"

"There must be another way," Jack said desperately.

"Not if you want to see your wife alive," Kaufman said brutally.

I knew he was right. It was the *only* way. We spent the next half hour pretending to look for alternatives, but I knew it would come back to that in the end . . . and it did.

Kaufman summed up. "Don't forget. You'll be under surveillance. Them and us—we'll both be watching. You park the VW then go and sit in the Café Cordina. Then you wait. Whatever happens just sit there—understand? Don't do a goddam thing—just wait. *Someone* will make contact, and you'll do whatever they say. They think you've got a list of names big enough to wrap them up for good. They *believe* that. They're afraid of you, Sam—don't forget that."

THE *MIRANDA* DROPPED anchor at eleven o'clock. Jack had stopped objecting to the plan. I suppose he had no alternative once I accepted it. Bonello went ashore. He had changed his clothes and shaved. We wished each other luck and I waved him goodbye from the rails—a slightly built, narrow shouldered man, sitting upright in the prow of the tender as it spluttered across the bay.

We ate a light lunch, served under a canopy on deck. It should have been soothing sitting there, watching the sunlight play on the water, but conversation was minimal and what there was sounded stilted and false. Eventually Kaufman gave up and went off to check the radio equipment, and I went to my cabin—saying I needed to change into the clothes I would wear ashore.

I sat there for an hour. Then Kaufman came in. He clutched a sheaf of radio messages in one hand and wore an excited look on his face. "We found out the name of Lew Douglas's partner," he said. "The one in the hotel business." He sat on the end of the bunk and offered his cigarettes. "Are you *sure* you never knew?"

I shook my head and wondered why he was so excited. I had never believed Edgar guilty—never—but if not Edgar, who? A shadowy idea haunted the back of my mind. Suddenly a shudder ran up my spine, and the words just spilled out. "I know what Bonello's agent was trying to say when he was shot down in that hotel room. He was trying to tell Bonello about the *tankers*. Hardman's Wine is what he would have said—if he had time."

Kaufman nodded excitedly.

"The tankers never belonged to Hardman," I said in a rush. "He subcontracted transport to his haulage contractor." Suddenly I was *certain*. I laughed aloud, but the sound rang sour. "My God! Of course—even the name—The Ferryman! Charlie Weston, alias The Ferryman. God! They set me up didn't they? And then poor old Edgar played right into their hands. Once he guaranteed a price for their shares they were safe. All they had to do was wreck Apex and pick up the pieces from the Receiver, for sweet damn all."

"And Lew Douglas—"

"Sold off the hotels and pulled out of the UK." I was sure I was right. Suddenly it all made sense. I said: "Once they'd got the night clubs and casinos from the Receiver, they no longer needed places like The Fisherman. They had far better outlets—"

"And Douglas didn't die—"

"That's what I'm saying. It was a smokescreen. Your boys were nosing around by then so Douglas fakes a heart attack—"

"Your ex-wife must have guessed about Weston. Maybe when Hardman told her about that meeting—when he put the squeeze on Weston and threatened to cancel the wine shipping contracts—"

I laughed bitterly. "I bet that frightened them."

"That's why she went to Malta," Kaufman said quickly. "She guessed something. She must have known Douglas was in the drugs racket. Maybe she issued an ultimatum—either Douglas supported her pa against the Receiver or she blew the whistle—"

"She did it for me," I said bleakly. "And that bastard Douglas murdered her."

"And this Tuskers crowd in Cardiff—"

"Charlie Weston actually *started* in Cardiff. And Tuskers started in Cardiff. I bet they met there and . . ." I clasped my hands together in an effort to stop trembling. I swear to God that I would have killed with my bare hands at that moment.

Kaufman cleared his throat. "Charlie Weston's not at his London office, or his home—or his office in Cardiff."

"Charlie Weston is in Alcamo," I said positively. "With Lew Douglas and Serracino—waiting for me."

"With Maria," he said quietly.

IT WAS ALMOST six o'clock when the tender took Jack and me ashore. Bonello was right—Castellammare was like a picture postcard, the pink and white houses set against a background of lush green vegetation topped by purple mountain peaks. The *Miranda* fell astern, Castellammare drew nearer. I picked out the wine warehouses on the far side of town. Nearer at hand a few fishing boats bobbed at rest. The place looked deserted. The end of siesta time. We reached the steps and scrambled ashore. At the top of the steps we turned right away from the town. The road climbed gently, parallel to the shore line—but only for a mile, then it turned inland.

Jack eased the pack on his shoulders. We were dressed as hikers—strong shoes, faded blue trousers, white shirts—and each

411

carried a backpack. We were both uncomfortable in the role—twenty years too old for it and even in our youth the open air life had never appealed.

"Bloody Kaufman," Jack grumbled. "Right little boy scout—I half expected him to tell us to start a fire with two sticks of wood."

The road was flanked with trees on the inland side—olives and pines twisted into bizarre shapes by the wind. The olive trees were stunted but the pines provided some shade. Climbing that hill was like crossing a chess board—black shade one moment, blazing white heat the next. The sun was still high in the sky. A cricket startled me by its sudden noise and there were a lot of flies about.

Soon the trees thinned out, and the track dragged inland, less than a couple of yards wide in places. We reached our rendezvous at the cemetery early. We wandered around, pretending to be interested in the tombstones—so many stark blocks of marble, the shimmering blue sea in the background. Some graves bore faded photographs. Many headstones were split down the middle—the customary way to mark the grave of a murdered man. No need to speak Italian to read the inscriptions—even I understood *Da maso assassina*.

Ten minutes later came the sound of an engine, in low gear, protesting a bit. Then a VW van lurched into sight. Jack stepped onto the track and waved it down. "Where you heading?" a man asked from the passenger's window. Maria would never mistake him for Jack, neither would I, but a stranger might.

"Alcamo." Jack looked round, but nobody was watching our game of charades.

The man jumped down. "Get in quick."

Jack and I squeezed into the back of the van and sat on padded benches opposite each other. The man climbed in and slammed the door.

The driver resembled me slightly. He re-started the engine. "Your cases are under the benches," he said over his shoulder. "Hurry up and get changed." It was difficult undressing in that confined space. Jack and I bumped each other, cursing the unpredictable motion of the van. The driver glanced at me in his mirror. "Papers are in the glove compartment. It's a rented van, rented in Salerno. Everything's in order."

I looked around for the microphones. Kaufman had told us everything we said would be heard in one of the film company's jeeps. And the van was also bugged with an electronic locating device which transmitted a signal not only to the jeep but to the radio room on board the *Miranda*. The man who looked like Jack was watching me. "You'll never find it."

"Can they call us?"

He shook his head. "They've only got a receiver—they can't transmit. Want to run through the procedure again?"

Jack finished tying his shoes and said: "If the plan works and they release Maria, I'm to drive her back to Castellammare in this. If we're alone I get her to talk about everything she's seen—how many men they've got, security systems, everything."

The man nodded. "And if they send someone with you just do the best you can."

The driver interrupted. "Hurry up. You've only got four minutes—then it's our turn. Get ready to swap places."

At least he stopped the van for that, pulling off the road into the shade of an olive grove. We dealt with the wine-coloured briefcase before we did anything else. I took it out of my backpack and the man who looked like Jack handcuffed it to my left wrist. "You won't need a key," he told me. "That way they can't take it away from you. The locating bug in there has the same range as the one on the van—twenty kilometres. It's well hidden."

Then we exchanged places. Jack pulled himself up behind the wheel, and we were off again. "Don't forget, Sam," said the man like Jack, "we allow half an hour for the first part. That's for you to talk them into swapping Jack and Maria for the list. But an hour after you go in we're coming after you—whatever happens. And Jack," he went on, "don't worry if they send you and Maria back to Castellammare in a different vehicle. We're ready for that. But if they let you use this it will be a bonus."

We approached Alcamo Marina, a noisy, steamy jungle of summer houses sandwiched between the road and the railway, built by Mafia money, hugely profitable for the owners and hell to live in.

"Don't forget," said the man who looked like me, "parking in the Piazza Ciullo is a right cow. It's always crowded. So we've got a car there waiting for you. A blue Datsun. He'll pull out as you drive into the square. Park in his place, lock up, then walk across to the Café Cordina."

We set them down on the outskirts of Alcamo. They stood at the

413

roadside and waved goodbye—two hikers calling thanks for the lift we had given them. I glanced over my shoulder. The clothes they had worn earlier—suits similar to the ones we now wore—were in their backpacks, and our suitcases were under the benches behind me. The change of identities had been completed in minutes.

"No more decoys," Jack grunted. "We're the hunted now."

"Wrong. We're the *hunters* and don't you forget it. Jack, *I* called this meeting. They snatched Maria to level the odds, that's all. But it's still my meeting and by God we'll run it that way."

Then we were there. The main square—the Piazza Ciullo. Cars were parked in front of the Jesuit Church. The blue Datsun waited until we were a few yards away, then reversed at speed. Jack slotted the VW into the space a second ahead of a battered Volvo.

I took a deep breath. Alcamo. Forty-eight hours ago I had never heard of it. Since then I had thought of little else.

Jack reached across to shake hands, a clumsily embarrassed gesture. "Good luck, Sam," he said. "If . . . if we get Maria out I'll be straight back. Whatever happens. You know that—"

I punched his arm. "Who else would lend me a hundred grand?"

He smiled and opened the door.

The Café Cordina was crowded, but so was the whole of the Piazza Ciullo. Street vendors called from the fish market fifty yards away. Rubbish littered the pavements, dumped there by the owners of shops and cafés. The warm evening air was scented with cooking smells, and the sky began to turn that shade of blue-black velvet I was beginning to recognize as Mediterranean. It was eight o'clock.

Most of the tables were occupied, but we found one eventually against the back inside wall. It suited us. From where we sat we could see not only the entrance but most of the café. We ordered pizzas and lemon *granita*, and settled back to wait.

Maria was not there. Nor was any other woman. The Café Cordina was strictly men only. And they were a mixed bunch. Some played cards at a nearby table, and beyond them four men in black suits talked earnestly over a meal of charcoal grilled fish. Near the door four men draped their jackets over the backs of their chairs. I strained my hearing to eavesdrop on the conversation. Two of the men were American. Brief snatches of their talk reached me—all about camera angles and shooting schedules and problems with the light. They were good, I had to admit that.

414

We ate our food, drank our wine and watched the clock. Eating was difficult with the case chained to my wrist. I tried putting it on the floor next to me, but that made me sit all lopsided—so in the end I rested it in my lap.

Nine o'clock came and went. Quarter past. Then, at nine twenty, it happened. Jack went to relieve himself and as soon as he vacated his chair a man sat down. "Give me the case," he said softly.

He spoke English with an American accent. I recognized him. He was one of the fish supper crowd—but when I looked their table was empty. I eased back to show him the chain connecting the case to my wrist. "Take it off," he said.

I shook my head. "I don't have a key," I said. I remembered Kaufman's pep talk about taking the initiative, so I added: "I came here for an important meeting. Don't waste my time—"

"You'll do as you're told," he snapped, breaking off as Jack came out of the Gents. Jack walked straight past me, towards the door. Two men stayed very close behind him. I pushed my chair back but the man at the table restrained me. "One moment," he said, "we don't want to attract attention."

Kaufman's voice rang in my ears—*Do whatever the man says, Sam*—I stared at him. He smiled. "Your bill has been taken care of—just get up and walk outside—slowly."

"We've got a van in the square," I said stupidly. "A VW."

"I know. It's being looked after. Your friend had the keys." We passed the film crowd on the way out. One of them told a joke and they all roared with laughter. Another beckoned a waiter for some more wine. They looked like making a night of it.

It was warm outside. I wondered what would happen to the VW. We needed that—it was part of the plan. Jack was climbing into an Audi ten yards away. I turned towards it but the man at my side put a hand on my arm. A Mercedes pulled away from the church steps opposite and slid towards us. I panicked. Jack and I were being separated. "Jack—wait a minute. I'm coming with you—"

He turned towards me, but then he was bundled into the car. Two men leaped out of the Mercedes and a second later I was in the back seat with a man either side of me. The man from the Café Cordina jumped into the front as the driver gunned the engine.

There were plenty of people about, but nobody spared us as much as a glance. I was sweating. *God, it had all gone wrong!* Jack and I had been separated! We had lost the VW! And Kaufman's bloody army were still in the Café Cordina drinking themselves silly.

"Where's Corrao?" I demanded. The man on my right hammered his elbow into my ribs. I jerked forward. Then he wrenched my right arm so far up my back that my head touched my knees. I spent the next twenty minutes like that, worried sick about being parted from Jack. Our plan *depended* on us staying together.

Then the gunfire broke out. We had been climbing—the tilt of the car told me that. I guessed we were making for the farm in the hills. Suddenly all hell broke loose. The driver screamed. Shots rang in my ears. The man on my left collapsed over me; warm, sticky blood seeped down my arm. The man to my right leaped out of the door. The car was out of control. Then we hit a stone wall . . . head-on. . . . The driver was impaled on the steering wheel, the man from Cordina's went through the windscreen—I damn near dug my eye out with that case, then my head cracked on the door pillar and I was being pulled out of the wreckage. My rescuer was Henderson.

"It's all gone wrong!" he shouted. "They've got Bonello. For God's sake, keep down!"

We were crouched behind a low wall next to some men dressed as Mexican soldiers. Beyond them were some arc lamps and a searchlight was being swivelled on the back of a jeep. Henderson shouted: "Bonello went off with an undercover man at two thirty. He thought he could guess which farmhouse. They went to scout it out—then they were jumped. They've got Bonello in there somewhere."

There was the farmhouse. At least I assumed it was. About thirty yards from where we crouched. Away to my right the Audi was on its side in flames. I saw Jack in the flickering glare; blood ran down his face and he was clutching his right shoulder.

"What's happening?" I shouted.

Henderson grabbed my shoulders and shook me. "Dammit, I just told you. For God's sake, keep down!"

Then Kaufman arrived. He raced across the open ground to the stone wall, ducking and weaving as he ran, to throw himself down beside me. "They knew we were coming," he gasped. "Bonello's in there! They've had him six hours. The guy he was with escaped and hid till he could get back to us. We came immediately—"

My head began to clear. "You mean you've changed the plan—"

But Kaufman was no longer listening. Instead he was shouting at a man who emerged from behind the blazing Audi. Henderson was still trying to make me understand. "Sam, they *know!* They know Enrico. Who he is, what he does—they'll have worked him over."

I felt sick. Poor devil—poor helpless devil. A jeep skidded to a halt behind me. Kaufman was across to it in a flash and instinct took me with him. I recognized the Mexican in the passenger seat: it was Lucia and she was clutching a microphone in her hand. "They're in the villa," she told Kaufman breathlessly. "At least four of them. They've got Maria . . . she's *alive* . . . she's in the villa—"

Kaufman snatched the microphone. "Murphy, you hear me?"

A man's voice boomed across the static. "Receiving you."

"Did you see the woman? Was she with them? *Definitely?*"

"Positively. Two of them dragged her between them. We identified Serracino—"

"You got *that* close! Without stopping them—"

"They had a gun at her head. But they've bought a one-way ticket. They can't get out. We've got the back and sides of the villa surrounded. Johnson's rigging up floodlights—"

"All right, this is what you do. Just stay put. Don't try to flush them out. We'll do that from here. You got that?"

Jack gripped my arm. "Sam, she's *alive!*" he whispered.

I hoped my shaky grin concealed that I was wondering how much longer Maria could *stay* alive, with this circus camped outside the door.

"That's the front entrance to the villa," Kaufman said, indicating the biggest pair of wrought iron gates I ever saw in my life. "This wall runs right round it." Two more jeeps were parked yards to the right. Searchlights on them were trained through the iron gates towards the villa. Mexican-type soldiers were everywhere, some at the entrance to the farmhouse, but most near the big gates. The driver of our jeep was the man who looked like Jack.

"We found the manufacturing plant," Kaufman was telling Henderson. "Big barn, back of the farmhouse. No sign of Enrico— no sign of the poor bastard anywhere."

Suddenly a shout drew our attention to the gates. Kaufman set off at a run, the rest of us on his heels. The villa was about fifty yards away, at the end of a drive. It was long and rambling, bathed in brilliant white light, fronted by a wide terrace, with a sweep of steps rising to a central front door, flanked either side by shuttered windows. A swimming pool was set into the right-hand side of the terrace and on the left-hand side of the house were some big doors I assumed to be an integral garage.

Someone was saying to Kaufman: "The front door opened, but it closed again, almost immediately."

Jack grabbed Kaufman's arm. "You're not going to rush the house. There's no way we can storm that place without Maria getting killed—"

Kaufman hurled him away. "For Chrissake, Jack, take hold of yourself!"

It fell so quiet I heard water splashing into the swimming pool from the fountains that fed it. Then Kaufman's breath rasped as he struggled to control his temper. "Now listen, Jack, I'm going to *try* to talk them out. I'm going to *try* to persuade them to give themselves up. But I don't want another outburst from you until this is all over. You better understand that."

He turned and walked towards the gates, in full view of the house. He pushed one gate, until it swung open a yard, then stood like a general surveying the field of battle. We all expected a shot to ring out, but nothing happened. A soft wind rustled the warm air. He turned to the jeep on his right and lifted a megaphone from the seat. "Serracino," he shouted. The name boomed from the megaphone, bringing an echo—"Serracino . . . cino . . . no. You are surrounded . . . rounded . . ded . . Come on out . . . on out . . out."

It brought no response. We held our breath.

"Come out with your hands up . . . hands up . . up." Kaufman replaced the megaphone in the jeep and returned to us. "I'm going to send two men in. Just halfway up the drive, that's all, just as a probe. When they're in place I'll try again."

He called two men over. "I'll douse those lights for twenty seconds. When I do I want you up that drive. See those statues about twenty yards in—take cover there. And keep your heads down when the lights go back on. Got that?"

The men gauged the distance, then glanced at each other before nodding. Kaufman walked back to the gates and spoke to the men manning the searchlights.

My fists bunched as the lights went out. Blindness. I tried to visualize the happenings inside the villa. If Serracino was there so were Weston and Douglas. I felt sure of that somehow. *Then came the explosions!* Followed by a man's scream. "Mined!" Henderson shouted. "The bloody place is mined!" The lights came back on. Neither of the two men had reached the statues. Both were only about fifteen yards from the gate, bloodied and motionless.

Then, at the top of the steps by the open front door we saw Maria! She was held firmly from behind, her feet were hobbled, she was too far away for me to tell if she was bruised or hurt, but at least she could stand upright. And that was Lew Douglas behind her, I was *sure* it was. "Harris!" he shouted. "Harris!"

It *was* Douglas.

I came to life and dashed to the gates, side by side with Jack. My movements were clumsy, hampered by that wretched briefcase still clamped to my left wrist. "I'm here," I shouted at the top of my voice. "I'm here. This is Sam Harris."

Douglas shouted from just inside the open door. "We'll negotiate with you, Harris. You hear that? We'll negotiate with you. Stay there until you read our terms." Then the door banged shut just as another opened, the garage door, at the top of the drive. It only opened a fraction, then a shade wider, and a donkey came out. A donkey! With a sack thrown across its back. It blinked nervously at the strong lights, backing away, but someone in the garage must have hit it because it turned again and started towards us.

"No way," Kaufman was whispering to himself, "no way that animal can walk through a minefield, unless—"

Suddenly Lucia screamed. "*No!* Oh God, please no."

It was Bonello. The *sack* was Bonello.

The donkey passed the statues and reached the dead soldiers. It paused a moment, then resumed its slow advance. Lucia turned her head away and sobbed helplessly in my arms. A note was pinned to the mutilated body roped to the donkey's back. I was conscious of an incredulous revulsion that men were alive who could bear to do such things to a human being. Kaufman untied the ropes, read the note quickly, then passed it to me without a word. Maria had written—"*The grounds are mined. They control them by radio from in here. They say they will switch the mines off long enough for Sam to come up to the house. They want to negotiate. Unless Sam comes in ten minutes they will kill me.*"

Kaufman started saying something when his words were lost in a new, unexpected noise, a clattering sound on the night air. Suddenly a searchlight came out of the sky, red and green navigation lights appeared, and a second later the whirling rotor blades of a helicopter cleared the ridge behind the villa to swoop over us. For an instant the machine hovered, then it came to rest on the terrace.

Its arrival was so sudden, so completely without warning that we were all knocked off balance, mesmerized. Then I was running back towards the other jeep, not of my own volition. Kaufman was dragging me and shouting at the same time. "That's how they plan to get out. That's their escape route."

Ten minutes remained, ten precious minutes before I was to walk up the drive and into that house to *negotiate*. Kaufman unlocked the chain on my wrist and handed the briefcase to the man who looked like Jack, who rushed away with it. "Just catch your breath," Kaufman said, "and listen. . . ." He sounded like a fighter's manager when the poor dumb boxer reels back to his corner at the end of a rough round. But gradually what he was saying got through to me. I thought he was mad at first. But what he said made sense—*if* it worked right. If it didn't I would be dead . . . so would Jack and Maria.

Kaufman wired me up with miniaturized radio-transmission equipment from the jeep. "We'll hear every damn word said in there, Sam. It's our best chance. It's our *only* chance." He hurried me back to the gates. I glanced at my watch. The ten minutes were up. Looking up the drive I saw the pilot still inside the helicopter.

Every eye focused on the house. Maria stood at the top of the steps, held from behind as before, her feet still hobbled. "Harris?" came a shout. I stood between the gates and waved.

"I'm ready. Jack Green is with me. We're coming in now."

Then I started to walk. We passed the statues. The helicopter's blades had stopped spinning but the motor was still running. The pilot watched us every step of the way—dark glasses shielding his eyes from the glare, an automatic rifle cradled in his arms. I reached the edge of the terrace before it occurred to me that we had walked through a minefield. I passed the helicopter and skirted the edge of the swimming pool. Then I was there.

We climbed the steps shoulder to shoulder. The entrance was empty now, the deserted lobby full of menacing shadows, and the smell of petrol was everywhere—the place reeked of it.

"Stop! That's far enough." A man's voice. A voice I knew. *Charlie Weston!* "Shut the door behind you."

He was in a room ahead of us. On the right-hand side light escaped through a half-open door. I saw his shadow on the far wall, a gun in his hand. I did as I was told. "You're not armed I take it?"

"Of course I'm bloody well not armed," I snapped. "For God's sake—"

"Stay where you are," Weston snapped, still standing in the room ahead. "Face the wall and put your hands above your heads."

I nodded to Jack and we turned together, resting our hands high on the wall. Footsteps sounded behind us. A hand patted my jacket, then each trouser leg, one-handed—as if whoever it was held a gun in the other. But when I turned I saw the man only had one effective hand. It was Corrao. And beyond him stood Charlie.

He was exactly as I remembered him, except for the gun in his hand. He stepped into the hall and jerked his head towards the room. "Walk slowly," he said. "And Mr. Green—remember that another gun is pointing at your wife's head."

I turned into the room and saw Maria. She sat at a table, chalk white, rigid with tension. Jack was across the room as soon as he saw her, ignoring Weston's warning, oblivious of the gun Douglas levelled at her. But nobody pulled a trigger. Jack swept her into his arms. She clung to him then, sobbing uncontrollably.

"For God's sake!" Douglas snarled. "Shut her up." It was my first close look at him. Douglas had changed. He looked twenty years older. The spoiled little rich boy had grown into an old man.

Suddenly someone brushed past me to wrench Jack and Maria apart. A big man, shirt-sleeved, bull-necked. A backhanded slap across Maria's face sent her staggering backwards. Jack roared but the man chopped him down so fast that I doubt Jack even saw the blows. He was halfway to the floor by the time I leaped forward. Maria screamed. Douglas had his gun at her head. And I hesitated just long enough to be hit in the face. The room turned over. Weston had his gun in my neck. Then the man in front of me sank his fist into my stomach.

"We haven't got time for games," he shouted. "You should be grateful for that." He looked beyond me to Weston. "Get on with it. Every minute is crucial."

"OK, Fiore," Weston said as the man left the room.

So *that* was Serracino. Jack coughed and spluttered to his feet, then helped Maria into a chair, her movements hampered by the rope around her ankles. I fought back my nausea and began: "This place is surrounded—"

"By mines," he interrupted with a smile. "Every yard of ground

421

beyond the edge of the terrace is mined. We control it from over there." He jerked his head. For the first time I spared a glance for the rest of the room. Corrao had followed us in from the hall and now sat at some kind of console which housed three video screens and a radio-transmitter, beyond which was another box which presumably activated the minefield. On one of the screens I could see Henderson down by the front gates amidst the blaze from the arc lamps. The sophistication of their defences sickened me when I remembered Kaufman's plan to rush the place with stun grenades.

"Twenty-five minutes left," Douglas said from his side of the room, his gun still pointing at Maria.

Weston turned to me. "This is what you are going to do. Go back to Kaufman and tell him to withdraw his men to the other side of the olive grove. That's almost a thousand yards. We want them there by eleven o'clock—*all* of his men, and their searchlights."

I don't know what surprised me the most. Finally I blurted out, "So you know Kaufman too?"

"Bonello was stubborn, but after three hours with Fiore . . ." he shrugged. "The word's out. We've alerted most of the Pipeline by radio. And we'll be away ourselves in a minute."

"But we'll take the list with us anyway," Douglas smirked.

"An exchange," I parried. "I'll take Jack and Maria—"

"Don't be a fool. They stay here until we lift off. Then they'd better move—this whole place will be ablaze within minutes."

Petrol! Suddenly the smell made sense. *That* was the plan. To set a torch to the villa as they left. Then another thought struck me. "But what about the minefield? How will they get past that—"

Weston shot Douglas a quick glance. "We'll switch it off. *If* Kaufman pulls back."

He was lying—as plain as day. "What if Kaufman stays put?"

"Then we shall kill our hostages and take our chances."

They would kill Jack and Maria anyway—I felt sure of it. But I wondered what Kaufman was thinking. If the radio was working he was listening to every word. *What would he do?* Immobilize the helicopter? But good God, if he did that . . .

"The list," Douglas was saying, "we'll take the list now."

It was hard not to panic. "Kaufman's still got it," I said quickly. "I came to negotiate, not to hand you everything on a plate."

Weston raised his revolver until it was level with my eyes. "Then when you've delivered the message you'll come back. And Sam, bring the list this time, there's a good chap, otherwise your friends—"

I tried one last gambit. "Send Maria. It makes no difference to you. She can tell Kaufman—"

But he shook his head. "She's served us well. Why part with a lucky mascot?"

"It's almost ten forty," Douglas interrupted.

"Walk." Weston jerked his gun. "You've got twenty minutes."

I threw Jack a quick look. "I'll be back," I promised. Serracino appeared in the doorway, carrying a suitcase. "Put this in the helicopter on the way past," he ordered. He was so *in control*.

The hall lights died as I reached the door. I started down the steps, reached the helicopter, needlessly ducking my head—the pilot stretched a hand for the case. Then I skirted the swimming pool and crossed to the edge of the terrace, raising my right arm to shield my eyes from the glare. Then I was at the gates and Henderson was pulling me down behind the wall.

Kaufman pounced on me. "You did great, Sam. You did marvellous in there." Some of the remaining Mexicans were working furiously behind the wall, either side of the big gates, burying something beneath the pillars. "Sam, it will *work*," Kaufman insisted. "What else can they do? You heard them—they're leaving on the dot of eleven. They've *got* to leave then by the sound of it."

The man who looked like Jack arrived back with the briefcase, and handed it to me. Henderson ran over. "We've finished at the gates. It's five to eleven."

Behind him one of the jeeps lurched into gear and trundled past us to bounce down the track towards the olive grove. The last arc lamp was dismantled. Suddenly the night seemed very dark. The headlights of the remaining jeeps sliced through the blackness as they backed up and prepared to depart. Soldiers clambered aboard. Kaufman was still giving me last-minute instructions as we walked back to the gates. Then he slapped me across the shoulder and scrambled up into the nearest vehicle. "You can do it, Sam. You can do it! Good luck."

And then I was alone, watching their red tail-lights bounce down the hill, the noise of their engines already fading. I turned to face the house, clutching the case. A single lantern shone above the front door. There was no light on the swimming pool. I told myself that at least we had a chance while there was no light on the swimming pool. Some chance.

My watch showed two minutes to eleven. I shouted and waved my left hand, gripping the case tightly in my right. "Weston! They've gone. Weston—can you hear me? OK to come back now?"

For answer the helicopter flashed its navigation lights. So the pilot was still aboard. I shouted again. "I'm coming up now. Switch those blasted mines off for God's sake!"

Then I drew a deep breath and started to walk. It seemed twice as far as before. The statues loomed out of the darkness. I passed them, my eyes straight ahead. The white paved edge of the terrace showed twenty yards away.

The noise from the helicopter was deafening as the rotors gathered momentum. I reached the edge of the terrace. Then the front door opened and Jack and Maria stood framed in the entrance, exactly as Kaufman had forecast. "They'll use Jack and Maria as a screen when they come out," he had said. "They won't trust me not to leave a sniper."

I ducked away from the rotor blades and skirted the swimming pool. Jack and Maria were already halfway down the steps. Serracino was behind Jack. Douglas and Weston were further back. I glimpsed a gun in Douglas's hand. Suddenly a huge flash of flame filled the entire lobby. Corrao ran out and started down the steps. Black smoke billowed from the door behind him. They were all out now, moving cautiously to the bottom step.

Kaufman had promised a diversion—*when, where, how?* Weston was armed too, I saw that now—he would shoot Jack as soon as they reached the helicopter. Douglas would shoot Maria, then me, once he got the case. I had my back to the pool, the open door of the helicopter less than two yards to my left. The noise was deafening— the screaming slipstream of wind tore at Maria's hair as she crossed towards me. I held the case up high for Douglas to see. *God, where was Kaufman's bloody diversion?* Suddenly Serracino shoved Jack aside and made a run for the helicopter—he was there, climbing on board, almost in. Weston was close behind, his gun arm swivelling towards me. Douglas grabbed the case and swung it aboard the machine, using the same hand to pull himself in after it, his gun hand already turning back for Maria. *He was going to shoot!* Weston's gun was on me. Then Corrao jogged everyone as he heaved himself upwards.

"JUMP!" I screamed, dragging Maria over the edge of the pool, "Jack, *jump!"*

"Water is the best shield there is against a bullet," Kaufman had said. "Water deflects a modern high velocity bullet better than anything I know. Hit the bottom of that pool and stay there."

Then Kaufman's landmines exploded under the front gates. The flash turned the night sky into daylight. I was falling backwards, Maria's hand still clasped in mine. I glimpsed the shock on Weston's face as he twisted towards the explosion. I hit the water.

When I surfaced the helicopter was almost on top of me, skimming the pool, Douglas leaning out, his gun flashing as I went under again. Jack came from nowhere to carry me spluttering to the surface. He kept shouting, "Sam, you're hit," but I was watching the helicopter. It was almost over the ridge. I saw the red navigation light quite clearly. Then the machine was surrounded by a ball of fire. For a fraction of a second its entire structure stood out like so many black lines in the centre of this huge orange glow. Then it blew apart. As I sank beneath the surface Kaufman's chuckle echoed in my ears, "Two can play with radio-detonated bombs."

Something was wrong with my left arm. Maria got her hands under my chin and dragged me kicking upwards. Jack was splashing wildly on the other side of me. I heard Maria crying: "Jack, your leg, your leg." Then I went under again.

We reached the side eventually. I clung onto the rail with my right hand. Jack was shouting, "Thank God, Maria, thank God!" and I remember shouting that I couldn't swim and all of us roaring with laughter as if that was the funniest joke we had heard in the whole of our lives.

The next explosion stopped us laughing. Kaufman was coming through the gates—except the gates weren't there any more—his diversion had ripped them from the walls and now they were chained to the front of the two jeeps, brushing the ground in front. The first driverless vehicle, jammed into gear with its steering locked, had made twenty yards before being blown up. That was the noise we had heard. And by the time we were peering over the edge of the pool the second jeep, similarly equipped, lurched towards the terrace. It almost made it, too. Then came another explosion and the jeep was upended. But the leading edge of the gate had reached the terrace. They had breached the minefield!

Jack was out of the pool by now, reaching down for me, Maria shoving from behind. Jack's leg was a mess. Even as he stood there blood pumped out from below his knee. I banged my arm on the way out, my left arm—the knock made me so sick and giddy that I nearly passed out. Then Jack was lifting me clear and stretching me out on the terrace—and a moment later Maria was trying to get me out of my sodden jacket. Behind her flames from the villa's shuttered windows licked up into the sky.

Suddenly there was a rush of running footsteps and Lucia arrived with Henderson. I was made to sit up while a tourniquet was applied to my arm, then my head was in Lucia's lap. "It's all over," I was assuring her. "The nightmare is over, Lucia. We beat the bastards in the end. We won, didn't we?"

Behind her Henderson was shouting for a stretcher. Maria wrapped her arms round Jack's neck and Lucia kissed me. "Will you look at that," Kaufman said from a long way away. "I ask you—is it any wonder they call him *Winner* Harris?"

Ian St. James

Ian St. James is something of a gambler himself. In 1977 he retired from the business world to become a full-time author—without ever having tried his hand at writing before! During the sixties he had served as a management consultant on the boards of several companies, and life had become unbearably hectic; rarely was he able to spend any length of time with his family. Suddenly he realized there had to be a more fulfilling way of life: "All the fun had been taken out of business anyway by the dead hand of bureaucracy. Writing seemed to be the last refuge of the individual." His wife, Pat, was a great support—she had obviously detected his tremendous skills as a storyteller—and she encouraged him to sell their Wiltshire farmhouse and move to Malta to escape completely from the distractions of the business world. Fortunately writing came easily to him. *Winner Harris* is his third novel to be published following his successes with *The Money Stones* and *The Balfour Conspiracy*.

The idea for *Winner* came to him as a result of occasional visits paid to nightclubs and casinos when he was a businessman. He enjoys gambling, although he has never been a compulsive gambler, and felt that the casino world would make a gripping stage for a novel, particularly as he believes that undesirable elements, not necessarily the Mafia, have penetrated the nightclub and casino scene in recent years.

At the present time Ian St. James is working on an immense family saga which is set in Ireland. He likes to immerse himself in the country about which he is writing, and so a year ago he and his family moved to Dublin. Although he is only twenty minutes out of the city of Dublin, his home is in the middle of beautiful countryside—and a million miles away from the world of Winner Harris. He plans to stay there another year and then, depending on the location of his next novel, the St. James family, including Henry their cat, will be moving on once again!

Sadie Shapiro, Matchmaker

A CONDENSATION OF THE BOOK BY

Robert Kimmel Smith

Illustrated by Bob Berran
Published by Simon & Schuster, New York

When sprightly grandmother Sadie
Shapiro attempts the impossible,
miracles are *bound* to happen. She has
inherited from her old friend Sarah
the job of "matchmaker". For her it is
an irresistible challenge: to find mates
for a trio of seemingly hopeless cases.

There is Doris, a fussy Manhattan
widow who has spurned a dozen
suitors in her quest for an exact
duplicate of her departed husband;
Harry, a lonely greengrocer who wants
only a duplicate of *his* departed wife;
and Brenda, an unkempt feminist
sculptor who doesn't want anybody.

With indomitable optimism Sadie
tackles this stubborn task. And somehow her campaign for love and marriage
is sure to have a happy ending.

Chapter 1

Somewhere on the avenue there had to be a taxi.

Sam Beck, his natty tan trench coat buckled tight against the breeze, stood at the curb in front of the Montana apartment house, a rather pallid imitation of the famous Dakota, two blocks farther south. Across the street, in Central Park, the huge Norway maple tree he and Sadie looked down on from their ninth-floor apartment was just coming into leaf. Spring in New York. Yesterday there had been hail and thunderstorms.

"Taxi!" Down the street a slow-moving Checker cab spotted Sam's upraised arm, cut across two lanes of traffic, and screeched to a halt. As Sam started forward, a woman brushed past him, yanked open the cab door, and leaped inside. "I'm awfully late—very important—I'm sure you don't mind—thank you!" she threw at Sam in one unbroken sentence.

"Slow down, you'll live longer." Sam managed a grin.

"Have a nice day," the woman said as the cab pulled away.

New York, New York, Sam thought, where your pulse rate's up and your battery runs down. Still, he loved this city. You knew you were alive here—in fact, no one would let you forget it.

"Taxi!" A Yellow cab pulled to the curb and Sam got in. "I want to go to Brooklyn. Court Street."

The driver turned around and opened the plastic partition. He was a young Oriental with thick glasses. "Brooklyn? Where is Brooklyn?"

"You go down to lower Manhattan and turn left," Sam said. "You can't miss it. Don't worry, I know the way."

Sam directed the driver through the park, across the East Side, and onto the FDR Drive. With only the Brooklyn Bridge ahead to navigate, he relaxed. His hand kept reaching to his breast pocket, feeling the cigars there, but he resisted taking one out. "You've got to cut down," Dr. Feingold had told him last week when he went for his checkup. "Twenty cigars a day is too much for a man your age."

"It's too much for a man *your* age, too," Sam had replied. Still, he would try. From now on, only nineteen a day.

He finally took out an Upmann Special and lit up. After all, how could he visit Brooklyn without making something special of it? He'd been born there seventy-eight years ago on a freezing winter's day in a cold-water flat on Gerry Street.

Sam took a long pull on his cigar as the taxi sped across the Brooklyn Bridge, the East River sparkling below. He wished that Sadie had come with him. After visiting the lawyer, he would have taken her down to Coney Island for some sunning on the boardwalk, maybe a frozen custard. But Sadie was busy. (When wasn't she busy?) This morning she was up in Central Park taping some promotional spots for a new public broadcasting TV program, "Fitness and Health," on which she had agreed to appear.

My wife the television star, Sam thought to himself. Sadie Shapiro—she kept her first husband's name in her work—had come a long way since the publication of her first knitting book. Now she was a regular guest on TV talk shows, had toured the country on the publication of her second knitting book, and her efforts as a jogger had been featured in magazines and television's "Wide World of Sports." Sadie was warm, Sadie was real, and people took to her, respecting her grandmotherly wisdom. For a woman who jogged a mile in an hour, she'd been moving very fast.

Sam took the lawyer's card from his pocket. Joseph S. Levine, Attorney-at-law, 16 Court Street.

Levine had sounded very young on the telephone. "It's a bequest, Mr. Beck, that I'm handling unofficially. An aunt of mine, a Mrs. Sarah Barish, passed away last week, and she left something for Sadie Shapiro. Apparently my aunt and your wife were good friends many years ago, when they were next-door neighbors."

"She left Sadie something in her will?"

Levine laughed. "Just a little package, not very valuable. But why don't you come by and pick it up?"

At Sam's direction the cabdriver pulled up in front of 16 Court Street. "Now you know where Brooklyn is," said Sam.

JOSEPH LEVINE led Sam to a conference room that overlooked New York Bay. Levine was a good-looking young man with thick, wavy black hair. "I appreciate your coming," he said. "I'm so busy I can't even get out for lunch. I've been writing briefs since seven o'clock this morning."

"And I've been wearing them since nine," Sam said.

Levine gave a wary smile, as if something had passed by he hadn't quite caught. Then he took a bulky manila envelope off a bookshelf and seated himself across the conference table from Sam. "I have some explaining to do," he said. "Does Sadie know anything about my aunt Sarah's later life?"

"Nothing. They hadn't seen each other in years."

Levine nodded. "For the past ten years my aunt Sarah was a matchmaker."

"No kidding." Sam grinned. "I didn't realize matchmakers still existed."

"Oh, yes. Of course, my aunt Sarah didn't make a business of it. She did it for the *mitzvah*, the joy of doing a good deed. She started with a neighbor who asked her to be on the lookout for a nice young boy for her daughter. Sarah found a fellow, matched him with the daughter, the two of them clicked and got married. After that, word got around and people started coming to her. In ten years she matched forty couples."

Sam lit a cigar and put the dead match in an ashtray. "And where does Sadie come into this?"

"I'm getting there." The young attorney rubbed his chin. "Sarah knew she was dying about six months ago. And she was worried—not so much for herself but for the people she was trying to match up. She passed most of them on to other matchmakers, all except her special-specials—people other matchmakers wouldn't take. Just before she died, Sarah gave me this package. 'For Sadie Shapiro,' she said, 'and make sure it gets into her hands.'" Levine pushed the bulky envelope across the table.

Sam unfastened the clasp and withdrew a tin box, brightly colored, that used to contain Swee-Touch-Nee tea. Inside the box

433

he saw three index cards with notations written in a small spidery hand. "Her special-specials," he said.

Levine nodded. "There's also a note."

Sam took a piece of pink notepaper from the tea box. Unfolding it he read:

Dear Sadie:

Here is a hello that is also a good-by. From your friend Sarah Barish who lived next door to you on Carroll Street for so many years. By now you know about my matchmaking and why I can't continue. Sadie—I had so much joy from this. It's like doing God's work.

Somehow I always thought that when I matched up my last person and took the name out of my tea box, that then I would find my final rest. But, Sadie, the end is coming sooner than I thought. I still got three names left—people I couldn't match up—and I turn to you to finish my work.

Please, Sadie, take care of them. Find them husbands and wives to make them happy. I know you'll do this, because you always said "a Shapiro never quits."

With love, your friend,
Sarah

Sam refolded the letter and put it into the tea box.

"Sarah was a sweet lady," Levine said.

"I can see that." There was a long silence as Sam and the young attorney sat quietly. Then Sam put the box back into the envelope.

"So," Levine said, getting up, "you'll take the box to Sadie?"

Sam nodded. "She'll have it this evening."

"Good." Levine walked with him to the door. He shook Sam's hand, then drew him closer. "Look," he said, "Sadie doesn't have to do this. I mean . . . there's nothing legally binding here. There's no obligation."

Sam's smile was thin and fleeting. "Counselor," he said, "I think you still have a few things to learn about obligation."

SHE CAME JOGGING ALONG the macadam path, heading for the vast meadow in Central Park. A slightly built woman of undetermined age, moving in a rhythm peculiar to herself, bouncing along at a crisp one mile per hour, feet lifting high, giving the overall effect of a child riding a pogo stick. She was wearing a bright pink hand-knitted sweat suit of her own design. On her head, a matching tam-o'-shanter. On her feet, well-worn running shoes. On her back, concealed beneath her sweat suit, a battery pack to power the wireless microphone clipped to her collar.

Inside a television tape truck parked some distance away, five people sat watching Sadie Shapiro's jogging figure on half a dozen color TV monitors. "Looking good," said the director, Fred Dubin. "Stay with her, camera two."

A wheezing sound, something like air being forced from a punctured balloon, came through the speaker system. "What's that noise?" Dubin snapped.

The sound engineer shrugged. "It must be the old lady."

"Why is she doing that?" Dubin demanded.

"It's just her breathing," said a young woman with a Modigliani nose. "We'll edit it out later." Maxine Morris looked over at Dubin, whose low boiling point was well known in the industry. As producer of the upcoming series "Fitness and Health," Maxine was responsible for taping spots to promote the show. Fred Dubin had not been her first choice as director, nor her tenth, for that matter. He was difficult to work with, although brilliant, and she meant to ride herd on his temper.

Over the loudspeaker in the truck came a different sound. "Train the body, don't strain the body," Sadie Shapiro was saying, "and jog straight ahead across the horse path. . . ."

"Amateur night," Dubin muttered.

"And when I jog up to the little piece of green tape on the grass, I stop and say what they told me, who knows if I'll remember, but I'll do my best and remember to smile, like they said, and then I jog away and across the meadow."

"She's nuts!" Dubin exploded.

"It's okay, Fred," Maxine said. "We'll be covering this part with music, anyway. Calm down." Gold flecks danced in her green eyes as her own temper began to rise.

"Feet, you're doing splendid," Sadie was saying. "Lungs, just keep breathing." But now, in addition to Sadie's voice, a new sound was coming over the speaker.

The engineer listened closely. "Sounds like . . . *hoofbeats?*"

"Oh, no!" Maxine exclaimed. "The horse path!"

The middle TV monitor showed what was happening. There was Sadie Shapiro, jogging for all she was worth, about to cross the bridle path. And there, emerging from a copse of trees, were a snow-white horse and rider coming at a rapid canter on a collision course.

"Stop tape!" Dubin shouted.

"Stop Sadie!" Maxine shouted. "Camera three—*stop her!*"

On the TV screen the action was being played out in living color. Sadie was on the cinder path now, the horse a stride away. With a thump that was audible in the truck, they met, and Sadie was suddenly and violently thrown to the ground.

Maxine ripped off her headset and was out of the truck and running. Behind her, Fred Dubin and the sound man gave chase. Sadie was not moving, and the horse and rider were gone.

Breathless, Maxine reached the inert form and knelt beside it. Sadie's eyelids fluttered. She groaned and opened her cornflower-blue eyes. "Hello," she said. "Where am I?"

"Take it easy," Maxine said, rubbing Sadie's hand.

"What hit me?"

"A horse," Maxine answered. "He ran away. How are you?"

"Hit by a hit-and-run horse," Sadie said. "Every day, a new adventure."

"How do you feel?" Fred Dubin asked.

"I don't know," Sadie replied. "All the pieces are here, but right now they don't feel like they belong to the same person, if you get my drift." She grasped Maxine's hand and sat up, patting herself all over. "Two arms, two legs, one body, and one head. So far, so good."

"Sadie," Maxine said, "you shouldn't move yet. Something might be broken."

"If you only knew how many parts are already broken from years ago," Sadie said with a grin. Slowly she got to her feet. "There you are, fat as a fiddler and good as new."

Suddenly she swayed, and Maxine took hold of her. "Sadie! Are you all right?"

"Fine, perfect. In a hundred years I'll feel better."

From out of the trees came a white horse, cantering sideways as the rider brought him near. "Easy, Silver," the rider called out. He was a young, good-looking man, wearing faded jeans and scuffed boots. He reined in the horse and dismounted. "I'm sorry," he began, but Maxine interrupted.

"Idiot! Are you insane?"

"I'm sorry. I didn't see her," the young man replied. "And I didn't

436

mean to run off, but Silver bolted and it took some time to bring him in check."

"Is that the horse's name?" Sadie asked. "Silver?"

"And this is the Lone Ranger, obviously," Maxine said.

"I'm Michael Newman," the young man said, smiling, "but you can call me Lone."

Maxine stared hard at Newman. "This is no time for jokes."

"You're right," Newman said pleasantly. He turned to Sadie. "Let me apologize again. It was stupid of me not to see you."

"Apology accepted," Sadie said. There was something very winning about Michael Newman, his smile perhaps, or the honest look in his deep brown eyes. Sadie warmed to him instantly.

"May I examine you?" he asked Sadie, and without waiting for an answer began feeling her arms and legs.

"Just a second here," Sadie protested.

"I'm a doctor," Newman said. "A plastic surgeon. It's all right." He unzipped Sadie's jacket and bared her left shoulder.

"How do we know you're really a doctor?" Maxine asked.

"You don't," Newman said matter-of-factly. He looked closely at Sadie's shoulder, then manipulated her arm. "Does that hurt?"

"No."

"Good. You'll have a nasty bruise, but I don't think any bones are broken. Come to my office. I'll take some X-rays."

"No," Sadie said. "I'm fine. As well as anybody hit by a horse. Just for a minute there I was a little *nonpulsed*."

Newman smiled at Sadie. "I think you'll be fine."

"No thanks to you," Maxine said.

Michael Newman had heard enough from the young woman at his side. He turned, intending to say something nasty, but his expression softened at once. He looked into her deep-set green eyes, saw her auburn hair, her generous lips, and firm upthrust chin, and something stirred inside him. What a nose she had, so long and straight. He wanted to plant a gentle kiss on it. For noses were a good part of the surgery Newman performed, and always the women involved wanted them shaped into a snub, a pug, a tiny peninsula. This girl had a nose that was a nose. And she wore it like a queen. "Don't ever change that nose," he said.

Maxine stared, not sure she had heard correctly.

"It's beautiful," he said, "and so are you. What's your name?"

Sadie made introductions, but Newman couldn't take his eyes

437

from Maxine's face. "Can I buy you a cup of coffee?" he asked.
"No."

"Can I see you sometime?"

Maxine shook her head. "Now run along."

"I'll be in touch," Michael Newman declared. He shook Sadie's hand, apologized once more, and mounted Silver.

"It was very nice running into you," Sadie said.

"Same here." Newman grinned at Maxine and rode away.

"What a nice young man," Sadie said. "And so handsome."

"He's an idiot," Maxine stated.

"Sha-sha," Sadie shushed. "That's no way to talk about the man you're going to marry."

SHE HAD BATHED and had dinner and now, dressed in her favorite flannel nightgown, she was rereading the letter for the third time. Sarah Barish . . . a voice from the past she would hear no more. How many years ago had they been close friends? Too many.

"So I told this Levine I would give you the package," Sam was saying, "and that knowing you, you would do what Sarah asked."

"Of course." Sadie nodded, sighing. "Sarah was a friend only your best friends should have."

Sam took a long pull on his Upmann Special. "So it looks like you're in the matchmaking business."

"For a friend you've got to do," Sadie said, "especially when your friend is dead and you're not." She put the letter down on the lamp table and thought a moment. "But matchmaking, who knows from matchmaking?"

Sam couldn't believe his ears. "Do you have to teach a duck to swim? Matchmaking is your middle name, my love."

"Oh, that reminds me," said Sadie. "I forgot to tell you what happened today in the park when the horse knocked me down."

Sam looked at Sadie. "Horse?"

"The nicest young man, Michael Newman, a doctor, and I could just see by his face what he was thinking about our own Maxine, from the TV show. And Maxine, you know her temper, she got up on her high horse and off on the wrong foot with him right away."

"Whoa there!" Sam said, holding up a hand. When Sadie got started, the words could flow like Niagara. "You got hit by a horse today?"

"Oh, that." Sadie shrugged. "A little accident, a piffle. I just ran

438

into a horse, and he almost killed me, that's all. Not worth talking about. But for Maxine I think it's the beginning of a beautiful tomorrow, if you take my meaning, and if she were smart she would, too. How many girls have a future husband come riding up on a big white horse?"

"Very few," Sam said, "except in cowboy pictures. But I've got news for you. I don't think Maxine Morris is crazy to find a husband. She's got her career and all, and I think she's happy the way she is."

"Wrong," Sadie said. "In their heart of hearts, every girl wants a husband, and Maxine is no exception. And Michael Newman is already in love with her."

"So fast you could tell?"

"Do you have to step outside and get wet to know it's raining? Of course I could tell."

"Then Maxine had better watch out." Sam took hold of the old tin tea box and handed it to Sadie. "All right, matchmaker," he said, "do your stuff."

Sadie took the three index cards out of the box and they began reading them together. "The widow Mandelbaum, age fifty plus," Sam said. "On Park Avenue. If she lives there, she must be rich."

"And Sarah wrote down she's good-looking."

Sam nodded. "A rich, good-looking widow. I don't think you'll have any trouble finding someone for her."

Sadie's bony finger ticked the bottom of the card. "Twelve men she already said no to, Sam. That's trouble right there."

Sadie turned to the next card. "Harry Wald. Fifty-six. Brooklyn Heights, not a bad neighborhood," said Sam. "What do you think Sarah meant when she wrote here 'plain-looking'?"

"Not Cary Grant."

"Aha. And 'poor dresser'?" Sam smiled thinly. "So Mr. Harry Wald is probably some kind of poor schnook, not your ideal matchmaker material. Oh well. I see here on the card he met one woman he liked. That's a hopeful sign."

"I also see that the woman he liked didn't like him. And six others this Mr. Wald didn't like."

"So Harry Wald is problem number two."

Sadie nodded, and turned over the next index card. After reading it, she uttered a quiet sigh. Why did Sarah take on Brenda Fogelman, a young girl who had told her she did not want to get married? Sadie glanced at the card again.

"It says, 'Try—as favor for Cousin Leah.' "

Sam groaned. "It also says that Sarah sent this Brenda Fogelman three fellas. One of them argued with her, another couldn't get to see her, and the third one thought she looked like a man. Oh, boy!" He shook his head. "She lives down in SoHo, probably in a cage. And no telephone. What's this note: 'Call doll factory'?"

Sadie shrugged. "So these are Sarah's special-specials. . . ."

"A rich widow who's rejected twelve men, a poor schnook from Brooklyn, and a girl who doesn't want to get married." Sam chuckled at such a collection.

"I'm beginning to see that being a real matchmaker is not so easy," Sadie said. "I mean, everybody else I matched up I already knew the two people involved. But what do I have here? People I don't know from a whole wall."

"Okay. Number one, you've got to meet them. I got an idea. Why don't you invite them all here?"

Sadie's face brightened. "Terrific! Why don't we have a party? Invite all three of them up here and *also* invite some nice eligible people for them to meet!"

"Now you're talking," Sam said.

"So while we're all saying how-do-you-do and all that, maybe lightning will strike and they'll meet somebody right away, they should be so lucky. Wouldn't that be a blessing?"

"It'd be a miracle."

A sudden dark cloud passed over Sadie's face. "Ay-yi-yi. I just realized what kind of problem we got. Where am I going to find a whole bunch of eligible people? Especially for Mrs. Mandelbaum and Harry Wald, who are over fifty."

Sam flicked an inch of ash into the marble ashtray. "You're right," he said, his forehead wrinkling. "You not only got to have index cards of people wanting to get married, you got to have real live people to match them up with."

"Exactly. So start thinking," Sadie said. She looked at Sam and giggled. "Abe Farkas?"

Sam looked scornfully over his cigar. "Abe Farkas is almost seventy years old, Sadie. It's true he's a widower, and a fine man, but he's a little old for Mrs. Mandelbaum, don't you think?"

"He's alive and breathing," Sadie said. "Call him."

Before Sam could reply, the doorbell rang. He rose and walked through the foyer to the door. It was Bryna Pernik, the young woman who lived in an apartment down the hall. In her hand she carried a plate with a slice of cake on it.

"Again with the fruitcake?" Sam asked.

"It's only the curse of my life," Bryna replied. "Is Sadie in?"

Nodding, Sam followed the short Hungarian émigré into the living room. Bryna Pernik had been three years old when she came to New York in 1956 after the brief revolution in Budapest. She was a bright, hardworking girl with a quicksilver smile, and Sadie liked her very much. Bryna was an outstanding cook, and she operated a party catering business from her apartment.

"Another fruitcake?" Sadie asked Bryna.

"Try it," Bryna said. She handed the plate and a fork to Sadie, and watched while she tasted it. "Too dry, right?"

"Yes," answered Sadie, "and it's missing something."

"I'll kill her," Bryna said. "I'll murder her."

"Don't kill," Sadie said, "especially not your grandmother."

"Can you tell me why she's keeping it a secret?" Bryna demanded. "My grandmother makes a fruitcake like no other in the world. Fantastic! Delicious! It could make me a household word for catering! And will she give me her recipe? Not on your life."

Sam took Sadie's fork and tasted the cake. "Dry is right," he said. "I liked yesterday's better."

"That was lousy, too," Bryna said, scowling. "And the three I made last week were awful. I'm going out of my mind, baking fruitcakes, when my grandmother already has the recipe for the best one I ever tasted." She raised her fist and shook it in the direction of her grandmother's apartment, across Central Park. "Back to the drawing board," she said, and marched out of Sadie's apartment.

"Eight million stories in the naked city, and we get a Hungarian fruitcake," Sam said. "But if we ever find people to come to your matchmaking party, she can cater it."

"Right." Sadie nodded. "So invite the first guest, Abe Farkas, and tell him to bring a friend."

Chapter 2

Harry Wald sat in a faded club chair, watching a freighter cross New York Bay. Otto, the tabby cat, sat on his lap, purring as Harry slowly stroked the back of his neck. So, he thought, the old matchmaker is dead, which is why he hadn't heard from her in weeks. And the woman he had just spoken with on the telephone, Sadie Shapiro . . . he knew her from somewhere. Wait a minute . . . the lady with the knitting books! He'd seen her on television, of course. . . .

"So what do you think, Otto?" he asked the cat. "Should we go to that party? Do I need a wife?" Could anyone ever take the place of his Emily? For twenty-seven years she had brightened his life. Emily with the quick smile, the dark hair, the gentle hands that stroked his neck, even as he stroked the cat. To lose a woman like that, so young, still with years to live and laugh and be happy. . . .

Living alone was not living. A man should have a wife, a soul must have a soul. The silence in this old apartment was deafening. To come home and not say a word to anyone from night till morning was not natural. He would go to Sadie Shapiro's party. Maybe, *maybe*, there would be a woman there.

DORIS MANDELBAUM circled the date on the calendar by the telephone. She was still smiling to herself over her conversation with Sadie Shapiro. Imagine, *the* Sadie Shapiro was going to search out a husband for Doris Mandelbaum! One pastime she had taken up in her widowhood was knitting. Which had led her to Sadie's first knitting book, then her second, and then to a knitting demonstration at Bloomingdale's, where she had seen Sadie herself.

She thought for a moment of the old matchmaker. How many candidates had Sarah Barish sent; how many had she cast away? No one measured up to her Jacob, may he rest in eternal peace.

Jacob . . . what a fine man he had been. So tall, so filled with life and energy. His fine taste in music, in art, in the clothes he wore. The joy of strolling with Jacob on a Sunday afternoon, looking into galleries on Madison Avenue, discussing pictures in the museum.

To have a Jacob once in your life was already a miracle. But maybe there was someone to fill Jacob's shadow and give meaning to the rest of her life. . . . Thinking thus, she wandered through the apartment, ending at the closet in the bedroom. The black wool sheath, of course. She would wear that to Sadie Shapiro's party. With the Buccellati choker Jacob had bought for her in Florence.

THE CAB DREW UP on an industrial street in lower Manhattan. "This is where Brenda Fogelman lives?" Sadie's eyes scanned the neighborhood. "It's all factories here."

442

"This is it," Sam said, and paid the driver. "Why, in this day and age, doesn't she have a telephone? Making us schlepp down here."

"She's probably a poor girl and can't afford one," Sadie said.

Grumbling, Sam led Sadie to the door. There was a metal sign listing the occupants of the building: ACKERMAN ELECTRICAL, BITSEY BABY DOLLS, TAUBER PRINTING. Sam opened the door, walked down the dark and dusty hall, and stuck his head inside Ackerman Electrical. A clerk sat behind a counter, reading the *Daily News*. "Is there a Brenda Fogelman in this building?"

The clerk turned toward the rear and shouted at the top of his voice, "Hey, Charlie! You know a Brenda Fogelman?"

A voice shouted back, "The weirdo on the top floor!"

"Thank you," Sam said. The clerk went back to his newspaper and Sam went back to Sadie in the hall. "She's on the top floor."

"I heard. And she's also a weirdo."

Sam walked to the end of the hallway and then returned. "I got news for you," he said. "There's no elevator."

"Then we go up the stairs."

"Six flights?" Sam stared at Sadie. "I wouldn't climb six flights for the Pope."

"Popes don't get married," Sadie said. "Come."

The stairs were as dimly lit and dirty as the rest of the building. On the fourth-floor landing Sam was puffing, and by the fifth floor he was ready to quit. "I think my ears just closed," he gasped, then hurried to catch up with Sadie. Gaining the top floor, Sam held on to an iron banister for support. Across the landing was a door, painted black, and on it a piece of masking tape on which Brenda Fogelman had scrawled her name.

"I hope she's home," Sadie said.

"If not, I kill myself," Sam panted. Twenty cigars a day and no exercise, dummy, he said to himself. Sadie the jogger looked as if she could climb another six flights and then dance a jig at the top.

Sadie knocked and a voice shouted come in. She opened the door to a vast open space, with grimy skylights flooding the room with sunlight. Thirty feet away a figure in coveralls and a black welding mask stood hunched over a piece of metal, making sparks fly as the welding torch hissed and flamed. "Excuse me, mister," Sadie said. "I'm looking for Brenda Fogelman."

The figure stood straight, extinguished the torch, and turned up the mask. "That's me. What the hell do you want?"

Sadie regarded her with disbelief. An oval face was revealed beneath the welding mask, with wide, heavy eyebrows and coal-black eyes. If you disregarded the smudged cheeks, the wild tangle of black hair peeking out from under the mask, and the total lack of makeup, Brenda Fogelman had the makings of an attractive young lady.

"I said what do you want!" Brenda barked.

"You said worse than that," Sadie replied, "and you should watch your language, because if you talk like that, others talk back to you that way and then we got half the world cursing, if you get my drift, and I see you do because of the look on your face."

Brenda blinked and looked at Sam. "Is she with you?"

"Forever, I hope," Sam said, his breath starting to return.

"I'm Sadie Shapiro," said Sadie Shapiro, "and I came to see you because the matchmaker, Sarah Barish, passed away, let her rest in peace, and she gave me your name to find a husband, and if you're willing, I'm willing, so why don't we get to know each other a little."

"So that's it." Brenda put down her welding torch, wiped her hands on a rag, and walked over to Sadie. "Look—I told Sarah Barish—leave me alone with the matchmaking. I'm not interested in finding a husband. I just want to be left in peace to do my work, okay?" She brushed her smudged cheek with the back of her hand, which spread the dirt as far back as her ear.

"Wouldn't dream of interrupting your work," Sadie said. She glanced at the jumble of metal littering the floor. "What is your work, anyway? It looks like you're making a car."

"I'm a sculptor," Brenda said.

Sadie's smile was wide. "How do you like that, an artist! Always glad to meet an artist, because I'm in that line myself, what with designing my own knitting patterns and everything."

A look of recognition crossed Brenda's face. "Oh, you're *that* Sadie Shapiro! The knitting books. I've seen you on television." She thrust out her dirty hand and took Sadie's in a grip of steel. "Glad to meet you. Hey, would you like to see my work?"

"Why not?" Sadie said. The more she knew about Brenda, the easier it would be to find the right man for her. At the moment, she thought, that would be a man who liked a girl who looked like a man. Also, he'd have to not mind living in a field of rubble.

Brenda pointed at a structure of smooth metal as high as Sadie's chin. "I call this *American Rustic*," she said.

"Of course." Sadie nodded. "It's very rusted. Maybe a Brillo pad, a little soap and water . . ."

"Sure." Brenda nodded, although she didn't know why. She led Sadie through her collection, pride in her voice as she explained the workmanship that had gone into each piece. To Sadie they all looked very much alike: twisted pieces of metal heaped together. That they represented art was beyond comprehension.

"Very nice," Sadie said, "and I wish you a lot of luck."

"Thanks." Brenda grinned. "I'm going nonstop because I'm having a one-woman show at a gallery next month. I've got half a dozen pieces to finish. That doesn't leave time for anything else."

"You could take one evening out," Sadie said. "I'm having this party and inviting a lot of people, and you never know—there could just be someone you'll meet there."

"Not interested," Brenda declared. "Look, I'm not into men right now. My work is everything. Men . . . they just get in the way."

"What are you talking?" Sadie said. "Men are terrific, especially ones you marry. If it wasn't for my Reuben, let him rest, and my wonderful Sam, who knows where I'd be today."

"Marriage is for the birds," Brenda said.

"And for the bees, and for all the animals, too, if you'll remember in the Bible how they got on the ark two by two. Not another word against marriage, Brenda please, because without marriage you wouldn't be here and neither would I. Marriage is what holds this whole world together, and don't you forget it, and plenty of women wouldn't have done what they did without help from a man, believe me. That Madame Curie got plenty of help from her husband when she was discovering radium, if you remember that picture. Yes, sir, every married woman should have a husband to help her."

Brenda Fogelman stared at Sadie and Sam, then pointed a finger at the door. "Out!" she cried. "I don't need interruptions, especially from someone trying to marry me off. Scram!"

Sam tugged at Sadie's elbow. "I think she'd like us to leave."

"That message I got." Sadie opened her handbag and took out a card. "Here's where to find me," she said, handing it to Brenda. "When you calm down a little, we'll talk."

Brenda put the card into the pocket of her coveralls and walked back to her work. It was clear that the interview was over. Going down six flights was easier than going up, and they were soon outside. "Did you see that face?" Sadie asked. "A beauty in disguise."

Sam's eyebrows raised and met in the middle of his forehead.
"Didn't you hear what she said, Sadie? She's not interested."

"Pish-tosh! With the right man she'll be interested."

"Not unless he looked like a piece of metal," Sam said.

"A Shapiro never quits, and neither does a Mrs. Sam Beck," said
Sadie. "You know me—I grab a bulb by the horns, stick it in the
ground, and make a flower grow."

"That you do." Sam grinned. "Brenda Fogelman, you'd better
start buying your trousseau."

FRED DUBIN was in a snit. The tall, lean TV director reached across
the conference-room table and grabbed a glass ashtray. What he
wanted to do was throw it at the two women seated opposite him. At
Sadie Shapiro, the primary cause of his headache, or perhaps a bank
shot off Sadie onto the long nose of Maxine Morris. What he did,
instead, was light a cigarette. "Look," he said roughly, "the idea
stinks. What we have is another static discussion program, four
people sitting around a table and talking their heads off. I mean,
there is nothing visually interesting about talking heads."

Maxine nodded. "Yes. But how else are we going to get our
message across? All the information—"

"Give me a chance!" Dubin snapped, getting up to pace the
room. "The message is fitness and health, and exercise. We have
Frank Shorter, the marathon runner, and Dr. Martin Shedley, the
guru of long-distance runners. I have about ten miles of film of those
two guys in action. Good running stuff, *which we can show as they
talk!* Got the picture? We let them say what they damn please about
exercise, but we run film over it, which is a damn sight better than
talking heads." He looked at Sadie and snapped, "That's two damns.
Forgive me, forgive me."

"I excuse you because you were angry," Sadie said.

"He's always angry," Maxine said. "Okay, Fred. But what do we
do when Sadie speaks? Or Haj Lothar, the man with the exercise
classes?"

"Damnation!" Dubin expostulated. "Sorry, Sadie. Use your
imagination, Max! I'll take Sadie to the park again and shoot her
jogging. For Lothar we'll take a crew up to his class of ladies and
shoot deep knee bends, or whatever the hell—sorry—they do."

Maxine's brow furrowed. "That's two additional days of shooting,
Fred. I don't think we have the money for it."

"How did I get into this nickel-and-dime outfit!" Dubin said. "Look, I'll shoot both Sadie and Lothar in one day. How's that?"

Maxine's long fingers drummed on the tabletop. "All right." She sighed. "We'll go over budget again. But only one day, Fred."

"Hallelujah!" Dubin's grin spread his mustache across his craggy face. Impulsively he grabbed Maxine in a hug and then, for good measure, he kissed Sadie's cheek. "This may not be such a dumb show after all." With a mock salute he left the room.

Maxine began gathering the papers in front of her. "Fred Dubin is my cross to bear," she said to Sadie.

"He's not a bad person," Sadie said. "If he learned to say heck and darn, he'd be all right. He's very talented, isn't he?"

"That he is"—Maxine nodded—"but so overbearing no one wants to work with him. Come to my office and let's talk about your part in the show."

"LISTEN, CHARLIE," Fred Dubin was saying to the TV station manager. "I want off this stupid health program, and pronto. I can't stand it." He put a look of despair on his face and stared at the station manager from under his heavy eyebrows. There wasn't a chance in the world that the manager would grant his request, Dubin knew, but that was not what he was after.

"Really, Fred?" the manager said. "I'm sorry to hear that, but you're too far along now for me to relieve you." He smiled and sat back, waiting for the request he knew was coming.

"Okay," Dubin said, "I'll be a good soldier. But I have some free time. Isn't there something new I could pitch in on?"

The manager thought for a moment. "Let's see. There's 'World Forum,' that discussion show we're launching."

"Talking heads," Dubin said. "What else?"

"We're planning a show called 'This Week in Business.'"

"Don't tell me. Stock tables, market reports, more talking heads. What else?"

"We're thinking about a weekly show on art. A kind of survey of new artists, their work, gallery showings—"

"Hey, that's all right," Dubin said. Images of colorful paintings popped into his head, the camera focusing on a still life, bright flowers, nudes. "I like it, Charlie."

"Thought you might," the station manager said, having planned to assign Dubin to the new show some three weeks ago. "I warn you, it's very low budget. You'll have to produce it, too. Just a couple of researchers, and a crew, of course."

"I want it."

"Fine." The station manager nodded. "And you'll plug along on 'Fitness and Health,' won't you?"

"No problem." As he left the office, Dubin was congratulating himself. At last a show he could use his full talents on. He didn't know much about the art world, but he would learn.

TWO FLOORS BELOW, Sadie was just entering Maxine Morris' tiny office, now made even smaller by three large floral bouquets on the floor, the desk, and the windowsill. "Very nice," she said. "Is it your birthday or something?"

Maxine sat down behind her desk. "What? Oh, the flowers. No. That idiot with the horse keeps sending them."

It took a few seconds for the connections to click in Sadie's mind. "Michael Newman? He's sending you flowers?"

"Every day."

"I knew it!" Sadie crowed. "Such a gentleman, so handsome, and a doctor, besides. Maxine, you must be thrilled."

"Why should I be thrilled?" Maxine asked. "Just because some rich plastic surgeon wants to throw his money away?"

Sadie blinked twice, not believing her ears. "Maxine, he's very interested in you."

"I know that, Sadie. He telephones every day, too."

"There, you see? I knew it. Love at first sight. A lot of people don't believe in it, but I do, because I know how crazy love can make even the sanest person. Your heart gets a message from your eyes and your mind stops working. I remember when I first saw my Reuben, let him rest, I almost fainted. Almost fell on the floor, he looked so handsome standing there in his uniform."

"He was in the army?"

"No, a mailman. With a leather pouch so new and shiny you could almost see yourself in it, which I never did because I couldn't take my eyes off his face. And that was the exact same look on Michael Newman's face when he saw you, cookie—the same!"

"Right." Maxine opened her desk drawer and took out a yellow pad. "Now let's talk about the program."

"Don't change the subject. Tell me why you're running away from him. For heaven's sake, Maxine, the man is a catch!"

449

"He's not my type." Maxine shrugged. "Look, Sadie, you've already told me you have three people on your matchmaking list—please don't include me."

"They're an obligation. You I'm helping as a friend."

"Well, stop. I'm too busy for romantic complications right now."

"Too busy for love?" Sadie said, smiling.

"You're worse than my mother!" Maxine stared at the small woman who, in a few short months, had become a friend, confidante, and adviser. "All right, here's the truth. One, I'm not impressed by men on horseback. Two, every doctor I've ever heard of wants a sweet little stay-at-home wife and that's not me. Three, the man is just too sure of himself for my taste."

"You never spent two minutes with him." Sadie wagged her head. "You can't judge a book by its cover. Or a man by his horse."

The telephone rang and Maxine was grateful for the interruption. Until she heard the voice at the other end. "Is this the lovely Maxine Morris?" Michael Newman asked. "I can get two tickets to the hockey game at the Garden. Dinner before or after?"

"Neither."

"Fine," Newman said imperturbably. "A concert? Broadway show? How about the new Woody Allen film?"

"Nope. Look, I'm busy right now."

"So am I. Did today's flowers arrive? How are they?"

"You're wasting your money, you know."

"No, I'm not," Newman said. "I steal them from patients in the hospital. Doesn't cost me a penny."

"Good-by," Maxine said, chuckling.

"Speak to you tomorrow," said Michael Newman.

Maxine put the telephone down slowly.

"That was him, right?" Sadie said. Maxine nodded. "He's not for you, right?"

"Right."

"So tell me, cookie, why are you blushing?"

Chapter 3

Harry Wald was unwrapping tomatoes and piling them onto a mass display inside the store. He wore a light Windbreaker that once might have been clean. There was a tear below the pocket on the right side, and the zipper had long since given up the ghost. He thought of it as a work jacket, something to protect him against the cold, especially out on the loading dock of the wholesale market at five in the morning. When his Emily was alive, he remembered, she always saw to it that his clothes were clean. And when a shirt or jacket had seen its day, she would make him throw it away. But there was no longer an Emily to look after him.

"You call these eggplants?" Mrs. Petrullio said, squeezing a small purple one. "This is garbage, Wald."

"It's a little early in the season." Wald put the last tomato on the display and turned to his customer. For twenty years Mrs. Petrullio had been calling his produce garbage. It was as natural to her as saying good morning. "How many pounds?" he asked.

"Three," she replied, "and ripe ones."

"For you, only the best," Wald said, picking them out.

"You don't mind my saying, you look terrible," declared the old woman. "You look like you're not sleeping." She moved to the tomatoes. "These won't be ripe until next Christmas."

"A few days on your windowsill," said Wald.

"Four pounds," said Mrs. Petrullio. "You ought to get married again. A woman can get along alone, but a man . . ." She nodded approval at the tomatoes Wald put on the scale. "Are you looking?"

"I'm looking." Wald put the tomatoes into a bag. After a woman like Emily, no one measured up. Even with this party tonight at Sadie Shapiro's, he had no real hope of finding someone.

At that same instant, far uptown, Doris Mandelbaum stepped out of her shower and took a large blue bath towel from the rack. In her mind's eye she saw herself already dressed. The black sheath, the gold choker. And for what? Maybe, maybe, she told herself.

She put on a terry-cloth robe and moved to the bedroom. A nice long nap now, what Jacob used to call her beauty sleep. Jacob, she thought, as she turned the sheets down. Jacob nestling next to her. Jacob laughing. . . . Tears came and she let them fall.

THE TRANSFORMATION of Sadie's apartment into a party setting was going splendidly. A bartender and a waiter had moved furniture aside and set up a buffet table and a bar. Bryna had organized the kitchen, and a massive turkey was cooking in the oven.

Beside Sam stood Abe Farkas, his friend of many years, who resided at the Mount Eden Senior Citizens Hotel in Hollis,

Queens. "I got twenty people on my list," Sadie was saying. "Single people from my TV show, from my book publisher, and others I know and they know."

"And I got thirty on my list," Sam said. "Relatives and friends of people from Mount Eden that Abe rounded up."

"How did you get thirty single people, Abe?" Sadie asked.

"It was like a bombshell out there, Sadie," Abe replied. "I put a notice on the bulletin board, Mildred Futterman and Bessie Frankel went to work, and everybody knew somebody looking to get married. So I invited them all."

"There's still something bothering me," Sadie said. "One of the main guests is not coming, Brenda Fogelman."

"Forget Brenda Fogelman," said Sam. "You want to make her happy, buy her a new welding torch. A husband you'll never get her." Seeing the distracted look on Sadie's face, Sam squeezed her arm. "What else is worrying you?"

"Harry Wald and Doris Mandelbaum. With so many people coming, I hope I'll be able to find them in the mob scene."

"You will," Sam said. "And you'll find them each a husband and wife, and we'll all live happily ever after. Okay?"

"From your mouth to God's ears," Sadie said.

"That's fine with me," Sam declared. He turned to Abe Farkas. "The bar is now officially open. Let's get this party on the road."

THE FIRST GUEST rang Sadie's doorbell a full half hour before eight o'clock, and by half past eight the living room was filled with men straightening ties and women patting each last hair into place. But soon there was laughter and loud conversation, and by the time Augie Donatello struck up "Lady of Spain" on his accordion, the party was rolling merrily along.

Sadie was having a wonderful time. Wearing a bright knit dress of her own design, she moved through the room exchanging hugs and pecks on the cheek with many women, including a large lady from Ozone Park who was wearing a dress she had made from instructions in Sadie's first knitting book. And it took the combined efforts of Sam and Abe Farkas to rescue her from a small birdlike woman whose bony fingers kept picking at Sadie's dress while she demanded complete knitting instructions on the spot.

Sam handed Sadie a glass. "Wet your whistle," he said, "and relax a little. The party is going great."

452

Sadie's eyes scanned the room. "I wish Doris Mandelbaum and Mr. Wald would show up. They're the reason for this whole party."

At that moment the front door opened and Maxine Morris entered, accompanied by Fred Dubin. Maxine made her way to Sadie. "What a bash! I didn't think you'd have so many people."

"Neither did I." Sadie grinned. "So what if people are belly button to belly button? With all this closeness maybe one couple will click and then it will all be worthwhile."

"Spoken like a true matchmaker," Maxine said. "I'll only stay a few minutes and then get out of your hair."

"Oh, no, Maxine!" Sadie protested. "You got to stay!"

The pleading note in Sadie's voice was not one that Maxine had heard before. "All right," she said, "if it's that important."

"Don't make a move," Sadie said mysteriously, and disappeared into the crowd.

Sam Beck was standing near the front door when a small voice at his elbow said, "Excuse me." Sam turned and saw a slightly built man, in his fifties perhaps, with thinning gray hair. "Harry Wald," the man said.

"You made it!" Sam beamed. He pumped Wald's hand and looked him over. An honest face, sad-looking brown eyes. Wald's suit was a three-button plaid number, with narrow lapels, and the tie was not quite appropriate with it. His shirt was white and clean, which, Sam decided, was about the best thing you could say about it.

"Come, have a drink," Sam said to Wald. "Tell me about yourself." He moved the smaller man to the bar, put a rye and ginger ale in his hand, and raised his glass in a toast. "Here's to you—can I call you Harry?—one of our guests of honor."

"*L'chayim,*" Wald said, taking a sip of his drink.

"In the fruit business, right? My father was in that business," Sam said. "Had a horse and wagon. Worked out of the old Wall-about Market in Brooklyn."

"How do you like that?" Wald said, smiling. "So did mine."

Sam raised his glass again. "*Landsman!*"

"I'm still in that business," Wald said. "More than forty years."

"How long were you married?" Sam asked.

"Not long enough. I've got a son in California, and another in Michigan, three grandchildren . . ."

"All gorgeous and very smart," Sam said.

"Of course."

Wald looked down at the floor for a moment. Sam lit a cigar. A plain guy, he decided, nice, keeping his head above water, like a million others. "How long has it been?" Sam asked softly.

"Two years." Wald gave a small sigh. "Two very long years."

"This I know about," Sam said. "Took me a lot of years to get over losing my first wife, believe me. And then I met that little person who knits, and the world lit up for me again."

"I should be so lucky," Wald said.

Across the room, Maxine Morris felt a hand touch her sleeve, and a familiar voice said hello. "You!" she gasped, turning around.

"Me," Michael Newman said, smiling. "A little bird told me you'd be here."

"A Sadie Shapiro bird," Maxine sputtered. "That *woman!*"

"Is wonderful," Newman said, "and so are you." He took Maxine's hand and held it firmly. Looking at her, he realized he must be grinning like an idiot. And that feeling he had upon first seeing her in the park returned: a hammering in his heart, a loss of breath, the sense that there might be a halo shining behind her auburn hair. Caring about nothing, he smiled on. "That dress looks wonderful on you," he said. "And your hair is marvelous—and I think I love you."

The young doctor's glassy-eyed stare put Maxine on her guard. "Look, take it easy, okay?" she said. "You don't know a single thing about me, so let's not start talking about love."

Newman took a breath and slowed his heart. "You're twenty-eight, single, born in Mount Vernon, New York, April nineteenth, father is a retired professor of English at Oberlin College, mother worked for the Red Cross, you graduated magna cum laude from New York University six years ago, worked at CBS, your favorite color is blue, and you're going to marry me."

"You're crazy," Maxine said.

"About you, yes."

"And you've been spying on me."

"Sadie helped. You'd be surprised how much she knows about you. And the rest I found out on my own. Ask me why."

Maxine pursed her lips and half smiled. "Why?"

"Because you're the most important thing that ever happened to me," Michael said.

In spite of herself, Maxine giggled. Michael Newman was very good-looking, and persuasive. His brown eyes looked soft and vulnerable, his smile warm. She didn't want to be rude.

"Newman," she said, "I could use another drink."

A woman wearing a black sheath dress touched Sadie on the arm. "You're Sadie Shapiro, aren't you? Doris Mandelbaum."

"Hello, hello!" Sadie beamed. "Look at you! A beauty!" She stepped back to admire her. "A face sweet like sugar and a figure to match. Such a good-looking woman, my best friends should have your shape. I love your dress, and that necklace, perfect!"

Doris Mandelbaum blushed under Sadie's gaze and the warm tribute to her looks. No one had complimented her in this fashion in years. "Please," she said. "In front of all these people . . ."

"Don't be a blushing varlet," Sadie went on. "I'm only saying what anyone with eyes in her head can see. You're having trouble finding a husband? *Um-possible!*"

"Thank you," Doris said.

"So how come you're not married?" Sadie asked. "It says on my little card from the matchmaker, let her rest, that she sent a dozen men to see you. But nothing clicked, right?"

"Here I am," Doris said with a smile. "Maybe it's still too soon after Jacob. I go out with them, but . . ."

"You had a happy marriage, I can tell," Sadie said.

"As close to perfect as it could be."

Sadie nodded. "If it was bad, you wouldn't want any part of another man. When you're happy in a marriage, it's the best that life can be. The state of happy matrimony, it's a better state than California or New Jersey or any of them, believe me."

"So where is he?" Doris asked, smiling gently.

"He's somewhere. You mustn't give up hope. You got to believe it's going to be. I never thought, after my dear Reuben passed away, that I would ever marry again. But Sam came along, and I got used to his ways, and pretty soon I knew that I wanted to be with him forever, because he makes every day a little sweeter. This is what I wish for you. Now tell me what kind of man I should find for you."

"Like Jacob. Gentle, with a kind of inner strength. It would be nice if we shared the same interests. Books, the theater, music . . ."

"What about money?" Sadie asked. "It said on your card you were very interested that the man should have money."

"I've got to be sensible, Sadie," Doris said. "I don't want someone who wants me for my money."

"Of course not," Sadie said. "I wouldn't introduce you to a fortune grabber. But there are a lot of wonderful men who aren't rich."

"I couldn't be comfortable with a poor man, Sadie, I know it. Sooner or later I'd wonder—Is it me, or my money?"

"All right," Sadie said. "I get the picture. But when I send a nice man to see you, what are you going to do—ask to look at his bankbook before he takes his hat off?"

"No," Doris said, "you are."

"DON'T GIVE UP," Sam was saying to Harry Wald as they fought their way across the room. "Aha, I see Sadie. We make a right turn at the plaid sport jacket and we'll be there."

"Good," Wald said. "A couple more people come in and we'll have to start breathing in unison."

"Hello," Sadie called as Sam came into view. "This beautiful person with me is *the* Doris Mandelbaum, from the card."

"How do you do," Sam nodded. "And this is Harry Wald."

"Hello, hello," Sadie bubbled. This is a man looking to meet a wife? she wondered as she took him in. How could he have dressed so poorly on such an occasion? "Let me say how happy I am to meet you. And I'd like to introduce you to Doris, here."

"We've met." Wald's eyes locked with Doris Mandelbaum's.

"You have?" Sadie was astonished.

"About a year ago," Doris replied.

"Fifteen months if you want to be exact," Harry added. "We dated. Only once."

"Which was enough," said Doris.

"I said I was sorry," Harry continued. Doris looked away. "And I kept calling, but you wouldn't go out again."

"She fixed you up, then?" Sadie asked. "The matchmaker, Sarah Barish?"

Doris nodded.

"Look," Harry began, "I know we got off on the wrong foot. But what did I do?" he asked, as much to Sam and Sadie as to Doris. "I took her to a sporting event."

"Is that what it was?" Doris said in a sweet voice.

"All right, it was the fights. Ringside seats at the Garden. Thousands of people like fights. How did I know you hated them?"

"Let's not discuss it, all right?" Doris said.

"Why not?" Wald said. "Fifteen months I've been walking around burning up at the way you acted that night. You were like an icicle the minute I walked in the door."

456

"You were half an hour late."

"Did you ever try to park a car in your neighborhood?"

To Sadie's eyes, it looked like an argument was building. "Why don't we get some food?" she said. "Isn't that a good idea?"

But Harry Wald had things to say to Doris Mandelbaum and nothing could stop him. "You hated the restaurant, too, right?"

"I don't eat seafood."

"I'm not a mind reader. All you had to do was tell me; we could have gone someplace else. Instead you sat there and sulked."

"I didn't sulk," Doris said with some heat. "I was upset because that old car of yours broke down."

"What old car?" Wald said, astonished. "A Buick, two years old— that's an old car?" He looked to Sam for confirmation.

"Sounds like you both had a wonderful evening," Sam said.

"And it was a flat tire," Wald continued. "It could happen to a brand-new car. You were very snobby about it."

"Oh, was I?" Doris said meanly. "I sulked and I was snobby. Any other nice things you have to say about me?"

"You're a little spoiled, but otherwise okay," Wald said.

"Thank you." Doris nodded.

"So how about one more chance?" Wald asked. "We couldn't have another night like that in a million years. What do you say?"

"I say no. And I also say good night." Doris Mandelbaum turned and began to make her way into the wall of people.

"So fast you're running away?" Sadie asked. "Stay awhile."

"I'll call you," Doris said, before she was lost to view.

"Fantastic woman," Wald said. "Fantastic."

"She's terrific, but not for you, Mr. Wald, if you don't mind my saying," Sadie said.

"I don't mind," Wald replied easily, "but you're wrong."

Sam caught Sadie's attention and rolled his eyes, as if to say Wald was around the bend.

"Listen," Sadie said, "there's a lot of peas in a pond. Doesn't have to be Doris Mandelbaum."

"Oh, but it does," Wald said. "She's exactly the kind of woman I could marry."

"The kind, yes, but not the actual person," Sadie said.

"Why not?"

"She doesn't like your car, or your first date, or how you called her snobby, which is never a good word to say to people. I mean, give me a week and maybe I'll think of something about you Doris could like, but out of all the people in the immediate world I don't think you got much of a chance with her."

"Listen," Wald said, grinning, "you're just beginning as a matchmaker. You didn't think it was going to be easy, did you?"

HARRY WALD left the party at two o'clock in the morning. After Doris Mandelbaum made her dramatic exit, Harry had spent the rest of the evening laughing and telling stories with Sam and Abe Farkas. Not once had he even looked at another woman.

Now Sam was sitting in a yellow club chair, surveying the litter that Bryna's crew was clearing away. Abe Farkas plopped himself down on the couch and opened his collar button. "This was some terrific blowout, kiddo," he said.

Sam removed a shoe and began massaging his toes. "The man who invented cocktail parties had no feet. Six hours standing up, I may never tap dance again."

"Thank goodness you don't have to," Farkas said. He took a sip of his drink. "That Harry Wald is all right."

"That he is." Sam removed his other shoe and winced as he wiggled his toes. "Terminal bunions."

"He's going after that Mandelbaum woman. She's number one on his hit parade."

"It takes two to tango, or even fox-trot," Sam said. "How do you tell a guy he's banging his head against the wall? Harry's a nice guy, but he's not for Doris Mandelbaum."

At that very moment in a West Side apartment close to mid-town, Michael Newman was floating somewhere south of Eden, his arms about Maxine Morris, his lips pressed on hers, his mind in the limbo of lovers. He had taken Maxine from the party to an East Side restaurant, and now they were in her two-and-a-half-room flat, on her couch to be exact. Maxine put a hand on Michael's chest and gave herself breathing room. "Take a break," she said. "As I was saying before I was so nicely interrupted, this is not going to work."

"This isn't work," Michael murmured. "This is a pleasure, Max, a whole different thing."

"Be serious, Michael. I mean it."

"Okay." Michael sat up straight, folded his hands in his lap.

Maxine shook her head. "Michael, I am not in love with you."

"Soon will be," said Michael. "Proceed."

"You goose," Maxine said. "Look, you're a nice person. I like you a lot, okay? But you told me before—you're thirty, you want to settle down, get married, have children. . . ."

"We could have children first and then get married, but my mother would be very upset."

"And I, on the other hand, do not—repeat not—want to get married. Not now. I'm at the beginning of something good in my career. I don't have room in my life for someone like you."

"Marry me," Michael said. "It'll be all right."

Maxine lit a cigarette and took a long puff. "Look, I almost married a doctor five years ago. I know all about doctors," she said. "Every one a prince. Office hours, hospital rounds, dinner on the table at six every night. You run everything by the clock. Talking to you now is a woman whose life is a shambles. *And I like it that way*."

"Listen, I can be just as disorganized as the next person."

"But you're not, don't you see? You ride your horse at the same time each day—you told me so yourself. Your life is too orderly. I like spending rainy Sundays reading the paper in my pajamas, staying up till three in the morning to finish a good book, blowing a whole Saturday by going to three movies in a row and eating nothing but popcorn. You're not like that."

"I want you, Max," Michael said, "and just the way you are."

"You don't, Michael. Sooner or later, if we got together, you'd start to organize me. I'd become your satellite. And I won't."

"You don't know me at all," Michael said. "I'm not that kind of guy, Max. Really, I'm not."

"It wouldn't work," Maxine said.

Michael moved forward to hold her in his arms again. "You have only one flaw," he said, then kissed the tip of her nose. "You talk too much." So saying, he closed her mouth with his own.

Chapter 4

"*Two minutes to tape!*" a voice called through the studio.

"So what happened with you and Michael?" Sadie was asking Maxine Morris. Sadie was dressed in her favorite pink hand-knitted sweat suit, a baby-blue scarf about her neck for color. A makeup woman was applying a thin coat of orange pancake to her forehead.

"Never mind," Maxine said. "Are you ready to start taping now?"

459

"Of course. But first tell me about Michael. Don't think I didn't see the two of you leave together. So what happened, cookie?"

"It was very nice," Maxine said.

"Excellent!" Sadie grinned. "Did you get lovey-dovey, or what?"

"Sadie!" Maxine was beginning to blush.

"Aha! I knew it!"

"*One minute to tape!*" the voice cried.

"Knowing him," Sadie went on, "he's proposed already, right?"

"Sadie, we have a show to do."

"Show, shmow. So did you say okay?"

"*Stand by! Ten seconds to tape!*"

Maxine ran into the control booth as the count-down ended.

"Cue music!" Fred Dubin ordered, and the show's perky theme was heard in the booth. Camera number one focused on the credit crawl, then the floor manager pointed a heavy finger, and Sadie began to talk.

"Hello, it's me again, Sadie Shapiro, the jogging lady, talking to all of you but especially people over sixty-five. I'm talking exercise, taking care of your body so it can take care of you. Lots of people over sixty-five think taking out the garbage is enough exercise. Or moving from their chair to the TV set and back. Couldn't be more wrong. The body is a machine, with a lot of working parts. And if you don't exercise that machine and let it do some work, you're going to wind up in the garage for repairs.

"Okay, let's talk jogging, which is what I know about. I started jogging twenty-five years ago. In those days people thought I was some kind of nut case. But now we know jogging is terrific exercise for your heart and lungs and liver and who knows what else. It's also a wonderful thing for your mind. Get your body feeling good and your mind will follow. What else can it do, stand there?

"We've got a little film of me jogging through Central Park. I'd like you to see how I do it, while I tell you some more. Okay?"

"Cue film!" said Fred Dubin in the control booth. He looked at his stopwatch and grinned. "What a pro! She hit that cue right on the second."

"And another thing," Sadie was saying.

DORIS MANDELBAUM WAS about to prepare her lunch when the apartment house intercom buzzed. She walked to the speaker. "Package for you," the doorman said. "I'll bring it up."

460

A few minutes later, he handed her a large basket of fruit. She brought it to the kitchen and put it down on the table. Mystified, she searched for a card. Between a Golden Delicious apple and a large tangerine there was a wrinkled piece of paper. She unfolded it and read: "Terrific seeing you the other night. I'll be calling. Meanwhile, have a piece of fruit. Harry Wald."

In spite of her feelings about him, Doris found herself smiling. She had not had a gift from a man in a long time. She looked at the fruit. The basket was clean and well packed, but the note was scribbled on a smudged piece of paper. It was so like Harry Wald.

Two hours later the phone rang. "Doris? Did you get the basket?" Harry Wald asked.

"Yes. Thank you."

"You're welcome." There was a long pause. Harry thought of three things to say and said none of them. "What happened was, I got those tangelos in this morning. From Arizona. Very special, so I thought of you right away."

"Harry . . ." Doris began.

"What I mean is—your usual tangelo is an Orlando. Or some people grow Minneolas. Down in Florida. But these are Sampson tangelos, the sweetest variety. Believe me, you don't see them in New York too often."

"Well, thanks again," Doris said.

Harry paused once more. Doris sounded cold and distant. "The grapefruits are special, too," he said miserably. "They're Thompsons, pink and sweet. Some people think the Rubys are better grapefruits, but I always found them not as tasty . . . as the Thompsons, I mean." You sound like a moron, Harry thought to himself.

"I'm sure they're very nice," Doris said.

"Listen, Doris," Harry blurted out. "I wish they were diamonds! Honest I do. I've been thinking about you since we met again. There's something about you. . . . I mean—"

"Harry," Doris interjected, "don't . . ."

"Doris, please, give me a chance, will you? I'm just saying what's on my mind. You can't shoot me for that."

"I don't want to shoot you," Doris said.

"So listen, then. There's a concert next Saturday at Lincoln Center. Tchaikovsky. And afterward we could go eat somewhere. This time *you* pick the place. Anywhere, Doris."

461

"Harry, no," Doris said firmly.

"Why not?" Harry asked. "Are you busy—or what?" He waited, and when she didn't speak, went on. "I promise, it won't be like last time. And what's the worst that could happen? You'd spend another evening with me. Am I so bad? I mean, really?"

"Harry, I'm sorry. Don't make this difficult."

"It's already difficult. I'm standing here like a sixteen-year-old, shaking in my boots. Tell me why you hate me."

"I don't hate you."

"I don't hate you, either. In fact, I'm beginning to be crazy about you. Of all the women I've met in the past couple of years, you got something none of them has—"

"I don't want to hear this, Harry. Good-by. I'm hanging up." Doris placed the receiver on its cradle.

"I'll call again," Harry said, but no one was listening.

FRED DUBIN was whistling as he walked along the dirty street in lower Manhattan. The director and producer of the upcoming "This Week in Art" was finding the tracking-down of new young artists a welcome relief from the exercise show. It got him out of the studio, for one thing. And he was beginning to have an appreciation of the new and varied work he was seeing. Some of it was worthless, of course, and a lot of it was pretentious. But now and then he would see something worthwhile, something fresh and alive, and that gave appetite to his searching.

He looked at the number of the building, checked the note in his hand, then took the steps two at a time. He strode down a dark hallway and thrust his head inside Ackerman Electrical. "Is Brenda Fogelman in this building?"

The clerk behind the counter did not look up from his newspaper. "The weirdo on the top floor."

The lanky director was in good physical condition, but even he was winded by the time he reached the sixth floor. The sound of a heavy hammer on metal led him to Brenda Fogelman's studio. He knocked twice, waited for a reply, and when none came he opened the black door. After several days of visiting artists at work he was somewhat used to seedy, unkempt places, but the sight of Brenda Fogelman's littered studio shocked him.

A figure in dirty coveralls was bent over a low workstand, hammering a piece of brass. "Brenda Fogelman?" Dubin called out.

462

The figure straightened up and looked in Dubin's direction. "What do you want?" Brenda said. "Can't you see I'm working?"

"You *are* Brenda Fogelman?"

"No, I'm the Queen of Sheba," Brenda said, and turned back to her hammering, as if Fred Dubin did not exist.

Dubin was amused. He had seen artist's temperament before; indeed, he had an ample supply of it himself. Stepping carefully around the detritus on the floor, he approached Brenda.

"Still here?" she said, looking up. "Who the hell are you?"

"Fred Dubin."

"Never heard of you."

"Ah, but I have heard of you." He told her about meeting Hymie Farrel, the gallery owner who was preparing Brenda's show, and how Farrel had recommended that he come and see her. As he talked, Brenda listened, her eyes taking in this tall, well-dressed stranger whose craggy face was oddly attractive. She looked into Dubin's slate-gray eyes, saw the dark slash of his mustache, the rough slant of his generous and strong nose. "And that's why I'm here—to take a look at your work," he said.

"I hate interruptions," Brenda said. A curse came to her tongue, but she checked it, wondering even as she did why this Dubin was having such an odd effect on her.

"Get used to it," Dubin said. "New York is not a monastery, and you live in the real world. Consider it a part of your work."

"Now look," Brenda said, almost by rote, "I don't need this and I don't need you."

"Perhaps not," Dubin said calmly. "But if I get a look at your work, and if I like it, then maybe I can help you. In one night, on television, I can present your work to hundreds of thousands of people. You do want people to look at your sculpture, don't you?" Brenda nodded. "Excellent. Now where is it?"

Brenda stared at Dubin for a moment, caught up in the spell and the authority of his voice. Then silently she led him across the studio and pointed out her finished sculptures.

Dubin took a long time inspecting them. They were no better and no worse than many he had recently seen. A few showed real insight and talent. The girl was by no means a great artist, but she was an original. He looked away from the work and stared at Brenda. She had an interesting face, complete with dirty smudges across her cheek. In her eyes there was intelligence, and something else—a

463

kind of liberated look. Brenda Fogelman was her own woman, without doubt.

Dubin took her arm. "Stand behind your work for a moment. There's a good girl."

"Woman, you mean, good *woman*," Brenda said.

"My dear woman, I never doubted it. Now, please, shut up."

Dubin took a few paces back and brought his hands up to frame the picture in his mind. Shapes and images floated—he saw a dirty, unkempt girl and her shining metal sculpture, beauty in the work and not in the artist. Yes, it was good. He could do an entire show on Brenda Fogelman. Better still, he could cover the opening of her exhibition at the gallery. Yes, that was it. Well-dressed people crowding around this wild artiste, the clean lines of her sculpture making a statement of the New York artist's world.

"Listen, Dubin," Brenda said, "who are you, anyway? Tell me about yourself."

"Why?"

Brenda looked at her work boots. "I don't know." She shrugged. "You interest me."

"Let's keep this professional and not personal, shall we?"

"Are you married?" Brenda asked.

"Certainly not."

"Good." Brenda nodded. "Good."

Dubin looked at her shrewdly and shook his head. "I'm not interested in you that way. But I do like your work."

For the first time in years Brenda used a word she had almost forgotten. "Thanks."

"Don't thank me now," Dubin said. "Wait. Brenda, my dear, I think I'm going to make you a star."

"COME ON NOW, be nice," Sam Beck was saying to the crossword puzzle of *The New York Times*. He had sailed through the upper left-hand corner, then zipped down almost to the bottom. But now they were throwing him a curveball. A four-letter word for a range of mountains in India. He knew of the Himalayas, and the female version, the Heralayas. Or were those in Nepal?

When the telephone rang, he was happy for the interruption.

"Sam? This is Harry Wald. Is Sadie there?"

"Hello, Harry. No, Sadie is off in television land. What's the problem?"

"Doris Mandelbaum, what else? The woman won't give me a tumble. Listen, Sam, can I talk to you?"

"We're talking now."

"I mean, can I see you? I'll buy you lunch, okay?"

"Fine," Sam said. "Harry, you wouldn't know a four-letter word for a range of mountains in India, would you?"

There was a short silence. "Kush, the Hindu Kush."

Sam looked down at the puzzle. "Son of a gun, it fits! Thanks, Harry. There's a good Chinese joint on Broadway, the Szechuan Hot Pot. I'll meet you there in half an hour."

Thirty-five minutes later, Sam met Wald at the restaurant's door. "You made pretty good time from Brooklyn," Sam said.

"I wasn't there," said Wald. "I was in my Manhattan store."

"I see." Sam eyed Wald's jacket. "Where do you get your clothes, the Salvation Army?"

Wald grinned. "I don't pay attention to clothes. I'm in a kind of rough-and-tumble business."

"Right," said Sam. He held the door for Wald, then led him to a booth along the far wall. They seated themselves, and Sam ordered two bottles of beer. "Can you eat hot food?"

Wald shrugged. "I'll take a chance."

"Good." Sam ordered spicy eggplant and a chicken dish called Emperor's Fire. Then he sat back and took a long sip of his beer. "Tell me about Doris. You sounded upset on the phone."

"Upset? I'm only going bananas, that's all. She's a hard case, Sam." Wald told him of the basket of fruit he had sent Doris. "So that's the thanks I get. She hangs up the phone on me."

"It happens." Sam shrugged. "Maybe you shouldn't have sent her fruit. Sometimes when you send people something from your own business, they think it doesn't cost you anything."

"So what should I have sent her?"

"Flowers . . . chocolates, maybe. From a fancy shop. The idea isn't the gift, you know, it's the impression it makes."

"Okay." Wald nodded. "Next time she gets flowers."

A waiter approached the table and set down the serving dishes. Sam doled out portions for Wald and himself. "Eggplant and chicken," he told Wald. "Be careful, and don't eat those hornshaped things. They're peppers."

"Hot stuff, eh?" Wald surveyed the food with a suspicious eye. He took a small forkful of eggplant, chewed gingerly, then

465

swallowed. Suddenly his eyes grew large, and, choking, he grabbed his beer and downed it.

"Isn't it great?" Sam said between mouthfuls.

Tears stood in Wald's eyes. He felt as if someone had scorched his throat with a blowtorch. Sam served himself another portion of the eggplant. "Wait'll you taste the chicken. *Fantastic.*"

Harry Wald knew he would not live to taste the chicken. He drank his glass of ice water, then stared at Sam through tear-filled eyes. "You mean," he gasped, "people actually pay to eat this?"

Sam nodded, his face a picture of bliss. "It is a little hotter than usual."

"Hot, he says." Wald sucked air down his incinerated throat. "What I left on my plate could warm Pittsburgh for the winter."

Sam laughed, then signaled the waiter. "Would you like something else, Harry? Maybe not so spicy?"

"Who can eat?" Wald shrugged. "I feel like I just had my tonsils removed. Without anesthesia."

"Then you'd better have some ice cream."

"Make it vanilla."

Sam ordered, then sat back and lit a cigar. What about Harry Wald and Doris Mandelbaum? He didn't rate the fruiterer more than a ten-to-one shot to even get a second date with the classy lady in question. He looked at the faded flannel shirt Wald was wearing under his torn jacket, and the faded khaki pants stained with grease. A picture of sartorial splendor the man was not.

Sam took a long pull on his cigar. But Wald was warm, had a sense of humor. And he was no dummy. Anyone who could come up with a four-letter Indian mountain range was okay. But Doris Mandelbaum had been married to a man who obviously was in another league. And she had rejected Harry at least three times. Three strikes is out in baseball, and many other games.

"So what should I do about Doris?" Wald asked.

"Do?" Sam looked speculatively at Wald. "Can I speak honestly? I don't want to hurt your feelings, Harry."

"Go ahead," Wald said with a wave. "My feelings have been hurt by the best of them."

"All right. Let's take a good look at Harry Wald, the way Doris Mandelbaum sees him, perhaps. Tall enough, still has his hair. Face . . . no Gregory Peck, but not a bad-looking guy. Clean-shaven if not clean-cut, let's say."

"So far, so good."

"Right," Sam said. "Now let's get to clothing—"

"I know what you're going to say," Wald interrupted. "I've let my wardrobe run down, Sam. My suits are old, my shirts are old, I haven't spent anything on clothing since Emily died."

"If you'll excuse me, Harry, your clothes were not terrific when they were new. Have you noticed the style Doris dresses with? You'll have to match that, I'm afraid. You have to look like you belong together when you take her out."

"*If* I ever take her out again," Wald said.

Sam took another sip of beer. "The next part is something you have to face. Has it occurred to you that you just might not be Doris' type? She's a cultured lady, Harry, with refined tastes."

"So am I," Wald said, "or I used to be. Once upon a time I read books, went to concerts, shows. With Emily. But these last couple of years . . . I sit in front of the television and watch any sport show going. Wrestling, the roller derby . . ."

"Which is why you took Doris to a prizefight."

"A mistake I'm still paying for. I'm not stupid, Sam, although sometimes it's hard to tell. I went to college for eight years," he said, smiling. "That's counting four years out in the middle to help Patton win the war. I run a successful business, too."

"That you do," Sam agreed, "which brings me to your biggest problem. Doris Mandelbaum is a very wealthy widow. She won't have anything to do with a man who might be a fortune hunter." Sam looked directly into Harry Wald's brown eyes.

"I have money."

"Of course, but there's money, and there's money. You've got a store in Brooklyn, and one in Manhattan you mentioned. With two fruit stores you probably make a pretty good living."

"I don't have *two* fruit stores," Harry Wald said. "I have *forty-eight* of them."

"What?" Sam's cigar almost dropped from his fingers.

"And I own a piece of the wholesale operation up in the Bronx," Wald went on, "plus orange and grapefruit groves in Arizona, California, and Florida. I'm comfortable, believe me."

"But the way you look," Sam said, "the way you live . . ."

"I've never had a problem making money. *Spending* it, that's what I don't know about."

"That," Sam said, smiling, "you can learn."

OUTSIDE THE KITCHEN WINDOW the sun was going down. Inside the kitchen Sam's temper was going up. "So you see, Sadie," he was saying for the third time, "Harry Wald is no shlemiel. He's probably got as much money as Doris."

Sadie stood by the window, practicing the deep-breathing exercise she had learned only yesterday. A yogi she had interviewed on the TV show had demonstrated it: take a very deep breath, hold it for ten seconds, then slowly exhale for ten seconds. It seemed to have done wonders for the yogi, who claimed to be one hundred and twenty years old. "You don't look a day over a hundred and one," Sadie had marveled.

"So isn't that terrific about Wald?" Sam said. "Sadie? I know you're alive because your face is turning pink. Hello?"

Seven, eight, nine, ten, Sadie counted in her head. "Listen," Sam said, "if we're going to talk, you'll have to stop breathing."

"All right," Sadie said. "Finished breathing." Panting a little, she sat down at the table.

"So what I figure is this," Sam said. "Harry is back in the ball-game. With Doris, that is."

"That would be nice, but I'm not too sure. To Doris, Harry Wald is a lost gauze. Like a bandage that falls off a finger and you throw away. I already called her to ask if she'd give Harry another chance."

"And?"

"Wouldn't budge an inch, and if I said two more words, I got the feeling she wouldn't talk to *me* again, either."

"Poor Harry. He's going to be very disappointed."

"I'm disappointed, too," Sadie said. "The man is a sweet person and he'd be very good for Doris. The same as her first husband, only different. What Doris wants is her Jacob all over again, and you can't find two people the same in one lifetime."

"Maybe you could talk to Doris again," Sam said.

"And maybe if I grew wheels, I could be a trolley car," Sadie countered. "No, I don't think she'd listen to me. Not even if I told her he was rich. He's what you call a persona au gratin with her. Sam, we got to do it the hard way. I've got to find a nice woman for Harry and another Jacob for Doris."

"That should only take seven or eight years. And what about Brenda Fogelman?"

"Don't remind me. I'm still trying to figure that girl out."

Sam looked up as the doorbell rang. "I'll bet that's our resident fruitcake," he said as he went to the door.

Bryna Pernik walked in, sniffling into a handkerchief. "Sadie," she said, her voice breaking, "she has to help me. . . ."

"In the kitchen," Sadie called. She rose to meet Bryna, who fell into her arms, sobbing.

"Now, now," Sadie said, hugging her. "It can't be that bad."

"My grandmother . . ." Bryna sobbed.

Sadie sat Bryna down in a chair at the table and, fetching a tissue, dabbed at the girl's mascara-streaked cheeks. "Stop crying now, cookie, and tell me everything."

Bryna sniffled. "We had a fight," she managed to say.

"Over the fruitcake," Sam said.

Bryna nodded. "I brought her my last one. She tasted it and smiled in a funny way and I got so angry. Then I pleaded with her to give me the recipe and she refused. I began to yell at her. . . . I said something awful. She got very mad and told me she's never talking to me again!" Bryna began sobbing once more. "What'll I do, Sadie? She's so sweet . . . and I've made an enemy of her."

"First calm yourself. Crying doesn't help, except for exercising your eyes." Sadie sat down next to her.

"For months now," Bryna said, "I've been trying to figure out why she won't part with her recipe. And I can't. It's a mystery."

Sadie looked into Bryna's tear-rimmed eyes, then took out her pen and a blank index card. "Write down her name and address."

"You'll see her?" Bryna leaned over and kissed Sadie's cheek.

"Sometime tomorrow," Sadie said, "I'm going to get to the bottom of your Hungarian fruitcake."

"ARE YOU SURE you have to go?" Maxine Morris was saying. She put her hands on Michael's cheeks and gently kissed his chin.

Michael squeezed her to him. "Duty calls, Max. I have to be in the operating room at six, and I need sleep. So, good night." Releasing her, he went to the coat closet.

Maxine followed and watched as he put on his topcoat. "Stay ten more minutes."

Michael buttoned his coat. "I'm going to go downstairs, drive across the park, put my car in the garage, go upstairs, and get into bed." He looked at her eyes. "That's what I'm going to do." He stood unmoving. "Soon I'm going to do that."

She put her arms about him. Then she unbuttoned the top button of his topcoat.

"You're impossible." Michael sighed. Maxine began to giggle.

Chapter 5

Fred Dubin was already seated at a table when Brenda Fogelman entered the chic restaurant in SoHo. He stood, appraising Brenda as she made her way through the dining room. She had taken some pains with her appearance, he could see. Her coveralls had no patches and the flannel shirt she wore underneath was clean. Her black hair was in a ponytail, held back by a red rubber band.

Dubin held the chair for her as she sat down. "I wasn't sure you'd come. It's not easy to get a message to you."

"You called Hymie Farrel, right? He called the doll factory on the floor below me. Next time you want me, call them direct—Bitsey Baby Dolls—and they'll come up and call me to the phone."

"Fine." Dubin held up a hand and a waiter appeared. "Two Americanos, please, on the rocks."

"I don't drink," Brenda said. "Don't waste your money."

"I'm on an expense account. And we'll be talking business."

"Okay. What's an Americano, anyway?"

"Vermouth, soda, and bitters. You may like it. If not, just stare at it." Dubin looked at Brenda's hands, which were drumming nervously at the edge of the table. They showed signs of recent exposure to soap and water, although her fingernails were edged in black. "Have you finished that large piece you were working on? Farrel says he's going to make it the centerpiece of the show."

"Almost. I still have some soldering to do. Maybe you could come up and see it after lunch."

"Some other time. I have an appointment after this."

"Okay." There was a short silence. Brenda stared at her hands. "I've been thinking about you a lot," she said.

"For heaven's sake, why?"

Brenda shrugged. "I don't know. I just have."

"Don't get any ideas. This is strictly business."

"Yeah, I know." She smiled nervously. "Listen, I'm more surprised than you are. I'm not terrific in the boy-girl department."

The waiter placed their drinks down before them. Dubin picked his up and held it before his eyes. "Here's to your work, and a fantastic opening."

Brenda smiled and took a cautious sip. "Hey, not bad." She took a healthy slug. "Nice."

"Easy," Dubin cautioned. "This isn't Coca-Cola."

"Sorry." Brenda put her drink down. "Listen, Dubin, what do people call you? I keep thinking of you as Freddie. Do you mind?"

"Whatever you like," he said. "Let's talk about the opening. I've suggested to Farrel that it be formal, in terms of dress. No jeans, coveralls, things like that. I want the crowd to look elegant."

"Why do you want that?" Brenda said. "My friends don't own evening clothes!"

"Then let them rent." He held up a hand to still Brenda's protest. "Listen to me now. I know precisely what I'm doing. It's contrast, don't you see? Your work spotlighted—rough-hewn, hard-edged metal, unfinished really but full of a terrible energy and vitality. And all around, elegant ladies and gents, the avant-garde, perhaps a few recognizable jet-setters, if we're lucky. And then you, the artist, in your usual costume. And not the way you are today. I want you wearing the filthy shirt and those dirty coveralls I saw you wearing last time. And your hair must be wild—not tied back so neatly."

Brenda finished her drink. "You're out of your gourd."

"Like a fox, my dear. Trust me. I know what I'm creating."

"A Frankenstein," Brenda said. "A freak. Is that it?"

"A freak? No, not at all. The picture I see is of a dedicated artist—young, daring, putting all of herself into her work, caring nothing for society's normal code of behavior. In other words, the real Brenda Fogelman."

Brenda stared at the director in the handsome suede jacket, noting the wicked slash of his mustache, the thrust of his chin. And that strange feeling she had inside, that knot of tension, tightened. "Holy mackerel," she said. "You're some hunk, you know that?"

Dubin laughed. "I don't think you'd better drink any more of that," he said.

SADIE WALKED PAST the little Budapest Restaurant and looked at the address Bryna had given her. Maria Pernik, Bryna's grandmother, lived only a few doors away, over a delicatessen.

Ten minutes after Sadie knocked on the door, she and Mrs. Pernik were old friends. Mrs. Pernik had seen Sadie many times on television, and while the tea was steeping she wanted to know everything about the world of celebrities. "Merv Griffing I like," she said. "Is he okay?"

"A sweetheart."

"And Dr. Joyce Brothers?"

"A nice person," Sadie said, "and a terrific knitter, besides."

Maria served the tea and sat down next to Sadie. On the table was a plate of raisin-and-nut twists. "Eat something," Maria insisted. "Have a *ruggle*—I baked them only yesterday."

Sadie took one. "Mmm," she said, chewing. "This is special. Now I see where Bryna gets her cooking talent. From you, Maria."

"Of course, from me."

"She's always talking about what a wonderful baker you are."

Maria Pernik took a sip of her tea. "Now I know why Bryna send you here," she said. "It's about fighting with me . . . and fruitcake, yes?" A cloud passed over the old grandmother's face.

"Tell me, Maria," Sadie said, "why don't you give the recipe for that fruitcake to Bryna?"

Maria drew breath sharply. "This is not your business." The tall woman with a coif of silvery braided hair arose from the table and walked to the window. She stared out, then turned to Sadie. "Very personal, this thing," she said.

"Important things always are, Maria."

"Very difficult to speak about . . ."

"Tell me, then," Sadie said gently. "You know you always feel better when you tell someone a secret."

Maria nodded, then spoke quietly. "Why I do not give Bryna the recipe is this—there is no recipe to give her."

"No recipe?" Sadie asked.

"Back in Hungary, many years ago, my mother teach me to make that fruitcake. And, Sadie, that is the way I make it still, by memory. With only my eyes and my hands and my memory."

"A memory cake!" Sadie exclaimed. "I see now, Maria. There really is no written-down recipe to give to Bryna, is there?"

"No recipe," said Maria Pernik. "Only in my head."

Sadie thought for a moment. "Then tell me, why in all these years couldn't you make the cake and write down the recipe for Bryna? You know, measure the flour and make a note, put in the eggs and make a note. You could do that, Maria."

"Could not," said Mrs. Pernik. She lowered her eyes. "I cannot write," she said in a whisper, tears brimming behind her lashes.

Dear God, Sadie thought, I should have guessed. Quickly she rose and went to Maria, enfolding her in a gentle hug. In Sadie's arms, Maria let down her defenses and cried.

It took some time to calm her, but soon she was at the table again sipping her tea. "Cannot write, cannot read," she said. "Not Hungarian, and not English. This is my secret, Sadie, for many years. I keep it from everyone, and always I am so ashamed. What Bryna think of me if she know, eh? Stupid old woman, Maria Pernik, cannot write one word."

'Let's not talk stupid," Sadie said. "Listen, it's no crime not to be able to read and write English. If it was, they would have locked up my own mother."

"So ashamed I cannot give Bryna this recipe. What can I do?"

"You're going to make the fruitcake, Maria, and I'm going to do the writing down." Before Maria could say a word, Sadie had everything organized. They went down to the street to shop for all the necessary ingredients to make the cake. Sadie also purchased a set of measuring cups and spoons. After unloading the packages onto Maria's kitchen table, Sadie said, "Okeydokey, you be the baker, and I'll be your secretary." She found a pad and pencil in her knitting bag. "I'm calling it Maria Pernik's Hungarian Fruitcake. Now what's first?"

"Measure the flour." Maria went to the cabinet above the sink and took down an old blue china bowl. She showed it to Sadie. "This chip, you see? Right here? I fill with flour up to this chip." And with that, she reached for the sack of cake flour.

"Wait!" Sadie cried. "First we have to measure."

Maria looked sheepishly at Sadie. "Of course." She took the measuring cup and carefully leveled each cup of flour with the edge of a knife before dumping it into the old blue bowl.

"Scant four cups of cake flour," Sadie wrote on her pad when the flour was measured. "What's next?"

"Chop up cherries, raisins, and currants."

"And how do you measure those, Maria?"

"By handfuls."

"Fine," said Sadie, "but before you add them to the mixing bowl, let's put them into a measuring cup."

With Sadie and Maria working as a team, the handfuls and then the pinches of baking powder, salt, baking soda, and cinnamon were brought into measurable proportions and Sadie added them to the recipe. The liquid ingredients went smoothly, too, and in half an hour the two women had worked their way through the butter, sugar, egg yolks, cider, rum, tart jelly, molasses, and a secret ingredient—a full cup of yogurt.

"Next?" Sadie asked.

"Nuts. I make a mound high as my hand on table, then chop."

"Make me a mound and then I'll measure."

The rest was simple for Maria's practiced hands to do and for Sadie's to record. Sadie made sure of the baking pan's size and noted the oven temperature. "Baking very slow for good fruitcake," Maria said. "Must not be dry. Three hours about. Time I can read."

Sadie made a last note, then gave the recipe to Maria. "Now you got a cake in the oven and a recipe in your hand for Bryna."

The warmth reflected on Maria's face almost matched that of the oven. "Sweet Sadie," she said. "You are most wonderful in America. How I ever thank you enough?"

"That's easy," Sadie said. "By making up with Bryna again."

"Yes. I do that. And give her recipe, of course." Maria embraced Sadie and walked her to the door. The silver-haired grandmother had one more request. "My secret—you know? Please, you do not tell Bryna I cannot write so she think I am stupid."

"Not in a million years," Sadie said. She smiled. "And besides, who says you have to tell a granddaughter *everything*?"

"I ONLY HAVE FIVE MINUTES." Fred Dubin was grumbling as he slowly climbed the stairs behind Brenda. "Just time for a quick look at your new sculpture and then I'm off."

"Right," Brenda called back as she scampered up the last flight. On the landing she turned and shot a smile back at Dubin. "Come on, slowpoke." She opened the door and waited for him.

The loft looked very different. Dubin saw that the girl had made an effort to clean up the place. The floor was clear of litter; the large, grimy windows had been cleaned. Where Brenda's uncovered mattress used to be, there was a bright blue air mattress with a neatly rolled sleeping bag at its foot. New, too, were the small white table and matching directors' chairs arranged in a conversational grouping. The place looked livable, Dubin thought; not *House & Garden*, but suitable perhaps for a monk or an artist.

"What do you think?" Brenda asked.

"Not bad." Dubin nodded. "A start, anyway."

Brenda took Dubin's hand and led him to the table and chairs. "I wanted you to be the first to sit in my chairs. And this one is just for you." She turned one around and showed it to him. On the backrest the name Freddie had been stenciled in bright blue. "Sit down," she said, grinning.

Dubin hesitated, looking at the young artist. This is silly, he started to say and then stopped himself. Brenda looked so open, so expectant of something he could not give her. As hardened to life and to women as he was, he did not want to hurt this girl. She was so incredibly naïve and vulnerable. He sat down in the chair and smiled at her. "It was very sweet of you to do this."

"Sweet, hell. I'm nuts about you, Freddie. What do I have to do, draw you a picture?"

"Brenda . . . stop. We're friends, which is more than we were a few weeks ago. Let's be careful, please, not to go beyond that."

"Are you seeing someone? Is that it?"

"That's none—" Dubin caught himself. "Yes," he lied. "I am. For a long time now. I'm sorry."

Brenda nodded, her lips set. "Okay, so I've got competition. I'll handle it. Some old broad, huh?"

"Ancient. Practically a relic."

"I figured," Brenda said. "I'm going to be twenty-six in a couple of months. How old are you?"

"Thirty-nine," Dubin said, adding two years to his age.

"So when you're fifty, I'll be thirty-seven. That's not too old."

Dubin laughed at the intently serious expression on her face. "You're incredible. Is there anything I can say to turn you off?"

"I doubt it. I'm on your trail, Freddie, and I don't like to lose." She began moving toward him. Dubin stood up and, before he could fend her off, found himself encircled by her arms. He let her hug him, feeling the strength in her. "Aren't you even going to kiss me?" she asked.

With what might have been fatherly feeling, Dubin took Brenda's face in his hands, leaned down, and kissed her on the forehead. Then he gently pried himself out of her grasp. "Easy now," he said. "I do have to get moving." Calmly he walked to the door.

"Freddie," Brenda called, "that's not what I call a kiss."

"I'll call you." He looked puzzled. "Baby Bidey Dolls?"

"Bitsey Baby Dolls."

"Right." He stared at her for a moment. "Be good now and finish that piece for your show."

Brenda walked into the hall and listened to his tread on the stairs, then returned to her studio. A strikeout, she thought, a big fat zero. I'm about as sexy as a tree. Taking up her hammer, she approached her massive sculpture and whacked it five, six times in succession. "Darn it!" she cried, and there were tears in her eyes. Twenty-five years she'd spent keeping men at arm's length. Now there was a man she wanted, and she didn't know how to get him.

Kong! The sound reverberated through the studio as she struck the hollow metal. *Kong!* She'd thrown herself at Freddie, and he'd thrown her back like a fish too small to keep. There had to be other ways to make him want her, approaches beyond merely flinging herself into his arms. But who knew about such things? Who had the wisdom and experience to tell her what to do? Who?

Kong!

"So that was the secret of the Hungarian fruitcake," Sam was saying. "Now I understand why Mrs. Pernik was so upset."

Sadie was sitting in the yellow club chair, her slippered feet on an ottoman. It had been a long day. When the doorbell rang, Sam went to answer it.

Harry Wald stood in the hallway, looking grim and worried. "Can I come in?" he asked. Sam led the fruit man to the living room. He noticed that Wald looked somewhat neater than the last time he had seen him. The awful ripped jacket was gone, replaced by a new one in olive drab. Sam could tell it was new because the manufacturer's ticket was still stapled to the side pocket.

"I'm sorry to come crashing in on you," Wald said. "I've got to talk to you, Sadie."

"Of course. Sit down."

Wald handed the jacket to Sam, who quickly worked the stapled ticket free. "Your husband smartened me up," Wald said to Sadie. "You see, Sam, I got all new clothes. New jacket, sweat shirt, blue jeans, and new work boots."

"I see," Sam said. "We'll talk about that later. I'm sure you didn't come here for sartorial advice."

"No," Wald said. "I'm here because I'm going out of my mind. Sadie, you've got to help me. I can't eat, I can't sleep, thinking about her. All day long it's like there's a bell ringing in my mind,

476

'Man-del-*baum*, Man-del-*baum!*' You've got to make Doris give me one more chance!" In his passion, Wald's voice rose an octave, and there was a wild look in his eyes.

"Take it easy," Sadie cautioned. "You get all excited like that, your heart can decide to go take a walk and then where will you be? I'll make us all a nice cup of tea."

Wald sat silently on the couch, staring across the room, as Sadie busied herself in the kitchen. He looked so forlorn and lost that Sam felt sympathy for him. Not so long ago he had been in the same situation. For two years he had seen Sadie every day, coming to know and love her. And he had realized he would do anything to have her close to him. Of such feelings are marriages made. But poor Harry Wald had not even gone through a courtship with the icy Doris Mandelbaum. And yet the strong grip of love and need held him in its grasp.

Tea made, they seated themselves around the kitchen table and Sadie poured. A few moments later, Wald was pouring out his heart. "Honest and true now, Sadie, you got me figured for a nogoodnik as far as Doris is concerned. Isn't that so?"

Sadie measured her words. "Not completely true, no. You're a nice, sweet man. I, personally, like you. So does Sam. The problem is Doris would kill me if I sent you to see her again, that's all."

"And with me, it's Doris or nobody!"

Sadie sighed. "I understand," she said, "but Doris is being a real stubborn Susie."

"Speak to her again," Wald said. "Please."

"I did." Sadie remembered the conversation with a shudder.

Wald took a sip of his tea without tasting it, and there was a short silence before Sadie spoke again. "You know, the mystery is how Sarah Barish ever sent you to Doris in the first place. I mean, from what she wrote on your card, Doris would not be right for you."

"That card was written a long time ago," he said. "I've changed a lot since then."

Sadie got up and fetched the matchmaker's old tea tin from the top of the refrigerator. She took out Harry Wald's card and read it aloud. "It says you want a warm, quiet woman and she should be a good cook. A homebody, you asked for." Sadie smiled at the fruit man. "Does that sound like Doris Mandelbaum?"

Harry Wald sighed. "You know what that card is," he began. "A description of my Emily. That's the way she was. Quiet, a woman

477

happy to cook and clean and keep a nice home. And when I went to the matchmaker that's what I told her I was looking for—another Emily. But time passes, you learn a little. There can never be another Emily. I understand that now." Wald's voice tightened, and to Sadie it was clear he was on the verge of tears.

"Tell you what," she said brightly. "We'll start again." Before Wald could reply, she had left the room. She brought back a pen and a blank index card. "Okay," she announced, forcing gaiety into her voice. "Ipsy-pipsy and okeydokey, we'll make a brand-new card, and with luck you'll find a brand-new wife." She sat down at the table and uncapped her pen. "Give me your whole name."

"Herschel Benjamin Wald. But everyone calls me Harry."

Sadie wrote Wald's whole name on the card. "Age?"

"Fifty-eight. And my address and phone number are the same."

Sadie wrote the information in her small, neat hand. "Okay, now the hard part—all about you." She gazed at him critically. "I'd say you were a very pleasant-looking man."

"Pleasant? Who wants to be described as pleasant? Couldn't you stretch it a little to good-looking?"

Sam laughed. "I think he's *adorable*, myself."

Sadie grinned at Wald. "Okay, *attractive*." She wrote the word on Wald's new card. "What else should I put down for you?"

"How about *rich?*" Sam said.

Wald winced. "No, no, not rich," he protested. "I hate that word. I mean, if you're rich, you don't go around advertising it. I would say I'm . . . comfortable."

"Forty-eight fruit stores plus groves in Florida, California, and Arizona is more than comfortable," Sam insisted.

"I'm impressed," Sadie said. "Rich or poor, at least you've got money. But why didn't you tell the matchmaker all this?"

Wald shrugged. "Does Macy's tell Gimbels?"

"I'm putting down 'wealthy,' Mr. Wald, and I won't go around advertising it. Okay, now tell me more about yourself."

"College graduate," Wald said. "Member of the chamber of commerce in five states, Kiwanis. I'm a sponsor of the Brooklyn Academy of Music, the Brooklyn Museum . . ."

"An intellectual!" Sadie said warmly. "That's very good!"

Wald shrugged. "Well, Brooklyn's my hometown. What else? I belong to two book clubs . . ."

"A reader, terrific."

"Subscriber to *Time, The Wall Street Journal*, and the *Wholesale Fruiterer*. I like plays, music, and I'm crazy about sports."

"Unfortunately, Doris Mandelbaum hates sports," Sadie said. "How about opera? Doris loves opera."

"Then I love opera," Wald said.

Sadie turned the card over to write on the back. Herschel Benjamin Wald was growing in her estimation, minute by minute. An old suit, an old car, and Doris had pegged Harry as a schnook. As Sadie herself had, too. Harry Wald had been hiding his light under a basket, an old fruit basket at that.

"Next, Mr. Wald," Sadie said, "I got to ask you the sixty-four-dollar question. The kind of woman you're looking for."

Wald grinned. "Put down Doris Mandelbaum."

"This I know already," Sadie said. "But, you know, a piano has eighty-eight keys, you can't keep playing on one all the time. It's possible I can find another nice woman for you."

"Not interested," Wald said. "Doris or nothing."

Sadie looked over at Sam, who shrugged at her. The man was smitten and would not be budged.

"All right, I'll try," Sadie said at last. "She'll throw me out, lock, smock, and blankets, but I'll go to see her."

Wald reached across the table and patted Sadie's hand. "Thank you," he said. "Thank you very much."

The telephone rang and Sadie glanced at the kitchen clock. It was late for a telephone call. She got up and went to the wall phone near the window. Sam walked Harry Wald into the living room. "Listen to me," he told the fruit merchant. "I'm going to talk to you like a Dutch uncle. You're a well-off guy, Harry, but you throw money around like glue. If you're going to stand a chance with Doris, you've got to smarten up. Open up your wallet, kiddo, and let those moths fly out. You hear what I'm saying?"

Wald nodded, not looking very happy. "Years of habit, Sam. You're right. I guess I'll have to learn how to spend money."

"Exactly. Not throw it around, but spend it wisely. What are you doing tomorrow?"

"Working?"

"Wrong. I'm taking you shopping. You got credit cards? Good, bring 'em along. And your checkbook. And don't look so upset; you'll be another Valentino when I'm through with you." He shook Wald's hand, escorted him to the door, and closed it behind him.

Then he walked back to the kitchen. Sadie was looking dazed, her telephone call concluded. "You'll never believe who called," she said. "Brenda Fogelman."

"I don't believe it. What did she say?"

" '*Help!*' "

Chapter 6

The sun came peeping over the RCA Building, took one look at the sleeping city, and ducked behind a large gray cloud. In Central Park a small host of joggers was already circling the lake when Sadie entered the park. A group of runners waved to her, and one smiling youth called to her by name. Sadie waved and watched them disappear, wondering at the stamina and strength it took to move so fast. She started jogging across the grassy meadow, feeling the dampness of the dew under her tread. Let the young ones run a mile a minute; she had her own way. Slow and easy she jogged, one choppy step after another, her breath shortening as the exertion built, and the clarity coming into her head.

People were in her head this morning, and the twisted relationships they created for themselves. Love, love, love . . . Over on Park Avenue, Doris Mandelbaum was sleeping, probably still reaching out in dreams to touch the Jacob who was no longer there. How could she show Doris that love is never twice the same, and the only place she would find her Jacob again was in heaven? How was she going to make Doris date Harry? Well, she would go see her and lay her cards on the table. Maybe only one card, Harry Wald's. And what would happen? Doris would throw her out.

Out of breath now, Sadie walked, ignoring the little stitch in her side. Brenda Fogelman and Fred Dubin—talk about an odd couple. They were like oil and vinegar, those two. How could the wild woman of Lower Broadway capture as stylish a gentleman as Fred Dubin? Could she help her? Or should she try to talk her out of it? Maybe find someone more suitable for Brenda?

Suitable for Brenda . . . Sadie smiled, thinking of an ad in the newspapers. "Wanted, young man to marry a young girl who wears dirty clothes, hammers metal all day long, sleeps on the floor, and swears like a longshoreman." Ay-yi-yi, Sarah Barish, you passed along a few beauties to me.

Feeling her breath come back Sadie began to jog again. The sun came out from behind a cloud and sparkled on the wet grass. There was always hope, of course, as long as you could put one foot in front of the other. Love was a mystery, coming and going like the sun. But hope was cheap; even poor people could afford it, and it was something to hang on to till love came along again.

Brenda and Dubin, Harry and Doris, Maxine and Michael. Love to everybody, she thought, to come quick and strong and last forever. She could not wish for better than that. Feeling light and buoyant, she rounded the pathway and jogged for home.

Upstairs, in front of her apartment door, stretched out on the carpeted floor and fast asleep, lay Brenda Fogelman. Sadie knelt down and nudged the young artist's shoulder. Brenda's eyes opened wide. "Hello," she said, sitting up.

"Hello to you. Do you always sleep in hallways, or what?"

Brenda got to her feet. "You said to see you in the morning."

Sadie nodded, eyeing her critically as she fished in her pocket for the door key. Stained coveralls, washed-out flannel shirt, work boots—the height of fashion if you were a day laborer. No make-up, eyebrows as thick as John L. Lewis' and with a temper to match. A Brenda Fogelman and a half, as usual. "I'll make breakfast, but we'll have to be quiet. My Sam is still asleep."

She spirited Brenda into the kitchen and let her watch the water come to the boil while she slipped through the bedroom and into the shower. Dressed in her favorite housecoat and mules, she returned to the kitchen. Brenda was sitting at the table, eating from a plastic container. "This is terrific," Brenda said. "What is it?"

"Last night's lamb stew."

"I love it."

"I'm very glad," Sadie said. "You could put it on a plate."

"Nah," Brenda said, "it's okay."

"I'm glad you at least learned how to use a fork," Sadie said. She brought cottage cheese from the refrigerator and saltines from the cupboard. Then she spooned a dab of cottage cheese onto a saltine and chewed it slowly, watching Brenda eat. Lamb stew for breakfast, sleeping on the floor, fingernails that had never seen a file, let alone a coat of polish. and this wild child had set her cap for the stylish Fred Dubin. What could she possibly do for this misguided, mistaken, and completely *meshuggeneh* creature?

"All right." Sadie sighed. "Tell me about you and Fred Dubin."

481

"I'm loony about him," Brenda said.

"That's the easy part. Is he in love with you?"

"It's strictly business with Dubin. He likes my work, and I think, in some way, he likes me. Yesterday he kissed me. Like a father, Sadie. On the forehead." Brenda's dark eyes were sad.

"It's a start," Sadie said. "You'd be surprised sometimes how love can start. I had a friend once, hit this man with her pocketbook right in the subway because she thought he was getting fresh, and one thing led to another, and from that smack she gave him they were married and had three lovely children. You never can tell."

"I don't have patience, Sadie," Brenda said. "I can't wait and I don't know how to play those flirting games. I've been throwing myself at Dubin and he isn't interested."

"Your first mistake, Brenda. You don't throw yourself until you're sure there's someone there who wants to catch you."

"I can't help myself," the young artist protested. "I see him and it's like a light switches on inside me. I want to grab him and kiss him. . . . I want to rip his clothes off and—"

"Hold it!" Sadie said. "And don't talk ripping and stripping. If that's all you're interested in, you've come to the wrong lady. I'm not going to help you do *that*, and good-by, Brenda Fogelman." Sadie crossed her arms over her chest and looked away.

There was a long silence. "I'm sorry," Brenda said at last.

"You should be," Sadie said. "A matchmaker makes matches, and the people usually get married. If you just want to fool around, do that on your own time."

Brenda nodded. "I want to be with him. And I need your help."

"Right," Sadie said, feeling better. "So stand up and turn around; I want to take a look." Brenda walked to the refrigerator and back again. Sadie got up from the table and took a small tour around Brenda Fogelman, squinting slightly as she imagined the girl with makeup, a haircut, and nice clothes. "A definite beauty," she said, pinching Brenda's cheek, "if you fix yourself up a little. Are you willing to make a few changes?"

"What kind of changes?" Brenda asked cautiously.

"Improvements only, a touch here, a smidgen there . . ." Sadie took Brenda's hand in a friendly squeeze, her mind already working on the transformation. "When do you see Fred Dubin again?"

Brenda shrugged. "In a couple of weeks. When my show opens."

"Your opening, of course!" Sadie said. "This I know about already, from Maxine Morris. Sam and I are invited, so we'll be there. And Mr. Dubin is making a television show out of it, right?" Sadie's eyes grew brighter. "That's wonderful! A very exciting evening, you'll be together, who knows what can happen? And you'll be all dressed up for once, and—"

"I'll be dressed like this," Brenda said to Sadie's uncomprehending look. "It's Freddie's idea."

"Like this?" Sadie's mouth flew open. "He wants you to look like . . . like a *himpie* . . . when everyone else is going to be dressed up beautiful? For heaven's sake, why?"

Brenda shrugged. "He has a plan in mind, Sadie . . . to make me stand out from the crowd."

"You'll stand out all right, like Limburger cheese in a crowded bus."

"He wants the whole focus to be on my work, not me."

Sadie shook her head from side to side. "One thing I'm beginning to see, Brenda," she said. "Maybe you and Mr. Dubin belong together . . . *because he can be as crazy as you are.*"

THEY CAME UP Madison Avenue, Sam striding briskly in the sunshine and Harry Wald schlepping two paces behind. The shopping tour was in full swing and the fruit man was cranky. "How many more stores are we going to?" he asked as they paused for a traffic light at Forty-eighth Street. "My feet are killing me, Sam."

"Only six or seven more. The next one's a shoe store; they'll take care of your feet."

"Shoes I got," Wald complained. "Plenty of shoes. These I'm wearing, plus a pair of black wing tips and some brown loafers."

Sam shook his head. "The ones you're wearing, we let the salesman throw them away. On the next corner is an English shoe store. They make a half boot that can't be beat. Brown and black we'll buy you, then later we'll walk over to Bally and get serious."

Wald blanched. "How many pairs of shoes do I need?"

"Enough," Sam said. The shopping trip was going well, he reflected, but he had to keep pushing Harry all the way. For a rich man, he hated to part with a buck, which was maybe how he got rich. At Brooks Brothers he had been fitted for three conservative suits. Then they had shopped for sport clothes, plus shirts, ties, and two sweaters Sam insisted Wald buy. "And a blue blazer and gray slacks is like a uniform," he'd advised. "You got to have it."

Sam and Harry came out of the shoe store. "Such prices," Harry said, wagging his head.

"Good doesn't come cheap. How do they feel?"

"Soft as butter. It's funny, I didn't think they'd feel so good. Where to next?" The shiny brown half boots felt so light on his feet he skipped for a couple of steps. Looking at his reflection in a store window, he smiled at himself.

"To Saks Fifth Avenue for a raincoat and a topcoat."

For the first time that morning, Harry Wald did not complain.

SEVERAL BLOCKS EAST, Maxine Morris and Michael Newman were finishing lunch at Le Perigord. Michael's thoughts were as black as the espresso before him. "This is silly," he said, stirring his coffee. "We're arguing over trivialities."

Maxine lit a cigarette. The feeling she'd had for several weeks now was being confirmed. It wasn't going to work out between them, as she'd known from the first.

"Your apartment is just too inconvenient, Max. That's all." Michael sighed. "I love you and I want to marry you. But you won't give an inch."

"Why does it have to be your apartment?" Maxine asked.

"Because it'll be easier for *you* to move," Michael said. "And my apartment is larger, anyway."

"Yours is out of the question. I hate the East Side; it's so . . . chichi. Real people don't live on the East Side."

"What am I, a ghost? Come on, babe, don't be so obstinate."

Maxine stirred sugar into her coffee. "I'm not being obstinate. My apartment is very convenient for me. I can walk to my office in six minutes, and the studio is practically around the corner. I don't want to be across the park, where I'll have to depend on cabs every day, or some bus that never comes."

"How about all the things I mentioned?" Michael said evenly. He began ticking them off on his fingers. "The hospital is a block away, my office is around the corner. The telephones—I have a tie line to the hospital and one to my office, two phones hooked into my answering service, and an unlisted one for emergencies. You know what kind of mess it would be to change all those numbers?"

"My place is closer to your horse. How about that?"

Michael nodded. "True, but I've gotten used to jogging across the park before taking Silver out. In fact, I like it."

484

"A creature of habit, aren't you?" Maxine said. She knew the problems. Marry a doctor and do everything his way. Even this doctor, the one who could take her in his arms and make time stop.

She finished her coffee. "I have a meeting in half an hour. On the *West Side*," she added pointedly. "I have to go."

"Wait a minute. We should finish this. It's important."

"So is my meeting." Maxine put her cigarettes into her handbag and snapped it closed. Michael's face was a picture of misery, so much so that she had to reach out and clasp his hand.

"I told you it wasn't going to work out," she said. "I think we both like our comfort too much. Or something . . ." She felt a heaviness in her throat. She stood up and turned away.

"Max!" Michael called, stopping her. "What about tonight?"

"Eight o'clock," she said, "and bring some wine. . . ." Fighting back tears, she fled.

THEY CAME WALKING down Fifth Avenue, Harry Wald carrying the packages from Sulka under his arm.

"I love these silk ties, Sam," he said happily. "And it was a good idea, making those notes for me so I'll know which tie to wear with which suit."

"My pleasure. I think you went a little overboard with the silk underwear, though. I'm a Fruit of the Loom man, myself."

Wald was still chuckling as they reached the garage where he had left his car that morning. "I appreciate what you've done for me, Sam. It's really fun to spend money."

"Especially when you've got it."

Harry handed in his parking ticket and the two men waited. Far off, a squeal of tires sounded. "So what can I do for you, Sam? Please, let me do something."

"Wear your new clothes in good health," Sam said, "and make some woman happy. Doris, if you're lucky, or somebody else." A green Buick came up the ramp and screeched to a stop. There was a dent in the fender, the left rear hubcap was missing, and the car was scratched and badly needed a coat of wax. Wald walked to the car, and Sam got into the passenger seat. Two pieces of tissue paper that had once wrapped persimmons were under his foot. "This is the car you took Doris out in?" he asked as Wald pulled into the street.

Wald nodded. "Almost three years and sixty thousand miles on it. I give it a lot of use." He glanced at Sam. "Looks like hell, right?"

"Not terrific. Especially when you're trying to make a good impression."

Wald looked thoughtful. "There's a showroom over on First Avenue," he said. "Would you mind helping me shop for a car?"

"I DON'T WANT to talk about it, Sadie," Maxine was saying, "and I think it was very unfair of Michael to have called you."

"Why shouldn't he call me?" Sadie asked. "I'm an official matchmaker these days, don't forget."

Maxine shifted the papers on her desk. "Can we get down to work now? We do have three more programs to shoot."

"Shoot, shmoot," Sadie scoffed. "Love and happiness is more important. It sounds to me like you and Michael are both being very stubborn, and neither of you wants to give an inch. You both thought you could eat your bagel and have it, too. But now you found out the truth—when you eat the bagel, only the hole is left."

"You're impossible!" Maxine exclaimed. "Look, it just won't work with Michael and me because he's so stubborn."

"You don't love him?" Sadie asked quietly.

Maxine sighed. "That's not the point. I'm getting a preview of what our life together would be. We'd disagree all the time—"

"He doesn't love you?" Sadie interrupted.

Maxine threw up her hands. "You have a one-track mind, Sadie. Nothing but love, love, love."

"You know something more important?"

Maxine did not reply at once, but busied herself with her papers. How easy it was for Sadie to give advice, she thought. And how difficult it had been for herself to make the long journey through a man's world to this responsible job. Marry Michael, indeed. The man would not bend, would not see things her way, no matter how great his love for her.

"The subject is closed," Maxine said. And it was.

THE DAY WAS SUNNY but her feelings were dark. Sadie walked along Central Park South, on her way to see Doris Mandelbaum. She passed the great hotels that line the handsome, wide avenue, seeing couples meeting, dashing to lunch, to hold hands and glory in the sight of each other. Once again she thanked God for sending her a Sam after so many years of widowhood.

Sadie crossed Madison Avenue and walked toward Park. Doris

had promised lunch and a good long chat. But if I mention Harry Wald, Sadie thought, I'll be thrown out on my ear, even with Mrs. Mandelbaum's Park Avenue manners. In her handbag she carried the new card she had made for Herschel Benjamin Wald. Can a leopard change his spots, like a woman can change her mind? She felt a surge of pity for Harry. What good is love if you love alone?

A doorman in a bright green uniform opened the door, then called upstairs on the intercom. Sadie crossed a splendid lobby and rode up in an elevator shiny with brass and polished wood. On the twelfth floor, she walked down a carpeted hallway, and there was Doris Mandelbaum, looking out from a doorway.

"Sadie! Come in." She wore a pale tweed skirt and an ivory silk blouse. On her head, a silk scarf tied back. On her face, a smile as bright as the sunshine outside.

"Look at you!" Sadie exclaimed. "You've lost ten years somewhere since I last saw you." Smiling and pleased, Doris showed Sadie into a wide living room that opened onto a terrace. Sadie looked around, struck by the elegance of the room. The floors were richly carpeted, the furniture highly polished. A baby grand piano stood gleaming in a corner, topped with photographs in silver frames. Bookshelves ran floor to ceiling. "Beautiful!" Sadie said, a hand to her cheek in awe. "What a place. You must be some reader, so many books!"

Doris shrugged. "What else do I have to do?"

"Can I see the rest of your place?"

"Come." Doris led her into a bedroom dominated by a wide bed with an antique Chinese-looking headboard. Sadie stopped in front of a framed photograph standing on Doris' dresser. A man's face, very young and smiling. A strong face, not handsome but close to it, with square chin and curly hair.

"My Jacob," Doris said quietly. Sadie nodded. This face, this photograph on the dresser, was what Doris saw each morning when she opened her eyes. As if being alone all night wasn't enough to remind her that he was gone.

"We'll have lunch on the terrace, if that's all right."

"Fine and dandy," Sadie said.

The terrace sparkled in bright sunshine. In redwood window boxes young marigolds were coming into bloom. A glass-topped table had been laid with linen napkins, china, and silverware. "I made us a Niçoise salad, and I have fresh brioche," Doris said.

"Fresh what?"

488

"It's a kind of French roll. Sit down, Sadie, please. And relax. You look nervous."

"Who nervous, what nervous?" Sadie put a smile on her face and sat down. It wasn't nervousness she felt, but dread. Where did that fruit man, even though rich, fit in here? A chicken can look at a farmer, but he doesn't move into the house.

Sadie accepted her plate, poked through the salad, then put down her fork. Food was impossible. She had come here to plead Harry Wald's case, and she had better get on with it. "Got to talk to you about something," she began, "a someone who wants to get to know you better. A sweet, lovely man I got to know better lately and who I like a lot. Doris, he's crazy about you."

"Do I know him?" Doris asked.

"Of course you know him, but not very well. Not well at all, Doris, and that's the thing about it—"

"Wait a minute." Doris put down her fork. "Not Harry Wald?"

"Why not, for heaven's sake? You know somebody else in this world so in love with you?"

"The subject is closed!"

"The subject is love!" Sadie declared. "Which is something you need and only one man I know is ready to give you right away. Harry Wald. What have you got against the man? Is he a Bloombeard or something, a murderer? Give the man another chance."

Doris shook her head. "Not interested," she said.

"Then who would interest you? That's what I can't figure out, Doris. How many men have you met? Plenty, I'll bet. And so far, nothing. Right?"

"You can see that, can't you?" Doris said in an angry way. "Look, Sadie, please don't get too personal with me."

"Hoo-hah!" Sadie said, an edge in her own voice. "*Personal.* What could be more personal, my dear Doris Mandelbaum, than finding a husband for you? I'm a matchmaker. It's not like I'm a baker sending up a dozen French rolls, which if they put more butter in, you could die of cholesterol poisoning, you should excuse me. Someone to live with is the most personal thing there is."

"I won't see Harry Wald again. So don't waste your time."

"Better you should waste *your* time, right, looking for a man who died years ago to come back again?"

Doris blanched, her hands clutched the edge of the table. "How dare you?" she whispered.

"I dare, I dare," Sadie said, rising from the table to walk a few steps along the terrace, "because I know about being a widow, believe me, I know. How your heart breaks every day, thinking about what you lost, how you think when it's six o'clock the door will open and he'll come walking in, how you wake in the night and reach for him. . . . Only he's not there, Doris, and will never be again. Not your Jacob and not, let him rest, my dear Reuben."

Doris' chair scraped on the brick floor as she pulled back from the table. But Sadie walked to her and put a hand on her shoulder. "It's time to stop running away," she said. "Life goes on, even though you don't want it to. I cried for my husband a long time, Doris, like you for yours, and I looked for him in other men. But God is not as smart as we are. He hasn't invented a Xerox machine to send you a copy of your Jacob. If you don't open up your heart to someone new, you'll live a long time alone. Like I did."

Doris sat in her chair, her head turned away. If she was crying, it was somewhere deep inside. "I was lucky," Sadie said. "I found someone. As different from my Reuben as day from night. Reuben was small and quiet and soft-spoken. And then I met my Sam, who was big and funny and made jokes and smoked smelly cigars which I hated. But somehow, Doris, that very different man became my love, my husband, the greatest thing in my life. I've asked myself so many times, How could it happen? And the only answer I can find is that when I was ready to let myself love him, I found I did."

With a napkin pressed to her lips, Doris Mandelbaum ran from the terrace into the apartment. Sadie sighed, feeling sorry for Doris and also Harry Wald. She had failed, but she had said some things to Doris that needed saying. All right, Sadie said to herself, now you find out how a Park Avenue lady throws you out of her house. Who would come to haul her away—the doorman, a porter?

Waiting, she sat down again. She put her head back and closed her eyes, feeling the warm sun on her face. Sometime later Doris stepped onto the terrace. She carried a tray. "I think we could both use a cup of tea," she said.

Sadie looked at her as she fussed with the tea things. If Doris had been crying, repairs had been made. Her hands were steady as she poured tea through a silver strainer. She handed a cup to Sadie. "Friends again?"

"Friends still," Sadie said.

"And no more Harry Wald. Promise?"

490

Sadie had to smile. "Promise." Good-by, Harry Wald, she said to herself. I tried for you and failed. She thought of the card in her purse for the new Herschel Benjamin Wald and the fun they'd had writing it. And the answer came to her.

"It's definitely time for you to meet a new man," she began, "and I got just the fella for you. His name is Ben Forest."

Over her teacup Doris nodded, listening.

"Ben Forest," Sadie repeated. "He's in a lot of businesses and he owns land—out west, I think, something to do with agriculture. He's a little older than you and a widower. Sweet as anything and very nice, besides. I think you'd click with him."

"Wealthy?" Doris asked.

"He's very rich, but doesn't like to admit it, which shows you how rich he really is. He rides around in a brand-new car, shops only in the finest stores. Ben Forest," Sadie said, repeating the name to make it more real for herself, "is a terrific man."

"Is he bright?"

"Very. Listen, the man is a college graduate, and *two book clubs* he belongs to. I mean, is that an intellectual or not?"

"Ben Forest," Doris said. "I'd like to meet him."

"But, Doris, he's not like your Jacob. Can you accept that?"

Doris met Sadie's gaze. "Yes . . . I can."

"Good." Sadie beamed. "Wonderful." She put a spoonful of sugar in her tea. "Now all I got to do is talk *him* into meeting you."

Chapter 7

"*Ben Forest?*" an incredulous Sam Beck was saying. "Who the heck is Ben Forest?" He put his razor down and turned to look at Sadie, his face covered with lather.

"Ben Forest is Harry Wald," Sadie said easily. She ran a comb through her gray hair, twisting her head to check that it was lying flat in the back. "Forest, Wald—same thing. You know, a Rosen by any other name would still be Jewish."

"It's crazy," Sam said. "It'll never work, Sadie. Doris will be expecting to see some new guy at her door, and it's going to be Harry Wald, who she hates."

"She doesn't hate him," Sadie corrected. "She just hasn't had time to see all his fine qualities yet. And besides, you yourself said you've made a new man out of Harry." She turned and walked into the bedroom.

Sam hastily washed his face and followed after his true love. "You've gone too far," he said. "Harry Wald is still Harry Wald."

"Sometimes a leopard can change his spots," Sadie said. She was transferring items from yesterday's handbag into today's. Keys, tissues, lipstick, pillbox . . . "What did I do? A little white lie, a piffle, a nothing. I stretched the truth a little, God forgive me. Was there any other way to give Harry another chance?"

Sam sat down in the bentwoôd rocking chair. "What chance? She's going to slam the door in his face the minute she sees him."

Sadie snapped today's handbag closed. "I'm not so sure," she said. "I got a feeling she'll take pity on him, and the rest is up to Harry." She started for the living room. "Luck," she said, "that's what Harry needs. A little luck, that can drop right into your lap something you couldn't reach even with a hundred stepladders."

BRENDA FOGELMAN saw Sadie step out of a cab and start down the street. She called out to her and Sadie stopped, taking a moment to recognize Brenda. In another moment Sadie was upset.

"Look at the way you're dressed! Wear your best, I said, and you said okay." She looked at Brenda in horror. "Paint on your jeans, army boots, and a man's shirt with a hole in one elbow!"

Brenda looked down. "They were the cleanest, so I wore them."

Shooting pains went through Sadie's head. "We're going into a fine and beautiful place, and you're walking around like Tobacco Road. You don't own a dress?" Brenda shook her head. "I should have known," Sadie said, half to herself. "All right, they'll have to take you the way you are. Come on."

Brenda glowered. "I hate this hassling," she barked, "and I hate myself for agreeing to the idea of going in to be made beautiful."

"Beautiful is what you are already," Sadie said. "What they're going to do is make sure everyone can see it. So come on. And act like a lady, even if you don't know how."

Brenda glared at Sadie from under her overhanging eyebrows. "This is going to be one stupid day, so let's get it over with." Petulantly she brushed past Sadie and opened the pink door.

Sadie followed her into the foyer of the beauty salon. A young woman receptionist behind an elegant counter looked Brenda over. "Deliveries through the side entrance, please," she said.

Hastily Sadie spoke up. "Mrs. Beck and Miss Fogelman. We're here for your famous day of beauty."

The receptionist looked from Brenda to Sadie, then back again. She consulted a staff member with an appointment schedule, found their names, and flutteringly apologized, then ushered them into a consulting room. "One of our beauty counselors will be with you shortly," she said.

Sadie sat and Brenda sprawled in the chairs. Down a short corridor the receptionist sought out a young man wearing a white suit, white shoes, and flaming red socks. She brought him toward the consulting room, stopping a short distance away. The young man looked into the room and blanched. "Oh, no!"

The receptionist grinned. "Miss Fogelman and Mrs. Beck."

"The Amazon and her grandmother." The young man groaned. "Where does one start?"

"Think of it as a challenge." The receptionist marched off.

The beauty counselor introduced himself as Mr. Caswell. "You will enjoy your day of beauty with us, we hope, being pampered and cosseted and shown the essentials of a beautiful life in a beautiful body, from hairstyle to hand care." He smiled benignly, trying to keep his eyes on Sadie and not Brenda. "I suggest we proceed from the bottom up. A pedicure, then leg treatment, steam room, massage, mudpack, body oils, manicure, moisturizing, upper arm and shoulder analysis, cellulite inspection, and fanny shaping."

"My goodness!" Sadie exclaimed, trying to get Brenda to show some interest. "That's a full day, all right."

"That's only the morning," Caswell said. "After lunch we'll talk again." He led them to dressing rooms, where they changed into shapeless white tent dresses.

In the pedicure room, a middle-aged specialist inspected Brenda's feet. "Poor dear," she clucked sadly. "You look as if you've been wearing army boots."

"I have," Brenda said through gritted teeth, but she submitted to the treatment. Sadie, on the other foot, enjoyed it thoroughly.

In the legs boutique, the woman who worked on legs could not believe Brenda's. "Haven't you ever shaved your legs?" she asked. Brenda growled a no.

"Twenty-five years' worth of hair you got there," Sadie said.

"We're supposed to have hair on our legs; it's natural," Brenda said. "Why can't we leave my leg hair alone?"

"Because men leave women with hairy legs alone," Sadie said.

Brenda was not convinced. "European women don't shave their legs. They think leg hair is sexy."

"Fred Dubin is an American human being person," Sadie said.

Having said the magic name, Sadie stared down Brenda's withering look. The young girl grumbled on, but lay back and submitted, although she did cover her eyes. Her legs were washed with warm water and dried with a fluffy towel. Next, the operator began applying wax. Brenda sat bolt upright, unbelieving. "I'm being simonized!" she wailed.

The day of beauty ticked on. Sadie and Brenda were steamed, mudpacked, bathed in precious oils, and pummeled by a Swedish masseuse. Every pore open to the world, they napped briefly before moving on to the manicurist. This kindly soul was appalled by Brenda's hands. "Only once have I seen hands as bad as yours," she said. "On a lady from Tulsa who worked an oil rig. What kind of soap are you using?"

"Ajax cleanser. It's the only thing that gets off the grime."

"I'm surprised you have any skin left." The manicurist worked half an hour on each of Brenda's hands, noting that her cuticles could be fully restored only through surgery.

Sometime later Brenda and Sadie lunched in a charming, airy room, picking at salads and drinking herbal tea. Brenda looked much improved already, and Sadie said so. The steam and mudpacks had brought a glow to the young face. "This isn't as bad as I thought it'd be," Brenda confessed. "I liked that hard massage."

"You would." Sadie grinned.

Now there was only an afternoon of beauty left. A chic woman wearing a shirtwaist dress starched to within an inch of its life led them into her private salon. "Call me Tamara," she said in a vaguely European accent. She sat Brenda in a barber chair and turned on a bank of lights and illuminated her face. Tamara studied her, not speaking, walking around to view her face from all angles. She picked up a sketchbook and began to draw. Three minutes later a very good approximation of Brenda appeared on her pad. "A sensitive face," she said to Brenda. "You are artist?"

"Sculptor."

"Ah, sensitive but with great strength, too, yes?"

"Like a truck driver," Sadie agreed.

Tamara showed Brenda her sketch. "Cheekbones very good, eyes outstanding, chin is firm, strong. These we highlight. Eyebrows now . . ." Tamara stared into Brenda's face.

"Wait a minute," Brenda said. "You don't touch my eyebrows."

Tamara smiled. "I agree. They are your strongest feature. Only a little shaping, yes?" She took her pad and, using an eraser, changed her sketch. "You see, now eyebrows have a curve, shape."

Brenda studied the picture. Tamara was an artist in her own right and, with a few strokes, had shown Brenda how to keynote her entire face. "I like it," Brenda said.

"Good." Tamara smiled. "Now for hair, I think we do this." She walked behind Brenda and seized the wild tangle that tumbled to the girl's shoulder blades. She folded it in her hand and held it at shoulder length. "Cut to this length, you see, and still you are *you*— not someone else."

"I don't want to be anyone else," Brenda said firmly.

Tamara nodded. "Just so. You are unusual-looking girl. Wild and free, with gypsy dark eyes and hair. And this haircut, you only have to brush for a few moments."

For the next thirty minutes Tamara washed and cut Brenda's hair, then dried it and brushed it out. "Little work, and it stays," the beauty consultant said. She pushed a lever and Brenda was suddenly horizontal in the chair. Using a succession of instruments, some of them electrical, Tamara worked on Brenda's eyebrows until they looked exactly like the sketch. She levered the chair upright so Brenda could see herself.

Standing behind her, Sadie gasped at the face in the mirror. It was Brenda all right, but a new Brenda—sophisticated, confident, with bold dark eyes that leaped out and held her own. "Look!" Brenda exclaimed. "I'm gorgeous!"

Tamara roared with laughter. "You are, yes. Now for finishing touches." She took her makeup kit and seated herself before the girl. She applied a pale blusher to her cheeks, then covered her lips with a pale pink lipstick. The transformation was complete. Eyes that commanded attention, molded high cheekbones now shown to advantage, that confident chin wedded to generous lips that looked sweet and vulnerable, all held together by clear, ivory skin and a soft fall of shining black hair.

"Only these three things," Tamara said, "and you will always be so beautiful. Wash and brush your hair, a touch of makeup on your cheeks, so, and always a pale lipstick. Lucky girl, to need so little."

Brenda nodded dumbly, then squeezed Tamara's hand in thanks. The rest of the day of beauty was an anticlimax. It seemed to Sadie that Brenda had become a different person, accepting her stunning appearance as a queen accepts her station in life. She walked differently, her voice sounded quieter and less strident, her whole demeanor became softer, more womanly. From time to time she looked at herself in the mirror, smiling shyly, clearly pleased. The girl could walk out of here and appear on a fashion magazine cover, Sadie thought.

They left the beauty salon, and Brenda stopped to admire herself in a store window. "Sadie, I still can't believe it. It's really me, though, isn't it? Me, Brenda Fogelman?"

"You're the same Brenda, only different. Like a Dr. Jekyll was hiding in you, a beautiful person inside a plain brown wrapper." Smiling, Sadie gave Brenda a playful pinch. "Fred Dubin," she announced, *"look out!"*

"OF COURSE, I BELIEVE YOU," Sam was saying. "If you told me you taught Brenda Fogelman to fly, I'd believe you." He opened his closet door and snapped on the light. Somewhere, he hoped, he'd find his tuxedo. "Helping Harry Wald was nothing compared to changing Brenda. I hope Dubin notices."

Sadie was sitting on the edge of the bed, her fingers flying as she knitted quickly with thin white wool from a huge shopping bag. "If it won't be Dubin, it'll be somebody else. Men will fight over her like she's the last herring left in the barrel, that's how gorgeous she is."

"Let's hope she doesn't hit them on the head with her hammer." Sam pushed aside a couple of tweed suits and found his tuxedo.

"Do you have a nice shirt, Sam? You'll be on television, you know. Fred Dubin said he'd show the crowd at the opening."

"I'll pick one up this week. And a couple of pairs of silk underwear. Harry Wald—excuse me—*Ben Forest* recommends them."

Sadie looked up from her knitting. "Cross your fingers for Harry. Tonight's the night he's seeing Doris."

At that very moment the front doorbell rang.

Bryna Pernik and her grandmother were standing in the doorway, and Bryna carried a fruitcake on a tray. "Wait till you taste this," Bryna told Sam. "This is the genuine article!" Then she called to Sadie, "You have to try Maria Pernik's Special Hungarian Fruitcake, and I have to thank you for all you did."

Sadie emerged from the bedroom. She hugged Maria and kissed Bryna lightly on the cheek. "You don't have to thank me. Just seeing you two together is enough."

A few minutes later, they were seated around the kitchen table. Bryna made a small ceremony of cutting the cake, and passed the first piece to Sadie. It was, as Bryna said it would be, the best of fruitcakes—light, moist, and delicious.

"Wonderful," Sadie said, "and worth waiting for."

"Let me confess something," Sam said. "I hate fruitcake, but I have to admit, if I was going to like it, I'd like this one."

Bryna looked at her grandmother. "I've made four of them since she gave me her recipe." She reached out and took Maria's hand. "I have a small confession to make, though. I made one teeny-tiny change, Grandma. You use only rum in the cake, and while it was terrific, I thought it would be better if I added two tablespoons of brandy. I think it makes the cake more moist."

Maria Pernik took another piece of fruitcake on her fork and tasted it. She looked at Bryna. "It is more moist. Good."

Bryna's dark eyes were serious. "You're not upset that I made a change in your recipe?"

"Upset?" Maria shook her head. "Better is better. Two tablespoons of brandy." She winked at Sadie. "When I get home, I'll have to write that down."

Chapter 8

The new silver-gray Cadillac paused for a light on Park Avenue. Harry Wald's fingers drummed nervously on the steering wheel. In his pocket were two tickets to the Rubinstein piano recital at Lincoln Center. He had paid an outrageous amount for them, but they were worth it. They would be, that is, if Doris went out with him at all. The light changed, and Harry headed uptown. "When you've got it, enjoy it," Sam had said. Harry had to admit he was enjoying it. He'd worked hard to make it, that was for sure. So why had he denied himself all these years?

He approached Doris' apartment building and pulled the car to a smooth stop in front of the canopy. The curb was painted yellow, and a small sign announced: POSITIVELY NO PARKING. Harry switched off the ignition. He took two packages from the seat, then got out of the car. The doorman approached, but before he could say anything Harry reached into his pocket, found a bill, and handed it him. "I'll be a few minutes," he said. "Keep an eye on the car."

The doorman looked at the bill and smiled. "Yes, sir."

Harry checked himself in the vestibule mirror. Spotless blue blazer, gray slacks, high-gloss loafers, and the bright striped tie Sam had selected to go with the baby-blue chambray shirt. Automatically he centered his tie, smiling devilishly at himself. "Mrs. Mandelbaum, twelfth floor," he said. "Tell her Ben Forest is here."

A moment later, he was in the elevator. Ben Forest indeed. It was a trick but at least he had one more chance. He ran his hand down the sleeve of his blazer. It was amazing what new clothes and a new attitude could do. He stood tall, feeling thinner, elegant, and very sophisticated, as if he had inherited Fred Astaire's genes.

Humming to himself, he stepped off the elevator and walked down the carpeted hall. He paused in front of Doris' door, suddenly nervous. What if she turned him down—what then? The way you look, kid, he answered himself, not a chance. And if she does, came another thought, you'll find someone else. He pressed the doorbell.

He heard the clack of high heels inside as Doris came to the door. Three antiburglar locks clicked; the door opened. Doris was standing there in a bright red wool dress. Doris Mandelbaum with a totally surprised look on her face. "Hello, Doris."

She blinked twice, taking in his smile, the bright tie knotted perfectly, the cut of his jacket, his hair parted just so. "Where's Ben Forest?" she asked.

He handed her a gold box of chocolates. "A token," he said. "Doris, I'm a new man. So I took a new name."

She shifted from one foot to the other, trying to make a decision. She felt hurt, disappointed, and yet a part of her was intrigued. How could Harry have changed his appearance so much? How could he get younger, taller . . . better-looking?

"Sadie thought you couldn't see the Forest for the Wald," he said. "Doris, take a chance. I won't let you down."

"Harry . . ." she said, still undecided. He did seem different— confident and assured, no longer hangdog Harry.

He handed her a bouquet of pink camellias. "You'd better put these in water," he said. "They're very fragile."

She took the flowers, cradling them against her breast. "Yes," she said. "Well, I guess you'd better come in."

498

MUCH LATER THEY CAME BACK to the apartment laughing. Doris put her fur wrap on the hall table. She smiled. "What can I get you? Brandy? Coffee?"

"Coffee would be nice," Harry said.

"Sit down. I'll only be a minute." In the kitchen she measured out the water and coffee and put the percolator on the stove.

It had been a wonderful evening, full of surprises. Their seats at the recital had been perfect. She'd listened to Rubinstein play, her heart soaring with the music. Stealing glances at Harry, she saw that he had been moved as well. She remembered the light grip on her arm as he guided her up the aisle after the performance, the quietly subdued ride to the restaurant for supper. And his charming conversation—amusing, and delivered with a look in his eyes of pure adoration. He was an interesting man, Harry Wald turned Ben Forest, a very interesting man indeed.

"DO YOU KNOW, it's almost two o'clock in the morning?" Harry said. "Perhaps I'd better go." Doris was sitting on the couch, her legs tucked up beneath her skirt. Harry sat next to her.

"A few more minutes," she said. "You never finished telling me about the fruit groves."

"Well, they're in Florida, Arizona, Texas and California. And Hawaii. I forgot Hawaii." Harry chuckled.

To Harry's ears, Doris' laugh tinkled like crystal. "And I took you for a schnook," she said.

"I was, Doris, don't you see?" A frown creased his brow. "I never really woke up after Emily died. I was like a zombie, in a daze. Alive, but just walking around . . ."

Something stirred in Doris as she looked at the pain on his face. She put a hand on his arm. "Yes, I know. . . ."

"To lose someone so dear," he said in a husky voice, "so sweet, so loving . . . so young."

Doris sighed. "You never really get over it, do you?"

They sat in silence for a time, locked in the past. Harry's hand sought hers and held it. "It's really late," he said quietly.

"Yes." She gently squeezed his arm.

"But not too late," Harry said, turning to look at her. Their eyes met and held. Slowly he moved to her and kissed her gently on her cheek. She moved up against him, her head fitting perfectly under his chin, the scent of her hair a perfume that filled his heart. He held her in the circle of his arms, rocking gently, until her own arms reached out.

"Hold me," she whispered. "Harry, just hold me awhile."

THERE ARE FEW THINGS as satisfying as the beginning of a love affair, even someone else's. Sam was walking around singing "Joy to the Wald," and Sadie looked like the cat that had eaten the canary. Harry had dropped by the apartment to deliver a kiss, a hug, and a bouquet of flowers to Sadie. For Sam he had a dozen pairs of silk shorts. Happiness oozed from every pore as Harry spoke of Doris' plans for the coming week.

"Just tell me when the wedding is going to be," Sadie said.

"Soon, soon." Harry grinned. "You'll be the first to know."

"And remember Saturday night. You and Doris are invited to this sculpture showing."

"You got a tuxedo?" Sam asked.

Harry shook his head, and Sam walked him to the door, planning yet another shopping trip. He came back to Sadie and kissed her. "That's for being such a good matchmaker."

"Don't give congratulations yet, Sam. When the ring is on her finger, that's when I'll be sure. And speaking of fingers, keep them crossed for Brenda and Fred Dubin."

Sam blew a smoke ring at the ceiling. "Sadie, he's not the marrying kind."

"Every man is the marrying kind, it just takes the right girl."

"That's not Brenda."

Sadie shrugged. "How can you ever figure out who'll fall for who in this world? It's a mystery, Sam, to keep everybody on their toes. I'm telling you, God sits up in heaven and makes matches down here on earth, and that's the way it is."

It was just possible that God sitting in heaven was looking for a little help that week. For as well as things were going for Harry and Doris—they spent each evening together—that's how badly Michael and Maxine were getting along. They argued daily by telephone and passed a tense Tuesday night bickering over dinner at a little Italian restaurant. The strain was beginning to show on their faces. Maxine looked drawn and pale, Michael tense and nervous. From Michael's point of view, Maxine was making him jump through hoops to prove his love. For her part, Michael's stubborn insistence on having his own way was proof to Maxine that their relationship could not progress beyond dating. Doctors thought themselves princes, she knew, but Michael was acting like an emperor.

She would not discuss Michael with Sadie. Taping a show that week, Maxine met twice with her, but made sure it was strictly business, no matter how Sadie attempted to draw her out. She knew what Sadie's message was, having heard it often enough. Give in, bend a little, the important thing is to be together, right? Wrong. Not ever would she surrender her hard-won independence. Not even for a person as perfect as Dr. Michael Newman.

UNDER FRED DUBIN'S direction a crew of five was working at Hymie Farrel's SoHo Gallery. Lighting men were stringing lights, a sound man was setting up, and Dubin was in the back-room office, worrying. "Where is she?" he said for the tenth time.

"Artists," Hymie Farrel said. "They're all crazy. Don't fret, Dubin, she'll be here for the opening tomorrow. I haven't seen an artist yet would miss his own show."

Dubin sighed. "I wanted to have a run-through. Maybe I can call her. What was the name of that place? Baby Bidey Dolls?"

"Bitsey Baby Dolls. I'll call." The small, rotund gallery owner dialed the doll factory and asked them to call the weirdo on the top floor. "Brenda? Fred Dubin wants to talk to you." He handed the phone to Dubin.

"Where the hell are you?" Dubin asked angrily.

"Working," Brenda said. "Where else should I be?"

"Right here. I want to have a run-through with you, so you'll know what to do tomorrow night."

"I know what to do tomorrow night. Meanwhile I'm working and you're interrupting."

Dubin unleashed a string of expletives.

"Very nice, Dubin, is that the way you talk to a lady? You know, you could say heck and darn."

Dubin took the receiver from his ear and looked at it, not sure he had heard Brenda correctly. Then a light went on in his head. "You've been talking to Sadie Shapiro, haven't you?"

"Why not? She's a friend of mine."

"Oh, no!" Dubin exclaimed. "Listen, I get enough of Sadie Shapiro on the exercise show. I don't want her interfering in this. But you . . . I want you here early tomorrow evening, understand?

So I can show you the kind of stuff I want on-camera. Eight o'clock and not a minute later."

"I'll try."

"Try!" Dubin exploded. "Try! You get here by eight or else!"

"Good-by," Brenda said sweetly. Dubin heard a click at the other end of the line. Unbelieving, he stared at the phone. Brenda Fogelman had hung up on him.

DR. MICHAEL NEWMAN was changing from his white coat to his suit jacket when the intercom rang. "You have visitors, Doctor. . . . Sadie Shapiro and a Mr. Beck."

Michael greeted them at his office door. "Sam, Sadie—what brings you to see me? I'm delighted."

"Don't be too sure," Sam said mysteriously.

Michael seated them before his desk. "Is anything wrong?"

Sadie's lips were compressed into a thin line. "Wrong, he says. What could be wrong? Only a man and a woman made for each other like bagels and lox, and acting like two idiots, that's all. It hurts my heart to look at you, a couple of icebergs in the ocean, drifting apart."

Michael sat down in his high-backed leather chair. "It's not exactly like that, Sadie."

"I don't see things getting any warmer between you."

Michael shrugged. "We seem to have reached an impasse."

"If impasse means impossible, then I don't believe it. Anything in this world can be passed as long as there's love on both sides. You love her, this I know. And Maxine?"

"I'm sure she loves me, too," Michael said.

Sadie looked at Michael, then at Sam, then at the heavens. "So what's the big problem?" Slowly Michael filled in the details for Sadie. About the decision to share each other's lives, and the argument over which of their apartments would be home. When he finished, Sadie was staring at him, a look of astonishment on her face. "This is what the big fight was about? Your apartment or hers? If you'll excuse me, Michael, that's crazy, and it's also insane."

"Sadie, this decision has become a matter of principle. If I let Maxine have her way now, at great inconvenience to myself, will I always have to accede to her in the future? And vice versa for Maxine. Will she be putting power in my hands by giving in now? It's not so simple, you see."

"Wrong! Simple, but made complicated by two people who want to have a stubborn contest." Sadie stood up and gathered her coat around herself. "Let's go, Michael."

"Go where?"

"To your apartment and then to Maxine's. It's time you let someone else in on this great problem. So up from behind your desk, Doctor, and let's start rolling."

There are few things in life as powerful as a Sadie Shapiro with her mind made up. Michael found himself closing his office and walking around the corner with Sadie and Sam. Like an overeager customs agent, she nosed about his apartment, inspecting closets, peeking into cupboards, taking in the view from his living-room window. "Nice," she pronounced at last. "Not the best place I've ever seen in my life—not with such a small foyer and only one closet you could hang a shoe rack on—but okay."

"I'm glad you like it." Michael grinned.

"And I'm sorry you do," Sadie shot back. "Wouldn't it be simple if you hated it here?"

"My office is around the corner," Michael began to explain all over again, "and the telephones—"

"Enough with the telephones," Sadie interrupted. "I think you love Ma Bell more than Maxine, believe me."

"It would be very inconvenient to move, Sadie. Very."

"Oh, I'm sorry, I forgot. *In-con-ven-ient.*" She made the word sound like an Islamic curse. "All right, I've seen enough. On to Maxine's place."

Michael looked at Sam, who rolled his eyes and shrugged. A short time later, they were climbing the stairs in Maxine's brownstone. "A little more light they could use on the stairs," Sadie observed. "Wouldn't hurt."

"Hello," Maxine said as she saw Michael in her doorway. And then she said hello again as Sadie and Sam walked past him. "What a nice surprise! But you should have told me you were coming. I haven't shopped or cleaned today."

"Not here to eat or inspect for dust," Sadie said. She stood in the middle of the living room and took it in. "The high ceilings are nice, but I'll bet it also gets cold in the winter."

"A little drafty," Maxine said. "What is this?"

Sadie couldn't answer because she had walked into the tiny kitchen. Maxine went after her, looking in from the doorway.

"This is the kitchen?" Sadie opened and closed the broom closet.

"They call it a kitchenette," Maxine said.

"I can see why. There isn't room to swing a coat in here."

Sadie walked past Maxine, bedroom bound. Maxine hurried to catch up. "I haven't made the bed. Sadie, don't go in there!"

"I won't tell your mother." Sadie walked in, inspected the closet, shook her head, then disappeared into the bathroom.

"Are you moving, Sadie?" Maxine called after her. "Are you looking for an apartment?"

Sadie came into view again, nodding sagely. "Looking *at*, not for. Looking at two people having some kind of apartment contest, like a poker game. I see your living room and I raise you one stall shower. I bid my telephones and call your fireplace. Two crazy kids, that's what I'm looking at, Maxine."

Now Maxine knew which way the wind was blowing. "Wait a minute," she said. "I won't discuss my relationship with Michael."

"It's too late for that," Sam said from the doorway. "She's bigger than both of you."

Sadie shooed Maxine into the living room, made her sit down next to Michael on the couch. Maxine looked Sadie in the eye. "Now you're going to browbeat me, right?"

"Wouldn't lay one finger on you, cookie," Sadie said.

"As long as I give up my independence," Maxine shot back.

"Aha!" Sadie cried, one bony finger pointed aloft. "I knew we'd hear that word soon. Independence! Why does that have to mean alone, Maxine? Can't independence be two people together, independent, yes, but also depending on each other? Listen, this country was made by people who wanted independence, and most of them were married!"

Maxine began to answer, then realized she didn't know the question.

"I'll give you another word, *spoiled*. Spoiled rotten, the two of you, my big-shot television producer and my important doctor. You can't be inconvenienced for a minute, you have a hangnail you'll make a federal case out of it." She fixed her eyes on Michael. "You'd really rather have your telephones than be with Maxine?"

Michael shook his head. "That's not the point."

"Oh, excuse me," Sadie said mockingly. "You got a swell apartment, Michael—five beautiful rooms and you can be lonely in every one of them. So what good is it if one day you go out and win

504

the Noble Prize if there's nobody to tell when you come home? And you, Maxine—you want to live here or nowhere, right?"

"I like it here," Maxine said. "It's convenient and—"

"Again that word, convenient. You fixed this place up very nice, Maxine, but there'll come a time when you'll want more warmth than that fireplace can give you. Talking about sharing and caring, and don't tell me about independence and being a woman alone. A man doesn't have to be an enemy; he can be a help."

With a withering look at Maxine and Michael, Sadie turned away and began to pace. For a long moment she seemed to collect her thoughts. Then she spoke. "What you two need is not a matchmaker. You're made for each other, you belong together, and the children you'll have will be as smart and good-looking as the two of you. So what do you need? A *referee*. Someone to make a decision neither of you can make. Michael, do you love this girl?"

"Like the air I breathe."

"Maxine, the truth—do you love this man?"

The flush on her face answered for her.

"I now pronounce you man and apartment," Sam joked.

"Exactly," Sadie said, grinning. "A home is in your heart, not in four walls. So listen to me good. What you do is you *both move!* Into someplace new that suits you both. Halfway between, so both of you give up something. To get something even better."

"She's not a Sadie, she's a Solomon," Michael said. "Maxine, I'm willing. I'll do anything to spend the rest of my life with you."

"I don't know," Maxine said.

"Let's talk about it," said Michael.

Sam crossed the room and took Sadie by the hand. "My dear, I think it's time we took a walk." Gently he steered her toward the door. Looking back on their way out, they saw Michael and Maxine locked in each other's arms. "How do you like that?" Sam said. "What they really needed was a real estate agent."

Chapter 9

Hymie Farrel's SoHo Gallery was a double storefront on Lower Broadway. Formerly an ironmongery, it had been transformed by Farrel into an arena of avant-garde chic. The walls had been stripped down to the bare brick, a teak floor had been laid throughout. The tin ceilings had been covered with black paint and a grid system of theatrical lighting installed. And on Hymie's desk a card file listed names and telephone numbers of New York's Beautiful People. His velvet dinner jacket shining under the lights, Hymie Farrel made a last-minute inspection of the gallery. Two waiters manned the bar along one wall, champagne glasses filled with bubbly at the ready, the three-piece band was in place, the sound man and cameraman had tested their equipment, the sculptures were all arranged and gleaming, the large piece (now entitled *American Woman*) revolving on its platform; the printed brochures were stacked on the desk near the door, and Fred Dubin was out on the sidewalk going quietly crazy.

At a signal from Hymie the band began playing, and the doors were opened to admit the first guests. Hymie greeted them, put brochures in their hands, and headed out to corral Fred Dubin. He was at the curb, smoking a cigarette. "She's late," Dubin said.

"She's Brenda." Hymie shrugged. "Don't worry, she'll show up."

Dubin nervously straightened his velvet bow tie, looking over the long black limousine that had pulled to the curb. A recognizable blond tennis pro emerged, followed by two stunning young women. Hymie showed them to the door, then turned back to Dubin. "Wait inside, Fred," he said, smiling. "I don't want you to frighten away the customers."

Dubin walked into the gallery behind Hymie. "We'll shoot some background stuff," he said. "The key shots we can't get until the idiot girl gets here—*if* she gets here."

Half a mile north, Harry Wald turned his Cadillac onto Broadway. Sadie thought Sam and Harry looked splendid in their formal clothes, and the gleam in Harry's eyes whenever he looked at Doris gladdened her heart. Doris was giggly as a teenager. Two blocks away from the gallery they found themselves in a traffic jam. It was almost eight thirty by the time they parked and fought their way through the crush into the gallery. They smiled widely for Dubin's camera, and Sadie found herself stepping on the director's toes. "Where is Brenda?" she asked him. "I want to say hello."

"I wish I knew! I'd like to wring her neck!"

"Don't wring and don't get excited," Sadie said. "She'll be here."

A phalanx of dinner-jacketed Texans swept by, and Sadie was carried along with them to the center of the room. She looked about for Sam and found Michael and Maxine instead. Michael quarter-

506

backed their move to an unoccupied space near the bar. "What a mob scene," he said. "Fantastic."

"The sculptures are very good," Maxine said. "Strong stuff."

"If you knew the artist, you'd see why." Sadie grinned. She nudged Maxine with a finger. "So? Tell me things."

"About what?" Maxine said blandly.

"Cool like ice," Sadie said. "Come on, I'm dying to hear about you two. I would have called seventeen times already, but Sam said leave you alone. Now tell me this instant what you decided."

"We didn't decide much," Maxine said with a shrug.

"Except that we love each other," said Michael. "And we went looking at apartments today, and we may have found one."

"And one more thing," Maxine said. "We're getting married."

Suddenly, unaccountably, tears welled in Sadie's eyes. With a sob, she fell on Maxine and hugged her tight, and Maxine began crying too. While the band played a disco version of "April Showers," the two women clung to each other, crying with joy, until Michael's handkerchief began to pass between them.

A gray-bearded art critic for *The New York Times* walked by, accompanied by Fred Dubin, his cameraman, and sound man. "In the main," the critic said, "Miss Fogelman's use of texture and form is, unlike the present generation's thinking, very original."

"Which means?" Dubin asked, holding the microphone under the critic's beard.

"She might be quite a find. You can read the rest of my comments in my review." The critic turned and headed for the bar.

Dubin's eyes swept the room. Suddenly, through the bright lights and haze of tobacco smoke, he saw a vision enter the gallery, a finely made mantilla framing dark hair, a white knitted dress, beautiful in its simplicity, clinging to a stunning figure, a face so lovely that it made him draw breath. An instant later, he recognized her as Brenda Fogelman.

"Brenda!" Sadie Shapiro shouted. Sam had rejoined her and they moved through the crowd to the young girl's side.

"That dress," Sam said. "Sadie, it's the one you were knitting!"

"Better than I ever pictured," Sadie managed to say.

"Brenda!" Fred Dubin shouted from across the room. He began to shoulder his way angrily through the crowd. "Upstart! Imbecile!" he roared at her, oblivious to the stares around them. He grasped her firmly by the arm and began pulling her to the door.

A seething rage filled Dubin as he half dragged, half pushed Brenda outside the gallery and onto the street. His carefully planned show was kaput, killed by an idiot girl who had opted for glamor behind his back. How dare she be so conventional, so middle class? She was Brenda Fogelman, an artist, an original with a rare talent for being herself. Squeezing her arm tightly, he turned her to face him. "Who put you up to this?" he barked.

"Freddie . . ." she whispered. "I'm sorry. . . ."

A neon sign, blinking on and off, illuminated the light in Brenda's eyes. "You cut your hair," Dubin moaned. He fingered the tips of her hair as it lay just above her white shoulders. "And lipstick . . ." Only now did he see the rest of the transformation that had taken place. Those dark eyes, shining with tears, the finely wrought cheekbones, the tender, trembling mouth so vulnerable in pink. "You've ruined everything," he said. "Why?"

A single tear started down her cheek. "Freddie, please . . ."

"I ought to kill you," he said less roughly. One hand wiped gently at her tear. "Brenda," he said, and then, as he started to say more, found he could not. For a thickness had invaded his throat, a wave of feeling so sharp he could not speak.

"I love you," Brenda said.

He nodded, not knowing why; his hands framed her face. "Yes," he said. "Yes." His eyes were slightly glazed as he looked into her face, and for the first time in his thirty-seven years a shaft of love pierced his wildly beating heart. "Brenda," he croaked, his voice a stranger to his ears, "Brenda," and he swept her into his arms, the scent of her hair filling his senses, the feel of her body locked to his, the warmth of her hand caressing his cheek.

He kissed those pink lips softly, and then with ever-increasing feeling, and for a long time they did not say anything more.

THE FIRST COLD WIND of September rattled the windowpanes as it swept across Central Park. Sadie Shapiro poured water into the glass kettle and put it on the stove to boil. Sam had been sleeping for half an hour, but Sadie had too much on her mind this night to settle down beside him. Pictures kept coming to her, pictures collected over a warm and sunshiny summer.

How lovely Doris had looked that day in the rabbi's study as she and Harry were married. And how elegant and charming was the groom. How wonderful that love can come twice.

And just this afternoon, Sadie had seen Brenda and Fred off on their honeymoon. They were taking a tour of Italy, with plans to see every piece of sculpture from Milan to Rome. That is, if they could manage to stop looking at each other.

Not far away, Michael and Maxine were probably in their new apartment. It had hurt her heart to see them move in with each other without benefit of marriage, but soon, soon, Maxine would name the day and their marriage would take place. For the prince Maxine had feared would rule her life had proved to be a willing slave, doting on her every wish, and filling her days with joy. Before the year was out, Sadie would dance at their wedding.

The water on the stove began to boil and brought Sadie back to the world. She went to the cabinet and took down a box of tea bags. She poured the water into a mug, then put a tea bag into it.

Her eye fell on the old tin tea box atop the refrigerator and she brought it to the table along with her tea. She opened the box and took out the three cards Sarah Barish had passed along to her as a last bequest. Harry Wald. Doris Mandelbaum. Brenda Fogelman.

She looked for a moment at the three cards, then put them into the pocket of her robe. The box was empty now, the work of a lifetime completed.

Smiling, Sadie began to fill the old tin box with tea.